THE PRIME MINISTER is the fifth in Trollope's six-volume sequence of novels known as the Palliser series. They chart the career of Plantagenet Palliser, and his troubled marriage to Lady Glencora. The novels depict the social milieu of the aristocracy and upper middle-class of mid-Victorian England, with occasional forays into low life and the criminal underworld. They combine the machinations of politics with an intimate exploration of personal relationships to paint an unparalleled portrait of an age. The novels can be read independently and as part of a linked whole. They are:

NICHOLAS SHRIMPTON is Emeritus Fellow at Lady Margaret Hall, Oxford. His publications include *The Whole Music of Passion: New Essays on Swinburne* (1993) and *Matthew Arnold: Selected Poems* (1998).

OXFORD WORLD'S CLASSICS

For over 100 years Oxford World's Classics have brought readers closer to the world's great literature. Now with over 700 titles—from the 4,000-year-old myths of Mesopotamia to the twentieth century's greatest novels—the series makes available lesser-known as well as celebrated writing.

The pocket-sized hardbacks of the early years contained introductions by Virginia Woolf, T. S. Eliot, Graham Greene, and other literary figures which enriched the experience of reading. Today the series is recognized for its fine scholarship and reliability in texts that span world literature, drama and poetry, religion, philosophy and politics. Each edition includes perceptive commentary and essential background information to meet the changing needs of readers.

OXFORD WORLD'S CLASSICS

ANTHONY TROLLOPE

The Prime Minister

Edited with an Introduction and Notes by
NICHOLAS SHRIMPTON

OXFORD
UNIVERSITY PRESS

OXFORD

UNIVERSITY PRESS

Great Clarendon Street, Oxford OX2 6DP

Oxford University Press is a department of the University of Oxford.
It furthers the University's objective of excellence in research, scholarship,
and education by publishing worldwide in

Oxford New York

Auckland Cape Town Dar es Salaam Hong Kong Karachi
Kuala Lumpur Madrid Melbourne Mexico City Nairobi
New Delhi Shanghai Taipei Toronto

With offices in

Argentina Austria Brazil Chile Czech Republic France Greece
Guatemala Hungary Italy Japan Poland Portugal Singapore
South Korea Switzerland Thailand Turkey Ukraine Vietnam

Oxford is a registered trade mark of Oxford University Press
in the UK and in certain other countries

Published in the United States
by Oxford University Press Inc., New York

Introduction, Select Bibliography, Explanatory Notes, Appendix © Nicholas Shrimpton 2011
Biographical Preface, Chronology © Katherine Mullin and Francis O'Gorman 2011

The moral rights of the authors have been asserted
Database right Oxford University Press (maker)

First published as a World's Classics paperback 1983
Reissued as an Oxford World's Classics paperback 1999, 2008
New edition 2011

British Library Cataloguing in Publication Data

Data available

Library of Congress Cataloging in Publication Data

Data available

Typeset by Glyph International, Bangalore, India
Printed in Great Britain
on acid-free paper by
Clays Ltd, Elcograf S.p.A.

ISBN 978-0-19-958719-3

12

CONTENTS

BIOGRAPHICAL PREFACE

ANTHONY TROLLOPE was born on 24 April 1815 in London. He was the fourth surviving child of a failing barrister and gentleman farmer, Thomas Anthony Trollope, and his wife Frances (née Milton), who became a successful novelist and travel writer. Trollope's childhood was dominated by uncongenial schooling. He was sent to Harrow, the boys' public school in north London, as a day boy, then to Sunbury, Surrey, while awaiting a place at his father's former school, Winchester College. Trollope was admitted to Winchester in 1827, but his father's embarrassing inability to pay the fees became known to fellow pupils. He was moved back from Winchester to Harrow in 1830 for two further years, which he later described as 'the worst period of my life'.[1] Unsurprisingly, he did not shine academically, and when, in 1834, the whole family fled to Bruges in Belgium to avoid imprisonment for debt, he obtained a clerkship in the London headquarters of the newly-created Post Office through his mother's connections.

The beginning of Trollope's long Post Office career was not encouraging. He soon became known for unpunctuality, and was, by his own account, 'always on the eve of being dismissed'.[2] His scanty salary led him into debt, and travails with money-lenders would later inform the scrapes of many fictional characters. Trollope was sustained by a habit of imagination that was first acquired during his unhappy adolescence. Daydreaming not only allowed him 'to live in a world altogether outside the world of my own material life':[3] it served as an apprenticeship for fiction. Yet it took a change of scene from London to rural Ireland to persuade Trollope to express his imagination in writing.

In July 1841, aged 26, Trollope was appointed deputy postal surveyor's clerk, based in Banagher, King's County (now Co. Offaly). His new-found professional success helped him to grow in social confidence. Ireland prompted his lifelong enthusiasm for hunting with hounds, too. That enthusiasm was never far from his writing, and sometimes it made life difficult for him at work, not least because hounds and horses were an expensive pastime. Within a year, he became engaged to Rose Heseltine, the daughter of a Rotherham banker who was holidaying in what is now Dun Laoghaire. Trollope proposed after barely a fortnight's acquaintance. The wedding was, for

---

[1] Anthony Trollope, *An Autobiography* (Oxford: OUP, 1980), 11.
[2] Ibid. 46. [3] Ibid. 43.

financial reasons, postponed for two years until 11 June 1844. Marriage
and the birth of two sons, Henry Merivale in 1846 and Frederick James
Anthony in 1847, helped Trollope to find what he called the 'vigour
necessary to prosecute two professions at the same time'.[4] His first
novel, *The Macdermots of Ballycloran* (1847), sold far fewer than the
400 copies printed. But it was favourably reviewed and was followed
by a second Irish tale, *The Kellys and the O'Kellys* (1848). Both kept an
uneasy silence on the Famine, to which Trollope was a horrified witness, but his recollections of the famine years would inform the later
Castle Richmond (1860). The failure of *La Vendée* (1850), on the French
Revolution, together with the increasing demands of his Post Office
career, conspired to deflect Trollope from fiction for some years.

In 1851, he was sent to the south-west of England to investigate
ways of expanding the rural postal system. His successful development
of the pillar box, which he first tried out in St Helier in the Channel
Islands in 1852, led to the spread of post boxes throughout the UK.
The project won Trollope promotion to the surveyorship of the north
of Ireland in 1854, and his family settled in Donnybrook. During these
years, he composed the first novel to bring him real recognition, *The
Warden* (1855). The first of six 'Chronicles of Barsetshire', *The Warden*
was set, like its successors, in a fictional county, based on the south-
west England Trollope knew. Although they dramatized changes in the
ecclesiastical world, the 'Chronicles' were also secular in their interests.
While *The Warden* brought him less than £10, Trollope 'soon felt it
had not failed as the others had failed',[5] and began work on *Barchester
Towers* (1857). It was warmly reviewed. But it was not until the publication of *Dr Thorne* (1858) that he met with unmixed success. The novels
following—*Framley Parsonage* (1861), *The Small House at Allington*
(1864), and *The Last Chronicle of Barset* (1867)—established his reputation, his popularity, and his fortune.

During the twelve years between *The Warden* and *The Last Chronicle*,
Trollope published seventeen novels, numerous short stories, and several collections of travel writing. This extraordinary scale of produc-
tion was sustained by his habit of rising at five each morning to allow
three hours of writing—250 words each quarter of an hour, he boasted
in *An Autobiography*—before leaving for the office at nine. Other celebrated writers have written to a similar schedule, but Trollope's pride
in his achievement has never been entirely admired by critics. His
schedule made him an invaluable contributor to the *Cornhill Magazine*,
founded in 1859 by the novelist, William Makepeace Thackeray. The

serialization of *Framley Parsonage* in the *Cornhill*'s first issues did much to secure the magazine's and Trollope's reputation. Through the *Cornhill*, he made lasting friendships with major literary and artistic figures. By 1859, he was living in the north London suburb of Waltham Cross, after a promotion to Post Office surveyor of the eastern district. He was soon elected to the Garrick and Athenaeum Clubs, and became a stalwart of the Royal Literary Fund. These were marks of serious literary success. He also, in 1860, met a young American woman, Kate Field, with whom he fell in love. The nature of *that* relationship is known almost as little as Trollope's relationship with Rose. But Kate mattered to him—and would do till the end of his life.

Trollope concluded the Barsetshire Chronicles on a high note, considering *The Last Chronicle of Barset* to be his best novel. Following the model of Honoré de Balzac's *Comédie humaine*, Trollope saw realist fiction as capable of depicting a complex culture through a multivolume series. The Palliser volumes, beginning with *Can You Forgive Her?* (1865) and ending with *The Duke's Children* (1880), were his other major sequence. These novels, like the Barsetshire Chronicles, could be read separately and in different orders without irrecoverable loss—but they formed a continuous whole all the same. In the story of the Pallisers, Trollope developed one of his strongest themes—the difficult marriage and its negotiations. He also explored great political issues, including the 1867 Reform Bill and the disestablishment of the Irish Church, while inviting readers to map the Conservative leader Daubeny onto Disraeli, and the Liberal Gresham onto Gladstone. His portrayal of democratic politics has remained consequential for generations. The novels' political appeal, nonetheless, was carefully balanced against other enticements: 'If I wrote politics for my own sake, I must put in love and intrigue, social incidents, a dash of sport, for the sake of my readers',[6] he said, with characteristic pragmatism.

Trollope resigned from the Post Office in 1867. His earnings from writing had long outstripped his salary. The following year, feeling that 'to sit in the British Parliament should be the highest object of ambition to every educated Englishman',[7] he stood as the Liberal candidate for Beverley in the 1868 General Election. He was unsuccessful. That failure haunted his fiction as it must have haunted his private life. Trollope interspersed the Palliser series with other novels and studies. He was by this stage a professional writer whose commitment was broken significantly only by field sports and travel. Trollope's international voyages included Australia, where Frederick, his younger son, was a sheep

[6] Ibid. 317.   [7] Ibid. 290.

farmer: *Australia and New Zealand* (1873) was a result. Trollope and Rose left London in 1880 for South Harting in Sussex, hoping country air would ease his persistent asthma. This was no retirement: the last two years of his life saw a further six books, including *Mr Scarborough's Family* (1883), a study of parental domination, and the unfinished *The Landleaguers*, a return to Irish matters (published posthumously, 1883).

In early November 1882, Trollope suffered a stroke, and, on 6 December, he died in London at the age of 67. He had written forty-seven novels, five volumes of short stories, four travel books, three biographies, an autobiography, and two translations from the classics, together with uncollected pieces of journalism. His prodigious output included a biography of Thackeray, and a study of Cicero whose political judiciousness was often a silent model behind his admirable fictional politicians. Few who knew Trollope could avoid commenting on his loud and bluff persona in public: at 5 ft. 10 in., and around 16 stones, he struck those who met him as burly—a man of bodily appetites. It was difficult for many to imagine him dissecting the emotional complexities of his characters with such delicacy and sympathy.

Trollope's posthumous *An Autobiography* (1883) startled a large number of readers. Its dry discussion of how much money his fiction made denied any Romantic model of authorship. Here was no account of the creative flash of inspiration. Writing fiction was more like a trade, the result of well-applied skill and labour. But, knowing at first hand the cost of his father's failure, it was important to Trollope to demonstrate to his family, if to no one else, that he had made such a success of his life. He had no university degree, and was without the much-coveted honour of a seat in Parliament. He wished to demonstrate too, in a culture less familiar with the notion of a professional writer than ours, that writing could indeed be a life. His estate was valued at the huge sum of £25,892 19s. 3d.

Biographies of Trollope are always to some degree doomed to follow the sparse facts laid out in *An Autobiography*. The nature of his marriage, his feelings for Kate Field, his relationship with his sons, let alone the secrets of his inner life, are among the topics on which it is impossible to write with certainty. Trollope had no commitment to privacy—but private he remains. Declining to reveal himself in correspondence, he is, perhaps, only glimpsed in the astonishingly fertile novels about human lives, desires, and choices, which were his enduring bequest to English literature.

Katherine Mullin
Francis O'Gorman

INTRODUCTION

[Readers who are unfamiliar with the plot may prefer to treat the Introduction as an Afterword]

A NOVEL, in Trollope's own definition, should be 'a picture of common life, enlivened with humour and sweetened with pathos'.[1] Though *The Prime Minister* depicts the everyday life of nineteenth-century England with its author's customary fidelity, there is not much humour and very little sweetness about it. This is an important but uncomfortable book.

The Russian novelist Tolstoy read it in January 1877 and thought it 'splendid'.[2] Trollope's English contemporaries, however, failed to appreciate *The Prime Minister*. 'This is not one of Mr Trollope's pleasanter novels,' the *Spectator* observed on 22 July 1876: 'We should, in fact, be half-inclined to believe that Mr. Trollope's power itself had declined, that he was positively unable to give us the sketches in which we have taken such delight.' The *Saturday Review*, in October 1876, was similarly 'forced to the conclusion that *The Prime Minister* represents a decadence in Mr. Trollope's powers'.[3] At the age of 61, Trollope began to wonder whether his career as a novelist was over.

This controversial novel was the fifth in a sequence of six 'semi-political tales', published between January 1864 and July 1880, which later became known as the Palliser series. First seen as a backbench MP in the 'Barsetshire' novel *The Small House at Allington* (1862–4), Plantagenet Palliser rises through the political ranks in *Can You Forgive Her?* (where he becomes Chancellor of the Exchequer), *Phineas Finn*, *The Eustace Diamonds*, and *Phineas Redux*, where he inherits his uncle's title, moves to the House of Lords as Duke of Omnium, and drops briefly in cabinet seniority, first to Lord Privy Seal, and then to President of the Board of Trade. Now, in *The Prime Minister* (1875–6), he finally reaches the top of the greasy pole and becomes 'the greatest man in the greatest country in the world' (p. 544) as the leader of a coalition government. Trollope thought that he was depicting an ideal

---

[1] Anthony Trollope, *An Autobiography*, ed. M. Sadleir and F. Page (Oxford: OUP, 1999), 126.

[2] See N. J. Hall's review of C. P. Snow's *Trollope* in *Nineteenth-Century Fiction*, 31/2 (1976), 215, citing a translation by R. F. Christian and Patrick Waddington from the 90-volume Jubilee edition of Tolstoy, lxii. 302.

[3] Donald Smalley (ed.), *Anthony Trollope: The Critical Heritage* (London: Routledge & Kegan Paul, 1969), 422, 426.

statesman whose only faults were the personal sensitivity and moral fas-
tidiousness which hampered his ability to cut deals and make compromises.
The reviewers, crushingly, found the political scenes 'vulgar'.

But their deepest objection was actually to the love story which
Trollope used, in his familiar multiplot structure, to 'sweeten' the parliamentary narrative. 'If I wrote politics for my own sake,' he noted in
his *Autobiography*, 'I must put in love and intrigue, social incidents,
with perhaps a dash of sport, for the sake of my readers.'[4] Unfortunately,
the relationship between Emily Wharton and Ferdinand Lopez was not
something which readers in the 1870s found it easy to enjoy. Even *The
Times*, which praised other features of the book, was unhappy with this.
'We doubt', the reviewer declared, 'whether it will ever be numbered
among the favourites of those who delight in Mr Trollope for his love
stories.'[5] Trollope himself came quickly to believe that he had made a
mistake. In a letter to Mary Holmes in May 1876, he declared that,
'though I myself am prepared to stand up for the character of the Prime
Minister, and for all his surroundings, I acknowledge the story of the
soi-disant hero, Lopez, and all that has to do with him, to be bad'.[6]

The reason for this distaste is obvious enough. In previous novels,
Trollope had often used the plot motif of a young woman's attempts to
choose between a glamorous but dangerous suitor and a safer, less
exciting man who would make the better husband. Usually, however,
he had allowed his heroines to escape from danger. By the end of the
story they would reject temptation and move, either into a good match
like Alice Vavasor and Glencora M'Cluskie, or into self-sufficient independence like Lily Dale. In *The Prime Minister* he does something
more daring. There is no escape for Emily Wharton. She gets her way,
marries her dangerous man, and has to live with the consequences.

The result is a perceptive but painful study of an unhappy marriage.
Only very belatedly will Trollope be able to turn the romantic narrative
of *The Prime Minister* back towards 'sweetness', and by that time the
circumstances required for a happy ending are both improbable and
uncomfortable. A violent suicide and a dead baby are needed before
Emily can embark on a second courtship as a suitably unencumbered
widow. And if a second marriage of this kind is less troubling for modern readers than it seems to have been for Trollope's contemporaries,
we are likely to be more disturbed than they were by the anti-Semitic
quality of the book.

---

[4] *Autobiography*, 317.   [5] *Critical Heritage*, 425.
[6] *The Letters of Anthony Trollope*, ed. N. J. Hall, 2 vols. (Stanford, Calif.: Stanford
University Press, 1983), ii. 687.

Emily's father, Abel Wharton, does not hesitate to express his dislike of his daughter's unsuitable boyfriend in racial terms. Lopez is a 'swarthy son of Judah' (p. 30) and a 'Jew-boy' (p. 34). He is 'a "nasty foreigner", and probably of Jewish descent' (p. 97), 'a greasy Jew adventurer out of the gutter' (p. 111). For John Fletcher he is 'a greasy, black foreigner' (p. 125). In the view of John's mother, old Mrs Fletcher, Lopez is 'a black Portuguese nameless Jew', with, 'a bright eye, and a hook nose, and a glib tongue' (p. 120). Even for Lady Glencora, who initially finds him attractive, he is 'half foreigner half Jew' (p. 585).

Though remarks of this kind are disturbingly frequent, they are the reported views of characters within the novel, not the opinions of its author. Trollope shared many of the customary prejudices of his class and era. But it is hard to convict him, specifically, of anti-Semitism. In *Nina Balatka* (1866), he had used a sympathetic account of the courtship and marriage of a Christian woman and a Jewish man as his main plot. Within the Palliser series there are hints that Phineas Finn's delightful wife, Marie Goesler, is Jewish. In *The Prime Minister*, the authorial voice refers directly to Lopez's 'race' only once (p. 167), and in circumstances where it might well be disapproving of him, not as a Jew, but as the Portuguese he acknowledges himself to be ('some inferior Latin race' as Abel Wharton puts it on p. 109). It was foreigners in general, rather than Jews in particular, that Englishmen of Trollope's generation were accustomed to regard as lesser breeds.

In fact, the question of whether Lopez is, or is not, Jewish remains unsettled throughout the book. His comparison of himself with 'the Israelites' who 'despoiled the Egyptians' (p. 404) proves nothing beyond his knowledge of the Bible, and when he likens himself to Shylock (p. 353) his business partner dismisses the idea as ridiculous; earlier in the same chapter Lopez has allusively compared himself to Shakespeare's Christian merchant Antonio, rather than to his Jewish usurer. When Sir Alured Wharton remarks that Lopez is 'a nasty Jew-looking man', Arthur Fletcher replies, 'He's not that, Sir Alured. He's a handsome man, with a fine voice;—dark, and not just like an Englishman' (p. 113). The tendency on the part of those who dislike him to see him as a Jew is a reflection, in other words, less of his actual ethnicity than of the society in which he moves. Trollope's brand of dispassionate realism, with its rejection of preaching and polemic (or what we might nowadays call political correctness), requires him to depict the anti-Semitic temper of English middle-class society in the second half of the nineteenth century accurately and without comment. The result is true to life. But it is also unpleasant, and has the unfortunate effect of coarsening the presentation of the figure who is, despite the doubts expressed about him by Trollope and his reviewers, much the most interesting character in the novel.

In literal terms, Lopez is a financial speculator. Today he would probably be running a hedge fund, or spread-betting on the performance of the equity, commodity, and currency indices. In the financial industry of the 1870s, he is limited to taking heavily leveraged, long-only positions in the commodities market, buying cargoes of jute, guano, Kauri gum, sulphur, and the African tree bark used to make 'Bios', in the expectation of significant price rises between purchase and delivery. In Chapter 43 he explicitly regrets the fact that derivatives have not yet been invented (though he does not, of course, use that word), since it would be more convenient to trade in what we now call 'futures' than to own actual consignments of raw materials:

> If I buy a ton of coffee and keep it six weeks, why do I buy it and keep it, and why does the seller sell it instead of keeping it? The seller sells it because he thinks he can do best by parting with it now at a certain price. I buy it because I think I can make money by keeping it. It is just the same as though we were to back our opinions. He backs the fall. I back the rise. You needn't have coffee and you needn't have guano to do this. Indeed the possession of the coffee or the guano is only a very clumsy addition to the trouble of your profession. (p. 332)

More than a century ahead of his time ('the world was dull and would not learn the tricks of trade as taught by Ferdinand Lopez'), he backs his judgement with borrowed money and seems, initially, to have been doing so with great success.

An intelligent man, he has been educated at an English private school, rather than one of the 'public schools' favoured by the gentry and professional classes, and at a German university. As a consequence, he is a 'thorough linguist' (p. 32), able to operate confidently in the increasingly globalized (as we would now say) world of commerce. After training with a firm of London stockbrokers, he works as a private trader, though with so little capital that he relies on credit to back his deals. His pursuit of Emily Wharton is not, Trollope insists, merely a matter of financial calculation: 'In very truth he loved the girl and reverenced her' (p. 21). There is affection here, and a strong mutual attraction. But he has, none the less, a perfectly reasonable expectation that a wife from such a background will come with a substantial dowry. This money would give him the capital base he needs to become a more effective player in the commodity markets. His letter to Mr Wharton about his business affairs in Chapter 46 is (deliberately) far from clear. But it does suggest the relatively small scale on which he has hitherto been operating. At this point he is involved in speculative ventures totalling £26,000, yet it is hard to see how he could possibly make more than twelve or thirteen hundred pounds of profit from them. Half of the investment (£13,000) belongs to his partner, Sextus Parker, who has provided the only capital involved. Lopez's share is entirely borrowed so, even if the cargoes rise in value (as he hopes) to 'more than £30,000' (p. 349), there is not a great deal left once he has both repaid his loans and paid the interest on them. Given the risks involved, this is a modest return, and one can quite see why Lopez wishes to acquire more capital and enlarge the scope of his dealings. In the event—though rather improbably given the way in which the risk has sensibly been spread across a wide range of different commodities—every single one of the cargoes mentioned in this letter appears to fall in value, and Lopez is ruined.

Trollope can rightly be accused of not saying enough about Lopez's commercial failure. At the beginning of the novel he lives in a flat in Westminster, dresses exquisitely, has his own brougham, rides a fine horse, hunts in the winter, belongs to a good, if not quite top-notch, club, and, it seems, actually pays his tailor. By Chapter 58 he is penniless. He had not, of course, received the dowry he had hoped for. But that, in itself, does not explain the collapse of his financial career, In Chapter 54 we are told, rather feebly, that 'everything had gone badly with him since his marriage' (p. 409). A conscientious writer of realist novels needs to say a little more than that about the working life of his protagonist.

At a symbolic rather than realistic level, however, Trollope gives a full and fascinating account of Ferdinand Lopez. He is the orphan child of 'an English lady' (p. 27) and a Portuguese father who was 'little better than a travelling pedlar' (p. 443), both of whom died before he was old enough to know them. Educated at an English school, with the fees paid by 'an old gentleman who was not related to him' (p. 9), he has 'always belonged to the Church of England' (p. 29). But he has no relatives, an unfamiliar profession, and a foreign name. As such, he is an outsider—a man who moves confidently in English upper-middle-class and aristocratic society without ever feeling wholly part of it. Some critics have linked him to the heroic rebels and outsiders of nineteenth-century European fiction: Stendhal's Julien Sorel, Turgenev's Bazarov, or Dostoevsky's Raskolnikov. He can also be seen as an anticipation of the 'hollow men' of T. S. Eliot, alienated from traditional values but unable to replace them with anything but sensuality and materialism.

Lopez's unusual upbringing certainly means that he has missed the moral education supposedly provided by the (otherwise rather impractical) classical and theological syllabus of Victorian public schools and universities. Nor, as an orphan, has he absorbed such values at his mother's knee. For John Fletcher, in Chapter 16, 'He's too clever, too cosmopolitan, —a sort of man whitewashed of all prejudices' (p. 124). Trollope's own way of putting it is to insist that Lopez is not a 'gentleman'. Emily Wharton, herself a rebel, is attracted to him for that very reason:

She had once ventured to form a doctrine for herself, to preach to herself a sermon of her own, and to tell herself that this gift of gentle blood and of gentle nurture, of which her father thought so much, to which something of divinity was attributed down in Herefordshire, was after all but a weak, spiritless quality. It could exist without intellect, without heart, and with very moderate culture. (pp. 234–5)

Trollope's purpose, in the love plot of *The Prime Minister*, is to correct this heretical assumption. 'Though this man had lived nearly all his life in England,' we are told in Chapter 43, 'he had not quite acquired that knowledge of the way in which things are done which is so general among men of a certain class' (p. 327). In Chapter 58 that ignorance is reformulated as emptiness:

He had no inner appreciation whatsoever of what was really good or what was really bad in a man's conduct . . . In a sense he was what is called a gentleman. He knew how to speak, and how to look, how to use a knife and fork, how to dress himself, and how to walk. But he had not the faintest notion of the feelings of a gentleman. (p. 440)

Lopez is Trollope's uncomfortable image of a human being who behaves spontaneously, lacking the supposedly instinctual, though actually learnt, value system of the society in which he lives. Morally, as well as commercially, he is ahead of his time.

Lopez confirms that judgement by expressing his own understanding of himself in disturbingly material ways. In Chapter 60 he uses the relatively conventional analogy of a gambling game:

Fate was against him. He saw no reason why he should not have had the aces and kings continually, especially as fate had given him perhaps more than his share of them at first. He had, however, lost rubber after rubber,—not paying his stakes for some of the last rubbers lost,—till the players would play with him no longer. The misfortune might have happened to any man;—but it had happened to him. (p. 456)

In Chapter 54 he sees his life more originally and at a deeper, more metaphorical level, as a mere business enterprise:

should he cut his throat and have done at once with all his troubles, acknowledging to himself that his career had been a failure, and that, therefore, it might be brought with advantage to an end? 'After all,' said he to himself, 'that may be the best way of winding up a bankrupt concern.' (p. 411)

Human existence, in this post-religious understanding, is of no more significance than a temporary legal and commercial arrangement.

A character who can internalize or embody an idea in this way is clearly not the product merely of realistic observation. So it should come as no surprise that Trollope's sources for *The Prime Minister* were, in part, very literary. There is, of course, a widespread assumption that Trollope was a naive realist: Virginia Woolf argued that he gave us 'the same sort of refreshment and delight we get from seeing something actually happen in the street below'.[7] For Henry James, in 1866, he was 'a good observer' but 'literally nothing else'.[8] But Trollope's mode of realism was actually a rather more complex one than this suggests: 'the realistic', he insisted in his book on Thackeray, 'must not be true,—but just so far removed from truth as to suit the erroneous idea of truth which the reader may be supposed to entertain'.[9] As a consequence, he derived his plots and characters from books, as well as from looking out of the window. Lopez is, in part, a Byronic hero—who plays on Lizzie Eustace's well-known weakness for Byron's corsairs by attempting to seduce her with a quotation from *The Bride of Abydos*. Like Byron's Conrad (in *The Corsair*), he is a social and racial outsider who combines sexual allure with a piratical morality.

Trollope's most persistent literary enthusiasm, however, was for what the character John Fletcher, in Chapter 16, calls 'the old plays' (p. 122). He had a large collection of Elizabethan and Jacobean dramatic texts, and read them frequently and closely. His *Autobiography* (chiefly written in 1875–6) concludes with a revealing account of this consuming interest: 'Of late years . . . I have found my greatest pleasure in our old English dramatists,—not from any excessive love of their work, which often irritates me by its want of truth to nature, even while it charms me by its language,—but from curiosity in searching their

---

[7] Virginia Woolf, 'Phases of Fiction', in *The Essays of Virginia Woolf*, ed. Andrew McNeillie and Stuart N. Clarke, 5 vols. (London: The Hogarth Press, 1986–2009), v. 42.

[8] Henry James, review of *The Belton Estate*, in *The Nation*, 4 Jan. 1866 (*Critical Heritage*, 258).

[9] Anthony Trollope, *Thackeray* (London: Macmillan, 1895), 185.

plots and examining their characters.'[10] Between 1866 and 1882 he read
more than 270 such dramas, annotating his copies as he did so. In 1871
he took a volume of Shakespeare with him on his voyage to Australia
and wrote notes on twenty-eight of the plays. In 1874, the year in which
he was writing *The Prime Minister*, he read fifty-five 'old plays', including work by Webster, Tourneur, Bale, Chapman, Marmion, Shirley,
Middleton, and Marston. But his chief preoccupation at this date was
with Francis Beaumont and John Fletcher. He had read the 1647 Folio
of their *Comedies and Tragedies* between 1850 and 1853. Now, in
December 1873 he turned to Beaumont and Fletcher again, in a copy
of Alexander Dyce's modern edition of their *Works*. By December
1874, Trollope had read and annotated no fewer than forty-seven of
the plays which it contained.[11]

The text which seems to have been particularly important for the
composition of *The Prime Minister* was the play *Women Pleased* by
the dramatist John Fletcher (whose name Trollope appears to have
borrowed for his drama-loving character), first performed about 1620.
Though Trollope's summary endnote is dated '23 October 1874',
Geoffrey Harvey dates the marginal annotations of the play to
23 March 1874 and notes that he 'began to write *The Prime Minister*
on 2 April 1874, just ten days later, while the details of character
and plot were still fresh in his mind'.[12] One of the chief characters of
Women Pleased is 'Lopez, *A sordid Usurer, the jealous Husband of
Isabella*'.[13] Though his Spanish or Portuguese name marks him out as
an alien in the otherwise Italian setting of the play, Fletcher's Lopez is
not Jewish, and he is neither elderly nor unattractive: in the eventual
comic resolution of this plot he and his wife depart happily to bed
together. But he has married Isabella for her fortune and uses it to
build (like Trollope's Lopez) a stock of goods from distant and exotic
locations:

[10] *Autobiography*, 366–7.

[11] See Elizabeth R. Epperly, *Anthony Trollope's Notes on the Old Drama* (Victoria,
British Columbia: English Literary Studies, University of Victoria, 1988). Most of
Trollope's copies of Elizabethan and Jacobean plays are now in the Folger Shakespeare
Library, Washington DC. His copy of the 1647 Beaumont and Fletcher Folio is in the
Shakespeare Institute, Stratford-upon-Avon, and the catalogue of his library made in
1874 is in the Victoria and Albert Museum: on these see *Notes and Queries*, 204 (Apr.
1959) and 195 (Oct. 1950).

[12] Geoffrey Harvey, *The Art of Anthony Trollope* (London: Weidenfeld & Nicolson,
1980), 33. Harvey is citing Folger Library Marginalia, PR2421 D8 1843 As. Col., *The
Works of Beaumont and Fletcher*, ed. A. Dyce, 11 vols. (London, 1843–6), iv. 94.

[13] John Fletcher, *Women Pleased*, ed. Hans Walter Gabler, in Fredson Bowers, gen. ed.,
The Dramatic Works in the Beaumont and Fletcher Canon (Cambridge, CUP), v (1982), 448.

> Thus do I study to preserve my fortune,
> And hatch with care at home the wealth that Saints me.
> Here's Rubies of *Bengala*, rich, rich, glorious;
> These Diamonds of *Ormus* bought for little,
> Here vented at the price of Princes Ransomes;
> How bright they shine like constellations,
> The South seas treasure here, Pearle, faire and orient.

These are the seventeenth-century equivalents of jute, guano, Kauri gum, and Bios, bought 'for little' in the speculative hope that they will, in due course, sell for 'Princes Ransomes'. Like Trollope's Lopez, Fletcher's anti-hero combines a public reputation for wealth with a miserly private meanness: his wife lives like 'a Slave subject to wants and hungers' and his half-starved comic servant is called Penurio. Similarly, when Emily Wharton, as Mrs Lopez, spends a summer holiday at the seaside, her husband insists 'on a front seat in the Dovercourt church, paying half a guinea more for it'. But when he goes back to London on business, he leaves her 'absolutely penniless', without money to pay 'the butcher and baker' (p. 355). Even the wish by Fletcher's Lopez that he had 'Ferret-claw'd' a rival finds a curious echo in Mrs Parker's dismayed assertion, later in the same chapter (p. 356), that 'men, when they get on at money-making,—or money-losing, which makes 'em worse,—are like tigers clawing one another'.[14] Isabella eventually brings her domestic tyrant to heel by making him jealous. She allows him to catch her with a 'lover' who proves to be her brother in disguise, and a humiliated Lopez promises to be a more generous and less suspicious husband in the future.

At that point Fletcher's comedy might seem to have little in common with the grim domestic tragedy of *The Prime Minister*. If Trollope's interest in Jacobean drama consisted, in his own words, of 'searching their plots and examining their characters', perhaps only the latter process was relevant here? In fact, it was not just the name and nature of Lopez which Trollope took from *Women Pleased*, but a great deal of thematic material as well. As its title indicates, Fletcher's play is concerned with the question of what women want. Isabella seeks more power in her household, and greater access to her own fortune. In the main plot, Princess Belvidere, daughter of the Duchess of Florence, wishes to avoid an arranged match with the Duke of Siena, and to marry the man she loves, Silvio. Both women achieve their aims, and the argument is reinforced with some material borrowed from Chaucer's 'The Wife of Bath's Tale'. Silvio is condemned to death unless he can

[14] Ibid. 454, 455, 490.

answer the question of what it is that 'women . . . most desire'. The answer, of course, is 'mastry' (mastery), or 'to have their will'.[15] Belvidere, disguised as an aged 'Hag', reveals this to Silvio on condition that he marries her. He reluctantly consents, she removes her disguise, and all ends happily.

This topic of female will (or 'women pleased') is one with which Trollope had been concerned throughout the Palliser series. Alice Vavasor, in chapter 11 of *Can You Forgive Her?* (1864–5), had been

thinking . . . till her mind had become filled with some undefined idea of the importance to her of her own life. What should a woman do with her life? There had arisen round her a flock of learned ladies asking that question, to whom it seems that the proper answer has never yet occurred.

Trollope combines a sympathetic interest in the inner lives of women who believe they have a right to ask this question with (in the same chapter) a very traditional answer to it—in some ways a more reactionary answer than Fletcher had given, in different social circumstances, in the early seventeenth century:

Fall in love, marry the man, have two children, and live happy ever afterwards. I maintain that answer has as much wisdom in it as any other that can be given;—or perhaps more.

In *The Prime Minister* Emily Wharton defies patriarchal authority and asserts her 'will', not by seeking an alternative to marriage, but by insisting on marrying a man of whom her father profoundly disapproves. In Chapter 21 Lady Glencora, another female rebel, correctly predicts the outcome of this contest: 'the old gentleman may as well give way at once. Of course his daughter will be too many for him' (p. 162). Emily duly achieves what Fletcher had called 'mastry' over the wishes of her family, and becomes Mrs Lopez. But is this a good thing? Abel Wharton's objection to Lopez had been an instance of mere prejudice, an instinctual, partly racial distaste. But the novel shows that prejudice to be substantially correct. Lopez turns out to be (or develops into) a penniless adventurer who lacks even the gentlemanly code which has traditionally tempered the exercise of male authority. Emily is left bitterly regretting her failure to obey.

Lady Glencora is another, more interesting study of the same problem. A wealthy woman in her own right, she had flirted with the handsome wastrel Burgo Fitzgerald before being safely married off (in *The Small House at Allington*) to the respectable but unromantic

[15] Fletcher, *Women Pleased*, 529, 519.

Plantagenet Palliser. Now, at last, she finds herself with an opportunity for the exercise of her long-suppressed 'will'. She is the Prime Minister's wife. She will be a great political hostess in the tradition of Lady Holland, Lady Lansdowne, and Lady Palmerston:

She was not only rich but she had a popularity that was exclusively her own. The new Prime Minister and the new Prime Minister's wife should entertain after a fashion that had never yet been known even among the nobility of England. Both in town and country those great mansions should be kept open which were now rarely much used because she had found them dull, cold, and comfortless. In London there should not be a Member of Parliament whom she would not herself know and influence by her flattery and grace,— or if there were men whom she could not influence, they should live as men tabooed and unfortunate. (p. 46)

Palliser (by now the Duke of Omnium) reluctantly agrees, in part because he acknowledges, in his characteristically scrupulous way, that the money she proposes to spend is, by origin, her own:

Though they were to squander her fortune,—the money which she had brought,—. . . they might do so without touching the Palliser property. Of that she was quite sure. And the squandering was to be all for his glory,—so that he might retain his position as a popular Prime Minister . . . 'Of course we are spending money,' she said. 'If you give me a hint to hold my hand, I will hold it.'
   He had looked at her, and read it all in her face. 'God knows,' he said, 'you've a right to do it if it pleases you.' (p. 79)

The town house in Carlton House Terrace and the uncomfortable mansion in Barsetshire, Gatherum Castle, are duly thrown open for lavish receptions and parties. Initially these performances 'please' her. But the results are very disappointing. The Duke, who hates fuss, fails to attend his own social events and describes the extravagance as 'vulgarity' (p. 139). The Duchess's handling of Palliser's key political allies is tactless, her choice of guests ill-judged. Above all, she strays across the line which separates backstairs influence from direct political intervention by encouraging Lopez to stand for parliament in a constituency which her husband has insisted should no longer be treated as one of the Palliser family's pocket boroughs. The gutter press gets hold of the story and almost destroys the Prime Minister with it. Once again, as in Emily Wharton's case, the expression of female will seems to be condemned.
   What makes the Glencora plot the more interesting of the two is the way in which this condemnation of the Duchess is qualified by a corresponding criticism of the Duke. In many ways his judgement is

better than hers. But he is not an ideal Prime Minister, especially in the difficult circumstances of a coalition government. He lacks the human touch, the hail-fellow-well-met affability, the ability to compromise, which are needed to hold together a group of ministers who lack a common political doctrine. In this context, Glencora's failed endeavours are not entirely inappropriate. When she first thinks of herself as 'a Prime Ministress' in Chapter 28 (p. 215), there is a hint of impropriety about the term. But when the topic recurs in Chapter 56 we are prepared to take the idea much more seriously:

Her heart was full, and out of a full heart the mouth speaks. 'They should have made me Prime Minister, and have let him be Chancellor of the Exchequer. I begin to see the ways of Government now. I could have done all the dirty work. I could have given away garters and ribbons, and made my bargains while giving them . . . I could brazen out a job and let the "People's Banner" and the Slides make their worst of it. And I think I could make myself popular with my party, and do the high-flowing patriotic talk for the benefit of the Provinces.' (pp. 429–30)

The impulsive and poorly educated Lady Glencora is no Margaret Thatcher. But we do at least begin to glimpse here a new possibility for what women might 'do with their lives'.

It remains the case that Trollope is reacting against the cheerful celebration of women's right to 'be pleased' in Fletcher's play, rather than endorsing it. But *Women Pleased* is still an important stimulus for the novel. Christopher Herbert, discussing Trollope's work as a whole rather than just this book, remarks that it 'comes as a surprise to discover just how pervasive are the arch-realist Trollope's borrowings from the artificial and extravagant world of Jacobean comedy'.[16] And if Fletcher helped to shape the sexual politics of *The Prime Minister*, it was Trollope's Shakespeare reading in 1871 which gave depth and definition to his parliamentary plot.

Glencora's attempts to make her husband a more ruthlessly ambitious politician are a modern, serio-comic version of Lady Macbeth's endeavours to push her husband onto the throne of Scotland. This is a parallel of which the Duchess of Omnium is fully conscious:

she felt in regard to him somewhat as did Lady Macbeth towards her lord.

> 'What thou would'st highly,
> That would'st thou holily.'

[16] Christopher Herbert, *Trollope and Comic Pleasure* (Chicago: University of Chicago Press, 1987), 6.

She knew him to be full of scruples, unable to bend when aught was to be got by bending, unwilling to domineer when men might be brought to subjection only by domination. (p. 45)

The idea is repeated, more explicitly, in Chapter 11:

'I feel myself to be a Lady Macbeth, prepared for the murder of any Duncan or any Daubeny who may stand in my lord's way. In the meantime, like Lady Macbeth herself, we must attend to the banqueting. Her lord appeared and misbehaved himself; my lord won't show himself at all,—which I think is worse.' (p. 81)

Three years later, after the fall of Omnium's coalition ministry, she is still thinking in these terms:

'I was the Lady Macbeth of the occasion all over;—whereas he was so scrupulous, so burdened with conscience! As for me I would have taken it by any means. Then it was that the old Duke played the part of the three witches to a nicety. Well, there hasn't been any absolute murder, and I haven't quite gone mad.' (p. 609)

It should, I think, come as no surprise that the note which Trollope made on *Macbeth* on 28 July 1871 should have read, 'I regard Macbeth as being on the whole the finest play of Shakespeare.'[17]

If Glencora is Lady Macbeth, her husband is based on two rather different Shakespearean characters. On 22 July 1871 Trollope had read and annotated *Julius Caesar*:

In this play is perhaps the finest character ever drawn by Shakespeare. Nowhere is greater skill in delineation and a closer knowledge of human nature shewn than in Brutus. The honesty of the man, and the ill adaptation of the man's honesty to political exigencies and the purposes of conspiracy would hardly seem to be a subject for poetry; but the poetry is as grand as the character-painting is minute.

Antony's last speech is a magnificent description of Brutus—'This was the noblest Roman of them all . . . Nature might stand up; And say to all the world There was a man.'[18]

This corresponds very closely with Trollope's account, in his *Autobiography*, of what he was seeking to make of the character of Plantagenet Palliser:

The Statesman of whom I was thinking . . . should have rank, and intellect, and parliamentary habits . . . and . . . unblemished, inextinguishable, inexhaustible love of country . . . But he should be scrupulous, and, as being

---

[17] Epperly, *Trollope's Notes on the Old Drama*, 120.
[18] Ibid.

scrupulous, weak . . . I think that Plantagenet Palliser, Duke of Omnium, is a perfect gentleman.[19]

But since Palliser is not involved in a 'conspiracy', Brutus alone is not a sufficient model. In Chapter 19, having been accused of 'vulgarity' by her husband, Glencora indignantly invokes another precedent: Coriolanus, the aristocratic leader who lacked the ability to stoop to the vulgar contrivances required of democratic politicians:

When a man wants to be Prime Minister he has to submit to vulgarity, and must give up his ambition if the task be too disagreeable to him. The Duchess thought that that had been understood, at any rate ever since the days of Coriolanus. (p. 145)

Trollope's note on *Coriolanus*, written on 27 June 1871, makes his admiration plain:

The conception of the character of Coriolanus is magnificently grand . . . Coriolanus, because of the greatness of the great Roman's character, is a very great play.[20]

The Duke of St Bungay congratulates Palliser on the fact that his coalition has 'Carried on the Queen's Government prosperously for three years' (p. 549). But this has been a merely 'caretaker' administration, unable to pass any significant legislation. As a consequence, its leader cannot escape the feeling that he has been a 'fainéant' Prime Minister. Too good a man for the sordid reality of the political process, he is, like Brutus and Coriolanus, a magnificent failure.

These references to Jacobean drama hold the novel together, and give it intellectual depth. Though mid-twentieth-century critics, anxious to rescue Trollope from his reputation as a cheerfully pedestrian realist, tended to do so by stressing the 'pessimism' of his later novels, artistry, of the kind shown in this complex network of literary allusions, is perhaps an even more important quality of Trollope's best work. The text remains, none the less, rather sombre. A dark love story and a political narrative of disappointment produce a book which lacks, as the original reviewers complained, the 'delight' which readers expected from Trollope. Tolstoy's view of the novel as 'splendid' reminds us that this effect may be the result, not of negligence or misjudgement, but of a greater artistic seriousness. It is in *The Prime Minister* that Trollope comes closest to writing a novel of political ideas, rather than simply a novel about people living in a political

[19] *Autobiography*, 359–61.
[20] Epperly, *Trollope's Notes on the Old Drama*, 119.

environment: in Chapter 68 he puts into the mouth of the Duke of Omnium a reasoned defence of his own Whig, or Liberal-Conservative, political creed. And the uniformity of tone could itself be seen as an anticipation of the newly ambitious conception of the novel as an art form which avant-garde critics began to express in the 1870s.

Though Henry James would not publish his famous essay 'The Art of the Novel' until 1884, he had started to formulate some of its key ideas rather earlier. In his review of *Middlemarch*, in 1873, he described George Eliot's novel as 'a treasure-house of details, but . . . an indifferent whole'. A novel, he suggested, should not be 'a mere chain of episodes, broken into accidental lengths and unconscious of the influence of a plan'. Rather, it should be 'an organized, moulded, balanced composition, gratifying the reader with a sense of design and construction'.[21] English novels had tended to be 'large loose baggy monsters'.[22] What they needed was unity of effect. James's new criterion would be immensely influential for more than a hundred years, both in the 'art novels' written by James and his imitators in the late nineteenth century, and in the work of Modernists like Conrad and Virginia Woolf. The eventual reaction against this view would be led by Peter Garrett, who in 1980 rightly argued that the search for unity could be misleading and unnecessary. We can enjoy the 'play of differences', the decentred 'dialogical form' of the Victorian multiplot novel as much as the single impression created by its art-novel alternative.[23]

But even Garrett allowed that the multiple plots of *The Prime Minister* (written in 1874, the year after James's *Middlemarch* review) were unusually integrated. Here there is a 'full doubling . . . which produces greater complexity of structure and meaning', with 'detailed parallels' between the different narratives.[24] The Duke of Omnium's inability to reach acceptable compromises with his coalition partners, for example, is echoed in Abel Wharton's failure to make a sensible settlement with his son-in-law over his daughter's dowry. The Palliser marriage and the Lopez marriage (both, in part, mercenary arrangements) have a curious mirror-image resemblance. Above all, Lopez's experience as an outsider is thrown into vivid relief by its juxtaposition with the career of the ultimate insider, the Duke of Omnium: immensely rich, immensely aristocratic, and the holder of the highest office in the

[21] *The Galaxy*, Mar. 1873.
[22] Henry James, Preface to the New York edn. (1908) of *The Tragic Muse*.
[23] See Peter K. Garrett, *The Victorian Multiplot Novel: Studies in Dialogical Form* (New Haven: Yale University Press, 1980), 181, 9–10.
[24] Ibid. 216.

land, yet ultimately unsatisfied by what he has achieved. In Garrett's words, again, 'Without blurring the distinction between Lopez's faults and Palliser's virtues, Trollope uses both to present an ironic portrait of a world whose social and political conventions enforce a complacent mediocrity that excludes them.'[25]

In his next two novels Trollope would recover his capacity to 'delight' and thus restore his damaged popularity. But were these entertaining texts better than *The Prime Minister*? He did not think so:

The American Senator and *Popenjoy* have appeared, each with fair success. Neither of them have encountered that reproach which, in regard to *The Prime Minister*, seemed to tell me that my work as a novelist should be brought to a close. And yet I feel assured that they are very inferior to *The Prime Minister*.[26]

In *The Prime Minister* Trollope had been taking risks. Rather than repeating his successful formulas, he was innovating and, in the process, coming very close to the most avant-garde conception of the novel in his era. Without sacrificing his customary psychological shrewdness and delicacy, or abandoning his capacity to construct absorbing plots, he produced a highly integrated novel of ideas. In *The Prime Minister* Trollope was working at the top of his powers. It is a book for when one wishes to be challenged, rather than merely charmed, by a novel.

[25] Garrett, *The Victorian Multiplot Novel*, 217.   [26] *Autobiography*, 362.

NOTE ON THE TEXT

TROLLOPE wrote *The Prime Minister* between 2 April and 15 September 1874. His worksheet for the novel is in the Bodleian Library, Oxford (MS Don. c.9–10) and is summarized (with the permission of the copyright holder, Lloyds Bank plc, Trust Division) by Juliet McMaster in the footnotes to her *Trollope's Palliser Novels: Theme and Pattern* (1978), 228. He planned to write a little over three chapters a week for twenty-four weeks and kept to that schedule. The manuscript is in the Arents Collection in the New York Public Library.

Trollope returned the last of the corrected proofs to his publisher, Chapman & Hall, on 26 February 1875, reminding them as he did so that 'The work is to come out in 8 parts, and each part is to contain 10 chapters . . . The first part is to appear in October' (*Letters*, ii. 650). In the event, Chapman & Hall issued the first of the eight part-issues in November 1875 and it ran until June 1876. Each monthly part contained ten chapters and cost five shillings: these were the units in which Trollope expected his original audience to read the novel. This unusual format of 'half-volume parts' had been invented by G. H. Lewes for George Eliot's *Middlemarch* in 1871–2 (though the parts here were initially bimonthly) and would be used again for *Daniel Deronda* in 1876. It was convenient for novels so long that they would require subsequent book publication in four volumes, rather than the usual three, and suited Eliot and Trollope at a stage in their careers when they wished to construct their novels in extended sections. Lewes also thought that it would make piracy by unauthorized American publishers more difficult (see John Sutherland, 'Marketing *Middlemarch*', in his *Victorian Novelists and Publishers* (Chicago: University of Chicago Press, 1976)). Trollope would not, however, use the format again: though he originally wrote *The Duke's Children* in 1876 at four-volume length, he would cut it down before publication.

The Prime Minister appeared as a book, in four volumes, in May or June 1876, with the chapters freshly numbered from 1 to 20 in each volume. In the same year it was published in four volumes by Tauchnitz of Leipzig, and in one volume by Harper in New York and Belford Brothers in Toronto. The text appears not to have been reset between part-issue and book publication and 'the proof-reading was not very stringent' (see Michael Sadleir, *Trollope: A Bibliography* (London: Constable, 1928), 155, noting misprints common to both versions).

In 1877 Chapman & Hall reissued it in one volume; in the same year it was pirated in both Philadelphia and New York, and published in Russian in St Petersburg as *Premer Ministr*. It also appeared, in Trollope's lifetime, in Chapman & Hall's Select Library of Fiction (no. 362) in 1877 and 1878, and in Ward Lock's Select Library of Fiction (no. 28) in 1881. The text used in this edition is that established for the Oxford Trollope, first published under the general editorship of Michael Sadleir and Frederick Page in 1952, with a few obvious errors silently corrected.

SELECT BIBLIOGRAPHY

Life and Letters

Trollope, Anthony, *An Autobiography*, ed. Michael Sadleir and Frederick Page, with introd. and notes by P. D. Edwards, Oxford World's Classics (Oxford: Oxford University Press, 1999).

The Letters of Anthony Trollope, ed. N. John Hall, 2 vols. (Stanford, Calif.: Stanford University Press, 1983).

Glendinning, Victoria, *Trollope* (London: Hutchinson, 1992).

Hall, N. John, *Trollope: A Biography* (Oxford: Clarendon Press, 1991).

Mullen, Richard, *Anthony Trollope: A Victorian in His World* (London: Duckworth, 1990).

Super, R. H., *The Chronicler of Barsetshire: A Life of Anthony Trollope* (Ann Arbor: University of Michigan Press, 1988).

Information about Trollope's Work and Context

Clark, J. W., *The Language and Style of Anthony Trollope* (London: André Deutsch, 1975).

Collins, Philip, *Trollope's London* (Leicester: University of Leicester Victorian Studies Centre, 1982).

Epperly, Elizabeth R., *Anthony Trollope's Notes on the Old Drama* (Victoria, British Columbia: English Literary Studies, University of Victoria, 1988).

Garrett, Peter K., *The Victorian Multiplot Novel: Studies in Dialogical Form* (New Haven: Yale University Press, 1980).

Levine, George, *The Realistic Imagination* (Chicago: University of Chicago Press, 1981).

Mullen, Richard, with Munson, James, *The Penguin Companion to Trollope* (London: Penguin, 1996).

Sadleir, Michael, *Trollope: A Bibliography* (London: Constable, 1928; repr. with addenda and corrigenda, 1934).

Skilton, David, *Anthony Trollope and His Contemporaries* (Harlow: Longman, 1972).

——'Schoolboy Latin and the Mid-Victorian Novelist: A Study in Reader Competence', *Browning Institute Studies*, 16 (1988), 39–55.

Smalley, Donald (ed.), *Anthony Trollope: The Critical Heritage* (London: Routledge & Kegan Paul, 1969).

Stone, Donald D., *The Romantic Impulse in Victorian Fiction* (Cambridge, Mass.: Harvard University Press, 1980).

Swingle, L. J., *Romanticism and Anthony Trollope: A Study in the Continuities of Nineteenth-Century Literary Thought* (Ann Arbor: University of Michigan Press, 1990).

Terry, R. C. (ed.), *Oxford Reader's Companion to Trollope* (Oxford: Oxford University Press, 1999).

[Tingay, Lance, Skilton, David, Connolly, Claire, and Edwards, Christopher, (eds.)], *Anthony Trollope: A Collector's Catalogue 1847–1990* (London: The Trollope Society, 1992).

General Critical Studies

apRoberts, Ruth, *Trollope, Artist and Moralist* (published in America as *The Moral Trollope*) (London: Chatto & Windus/Athens, Ohio: Ohio University Press, 1971).

Cockshut, A. O. J., *Anthony Trollope: A Critical Study* (London: Collins, 1955).

Edwards, P. D., *Anthony Trollope: His Art and Scope* (Brighton: Harvester Press, 1978).

Harvey, Geoffrey, *The Art of Anthony Trollope* (London: Weidenfeld & Nicholson, 1980).

Herbert, Christopher, *Trollope and Comic Pleasure* (Chicago: University of Chicago Press, 1987).

Kincaid, James R., *The Novels of Anthony Trollope* (Oxford: Clarendon Press, 1977).

Letwin, Shirley Robin, *The Gentleman in Trollope: Individuality and Moral Conduct* (Cambridge, Mass.: Harvard University Press, 1982).

Nardin, Jane, *Trollope and Victorian Moral Philosophy* (Athens, Ohio: Ohio University Press, 1996).

Polhemus, Robert M., *The Changing World of Anthony Trollope* (Berkeley and Los Angeles: University of California Press, 1968).

Tracy, Robert, *Trollope's Later Novels* (Berkeley and Los Angeles: University of California Press, 1978).

Wright, Andrew, *Anthony Trollope: Dream and Art* (Chicago: Chicago University Press, 1983).

The Palliser Series and 'The Prime Minister'

Briggs, Asa, 'Trollope, Bagehot and the English Constitution', originally in *Cambridge Journal* 5 (1952); repr. in his *Victorian People* (London: Odhams, 1954; Chicago: University of Chicago Press, 1955; London: Pelican Books, 1965).

Butte, George, 'Trollope's Duke of Omnium and "The Pain of History": A Study of the Novelist's Politics', *Victorian Studies*, 24/2 (Winter 1981), 209–27.

Cockshut, A. O. J., 'Trollope's Liberalism', in Tony Bareham (ed.), *Anthony Trollope* (London: Vision Press, 1980).

Delany, Paul, 'Land, Money, and the Jews in the Later Trollope', *Studies in English Literature*, 32 (1992), 765–87.

Halperin, John, *Trollope and Politics: A Study of the Pallisers and Others* (London: Macmillan, 1977).

Jaffe, Audrey, 'Trollope in the Stock Market: Irrational Exuberance and *The Prime Minister*', *Victorian Studies*, 45/1 (2002), 43–64.

McMaster, Juliet, *Trollope's Palliser Novels: Theme and Pattern* (London: Macmillan, 1978).

Mizener, Arthur, 'Anthony Trollope: The Palliser novels', in R. C. Rathburn and M. Steinmann (eds.), *From Jane Austen to Joseph Conrad* (Minneapolis: University of Minnesota Press, 1958).

Pollard, Arthur, *Trollope's Political Novels* (Hull: University of Hull, 1968).

Robbins, Frank E., 'Chronology and History in Trollope's Barset and Parliamentary Novels', *Nineteenth-Century Fiction*, 5/4 (Mar. 1951), 303–16.

Trollope, Anthony, review of Charles Buxton, *The Ideas of the Day on Policy* (London: John Murray, 1866) in *Fortnightly Review*, 3 (15 Jan. 1866), 650–1.

Useful websites

http://www.trollopesociety.org/
http://www.anthonytrollope.com/
http://www.trollope.org/

A CHRONOLOGY OF ANTHONY TROLLOPE

(Selected publications are noted here only; volume publication is given in all cases.)

Life	*Historical and Cultural Background*
1815 (24 April) AT born in London.	Battle of Waterloo and final defeat of Napoleon.
1823 Enters Harrow Boys' School.	Monroe doctrine formulated to protect American interests in relation to Europe.
1825 At school in Sunbury.	Stockton and Darlington Railway, first public railway, opens.
1827 Admitted to Winchester College.	
1830 Back at home in poverty then to Harrow School again.	Accession of William IV in Britain; in France, rioting sees overthrow of the Bourbons and accession of Louis Philippe.
1832	First Reform Act increases electorate to *c*.700,000 men.
1834 Trollope family flee creditors to Bruges; AT takes up clerkship at London Post Office; a period of poverty and an unpromising start to work.	'New Poor Law'; Tolpuddle martyrs (early example of, in effect, trade union membership).
1839	First commercial telegraph in UK.
1841 After much misery, AT is offered the post of deputy postal surveyor's clerk at Banagher, King's county, Ireland; begins to hunt.	British occupation of Hong Kong; Robert Peel becomes Prime Minister.
1843 Begins *The Macdermots of Ballycloran.*	Wordsworth becomes Poet Laureate.
1844 Marries Rose Heseltine from Rotherham (d. 1917).	Factory Act shortens working day, increases minimum hours of schooling.
1845	Great Famine begins in Ireland (–1850).
1846 Henry Merivale Trollope born (d. 1926).	Repeal of Corn Laws, major achievement for free trade; Lord John Russell becomes Prime Minister.
1847 Frederick James Anthony Trollope born (d. 1910); *The Macdermots of Ballycloran.*	Ten Hours Factory Act (cuts working day to 10 hours for women and children).

Life	*Historical and Cultural Background*
1848 *The Kellys and the O'Kellys.*	European revolutions; second Chartist petition.
1850 *La Vendée*, a failure.	Tennyson becomes Poet Laureate; restoration of Catholic ecclesiastical hierarchy.
1851 Working for the Post Office in England.	Great Exhibition, evidence of British dominance in trade.
1852 Suggests the new pillar box for post on the Channel Islands.	Opening of new Palace of Westminster; Earl of Derby becomes Prime Minister followed by Earl of Aberdeen.
1853	Crimean War (–1856).
1854 Post Office surveyor for the north of Ireland: family in Donnybrook.	
1855 *The Warden*, first of the 'Chronicles of Barsetshire'; thereafter, he sets himself writing targets (usually 10,000 words a week).	Abolition of final newspaper tax leads to growth of new journalism and newspaper titles; Palmerston becomes Prime Minister.
1857 *Barchester Towers*, a success.	Indian Mutiny; Matrimonial Causes Act extends availability of divorce.
1858 *Doctor Thorne* (Barsetshire).	Jewish Disabilities Act; abolition of property qualification for MPs; Earl of Derby is Prime Minister, then Palmerston again.
1860 Beginning of instalments of *Framley Parsonage*; moves to London as Post Office surveyor; meets Kate Field, an American woman, in Florence, with whom he forms a strong attachment.	Wilberforce–Huxley debate on evolution.
1861	American Civil War begins.
1862 Elected to Garrick Club.	London Exposition; Lincoln's Emancipation proclamation.
1864 Elected to the Athenaeum. *The Small House at Allington* (Barsetshire, but introduces Plantagenet and Glencora Palliser).	
1864–5 *Can You Forgive Her?* (first of the Palliser novels; vol. 1, Sept. 1864; vol. 2, July 1865).	

Life	Historical and Cultural Background
1865	Abolition of slavery in North America; Earl Russell becomes Prime Minister.
1866	Success with commercial transatlantic cable; Earl of Derby becomes Prime Minister.
1867 *The Last Chronicle of Barset.* Resigns from the Post Office to edit *Saint Pauls: A Monthly Magazine* with illustrations by Millais.	Second Reform Act (further extension of franchise to about 2 million electors).
1868 Defeated as Liberal candidate for Beverley in the General Election.	Trades Union Congress formed; Disraeli becomes Prime Minister followed by Gladstone.
1869 *He Knew He Was Right*; *Phineas Finn* (Palliser).	Suez Canal opened; first issue of *Nature*.
1870 *The Vicar of Bullhampton.*	Forster's Education Act, widely extending provision of primary education; first Married Women's Property Act, granting married women the right to their own earnings and to inherit property in their own name.
1871 Travels in Australasia.	Paris Commune; legalization of Trade Unions.
1872 *The Eustace Diamonds* (Palliser).	
1873 *Phineas Redux* (Palliser); *Australia and New Zealand.*	Financial crisis begins US Long Depression.
1874	First Impressionist Exhibition (Paris); Disraeli becomes Prime Minister.
1875 *The Way We Live Now.*	Third Republic in France; Theosophical Society founded.
1876 *The Prime Minister* (Palliser).	The telephone patented.
1877 *The American Senator.*	
1878 *Is He Popenjoy?*; *South Africa.*	Exposition Universelle (Paris), including arts and machinery.
1879 *Thackeray* in the English Men of Letters series.	
1880 Moves to South Harting, Sussex. *The Duke's Children* (Palliser); *Life of Cicero.*	First Anglo-Boer War (–1881); Gladstone becomes Prime Minister.
1881 *Dr Wortle's School.*	Assassination of US President James Garfield.

Life	Historical and Cultural Background
1882 *Lord Palmerston*; *The Fixed Period*, a futuristic novel. Suffers a stroke; (6 Dec.), dies in nursing home. Buried in Kensal Green (his grave reads: 'He was a loving husband, a loving father, and a true friend'); leaves estate worth £25,892 19s. 3d.	Phoenix Park Murders; Egypt now British protectorate; second Married Women's Property Act allowing married women to own and control their own property.
1883 *Mr Scarborough's Family*; *An Autobiography*.	Death of Richard Wagner.
1887 Publication of AT's brother, Thomas Adolphus Trollope's *What I Remember*, with alternative account of the family upbringing.	

THE PRIME MINISTER

CONTENTS

VOLUME III

VOLUME I

CHAPTER 1
FERDINAND LOPEZ

IT is certainly of service to a man to know who were his grandfathers and who were his grandmothers if he entertain an ambition to move in the upper circles of society, and also of service to be able to speak of them as of persons who were themselves somebodies in their time. No doubt we all entertain great respect for those who by their own energies have raised themselves in the world; and when we hear that the son of a washerwoman has become Lord Chancellor or Archbishop of Canterbury we do, theoretically and abstractedly, feel a higher reverence for such self-made magnate than for one who has been as it were born into forensic or ecclesiastical purple. But not the less must the offspring of the washerwoman have had very much trouble on the subject of his birth, unless he has been, when young as well as when old, a very great man indeed. After the goal has been absolutely reached, and the honour and the titles and the wealth actually won, a man may talk with some humour, even with some affection, of the maternal tub;—but while the struggle is going on, with the conviction strong upon the struggler that he cannot be altogether successful unless he be esteemed a gentleman, not to be ashamed, not to conceal the old family circumstances, not at any rate to be silent, is difficult. And the difficulty is certainly not less if fortunate circumstances rather than hard work and intrinsic merit have raised above his natural place an aspirant to high social position. Can it be expected that such a one when dining with a duchess shall speak of his father's small shop, or bring into the light of day his grandfather's cobbler's awl? And yet it is difficult to be altogether silent! It may not be necessary for any of us to be always talking of our own parentage. We may be generally reticent as to our uncles and aunts, and may drop even our brothers and sisters in our ordinary conversation. But if a man never mentions his belongings among those with whom he lives, he becomes mysterious, and almost open to suspicion. It begins to be known that nobody knows anything of such a man, and even friends become afraid. It is certainly convenient to be able to allude, if it be but once in a year, to some blood relation.

Ferdinand Lopez, who in other respects had much in his circumstances on which to congratulate himself, suffered trouble in his mind respecting his ancestors such as I have endeavoured to describe. He did not know very much himself, but what little he did know he kept altogether to himself. He had no father or mother, no uncle, aunt, brother or sister, no cousin even whom he could mention in a cursory way to his dearest friend. He suffered, no doubt;—but with Spartan consistency he so hid his trouble from the world that no one knew that he suffered. Those with whom he lived, and who speculated often and wondered much as to who he was, never dreamed that the silent man's reticence was a burden to himself. At no special conjuncture of his life, at no period which could be marked with the finger of the observer, did he glaringly abstain from any statement which at the moment might be natural. He never hesitated, blushed, or palpably laboured at concealment; but the fact remained that though a great many men and not a few women knew Ferdinand Lopez very well, none of them knew whence he had come, or what was his family.

He was a man, however, naturally reticent, who never alluded to his own affairs unless in pursuit of some object the way to which was clear before his eyes. Silence therefore on a matter which is common in the mouths of most men was less difficult to him than to another, and the result less embarrassing. Dear old Jones, who tells his friends at the club of every pound that he loses or wins at the races, who boasts of Mary's favours and mourns over Lucy's coldness almost in public, who issues bulletins on the state of his purse, his stomach, his stable, and his debts, could not with any amount of care keep from us the fact that his father was an attorney's clerk, and made his first money by discounting small bills. Everybody knows it, and Jones, who likes popularity, grieves at the unfortunate publicity. But Jones is relieved from a burden which would have broken his poor shoulders, and which even Ferdinand Lopez, who is a strong man, often finds it hard to bear without wincing.

It was admitted on all sides that Ferdinand Lopez was a 'gentleman'. Johnson* says that any other derivation of this difficult word than that which causes it to signify 'a man of ancestry' is whimsical. There are many, who in defining the term for their own use, still adhere to Johnson's dictum;—but they adhere to it with certain unexpressed allowances for possible exceptions. The chances are very much in favour of the well-born man, but exceptions may exist. It was not generally believed that Ferdinand Lopez was well born;—but he was a gentleman. And this most precious rank was acceded to him although he was employed,—or at least had been employed,—on business which does not of itself give such a warrant of position as is supposed to be afforded by the bar and the church, by the military services and by physic. He had been on the Stock Exchange, and still in some manner, not clearly understood by his friends, did business in the City.

At the time with which we are now concerned* Ferdinand Lopez was thirty-three years old, and as he had begun life early he had been long before the world. It was known of him that he had been at a good English private school, and it was reported, on the solitary evidence of one who had there been his schoolfellow, that a rumour was current in the school that his school bills were paid by an old gentleman who was not related to him. Thence at the age of seventeen he had been sent to a German University,* and at the age of twenty-one had appeared in London, in a stockbroker's office, where he was soon known as an accomplished linguist, and as a very clever fellow,—precocious, not given to many pleasures, apt for work, but hardly trustworthy by employers, not as being dishonest, but as having a taste for being a master rather than a servant. Indeed his period of servitude was very short. It was not in his nature to be active on behalf of others. He was soon active for himself, and at one time it was supposed that he was making a fortune. Then it was known that he had left his regular business, and it was supposed that he had lost all that he had ever made or had ever possessed. But nobody, not even his own bankers or his own lawyer,—not even the old woman who looked after his linen,—ever really knew the state of his affairs.

He was certainly a handsome man,—his beauty being of a sort which men are apt to deny and women to admit lavishly. He was nearly six feet tall, very dark, and very thin, with regular, well-cut features indicating little to the physiognomist unless it be the great gift of self-possession. His hair was cut short, and he wore no beard beyond an absolutely black moustache. His teeth were perfect in form and whiteness,—a characteristic which, though it may be a valued item in a general catalogue of personal attraction, does not generally recommend a man to the unconscious judgement of his acquaintance. But about the mouth and chin of this man there was a something of softness, perhaps in the play of the lips, perhaps in the dimple, which in some degree lessened the feeling of hardness which was produced by the square brow and bold, unflinching, combative eyes. They who knew him and liked him were reconciled by the lower face. The greater number who knew him and did not like him felt and resented,—even though in nine cases out of ten they might express no resentment even to themselves,—the pugnacity of his steady glance.

For he was essentially one of those men who are always, in the inner workings of their minds, defending themselves and attacking others. He could not give a penny to a woman at a crossing without a look which argued at full length her injustice in making her demand, and his freedom from all liability let him walk the crossing as often as he might. He could not seat himself in a railway carriage without a lesson to his opposite neighbour that in all the mutual affairs of travelling, arrangement of feet, disposition of bags, and opening of windows, it would be that neighbour's duty to submit and his to exact. It was, however, for the spirit rather than for the thing itself that he combated. The woman with the broom got her penny. The opposite gentleman when once by a glance he had expressed submission was allowed his own way with his legs and with the window. I would not say that Ferdinand Lopez was prone to do ill-natured things; but he was imperious, and he had learned to carry his empire in his eye.

The reader must submit to be told one or two further and still smaller details respecting the man, and then the man shall be allowed to make his own way. No one of those around him knew how much care he took to dress himself well, or how careful he was that no one should know it. His very tailor regarded him as being simply extravagant in the number of his coats and trousers, and his friends looked upon him as one of those fortunate beings to whose nature belongs a facility of being well dressed, or almost an impossibility of being ill dressed. We all know the man,—a little man generally who moves seldom and softly,—who looks always as though he had just been sent home in a bandbox. Ferdinand Lopez was not a little man, and moved freely enough; but never, at any moment,—going into the city or coming out of it, on horseback or on foot, at home over his book or after the mazes of the dance,—was he dressed otherwise than with perfect care. Money and time did it, but folk thought that it grew with him, as did his hair and his nails. And he always rode a horse which charmed good judges of what a park nag* should be;—not a prancing, restless, giggling, sideway-going, useless garran,* but an animal well made, well bitted, with perfect paces, on whom a rider if it pleased him could be as quiet as a statue on a monument. It often did please Ferdinand Lopez to be quiet on horseback; and yet he did not look like a statue, for it was acknowledged through all London that he was a good horseman. He lived luxuriously too,—though whether at his ease or not nobody knew,—for he kept a brougham* of his own, and during the hunting season he had two horses down at Leighton.* There had once been a belief abroad that he was ruined, but they who interest themselves in such matters had found out,—or at any rate believed that they had found out,—that he paid his tailor regularly: and now there prevailed an opinion that Ferdinand Lopez was a monied man.

It was known to some few that he occupied rooms in a flat at Westminster,—but to very few exactly where the rooms were situate. Among all his friends no one was known to have entered them. In a moderate way he was given to hospitality,—that is to infrequent but, when the occasion came, to graceful hospitality. Some club, however, or tavern, or perhaps, in the summer, some river bank would be chosen as the scene of these festivities. To a few—if, as suggested, amidst summer flowers on the water's edge to men and women mixed,—he would be a courtly and efficient host; for he had the rare gift of doing such things well.

Hunting was over, and the east wind was still blowing, and a great portion of the London world was out of town taking its Easter holiday, when, on an unpleasant morning, Ferdinand Lopez travelled into the city by the Metropolitan railway* from Westminster Bridge. It was his custom to go thither when he did go,—not daily like a man of business, but as chance might require, like a capitalist or a man of pleasure,—in his own brougham. But on this occasion he walked down to the river side, and then walked from the Mansion House into a dingy little court called Little Tankard Yard,* near the Bank of England, and going through a narrow dark long passage got into a little office at the back of a building, in which there sat at a desk a greasy gentleman with a new hat on one side of his head, who might perhaps be about forty years old. The place was very dark, and the man was turning over the leaves of a ledger. A stranger to city ways might probably have said that he was idle, but he was no doubt filling his mind with that erudition which would enable him to earn his bread. On the other side of the desk there was a little boy copying letters. These were Mr Sextus Parker,—commonly called Sexty Parker,—and his clerk. Mr Parker was a gentleman very well known and at the present moment favourably esteemed on the Stock Exchange. 'What, Lopez!' said he. 'Uncommon glad to see you. What can I do for you?'

'Just come inside,—will you?' said Lopez. Now within Mr Parker's very small office there was a smaller office in which there were a safe, a small rickety Pembroke table, two chairs, and an old washing-stand with a tumbled towel. Lopez led the way into this sanctum as though he knew the place well, and Sexty Parker followed him.

'Beastly day, isn't it?' said Sexty.

'Yes,—a nasty east wind.'

'Cutting one in two, with a hot sun at the same time. One ought to hybernate at this time of the year.'

'Then why don't you hybernate?' said Lopez.

'Business is too good. That's about it. A man has to stick to it when it does come. Everybody can't do like you;—give up regular work, and make a better thing of an hour now and an hour then, just as it pleases you. I shouldn't dare go in for that kind of thing.'

'I don't suppose you or any one else know what I go in for,' said Lopez, with a look that indicated offence.

'Nor don't care,' said Sexty;—'only hope it's something good for your sake.' Sexty Parker had known Mr Lopez well, now for some years, and being an overbearing man himself,—somewhat even of a bully if the truth be spoken,—and by no means apt to give way unless hard pressed, had often tried his 'hand' on his friend, as he himself would have said. But I doubt whether he could remember any instance in which he could congratulate himself on success. He was trying his hand again now, but did it with a faltering voice, having caught a glance of his friend's eye.

'I dare say not,' said Lopez. Then he continued without changing his voice or the nature of his eye, 'I'll tell you what I want you to do now. I want your name to this bill for three months.'*

Sexty Parker opened his mouth and his eyes, and took the bit of paper that was tendered to him. It was a promissory note for £750, which, if signed by him, would at the end of the specified period make him liable for that sum were it not otherwise paid. His friend Mr Lopez was indeed applying to him for the assistance of his name in raising a loan to the amount of the sum named. This was a kind of favour which a man should ask almost on his knees,—and which, if so asked, Mr Sextus Parker would certainly refuse. And here was Ferdinand Lopez asking it,—whom Sextus Parker had latterly regarded as an opulent man,—and asking it not at all on his knees, but, as one might say, at the muzzle of a pistol. 'Accommodation bill!'* said Sexty. 'Why, you ain't hard up; are you?'

'I'm not going just at present to tell you much about my affairs, and yet I expect you to do what I ask you. I don't suppose you doubt my ability to raise £750.'

'Oh, dear no,' said Sexty, who had been looked at and who had not borne the inspection well.

'And I don't suppose you would refuse me even if I were hard up, as you call it.' There had been affairs before between the two men in which Lopez had probably been the stronger, and the memory of them, added to the inspection which was still going on, was heavy upon poor Sexty.

'Oh, dear no;—I wasn't thinking of refusing. I suppose a fellow may be a little surprised at such a thing.'

'I don't know why you need be surprised, as such things are very common. I happen to have taken a share in a loan a little beyond my immediate means, and therefore want a few hundreds. There is no one I can ask with a better grace than you. If you ain't—afraid about it, just sign it.'

'Oh, I ain't afraid,' said Sexty, taking his pen and writing his name across the bill. But even before the signature was finished, when his eye was taken away from the face of his companion and fixed upon the disagreeable piece of paper beneath his hand, he repented of what he was doing. He almost arrested his signature half-way. He did hesitate, but had not pluck enough to stop his hand. 'It does seem to be a d——d odd transaction all the same,' he said as he leaned back in his chair.

'It's the commonest thing in the world,' said Lopez picking up the bill in a leisurely way, folding it and putting it into his pocket-book. 'Have our names never been together on a bit of paper before?'

'When we both had something to make by it.'

'You've nothing to make and nothing to lose by this. Good day and many thanks;—though I don't think so much of the affair as you seem to do.' Then Ferdinand Lopez took his departure and Sexty Parker was left alone in his bewilderment.

'By George,—that's queer,' he said to himself. 'Who'd have thought of Lopez being hard up for a few hundred pounds? But it must be all right. He wouldn't have come in that fashion, if it hadn't been all right. I oughtn't to have done it though! A man ought never to do that kind of thing;—never,—never!' And Mr Sextus Parker was much discontented with himself, so that when he got home that evening to the wife of his bosom and his little family at Ponders End,* he by no means made himself agreeable to them. For that sum of £750 sat upon his bosom as he ate his supper, and lay upon his chest as he slept,—like a nightmare.

CHAPTER 2

EVERETT WHARTON

ON that same day Lopez dined with his friend Everett Wharton at a new club called the Progress,* of which they were both members. The Progress was certainly a new club, having as yet been open hardly more than three years; but still it was old enough to have seen many of the hopes of its early youth become dim with age and inaction. For the Progress had intended to do great things for the Liberal party,—or rather for political liberality in general,—and had in truth done little or nothing. It had been got up with considerable enthusiasm, and for a while certain fiery politicians had believed that through the instrumentality of this institution men of genius, and spirit, and natural power, but without wealth,—meaning always themselves,—would be supplied with sure seats in Parliament and a probable share in the Government. But no such results had been achieved. There had been a want of something,—some deficiency felt but not yet defined,—which had hitherto been fatal. The young men said it was because no old stager who knew the way of pulling the wires would come forward and put the club in the proper groove. The old men said it was because the young men were pretentious puppies. It was, however, not to be doubted that the party of Progress had become slack, and that the Liberal politicians of the country, although a special new club had been opened for the furtherance of their views, were not at present making much way. 'What we want is organization,' said one of the leading young men. But the organization was not as yet forthcoming.

The club, nevertheless, went on its way, like other clubs, and men dined and smoked and played billiards and pretended to read. Some few energetic members still hoped that a good day would come in which their grand ideas might be realized,—but as regarded the members generally, they were content to eat and drink and play billiards. It was a fairly good club,—with a sprinkling of Liberal lordlings, a couple of dozen of members of Parliament who had been made to believe that they would neglect their party duties unless they paid their money, and the usual assortment of barristers, attorneys, city merchants and idle men. It was good enough at any rate for Ferdinand Lopez, who was particular about his dinner, and had an opinion of his own about wines. He had been heard to assert that, for real quiet comfort, there was not a club in London equal to it; but his hearers were not aware that in past days he had been blackballed at the T—— and the G——.* These were accidents which Lopez had a gift of keeping in the background.

His present companion, Everett Wharton, had, as well as himself, been an original member;—and Wharton had been one of those who had hoped to find in the club a stepping-stone to high political life, and who now talked often with idle energy of the need of organization.

'For myself,' said Lopez, 'I can conceive no vainer object of ambition than a seat in the British Parliament. What does any man gain by it? The few who are successful work very hard for little pay and no thanks,—or nearly equally hard for no pay and as little thanks. The many who fail sit idly for hours, undergoing the weary task of listening to platitudes, and enjoy in return the now absolutely valueless privilege of having M.P. written on their letters.'

'Somebody must make laws for the country.'

'I don't see the necessity. I think the country would do uncommonly well if it were to know that no old law would be altered or new law made for the next twenty years.'

'You wouldn't have repealed the corn laws?'

'There are no corn laws to repeal now.'

'Nor modify the income tax?'*

'I would modify nothing. But at any rate, whether laws are to be altered or to be left, it is a comfort to me that I need not put my finger into that pie. There is one benefit indeed in being in the House.'

'You can't be arrested.'

'Well;—that, as far as it goes; and one other. It assists a man in getting a seat as the director of certain companies. People are still such asses that they trust a Board of Directors made up of members of Parliament, and therefore of course members are made welcome. But if you want to get into the House why don't you arrange it with your father, instead of waiting for what the club may do for you?'

'My father wouldn't pay a shilling for such a purpose. He was never in the House himself.'

'And therefore despises it.'

'A little of that, perhaps. No man ever worked harder than he did, or, in his way, more successfully; and having seen one after another of his juniors become members of Parliament, while he stuck to the attorneys, there is perhaps a little jealousy about it.'

'From what I see of the way you live at home, I should think your father would do anything for you,—with proper management. There is no doubt, I suppose, that he could afford it?'

'My father never in his life said anything to me about his own money affairs, though he says a great deal about mine. No man ever was closer than my father. But I believe that he could afford almost anything.'

'I wish I had such a father,' said Ferdinand Lopez. 'I think that I should succeed in ascertaining the extent of his capabilities, and in making some use of them too.'

Wharton nearly asked his friend,—almost summoned courage to ask him,—whether his father had done much for him. They were very intimate; and on one subject, in which Lopez was much interested, their confidence had been very close. But the younger and the weaker man of the two could not quite bring himself to the point of making an inquiry which he thought would be disagreeable. Lopez had never before, in all their intercourse, hinted at the possibility of his having or having had filial aspirations. He had been as though he had been created self-sufficient, independent of mother's milk or father's money. Now the question might have been asked almost naturally. But it was not asked.

Everett Wharton was a trouble to his father,—but not an agonizing trouble, as are some sons. His faults were not of a nature to rob his father's cup of all its sweetness and to bring his grey hairs with sorrow to the grave.* Old Wharton had never had to ask himself whether he should now, at length, let his son fall into the lowest abysses, or whether he should yet again struggle to put him on his legs, again forgive him, again pay his debts, again endeavour to forget dishonour, and place it all to the score of thoughtless youth. Had it been so, I think that, if not on the first or second fall, certainly on the third, the young man would have gone into the abyss; for Mr Wharton was a stern man, and capable of coming to a clear conclusion on things that were nearest and even dearest to himself. But Everett Wharton had simply shown himself to be inefficient to earn his own bread. He had never declined even to do this,—but had simply been inefficient. He had not declared either by words or by actions that as his father was a rich man, and as he was an only son, he would therefore do nothing. But he had tried his hand thrice, and in each case, after but short trial, had assured his father and his friends that the thing had not suited him. Leaving Oxford without a degree,—for the reading of the schools* did not suit him,—he had gone into a banking-house, by no means as a mere clerk, but with an expressed proposition from his father, backed by the assent of a partner, that he should work his way up to wealth and a great commercial position. But six months taught him that banking was 'an abomination', and he at once went into a course of reading with a barrister. He remained at this till he was called,—for a man may be called with very little continuous work. But after he was called the solitude of his chambers was too much for him, and at twenty-five he found that the Stock

Exchange was the mart in the world for such talents and energies as he possessed. What was the nature of his failure during the year that he went into the city, was known only to himself and his father,—unless Ferdinand Lopez knew something of it also. But at six-and-twenty the Stock Exchange was also abandoned; and now, at eight-and-twenty, Everett Wharton had discovered that a parliamentary career was that for which nature and his special genius had intended him. He had probably suggested this to his father, and had met with some cold rebuff.

Everett Wharton was a good-looking, manly fellow, six feet high, with broad shoulders, with light hair, wearing a large silky bushy beard, which made him look older than his years, who neither by his speech nor by his appearance would ever be taken for a fool, but who showed by the very actions of his body as well as by the play of his face, that he lacked firmness of purpose. He certainly was no fool. He had read much, and, though he generally forgot what he read, there were left with him from his readings certain nebulous lights, begotten by other men's thinking, which enabled him to talk on most subjects. It cannot be said of him that he did much thinking for himself;—but he thought that he thought. He believed of himself that he had gone rather deep into politics, and that he was entitled to call many statesmen asses because they did not see the things which he saw. He had the great question of labour, and all that refers to unions, strikes, and lock-outs, quite at his fingers' ends. He knew how the Church of England should be disestablished and recomposed. He was quite clear on questions of finance, and saw to a 't' how progress should be made towards communism,* so that no violence should disturb that progress, and that in the due course of centuries all desire for personal property should be conquered and annihilated by a philanthropy so general as hardly to be accounted a virtue. In the meantime he could never contrive to pay his tailor's bill regularly out of the allowance of £400 a year* which his father made him, and was always dreaming of the comforts of a handsome income.

He was a popular man certainly,—very popular with women, to whom he was always courteous, and generally liked by men, to whom he was genial and good-natured. Though he was not himself aware of the fact, he was very dear to his father, who in his own silent way almost admired and certainly liked the openness and guileless freedom of a character which was very opposite to his own. The father, though he had never said a word to flatter the son, did in truth give his offspring credit for greater talent than he possessed, and, even when appearing to scorn them, would listen to the young man's diatribes almost with satisfaction. And Everett was very dear also to a sister, who was the only other living member of this branch of the Wharton family. Much will be said of her in these pages, and it is hoped that the reader may take an interest in her fate. But here, in speaking of the brother, it may suffice to say, that the sister, who was endowed with infinitely finer gifts than his, did give credit to the somewhat pretentious claims of her less noble brother.

Indeed it had been perhaps a misfortune with Everett Wharton that some people had believed in him,—and a further misfortune that some others had thought it worth their while to pretend to believe in him. Among the latter might probably be reckoned the friend with whom he was now dining at the Progress. A man may flatter another, as Lopez occasionally did flatter Wharton, without preconcerted falsehood. It suits one man to be well with another, and the one learns gradually and perhaps unconsciously the way to take advantage of the foibles of the other. Now it was most material to Lopez that he should stand well with all the members of the Wharton family, as he aspired to the hand of the daughter of the house. Of her regard he had already thought himself nearly sure. Of the father's sanction to such a marriage he had reason to be almost more than doubtful. But the brother was his friend,—and in such circumstances a man is almost justified in flattering a brother.

'I'll tell you what it is, Lopez,' said Wharton, as they strolled out of the club together, a little after ten o'clock, 'the men of the present day won't give themselves the trouble to occupy their minds with matters which have, or should have, real interest. Pope* knew all about it when he said that "The proper study of mankind is man." But people don't read Pope now, or if they do they don't take the trouble to understand him.'

'Men are too busy making money, my dear fellow.'

'That's just it. Money's a very nice thing.'

'Very nice,' said Lopez.

'But the search after it is debasing. If a man could make money for four, or six, or even eight hours a day, and then wash his mind of the pursuit, as a clerk in an office washes the copies and ledgers out of his mind, then——'

'He would never make money in that way,—and keep it.'

'And therefore the whole thing is debasing. A man ceases to care for the great interests of the world, or even to be aware of their existence, when his whole soul is in Spanish bonds. They wanted to make a banker of me, but I found that it would kill me.'

'It would kill me, I think, if I had to confine myself to Spanish bonds.'

'You know what I mean. You at any rate can understand me, though I fear you are too far gone to abandon the idea of making a fortune.'

'I would abandon it to-morrow if I could come into a fortune ready made. A man must at any rate eat.'

'Yes;—he must eat. But I am not quite sure,' said Wharton thoughtfully, 'that he need think about what he eats.'

'Unless the beef is sent up without horse radish!' It had happened that when the two men sat down to their dinner the insufficient quantity of that vegetable supplied by the steward of the club had been all consumed, and Wharton had complained of the grievance.

'A man has a right to that for which he has paid,' said Wharton, with mock solemnity, 'and if he passes over laches of that nature without observation, he does an injury to humanity at large. I'm not going to be caught in a trap, you know, because I like horse radish with my beef. Well, I can't go farther out of my way, as I have a deal of reading to do before I court my Morpheus.* If you'll take my advice, you'll go straight to the governor. Whatever Emily may feel I don't think she'll say much to encourage you unless you go about it after that fashion. She has prim notions of her own, which perhaps are not after all so much amiss when a man wants to marry a girl.'

'God forbid that I should think that anything about your sister was amiss!'

'I don't think there is much myself. Women are generally superficial,—but some are honestly superficial and some dishonestly. Emily at any rate is honest.'

'Stop half a moment.' Then they sauntered arm in arm down the broad pavement leading from Pall Mall to the Duke of York's column. 'I wish I could make out your father more clearly. He is always civil to me, but he has a cold way of looking at me which makes me think I am not in his good books.'

'He is like that to everybody.'

'I never seem to get beyond the skin with him. You must have heard him speak of me in my absence?'

'He never says very much about anybody.'

'But a word would let me know how the land lies. You know me well enough to be aware that I am the last man to be curious as to what others think of me. Indeed I do not care about it as much as a man should do. I am utterly indifferent to the opinion of the world at large, and would never object to the company of a pleasant person because the pleasant person abused me behind my back. What I value is the pleasantness of the man and not the liking or disliking for myself. But here the dearest aim of my life is concerned, and I might be guided either this way or that, to my great advantage, by knowing whether I stand well or ill with him.'

'You have dined three times within the last three months in Manchester Square, and I don't know any other man,—certainly no other young man,—who has had such strong proof of intimacy from my father.'

'Yes, and I know my advantages. But I have been there as your friend, not as his.'

'He doesn't care twopence about my friends. I wanted to give Charlie Skate a dinner, but my father wouldn't have him at any price.'

'Charlie Skate is out at elbows, and bets at billiards. I am respectable,—or at any rate your father thinks so. Your father is more anxious about you than you are aware of, and wishes to make his house pleasant to you as long as he can do so to your advantage. As far as you are concerned he rather approves of me, fancying that my turn for making money is stronger than my turn for spending it. Nevertheless, he looks upon me as a friend of yours rather than his own. Though he has given me three dinners in three months,—and I own the greatness of his hospitality,—I don't suppose he ever said a word in my favour. I wish I knew what he does say.'

'He says he knows nothing about you.'

'Oh;—that's it, is it? Then he can know no harm. When next he says so ask him of how many of the men who dine at his house he can say as much. Good night;—I won't keep you any longer. But I can tell you this;—if between us we can manage to handle him rightly, you may get your seat in Parliament and I may get my wife;——that is, of course, if she will have me.'

Then they parted, but Lopez remained in the pathway walking up and down by the side of the old military club,* thinking of things. He certainly knew his friend, the younger Wharton, intimately, appreciating the man's good qualities, and being fully aware of the man's weakness. By his questions he had extracted quite enough to assure himself that Emily's father would be adverse to his proposition. He had not felt much doubt before, but now he was certain. 'He doesn't know much about me,' he said, musing to himself. 'Well, no; he doesn't;—and there isn't very much that I can tell him. Of course he's wise,—as wisdom goes. But then, wise men do do foolish things at intervals. The discreetest of city bankers are talked out of their money; the most scrupulous of matrons are talked out of their virtue; the most experienced of statesmen are talked out of their principles. And who can really calculate chances? Men who lead forlorn hopes generally push through without being wounded;—and the fifth or sixth heir comes to a title.' So much he said, palpably, though to himself, with his inner voice. Then—impalpably, with no even inner voice,—he asked himself what chance he might have of prevailing with the girl herself; and he almost ventured to tell himself that in that direction he need not despair.

In very truth he loved the girl and reverenced her, believing her to be better and higher and nobler than other human beings,—as a man does when he is in love; and so believing, he had those doubts as to his own success which such reverence produces.

CHAPTER 3

MR ABEL WHARTON, Q.C.

LOPEZ was not a man to let grass grow under his feet when he had anything to do. When he was tired of walking backwards and forwards over the same bit of pavement, subject all the while to a cold east wind, he went home and thought of the same matter while he lay in bed. Even were he to get the girl's assurances of love, without the father's consent he might find himself farther from his object than ever. Mr Wharton was a man of old fashions, who would think himself ill-used and his daughter ill-used, and who would think also that a general offence would have been committed against good social manners, if his daughter were to be asked for her hand without his previous consent. Should he absolutely refuse,—why then the battle, though it would be a desperate battle, might perhaps be fought with other strategy; but, giving to the matter his best consideration, Lopez thought it expedient to go at once to the father. In doing this he would have no silly tremors. Whatever he might feel in speaking to the girl, he had sufficient self-confidence to be able to ask the father, if not with assurance, at any rate without trepidation. It was, he thought, probable that the father, at the first attack, would neither altogether accede, or altogether refuse. The disposition of the man was averse to the probability of an absolute reply at the first moment. The lover imagined that it might be possible for him to take advantage of the period of doubt which would thus be created.

Mr Wharton was and had for a great many years been a barrister practising in the Equity Courts,*—or rather in one Equity Court, for throughout a life's work now extending to nearly fifty years, he had hardly ever gone out of the single Vice-Chancellor's Court which was much better known by Mr Wharton's name than by that of the less eminent judge who now sat there. His had been a very peculiar, a very toilsome, but yet probably a very satisfactory life. He had begun his practice early, and had worked in a stuff gown* till he was nearly sixty. At that time he had amassed a large fortune, mainly from his profession, but partly also by the careful use of his own small patrimony and by his wife's money. Men knew that he was rich, but no one knew the extent of his wealth. When he submitted to take a silk gown, he declared among his friends that he did so as a step preparatory to his retirement. The altered method of work would not suit him at his age, nor,—as he said,—would it be profitable. He would take his silk as an honour for his declining years, so that he might become a bencher at his Inn.* But he had now been working for the last twelve or fourteen years with his silk gown,—almost as hard as in younger days, and with pecuniary results almost as serviceable: and though from month to month he declared his intention of taking no fresh briefs, and though he did now occasionally refuse to work, still he was there with his mind as clear as ever, and with his body apparently as little affected by fatigue.

Mr Wharton had not married till he was forty, and his wife had now been two years dead. He had had six children,—of whom but two were now left to make a household for his old age. He had been nearly fifty when his youngest daughter was born, and was therefore now an old father of a young child. But he was one of those men who, as in youth they are never very young, so in age are they never very old. He could still ride his cob* in the park jauntily; and did so carefully every morning in his life, after an early cup of tea and before his breakfast. And he could walk home from his chambers every day, and on Sundays could do the round of the parks on foot. Twice a week, on Wednesdays and Saturdays, he dined at that old law club, the Eldon,* and played whist after dinner till twelve o'clock. This was the great dissipation and, I think, the chief charm of his life. In the middle of August he and his daughter usually went for a month to Wharton Hall in Herefordshire, the seat of his cousin Sir Alured Wharton;—and this was the one duty of his life which was a burthen to him. But he had been made to believe that it was essential to his health, and to his wife's, and then to his girl's health, that he should every summer leave town for a time,—and where else was he to go? Sir Alured was a relation and a gentleman. Emily liked Wharton Hall. It was the proper thing. He hated Wharton Hall, but then he did not know any place out of London that he would not hate worse. He had once been induced to go up the Rhine; but had never repeated the experiment of foreign travel. Emily sometimes went abroad with her cousins, during which periods it was supposed that the old lawyer spent a good deal of his time at the Eldon. He was a spare, thin, strongly made man, with spare light brown hair, hardly yet grizzled, with small grey whiskers, clear eyes, bushy eyebrows, with a long ugly nose, on which young barristers had been heard to declare that you might hang a small kettle, and with considerable vehemence of talk when he was opposed in argument. For, with all his well-known coolness of temper, Mr Wharton could become very hot in an argument, when the nature of the case in hand required heat. On one subject all who knew him were agreed. He was a thorough lawyer. Many doubted his eloquence, and some declared that he had known well the extent of his own powers in abstaining from seeking the higher honours of his profession; but no one doubted his law. He had once written a book,—on the mortgage of stocks in trade; but that had been in early life, and he had never since dabbled in literature.

He was certainly a man of whom men were generally afraid. At the whist-table no one would venture to scold him. In the court no one ever contradicted him. In his own house, though he was very quiet, the servants dreaded to offend him, and were attentive to his slightest behests. When he condescended to ride with any acquaintance in the park, it was always acknowledged that old Wharton was to regulate the pace. His name was Abel, and all his life he had been known as able Abe;—a silent, far-seeing, close-fisted, just old man, who was not, however, by any means deficient in sympathy either with the sufferings or with the joys of humanity.

It was Easter time and the courts were not sitting, but Mr Wharton was in his chamber as a matter of course at ten o'clock. He knew no real homely comforts elsewhere,—unless at the whist-table at the Eldon. He ate and drank and slept in his own house in Manchester Square,* but he could hardly be said to live there. It was not there that his mind was awake, and that the powers of the man were exercised. When he came up from the dining-room to join his daughter after dinner, he would get her to sing him a song, and would then seat himself with a book. But he never read in his own house, invariably falling into a sweet and placid slumber, from which he was never disturbed till his daughter kissed him as she went to bed. Then he would walk about the room, and look at his watch, and shuffle uneasily through half an hour till his conscience allowed him to take himself to his chamber. He was a man of no pursuits in his own house. But from ten in the morning till five, or often till six, in the evening, his mind was active in some work. It was not now all law, as it used to be. In the drawer of the old piece of furniture which stood just at the right hand of his own arm-chair there were various books hidden away, which he was sometimes ashamed to have seen by his clients,—poetry and novels and even fairy tales. For there was nothing Mr Wharton could not read in his chambers, though there was nothing that he could read in his own house. He had a large pleasant room in which to sit, looking out from the ground floor of Stone Buildings* on to the gardens belonging to the Inn,—and here, in the centre of the metropolis, but in perfect quiet as far as the outside world was concerned, he had lived and still lived his life.

At about noon on the day following that on which Lopez had made his sudden swoop on Mr Parker and had then dined with Everett Wharton, he called at Stone Buildings, and was shown into the lawyer's room. His quick eye at once discovered the book which Mr Wharton half hid away, and saw upon it Mr Mudie's suspicious ticket.* Barristers certainly never get their law books from Mudie, and Lopez at once knew that his hoped-for father-in-law had been reading a novel. He had not suspected such weakness, but argued well from it for the business he had in hand. There must be a soft spot to be found about the heart of an old lawyer who spent his mornings in such occupation. 'How do you do, sir?' said Mr Wharton rising from his seat. 'I hope I see you well, sir.' Though he had been reading a novel his tone and manner were very cold. Lopez had never been in Stone Buildings before, and was not quite sure that he might not have committed some offence in coming there. 'Take a seat, Mr Lopez. Is there anything I can do for you in my way?'

There was a great deal that could be done 'in his way' as father;—but how was it to be introduced and the case made clear? Lopez did not know whether the old man had as yet ever suspected such a feeling as that which he now intended to declare. He had been intimate at the house in Manchester Square, and had certainly ingratiated himself very closely with a certain Mrs Roby, who had been Mrs Wharton's sister and constant companion, who lived in Berkeley Street,* close round the corner from Manchester Square, and spent very much of her time with Emily Wharton. They were together daily, as though Mrs Roby had assumed the part of a second mother, and Lopez was well aware that Mrs Roby knew of his love. If there was real confidence between Mrs Roby and the old man, the old lawyer must know it also;—but as to that Lopez felt that he was in the dark.

The task of speaking to an old father is not unpleasant when the lover knows that he has been smiled upon, and, in fact, approved for the last six months. He is going to be patted on the back, and made much of, and received into the family. He is to be told that his Mary or his Augusta has been the best daughter in the world and will therefore certainly be the best wife, and he himself will probably on that special occasion be spoken of with unqualified praise,—and all will be pleasant. But the subject is one very difficult to broach when no previous light has been thrown on it. Ferdinand Lopez, however, was not the man to stand shivering on the brink when a plunge was necessary,—and therefore he made his plunge. 'Mr Wharton, I have taken the liberty to call upon you here, because I want to speak to you about your daughter.'

'About my daughter!' The old man's surprise was quite genuine. Of course when he had given himself a moment to think, he knew what must be the nature of his visitor's communication. But up to that moment he had never mixed his daughter and Ferdinand Lopez in his thoughts together. And now, the idea having come upon him, he looked at the aspirant with severe and unpleasant eyes. It was manifest to the aspirant that the first flash of the thing was painful to the father.

'Yes, sir. I know how great is my presumption. But, yet, having ventured, I will hardly say to entertain any hope, but to have come to such a state that I can only be happy by hoping, I have thought it best to come to you at once.'

'Does she know anything of this?'

'Of my visit to you? Nothing.'

'Of your intentions;—of your suit generally? Am I to understand that this has any sanction from her?'

'None at all.'

'Have you told her anything of it?'

'Not a word. I come to ask you for your permission to address her.'

'You mean that she has no knowledge whatever of your,—your preference for her.'

'I cannot say that. It is hardly possible that I should have learned to love her as I do without some consciousness on her part that it is so.'

'What I mean is, without any beating about the bush,—have you been making love to her?'

'Who is to say in what making love consists, Mr Wharton?'

'D—— it, sir, a gentleman knows. A gentleman knows whether he has been playing on a girl's feelings, and a gentleman, when he is asked as I have asked you, will at any rate tell the truth. I don't want any definitions. Have you been making love to her?'

'I think, Mr Wharton, that I have behaved like a gentleman; and that you will acknowledge at least so much when you come to know exactly what I have done and what I have not done. I have endeavoured to commend myself to your daughter, but I have never spoken a word of love to her.'

'Does Everett know of all this?'

'Yes.'

'And has he encouraged it?'

'He knows of it, because he is my most intimate friend. Whoever the lady might have been, I should have told him. He is attached to me, and would not, I think, on his own account, object to call me his brother. I spoke to him yesterday on the matter very plainly, and he told me that I ought certainly to see you first. I quite agreed with him, and therefore I am here. There has certainly been nothing in his conduct to make you angry, and I do not think that there has been anything in mine.'

There was a dignity of demeanour and a quiet assured courage which had its effect upon the old lawyer. He felt that he could not storm and talk in ambiguous language of what a 'gentleman' would or would not do. He might disapprove of this man altogether as a son-in-law,—and at the present moment he thought that he did,—but still the man was entitled to a civil answer. How were lovers to approach the ladies of their love in any manner more respectful than this? 'Mr Lopez,' he said, 'you must forgive me if I say that you are comparatively a stranger to us.'

'That is an accident which would be easily cured if your will in that direction were as good as mine.'

'But, perhaps, it isn't. One has to be explicit in these matters. A daughter's happiness is a very serious consideration—and some people, among whom I confess that I am one, consider that like should marry like. I should wish to see my daughter marry,—not only in my own sphere, neither higher nor lower,—but with some one of my own class.'

'I hardly know, Mr Wharton, whether that is intended to exclude me.'

'Well,—to tell you the truth I know nothing about you. I don't know who your father was,—whether he was an Englishman, whether he was a Christian, whether he was a Protestant,—not even whether he was a gentleman. These are questions which I should not dream of asking under any other circumstances;—would be matters with which I should have no possible concern, if you were simply an acquaintance. But when you talk to a man about his daughter——!'

'I acknowledge freely your right of inquiry.'

'And I know nothing of your means;—nothing whatever. I understand that you live as a man of fortune, but I presume that you earn your bread. I know nothing of the way in which you earn it, nothing of the certainty or amount of your means.'

'Those things are of course matters for inquiry; but may I presume that you have no objection which satisfactory answers to such questions may not remove?'

'I shall never willingly give my daughter to anyone who is not the son of an English gentleman. It may be a prejudice, but that is my feeling.'

'My father was certainly not an English gentleman. He was a Portuguese.'* In admitting this, and in thus subjecting himself at once to one clearly-stated ground of objection,—the objection being one which, though admitted, carried with it neither fault nor disgrace,— Lopez felt that he had got a certain advantage. He could not get over the fact that he was the son of a Portuguese parent, but by admitting that openly he thought he might avoid present discussion on matters which might, perhaps, be more disagreeable, but to which he need not allude if the accident of his birth were to be taken by the father as settling the question. 'My mother was an English lady,' he added, 'but my father certainly was not an Englishman. I never had the common happiness of knowing either of them. I was an orphan before I understood what it was to have a parent.'

This was said with a pathos, which for the moment stopped the expression of any further harsh criticism from the lawyer. Mr Wharton could not instantly repeat his objection to a parentage which was matter for such melancholy reflections; but he felt at the same time that as he had luckily landed himself on a positive and undeniable ground of objection to a match which was distasteful to him, it would be unwise for him to go to other matters in which he might be less successful. By doing so, he would seem to abandon the ground which he had already made good. He thought it probable that the man might have an adequate income, and yet he did not wish to welcome him as a son-in-law. He thought it possible that the Portuguese father might be a Portuguese nobleman, and therefore one whom he would be driven to admit to have been some sort of a gentleman;—but yet this man who was now in his presence and whom he continued to scan with the closest observation, was not what he called a gentleman. The foreign blood was proved, and that would suffice. As he looked at Lopez, he thought that he detected Jewish signs, but he was afraid to make any allusion to religion, lest Lopez should declare that his ancestors had been noted as Christians since St James first preached in the Peninsula.

'I was educated altogether in England,' continued Lopez, 'till I was sent to a German university in the idea· that the languages of the continent are not generally well learned in this country. I can never be sufficiently thankful to my guardian for doing so.'

'I dare say;—I dare say. French and German are very useful. I have a prejudice of my own in favour of Greek and Latin.'

'But I rather fancy I picked up more Greek and Latin at Bohn* than I should have got here, had I stuck to nothing else.'

'I dare say;—I dare say. You may be an Admirable Crichton* for what I know.'

'I have not intended to make any boast, sir, but simply to vindicate those who had the care of my education. If you have no objection except that founded on my birth, which is an accident——'

'When one man is a peer and another a ploughman, that is an accident. One doesn't find fault with the ploughman, but one doesn't ask him to dinner.'

'But my accident,' said Lopez smiling, 'is one which you would hardly discover unless you were told. Had I called myself Talbot you would not know but that I was as good an Englishman as yourself.'

'A man of course may be taken in by falsehoods,' said the lawyer.

'If you have no other objection than that raised, I hope you will allow me to visit in Manchester Square.'

'There may be ten thousand other objections, Mr Lopez, but I really think that the one is enough. Of course I know nothing of my daughter's feelings. I should imagine that the matter is as strange to her as it is to me. But I cannot give you anything like encouragement. If I am ever to have a son-in-law I should wish to have an English son-in-law. I do not even know what your profession is.'

'I am engaged in foreign loans.'*

'Very precarious I should think. A sort of gambling; isn't it?'

'It is the business by which many of the greatest mercantile houses in the city have been made.'

'I dare say;—I dare say;—and by which they come to ruin. I have the greatest respect in the world for mercantile enterprise, and have had as much to do as most men with mercantile questions. But I ain't sure that I wish to marry my daughter in the City. Of course it's all prejudice.

I won't deny that on general subjects I can give as much latitude as any man; but when one's own hearth is attacked——'

'Surely such a proposition as mine, Mr Wharton, is no attack!'

'In my sense it is. When a man proposes to assault and invade the very kernel of another man's heart, to share with him, and indeed to take from him, the very dearest of his possessions, to become part and parcel with him either for infinite good or infinite evil, then a man has a right to guard even his prejudices as precious bulwarks.' Mr Wharton as he said this was walking about the room with his hands in his trowsers pockets. 'I have always been for absolute toleration in matters of religion,—have always advocated admission of Roman Catholics and Jews into Parliament, and even to the Bench.* In ordinary life I never question a man's religion. It is nothing to me whether he believes in Mahomet, or has no belief at all. But when a man comes to me for my daughter——'

'I have always belonged to the Church of England,' said Ferdinand Lopez.

'Lopez is at any rate a bad name to go to a Protestant church with, and I don't want my daughter to bear it. I am very frank with you, as in such a matter men ought to understand each other. Personally I have liked you well enough and have been glad to see you at my house. Everett and you have seemed to be friends, and I have had no objection to make. But marrying into a family is a very serious thing indeed.'

'No man feels that more strongly than I do, Mr Wharton.'

'There had better be an end of it.'

'Even though I should be happy enough to obtain her favour?'

'I can't think that she cares about you. I don't think it for a moment. You say that you haven't spoken to her, and I am sure she's not a girl to throw herself at a man's head. I don't approve it, and I think it had better fall to the ground. It must fall to the ground.'

'I wish you would give me a reason.'

'Because you are not English.'

'But I am English. My father was a foreigner.'

'It doesn't suit my ideas. I suppose I may have my own ideas about my own family, Mr Lopez? I feel perfectly certain that my child will do nothing to displease me, and this would displease me. If we were to talk for an hour I could say nothing further.'

'I hope that I may be able to present things to you in an aspect so altered,' said Lopez as he prepared to take his leave, 'as to make you change your mind.'

'Possibly;—possibly,' said Wharton, 'but I do not think it probable. Good morning to you, sir. If I have said anything that has seemed to be unkind put it down to my anxiety as a father and not to my conduct as a man.' Then the door was closed behind his visitor, and Mr Wharton was left walking up and down his room alone. He was by no means satisfied with himself. He felt that he had been rude and at the same time not decisive. He had not explained to the man as he would wish to have done, that it was monstrous and out of the question that a daughter of the Whartons, one of the oldest families in England, should be given to a friendless Portuguese,—a probable Jew,—about whom nobody knew anything. Then he remembered that sooner or later his girl would have at least £60,000,* a fact of which no human being but himself was aware. Would it not be well that somebody should be made aware of it, so that his girl might have the chance of suitors preferable to the swarthy son of Judah? He began to be afraid, as he thought of it, that he was not managing his matters well. How would it be with him if he should find that the girl was really in love with this swarthy son of Judah? He had never inquired about his girl's heart, though there was one to whom he hoped that his girl's heart might some day be given. He almost made up his mind to go home at once, so anxious was he. But the prospect of having to spend an entire afternoon in Manchester Square was too much for him, and he remained in his chamber till the usual hour.

Lopez, as he returned from Lincoln's Inn, westward to his club, was, on the whole, contented with the interview. He had expected opposition. He had not thought that the cherry would fall easily into his mouth. But the conversation generally had not taken those turns which he had thought would be most detrimental to him.

CHAPTER 4

MRS ROBY

MR WHARTON as he walked home, remembered that Mrs Roby was to dine at his house on that evening. During the remainder of the day, after the departure of Lopez, he had been unable to take his mind from the consideration of the proposition made to him. He had tried the novel, and he had tried Huggins *v.* the Trustees of the Charity of St Ambox, a case of undeniable importance in which he was engaged on the part of Huggins, but neither was sufficiently powerful to divert his thoughts. Throughout the morning he was imagining what he would say to Emily about this lover of hers,—in what way he would commence the conversation, and how he would express his own opinion should he find that she was in any degree favourable to the man. Should she altogether ignore the man's pretensions, there would be no difficulty. But if she hesitated,— if, as was certainly possible, she should show any partiality for the man, then there would be a knot which would require untying. Hitherto the intercourse between the father and daughter had been simple and pleasant. He had given her everything she had asked for, and she had obeyed him in all the very few matters as to which he had demanded obedience. Questions of discipline, as far as there had been any discipline, had generally been left to Mrs Roby. Mrs Roby was to dine in Manchester Square to-day, and perhaps it would be well that he should have a few words with Mrs Roby before he spoke to his daughter.

Mrs Roby had a husband, but Mr Roby had not been asked to dine in the Square on this occasion. Mrs Roby dined in the Square very often, but Mr Roby very seldom,—not probably above once a year, on some special occasion. He and Mr Wharton had married sisters, but they were quite unlike in character and had never become friends. Mrs Wharton had been nearly twenty years younger than her husband; Mrs Roby had been six or seven years younger than her sister; and Mr Roby was a year or two younger than his wife. The two men therefore belonged to different periods of life, Mr Roby at the present time being a florid youth of forty. He had a moderate fortune, inherited from his mother, of which he was sufficiently careful; but he loved races, and read sporting papers; he was addicted to hunting and billiards; he shot pigeons, and,—so Mr Wharton had declared calumniously more than once to an intimate friend,—had not an H in his vocabulary. The poor man did drop an aspirate now and again; but he knew his defect and strove hard, and with fair average success, to overcome it. But Mr Wharton did not love him and they were not friends. Perhaps neither did Mrs Roby love him very ardently. She was at any rate almost always willing to leave her own house to come to the Square, and on such occasions Mr Roby was always willing to dine at the Nimrod,* the club which it delighted him to frequent.

Mr Wharton, on entering his own house, met his son on the staircase. 'Do you dine at home to-day, Everett?'

'Well, sir; no, sir. I don't think I do. I think I half promised to dine with a fellow at the club.'

'Don't you think you'd make things meet more easily about the end of the year if you dined oftener here where you have nothing to pay, and less frequently at the club, where you pay for everything?'

'But what I should save you would lose, sir. That's the way I look at it.'

'Then I advise you to look at it the other way, and leave me to take care of myself. Come in here, I want to speak to you.' Everett followed his father into a dingy back parlour, which was fitted up with book shelves and was generally called the study, but which was gloomy and comfortless because it was seldom used. 'I have had your friend Lopez with me at my chambers to-day. I don't like your friend Lopez.'

'I am sorry for that, sir.'

'He is a man as to whom I should wish to have a good deal of evidence before I would trust him to be what he seems to be. I dare say he's clever.'

'I think he's more than clever.'

'I dare say;—and well instructed in some respects.'

'I believe him to be a thorough linguist, sir.'

'I dare say. I remember a waiter in a hotel in Holborn who could speak seven languages. It's an accomplishment very necessary for a Courier or a Queen's Messenger.'

'You don't mean to say, sir, that you disregard foreign languages?'

'I have said nothing of the kind. But in my estimation they don't stand in the place of principles, or a profession, or birth, or country. I fancy there has been some conversation between you about your sister.'

'Certainly there has.'

'A young man should be very chary about how he speaks to another man, to a stranger, about his sister. A sister's name should be too sacred for club talk.'

'Club talk! Good heavens, sir, you don't think that I have spoken of Emily in that way? There isn't a man in London has a higher respect for his sister than I have for mine. This man, by no means in a light way but with all seriousness, has told me that he was attached to Emily; and I, believing him to be a gentleman and well to do in the world, have referred him to you. Can that have been wrong?'

'I don't know how he's "to do", as you call it. I haven't asked, and I don't mean to ask. But I doubt his being a gentleman. He is not an English gentleman. What was his father?'

'I haven't the least idea.'

'Or his mother?'

'He has never mentioned her to me.'

'Nor his family; nor anything of their antecedents? He is a man fallen out of the moon. All that is nothing to us as passing acquaintances. Between men such ignorance should I think bar absolute intimacy;—but that may be a matter of taste. But it should be held to be utterly antagonistic to any such alliance as that of marriage. He seems to be a friend of yours. You had better make him understand that it is quite out of the question. I have told him so, and you had better repeat it.' So saying, Mr Wharton went upstairs to dress, and Everett, having received his father's instructions, went away to the club.

When Mr Wharton reached the drawing-room, he found Mrs Roby alone, and he at once resolved to discuss the matter with her before he spoke to his daughter. 'Harriet,' he said abruptly, 'do you know anything of one Mr Lopez?'

'Mr Lopez! Oh yes, I know him.'

'Do you mean that he is an intimate friend?'

'As friends go in London, he is. He comes to our house, and I think that he hunts with Dick.' Dick was Mr Roby.

'That's a recommendation.'

'Well, Mr Wharton, I hardly know what you mean by that,' said Mrs Roby, smiling. 'I don't think my husband will do Mr Lopez any harm; and I am sure Mr Lopez won't do my husband any.'

'I dare say not. But that's not the question. Roby can take care of himself.'

'Quite so.'

'And so I dare say can Mr Lopez.' At this moment Emily entered the room. 'My dear,' said her father, 'I am speaking to your aunt. Would you mind going downstairs and waiting for us? Tell them we shall be ready for dinner in ten minutes.' Then Emily passed out of the room, and Mrs Roby assumed a grave demeanour. 'The man we are speaking of has been to me and has made an offer for Emily.' As he said this he looked anxiously into his sister-in-law's face, in order that he might tell from that how far she favoured the idea of such a marriage,—and he thought that he perceived at once that she was not averse to it. 'You know it is quite out of the question,' he continued.

'I don't know why it should be out of the question. But of course your opinion would have great weight with Emily.'

'Great weight! Well;—I should hope so. If not, I do not know whose opinion is to have weight. In the first place, the man is a foreigner.'

'Oh no;—he is English. But if he were a foreigner: many English girls marry foreigners.'

'My daughter shall not;—not with my permission. You have not encouraged him, I hope.'

'I have not interfered at all,' said Mrs Roby. But this was a lie. Mrs Roby had interfered. Mrs Roby, in discussing the merits and character of the lover with the young lady, had always lent herself to the lover's aid,—and had condescended to accept from the lover various presents which she could hardly have taken had she been hostile to him.

'And now tell me about herself. Has she seen him often?'

'Why, Mr Wharton, he has dined here, in the house, over and over again. I thought that you were encouraging him.'

'Heavens and earth!'

'Of course she has seen him. When a man dines at a house he is bound to call. Of course he has called,—I don't know how often. And she has met him round the corner.'—'Round the corner,' in Manchester Square, meant Mrs Roby's house in Berkeley Street.—'Last Sunday they were at the Zoo together. Dick got them tickets. I thought you knew all about it.'

'Do you mean that my daughter went to the Zoological Gardens alone with this man?' the father asked in dismay.

'Dick was with them. I should have gone, only I had a headache. Did you not know she went?'

'Yes;—I heard about the Gardens. But I heard nothing about the man.'

'I thought, Mr Wharton, you were all in his favour.'

'I am not at all in his favour. I dislike him particularly. For anything I know he may have sold pencils about the streets like any other Jew-boy.'

'He goes to church just as you do,—that is, if he goes anywhere; which I dare say he does about as often as yourself, Mr Wharton.' Now Mr Wharton, though he was a thorough and perhaps a bigoted member of the Church of England, was not fond of going to church.

'Do you mean to tell me,' he said, pressing his hands together, and looking very seriously into his sister-in-law's face; 'do you mean to tell me that she—likes him?'

'Yes;—I think she does like him.'

'You don't mean to say—she's in love with him?'

'She has never told me that she is. Young ladies are shy of making such assertions as to their own feelings before the due time for doing so has come. I think she prefers him to anybody else; and that were he to propose to herself, she would give him her consent to go to you.'

'He shall never enter this house again,' said Mr Wharton passionately.

'You must arrange that with her. If you have so strong an objection to him, I wonder that you should have had him here at all.'

'How was I to know? God bless my soul!—just because a man was allowed to dine here once or twice! Upon my word, it's too bad!'

'Papa, won't you and aunt come down to dinner?' said Emily, opening the door gently. Then they went down to dinner, and during the meal nothing was said about Mr Lopez. But they were not very merry together, and poor Emily felt sure that her own affairs had been discussed in a troublesome manner.

CHAPTER 5

'NO ONE KNOWS ANYTHING ABOUT HIM'

NEITHER at dinner, on that evening at Manchester Square, nor after dinner, as long as Mrs Roby remained in the house, was a word said about Lopez by Mr Wharton. He remained longer than usual with his bottle of port-wine in the dining-room; and when he went upstairs, he sat himself down and fell asleep, almost without a sign. He did not ask for a song, nor did Emily offer to sing. But as soon as Mrs Roby was gone,—and Mrs Roby went home, round the corner, somewhat earlier than usual,—then Mr Wharton woke up instantly and made inquiry of his daughter.

There had, however, been a few words spoken on the subject between Mrs Roby and her niece which had served to prepare Emily for what was coming. 'Lopez has been to your father,' said Mrs Roby, in a voice not specially encouraging for such an occasion. Then she paused a moment; but her niece said nothing, and she continued, 'Yes,—and your father has been blaming me,—as if I had done anything! If he did not mean you to choose for yourself, why didn't he keep a closer look-out?'

'I haven't chosen any one, Aunt Harriet.'

'Well;—to speak fairly, I thought you had; and I have nothing to say against your choice. As young men go, I think Mr Lopez is as good as the best of them. I don't know why you shouldn't have him. Of course you'll have money, but then I suppose he makes a large income himself. As to Mr Fletcher, you don't care a bit about him.'

'Not in that way certainly.'

'No doubt your papa will have it out with you just now; so you had better make up your mind what you will say to him. If you really like the man, I don't see why you shouldn't say so, and stick to it. He has made a regular offer, and girls in these days are not expected to be their father's slaves.' Emily said nothing further to her aunt on that occasion, but finding that she must in truth 'have it out' with her father presently, gave herself up to reflection. It might probably be the case that the whole condition of her future life would depend on the way in which she might now 'have it out' with her father.

I would not wish the reader to be prejudiced against Miss Wharton by the not unnatural feeling which may perhaps be felt in regard to the aunt. Mrs Roby was pleased with little intrigues, was addicted to the amusement of fostering love affairs, was fond of being thought to be useful in such matters, and was not averse to having presents given to her. She had married a vulgar man; and though she had not become like the man, she had become vulgar. She was not an eligible companion for Mr Wharton's daughter,—a matter as to which the father had not given himself proper opportunities of learning the facts. An aunt in his close neighbourhood was so great a comfort to him,—so ready and so natural an assistance to him in his difficulties! But Emily Wharton was not in the least like her aunt, nor had Mrs Wharton been at all like Mrs Roby. No doubt the contact was dangerous. Injury had perhaps already been done. It may be that some slightest soil had already marred the pure white of the girl's natural character. But if so, the stain was as yet too impalpable to be visible to ordinary eyes.

Emily Wharton was a tall, fair girl, with grey eyes, rather exceeding the average proportions as well as height of women. Her features were regular and handsome, and her form was perfect, but it was by her manner and her voice that she conquered rather than by her beauty,—by those gifts and by a clearness of intellect joined with that feminine sweetness which has its most frequent foundation in self-denial. Those who knew her well, and had become attached to her, were apt to endow her with all virtues, and to give her credit for a loveliness which strangers did not find on her face. But as we do not light up our houses with our brightest lamps for all comers, so neither did she emit from her eyes their brightest sparks till special occasion for such shining had arisen. To those who were allowed to love her no woman was more lovable. There was innate in her an appreciation of her own position as a woman, and with it a principle of self-denial as a human being, which it was beyond the power of any Mrs Roby to destroy or even defile by small stains.

Like other girls she had been taught to presume that it was her destiny to be married, and like other girls she had thought much about her destiny. A young man generally regards it as his destiny either to succeed or to fail in the world, and he thinks about that. To him marriage, when it comes, is an accident to which he has hardly as yet given a thought. But to the girl the matrimony which is or is not to be her destiny contains within itself the only success or failure which she anticipates. The young man may become Lord Chancellor, or at any rate earn his bread comfortably as a county court judge. But the girl can look forward to little else than the chance of having a good man for her husband;—a good man, or if her tastes lie in that direction, a rich man. Emily Wharton had doubtless thought about these things, and she sincerely believed that she had found the good man in Ferdinand Lopez.

The man, certainly, was one strangely endowed with the power of creating a belief. When going to Mr Wharton at his chambers he had not intended to cheat the lawyer into any erroneous idea about his family, but he had resolved that he would so discuss the questions of his own condition, which would probably be raised, as to leave upon the old man's mind an unfounded conviction that in regard to money and income he had no reason to fear question. Not a word had been said about his money or his income. And Mr Wharton had felt himself bound to abstain from allusion to such matters from an assured feeling that he could not in that direction plant an enduring objection. In this way Lopez had carried his point with Mr Wharton. He had convinced Mrs Roby that among all the girl's attractions the greatest attraction for him was the fact that she was Mrs Roby's niece. He had made Emily herself believe that the one strong passion of his life was his love for her, and this he had done without ever having asked for her love. And he had even taken the trouble to allure Dick, and had listened to and had talked whole pages out of *Bell's Life*.* On his own behalf it must be acknowledged that he did love the girl, as well perhaps as he was capable of loving anyone;—but he had found out many particulars as to Mr Wharton's money before he had allowed himself to love her.

As soon as Mrs Roby had gathered up her knitting, and declared, as she always did on such occasions, that she could go round the corner without having anyone to look after her, Mr Wharton began, 'Emily, my dear, come here.' Then she came and sat on a footstool at his feet, and looked up into his face. 'Do you know what I am going to speak to you about, my darling?'

'Yes, papa; I think I do. It is about—Mr Lopez.'

'Your aunt has told you, I suppose. Yes; it is about Mr Lopez. I have been very much astonished to-day by Mr Lopez,—a man of whom I have seen very little and know less. He came to me to-day and asked for my permission—to address you.' She sat perfectly quiet, still looking at him, but she did not say a word. 'Of course I did not give him permission.'

'Why of course, papa?'

'Because he is a stranger and a foreigner. Would you have wished me to tell him that he might come?'

'Yes, papa.' He was sitting on a sofa and shrank back a little from her as she made this free avowal. 'In that case I could have judged for myself. I suppose every girl would like to do that.'

'But should you have accepted him?'

'I think I should have consulted you before I did that. But I should have wished to accept him. Papa, I do love him. I have never said so before to anyone. I would not say so to you now, if he had not—spoken to you as he has done.'

'Emily, it must not be.'

'Why not, papa? If you say it shall not be so, it shall not. I will do as you bid me.' Then he put out his hand and caressed her, stroking down her hair. 'But I think you ought to tell me why it must not be,—as I do love him.'

'He is a foreigner.'

'But is he? And why should not a foreigner be as good as an Englishman? His name is foreign, but he talks English and lives as an Englishman.'

'He has no relatives, no family, no belongings. He is what we call an adventurer. Marriage, my dear, is a most serious thing.'

'Yes, papa, I know that.'

'One is bound to be very careful. How can I give you to a man I know nothing about,—an adventurer? What would they say in Herefordshire?'

'I don't know why they should say anything, but if they did I shouldn't much care.'

'I should, my dear. I should care very much. One is bound to think of one's family. Suppose it should turn out afterwards that he was—disreputable!'

'You may say that of any man, papa.'

'But when a man has connections, a father and mother, or uncles and aunts, people that everybody knows about, then there is some guarantee of security. Did you ever hear this man speak of his father?'

'I don't know that I ever did.'

'Or his mother,—or his family? Don't you think that is suspicious?'

'I will ask him, papa, if you wish.'

'No, I would have you ask him nothing. I would not wish that there should be opportunity for such asking. If there has been intimacy between you, such information should have come naturally,—as a thing of course. You have made him no promise?'

'Oh no, papa.'

'Nor spoken to him—of your regard for him?'

'Never;—not a word. Nor he to me,—except in such words as one understands even though they say nothing.'

'I wish he had never seen you.'

'Is he a bad man, papa?'

'Who knows? I cannot tell. He may be ever so bad. How is one to know whether a man be bad or good when one knows nothing about him?' At this point the father got up and walked about the room. 'The long and the short of it is that you must not see him any more.'

'Did you tell him so?'

'Yes;—well; I don't know whether I said exactly that, but I told him that the whole thing must come to an end. And it must. Luckily it seems that nothing has been said on either side.'

'But papa——; is there to be no reason?'

'Haven't I given reasons? I will not have my daughter encourage an adventurer,—a man of whom nobody knows anything. That is reason sufficient.'

'He has a business, and he lives with gentlemen. He is Everett's friend. He is well educated;—oh, so much better than most men that one meets. And he is clever. Papa, I wish you knew him better than you do.'

'I do not want to know him better.'

'Is not that prejudice, papa?'

'My dear Emily,' said Mr Wharton, striving to wax into anger that he might be firm against her. 'I don't think that it becomes you to ask your father such a question as that. You ought to believe that it is the chief object of my life to do the best I can for my children.'

'I am sure it is.'

'And you ought to feel that, as I have had a long experience in the world, my judgement about a young man might be trusted.'

That was a statement which Miss Wharton was not prepared to admit. She had already professed herself willing to submit to her father's judgement, and did not now by any means contemplate rebellion against parental authority. But she did feel that on a matter so vital to her she had a right to plead her cause before judgement should be given, and she was not slow to assure herself, even as this interview went on, that her love for the man was strong enough to entitle her to assure her father that her happiness depended on his reversal of the sentence already pronounced. 'You know, papa, that I trust you,' she said.

'And I have promised you that I will not disobey you. If you tell me that I am never to see Mr Lopez again, I will not see him.'

'You are a good girl. You were always a good girl.'

'But I think that you ought to hear me.' Then he stood still with his hands in his trowsers pockets looking at her. He did not want to hear a word, but he felt that he would be a tyrant if he refused. 'If you tell me that I am not to see him, I shall not see him. But I shall be very unhappy. I do love him, and I shall never love anyone else in the same way.'

'That is nonsense, Emily. There is Arthur Fletcher.'

'I am sure you will never ask me to marry a man I do not love, and I shall never love Arthur Fletcher. If this is to be as you say, it will make me very, very wretched. It is right that you should know the truth. If it is only because Mr Lopez has a foreign name——'

'It isn't only that; no one knows anything about him, or where to inquire even.'

'I think you should inquire, papa, and be quite certain before you pronounce such a sentence against me. It will be a crushing blow.' He looked at her, and saw that there was a fixed purpose in her countenance of which he had never before seen similar signs. 'You claim a right to my obedience, and I acknowledge it. I am sure you believe me when I promise not to see him without your permission.'

'I do believe you. Of course I believe you.'

'But if I do that for you, papa, I think that you ought to be very sure, on my account, that I haven't to bear such unhappiness for nothing. You'll think about it, papa,—will you not, before you quite decide?' She leaned against him as she spoke, and he kissed her. 'Good night, now, papa. You will think about it?'

'I will. I will. Of course I will.'

And he began the process of thinking about it immediately,— before the door was closed behind her. But what was there to think about? Nothing that she had said altered in the least his idea about the man. He was convinced as ever that unless there was much to conceal there would not be so much concealment. But a feeling began to grow upon him already that his daughter had a mode of pleading with him which he would not ultimately be able to resist. He had the power, he knew, of putting an end to the thing altogether. He had only to say resolutely and unchangeably that the thing shouldn't be, and it wouldn't be. If he could steel his heart against his daughter's sorrow for, say, a twelvemonth, the victory would be won. But he already began to fear that he lacked the power to steel his heart against his daughter.

CHAPTER 6

AN OLD FRIEND GOES TO WINDSOR

'AND what are they going to make you now?'

This question was asked of her husband by a lady with whom perhaps the readers of this volume may have already formed some acquaintance. Chronicles of her early life* have been written, at any rate copiously. The lady was the Duchess of Omnium, and her husband was of course the Duke. In order that the nature of the question asked by the duchess may be explained, it must be stated that just at this time the political affairs of the nation had got themselves tied up into one of those truly desperate knots from which even the wisdom and experience of septuagenarian statesmen can see no unravelment. The heads of parties were at a standstill. In the House of Commons, there was, so to say, no majority on either side. The minds of members were so astray that, according to the best calculation that could be made, there would be a majority of about ten against any possible Cabinet. There would certainly be a majority against either of those well-tried, but, at this moment, little trusted Prime Ministers, Mr Gresham and Mr Daubeny.* There were certain men, nominally belonging to this or to the other party, who would certainly within a week of the nomination of a Cabinet in the House, oppose the Cabinet which they ought to support. Mr Daubeny had been in power,—nay, was in power, though he had twice resigned. Mr Gresham had been twice sent for to Windsor,* and had on one occasion undertaken and on another had refused to undertake to form a Ministry. Mr Daubeny had tried two or three combinations, and had been at his wits' end. He was no doubt still in power,—could appoint bishops, and make peers, and give away ribbons. But he couldn't pass a law, and certainly continued to hold his present uncomfortable position by no will of his own. But a Prime Minister cannot escape till he has succeeded in finding a successor; and though the successor be found and consents to make an attempt, the old unfortunate cannot be allowed to go free when that attempt is shown to be a failure. He has not absolutely given up the keys of his boxes,* and no one will take them from him. Even a sovereign can abdicate; but the Prime Minister of a constitutional government is in bonds. The reader may therefore understand that the Duchess was asking her husband what place among the political rulers of the country had been offered to him by the last aspirant to the leadership of the Government.

But the reader should understand more than this, and may perhaps do so, if he has ever seen those former chronicles to which allusion has been made. The Duke, before he became a duke, had held very high office, having been Chancellor of the Exchequer. When he was transferred, perforce, to the House of Lords, he had,—as is not uncommon in such cases,—accepted a lower political station. This had displeased the Duchess, who was ambitious both on her own behalf and that of her lord,—and who thought that a Duke of Omnium should be nothing in the Government if not at any rate near the top. But after that, with the simple and single object of doing some special piece of work for the nation,*—something which he fancied that nobody else would do if he didn't do it,—his Grace, of his own motion, at his own solicitation, had encountered further official degradation, very much to the disgust of the Duchess. And it was not the way with her Grace to hide such sorrows in the depth of her bosom. When affronted she would speak out, whether to her husband, or to another,—using irony rather than argument to support her cause and to vindicate her ways. The shafts of ridicule hurled by her against her husband in regard to his voluntary abasement had been many and sharp. They stung him, but never for a moment influenced him. And though they stung him, they did not even anger him. It was her nature to say such things,—and he knew that they came rather from her uncontrolled spirit than from any malice. She was his wife too, and he had an idea that of little injuries of that sort there should be no end of bearing on the part of a husband. Sometimes he would endeavour to explain to her the motives which actuated him; but he had come to fear that they were and must ever be unintelligible to her. But he credited her with less than her real intelligence. She did understand the nature of his work and his reasons for doing it; and, after her own fashion, did what she conceived to be her own work in endeavouring to create within his bosom a desire for higher things. 'Surely,' she said to herself, 'if a man of his rank is to be a minister he should be a great minister;—at any rate as great as his circumstances will make him. A man never can save his country by degrading himself.' In this he would probably have agreed; but his idea of degradation and hers hardly tallied.

When therefore she asked him what they were going to make him, it was as though some sarcastic housekeeper in a great establishment should ask the butler,—some butler too prone to yield in such matters,—whether the master had appointed him lately to the cleaning of shoes or the carrying of coals. Since these knots had become so very tight, and since the journeys to Windsor had become so very frequent, her Grace had asked many such questions, and had received but very indifferent replies. The Duke had sometimes declared that the matter was not ripe enough to allow him to make any answer. 'Of course,' said the Duchess, 'you should keep the secret. The editors of the evening papers haven't known it for above an hour.' At another time he told her that he had undertaken to give Mr Gresham his assistance in any way in which it might be asked. 'Joint Under-Secretary with Lord Fawn,* I should say,' answered the Duchess. Then he told her that he believed an attempt would be made at a mixed ministry, but that he did not in the least know to whom the work of doing so would be confided. 'You will be about the last man who will be told,' replied the Duchess. Now, at this moment, he had, as she knew, come direct from the house of Mr Gresham, and she asked her question in her usual spirit. 'And what are they going to make you now?'

But he did not answer the question in his usual manner. He would customarily smile gently at her badinage, and perhaps say a word intended to show that he was not in the least moved by her raillery. But in this instance he was very grave, and stood before her a moment making no answer at all, looking at her in a sad and almost solemn manner. 'They have told you that they can do without you,' she said, breaking out almost into a passion. 'I knew how it would be. Men are always valued by others as they value themselves.'

'I wish it were so,' he replied. 'I should sleep easier to-night.'

'What is it, Plantagenet?' she exclaimed, jumping up from her chair.

'I never cared for your ridicule hitherto, Cora; but now I feel that I want your sympathy.'

'If you are going to do anything,—to do really anything, you shall have it. Oh, how you shall have it!'

'I have received her Majesty's orders to go down to Windsor at once. I must start within half-an-hour.'

'You are going to be Prime Minister!' she exclaimed. As she spoke she threw her arms up, and then rushed into his embrace. Never since their first union had she been so demonstrative either of love or admiration. 'Oh, Plantagenet,' she said, 'if I can only do anything I will slave for you.' As he put his arm round her waist he already felt the pleasantness of her altered way to him. She had never worshipped him yet, and therefore her worship when it did come had all the delight to him which it ordinarily has to the newly married hero.

'Stop a moment, Cora. I do not know how it may be yet. But this I know, that if without cowardice I could avoid this task, I would certainly avoid it.'

'Oh no! And there would be cowardice; of course there would,' said the Duchess, not much caring what might be the bonds which bound him to the task so long as he should certainly feel himself to be bound.

'He has told me that he thinks it my duty to make the attempt.'

'Who is he?'

'Mr Gresham. I do not know that I should have felt myself bound by him, but the Duke said so also.' This duke was our duke's old friend, the Duke of St Bungay.*

'Was he there? And who else?'

'No one else. It is no case for exultation, Cora, for the chances are that I shall fail. The Duke has promised to help me, on condition that one or two he has named are included, and that one or two whom he has also named are not. In each case, I should myself have done exactly as he proposes.'

'And Mr Gresham?'

'He will retire. That is a matter of course. He will intend to support us; but all that is veiled in the obscurity which is always, I think, darker as to the future of politics than any other future. Clouds arise, one knows not why or whence, and create darkness when one expected light. But as yet, you must understand, nothing is settled. I cannot even say what answer I may make to her Majesty, till I know what commands her Majesty may lay upon me.'

'You must keep a hold of it now, Plantagenet,' said the Duchess clenching her own fist.

'I will not even close a finger on it with any personal ambition,' said the Duke. 'If I could be relieved from the burden this moment it would be an ease to my heart. I remember once,' he said,—and as he spoke he again put his arm around her waist, 'when I was debarred from taking office by a domestic circumstance.'*

'I remember that too,' she said, speaking very gently and looking up at him.

'It was a grief to me at the time, though it turned out so well,— because the office then suggested to me was one which I thought I could fill with credit to the country. I believed in myself then as far as that work went. But for this attempt I have no belief in myself. I doubt whether I have any gift for governing men.'

'It will come.'

'It may be that I must try;—and it may be that I must break my heart because I fail. But I shall make the attempt if I am directed to do so in any manner that shall seem feasible. I must be off now. The Duke is to be here this evening. They had better have dinner ready for me whenever I may be able to eat it.' Then he took his departure before she could say another word.

When the Duchess was alone she took to thinking of the whole thing in a manner which they who best knew her would have thought to be very unusual with her. She already possessed all that rank and wealth could give her, and together with those good things a peculiar position of her own, of which she was proud, and which she had made her own not by her wealth and rank, but by a certain fearless energy and power of raillery which never deserted her. Many feared her and she was afraid of none, and many also loved her,—whom she also loved, for her nature was affectionate. She was happy with her children, happy with her friends, in the enjoyment of perfect health, and capable of taking an exaggerated interest in anything that might come uppermost for the moment. One would have been inclined to say that politics were altogether unnecessary to her, and that as Duchess of Omnium, lately known as Lady Glencora Palliser, she had a wider and pleasanter influence than could belong to any woman as wife of a Prime Minister. And she was essentially one of those women who are not contented to be known simply as the wives of their husbands. She had a celebrity of her own, quite independent of his position, and which could not be enhanced by any glory or any power added to him. Nevertheless when he left her to go down to the Queen with the prospect of being called upon to act as chief of the incoming ministry, her heart throbbed with excitement. It had come at last, and he would be, to her thinking, the leading man in the greatest kingdom in the world.

But she felt in regard to him somewhat as did Lady Macbeth* towards her lord.

'What thou would'st highly,
That would'st thou holily.'

She knew him to be full of scruples, unable to bend when aught was to be got by bending, unwilling to domineer when men might be brought to subjection only by domination. The first duty never could be taught to him. To win support by smiles when his heart was bitter within him would never be within the power of her husband. He could never be brought to buy an enemy by political gifts,—would never be prone to silence his keenest opponent by making him his right hand supporter. But the other lesson was easier and might she thought be learned. Power is so pleasant that men quickly learn to be greedy in the enjoyment of it, and to flatter themselves that patriotism requires them to be imperious. She would be constant with him day and night to make him understand that his duty to his country required him to be in very truth its chief ruler. And then with some knowledge of things as they are,—and also with much ignorance,—she reflected that he had at his command a means of obtaining popularity and securing power, which had not belonged to his immediate predecessors, and had perhaps never to the same extent been at the command of any minister in England. His wealth as Duke of Omnium had been great; but hers, as available for immediate purposes, had been greater even than his. After some fashion, of which she was profoundly ignorant, her own property was separated from his* and reserved to herself and her children. Since her marriage she had never said a word to him about her money,— unless it were to ask that something out of the common course might be spent on some, generally absurd, object. But now had come the time for squandering money. She was not only rich but she had a popularity that was exclusively her own. The new Prime Minister and the new Prime Minister's wife should entertain after a fashion that had never yet been known even among the nobility of England. Both in town and country those great mansions should be kept open which were now rarely much used because she had found them dull, cold, and comfortless. In London there should not be a Member of Parliament whom she would not herself know and influence by her flattery and grace,—or if there were men whom she could not influence, they should live as men tabooed and unfortunate. Money mattered nothing. Their income was enormous, and for a series of years,—for half-a-dozen years if the game could be kept up so long,—they could spend treble what they called their income without real injury to their children. Visions passed through her brain of wondrous things which might be done,—if only her husband would be true to his own greatness.

The Duke had left her about two. She did not stir out of the house that day, but in the course of the afternoon she wrote a line to a friend who lived not very far from her. The Duchess dwelt in Carlton Terrace, and her friend in Park Lane. The note was as follows:—

'Dear M.,
    'Come to me at once. I am too excited to go to you.
                                                'Yours,
                                                                'G.'

This was addressed to one Mrs Finn,* a lady as to whom chronicles also have been written, and who has been known to the readers of such chronicles as a friend dearly loved by the Duchess. As quickly as she could put on her carriage garments and get herself to Carlton Terrace, Mrs Finn was there. 'Well, my dear, how do you think it's all settled at last?' said the Duchess. It will probably be felt that the new Prime Minister's wife was indiscreet, and hardly worthy of the confidence placed in her by her husband. But surely we all have some one friend to whom we tell everything, and with the Duchess Mrs Finn was that one friend.

'Is the Duke to be Prime Minister?'

'How on earth should you have guessed that?'

'What else could make you so excited? Besides it is by no means strange. I understand that they have gone on trying the two old stagers till it is useless to try them any longer; and if there is to be a fresh man, no one would be more likely than the Duke.'

'Do you think so?'

'Certainly. Why not?'

'He has frittered away his political position by such meaningless concessions. And then he had never done anything to put himself forward,—at any rate since he left the House of Commons. Perhaps I haven't read things right,—but I was surprised, very much surprised.'

'And gratified?'

'Oh yes. I can tell you everything, because you will neither misunderstand me nor tell tales of me. Yes,—I shall like him to be Prime Minister, though I know that I shall have a bad time of it myself.'

'Why a bad time?'

'He is so hard to manage. Of course I don't mean about politics. Of course it must be a mixed kind of thing at first, and I don't care a straw whether it run to Radicalism or Toryism. The country goes on its own way; either for better or for worse, whichever of them are in. I don't think it makes any difference as to what sort of laws are passed. But among ourselves, in our set, it makes a deal of difference who gets the garters, and the counties, who are made barons and then earls, and whose name stands at the head of everything.'

'That is your way of looking at politics?'

'I own it to you;—and I must teach it to him.'

'You never will do that, Lady Glen.'

'Never is a long word. I mean to try. For look back and tell me of any Prime Minister who has become sick of his power. They become sick of the want of power when it's falling away from them,—and then they affect to disdain and put aside the thing they can no longer enjoy. Love of power is a kind of feeling which comes to a man as he grows older.'

'Politics with the Duke have been simple patriotism,' said Mrs Finn.

'The patriotism may remain, my dear, but not the simplicity. I don't want him to sell his country to Germany, or to turn it into an American republic in order that he may be president. But when he gets the reins in his hands, I want him to keep them there. If he's so much honester than other people, of course he's the best man for the place. We must make him believe that the very existence of the country depends on his firmness.'

'To tell you the truth, Lady Glen, I don't think you'll ever make the Duke believe anything. What he believes, he believes either from very old habit, or from the working of his own mind.'

'You're always singing his praises, Marie.'

'I don't know that there is any special praise in what I say; but as far as I can see, it is the man's character.'

'Mr Finn will come in, of course,' said the Duchess.

'Mr Finn will be like the Duke in one thing. He'll take his own way as to being in or out quite independently of his wife.'

'You'd like him to be in office?'

'No, indeed! Why should I? He would be more often at the House, and keep later hours, and be always away all the morning into the bargain. But I shall like him to do as he likes himself.'

'Fancy thinking of all that. I'd sit up all night every night of my life,—I'd listen to every debate in the House myself,—to have Plantagenet Prime Minister. I like to be busy. Well now, if it does come off——'

'It isn't settled then?'

'How can one hope that a single journey will settle it, when those other men have been going backwards and forwards between Windsor and London, like buckets in a well, for the last three weeks? But if it is settled, I mean to have a cabinet of my own, and I mean that you shall do the foreign affairs.'

'You'd better let me be at the exchequer. I'm very good at accounts.'

'I'll do that myself. The accounts that I intend to set a-going would frighten any one less audacious. And I mean to be my own home secretary, and to keep my own conscience,—and to be my own master of the ceremonies certainly. I think a small cabinet gets on best. Do you know,—I should like to put the Queen down.'

'What on earth do you mean?'

'No treason; nothing of that kind. But I should like to make Buckingham Palace second-rate; and I'm not quite sure but I can. I dare say you don't quite understand me.'

'I don't think that I do, Lady Glen.'

'You will some of these days. Come in to-morrow before lunch. I suppose I shall know all about it then, and shall have found that my basket of crockery has been kicked over and everything smashed.'

CHAPTER 7

ANOTHER OLD FRIEND

AT about nine the Duke had returned, and was eating his very simple dinner in the breakfast-room,—a beefsteak and a potato, with a glass of sherry and Apollinaris water.* No man more easily satisfied as to what he eat and drank lived in London in those days. As regarded the eating and drinking he dined alone, but his wife sat with him and waited on him, having sent the servant out of the room. 'I have told her Majesty that I would do the best I could,' said the Duke.

'Then you are Prime Minister.'

'Not at all. Mr Daubeny is Prime Minister. I have undertaken to form a ministry, if I find it practicable, with the assistance of such friends as I possess. I never felt before that I had to lean so entirely on others as I do now.'

'Lean on yourself only. Be enough for yourself.'

'Those are empty words, Cora;—words that are quite empty. In one sense a man should always be enough for himself. He should have enough of principle and enough of conscience to restrain him from doing what he knows to be wrong. But can a ship-builder build his ship single-handed, or the watchmaker make his watch without assistance? On former occasions such as this, I could say, with little or no help from without, whether I would or would not undertake the work that was proposed to me, because I had only a bit of the ship to build, or a wheel of the watch to make. My own efficacy for my present task depends entirely on the co-operation of others, and unfortunately upon that of some others with whom I have no sympathy, nor have they with me.'

'Leave them out,' said the Duchess boldly.

'But they are men who will not be left out, and whose services the country has a right to expect.'

'Then bring them in, and think no more about it. It is no good crying for pain that cannot be cured.'

'Co-operation is difficult without community of feeling. I find myself to be too stubborn-hearted for the place. It was nothing to me to sit in the same Cabinet with a man I disliked when I had not put him there myself. But now——. As I have travelled up I have almost felt that I could not do it! I did not know before how much I might dislike a man.'

'Who is the one man?'

'Nay;—whoever he be, he will have to be a friend now, and therefore I will not name him, even to you. But it is not one only. If it were one, absolutely marked and recognized, I might avoid him. But my friends, real friends, are so few! Who is there besides the Duke on whom I can lean with both confidence and love?'

'Lord Cantrip.'

'Hardly so, Cora. But Lord Cantrip goes out with Mr Gresham. They will always cling together.'

'You used to like Mr Mildmay.'

'Mr Mildmay,—yes! If there could be a Mr Mildmay in the Cabinet, this trouble would not come upon my shoulders.'

'Then I'm very glad that there can't be a Mr Mildmay. Why shouldn't there be as good fish in the sea as ever were caught out of it?'

'When you've got a good fish you like to make as much of it as you can.'

'I suppose Mr Monk* will join you.'

'I think we shall ask him. But I am not prepared to discuss men's names as yet.'

'You must discuss them with the Duke immediately.'

'Probably;—but I had better discuss them with him before I fix my own mind by naming them even to you.'

'You'll bring Mr Finn in, Plantagenet?'

'Mr Finn!'

'Yes;—Phineas Finn,—the man who was tried.'

'My dear Cora, we haven't come down to that yet. We need not at any rate trouble ourselves about the small fishes till we are sure that we can get the big fishes to join us.'

'I don't know why he should be a small fish. No man has done better than he has; and if you want a man to stick to you——'

'I don't want a man to stick to me. I want a man to stick to his country.'

'You were talking about sympathy.'

'Well, yes;—I was. But do not name anyone else just at present. The Duke will be here soon, and I would be alone till he comes.'

'There is one thing I want to say, Plantagenet.'

'What is it?'

'One favour I want to ask.'

'Pray do not ask anything for any man at present.'

'It is not anything for any man.'

'Nor for any woman.'

'It is for a woman,—but one whom I think you would wish to oblige.'

'Who is it?' Then she curtseyed, smiling at him drolly, and put her hand upon her breast. 'Something for you! What on earth can you want that I can do for you?'

'Will you do it,—if it be reasonable?'

'If I think it reasonable, I certainly will do it.'

Then her manner changed altogether, and she became serious and almost solemn. 'If, as I suppose, all the great places about her Majesty be changed, I should like to be Mistress of the Robes.'*

'You!' said he, almost startled out of his usual quiet demeanour.

'Why not I? Is not my rank high enough?'

'You burden yourself with the intricacies and subserviences, with the tedium and pomposities of Court life! Cora, you do not know what you are talking about, or what you are proposing for yourself.'

'If I am willing to try to undertake a duty, why should I be debarred from it any more than you?'

'Because I have put myself into a groove, and ground myself into a mould, and clipped and pared and pinched myself all round,—very ineffectually, as I fear,—to fit myself for this thing. You have lived as free as air. You have disdained,—and though I may have grumbled I have still been proud to see you disdain,—to wrap yourself in the swaddling bandages of Court life. You have ridiculed all those who have been near her Majesty as Court ladies.'

'The individuals, Plantagenet, perhaps; but not the office. I am getting older now, and I do not see why I should not begin a new life.' She had been somewhat quelled by his unexpected energy, and was at the moment hardly able to answer him with her usual spirit.

'Do not think of it, my dear. You asked whether your rank was high enough. It must be so, as there is, as it happens, none higher. But your position, should it come to pass that your husband is the head of the Government, will be too high. I may say that in no condition should I wish my wife to be subject to other restraint than that which is common to all married women. I should not choose that she should have any duties unconnected with our joint family and home. But as First Minister of the Crown I would altogether object to her holding an office believed to be at my disposal.' She looked at him with her large eyes wide open, and then left him without a word. She had no other way of showing her displeasure, for she knew that when he spoke as he had spoken now all argument was unavailing.

The Duke remained an hour alone before he was joined by the other Duke, during which he did not for a moment apply his mind to the subject which might be thought to be most prominent in his thoughts,— the filling up, namely, of a list of his new government. All that he could do in that direction without further assistance had been already done very easily. There were four or five certain names,—names that is of certain political friends, and three or four almost equally certain of men who had been political enemies, but who would now clearly be asked to join the ministry. Sir Gregory Grogram, the late Attorney-General, would of course be asked to resume his place; but Sir Timothy Beeswax,* who was up to this moment Solicitor-General for the Conservatives, would also be invited to retain that which he held. Many details were known, not only to the two dukes who were about to patch up the ministry between them, but to the political world at large,—and were facts upon which the newspapers were able to display their wonderful foresight and general omniscience with their usual confidence. And as to the points which were in doubt,—whether or not, for instance, that consistent old Tory Sir Orlando Drought* should be asked to put up with the Post-office or should be allowed to remain at the Colonies,— the younger Duke did not care to trouble himself till the elder should have come to his assistance. But his own position and his questionable capacity for filling it,—that occupied all his mind. If nominally first he would be really first. Of so much it seemed to him that his honour required him to assure himself. To be a *fainéant** ruler was in direct antagonism both to his conscience and to his predilections. To call himself by a great name before the world, and then to be something infinitely less than that name, would be to him a degradation. But though he felt fixed as to that, he was by no means assured as to that other point, which to most men firm in their resolves as he was, and backed up as he had been by the confidence of others, would be cause of small hesitation. He did doubt his ability to fill that place which it would now be his duty to occupy. He more than doubted. He told himself again and again that there was wanting to him a certain noble capacity for commanding support and homage from other men. With things and facts he could deal, but human beings had not opened themselves to him. But now it was too late! and yet,—as he said to his wife,—to fail would break his heart! No ambition had prompted him.

He was sure of himself there. One only consideration had forced him into this great danger, and that had been the assurance of others that it was his manifest duty to encounter it. And now there was clearly no escape,—no escape compatible with that clean-handed truth from which it was not possible for him to swerve. He might create difficulties in order that through them a way might still be opened to him of restoring to the Queen the commission which had been entrusted to him. He might insist on this or that impossible concession. But the memory of escape such as that would break his heart as surely as the failure.

When the Duke was announced he rose to greet his old friend almost with fervour. 'It is a shame,' he said, 'to bring you out so late. I ought to have gone to you.'

'Not at all. It is always the rule in these cases that the man who has most to do should fix himself as well as he can where others may be able to find him.' The Duke of St Bungay was an old man, between seventy and eighty, with hair nearly white, and who on entering the room had to unfold himself out of various coats and comforters. But he was in full possession not only of his intellects but of his bodily power, showing, as many politicians do show, that the cares of the nation may sit upon a man's shoulders for many years without breaking or even bending them. For the Duke had belonged to ministries for nearly the last half century. As the chronicles have also dealt with him, no further records of his past life shall now be given.

He had said something about the Queen, expressing gracious wishes for the comfort of her Majesty in all these matters, something of the inconvenience of these political journeys to and fro, something also of the delicacy and difficulty of the operations on hand which were enhanced by the necessity of bringing men together as cordial allies who had hitherto acted with bitter animosity one to another, before the younger Duke said a word. 'We may as well,' said the elder, 'make out some small provisional list, and you can ask those you name to be with you early to-morrow. But perhaps you have already made a list.'

'No indeed. I have not even had a pencil in my hand.'

'We may as well begin then,' said the elder, facing the table when he saw that his less-experienced companion made no attempt at beginning.

'There is something horrible to me in the idea of writing down men's names for such a work as this, just as boys at school used to draw out the elevens for a cricket match.' The old stager turned round and stared at the younger politician. 'The thing itself is so momentous that one ought to have aid from heaven.'

Plantagenet Palliser was the last man from whom the Duke of St Bungay would have expected romance at any time, and, least of all, at such a time as this. 'Aid from heaven you may have,' he said, 'by saying your prayers; and I don't doubt you ask it for this and all other things generally. But an angel won't come to tell you who ought to be Chancellor of the Exchequer.'

'No angel will, and therefore I wish that I could wash my hands of it.' His old friend still stared at him. 'It is like sacrilege to me, attempting this without feeling one's own fitness for the work. It unmans me,—this necessity of doing that which I know I cannot do with fitting judgement.'

'Your mind has been a little too hard at work to-day.'

'It hasn't been at work at all. I've had nothing to do, and have been unable really to think of work. But I feel that chance circumstances have put me into a position for which I am unfit, and which yet I have been unable to avoid. How much better would it be that you should do this alone,—you yourself.'

'Utterly out of the question. I do know and think that I always have known my own powers. Neither has my aptitude in debate nor my capacity for work justified me in looking to the premiership. But that, forgive me, is now not worthy of consideration. It is because you do work and can work, and because you have fitted yourself for that continued course of lucid explanation which we now call debate, that men on both sides have called upon you as the best man to come forward in this difficulty. Excuse me, my friend, again, if I say that I expect to find your manliness equal to your capacity.'

'If I could only escape from it!'

'Psha;—nonsense!' said the old Duke, getting up. 'There is such a thing as a conscience with so fine an edge that it will allow a man to do nothing. You've got to serve your country. On such assistance as I can give you you know that you may depend with absolute assurance. Now let us get to work. I suppose you would wish that I should take the chair at the Council.'*

'Certainly;—of course,' said the Duke of Omnium, turning to the table. The one practical suggestion had fixed him, and from that moment he gave himself to the work in hand with all his energies. It was not very difficult, nor did it take them a very long time. If the future Prime Minister had not his names at his fingers' ends, the future President of the Council had them. Eight men were soon named whom it was thought well that the Duke of Omnium should consult early in the morning as to their willingness to fill certain places.*

'Each one of them may have some other one or some two whom he may insist on bringing with him,' said the elder Duke; 'and though of course you cannot yield to the pressure in every such case, it will be wise to allow yourself scope for some amount of concession. You'll find they'll shake down after the usual amount of resistance and compliance. No;—don't you leave your house to-morrow to see anybody unless it be Mr Daubeny or Her Majesty. I'll come to you at two, and if her Grace will give me luncheon, I'll lunch with her. Good night, and don't think too much of the bigness of the thing. I remember dear old Lord Brock* telling me how much more difficult it was to find a good coachman than a good Secretary of State.' The Duke of Omnium, as he sat thinking of things for the next hour in his chair, succeeded only in proving to himself that Lord Brock never ought to have been Prime Minister of England after having ventured to make so poor a joke on so solemn a subject.

CHAPTER 8

THE BEGINNING OF A NEW CAREER

By the time that the Easter holidays were over,—holidays which had been used so conveniently for the making of a new government,—the work of getting a team together had been accomplished by the united energy of the two dukes and other friends. The filling up of the great places had been by no means so difficult or so tedious,—nor indeed the cause of half so many heartburns,—as the completion of the list of subordinates. *Noblesse oblige.** The Secretaries of State, and the Chancellors, and the First Lords, selected from this or the other party, felt that the eyes of mankind were upon them, and that it behoved them to assume a virtue* if they had it not. They were habitually indifferent to self-exaltation, and allowed themselves to be thrust into this or that unfitting role, professing that the Queen's Government and the good of the country were their only considerations. Lord Thrift made way for Sir Orlando Drought at the Admiralty, because it was felt on all sides that Sir Orlando could not join the new composite party without high place. And the same grace was shown in regard to Lord Drummond, who remained at the Colonies, keeping the office to which he had been lately transferred under Mr Daubeny. And Sir Gregory Grogram said not a word, whatever he may have thought, when he was told that Mr Daubeny's Lord Chancellor, Lord Ramsden, was to keep the seals.* Sir Gregory did, no doubt, think very much about it; for legal offices have a signification differing much from that which attaches itself to places simply political. A Lord Chancellor becomes a peer, and on going out of office enjoys a large pension. When the woolsack has been reached there comes an end of doubt, and a beginning of ease. Sir Gregory was not a young man, and this was a terrible blow. But he bore it manfully, saying not a word when the Duke spoke to him; but he became convinced from that moment that no more inefficient lawyer ever sat upon the English bench, or a more presumptuous politician in the British Parliament, than Lord Ramsden.

The real struggle, however, lay in the appropriate distribution of the Rattlers and the Robys, the Fitzgibbons and the Macphersons among the subordinate offices of State. Mr Macpherson and Mr Roby, with a host of others who had belonged to Mr Daubeny, were prepared, as they declared from the first, to lend their assistance to the Duke. They had consulted Mr Daubeny on the subject, and Mr Daubeny told them that their duty lay in that direction. At the first blush of the matter the arrangement took the form of a gracious tender from themselves to a statesman called upon to act in very difficult circumstances,—and they were thanked accordingly by the Duke, with something of real cordial gratitude. But when the actual adjustment of things was in hand, the Duke, having but little power of assuming a soft countenance and using soft words while his heart was bitter, felt on more than one occasion inclined to withdraw his thanks. He was astounded not so much by the pretensions as by the unblushing assertion of these pretensions in reference to places which he had been innocent enough to think were always bestowed at any rate without direct application. He had measured himself rightly when he told the older duke in one of those anxious conversations which had been held before the attempt was made, that long as he had been in office himself he did not know what was the way of bestowing office. 'Two gentlemen have been here this morning,' he said one day to the Duke of St Bungay, 'one on the heels of the other, each assuring me not only that the whole stability of the enterprise depends on my giving a certain office to him,—but actually telling me to my face that I had promised it to him!' The old statesman laughed. 'To be told within the same half-hour by two men that I had made promises to each of them inconsistent with each other!'

'Who were the two men?'

'Mr Rattler and Mr Roby.'

'I am assured that they are inseparable since the work was begun. They always had a leaning to each other, and now I hear they pass their time between the steps of the Carlton and Reform Clubs.'*

'But what am I to do? One must be Patronage Secretary,* no doubt.'

'They're both good men in their way, you know.'

'But why do they come to me with their mouths open, like dogs craving a bone? It used not to be so. Of course men were always anxious for office as they are now.'

'Well; yes. We've heard of that before to-day, I think.'

'But I don't think any man ever ventured to ask Mr Mildmay.'

'Time had done much for him in consolidating his authority, and perhaps the present world is less reticent in its eagerness than it was in his younger days. I doubt, however, whether it is more dishonest, and whether struggles were not made quite as disgraceful to the strugglers as anything that is done now. You can't alter the men, and you must use them.' The younger Duke sat down and sighed over the degenerate patriotism of the age.

But at last even the Rattlers and Robys were fixed, if not satisfied, and a complete list of the ministry appeared in all the newspapers. Though the thing had been long a-doing, still it had come suddenly,—so that at the first proposition to form a coalition ministry, the newspapers had hardly known whether to assist or to oppose the scheme. There was no doubt, in the minds of all these editors and contributors, the teaching of a tradition that coalitions of this kind have been generally feeble, sometimes disastrous, and on occasions even disgraceful. When a man, perhaps through a long political life, has bound himself to a certain code of opinions, how can he change that code at a moment? And when at the same moment, together with the change, he secures power, patronage, and pay, how shall the public voice absolve him? But then again, men, who have by the work of their lives grown into a certain position in the country, and have unconsciously but not therefore less actually made themselves indispensable either to this side in politics or to that, cannot free themselves altogether from the responsibility of managing them when a period comes such as that now reached. This also the newspapers perceived; and having, since the commencement of the session, been very loud in exposing the disgraceful collapse of government affairs, could hardly refuse their support to any attempt at a feasible arrangement. When it was first known that the Duke of Omnium had consented to make the attempt, they had both on one side and the other been loud in his praise, going so far as to say that he was the only man in England who could do the work. It was probably this encouragement which had enabled the new Premier to go on with an undertaking which was personally distasteful to him, and for which from day to day he believed himself to be less and less fit. But when the newspapers told him that he was the only man for the occasion, how could he be justified in crediting himself in preference to them?

The work in Parliament began under the new auspices with great tranquillity. That there would soon come causes of hot blood,—the English Church, the county suffrage, the income tax, and further education questions,*—all men knew who knew anything. But for the moment, for the month even, perhaps for the session, there was to be peace, with full latitude for the performance of routine duties. There was so to say no opposition, and at first it seemed that one special bench* in the House of Commons would remain unoccupied. But after a day or two,—on one of which Mr Daubeny had been seen sitting just below the gangway,—that gentleman returned to the place usually held by the Prime Minister's rival, saying with a smile that it might be for the convenience of the House that the seat should be utilized. Mr Gresham, at this time had, with declared purpose, asked and obtained the Speaker's leave of absence, and was abroad. Who should lead the House? That had been a great question, caused by the fact that the Prime Minister was in the House of Lords;—and what office should the leader hold? Mr Monk had consented to take the Exchequer, but the right to sit opposite to the Treasury Box and to consider himself for the time the principal spirit in that chamber was at last assigned to Sir Orlando Drought. 'It will never do,' said Mr Rattler to Mr Roby. 'I don't mean to say anything against Drought, who has always been a very useful man to your party;—but he lacks something of the position.'

'The fact is,' said Roby, 'that we've trusted to two men so long that we don't know how to suppose any one else big enough to fill their places. Monk wouldn't have done. The House doesn't care about Monk.'

'I always thought it should have been Wilson,* and so I told the Duke. He had an idea that it should be one of your men.'

'I think he's right there,' said Roby. 'There ought to be something like a fair division. Individuals might be content, but the party would be dissatisfied. For myself, I'd have sooner stayed out as an independent member, but Daubeny said that he thought I was bound to make myself useful.'

'I told the Duke from the beginning,' said Rattler, 'that I didn't think that I could be of any service to him. Of course I would support him, but I had been too thoroughly a party man for a new movement of this kind. But he said just the same!—that he considered I was bound to join him. I asked Gresham, and when Gresham said so too, of course I had no help for it.'

Neither of these excellent public servants had told a lie in this. Some such conversations as those reported had passed;—but a man doesn't lie when he exaggerates an emphasis, or even when he gives by a tone a meaning to a man's words exactly opposite to that which another tone would convey. Or, if he does lie in doing so, he does not know that he lies. Mr Rattler had gone back to his old office at the Treasury and Mr Roby had been forced to content himself with the Secretaryship at the Admiralty. But, as the old Duke had said, they were close friends, and prepared to fight together any battle which might keep them in their present position.

Many of the cares of office the Prime Minister did succeed in shuffling off altogether on to the shoulders of his elder friend. He would not concern himself with the appointment of ladies, about whom he said he knew nothing, and as to whose fitness and claims he professed himself to be as ignorant as the office messenger. The offers were of course made in the usual form, as though coming direct from the Queen, through the Prime Minister;—but the selections were in truth effected by the old Duke in council with —— an illustrious personage. The matter affected our Duke,—only in so far that he could not get out of his mind that strange application from his own wife. 'That she should have even dreamed of it!' he would say to himself, not yet having acquired sufficient experience of his fellow creatures to be aware how wonderfully temptations will affect even those who appear to be least subject to them. The town horse, used to gaudy trappings, no doubt despises the work of his country brother; but yet, now and again, there comes upon him a sudden desire to plough. The desire for ploughing had come upon the Duchess, but the Duke could not understand it.

He perceived, however, in spite of the multiplicity of his official work, that his refusal sat heavily on his wife's breast, and that, though she spoke no further word, she brooded over her injury. And his heart was sad within him when he thought that he had vexed her,—loving her as he did with all his heart, but with a heart that was never demonstrative. When she was unhappy he was miserable, though he would hardly know the cause of his misery. Her ridicule and raillery he could bear, though they stung him; but her sorrow, if ever she were sorrowful, or her sullenness, if ever she were sullen, upset him altogether. He was in truth so soft of heart that he could not bear the discomfort of the one person in the world who seemed to him to be near to him. He had expressly asked her for her sympathy in the business he had on hand,—thereby going much beyond his usual coldness of manner. She, with an eagerness which might have been expected from her, had promised that she would slave for him, if slavery were necessary. Then she had made her request, had been refused, and was now moody. 'The Duchess of —— is to be Mistress of the Robes,' he said to her one day. He had gone to her, up to her own room, before he dressed for dinner, having devoted much more time than as Prime Minister he ought to have done to a resolution that he would make things straight with her, and to the best way of doing it.

'So I am told. She ought to know her way about the place, as I remember she was at the same work when I was a girl of eleven.'

'That's not so very long ago, Cora.'

'Silverbridge is older now than I was then, and I think that makes it a very long time ago.' Lord Silverbridge was the Duke's eldest son.

'But what does it matter? If she began her career in the time of George the Fourth, what is it to you?'

'Nothing on earth,—only that she did in truth begin her career in the time of George the Third. I'm sure she's nearer sixty than fifty.'

'I'm glad to see you remember your dates so well.'

'It's a pity she should not remember hers in the way she dresses,' said the Duchess.

This was marvellous to him,—that his wife who as Lady Glencora Palliser had been so conspicuous for a wild disregard of social rules as to be looked upon by many as an enemy of her own class, should be so depressed by not being allowed to be the Queen's head servant as to descend to personal invective! 'I'm afraid,' said he, attempting to smile, 'that it won't come within the compass of my office to effect or even to propose any radical change in her Grace's apparel. But don't you think that you and I can afford to ignore all that?'

'I can certainly. She may be an antiquated Eve for me.'

'I hope, Cora, you are not still disappointed because I did not agree with you when you spoke about the place for yourself.'

'Not because you did not agree with me,—but because you did not think me fit to be trusted with any judgement of my own. I don't know why I'm always to be looked upon as different from other women,—as though I were half a savage.'

'You are what you have made yourself, and I have always rejoiced that you are as you are, fresh, untrammelled, without many prejudices which afflict other ladies, and free from bonds by which they are cramped and confined. Of course such a turn of character is subject to certain dangers of its own.'

'There is no doubt about the dangers. The chances are that when I see her Grace, I shall tell her what I think about her.'

'You will I am sure say nothing unkind to a lady who is supposed to be in the place she now fills by my authority. But do not let us quarrel about an old woman.'

'I won't quarrel with you even about a young one.'

'I cannot be at ease within myself while I think you are resenting my refusal. You do not know how constantly I carry you about with me.'

'You carry a very unnecessary burden then,' she said. But he could tell at once from the altered tone of her voice, and from the light of her eye as he glanced into her face, that her anger about 'The Robes' was appeased.

'I have done as you have asked about a friend of yours,' he said. This occurred just before the final and perfected list of the new men had appeared in all the newspapers.

'What friend?'

'Mr Finn is to go to Ireland.'

'Go to Ireland!—How do you mean?'

'It is looked upon as being a very great promotion. Indeed I am told that he is considered to be the luckiest man in all the scramble.'

'You don't mean as Chief Secretary?'*

'Yes, I do. He certainly couldn't go as Lord Lieutenant.'

'But they said that Barrington Erle was going to Ireland.'

'Well; yes. I don't know that you'd be interested by all the ins and outs of it. But Mr Erle declined. It seems that Mr Erle is after all the one man in Parliament modest enough not to consider himself to be fit for any place that can be offered to him.'

'Poor Barrington! He does not like the idea of crossing the Channel so often. I quite sympathize with him. And so Phineas is to be Secretary for Ireland! Not in the Cabinet?'

'No;—not in the Cabinet. It is not by any means usual that he should be.'

'That is promotion, and I am glad! Poor Phineas! I hope they won't murder him, or anything of that kind. They do murder people, you know, sometimes.'

'He's an Irishman himself.'

'That just the reason why they should. He must put up with that of course. I wonder whether she'll like going. They'll be able to spend money, which they always like, over there. He comes backwards and forwards every week,—doesn't he?'

'Not quite that, I believe.'

'I shall miss her, if she has to stay away so long. I know you don't like her.'

'I do like her. She has always behaved well, both to me and to my uncle.'

'She was an angel to him,—and to you too, if you only knew it. I dare say you're sending him to Ireland so as to get her away from me.' This she said with a smile, as though not meaning it altogether, but yet half meaning it.

'I have asked him to undertake the office,' said the Duke solemnly, 'because I am told that he is fit for it. But I did have some pleasure in proposing it to him because I thought that it would please you.'

'It does please me, and I won't be cross any more, and the Duchess of —— may wear her clothes just as she pleases, or go without them. And as for Mrs Finn, I don't see why she should be with him always when he goes. You can quite understand how necessary she is to me. But she is in truth the only woman in London, to whom I can say what I think. And it is a comfort, you know, to have some one.'

In this way the domestic peace of the Prime Minister was readjusted, and that sympathy and co-operation for which he had first asked was accorded to him. It may be a question whether on the whole the Duchess did not work harder than he did. She did not at first dare to expound to him those grand ideas which she had conceived in regard to magnificence and hospitality. She said nothing of any extraordinary expenditure of money. But she set herself to work after her own fashion, making to him suggestions as to dinners and evening receptions, to which he objected only on the score of time. 'You must eat your dinner somewhere,' she said, 'and you need only come in just before we sit down, and go into your own room if you please without coming upstairs at all. I can at any rate do that part of it for you.' And she did do that part of it with marvellous energy all through the month of May,—so that by the end of the month, within six weeks of the time at which she first heard of the Coalition Ministry, all the world had begun to talk of the Prime Minister's dinners, and of the receptions given by the Prime Minister's wife.

CHAPTER 9

MRS DICK'S DINNER PARTY.—NO. 1

OUR readers must not forget the troubles of poor Emily Wharton amidst the gorgeous festivities of the new Prime Minister. Throughout April and May she did not see Ferdinand Lopez. It may be remembered that on the night when the matter was discussed between her and her father, she promised him that she would not do so without his permission,—saying, however, at the same time very openly that her happiness depended on such permission being given to her. For two or three weeks not a word further was said between her and her father on the subject, and he had endeavoured to banish the subject from his mind,—feeling no doubt that if nothing further were ever said it would be so much the better. But then his daughter referred to the matter,—very plainly, with a simple question, and without disguise of her own feeling, but still in a manner which he could not bring himself to rebuke. 'Aunt Harriet has asked me once or twice to go there of an evening, when you have been out. I have declined because I thought Mr Lopez would be there. Must I tell her that I am not to meet Mr Lopez, papa?'

'If she has him there on purpose to throw him in your way, I shall think very badly of her.'

'But he has been in the habit of being there, papa. Of course if you are decided about this, it is better that I should not see him.'

'Did I not tell you that I was decided?'

'You said you would make some further inquiry and speak to me again.' Now Mr Wharton had made inquiry, but had learned nothing to reassure himself;—neither had he been able to learn any fact, putting his finger on which he could point out to his daughter clearly that the marriage would be unsuitable for her. Of the man's ability and position, as certainly also of his manners, the world at large seemed to speak well. He had been blackballed at two clubs, but apparently without any defined reason. He lived as though he possessed a handsome income, and yet was in no degree fast or flashy. He was supposed to be an intimate friend of Mr Mills Happerton, one of the partners in the world-famous commercial house of Hunky and Sons, which dealt in millions. Indeed there had been at one time a rumour that he was going to be taken into the house of Hunky and Sons as a junior partner. It was evident that many people had been favourably impressed by his outward demeanour, by his mode of talk, and by his way of living. But no one knew anything about him. With regard to his material position Mr Wharton could of course ask direct questions if he pleased, and require evidence as to his alleged property. But he felt that by doing so he would abandon his right to object to the man as being a Portuguese stranger, and he did not wish to have Ferdinand Lopez as a son-in-law, even though he should be a partner in Hunky and Sons, and able to maintain a gorgeous palace at South Kensington.

'I have made inquiry.'

'Well, papa?'

'I don't know anything about him. Nobody knows anything about him.'

'Could you not ask himself anything you want to know? If I might see him I would ask him.'

'That would not do at all.'

'It comes to this, papa, that I am to sever myself from a man to whom I am attached, and whom you must admit that I have been allowed to meet from day to day with no caution that his intimacy was unpleasant to you, because he is called—Lopez.'

'It isn't that at all. There are English people of that name;* but he isn't an Englishman.'

'Of course if you say so, papa, it must be so. I have told Aunt Harriet that I consider myself to be prohibited from meeting Mr Lopez by what you have said; but I think, papa, you are a little—cruel to me.'

'Cruel to you!' said Mr Wharton, almost bursting into tears.

'I am as ready to obey as a child;—but, not being a child, I think I ought to have a reason.' To this Mr Wharton made no further immediate answer, but pulled his hair, and shuffled his feet about, and then escaped out of the room.

A few days afterwards his sister-in-law attacked him. 'Are we to understand, Mr Wharton, that Emily is not to meet Mr Lopez again? It makes it very unpleasant, because he had been intimate at our house.'

'I never said a word about her not meeting him. Of course I do not wish that any meeting should be contrived between them.'

'As it stands now it is prejudicial to her. Of course it cannot but be observed, and it is so odd that a young lady should be forbidden to meet a certain man. It looks so unpleasant for her,—as though she had misbehaved herself.'

'I have never thought so for a moment.'

'Of course you have not. How could you have thought so, Mr Wharton?'

'I say that I never did.'

'What must he think when he knows,—as of course he does know,—that she has been forbidden to meet him? It must make him fancy that he is made very much of. All that is so very bad for a girl! Indeed it is, Mr Wharton.' Of course there was absolute dishonesty in all this on the part of Mrs Roby. She was true enough to Emily's lover,—too true to him; but she was false to Emily's father. If Emily would have yielded to her she would have arranged meetings at her own house between the lovers altogether in opposition to the father. Nevertheless, there was a show of reason about what she said which Mr Wharton was unable to overcome. And at the same time there was a reality about his girl's sorrow which overcame him. He had never hitherto consulted anyone about anything in his family, having always found his own information and intellect sufficient for his own affairs. But now he felt grievously in want of some pillar,—some female pillar on which he could lean. He did not know all Mrs Roby's iniquities; but still he felt that she was not the pillar of which he was in need. There was no such pillar for his use, and he was driven to acknowledge to himself that in this distressing position he must be guided by his own strength, and his own lights. He thought it all out as well as he could in his own chamber, allowing his book or his brief to lie idle beside him for many a half-hour. But he was much puzzled both as to the extent of his own authority and the manner in which it should be used. He certainly had not desired his daughter not to meet the man. He could understand that unless some affront had been offered such an edict enforced as to the conduct of a young lady would induce all her acquaintance to suppose that she was either very much in love or else very prone to misbehave herself. He feared, indeed, that she was very much in love, but it would not be prudent to tell her secret to all the world. Perhaps it would be better that she should meet him,—always with the understanding that she was not to accept from him any peculiar attention. If she would be obedient in one particular, she would probably be so in the other;—and, indeed, he did not at all doubt her obedience. She would obey, but would take care to show him that she was made miserable by obeying. He began to foresee that he had a bad time before him.

And then as he still sat idle, thinking of it all, his mind wandered off to another view of the subject. Could he be happy, or even comfortable, if she were unhappy? Of course he endeavoured to convince himself that if he were bold, determined, and dictatorial with her, it would only be in order that her future happiness might be secured. A parent is often bound to disregard the immediate comfort of a child. But then was he sure that he was right? He of course had his own way of looking at life, but was it reasonable that he should force his girl to look at things with his eyes? The man was distasteful to him as being unlike his idea of an English gentleman, and as being without those far-reaching fibres and roots by which he thought that the solidity and stability of a human tree should be assured. But the world was changing around him every day. Royalty was marrying out of its degree. Peers' sons were looking only for money. And, more than that, peers' daughters were bestowing themselves on Jews and shopkeepers. Had he not better make the usual inquiry about the man's means, and, if satisfied on that head, let the girl do as she would? Added to all this there was growing on him a feeling that ultimately youth would as usual triumph over age, and that he would be beaten. If that were so, why worry himself, or why worry her?

On the day after Mrs Roby's attack upon him he again saw that lady, having on this occasion sent round to ask her to come to him. 'I want you to understand that I put no embargo on Emily as to meeting Mr Lopez. I can trust her fully. I do not wish her to encourage his attentions, but I by no means wish her to avoid him.'

'Am I to tell Emily what you say?'

'I will tell her myself. I think it better to say as much to you, as you seemed to be embarrassed by the fear that they might happen to see each other in your drawing-room.'

'It was rather awkward;—wasn't it?'

'I have spoken now because you seemed to think so.' His manner to her was not very pleasant, but Mrs Roby had known him for many years, and did not care very much for his manner. She had an object to gain, and could put up with a good deal for the sake of her object.

'Very well. Then I shall know how to act. But, Mr Wharton, I must say this, you know Emily has a will of her own, and you must not hold me responsible for anything that may occur.' As soon as he heard this he almost resolved to withdraw the concession he had made,—but he did not do so.

Very soon after this there came a special invitation from Mr and Mrs Roby, asking the Whartons, father and daughter, to dine with them round the corner. It was quite a special invitation, because it came in the form of a card,—which was unusual between the two families. But the dinner was too, in some degree, a special dinner,—as Emily was enabled to explain to her father, the whole speciality having been fully detailed to herself by her aunt. Mr Roby, whose belongings were not generally aristocratic, had one great connection with whom, after many years of quarrelling, he had lately come into amity. This was his half-brother, considerably older than himself, and was no other than that Mr Roby who was now Secretary to the Admiralty, and who in the last Conservative Government had been one of the Secretaries to the Treasury. The oldest Mr Roby of all, now long since gathered to his fathers, had had two wives and two sons. The elder son had not been left as well off as friends, or perhaps as he himself, could have wished.

But he had risen in the world by his wits, had made his way into Parliament, and had become, as all readers of these chronicles know, a staff of great strength to his party. But he had always been a poor man. His periods of office had been much shorter than those of his friend Rattler, and his other sources of income had not been certain. His younger half-brother, who, as far as the great world was concerned, had none of his elder brother's advantages, had been endowed with some fortune from his mother, and,—in an evil hour for both of them,—had lent the politician money. As one consequence of this transaction, they had not spoken to each other for years. On this quarrel Mrs Roby was always harping with her own husband,—not taking his part. Her Roby, her Dick, had indeed the means of supporting her with a fair comfort, but had, of his own, no power of introducing her to that sort of society for which her soul craved. But Mr Thomas Roby was a great man,—though unfortunately poor,—and moved in high circles. Because they had lent their money,—which no doubt was lost for ever,—why should they also lose the advantages of such a connection? Would it not be wiser rather to take the debt as a basis whereon to found a claim for special fraternal observation and kindred social intercourse? Dick, who was fond of his money, would not for a long time look at the matter in this light, but harassed his brother from time to time by applications which were quite useless, and which by the acerbity of their language altogether shut Mrs Roby out from the good things which might have accrued to her from so distinguished a brother-in-law. But when it came to pass that Thomas Roby was confirmed in office by the coalition which has been mentioned, Mrs Dick became very energetic. She went herself to the official hero and told him how desirous she was of peace. Nothing more should be said about the money,—at any rate for the present. Let brothers be brothers. And so it came to pass that the Secretary to the Admiralty with his wife were to dine in Berkeley Street, and that Mr Wharton was asked to meet them.

'I don't particularly want to meet Mr Thomas Roby,' the old barrister said.

'They want you to come,' said Emily, 'because there has been some family reconciliation. You usually do go once or twice a year.'

'I suppose it may as well be done,' said Mr Wharton.

'I think, papa, that they mean to ask Mr Lopez,' said Emily demurely.

'I told you before that I don't want to have you banished from your aunt's home by any man,' said the father. So the matter was settled, and the invitation was accepted. This was just at the end of May, at which time people were beginning to say that the coalition was a success, and some wise men to predict that at last fortuitous parliamentary atoms had so come together by accidental connection, that a ministry had been formed which might endure for a dozen years. Indeed there was no reason why there should be any end to a ministry built on such a foundation. Of course this was very comfortable to such men as Mr Roby, so that the Admiralty Secretary when he entered his sister-in-law's drawing-room was suffused with that rosy hue of human bliss which a feeling of triumph bestows. 'Yes,' said he, in answer to some would-be facetious remark from his brother, 'I think we have weathered that storm pretty well. It does seem rather odd, my sitting cheek by jowl with Mr Monk and gentlemen of that kidney; but they don't bite. I've got one of our own set at the head of our own office, and he leads the House. I think upon the whole we've got a little the best of it.' This was listened to by Mr Wharton with great disgust,—for Mr Wharton was a Tory of the old school, who hated compromises, and abhorred in his heart the clash of politicians to whom politics were a profession rather than a creed.

Mr Roby senior, having escaped from the House was of course the last, and had indeed kept all the other guests waiting half an hour,—as becomes a parliamentary magnate in the heat of the session. Mr Wharton, who had been early, saw all the other guests arrive, among them Mr Ferdinand Lopez. There was also Mr Mills Happerton,—partner in Hunky and Sons,—with his wife, respecting whom Mr Wharton at once concluded that he was there as being the friend of Ferdinand Lopez. If so, how much influence must Ferdinand Lopez have in that house! Nevertheless, Mr Mills Happerton was in his way a great man, and a credit to Mrs Roby. And there were Sir Damask and Lady Monogram,* who were people moving quite in the first circles. Sir Damask shot pigeons, and so did also Dick Roby,— whence had perhaps arisen an intimacy. But Lady Monogram was not at all a person to dine with Mrs Dick Roby without other cause than this. But a great official among one's acquaintance can do so much for one! It was probable that Lady Monogram's presence was among the first fruits of the happy family reconciliation that had taken place. Then there was Mrs Leslie, a pretty widow, rather poor, who was glad to receive civilities from Mrs Roby, and was Emily Wharton's pet aversion. Mrs Leslie had said impertinent things to her about Ferdinand Lopez, and she had snubbed Mrs Leslie. But Mrs Leslie was serviceable to Mrs Roby, and had now been asked to her great dinner party.

But the two most illustrious guests have not yet been mentioned. Mrs Roby had secured a lord,—an absolute peer of Parliament! This was no less a man than Lord Mongrober, whose father had been a great judge in the early part of the century, and had been made a peer. The Mongrober estates were not supposed to be large, nor was the Mongrober influence at this time extensive. But this nobleman was seen about a good deal in society when the dinners given were supposed to be worth eating. He was a fat, silent, red-faced, elderly gentleman, who said very little, and who when he did speak seemed always to be in an ill-humour. He would now and then make ill-natured remarks about his friends' wines, as suggesting '68 when a man would boast of his '48 claret; and when costly dainties were supplied for his use, would remark that such and such a dish was very well at some other time of the year. So that ladies attentive to their tables and hosts proud of their cellars would almost shake in their shoes before Lord Mongrober. And it may also be said that Lord Mongrober never gave any chance of retaliation by return dinners. There lived not the man or woman who had dined with Lord Mongrober. But yet the Robys of London were glad to entertain him; and the Mrs Robys, when he was coming, would urge their cooks to superhuman energies by the mention of his name.

And there was Lady Eustace!* Of Lady Eustace it was impossible to say whether her beauty, her wit, her wealth, or the remarkable history of her past life, most recommended her to such hosts and hostesses as Mr and Mrs Roby. As her history may already be known to some, no details of it shall be repeated here. At this moment she was free from all marital persecution, and was very much run after by a certain set in society. There were others again who declared that no decent man or woman ought to meet her. On the score of lovers there was really little or nothing to be said against her; but she had implicated herself in an unfortunate second marriage, and then there was that old story about the jewels! But there was no doubt about her money and her good looks, and some considered her to be clever. These completed the list of Mrs Roby's great dinner party.

Mr Wharton, who had arrived early, could not but take notice that Lopez, who soon followed him into the room, had at once fallen into conversation with Emily, as though there had never been any difficulty in the matter. The father, standing on the rug and pretending to answer the remarks made to him by Dick Roby, could see that Emily said but little. The man, however, was so much at his ease that there was no necessity for her to exert herself. Mr Wharton hated him for being at his ease. Had he appeared to have been rebuffed by the circumstances of his position the prejudices of the old man would have been lessened. By degrees the guests came. Lord Mongrober stood also on the rug, dumb, with a look of intense impatience for his food, hardly ever condescending to answer the little attempts at conversation made by Mrs Dick. Lady Eustace gushed into the room, kissing Mrs Dick and afterwards kissing her great friend of the moment, Mrs Leslie, who followed. She then looked as though she meant to kiss Lord Mongrober, whom she playfully and almost familiarly addressed. But Lord Mongrober only grunted. Then came Sir Damask and Lady Monogram, and Dick at once began about his pigeons. Sir Damask, who was the most good-natured man in the world, interested himself at once and became energetic, but Lady Monogram looked round the room carefully, and seeing Lady Eustace turned up her nose, nor did she care much for meeting Lord Mongrober. If she had been taken in as to the Admiralty Robys, then would she let the junior Robys know what she thought about it. Mills Happerton, with his wife, caused the frown on Lady Monogram's brow to loosen itself a little, for, so great was the wealth and power of the house of Hunky and Sons, that Mr Mills Happerton was no doubt a feature at any dinner party. Then came the Admiralty Secretary with his wife, and the order for dinner was given.

CHAPTER 10

MRS DICK'S DINNER PARTY.—NO. 2

DICK walked downstairs with Lady Monogram. There had been some doubt whether of right he should not have taken Lady Eustace, but it was held by Mrs Dick that her ladyship had somewhat impaired her rights by the eccentricities of her career, and also that she would amiably pardon any little wrong against her of that kind,—whereas Lady Monogram was a person to be much considered. Then followed Sir Damask with Lady Eustace. They seemed to be paired so well together that there could be no doubt about them. The ministerial Roby, who was really the hero of the night, took Mrs Happerton, and our friend Mr Wharton took the Secretary's wife. All that had been easy,—so easy that fate had good-naturedly arranged things which are sometimes difficult of management. But then there came an embarrassment. Of course it would in a usual way be right that a married man as was Mr Happerton should be assigned to the widow Mrs Leslie, and that the only two 'young' people,—in the usual sense of the word,—should go down to dinner together. But Mrs Roby was at first afraid of Mr Wharton, and planned it otherwise. When, however, the last moment came she plucked up courage, gave Mrs Leslie to the great commercial man, and with a brave smile asked Lopez to give his arm to the lady he loved. It is sometimes so hard to manage these 'little things,' said she to Lord Mongrober as she put her hand upon his arm. His lordship had been kept standing in that odious drawing-room for more than half an hour waiting for a man whom he regarded as a poor Treasury hack, and was by no means in a good humour. Dick Roby's wine was no doubt good, but he was not prepared to purchase it at such a price as this. 'Things always get confused when you have waited an hour for any one,' he said. 'What can one do, you know, when the House is sitting?' said the lady apologetically. 'Of course you lords can get away, but then you have nothing to do.' Lord Mongrober grunted, meaning to imply by his grunt that any one would be very much mistaken who supposed that he had any work to do because he was a peer of Parliament.

Lopez and Emily were seated next to each other, and immediately opposite to them was Mr Wharton. Certainly nothing fraudulent had been intended on this occasion,—or it would have been arranged that the father should sit on the same side of the table with the lover, so that he should see nothing of what was going on. But it seemed to Mr Wharton as though he had been positively swindled by his sister-in-law. There they sat opposite to him, talking to each other apparently with thoroughly mutual confidence, the very two persons whom he most especially desired to keep apart. He had not a word to say to either of the ladies near him. He endeavoured to keep his eyes away from his daughter as much as possible, and to divert his ears from their conversation;—but he could not but look and he could not but listen. Not that he really heard a sentence. Emily's voice hardly reached him, and Lopez understood the game he was playing much too well to allow his voice to travel. And he looked as though his position were the most commonplace in the world, and as though he had nothing of more than ordinary interest to say to his neighbour. Mr Wharton, as he sat there, almost made up his mind that he would leave his practice, give up his chambers, abandon even his club, and take his daughter at once to,— to;—it did not matter where, so that the place should be very distant from Manchester Square. There could be no other remedy for this evil.

Lopez, though he talked throughout the whole of dinner,—turning sometimes indeed to Mrs Leslie who sat at his left hand,—said very little that all the world might not have heard. But he did say one such word. 'It has been so dreary to me, the last month!' Emily of course had no answer to make to this. She could not tell him that her desolation had been infinitely worse than his, and that she had sometimes felt as though her very heart would break. 'I wonder whether it must always be like this with me,' he said,—and then he went back to the theatres and other ordinary conversation.

'I suppose you've got to the bottom of that champagne you used to have,' said Lord Mongrober roaring across the table to his host, holding his glass in his hand, and with strong marks of disapprobation on his face.

'The very same wine as we were drinking when your lordship last did me the honour of dining here,' said Dick. Lord Mongrober raised his eyebrows, shook his head and put down the glass.

'Shall we try another bottle?' asked Mrs Dick with solicitude.

'Oh no;—it'd be all the same, I know. I'll just take a little dry sherry if you have it.' The man came with the decanter. 'No, dry sherry;—dry sherry,' said his lordship. The man was confounded, Mrs Dick was at her wits' ends, and everything was in confusion. Lord Mongrober was not the man to be kept waiting by a government subordinate without exacting some penalty for such ill-treatment.

''Is lordship is a little out of sorts,' whispered Dick to Lady Monogram.

'Very much out of sorts, it seems.'

'And the worst of it is, there isn't a better glass of wine in London, and 'is lordship knows it.'

'I suppose that's what he comes for,' said Lady Monogram, being quite as uncivil in her way as the nobleman.

''E's like a good many others. He knows where he can get a good dinner. After all, there's no attraction like that. Of course, a 'ansome woman won't admit that, Lady Monogram.'

'I will not admit it, at any rate, Mr Roby.'

'But I don't doubt Monogram is as careful as any one else to get the best cook he can, and takes a good deal of trouble about his wine too. Mongrober is very unfair about that champagne. It came out of Madame Cliquot's* cellars before the war,* and I gave Sprott and Burlinghammer 110s. for it.'

'Indeed!'

'I don't think there are a dozen men in London can give you such a glass of wine as that. What do you say about that champagne, Monogram?'

'Very tidy wine,' said Sir Damask.

'I should think it is. I gave 110s. for it before the war. 'Is lordship's got a fit of the gout coming, I suppose.'

But Sir Damask was engaged with his neighbour Lady Eustace. 'Of all things I should so like to see a pigeon match,' said Lady Eustace. 'I have heard about them all my life. Only I suppose it isn't quite proper for a lady.'

'Oh, dear, yes.'

'The darling little pigeons! They do sometimes escape, don't they? I hope they escape sometimes. I'll go any day you'll make up a party,—if Lady Monogram will join us.' Sir Damask said that he would arrange it, making up his mind, however, at the same time, that this last stipulation, if insisted on, would make the thing impracticable.

Roby the ministerialist, sitting at the end of the table between his sister-in-law and Mrs Happerton, was very confidential respecting the Government and parliamentary affairs in general. 'Yes, indeed;—of course it's a coalition, but I don't see why we shouldn't go on very well. As to the Duke, I've always had the greatest possible respect for him. The truth is, there's nothing special to be done at the present moment, and there's no reason why we shouldn't agree and divide the good things between us. The Duke has got some craze of his own about decimal coinage. He'll amuse himself with that; but it won't come to anything, and it won't hurt us.'

'Isn't the Duchess giving a great many parties?' asked Mrs Happerton.

'Well;—yes. That kind of thing used to be done in old Lady Brock's time, and the Duchess is repeating it. There's no end to their money, you know. But it's rather a bore for the persons who have to go.' The ministerial Roby knew well how he would make his sister-in-law's mouth water by such an allusion as this to the great privilege of entering the Prime Minister's mansion in Carlton Terrace.

'I suppose you in the Government are always asked.'

'We are expected to go too, and are watched pretty close. Lady Glen, as we used to call her, has the eyes of Argus.* And of course we who used to be on the other side are especially bound to pay her observance.'

'Don't you like the Duchess?' asked Mrs Happerton.

'Oh, yes;—I like her very well. She's mad, you know,—mad as a hatter,—and no one can ever guess what freak may come next. One always feels that she'll do something sooner or later that will startle all the world.'

'There was a queer story* once,—wasn't there?' asked Mrs Dick.

'I never quite believed that,' said Roby. 'It was something about some lover she had before she was married. She went off to Switzerland. But the Duke,—he was Mr Palliser then,—followed her very soon and it all came right.'

'When ladies are going to be duchesses, things do come right; don't they?' said Mrs Happerton.

On the other side of Mrs Happerton was Mr Wharton, quite unable to talk to his right-hand neighbour, the Secretary's wife. The elder Mrs Roby had not, indeed, much to say for herself, and he during the whole dinner was in misery. He had resolved that there should be no intimacy of any kind between his daughter and Ferdinand Lopez,— nothing more than the merest acquaintance; and there they were, talking together before his very eyes, with more evident signs of understanding each other than were exhibited by any other two persons at the table. And yet he had no just ground of complaint against either of them. If people dine together at the same house, it may of course happen that they shall sit next to each other. And if people sit next to each other at dinner, it is expected that they shall talk. Nobody could accuse Emily of flirting; but then she was a girl who under no circumstances would condescend to flirt. But she had declared boldly to her father that she loved this man, and there she was in close conversation with him! Would it not be better for him to give up any further trouble, and let her marry the man? She would certainly do so sooner or later.

When the ladies went upstairs that misery was over for a time, but Mr Wharton was still not happy. Dick came round and took his wife's chair, so that he sat between the lord and his brother. Lopez and Happerton fell into City conversation, and Sir Damask tried to amuse himself with Mr Wharton. But the task was hopeless,—as it always is when the elements of a party have been ill-mixed. Mr Wharton had not even heard of the new Aldershot coach which Sir Damask had just started with Colonel Buskin and Sir Alfonso Blackbird. And when Sir Damask declared that he drove the coach up and down twice a week himself, Mr Wharton at any rate affected to believe that such a thing was impossible. Then when Sir Damask gave his opinion as to the cause of the failure of a certain horse at Northampton, Mr Wharton gave him no encouragement whatever. 'I never was at a racecourse in my life,' said the barrister. After that Sir Damask drank his wine in silence.

'You remember that claret, my lord?' said Dick, thinking that some little compensation was due to him for what had been said about the champagne.

But Lord Mongrober's dinner had not yet had the effect of mollifying the man sufficiently for Dick's purposes. 'Oh, yes. I remember the wine. You call it '57, don't you?'

'And it is '57;—'57, Leoville.'*

'Very likely,—very likely. If it hadn't been heated before the fire——'

'It hasn't been near the fire,' said Dick.

'Or put into a hot decanter——'

'Nothing of the kind.'

'Or treated after some other damnable fashion, it would be very good wine, I dare say.'

'You are hard to please, my lord, to-day,' said Dick, who was put beyond his bearing.

'What is a man to say? If you will talk about your wine I can only tell you what I think. Any man may get good wine,—that is if he can afford to pay the price,—but it isn't one out of ten who knows how to put it on the table.' Dick felt this to be very hard. When a man pays 110s. a dozen for his champagne, and then gives it to guests like Lord Mongrober who are not even expected to return the favour, then that man ought to be allowed to talk about his wine without fear of rebuke. One doesn't have an agreement to that effect written down on parchment and sealed; but it is as well understood and ought to be as faithfully kept as any legal contract. Dick, who could on occasions be awakened to a touch of manliness, gave the bottle a shove and threw himself back in his chair. 'If you ask me, I can only tell you,' repeated Lord Mongrober.

'I don't believe you ever had a bottle of wine put before you in better order in all your life,' said Dick. His lordship's face became very square and very red as he looked round at his host. 'And as for talking about my wine, of course I talk to a man about what he understands. I talk to Monogram about pigeons, to Tom there about politics, to 'Apperton and Lopez about the price of consols,* and to you about wine. If I asked you what you thought of the last new book, your lordship would be a little surprised.' Lord Mongrober grunted and looked redder and squarer than ever; but he made no attempt at reply, and the victory was evidently left with Dick,—very much to the general exaltation of his character. And he was proud of himself. 'We had a little tiff, me and Mongrober,' he said to his wife that night. ''E's a very good fellow, and of course he's a lord and all that. But he has to be put down occasionally, and, by George, I did it to-night. You ask Lopez.'

There were two drawing-rooms up-stairs, opening into each other, but still distinct. Emily had escaped into the back room, avoiding

the gushing sentiments and equivocal morals of Lady Eustace and
Mrs Leslie,—and here she was followed by Ferdinand Lopez.
Mr Wharton was in the front room, and though on entering it he did
look round furtively for his daughter, he was ashamed to wander about
in order that he might watch her. And there were others in the back
room,—Dick and Monogram standing on the rug, and the elder
Mrs Roby seated in a corner,—so that there was nothing peculiar in the
position of the two lovers.

'Must I understand,' said he, 'that I am banished from Manchester
Square?'

'Has papa banished you?'

'That's what I want you to tell me.'

'I know you had an interview with him, Mr Lopez.'

'Yes. I had.'

'And you must know best what he told you.'

'He would explain himself better to you than he did to me.'

'I doubt that very much. Papa, when he has anything to say, generally
says it plainly. However, I do think that he did intend to banish you.
I do not know why I should not tell you the truth.'

'I do not know either.'

'I think he did—intend to banish you.'

'And you?'

'I shall be guided by him in all things,—as far as I can.'

'Then I am banished by you also?'

'I did not say so. But if papa says that you are not to come there, of
course I cannot ask you to do so.'

'But I may see you here?'

'Mr Lopez, I will not be asked some questions. I will not indeed.'

'You know why I ask them. You know that to me you are more than
all the world.' She stood still for a moment after hearing this, and then
without any reply walked away into the other room. She felt half
ashamed of herself in that she had not rebuked him for speaking to her
in that fashion after his interview with her father, and yet his words had
filled her heart with delight. He had never before plainly declared his
love to her,—though she had been driven by her father's questions to
declare her own love to herself. She was quite sure of herself,—that the
man was and would always be to her the one being whom she would
prefer to all others. Her fate was in her father's hands. If he chose to
make her wretched he must do so. But on one point she had quite made
up her mind. She would make no concealment. To the world at large
she had nothing to say on the matter. But with her father there should

be no attempt on her part to keep back the truth. Were he to question her on the subject she would tell him, as far as her memory would serve her, the very words which Lopez had spoken to her this evening. She would ask nothing from him. He had already told her that the man was to be rejected, and had refused to give any other reason than his dislike to the absence of any English connection. She would not again ask even for a reason. But she would make her father understand that though she obeyed him she regarded the exercise of his authority as tyrannical and irrational.

They left the house before any of the other guests and walked round the corner together into the Square. 'What a very vulgar set of people!' said Mr Wharton as soon as they were down the steps.

'Some of them were,' said Emily, making a mental reservation of her own.

'Upon my word I don't know where to make the exception. Why on earth any one should want to know such a person as Lord Mongrober I can't understand. What does he bring into society?'

'A title.'

'But what does that do of itself? He is an insolent, bloated brute.'

'Papa, you are using strong language to-night.'

'And that Lady Eustace! Heaven and earth! Am I to be told that that creature is a lady?'

They had now come to their own door, and while that was being opened and as they went up into their own drawing-room, nothing was said, but then Emily began again. 'I wonder why you go to Aunt Harriet's at all. You don't like the people?'

'I didn't like any of them to-day.'

'Why do you go there? You don't like Aunt Harriet herself. You don't like Uncle Dick. You don't like Mr Lopez.'

'Certainly I do not.'

'I don't know who it is you do like.'

'I like Mr Fletcher.'

'It's no use saying that to me, papa.'

'You ask me a question, and I choose to answer it. I like Arthur Fletcher, because he is a gentleman,—because he is a gentleman of the class to which I belong myself; because he works; because I know all about him, so that I can be sure of him; because he had a decent father and mother; because I am safe with him, being quite sure that he will say to me neither awkward things nor impertinent things. He will not talk to me about driving a mail coach like that foolish baronet, nor tell me the price of all his wines like your uncle.' Nor would Ferdinand

Lopez do so, thought Emily to herself. 'But in all such matters, my dear, the great thing is like to like. I have spoken of a young person, merely because I wish you to understand that I can sympathize with others besides those of my own age. But to-night there was no one there at all like myself,—or, as I hope, like you. That man Roby is a chattering ass. How such a man can be useful to any government I can't conceive. Happerton was the best, but what had he to say for himself? I've always thought that there was very little wit wanted to make a fortune in the City.' In this frame of mind Mr Wharton went off to bed, but not a word more was spoken about Ferdinand Lopez.

CHAPTER 11

CARLTON TERRACE*

CERTAINLY the thing was done very well by Lady Glen,—as many in the political world persisted in calling her even in these days. She had not as yet quite carried out her plan,—the doing of which would have required her to reconcile her husband to some excessive abnormal expenditure, and to have obtained from him a deliberate sanction for appropriation and probable sale of property. She never could find the proper moment for doing this, having, with all her courage,—low down in some corner of her heart,—a wholesome fear of a certain quiet power which her husband possessed. She could not bring herself to make her proposition;—but she almost acted as though it had been made and approved. Her house was always gorgeous with flowers. Of course there would be the bill;—and he, when he saw the exotics, and the whole place turned into a bower of ever fresh blooming floral glories, must know that there would be the bill. And when he found that there was an archducal dinner-party every week, and an almost imperial reception twice a week; that at these receptions a banquet was always provided; when he was asked whether she might buy a magnificent pair of bay carriage-horses, as to which she assured him that nothing so lovely had ever as yet been seen stepping in the streets of London,—of course he must know that the bills would come. It was better, perhaps, to do it in this way, than to make any direct proposition. And then, early in June, she spoke to him as to the guests to be invited to Gatherum Castle* in August. 'Do you want to go to Gatherum in August?' he asked in surprise. For she hated the place, and had hardly been content to spend ten days there every year at Christmas.

'I think it should be done,' she said solemnly. 'One cannot quite consider just now what one likes oneself.'

'Why not?'

'You would hardly go to a small place like Matching in your present position. There are so many people whom you should entertain! You would probably have two or three of the foreign ministers down for a time.'

'We always used to find plenty of room at Matching.'

'But you did not always use to be Prime Minister. It is only for such a time as this that such a house as Gatherum is serviceable.'

He was silent for a moment, thinking about it, and then gave way without another word. She was probably right. There was the huge pile of magnificent buildings; and somebody, at any rate, had thought that it behoved a Duke of Omnium to live in such a palace. If it ought to be done at any time, it ought to be done now. In that his wife had been right. 'Very well. Let us go there.'

'I'll manage it all,' said the Duchess,—'I and Locock.' Locock was the house-steward.

'I remember once,' said the Duke, and he smiled as he spoke with a peculiarly sweet expression, which would at times come across his generally inexpressive face,—'I remember once that some First Minister of the Crown gave evidence as to the amount of his salary, saying that his place entailed upon him expenses higher than his stipend would defray. I begin to think that my experience will be the same.'

'Does that fret you?'

'No, Cora;—it certainly does not fret me, or I should not allow it. But I think there should be a limit. No man is ever rich enough to squander.'

Though they were to squander her fortune,—the money which she had brought,—for the next ten years at a much greater rate than she contemplated, they might do so without touching the Palliser property. Of that she was quite sure. And the squandering was to be all for his glory,—so that he might retain his position as a popular Prime Minister. For an instant it occurred to her that she would tell him all this. But she checked herself, and the idea of what she had been about to say brought the blood into her face. Never yet had she in talking to him alluded to her own wealth. 'Of course we are spending money,' she said. 'If you give me a hint to hold my hand, I will hold it.'

He had looked at her, and read it all in her face. 'God knows,' he said, 'you've a right to do it if it pleases you.'

'For your sake!' Then he stooped down and kissed her twice, and left her to arrange her parties as she pleased. After that she congratulated herself that she had not made the direct proposition, knowing that she might now do pretty much what she pleased.

Then there were solemn cabinets held, at which she presided, and Mrs Finn and Locock assisted. At other cabinets it is supposed that, let a leader be ever so autocratic by disposition and superior by intelligence, still he must not unfrequently yield to the opinion of his colleagues. But in this cabinet the Duchess always had her own way, though she was very persistent in asking for counsel. Locock was frightened about the money. Hitherto money had come without a word, out of the common, spoken to the Duke. The Duke had always signed certain cheques, but they had been normal cheques; and the money in its natural course had flown in to. meet them;—but now he must be asked to sign abnormal cheques. That, indeed, had already been done; but still the money had been there. A large balance, such as had always stood to his credit, would stand a bigger racket than had yet been made. But Locock was quite sure that the balance ought not to be much further reduced,—and that steps must be taken. Something must be sold! The idea of selling anything was dreadful to the mind of Locock! Or else money must be borrowed! Now the management of the Palliser property had always been conducted on principles antagonistic to borrowing. 'But his Grace has never spent his income,' said the Duchess. That was true. But the money, as it showed a tendency to heap itself up, had been used for the purchase of other bits of property, or for the amelioration of the estates generally. 'You don't mean to say that we can't get money if we want it!' Locock was profuse in his assurance that any amount of money could be obtained,—only that something must be done. 'Then let something be done,' said the Duchess, going on with her general plans. 'Many people are rich,' said the Duchess afterwards to her friend, 'and some people are very rich indeed; but nobody seems to be rich enough to have ready money to do just what he wishes. It all goes into a grand sum total, which is never to be touched without a feeling of sacrifice. I suppose you have always enough for everything.' It was well known that the present Mrs Finn, as Madame Goesler, had been a wealthy woman.

'Indeed, no;—very far from that. I haven't a shilling.'

'What has happened?' asked the Duchess, pretending to be frightened.

'You forget that I've got a husband of my own, and that he has to be consulted.'

'That must be nonsense. But don't you think women are fools to marry when they've got anything of their own, and could be their own mistresses? I couldn't have been. I was made to marry before I was old enough to assert myself.'

'And how well they did for you!'

'*Pas si mal.**—He's Prime Minister, which is a great thing, and I begin to find myself filled to the full with political ambition. I feel myself to be a Lady Macbeth,* prepared for the murder of any Duncan or any Daubeny who may stand in my lord's way. In the meantime, like Lady Macbeth herself, we must attend to the banqueting. Her lord appeared and misbehaved himself; my lord won't show himself at all,—which I think is worse.'

Our old friend Phineas Finn, who had now reached a higher place in politics than even his political dreams had assigned to him, though he was a Member of Parliament, was much away from London in these days. New brooms sweep clean; and official new brooms, I think, sweep cleaner than any other. Who has not watched at the commencement of a Ministry some Secretary, some Lord, or some Commissioner, who intends by fresh Herculean labours to cleanse the Augean stables* just committed to his care? Who does not know the gentleman at the Home Office, who means to reform the police and put an end to malefactors; or the new Minister at the Board of Works, who is to make London beautiful as by a magician's stroke,—or, above all, the new First Lord, who is resolved that he will really build a fleet, purge the dockyards, and save us half a million a year at the same time? Phineas Finn was bent on unriddling the Irish sphinx. Surely something might be done to prove to his susceptible countrymen that at the present moment no curse could be laid upon them so heavy as that of having to rule themselves apart from England; and he thought that this might be the easier, as he became from day to day more thoroughly convinced that those Home Rulers* who were all around him in the House were altogether of the same opinion. Had some inscrutable decree of fate ordained and made it certain,—with a certainty not to be disturbed,—that no candidate could be returned to Parliament who would not assert the earth to be triangular, there would rise immediately a clamorous assertion of triangularity among political aspirants. The test would be innocent. Candidates have swallowed, and daily do swallow, many a worse one. As might be this doctrine of a great triangle, so is the doctrine of Home Rule. Why is a gentleman of property to be kept out in the cold by some O'Mullins because he will not mutter an unmeaning shibboleth? 'Triangular? Yes,—or lozenge-shaped, if you please; but, gentlemen, I am the man for Tipperary.' Phineas Finn, having seen, or thought that he had seen, all this, began, from the very first moment of his appointment, to consider painfully within himself whether the genuine services of an honest and patriotic man might not compass some remedy for the present ill-boding ferment of the country. What was it that the Irish really did want;—what that they wanted, and had not got, and which might with propriety be conceded to them? What was it that the English really would refuse to sanction, even though it might not be wanted? He found himself beating about among rocks as to Catholic education and Papal interference,* the passage among which might be made clearer to him in Irish atmosphere than in that of Westminster. Therefore he was away a good deal in these days, travelling backwards and forwards as he might be wanted for any debate. But as his wife did not accompany him on these fitful journeys, she was able to give her time very much to the Duchess.

The Duchess was on the whole very successful with her parties. There were people who complained that she had everybody; that there was no selection whatever as to politics, principles, rank, morals,—or even manners. But in such a work as the Duchess had now taken in hand, it was impossible that she should escape censure. They who really knew what was being done were aware that nobody was asked to that house without an idea that his or her presence might be desirable,—in however remote a degree. Paragraphs in newspapers go for much, and therefore the writers and editors of such paragraphs were there,—sometimes with their wives. Mr Broune, of the 'Breakfast Table,' was to be seen there constantly, with his wife Lady Carbury, and poor old Booker* of the 'Literary Chronicle.' City men can make a budget popular or the reverse, and therefore the Mills Happertons of the day were welcome. Rising barristers might be wanted to become Solicitors-General. The pet Orpheus* of the hour, the young tragic actor who was thought to have a real Hamlet within him, the old painter who was growing rich on his reputation, and the young painter who was still strong with hope, even the little trilling poet though he trilled never so faintly, and the somewhat wooden novelist,* all had tongues of their own, and certain modes of expression, which might assist or injure the Palliser Coalition,—as the Duke's Ministry was now called.

'Who is that man? I've seen him here before. The Duchess was talking to him ever so long just now.' The question was asked by Mr Rattler of Mr Roby. About half an hour before this time Mr Rattler had essayed to get a few words with the Duchess, beginning with the communication of some small political secret. But the Duchess did not care much for the Rattlers attached to her husband's Government. They were men whose services could be had for a certain payment,—and when paid for were, the Duchess thought, at the Premier's command without further trouble. Of course they came to the receptions, and were entitled to a smile apiece as they entered. But they were entitled to nothing more, and on this occasion Rattler had felt himself to be snubbed. It did not occur to him to abuse the Duchess. The Duchess was too necessary for abuse,—just at present. But any friend of the Duchess,—any favourite for the moment,—was, of course, open to remark.

'He is a man named Lopez,' said Roby, 'a friend of Happerton;—a very clever fellow, they say.'

'Did you ever see him anywhere else?'

'Well, yes,—I have met him at dinner.'

'He was never in the House. What does he do?' Rattler was distressed to think that any drone should have made its way into the hive of working bees.

'Oh;—money, I fancy.'

'He's not a partner in Hunky's, is he?'

'I fancy not. I think I should have known if he was.'

'She ought to remember that people make a use of coming here,' said Rattler. She was, of course, the Duchess. 'It's not like a private house. And whatever influence outsiders get by coming, so much she loses. Somebody ought to explain that to her.'

'I don't think you or I could do that,' replied Mr Roby.

'I'll tell the Duke in a minute,' said Rattler. Perhaps he thought he could tell the Duke, but we may be allowed to doubt whether his prowess would not have fallen below the necessary pitch when he met the Duke's eye.

Lopez was there for the third time, about the middle of June, and had certainly contrived to make himself personally known to the Duchess. There had been a deputation from the City to the Prime Minister asking for a subsidized mail, via San Francisco, to Japan,* and Lopez, though he had no interest in Japan, had contrived to be one of the number. He had contrived also, as the deputation was departing, to say a word on his own account to the Minister, and had ingratiated himself. The Duke had remembered him, and had suggested that he should have a card. And now he was among the flowers and greatness, the beauty, the politics, and the fashion of the Duchess's gatherings for the third time. 'It is very well done,—very well, indeed,' said Mr Boffin to him. Lopez had been dining with Mr and Mrs Boffin, and had now again encountered his late host and hostess. Mr Boffin was a gentleman who had belonged to the late Ministry, but had somewhat out-Heroded Herod* in his Conservatism, so as to have been considered to be unfit for the Coalition. Of course he was proud of his own staunchness, and a little inclined to criticize the lax principles of men who, for the sake of carrying on her Majesty's Government, could be Conservatives one day and Liberals the next. He was a laborious, honest man,—but hardly of calibre sufficient not to regret his own honesty in such an emergency as the present. It is easy for most of us to keep our hands from picking and stealing when picking and stealing plainly lead to prison diet and prison garments. But when silks and satins come of it, and with the silks and satins general respect, the net result of honesty does not seem to be so secure. Whence will come the reward, and when? On whom the punishment, and where? A man will not, surely, be damned for belonging to a Coalition Ministry! Boffin was a little puzzled as he thought on all this, but in the meantime was very proud of his own consistency.

'I think it is so lovely,' said Mrs Boffin. 'You look down through an Elysium of rhododendrons into a Paradise of mirrors. I don't think there was ever anything like it in London before.'

'I don't know that we ever had anybody at the same time, rich enough to do this kind of thing as it is done now,' said Boffin, 'and powerful enough to get such people together. If the country can be ruled by flowers and looking-glasses, of course it is very well.'

'Flowers and looking-glasses won't prevent the country being ruled well,' said Lopez.

'I'm not so sure of that,' continued Boffin. 'We all know what bread and the games* came to in Rome.'

'What did they come to?' asked Mrs Boffin.

'To a man burning Rome, my dear, for his amusement, dressed in a satin petticoat and a wreath of roses.'*

'I don't think the Duke will dress himself like that,' said Mrs Boffin.

'And I don't think,' said Lopez, 'that the graceful expenditure of wealth in a rich man's house has any tendency to demoralize the people.'

'The attempt here,' said Boffin severely, 'is to demoralize the rulers of the people. I am glad to have come once to see how the thing is done; but as an independent member of the House of Commons I should not wish to be known to frequent the saloon of the Duchess.' Then Mr Boffin took away Mrs Boffin, much to that lady's regret.

'This is fairy land,' said Lopez to the Duchess, as he left the room.

'Come and be a fairy then,' she answered, very graciously. 'We are always on the wing about this hour on Wednesday night.' The words contained a general invitation for the season, and were esteemed by Lopez as an indication of great favour. It must be acknowledged of the Duchess that she was prone to make favourites, perhaps without adequate cause; though it must be conceded to her that she rarely altogether threw off from her any one whom she had once taken to her good graces. It must also be confessed that when she had allowed herself to hate either a man or a woman, she generally hated on to the end. No Paradise could be too charming for her friends; no Pandemonium* too frightful for her enemies. In reference to Mr Lopez she would have said, if interrogated, that she had taken the man up in obedience to her husband. But in truth she had liked the look and the voice of the man. Her husband before now had recommended men to her notice and kindness, whom at the first trial she had rejected from her good-will, and whom she had continued to reject ever afterwards, let her husband's urgency be what it might.

Another old friend, of whom former chronicles were not silent, was at the Duchess's that night, and there came across Mrs Finn. This was Barrington Erle,* a politician of long standing, who was still looked upon by many as a young man, because he had always been known as a young man, and because he had never done anything to compromise his position in that respect. He had not married, or settled himself down in a house of his own, or become subject to gout, or given up being careful about the fitting of his clothes. No doubt the grey hairs were getting the better of the black hairs, both on his head and face, and marks of coming crows' feet were to be seen if you looked close at him, and he had become careful about his great-coat and umbrella. He was in truth much nearer fifty than forty;—nevertheless he was felt in the House and among Cabinet Ministers, and among the wives of members and Cabinet Ministers, to be a young man still. And when he was invited to become Secretary for Ireland it was generally felt that he was too young for the place. He declined it, however; and when he went to the Post-office, the gentlemen there all felt that they had had a boy put over them. Phineas Finn, who had become Secretary for Ireland, was in truth ten years his junior. But Phineas Finn had been twice married, and had gone through other phases of life, such as make a man old. 'How does Phineas like it?' Erle asked. Phineas Finn and Barrington Erle had gone through some political struggles together, and had been very intimate.

'I hope not very much,' said the lady.

'Why so? Because he's away so much?'

'No;—not that. I should not grudge his absence if the work satisfied him. But I know him so well. The more he takes to it now,—the more sanguine he is as to some special thing to be done,—the more bitter will be the disappointment when he is disappointed. For there never really is anything special to be done;—is there, Mr Erle?'

'I think there is always a little too much zeal about Finn.'

'Of course there is. And then with zeal there always goes a thin skin,—and unjustifiable expectations, and biting despair, and contempt of others, and all the elements of unhappiness.'

'That is a sad programme for your husband.'

'He has recuperative faculties which bring him round at last:—but I really doubt whether he was made for a politician in this country. You remember Lord Brock?'

'Dear old Brock;—of course I do. How should I not, if you remember him?'

'Young men are boys at college, rowing in boats, when women have been ever so long out in the world. He was the very model of an English statesman. He loved his country dearly, and wished her to be, as he believed her to be, first among nations. But he had no belief in perpetuating her greatness by any grand improvements. Let things take their way naturally,—with a slight direction hither or thither as things might require. That was his method of ruling. He believed in men rather than measures. As long as he had loyalty around him, he could be personally happy, and quite confident as to the country. He never broke his heart because he could not carry this or that reform. What would have hurt him would have been to be worsted in personal conflict. But he could always hold his own, and he was always happy. Your man with a thin skin, a vehement ambition, a scrupulous conscience, and a sanguine desire for rapid improvement, is never a happy, and seldom a fortunate politician.'

'Mrs Finn, you understand it all better than any one else that I ever knew.'

'I have been watching it a long time, and of course very closely since I have been married.'

'But you have an eye trained to see it all. What a useful member you would have been in a government!'

'But I should never have had patience to sit all night upon that bench in the House of Commons. How men can do it! They mustn't read. They can't think because of the speaking. It doesn't do for them to talk. I don't believe they ever listen. It isn't in human nature to listen hour after hour to such platitudes. I believe they fall into a habit of half wakeful sleeping, which carries them through the hours; but even that can't be pleasant. I look upon the Treasury Bench in July as a sort of casual-ward* which we know to be necessary, but is almost too horrid to be contemplated.'

'Men do get bread and skilly there certainly; but, Mrs Finn, we can go into the library and smoking-room.'

'Oh, yes;—and a clerk in an office can read the newspapers instead of doing his duty. But there is a certain surveillance exercised, and a certain quantity of work exacted. I have met Lords of the Treasury out at dinner on Mondays and Thursdays, but we all regard them as boys who have shirked out of school. I think upon the whole, Mr Erle, we women have the best of it.'

'I don't suppose you will go in for your "rights."'*

'Not by Act of Parliament, or by platform meeting. I have a great idea of a woman's rights; but that is the way, I think, to throw them away. What do you think of the Duchess's evenings?'

'Lady Glen is in her way as great a woman as you are;—perhaps greater, because nothing ever stops her.'

'Whereas I have scruples.'

'Her Grace has none. She has feelings and convictions which keep her straight, but no scruples. Look at her now talking to Sir Orlando Drought, a man whom she both hates and despises. I am sure she is looking forward to some happy time in which the Duke may pitch Sir Orlando overboard, and rule supreme, with me or some other sub-ordinate leading the House of Commons simply as lieutenant. Such a time will never come, but that is her idea. But she is talking to Sir Orlando now as if she were pouring her full confidence into his ear, and Sir Orlando is believing her. Sir Orlando is in a seventh heaven, and she is measuring his credulity inch by inch.'

'She makes the place very bright.'

'And is spending an enormous deal of money,' said Barrington Erle.

'What does it matter?'

'Well, no;—if the Duke likes it. I had an idea that the Duke would not like the display of the thing. There he is. Do you see him in the corner with his brother duke? He doesn't look as if he were happy; does he? No one would think he was the master of everything here. He has got himself hidden almost behind the screen. I'm sure he doesn't like it.'

'He tries to like whatever she likes,' said Mrs Finn.

As her husband was away in Ireland, Mrs Finn was staying in the house in Carlton Gardens. The Duchess at present required so much of her time that this was found to be convenient. When, therefore, the guests on the present occasion had all gone the Duchess and Mrs Finn were left together. 'Did you ever see anything so hopeless as he is?' said the Duchess.

'Who is hopeless?'

'Heavens and earth! Plantagenet;—who else? Is there another man in the world would come into his own house, among his own guests, and speak only to one person? And, then, think of it! Popularity is the staff on which alone Ministers can lean in this country with security.'

'Political but not social popularity.'

'You know as well as I do that the two go together. We've seen enough of that even in our day. What broke up Mr Gresham's Ministry? If he had stayed away people might have thought that he was reading blue-books,* or calculating coinage, or preparing a speech. That would have been much better. But he comes in and sits for half an hour whispering to another duke! I hate dukes!'

'He talks to the Duke of St Bungay because there is no one he trusts so much. A few years ago it would have been Mr Mildmay.'

'My dear,' said the Duchess angrily, 'you treat me as though I were a child. Of course I know why he chooses that old man out of all the crowd. I don't suppose he does it from any stupid pride of rank. I know very well what set of ideas govern him. But that isn't the point. He has to reflect what others think of it, and to endeavour to do what will please them. There was I telling tarradiddles by the yard to that old oaf, Sir Orlando Drought, when a confidential word from Plantagenet would have had ten times more effect. And why can't he speak a word to the people's wives? They wouldn't bite him. He has got to say a few words to you sometimes,—to whom it doesn't signify, my dear——'

'I don't know about that.'

'But he never speaks to another woman. He was here this evening for exactly forty minutes, and he didn't open his lips to a female creature. I watched him. How on earth am I to pull him through if he goes on in that way? Yes, Locock, I'll go to bed, and I don't think I'll get up for a week.'

CHAPTER 12

THE GATHERING OF CLOUDS

THROUGHOUT June and the first week of July the affairs of the Ministry went on successfully, in spite of the social sins of the Duke and the occasional despair of the Duchess. There had been many politicians who had thought, or had, at any rate, predicted, that the Coalition Ministry would not live a month. There had been men, such as Lord Fawn on one side and Mr Boffin on the other, who had found themselves stranded disagreeably,—with no certain position,—unwilling to sit immediately behind a Treasury bench from which they were excluded, and too shy to place themselves immediately opposite. Seats beneath the gangway were, of course, open to such of them as were members of the Lower House, and those seats had to be used; but they were not accustomed to sit beneath the gangway. These gentlemen had expected that the seeds of weakness, of which they had perceived the scattering, would grow at once into an enormous crop of blunders, difficulties, and complications; but, for a while, the Ministry were saved from these dangers either by the energy of the Prime Minister, or the popularity of his wife, or perhaps by the sagacity of the elder Duke;—so that there grew up an idea that the Coalition was really the proper thing. In one respect it certainly was successful. The Home Rulers, or Irish party generally, were left without an inch of standing ground. Their support was not needed, and therefore they were not courted. For the moment there was not even a necessity to pretend that Home Rule was anything but an absurdity from beginning to end;—so much so that one or two leading Home Rulers, men who had taken up the cause not only that they might become Members of Parliament, but with some further ideas of speech-making and popularity, declared that the Coalition had been formed merely with a view of putting down Ireland. This capability of dispensing with a generally untractable element of support was felt to be a great comfort. Then, too, there was a set in the House,—at the moment not a very numerous set,—who had been troublesome friends to the old Liberal party, and which the Coalition was able, if not to ignore, at any rate to disregard. These were the staunch economists,* and argumentative philosophical Radicals,*— men of standing and repute, who are always in doubtful times individually flattered by Ministers, who have great privileges accorded to them of speaking and dividing, and who are not unfrequently even thanked for their rods by the very owners of the backs which bear the scourges.

These men could not be quite set aside by the Coalition as were the Home Rulers. It was not even yet, perhaps, wise to count them out, or to leave them to talk to benches absolutely empty;—but the tone of flattery with which they had been addressed became gradually less warm; and when the scourges were wielded, ministerial backs took themselves out of the way. There grew up unconsciously a feeling of security against attack which was distasteful to these gentlemen, and was in itself perhaps a little dangerous. Gentlemen bound to support the Government, when they perceived that there was comparatively but little to do, and that that little might easily be done, became careless, and, perhaps, a little contemptuous. So that the great popular orator, Mr Turnbull,* found himself compelled to rise in his seat, and ask whether the noble Duke at the head of the Government thought himself strong enough to rule without attention to Parliamentary details. The question was asked with an air of inexorable severity, and was intended to have deep signification. Mr Turnbull had disliked the Coalition from the beginning; but then Mr Turnbull always disliked everything. He had so accustomed himself to wield the constitutional cat-of-nine-tails, that heaven will hardly be happy to him unless he be allowed to flog the cherubim. Though the party with which he was presumed to act had generally been in power since he had been in the House, he had never allowed himself to agree with a Minister on any point. And as he had never been satisfied with a Liberal Government, it was not probable that he should endure a Coalition in silence. At the end of a rather lengthy speech, he repeated his question, and then sat down, taking his place with all that constitutional indignation which becomes the parliamentary flagellator of the day. The little jokes with which Sir Orlando answered him were very well in their way. Mr Turnbull did not care much whether he were answered or not. Perhaps the jauntiness of Sir Orlando, which implied that the Coalition was too strong to regard attack, somewhat irritated outsiders. But there certainly grew up from that moment a feeling among such men as Erle and Rattler that care was necessary, that the House, taken as a whole, was not in a condition to be manipulated with easy freedom, and that Sir Orlando must be made to understand that he was not strong enough to depend upon jauntiness. The jaunty statesman must be very sure of his personal following. There was a general opinion that Sir Orlando had not brought the Coalition well out of the first real attack which had been made upon it.

'Well, Phineas; how do you like the Phoenix?'* Phineas Finn had flown back to London at the instigation probably of Mr Rattler, and was now standing at the window of Brooks's club* with Barrington Erle. It was near nine one Thursday evening, and they were both about to return to the House.

'I don't like the Castle, if you mean that.'

'Tyrone isn't troublesome surely?' The Marquis of Tyrone was the Lord Lieutenant of the day, and had in his time been a very strong Conservative.

'He finds me troublesome, I fear.'

'I don't wonder at that, Phineas.'

'How should it be otherwise? What can he and I have in sympathy with one another? He has been brought up with all an Orangeman's* hatred for a Papist. Now that he is in high office, he can abandon the display of the feeling,—perhaps the feeling itself as regards the country at large. He knows that it doesn't become a Lord Lieutenant to be Orange. But how can he put himself into a boat with me?'

'All that kind of thing vanishes when a man is in office.'

'Yes, as a rule; because men go together into office with the same general predilections. Is it too hot to walk down?'

'I'll walk a little way,—till you make me hot by arguing.'

'I haven't an argument left in me,' said Phineas. 'Of course everything over there seems easy enough now,—so easy that Lord Tyrone evidently imagines that the good times are coming back in which governors may govern and not be governed.'

'You are pretty quiet in Ireland now, I suppose;—no martial law, suspension of the habeas corpus, or anything of that kind, just at present?'

'No; thank goodness!' said Phineas.

'I'm not quite sure whether a general suspension of the habeas corpus would not upon the whole be the most comfortable state of things for Irishmen themselves. But whether good or bad, you've nothing of that kind of thing now. You've no great measure that you wish to pass?'

'But they've a great measure that they wish to pass.'

'They know better than that. They don't want to kill their golden goose.'

'The people, who are infinitely ignorant of all political work, do want it. There are counties in which, if you were to poll the people, Home Rule would carry nearly every voter,—except the members themselves.'

'You wouldn't give it them?'

'Certainly not;—any more than I would allow a son to ruin himself because he asked me. But I would endeavour to teach them that they can get nothing by Home Rule,—that their taxes would be heavier, their property less secure, their lives less safe, their general position more debased, and their chances of national success more remote than ever.'

'You can never teach them, except by the slow lesson of habit. The Heptarchy* didn't mould itself into a nation in a day.'

'Men were governed then, and could be and were moulded. I feel sure that even in Ireland there is a stratum of men, above the working peasants, who would understand, and make those below them understand, the position of the country, if they could only be got to give up fighting about religion. Even now Home Rule is regarded by the multitude as a weapon to be used against Protestantism on behalf of the Pope.'

'I suppose the Pope is the great sinner?'

'They got over the Pope in France,—even in early days, before religion had become a farce in the country. They have done so in Italy.'

'Yes;—they have got over the Pope in Italy* certainly.'

'And yet,' said Phineas, 'the bulk of the people are staunch Catholics. Of course the same attempt to maintain a temporal influence, with the hope of recovering temporal power, is made in other countries. But while we see the attempt failing elsewhere,—so that we know the power of the Church is going to the wall,—yet in Ireland it is infinitely stronger now than it was fifty, or even twenty years ago.'

'Because we have been removing restraints on Papal aggression, while other nations have been imposing restraints. There are those at Rome who believe all England to be Romish at heart, because here in England a Roman Catholic can say what he will, and print what he will.'

'And yet,' said Phineas, 'all England does not return one Catholic to the House, while we have Jews in plenty. You have a Jew among your English judges, but at present not a single Roman Catholic. What do you suppose are the comparative numbers of the population here in England?'

'And you are going to cure all this;—while Tyrone thinks it ought to be left as it is? I rather agree with Tyrone.'

'No,' said Phineas wearily; 'I doubt whether I shall ever cure anything, or even make any real attempt. My patriotism just goes far enough to make me unhappy, and Lord Tyrone thinks that while Dublin ladies dance at the Castle, and the list of agrarian murders is kept low, the country is admirably managed. I don't quite agree with him;—that's all.'

Then there arose a legal difficulty, which caused much trouble to the Coalition Ministry. There fell vacant a certain seat on the bench of judges,*—a seat of considerable dignity and importance, but not quite of the highest rank. Sir Gregory Grogram, who was a rich, energetic man, determined to have a peerage, and convinced that, should the Coalition fall to pieces, the Liberal element would be in the ascendant,—so that the woolsack would then be opened to him,—declined to occupy the place. Sir Timothy Beeswax, the Solicitor-General, saw that it was exactly suited for him, and had no hesitation in expressing his opinion to that effect. But the place was not given to Sir Timothy. It was explained to Sir Timothy that the old rule,—or rather custom,—of offering certain high positions to the law officers of the Crown had been abrogated. Some Prime Minister, or, more probably, some collection of Cabinet Ministers, had asserted the custom to be a bad one,—and, as far as right went, Sir Timothy was declared not to have a leg to stand upon. He was informed that his services in the House were too valuable to be so lost. Some people said that his temper was against him. Others were of the opinion that he had risen from the ranks too quickly, and that Lord Ramsden, who had come from the same party, thought that Sir Timothy had not yet won his spurs. The Solicitor-General resigned in a huff, and then withdrew his resignation. Sir Gregory thought the withdrawal should not be accepted, having found Sir Timothy to be an unsympathetic colleague. Our Duke consulted the old Duke, among whose theories of official life forbearance to all colleagues and subordinates was conspicuous. The withdrawal was, therefore, allowed,—but the Coalition could not after that be said to be strong in regard to its Law Officers.

But the first concerted attack against the Ministry was made in reference to the budget. Mr Monk, who had consented to undertake the duties of Chancellor of the Exchequer under the urgent entreaties of the two dukes, was of course late with his budget. It was April before the Coalition had been formed. The budget when produced had been very popular. Budgets, like babies, are always little loves when first born. But as their infancy passes away, they also become subject to many stripes. The details are less pleasing than was the whole in the hands of the nurse. There was a certain 'interest', very influential both by general wealth and by the presence of many members in the House, which thought that Mr Monk had disregarded its just claims. Mr Monk had refused to relieve the Brewers from their licences. Now the Brewers had for some years been agitating about their licences,—and it is acknowledged in politics that any measure is to be carried, or to be left out in the cold uncarried and neglected, according to the number of deputations which may be got to press a Minister on the subject. Now the Brewers had had deputation after deputation to many Chancellors of the Exchequer; and these deputations had been most respectable,—we may almost say imperative. It was quite usual for a deputation to have four or five County members among its body, all Brewers; and the average wealth of a deputation of Brewers would buy up half London. All the Brewers in the House had been among the supporters of the Coalition, the number of Liberal and Conservative Brewers having been about equal. But now there was a fear that the 'interest' might put itself into opposition. Mr Monk had been firm. More than one of the Ministry had wished to yield;—but he had discussed the matter with his Chief, and they were both very firm. The Duke had never doubted. Mr Monk had never doubted. From day to day certain organs of the Press expressed an opinion, gradually increasing in strength, that however strong might be the Coalition as a body, it was weak as to finance. This was hard, because not very many years ago the Duke himself had been known as a particularly strong Minister of Finance. An amendment was moved in Committee as to the Brewers' Licences, and there was almost a general opinion that the Coalition would be broken up. Mr Monk would certainly not remain in office if the Brewers were to be relieved from their licences.

Then it was that Phineas Finn was recalled from Ireland in red-hot haste. The measure was debated for a couple of nights, and Mr Monk carried his point. The Brewers' Licences were allowed to remain, as one great gentleman from Burton* declared, a 'disgrace to the fiscal sagacity of the country'. The Coalition was so far victorious;—but there was a general feeling that its strength had been impaired.

CHAPTER 13

MR WHARTON COMPLAINS

'I THINK you have betrayed me.' This accusation was brought by Mr Wharton against Mrs Roby in that lady's drawing-room, and was occasioned by a report that had been made to the old lawyer by his daughter. He was very angry and almost violent;—so much so that by his manner, he gave a considerable advantage to the lady whom he was accusing.

Mrs Roby undoubtedly had betrayed her brother-in-law. She had been false to the trust reposed in her. He had explained his wishes to her in regard to his daughter, to whom she had in some sort assumed to stand in place of a mother, and she, while pretending to act in accordance with his wishes, had directly opposed them. But it was not likely that he would be able to prove her treachery though he might be sure of it. He had desired that his girl should see as little as possible of Ferdinand Lopez, but had hesitated to give a positive order that she should not meet him. He had indeed himself taken her to a dinner party at which he knew that she would meet him. But Mrs Roby had betrayed him. Since the dinner party she had arranged a meeting at her own house on behalf of the lover,—as to which arrangement Emily Wharton had herself been altogether innocent. Emily had met the man in her aunt's house, not expecting to meet him, and the lover had had an opportunity of speaking his mind freely. She also had spoken hers freely. She would not engage herself to him without her father's consent. With that consent she would do so,—oh, so willingly! She did not coy her love.* He might be certain that she would give herself to no one else. Her heart was entirely his. But she had pledged herself to her father, and on no consideration would she break that pledge. She went on to say that after what had passed she thought that they had better not meet. In such meetings there could be no satisfaction, and must be much pain. But he had her full permission to use any arguments that he could use with her father. On the evening of that day she told her father all that had passed,—omitting no detail either of what she had said or of what had been said to her,—adding a positive assurance of obedience, but doing so with a severe solemnity and apparent consciousness of ill-usage which almost broke her father's heart. 'Your aunt must have had him there on purpose,' Mr Wharton had said. But Emily would neither accuse nor defend her aunt. 'I at least knew nothing of it,' she said. 'I know that,' Mr Wharton had ejaculated. 'I know that. I don't accuse you of anything, my dear,—except of thinking that you understand the world better than I do.' Then Emily had retired and Mr Wharton had been left to pass half the night in perplexed reverie, feeling that he would be forced ultimately to give way, and yet certain that by doing so he would endanger his child's happiness.

He was very angry with his sister-in-law, and on the next day, early in the morning, he attacked her. 'I think you have betrayed me,' he said.

'What do you mean by that, Mr Wharton?'

'You have had this man here on purpose that he might make love to Emily.'

'I have done no such thing. You told me yourself that they were not to be kept apart. He comes here, and it would be very odd indeed if

I were to tell the servants that he is not to be admitted. If you want to quarrel with me, of course you can. I have always endeavoured to be a good friend to Emily.'

'It is not being a good friend to her, bringing her and this adventurer together.'

'I don't know why you call him an adventurer. But you are so very odd in your ideas! He is received everywhere, and is always at the Duchess of Omnium's.'

'I don't care a fig about the Duchess.'

'I dare say not. Only the Duke happens to be Prime Minister, and his house is considered to have the very best society that England, or indeed Europe, can give. And I think it is something in a young man's favour when it is known that he associates with such persons as the Duke of Omnium. I believe that most fathers would have a regard to the company which a man keeps when they think of their daughter's marrying.'

'I ain't thinking of her marrying. I don't want her to marry;—not this man at least. And I fancy the Duchess of Omnium is just as likely to have scamps in her drawing-room as any other lady in London.'

'And do such men as Mr Happerton associate with scamps?'

'I don't know anything about Mr Happerton,—and I don't care anything about him.'

'He has £20,000 a year out of his business. And does Everett associate with scamps?'

'Very likely.'

'I never knew any one so much prejudiced as you are, Mr Wharton. When you have a point to carry there's nothing you won't say. I suppose it comes from being in the courts.'

'The long and the short of it is this,' said the lawyer; 'if I find that Emily is brought here to meet Mr Lopez, I must forbid her to come at all.'

'You must do as you please about that. But to tell you the truth, Mr Wharton, I think the mischief is done. Such a girl as Emily, when she has taken it into her head to love a man, is not likely to give him up.'

'She has promised to have nothing to say to him without my sanction.'

'We all know what that means. You'll have to give way. You'll find that it will be so. The stern parent who dooms his daughter to perpetual seclusion because she won't marry the man he likes, doesn't belong to this age.'

'Who talks about seclusion?'

'Do you suppose that she'll give up the man she loves because you don't like him? Is that the way girls live now-a-days? She won't run away with him, because she's not one of that sort; but unless you're harder-hearted than I take you to be, she'll make your life a burden to you. And as for betraying you, that's nonsense. You've no right to say it. I'm not going to quarrel with you whatever you may say, but you've no right to say it.'

Mr Wharton, as he went away to Lincoln's Inn, bewailed himself because he knew that he was not hard-hearted. What his sister-in-law had said to him in that respect was true enough. If he could only rid himself of a certain internal ague which made him feel that his life was, indeed, a burden to him while his daughter was unhappy, he need only remain passive and simply not give the permission without which his daughter would not ever engage herself to this man. But the ague troubled every hour of his present life. That sister-in-law of his was a silly, vulgar, worldly, and most untrustworthy woman;—but she had understood what she was saying.

And there had been something in that argument about the Duchess of Omnium's parties, and Mr Happerton, which had its effect. If the man did live with the great and wealthy, it must be because they thought well of him and of his position. The fact of his being 'a nasty foreigner', and probably of Jewish descent, remained. To him, Wharton, the man must always be distasteful. But he could hardly maintain his opposition to one of whom the choice spirits of the world thought well. And he tried to be fair on the subject. It might be that it was a prejudice. Others probably did not find a man to be odious because he was of foreign extraction and known by a foreign name. Others would not suspect a man of being of Jewish blood because he was swarthy, or even object to him if he were a Jew by descent. But it was wonderful to him that his girl should like such a man,—should like such a man well enough to choose him as the one companion of her life. She had been brought up to prefer English men, and English thinking, and English ways,—and English ways, too, somewhat of a past time. He thought as did Brabantio,* that it could not be that without magic his daughter who had shunned—

> 'The wealthy curled darlings of our nation,
> Would ever have, to incur a general mock,
> Run from her guardage to the sooty bosom
> Of such a thing as'—

this distasteful Portuguese.

That evening he said nothing further to his daughter, but sat with her, silent and disconsolate. Later in the evening, after she had gone to her room, Everett came in while the old man was still walking up and down the drawing-room. 'Where have you been?' asked the father,—not caring a straw as to any reply when he asked the question, but roused almost to anger by the answer when it came.

'I have been dining with Lopez at the club.'

'I believe you live with that man.'

'Is there any reason, sir, why I should not?'

'You know that there is a good reason why there should be no peculiar intimacy. But I don't suppose that my wishes, or your sister's welfare, will interest you.'

'That is severe, sir.'

'I am not such a fool as to suppose that you are to quarrel with a man because I don't approve of his addressing your sister; but I do think that while this is going on, and while he perseveres in opposition to my distinct refusal, you need not associate with him in any special manner.'

'I don't understand your objection to him, sir.'

'I dare say not. There are a great many things you don't understand. But I do object.'

'He's a very rising man. Mr Roby was saying to me just now——'

'Who cares a straw what a fool like Roby says?'

'I don't mean Uncle Dick, but his brother,—who, I suppose, is somebody in the world. He was saying to me just now that he wondered why Lopez does not go into the House;—that he would be sure to get a seat if he chose, and safe to make a mark when he got there.'

'I dare say he could get into the House. I don't know any well-to-do blackguard of whom you might not predict as much. A seat in the House of Commons doesn't make a man a gentleman as far as I can see.'

'I think every one allows that Ferdinand Lopez is a gentleman.'

'Who was his father?'

'I didn't happen to know him, sir.'

'And who was his mother? I don't suppose you will credit anything because I say it, but as far as my experience goes, a man doesn't often become a gentleman in the first generation. A man may be very worthy, very clever, very rich,—very well worth knowing, if you will;—but when one talks of admitting a man into close family communion by marriage, one would, I fancy, wish to know something of his father and mother.' Then Everett escaped, and Mr Wharton was again left to his own meditations. Oh, what a peril, what a trouble, what a labyrinth of difficulties was a daughter! He must either be known as a stern, hardhearted parent, utterly indifferent to his child's feelings, using with tyranny the power over her which came to him only from her sense of filial duty,—or else he must give up his own judgement, and yield to her in a matter as to which he believed that such yielding would be most pernicious to her own interests.

Hitherto he really knew nothing of the man's means;—nor, if he could have his own way, did he want such information. But, as things were going now, he began to feel that if he could hear anything averse to the man he might thus strengthen his hands against him. On the following day he went into the city, and called on an old friend, a banker,—one whom he had known for nearly half a century, and of whom, therefore, he was not afraid to ask a question. For Mr Wharton was a man not prone, in the ordinary intercourse of life, either to ask or to answer questions. 'You don't know anything, do you, of a man named Ferdinand Lopez?'

'I have heard of him. But why do you ask?'

'Well; I have reason for asking. I don't know that I quite wish to say what my reason is.'

'I have heard of him as connected with Hunky's house,' said the banker,—'or rather with one of the partners in the house.'

'Is he a man of means?'

'I imagine him to be so;—but I know nothing. He has rather large dealings, I take it, in foreign stocks. Is he after my old friend, Miss Wharton?'

'Well;—yes.'

'You had better get more information than I can give you. But, of course, before anything of that kind was done you would see that money was settled.' This was all he heard in the city, and this was not satisfactory. He had not liked to tell his friend that he wished to hear that the foreigner was a needy adventurer,—altogether untrustworthy; but that had really been his desire. Then he thought of the £60,000 which he himself destined for his girl. If the man were to his liking there would be money enough. Though he had been careful to save money, he was not a greedy man, even for his children. Should his daughter insist on marrying this man he could take care that she should never want a sufficient income.

As a first step,—a thing to be done almost at once,—he must take her away from London. It was now July, and the custom of the family was that the house in Manchester Square should be left for two months, and that the flitting should take place about the middle of August. Mr Wharton usually liked to postpone the flitting, as he also liked to hasten the return. But now it was a question whether he had not better start at once,—start somewhither, and probably for a much longer period than the usual vacation. Should he take the bull by the horns, and declare his purpose of living for the next twelvemonth at——; well, it did not much matter where; Dresden, he thought, was a long way off, and would do as well as any place. Then it occurred to him that his cousin, Sir Alured, was in town, and that he had better see his cousin before he came to any decision. They were, as usual, expected at Wharton Hall this autumn, and that arrangement could not be abandoned without explanation.

Sir Alured Wharton was a baronet, with a handsome old family place on the Wye in Herefordshire, whose forefathers had been baronets since baronets* were first created, and whose earlier forefathers had lived at Wharton Hall much before that time. It may be imagined, therefore, that Sir Alured was proud of his name, of his estate, and of his rank. But there were drawbacks to his happiness. As regarded his name, it was to descend to a nephew whom he specially disliked,—and with good cause. As to his estate, delightful as it was in many respects, it was hardly sufficient to maintain his position with that plentiful hospitality which he would have loved;—and other property he had none. And as to his rank he had almost become ashamed of it, since,—as he was wont to declare was now the case,—every prosperous tallow-chandler throughout the country was made a baronet as a matter of course. So he lived at home through the year with his wife and daughters, not pretending to the luxury of a season in London for which his modest three or four thousand a year did not suffice;—and so living, apart from all the friction of clubs, parliaments, and mixed society, he did veritably believe that his dear country was going utterly to the dogs. He was so staunch in politics that during the doings of the last quarter of a century—from the repeal of the Corn Laws down to the Ballot,*—he had honestly declared one side to be as bad as the other. Thus he felt that all his happiness was to be drawn from the past. There was nothing of joy or glory to which he could look forward either on behalf of his country or his family. His nephew,—and alas, his heir,—was a needy spendthrift, with whom he would hold no communication. The family settlement for his wife and daughters would leave them but poorly off; and though he did struggle to save something, the duty of living as Sir Alured Wharton of Wharton Hall should live made those struggles very ineffective. He was a melancholy, proud, ignorant man, who could not endure a personal liberty, and who thought the assertion of social equality on the part of men of lower rank to amount to the taking of personal liberty;—who read little or nothing, and thought that he knew the history of his country because he was aware that Charles I had had his head cut off, and that the Georges had come from Hanover. If Charles I had never had his head cut off, and if the Georges had never come from Hanover, the Whartons would now probably be great people and Britain a great nation. But the Evil One had been allowed to prevail, and everything had gone astray, and Sir Alured now had nothing of this world to console him but a hazy retrospect of past glories, and a delight in the beauty of his own river, his own park, and his own house. Sir Alured, with all his foibles, and with all his faults, was a pure-minded, simple gentleman, who could not tell a lie, who could not do a wrong, and who was earnest in his desire to make those who were dependent on him comfortable, and, if possible, happy. Once a year he came up to London for a week, to see his lawyers, and get measured for a coat, and go to the dentist. These were the excuses which he gave, but it was fancied by some that his wig was the great moving cause. Sir Alured and Mr Wharton were second cousins, and close friends. Sir Alured trusted his cousin altogether in all things, believing him to be the great legal luminary of Great Britain, and Mr Wharton returned his cousin's affection, entertaining something akin to reverence for the man who was the head of his family. He dearly loved Sir Alured,—and loved Sir Alured's wife and two daughters. Nevertheless, the second week at Wharton Hall became always tedious to him, and the fourth, fifth, and sixth weeks frightful with ennui.

Perhaps it was with some unconscious dread of this tedium that he made a sudden suggestion to Sir Alured in reference to Dresden. Sir Alured had come to him at his chambers, and the two old men were sitting together near the open window. Sir Alured delighted in the privilege of sitting there, which seemed to confer upon him something of an insight into the inner ways of London life beyond what he could get at his hotel or his wigmaker's. 'Go to Dresden;—for the winter!' he exclaimed.

'Not only for the winter. We should go at once.'

'Not before you come to Wharton!' said the amazed baronet.

Mr Wharton replied in a low, sad voice, 'In that case we should not go down to Herefordshire at all.' The baronet looked hurt as well as unhappy. 'Yes, I know what you will say, and how kind you are.'

'It isn't kindness at all. You always come. It would be breaking up everything.'

'Everything has to be broken up sooner or later. One feels that as one grows older.'

'You and I, Abel, are just of an age. Why should you talk to me like this? You are strong enough, whatever I am. Why shouldn't you come? Dresden! I never heard of such a thing. I suppose it's some nonsense of Emily's.'

Then Mr Wharton told his whole story. 'Nonsense of Emily's!' he began. 'Yes, it is nonsense,—worse than you think. But she doesn't want to go abroad.' The father's plaint needn't be repeated to the reader as it was told to the baronet. Though it was necessary that he should explain himself, yet he tried to be reticent. Sir Alured listened in silence. He loved his cousin Emily, and, knowing that she would be rich, knowing her advantages of birth, and recognizing her beauty, had expected that she would make a match creditable to the Wharton family. But a Portuguese Jew! A man who had never been even known to allude to his own father! For by degrees Mr Wharton had been driven to confess all the sins of the lover, though he had endeavoured to conceal the extent of his daughter's love.

'Do you mean that Emily—favours him?'

'I am afraid so.'

'And would she,—would she—do anything without your sanction?' He was always thinking of the disgrace attaching to himself by reason of his nephew's vileness, and now, if a daughter of the family should also go astray, so as to be exiled from the bosom of the Whartons, how manifest would it be that all the glory was departing from their house!*

'No! She will do nothing without my sanction. She has given her word,—which is gospel.' As he spoke the old lawyer struck his hand upon the table.

'Then why should you run away to Dresden?'

'Because she is unhappy. She will not marry him,—or even see him, if I forbid it. But she is near him.'

'Herefordshire is a long way off,' said the baronet, pleading.

'Change of scene is what she should have,' said the father.

'There can't be more of a change than she'd get at Wharton. She always did like Wharton. It was there that she met Arthur Fletcher.' The father only shook his head as Arthur Fletcher's name was mentioned. 'Well,—that is sad. I always thought she'd give way about Arthur at last.'

'It is impossible to understand a young woman,' said the lawyer. With such an English gentleman as Arthur Fletcher on one side, and with this Portuguese Jew on the other, it was to him Hyperion to a Satyr.* A darkness had fallen over his girl's eyes, and for a time her power of judgement had left her.

'But I don't see why Wharton should not do just as well as Dresden,' continued the baronet.

Mr Wharton found himself quite unable to make his cousin understand that the greater disruption caused by a residence abroad, the feeling that a new kind of life had been considered necessary for her, and that she must submit to the new kind of life, might be gradually effective, while the journeyings and scenes which had been common to her year after year would have no effect. Nevertheless he gave way. They could hardly start to Germany at once, but the visit to Wharton might be accelerated; and the details of the residence abroad might be there arranged. It was fixed, therefore, that Mr Wharton and Emily should go down to Wharton Hall at any rate before the end of July.

'Why do you go earlier than usual, papa?' Emily asked him afterwards.

'Because I think it best,' he replied angrily. She ought at any rate to understand the reason.

'Of course I shall be ready, papa. You know that I always like Wharton. There is no place on earth I like so much, and this year it will be especially pleasant to me to go out of town. But——'

'But what?'

'I can't bear to think that I shall be taking you away.'

'I've got to bear worse things than that, my dear.'

'Oh, papa, do not speak to me like that! Of course I know what you mean. There is no real reason for your going. If you wish it I will promise you that I will not see him.' He only shook his head,—meaning to imply that a promise which could go no farther than that would not make him happy. 'It will be just the same, papa,—either here, or at Wharton, or elsewhere. You need not be afraid of me.'

'I am not afraid of you;—but I am afraid for you. I fear for your happiness,—and for my own.'

'So do I, papa. But what can be done? I suppose sometimes people must be unhappy. I can't change myself and I can't change you. I find myself to be as much bound to Mr Lopez as though I were his wife.'

'No, no! you shouldn't say so. You've no right to say so.'

'But I have given you a promise, and I certainly will keep it. If we must be unhappy, still we need not,—need not quarrel; need we, papa?' Then she came up to him and kissed him,—whereupon he went out of the room wiping his eyes.

That evening he again spoke to her, saying merely a word. 'I think, my dear, we'll have it fixed that we go on the 30th. Sir Alured seemed to wish it.'

'Very well, papa;—I shall be quite ready.'

CHAPTER 14

A LOVER'S PERSEVERANCE

FERDINAND LOPEZ learned immediately through Mrs Roby that the early departure for Herefordshire had been fixed. 'I should go to him and speak to him very plainly,' said Mrs Roby. 'He can't bite you.'

'I'm not in the least afraid of his biting me.'

'You can talk so well! I should tell him everything, especially about money,—which I'm sure is all right.'

'Yes,—that is all right,' said Lopez, smiling.

'And about your people.'

'Which I've no doubt you think is all wrong.'

'I don't know anything about it,' said Mrs Roby, 'and I don't much care. He has old-world notions. At any rate you should say something, so that he should not be able to complain to her that you had kept him in the dark. If there is anything to be known, it's much better to have it known.'

'But there is nothing to be known.'

'Then tell him nothing;—but still tell it to him. After that you must trust to her. I don't suppose she'd go off with you.'

'I'm sure she wouldn't.'

'But she's as obstinate as a mule. She'll get the better of him if you really mean it.' He assured her that he really did mean it, and determined that he would take her advice as to seeing, or endeavouring to see, Mr Wharton once again. But before doing so he thought it to be expedient to put his house into order, so that he might be able to make a statement of his affairs if asked to do so. Whether they were flourishing or the reverse, it might be necessary that he should have to speak of them,—with, at any rate, apparent candour.

The reader may, perhaps, remember that in the month of April Ferdinand Lopez had managed to extract a certain signature from his unfortunate city friend, Sexty Parker, which made that gentleman responsible for the payment of a considerable sum of money before the end of July. The transaction had been one of an unmixed painful nature to Mr Parker. As soon as he came to think of it, after Lopez had left him, he could not prevail upon himself to forgive himself for his folly. That he,—he, Sextus Parker,—should have been induced by a few empty words to give his name for seven hundred and fifty pounds without any consideration or possibility of benefit! And the more he thought of it the more sure he was that the money was lost. The next day he confirmed his own fears, and before a week was gone he had written down the sum as gone. He told nobody. He did not like to confess his folly. But he made some inquiry about his friend,—which was absolutely futile. No one that he knew seemed to know anything of the man's affairs. But he saw his friend from time to time in the city, shining as only successful men do shine, and he heard of him as one whose name was becoming known in the city. Still he suffered grievously. His money was surely gone. A man does not fly a kite* in that fashion till things with him have reached a bad pass.

So it was with Mr Parker all through May and to the end of June,—the load ever growing heavier and heavier as the time became nearer. Then, while he was still afflicted with a heaviness of spirits which had never left him since that fatal day, who but Ferdinand Lopez should walk into his office, wearing the gayest smile and with a hat splendid as hats are splendid only in the city. And nothing could be more 'jolly' than his friend's manner,—so much so that Sexty was almost lifted up into temporary jollity himself. Lopez, seating himself, almost at once began to describe a certain speculation into which he was going rather deeply, and as to which he invited his friend Parker's co-operation. He was intending, evidently, not to ask, but to confer, a favour.

'I rather think that steady business is best,' said Parker. 'I hope it's all right about that £750.'

'Ah; yes;—I meant to have told you. I didn't want the money, as it turned out, for much above a fortnight, and as there was no use in letting the bill run out, I settled it.' So saying he took out a pocket-book, extracted the bill, and showed it to Sexty. Sexty's heart fluttered in his bosom. There was his name still on the bit of paper, and it might still be used. Having it shown to him after this fashion in its mid career, of course he had strong ground for hope. But he could not bring himself to put out his hand for it. 'As to what you say about steady business, of course that's very well,' said Lopez. 'It depends upon whether a man wants to make a small income or a large fortune.' He still held the bill as though he were going to fold it up again, and the importance of it was so present to Sexty's mind that he could hardly digest the argument about the steady business. 'I own that I am not satisfied with

the former,' continued Lopez, 'and that I go in for the fortune.' As he
spoke he tore the bill into three or four bits, apparently without thinking of it, and let the fragments fall upon the floor. It was as though a
mountain had been taken off Sexty's bosom. He felt almost inclined to
send out for a bottle of champagne on the moment, and the arguments
of his friend rang in his ears with quite a different sound. The allurements of a steady income paled before his eyes, and he too began to tell
himself, as he had often told himself before, that if he would only keep
his eyes open and his heart high, there was no reason why he too should
not become a city millionaire. But on that occasion Lopez left him
soon, without saying very much about his favourite speculation. In a
few days, however, the same matter was brought before Sexty's eyes
from another direction. He learned from a side wind that the house of
Hunky and Sons was concerned largely in this business,—or at any
rate he thought that he had so learned. The ease with which Lopez had
destroyed that bill six weeks before it was due had had great effect upon
him. Those arguments about a large fortune or a small income still
clung to him. Lopez had come to him about the business in the first
instance, but it was now necessary that he should go to Lopez. He was,
however, very cautious. He managed to happen to meet Lopez in the
street, and introduced the subject in his own slap-dash, aery manner,—
the result of which was, that he had gone rather deep into two or three
American mines* before the end of July. But he had already made some
money out of them, and, though he would find himself sometimes
trembling before he had taken his daily allowance of port wine and
brandy-and-water, still he was buoyant, and hopeful of living in a park,
with a palace at the West End, and a seat in Parliament. Knowing also,
as he did, that his friend Lopez was intimate with the Duchess of
Omnium, he had much immediate satisfaction in the intimacy which
these relations created. He was getting in the thin edge of the wedge,
and would calculate as he went home to Ponders End how long it must
be before he could ask his friend to propose him at some West End
club. On one halcyon summer evening Lopez had dined with him at
Ponders End, had smiled on Mrs Parker, and played with the hopeful
little Parkers. On that occasion Sexty had assured his wife that he
regarded his friendship with Ferdinand Lopez as the most fortunate
circumstance of his life. 'Do be careful, Sexty,' the poor woman had
said. But Parker had simply told her that she understood nothing about
business. On that evening Lopez had thoroughly imbued him with the
conviction that if you will only set your mind that way, it is quite as
easy to amass a large fortune as to earn a small income.

About a week before the departure of the Whartons for Herefordshire, Lopez, in compliance with Mrs Roby's councils, called at the chambers in Stone Buildings. It is difficult to say that you will not see a man, when the man is standing just on the other side of an open door;—nor, in this case, was Mr Wharton quite clear that he had better decline to see the man. But while he was doubting,—at any rate before he had resolved upon denying his presence,—the man was there, inside his room. Mr Wharton got up from his chair, hesitated a moment, and then gave his hand to the intruder in that half-unwilling, unsatisfactory manner which most of us have experienced when shaking hands with some cold-blooded, ungenial acquaintance. 'Well, Mr Lopez,— what can I do for you?' he said, as he reseated himself. He looked as though he were at his ease and master of the situation. He had control over himself sufficient for assuming such a manner. But his heart was not high within his bosom. The more he looked at the man the less he liked him.

'There is one thing, and one thing only, you can do for me,' said Lopez. His voice was peculiarly sweet, and when he spoke his words seemed to mean more than when they came from other mouths. But Mr Wharton did not like sweet voices and mellow, soft words,—at least not from men's mouths.

'I do not think I can do anything for you, Mr Lopez,' he said. There was a slight pause, during which the visitor put down his hat and seemed to hesitate. 'I think your coming here can be of no avail. Did I not explain myself when I saw you before?'

'But, I fear, I did not explain myself. I hardly told my story.'

'You can tell it, of course,—if you think the telling will do you any good.'

'I was not able to say then, as I can say now, that your daughter has accepted my love.'

'You ought not to have spoken to my daughter on the subject after what passed between us. I told you my mind frankly.'

'Ah, Mr Wharton, how was obedience in such a matter possible? What would you yourself think of a man who in such a position would be obedient? I did not seek her secretly. I did nothing underhand. Before I had once directly asked her for her love, I came to you.'

'What's the use of that, if you go to her immediately afterwards in manifest opposition to my wishes? You found yourself bound, as would any gentleman, to ask a father's leave, and when it was refused, you went on just as though it had been granted! Don't you call that a mockery?'

'I can say now, sir, what I could not say then. We love each other. And I am as sure of her as I am of myself when I assert that we shall be true to each other. You must know her well enough to be sure of that also.'

'I am sure of nothing but of this;—that I will not give her my consent to become your wife.'

'What is your objection, Mr Wharton?'

'I explained it before as far as I found myself called upon to explain it.'

'Are we both to be sacrificed for some reason that we neither of us understand?'

'How dare you take upon yourself to say that she doesn't understand! Because I refuse to be more explicit to you, a stranger, do you suppose that I am equally silent to my own child?'

'In regard to money and social rank, I am able to place your daughter as my wife in a position as good as she now holds as Miss Wharton.'

'I care nothing about money, Mr Lopez, and our ideas of social rank are perhaps different. I have nothing further to say to you, and I do not think that you can have anything further to say to me that can be of any avail.' Then, having finished his speech, he got up from his chair and stood upright, thereby demanding of his visitor that he should depart.

'I think it no more than honest, Mr Wharton, to declare this one thing. I regard myself as irrevocably engaged to your daughter; and she, although she has refused to bind herself to me by that special word, is, I am certain, as firmly fixed in her choice as I am in mine. My happiness, as a matter of course, can be nothing to you.'

'Not much,' said the lawyer, with angry impatience.

Lopez smiled, but he put down the word in his memory and determined that he would treasure it there. 'Not much, at any rate as yet,' he said. 'But her happiness must be much to you.'

'It is everything. But in thinking of her happiness I must look beyond what might be the satisfaction of the present day. You must excuse me, Mr Lopez, if I say that I would rather not discuss the matter with you any further.' Then he rang the bell and passed quickly into an inner room. When the clerk came Lopez of course marched out of the chamber and went his way.

Mr Wharton had been very firm, and yet he was shaken. It was by degrees becoming a fixed idea in his mind that the man's material prosperity was assured. He was afraid even to allude to the subject when talking to the man himself, lest he should be overwhelmed by evidence on that subject. Then the man's manner, though it was distasteful to Wharton himself, would, he well knew, recommend him to others.

He was good-looking, he lived with people who were highly regarded, he could speak up for himself, and he was a favoured guest at Carlton House Terrace. So great had been the fame of the Duchess and her hospitality during the last two months, that the fact of the man's success in this respect had come home even to Mr Wharton. He feared that the world would be against him, and he already began to dread the joint opposition of the world and his own child. The world of this day did not, he thought, care whether its daughters' husbands had or had not any fathers or mothers. The world as it was now didn't care whether its sons-in-law were Christian or Jewish;—whether they had the fair skin and bold eyes and uncertain words of an English gentleman, or the swarthy colour and false grimace and glib tongue of some inferior Latin race. But he cared for these things;—and it was dreadful to him to think that his daughter should not care for them. 'I suppose I had better die and leave them to look after themselves,' he said, as he returned to his arm-chair.

Lopez himself was not altogether ill-satisfied with the interview, not having expected that Mr Wharton would have given way at once, and bestowed upon him then and there the kind father-in-law's 'bless you,—bless you!' Something yet had to be done before the blessing would come, or the girl,—or the money. He had to-day asserted his own material success, speaking of himself as of a moneyed man,—and the statement had been received with no contradiction,—even without the suggestion of a doubt. He did not therefore suppose that the difficulty was over; but he was clever enough to perceive that the aversion to him on another score might help to tide him over that difficulty. And if once he could call the girl his wife, he did not doubt but that he could build himself up with the old barrister's money. After leaving Lincoln's Inn he went at once to Berkeley Street, and was soon closeted with Mrs Roby. 'You can get her here before they go?' he said.

'She wouldn't come;—and if we arranged it without letting her know that you were to be here, she would tell her father. She hasn't a particle of female intrigue in her.'

'So much the better,' said the lover.

'That's all very well for you to say, but when a man makes such a tyrant of himself as Mr Wharton is doing, a girl is bound to look after herself. If it was me I'd go off with my young man before I'd stand such treatment.'

'You could give her a letter.'

'She'd only show it to her father. She is so perverse that I sometimes feel inclined to say that I'll have nothing further to do with her.'

'You'll give her a message at any rate?'

'Yes,—I can do that;—because I can do it in a way that won't seem to make it important.'

'But I want my message to be very important. Tell her that I've seen her father, and have offered to explain all my affairs to him,—so that he may know that there is nothing to fear on her behalf.'

'It isn't any thought of money that is troubling him.'

'But tell her what I say. He, however, would listen to nothing. Then I assured him that no consideration on earth would induce me to surrender her, and that I was as sure of her as I am of myself. Tell her that;—and tell her that I think she owes it to me to say one word to me before she goes into the country.'

CHAPTER 15

ARTHUR FLETCHER

IT may, I think, be a question whether the two old men acted wisely in having Arthur Fletcher at Wharton Hall when Emily arrived there. The story of his love for Miss Wharton, as far as it had as yet gone, must be shortly told. He had been the second son, as he was now the second brother, of a Herefordshire squire endowed with much larger property than that belonging to Sir Alured. John Fletcher, Esq., of Longbarns, some twelve miles from Wharton, was a considerable man in Herefordshire. This present squire had married Sir Alured's eldest daughter, and the younger brother had, almost since they were children together, been known to be in love with Emily Wharton. All the Fletchers and everything belonging to them were almost worshipped at Wharton Hall. There had been marriages between the two families certainly as far back as the time of Henry VII, and they were accustomed to speak, if not of alliances, at any rate of friendships, much anterior to that. As regards family, therefore, the pretensions of a Fletcher would always be held to be good by a Wharton. But this Fletcher was the very pearl of the Fletcher tribe. Though a younger brother, he had a very pleasant little fortune of his own. Though born to comfortable circumstances, he had worked so hard in his young days as to have already made for himself a name at the bar. He was a fair-haired, handsome fellow, with sharp, eager eyes, with an aquiline nose and just that shape of mouth and chin which such men as Abel Wharton regarded as characteristic of good blood. He was rather thin, about five feet ten in height, and had the character of being one of the best horsemen in the county. He was one of the most popular men in Herefordshire, and at Longbarns was almost as much thought of as the squire himself. He certainly was not the man to be taken, from his appearance, for a forlorn lover. He looked like one of those happy sons of the gods who are born to success. No young man of his age was more courted both by men and women. There was no one who in his youth had suffered fewer troubles from those causes of trouble which visit English young men,— occasional impecuniosity, sternness of parents, native shyness, fear of ridicule, inability of speech, and a general pervading sense of inferiority combined with an ardent desire to rise to a feeling of conscious superiority. So much had been done for him by nature that he was never called upon to pretend to anything. Throughout the county those were the lucky men,—and those too were the happy girls,—who were allowed to call him Arthur. And yet this paragon was vainly in love with Emily Wharton, who, in the way of love, would have nothing to say to him, preferring,—as her father once said in his extremest wrath,—a greasy Jew adventurer out of the gutter!

And now it had been thought expedient to have him down to Wharton, although the lawyer's regular summer vacation had not yet commenced. But there was some excuse made for this, over and above the emergency of his own love, in the fact that his brother John, with Mrs Fletcher, was also to be at the Hall,—so that there was gathered there a great family party of the Whartons and Fletchers; for there was present there also old Mrs Fletcher, a magnificently aristocratic and high-minded old lady, with snow-white hair, and lace worth fifty guineas a yard, who was as anxious as everybody else that her younger son should marry Emily Wharton. Something of the truth as to Emily Wharton's £60,000 was, of course, known to the Longbarns people. Not that I would have it inferred that they wanted their darling to sell himself for money. The Fletchers were great people, with great spirits, too good in every way for such baseness. But when love, old friendship, good birth, together with every other propriety as to age, manners, and conduct, can be joined to money, such a combination will always be thought pleasant.

When Arthur reached the Hall it was felt to be necessary that a word should be said to him as to that wretched interloper, Ferdinand Lopez. Arthur had not of late been often in Manchester Square. Though always most cordially welcomed there by old Wharton, and treated with every kindness by Emily Wharton short of that love which he desired, he had during the last three or four months abstained from frequenting the house. During the past winter, and early in the spring, he had pressed his suit,—but had been rejected, with warmest assurances of all friendship short of love. It had then been arranged between him and the elder Whartons that they should all meet down at the Hall, and there had been sympathetic expressions of hope that all might yet be well. But at that time little or nothing had been known of Ferdinand Lopez.

But now the old baronet spoke to him, the father having deputed the loathsome task to his friend,—being unwilling himself even to hint his daughter's disgrace. 'Oh, yes, I've heard of him,' said Arthur Fletcher. 'I met him with Everett, and I don't think I ever took a stronger dislike to a man. Everett seems very fond of him.' The baronet mournfully shook his head. It was sad to find that Whartons could go so far astray. 'He goes to Carlton House Terrace,—to the Duchess's,' continued the young man.

'I don't think that that is very much in his favour,' said the baronet.

'I don't know that it is, sir;—only they try to catch all fish in that net that are of any use.'

'Do you go there, Arthur?'

'I should if I were asked, I suppose. I don't know who wouldn't. You see it's a Coalition affair, so that everybody is able to feel that he is supporting his party by going to the Duchess's.'

'I hate Coalitions,' said the baronet. 'I think they are disgraceful.'

'Well;—yes; I don't know. The coach has to be driven somehow. You mustn't stick in the mud, you know. And after all, sir, the Duke of Omnium is a respectable man, though he is a Liberal. A Duke of Omnium can't want to send the country to the dogs.' The old man shook his head. He did not understand much about it, but he felt convinced that the Duke and his colleagues were sending the country to the dogs whatever might be their wishes. 'I shan't think of politics for the next ten years, and so I don't trouble myself about the Duchess's parties, but I suppose I should go if I were asked.'

Sir Alured felt that he had not as yet begun even to approach the difficult subject. 'I'm glad you don't like that man,' he said.

'I don't like him at all. Tell me, Sir Alured;—why is he always going to Manchester Square?'

'Ah;—that is it.'

'He has been there constantly;—has he not?'

'No;—no. I don't think that. Mr Wharton doesn't love him a bit better than you do. My cousin thinks him a most objectionable young man.'

'But Emily?'

'Ah——. That's where it is.'

'You don't mean to say she—cares about that man!'

'He has been encouraged by that aunt of hers, who, as far as I can make out, is a very unfit sort of person to be much with such a girl as our dear Emily. I never saw her but once, and then I didn't like her at all.'

'A vulgar, good-natured woman. But what can she have done? She can't have twisted Emily round her finger.'

'I don't suppose there is very much in it, but I thought it better to tell you. Girls take fancies into their heads,—just for a time.'

'He's a handsome fellow, too,' said Arthur Fletcher, musing in his sorrow.

'My cousin says he's a nasty Jew-looking man.'

'He's not that, Sir Alured. He's a handsome man with a fine voice;—dark, and not just like an Englishman; but still I can fancy——. That's bad news for me, Sir Alured.'

'I think she'll forget all about him down here.'

'She never forgets anything. I shall ask her, straight away. She knows my feeling about her, and I haven't a doubt but she'll tell me. She's too honest to be able to lie. Has he got any money?'

'My cousin seems to think he's rich.'

'I suppose he is. Oh, Lord! That's a blow. I wish I could have the pleasure of shooting him as a man might a few years ago.* But what would be the good? The girl would only hate me the more after it. The best thing to do would be to shoot myself.'

'Don't talk like that, Arthur.'

'I shan't throw up the sponge as long as there's a chance left, Sir Alured. But it will go badly with me if I'm beat at last. I shouldn't have thought it possible that I should have felt anything so much.' Then he pulled his hair, and thrust his hand into his waistcoat; and turned away, so that his old friend might not see the tear in his eye.

His old friend also was much moved. It was dreadful to him that the happiness of a Fletcher, and the comfort of the Whartons generally, should be marred by a man with such a name as Ferdinand Lopez. 'She'll never marry him without her father's consent,' said Sir Alured.

'If she means it, of course he'll consent.'

'That I'm sure he won't. He doesn't like the man a bit better than you do.' Fletcher shook his head. 'And he's as fond of you as though you were already his son.'

'What does it matter? If a girl sets her heart on marrying a man, of course she will marry him. If he had no money it might be different.

But if he's well off, of course he'll succeed. Well——; I suppose other men have borne the same sort of thing before and it hasn't killed them.'

'Let us hope, my boy. I think of her quite as much as of you.'

'Yes,—we can hope. I shan't give it up. As for her, I dare say she knows what will suit her best. I've nothing to say against the man,— excepting that I should like to cut him into four quarters.'

'But a foreigner!'

'Girls don't think about that,—not as you do and Mr Wharton. And I think they like dark, greasy men with slippery voices, who are up to dodges and full of secrets. Well, sir, I shall go to her at once and have it out.'

'You'll speak to my cousin?'

'Certainly I will. He has always been one of the best friends I ever had in my life. I know it hasn't been his fault. But what can a man do? Girls won't marry this man or that because they're told.'

Fletcher did speak to Emily's father, and learned more from him than had been told him by Sir Alured. Indeed he learned the whole truth. Lopez had been twice with the father pressing his suit and had been twice repulsed, with as absolute denial as words could convey. Emily, however, had declared her own feeling openly, expressing her wish to marry the odious man, promising not to do so without her father's consent, but evidently feeling that that consent ought not to be withheld from her. All this Mr Wharton told very plainly, walking with Arthur a little before dinner along a shaded, lonely path, which for half a mile ran along the very marge of the Wye at the bottom of the park. And then he went on to speak other words which seemed to rob his young friend of all hope. The old man was walking slowly, with his hands clasped behind his back and with his eyes fixed on the path as he went;—and he spoke slowly, evidently weighing his words as he uttered them, bringing home to his hearer a conviction that the matter discussed was one of supreme importance to the speaker,—as to which he had thought much, so as to be able to express his settled resolutions. 'I've told you all now, Arthur;—only this. I do not know how long I may be able to resist this man's claim if it be backed by Emily's entreaties. I am thinking very much about it. I do not know that I have really been able to think of anything else for the last two months. It is all the world to me,—what she and Everett do with themselves; and what she may do in this matter of marriage is of infinitely greater importance than anything that can befall him. If he makes a mistake, it may be put right. But with a woman's marrying——, vestigia nulla retrorsum.* She has put off all her old bonds and taken new ones, which must be her bonds for life. Feeling this very strongly, and disliking this man greatly,—disliking him, that is to say, in the view of this close relation,—I have felt myself to be justified in so far opposing my child by the use of a high hand. I have refused my sanction to the marriage both to him and to her,—though in truth I have been hard set to find any adequate reason for doing so. I have no right to fashion my girl's life by my prejudices. My life has been lived. Hers is to come. In this matter I should be cruel and unnatural were I to allow myself to be governed by any selfish inclination. Though I were to know that she would be lost to me for ever, I must give way,—if once brought to a conviction that by not giving way I should sacrifice her young happiness. In this matter, Arthur, I must not even think of you, though I love you well. I must consider only my child's welfare;—and in doing so I must try to sift my own feelings and my own judgement, and ascertain, if it be possible, whether my distaste to the man is reasonable or irrational;—whether I should serve her or sacrifice her by obstinacy of refusal. I can speak to you more plainly than to her. Indeed I have laid bare to you my whole heart and my whole mind. You have all my wishes, but you will understand that I do not promise you my continued assistance.' When he had so spoken he put out his hand and pressed his companion's arm. Then he turned slowly into a little by-path which led across the park up to the house, and left Arthur Fletcher standing alone by the river's bank.

And so by degrees the blow had come full home to him. He had been twice refused. Then rumours had reached him,—not at first that he had a rival, but that there was a man who might possibly become so. And now this rivalry, and its success, were declared to him plainly. He told himself from this moment that he had not a chance. Looking forward he could see it all. He understood the girl's character sufficiently to be sure that she would not be wafted about, from one lover to another, by change of scene. Taking her to Dresden,—or to New Zealand,—would only confirm in her passion such a girl as Emily Wharton. Nothing could shake her but the ascertained unworthiness of the man,—and not that unless it were ascertained beneath her own eyes. And then years must pass by before she would yield to another lover. There was a further question, too, which he did not fail to ask himself. Was the man necessarily unworthy because his name was Lopez, and because he had not come of English blood?

As he strove to think of this, if not coolly yet rationally, he sat himself down on the river's side and began to pitch stones off the path in among the rocks, among which at that spot the water made its way rapidly. There had been moments in which he had been almost ashamed of his love,—and now he did not know whether to be most ashamed or most proud of it. But he recognized the fact that it was crucifying him, and that it would continue to crucify him. He knew himself in London to be a popular man,—one of those for whom, according to general opinion, girls should sigh, rather than one who should break his heart sighing for a girl. He had often told himself that it was beneath his manliness to be despondent; that he should let such a trouble run from him like water from a duck's back, consoling himself with the reflection that if the girl had such bad taste she could hardly be worthy of him. He had almost tried to belong to that school which throws the heart away and rules by the head alone. He knew that others,—perhaps not those who knew him best, but who nevertheless were the companions of many of his hours,—gave him the credit for such power. Why should a man afflict himself by the inward burden of an unsatisfied craving, and allow his heart to sink into his very feet because a girl would not smile when he wooed her? 'If she be not fair for me, what care I how fair she be!'* He had repeated the lines to himself a score of times, and had been ashamed of himself because he could not make them come true to himself.

They had not come true in the least. There he was, Arthur Fletcher, whom all the world courted, with his heart in his very boots! There was a miserable load within him, absolutely palpable to his outward feeling,—a very physical pain,—which he could not shake off. As he threw the stones into the water he told himself that it must be so with him always. Though the world did pet him, though he was liked at his club, and courted in the hunting-field, and loved at balls and archery meetings, and reputed by old men to be a rising star, he told himself that he was so maimed and mutilated as to be only half a man. He could not reason about it. Nature had afflicted him with a certain weakness. One man has a hump;—another can hardly see out of his imperfect eyes;—a third can barely utter a few disjointed words. It was his fate to be constructed with some weak arrangement of the blood-vessels which left him in this plight. 'The whole damned thing is nothing to me,' he said bursting into absolute tears, after vainly trying to reassure himself by a recollection of the good things which the world still had in store for him.

Then he strove to console himself by thinking that he might take a pride in his love even though it were so intolerable a burden to him. Was it not something to be able to love as he loved? Was it not something at any rate that she to whom he had condescended to stoop was worthy of all love? But even here he could get no comfort,—being in truth unable to see very clearly into the condition of the thing. It was a disgrace to him,—to him within his own bosom,—that she should have preferred to him such a one as Ferdinand Lopez, and this disgrace he exaggerated, ignoring the fact that the girl herself might be deficient in judgement, or led away in her love by falsehood and counterfeit attractions. To him she was such a goddess that she must be right,— and therefore his own inferiority to such a one as Ferdinand Lopez was proved. He could take no pride in his rejected love. He would rid himself of it at a moment's notice if he knew the way. He would throw himself at the feet of some second-rate, tawdry, well-born, well-known beauty of the day,—only that there was not now left to him strength to pretend the feeling that would be necessary. Then he heard steps, and jumping up from his seat, stood just in the way of Emily Wharton and her cousin Mary. 'Ain't you going to dress for dinner, young man?' said the latter.

'I shall have time if you have, any way,' said Arthur, endeavouring to pluck up his spirits.

'That's nice of him;—isn't it?' said Mary. 'Why, we are dressed. What more do you want? We came out to look for you, though we didn't mean to come as far as this. It's past seven now, and we are supposed to dine at a quarter past.'

'Five minutes will do for me.'

'But you've got to get to the house. You needn't be in a tremendous hurry, because papa has only just come in from haymaking. They've got up the last load, and there has been the usual ceremony. Emily and I have been looking at them.'

'I wish I'd been here all the time,' said Emily. 'I do so hate London in July.'

'So do I,' said Arthur,—'in July and all other times.'

'You hate London!' said Mary.

'Yes,—and Herefordshire,—and other places generally. If I've got to dress I'd better get across the park as quick as I can go,' and so he left them. Mary turned round and looked at her cousin, but at the moment said nothing. Arthur's passion was well known to Mary Wharton, but Mary had as yet heard nothing of Ferdinand Lopez.

CHAPTER 16

NEVER RUN AWAY!

DURING the whole of that evening there was a forced attempt on the part of all the party at Wharton Hall to be merry,—which, however, as is the case whenever such attempts are forced, was a failure. There had been a haymaking harvest-home which was supposed to give the special occasion for mirth, as Sir Alured farmed the land around the park himself, and was great in hay. 'I don't think it pays very well,' he said with a gentle smile, 'but I like to employ some of the people myself. I think the old people find it easier with me than with the tenants.'

'I shouldn't wonder,' said his cousin;—'but that's charity; not employment.'

'No, no,' exclaimed the baronet. 'They work for their wages and do their best. Powell sees to that.' Powell was the bailiff, who knew the length of his master's foot to a quarter of an inch, and was quite aware that the Wharton haymakers were not to be overtasked. 'Powell doesn't keep any cats about the place, but what catch mice. But I am not quite sure that haymaking does pay.'

'How do the tenants manage?'

'Of course they look to things closer. You wouldn't wish me to let the land up to the house door.'

'I think,' said old Mrs Fletcher, 'that a landlord should consent to lose a little by his own farming. It does good in the long run.' Both Mr Wharton and Sir Alured felt that this might be very well at Longbarns, though it could hardly be afforded at Wharton.

'I don't think I lose much by my farming,' said the squire of Longbarns. 'I have about four hundred acres on hand, and I keep my accounts pretty regularly.'

'Johnson is a very good man, I dare say,' said the baronet.

'Like most of the others,' continued the squire, 'he's very well as long as he's looked after. I think I know as much about it as Johnson. Of course I don't expect a farmer's profit; but I do expect my rent, and I get it.'

'I don't think I manage it quite that way,' said the baronet in a melancholy tone.

'I'm afraid not,' said the barrister.

'John is as hard upon the men as any one of the tenants,' said John's wife, Mrs Fletcher of Longbarns.

'I'm not hard at all,' said John, 'and you understand nothing about it. I'm paying three shillings a week more to every man, and eighteen pence a week more to every woman, than I did three years ago.'

'That's because of the Unions,'* said the barrister.

'I don't care a straw for the Unions. If the Unions interfered with my comfort, I'd let the land and leave the place.'

'Oh, John!' ejaculated John's mother.

'I would not consent to be made a slave even for the sake of the country. But the wages had to be raised,—having raised them I expect to get proper value for my money. If anything has to be given away, let it be given away,—so that the people should know what it is that they receive.'

'That's just what we don't want to do here,' said Lady Wharton, who did not often join in any of these arguments.

'You're wrong, my lady,' said her stepson. 'You're only breeding idleness when you teach people to think that they are earning wages without working for their money. Whatever you do with 'em, let 'em know and feel the truth. It'll be the best in the long run.'

'I'm sometimes happy when I think that I shan't live to see the long run,' said the baronet. This was the manner in which they tried to be merry that evening after dinner at Wharton Hall. The two girls sat listening to their seniors in contented silence,—listening or perhaps thinking of their own peculiar troubles, while Arthur Fletcher held some book in his hand which he strove to read with all his might.

There was not one there in the room who did not know that it was the wish of the united families that Arthur Fletcher should marry Emily Wharton, and also that Emily had refused him. To Arthur of course the feeling that it was so could not but be an additional vexation; but the knowledge had grown up and had become common in the two families without any power on his part to prevent so disagreeable a condition of affairs. There was not one in that room, unless it was Mary Wharton, who was not more or less angry with Emily, thinking her to be perverse and unreasonable. Even to Mary her cousin's strange obstinacy was matter of surprise and sorrow,—for to her Arthur Fletcher was one of those demigods, who should never be refused, who are not expected to do more than express a wish and be accepted. Her own heart had not strayed that way because she thought but little of herself, knowing herself to be portionless, and believing from long thought on the subject that it was not her destiny to the wife of any man. She regarded Arthur Fletcher as being of all men the most lovable,—though, knowing her own condition, she did not dream of loving him.

It did not become her to be angry with another girl on such a cause;— but she was amazed that Arthur Fletcher should sigh in vain.

The girl's folly and perverseness on this head were known to them all,—but as yet her greater folly and worse perverseness, her vitiated taste and dreadful partiality for the Portuguese adventurer, were known but to the two old men and to poor Arthur himself. When that sternly magnificent old lady, Mrs Fletcher,—whose ancestors had been Welsh kings in the time of the Romans,—when she should hear this story, the roof of the old hall would hardly be able to hold her wrath and her dismay! The old kings had died away, but the Fletchers and the Vaughans,—of whom she had been one,—and the Whartons remained, a peculiar people in an age that was then surrendering itself to quick perdition, and with peculiar duties. Among these duties, the chiefest of them incumbent on females was that of so restraining their affections that they should never damage the good cause by leaving it. They might marry within the pale,—or remain single, as might be their lot. She would not take upon herself to say that Emily Wharton was bound to accept Arthur Fletcher, merely because such a marriage was fitting,—although she did think that there was much perverseness in the girl, who might have taught herself, had she not been stubborn, to comply with the wishes of the families. But to love one below herself, a man without a father, a foreigner, a black Portuguese nameless Jew, merely because he had a bright eye, and a hook nose, and a glib tongue,—that a girl from the Whartons should do this——! It was so unnatural to Mrs Fletcher that it would be hardly possible to her to be civil to the girl after she had heard that her mind and taste were so astray. All this Sir Alured knew and the barrister knew it,—and they feared her indignation the more because they sympathized with the old lady's feelings.

'Emily Wharton doesn't seem to me to be a bit more gracious than she used to be,' Mrs Fletcher said to Lady Wharton that night. The two old ladies were sitting together upstairs, and Mrs John Fletcher was with them. In such conferences Mrs Fletcher always domineered,—to the perfect contentment of old Lady Wharton, but not equally so to that of her daughter-in-law.

'I'm afraid she is not very happy,' said Lady Wharton.

'She has everything that ought to make a girl happy, and I don't know what it is she wants. It makes me quite angry to see her so discontented. She doesn't say a word, but sits there as glum as death. If I were Arthur I would leave her for six months, and never speak to her during the time.'

'I suppose, mother,' said the younger Mrs Fletcher,—who called her husband's mother, mother, and her own mother, mamma,—'a girl needn't marry a man unless she likes him.'

'But she should try to like him if it is suitable in other respects. I don't mean to take any trouble about it. Arthur needn't beg for any favour. Only I wouldn't have come here if I had thought that she had intended to sit silent like that always.'

'It makes her unhappy, I suppose,' said Lady Wharton, 'because she can't do what we all want.'

'Fall, lall! She'd have wanted it herself if nobody else had wished it. I'm surprised that Arthur should be so much taken with her.'

'You'd better say nothing more about it, mother.'

'I don't mean to say anything more about it. It's nothing to me. Arthur can do very well in the world without Emily Wharton. Only a girl like that will sometimes make a disgraceful match; and we should all feel that.'

'I don't think Emily will do anything disgraceful,' said Lady Wharton. And so they parted.

In the meantime the two brothers were smoking their pipes in the housekeeper's room, which, at Wharton, when the Fletchers or Everett were there, was freely used for that purpose.

'Isn't it rather quaint of you,' said the elder brother, 'coming down here in the middle of term time?'

'It doesn't matter much.'

'I should have thought it would matter;—that is, if you mean to go on with it.'

'I'm not going to make a slave of myself about it, if you mean that. I don't suppose I shall ever marry,—and as for rising to be a swell in the profession, I don't care about it.'

'You used to care about it,—very much. You used to say that if you didn't get to the top it shouldn't be your own fault.'

'And I have worked;—and I do work. But things get changed somehow. I've half a mind to give it all up,—to raise a lot of money, and to start off with a resolution to see every corner of the world. I suppose a man could do it in about thirty years if he lived so long. It's the kind of thing would suit me.'

'Exactly. I don't know any fellow who has been more into society, and therefore you are exactly the man to live alone for the rest of your life. You've always worked hard, I will say that for you;—and therefore you're just the man to be contented with idleness. You've always been ambitious and self-confident, and therefore it will suit you to a T, to be nobody and to do nothing.' Arthur sat silent, smoking his pipe with all his might, and his brother continued,—'Besides,—you read sometimes, I fancy.'

'I should read all the more.'

'Very likely. But what you have read, in the old plays,* for instance, must have taught you that when a man is cut up about a woman,—which I suppose is your case just at present,—he never does get over it. He never gets all right after a time,—does he? Such a one had better go and turn monk at once, as the world is over for him altogether;—isn't it? Men don't recover after a month or two, and go on just the same. You've never seen that kind of thing yourself?'

'I'm not going to cut my throat or turn monk either.'

'No. There are so many steamboats and railways now that travelling seems easier. Suppose you go as far as St Petersburg, and see if that does you any good. If it don't, you needn't go on, because it will be hopeless. If it does,—why, you can come back, because the second journey will do the rest.'

'There never was anything, John, that wasn't a matter for chaff with you.'

'And I hope there never will be. People understand it when logic would be thrown away. I suppose the truth is the girl cares for somebody else.' Arthur nodded his head. 'Who is it? Any one I know?'

'I think not.'

'Any one you know?'

'I have met the man.'

'Decent?'

'Disgustingly indecent, I should say.' John looked very black, for even with him the feeling about the Whartons and the Vaughans and the Fletchers was very strong. 'He's a man I should say you wouldn't let into Longbarns.'

'There might be various reasons for that. It might be that you wouldn't care to meet him.'

'Well;—no,—I don't suppose I should. But without that you wouldn't like him. I don't think he's an Englishman.'

'A foreigner!'

'He has got a foreign name.'

'An Italian nobleman?'

'I don't think he's noble in any country.'

'Who the d—— is he?'

'His name is——Lopez.'

'Everett's friend?'

'Yes;—Everett's friend. I ain't very much obliged to Master Everett for what he has done.'

'I've seen the man. Indeed, I may say I know him,—for I dined with him once in Manchester Square. Old Wharton himself must have asked him there.'

'He was there as Everett's friend. I only heard all this to-day, you know,—though I had heard about it before.'

'And therefore you want to set out on your travels. As far as I saw I should say he is a clever fellow.'

'I don't doubt that.'

'And a gentleman.'

'I don't know that he is not,' said Arthur. 'I've no right to say a word against him. From what Wharton says I suppose he's rich.'

'He's good looking too;—at least he's the sort of man that women like to look at.'

'Just so. I've no cause of quarrel with him,—nor with her. But——.'

'Yes, my friend. I see it all,' said the elder brother. 'I think I know all about it. But running away is not the thing. One may be pretty nearly sure that one is right when one says that a man shouldn't run away from anything.'

'The thing is to be happy if you can,' said Arthur.

'No;—that's not the thing. I'm not much of a philosopher, but as far as I can see there are two philosophies in the world. The one is to make one's self happy, and the other is to make other people happy. The latter answers the best.'

'I can't add to her happiness by hanging about London.'

'That's a quibble. It isn't her happiness we are talking about,—nor yet your hanging about London. Gird yourself up and go on with what you've got to do. Put your work before your feelings. What does a poor man do, who goes out hedging and ditching with a dead child lying in his house? If you get a blow in the face, return it if it ought to be returned, but never complain of the pain. If you must have your vitals eaten into,—have them eaten into like a man. But, mind you,—these ain't your vitals.'

'It goes pretty near.'

'These ain't your vitals. A man gets cured of it,—almost always. I believe always; though some men get hit so hard they can never bring themselves to try it again. But tell me this. Has old Wharton given his consent?'

'No. He has refused,' said Arthur with strong emphasis.

'How is it to be, then?'

'He has dealt very fairly by me. He has done all he could to get rid of the man,—both with him and with her. He has told Emily that he will have nothing to do with the man. And she will do nothing without his sanction.'

'Then it will remain just as it is.'

'No, John; it will not. He has gone on to say that though he has refused,—and has refused roughly enough,—he must give way if he sees that she has really set her heart upon him. And she has.'

'Has she told you so?'

'No;—but he has told me. I shall have it out with her to-morrow, if I can. And then I shall be off.'

'You'll be here for the shooting on the 1st?'

'No. I dare say you're right in what you say about sticking to my work. It does seem unmanly to run away because of a girl.'

'Because of anything! Stop and face it, whatever it is.'

'Just so;—but I can't stop and face her. It would do no good. For all our sakes I should be better away. I can get shooting with Musgrave and Carnegie in Perthshire. I dare say I shall go there, and take a share with them.'

'That's better than going into all the quarters of the globe.'

'I didn't mean that I was to surrender and start at once. You take a fellow up so short. I shall do very well, I've no doubt, and shall be hunting here as jolly as ever at Christmas. But a fellow must say it all to somebody.' The elder brother put his hand out and laid it affectionately upon the younger one's arm. 'I'm not going to whimper about the world like a whipped dog. The worst of it is so many people have known of this.'

'You mean down here.'

'Oh;—everywhere. I have never told them. It has been a kind of family affair and thought to be fit for general discussions.'

'That'll wear away.'

'In the mean time it's a bore. But that shall be the end of it. Don't you say another word to me about it, and I won't to you. And tell mother not to, or Sarah.' Sarah was John Fletcher's wife. 'It has got to be dropped, and let us drop it as quickly as we can. If she does marry this man, I don't suppose she'll be much at Longbarns or Wharton.'

'Not at Longbarns certainly, I should say,' replied John. 'Fancy mother having to curtsey to her as Mrs Lopez! And I doubt whether Sir Alured would like him. He isn't of our sort. He's too clever, too cosmopolitan,—a sort of man whitewashed of all prejudices, who wouldn't mind whether he ate horseflesh or beef if horseflesh were as good as beef, and never had an association in his life. I'm not sure that he's not on the safest side. Good night, old fellow. Pluck up, and send us plenty of grouse if you do go to Scotland.'

John Fletcher, as I hope may have been already seen, was by no means a weak man or an indifferent brother. He was warm-hearted, sharp-witted, and, though perhaps a little self-opinionated, considered throughout the county to be one of the most prudent in it. Indeed no one ever ventured to doubt his wisdom on all practical matters,—save his mother, who seeing him almost every day, had a stronger bias towards her younger son. 'Arthur has been hit hard about that girl,' he said to his wife that night.

'Emily Wharton?'

'Yes;—your cousin Emily. Don't say anything to him, but be as good to him as you know how.'

'Good to Arthur! Am I not always good to him?'

'Be a little more than usually tender with him. It makes one almost cry to see such a fellow hurt like that. I can understand it, though I never had anything of it myself.'

'You never had, John,' said the wife leaning close upon the husband's breast as she spoke. 'It all came very easily to you;—too easily perhaps.'

'If any girl had ever refused me, I should have taken her at her word I can tell you. There would have been no second "hop" to that ball.'

'Then I suppose I was right to catch it the first time?'

'I don't say how that may be.'

'I was right. Oh, dear me!—Suppose I had doubted, just for once, and you had gone off. You would have tried once more,—wouldn't you?'

'You'd have gone about like a broken-winged old hen, and have softened me in that way.'

'And now poor Arthur has had his wing broken.'

'You mustn't let on to know that it's broken, and the wing will be healed in due time. But what fools girls are!'

'Indeed they are, John;—particularly me.'

'Fancy a girl like Emily Wharton,' said he, not condescending to notice her little joke, 'throwing over a fellow like Arthur for a greasy, black foreigner.'

'A foreigner!'

'Yes;—a man named Lopez. Don't say anything about it at present. Won't she live to find out the difference, and to know what she has done! I can tell her of one that won't pity her.'

CHAPTER 17

GOOD-BYE

ARTHUR FLETCHER received his brother's teaching as true, and took his brother's advice in good part,—so that, before the morning following, he had resolved that however deep the wound might be, he would so live before the world, that the world should not see his wound. What people already knew they must know,—but they should learn nothing further either by words or signs from him. He would, as he had said to his brother, 'have it out with Emily'; and then, if she told him plainly that she loved the man, he would bid her adieu, simply expressing regret that their course for life should be divided. He was confident that she would tell him the entire truth. She would be restrained neither by false modesty, nor by any assumed unwillingness to discuss her own affairs with a friend so true to her as he had been. He knew her well enough to be sure that she recognized the value of his love though she could not bring herself to accept it. There are rejected lovers who, merely because they are lovers, become subject to the scorn and even to the disgust of the girls they love. But again there are men who, even when they are rejected, are almost loved, who are considered to be worthy of the reverence, almost of worship;—and yet the worshippers will not love them. Not analysing all this, but somewhat conscious of the light in which this girl regarded him, he knew that what he might say would be treated with deference. As to shaking her,—as to talking her out of one purpose and into another,—that to him did not for a moment seem to be practicable. There was no hope of that. He hardly knew why he should endeavour to say a word to her before he left Wharton. And yet he felt that it must be said. Were he to allow her to be married to this man, without any further previous word between them, it would appear that he had resolved to quarrel with her for ever. But now, at this very moment of time, as he lay in his bed, as he dressed himself in the morning, as he sauntered about among the new hay-stacks with his pipe in his mouth after breakfast, he came to some conclusion in his mind very much averse to such quarrelling.

He had loved her with all his heart. It had not been a mere drawing-room love begotten between a couple of waltzes, and fostered by five minutes in a crush. He knew himself to be a man of the world, and he did not wish to be other than he was. He could talk among men as men talked, and act as men acted;—and he could do the same with women. But there was one person who had been to him above all, and round everything, and under everything. There had been a private nook within him into which there had been no entrance but for the one image. There had been a holy of holies, which he had guarded within himself, keeping it free from all outer contamination for his own use. He had cherished the idea of a clear fountain of ever-running water which would at last be his, always ready for the comfort of his own lips. Now all his hope was shattered, his trust was gone, and his longing disappointed. But the person was the same person, though she could not be his. The nook was there, though she would not fill it. The holy of holies was not less holy, though he himself might not dare to lift the curtain. The fountain would still run,—still the clearest fountain of all,—though he might not put his lips to it. He would never allow himself to think of it with lessened reverence, or with changed ideas as to her nature.

And then, as he stood leaning against a ladder which still kept its place against one of the hay-ricks, and filled his second pipe unconsciously, he had to realize to himself the probable condition of his future life. Of course she would marry this man with very little further delay. Her father had already declared himself to be too weak to interfere much longer with her wishes. Of course Mr Wharton would give way. He had himself declared that he would give way. And then,—what sort of life would be her life? No one knew anything about the man. There was an idea that he was rich,—but wealth such as his, wealth that is subject to speculation, will fly away at a moment's notice. He might be cruel, a mere adventurer, or a thorough ruffian for all that was known of him. There should, thought Arthur Fletcher to himself, be more stability in the giving and taking of wives than could be reckoned upon here. He became old in that half hour, taking home to himself and appreciating many saws of wisdom and finger-directions of experience which hitherto had been to him matters almost of ridicule. But he could only come to this conclusion,—that as she was still to be to him his holy of holies though he might not lay his hand upon the altar, his fountain though he might not drink of it, the one image which alone could have filled that nook, he would not cease to regard her happiness when she should have become the wife of this stranger. With the stranger himself he never could be on friendly terms;—but for the stranger's wife there should always be a friend, if the friend were needed.

About an hour before lunch, John Fletcher, who had been hanging about the house all the morning in a manner very unusual to him, caught Emily Wharton as she was passing through the hall, and told her that Arthur was in a certain part of the grounds and wished to speak to her. 'Alone?' she asked. 'Yes, certainly alone.' 'Ought I to go

to him, John?' she asked again. 'Certainly I think you ought.' Then he
had done his commission and was able to apply himself to whatever
business he had on hand.

Emily at once put on her hat, took her parasol, and left the house.
There was something distasteful to her in the idea of this going out at
a lover's bidding, to meet him; but like all Whartons and all Fletchers,
she trusted John Fletcher. And then she was aware that there were
circumstances which might make such a meeting as this serviceable.
She knew nothing of what had taken place during the last four-and-
twenty hours. She had no idea that in consequence of words spoken to
him by her father and his brother, Arthur Fletcher was about to abandon his suit. There would have been no doubt about her going to meet
him had she thought this. She supposed that she would have to hear
again the old story. If so, she would hear it, and would then have an
opportunity of telling him that her heart had been given entirely to
another. She knew all that she owed to him. After a fashion she did love
him. He was entitled to all kindest consideration from her hands. But
he should be told the truth.

As she entered the shrubbery he came out to meet her, giving her his
hand with a frank, easy air and a pleasant smile. His smile was as bright
as the ripple of the sea, and his eye would then gleam, and the slightest
sparkle of his white teeth would be seen between his lips, and the
dimple of his chin would show itself deeper than at other times. 'It is
very good of you. I thought you'd come. John asked you, I suppose.'

'Yes;—he told me you were here, and he said I ought to come.'

'I don't know about ought, but I think it better. Will you mind walking on, as I've got something that I want to say?' Then he turned and
she turned with him into the little wood. 'I'm not going to bother you
any more, my darling,' he said. 'You are still my darling, though I will
not call you so after this.' Her heart sank almost in her bosom as she
heard this,—though it was exactly what she would have wished to hear.
But now there must be some close understanding between them and
some tenderness. She knew how much she had owed him, how good he
had been to her, how true had been his love; and she felt that words
would fail her to say that which ought to be said. 'So you have given
yourself to—one Ferdinand Lopez!'

'Yes,' she said, in a hard, dry voice. 'Yes; I have. I do not know who
told you; but I have.'

'Your father told me. It was better,—was it not?—that I should
know. You are not sorry that I should know?'

'It is better.'

'I am not going to say a word against him.'

'No;—do not do that.'

'Nor against you. I am simply here now to let you know that——I retire.'

'You will not quarrel with me, Arthur?'

'Quarrel with you! I could not quarrel with you, if I would. No;—there shall be no quarrel. But I do not suppose we shall see each other very often.'

'I hope we may.'

'Sometimes, perhaps. A man should not, I think, affect to be friends with a successful rival. I dare say he is an excellent fellow, but how is it possible that he and I should get on together? But you will always have one,—one besides him,—who will love you best in this world.'

'No;—no;—no.'

'It must be so. There will be nothing wrong in that. Every one has some dearest friend, and you will always be mine. If anything of evil should ever happen to you,—which of course there won't,—there would be some one who would——. But I don't want to talk buncum; I only want you to believe me. Good-bye, and God bless you.' Then he put out his right hand, holding his hat under his left arm.

'You are not going away?'

'To-morrow, perhaps. But I will say my real good-bye to you here, now, to-day. I hope you may be happy. I hope it with all my heart. Good-bye. God bless you!'

'Oh, Arthur!' Then she put her hand in his.

'Oh, I have loved you so dearly. It has been with my whole heart. You have never quite understood me, but it has been as true as heaven. I have thought sometimes that had I been a little less earnest about it, I should have been a little less stupid. A man shouldn't let it get the better of him, as I have done. Say good-bye to me, Emily.'

'Good-bye,' she said, still leaving her hand in his.

'I suppose that's about all. Don't let them quarrel with you here if you can help it. Of course at Longbarns they won't like it for a time. Oh,—if it could have been different!' Then he dropped her hand, and turning his back quickly upon her, went away along the path.

She had expected and had almost wished that he should kiss her. A girl's cheek is never so holy to herself as it is to her lover,—if he do love her. There would have been something of reconciliation, something of a promise of future kindness in a kiss, which even Ferdinand would not have grudged. It would, for her, have robbed the parting of that bitterness of pain which his words had given to it. As to all that, he had made no calculation; but the bitterness was there for him, and he could have done nothing that would have expelled it.

She wept bitterly as she returned to the house. There might have been cause for joy. It was clear enough that her father, though he had shown no sign of yielding, was nevertheless prepared to yield. It was her father who had caused Arthur Fletcher to take himself off, as a lover really dismissed. But, at this moment, she could not bring herself to look at that aspect of the affair. Her mind would revert to all those choicest moments in her early years in which she had been happy with Arthur Fletcher; in which she had first learned to love him, and had then taught herself to understand by some confused and perplexed lesson that she did not love him as men and women love. But why should she not so have loved him? Would she not have done so could she then have understood how true and firm he was? And then, independently of herself, throwing herself aside for the time as she was bound to do when thinking of one so good to her as Arthur Fletcher, she found that no personal joy could drown the grief which she shared with him. For a moment the idea of a comparison between the two men forced itself upon her,—but she drove it from her as she hurried back to the house.

CHAPTER 18

THE DUKE OF OMNIUM THINKS OF HIMSELF

THE blaze made by the Duchess of Omnium during the three months of the season up in London had been very great, but it was little in comparison with the social coruscation expected to be achieved at Gatherum Castle,—little at least as far as public report went, and the general opinion of the day. No doubt the house in Carlton Gardens had been thrown open as the house of no Prime Minister, perhaps of no duke, had been opened before in this country; but it had been done by degrees, and had not been accompanied by such a blowing of trumpets as was sounded with reference to the entertainments at Gatherum. I would not have it supposed that the trumpets were blown by the direct order of the Duchess. The trumpets were blown by the customary trumpeters as it became known that great things were to be done,—all newspapers and very many tongues lending their assistance, till the sounds of the instruments almost frightened the Duchess herself. 'Isn't it odd,' she said to her friend Mrs Finn, 'that one can't have a few friends down in the country without such a fuss about it as the people are making?' Mrs Finn did not think that it was odd, and so she said. Thousands of pounds were being spent in a very conspicuous way. Invitations to the place even for a couple of days,—for twenty-four hours,—had been begged for abjectly. It was understood everywhere that the Prime Minister was bidding for greatness and popularity. Of course the trumpets were blown very loudly. 'If people don't take care,' said the Duchess, 'I'll put everybody off and have the whole place shut up. I'd do it for sixpence, now.'

Perhaps of all the persons, much or little concerned, the one who heard the least of the trumpets,—or rather who was the last to hear them,—was the Duke himself. He could not fail to see something in the newspapers, but what he did see did not attract him so frequently or so strongly as it did the others. It was a pity, he thought, that a man's social and private life should be made subject to so many remarks, but this misfortune was one of those to which wealth and rank are liable. He had long recognized that fact, and for a time endeavoured to believe that his intended sojourn at Gatherum Castle was not more public than are the autumn doings of other dukes and other prime ministers. But gradually the trumpets did reach even his ears. Blind as he was to many things himself, he always had near to him that other duke who was never blind to anything. 'You are going to do great things at Gatherum this year,' said the Duke.

'Nothing particular, I hope,' said the Prime Minister, with an inward trepidation,—for gradually there had crept upon him a fear that his wife was making a mistake.

'I thought it was going to be very particular.'

'It's Glencora's doing.'

'I don't doubt but that her Grace is right. Don't suppose that I am criticizing your hospitality. We are to be at Gatherum ourselves about the end of the month. It will be the first time I shall have seen the place since your uncle's time.'

The Prime Minister at this moment was sitting in his own particular room at the Treasury Chambers, and before the entrance of his friend had been conscientiously endeavouring to define for himself, not a future policy, but the past policy of the last month or two. It had not been for him a very happy occupation. He had become the Head of the Government,—and had not failed, for there he was, still the Head of the Government, with a majority at his back, and the six months' vacation* before him. They who were entitled to speak to him confidentially as to his position, were almost vehement in declaring his success. Mr Rattler, about a week ago, had not seen any reason why the

Ministry should not endure at least for the next four years. Mr Roby, from the other side, was equally confident. But, on looking back at what he had done, and indeed on looking forward into his future intentions, he could not see why he, of all men, should be Prime Minister. He had once been Chancellor of the Exchequer, filling that office through two halcyon sessions, and he had known the reason why he had held it. He had ventured to assure himself at the time that he was the best man whom his party could then have found for that office, and he had been satisfied. But he had none of that satisfaction now. There were men under him who were really at work. The Lord Chancellor had legal reforms on foot. Mr Monk was busy, heart and soul, in regard to income tax and brewers' licences,—making our poor Prime Minister's mouth water. Lord Drummond was active among the colonies. Phineas Finn had at any rate his ideas about Ireland. But with the Prime Minister,—so at least the Duke told himself,—it was all a blank. The policy confided to him and expected at his hands was that of keeping together a Coalition Ministry. That was a task that did not satisfy him. And now, gradually,—very slowly indeed at first, but still with a sure step,—there was creeping upon him the idea that his power of cohesion was sought for, and perhaps found, not in his political capacity, but in his rank and wealth. It might, in fact, be the case that it was his wife the Duchess,—that Lady Glencora of whose wild impulses and general impracticability he had always been in dread,—that she with her dinner parties and receptions, with her crowded saloons, her music, her picnics, and social temptations, was Prime Minister rather than he himself. It might be that this had been understood by the coalesced parties,—by everybody, in fact, except himself. It had, perhaps, been found that in the state of things then existing, a ministry could be best kept together, not by parliamentary capacity, but by social arrangements, such as his Duchess, and his Duchess alone, could carry out. She and she only would have the spirit and the money and the sort of cleverness required. In such a state of things he of course, as her husband, must be the nominal Prime Minister.

There was no anger in his bosom as he thought of this. It would be hardly just to say that there was jealousy. His nature was essentially free from jealousy. But there was shame,—and self-accusation at having accepted so great an office with so little fixed purpose as to great work. It might be his duty to subordinate even his pride to the service of his country, and to consent to be a *fainéant* minister, a gilded Treasury log,* because by remaining in that position he would enable the Government to be carried on. But how base the position, how mean, how repugnant to that grand idea of public work which had hitherto been the motive power of all his life! How would he continue to live if this thing were to go on from year to year,—he pretending to govern while others governed,—stalking about from one public hall to another in a blue ribbon,* taking the highest place at all tables, receiving mock reverence, and known to all men as *fainéant* First Lord of the Treasury? Now, as he had been thinking of all this, the most trusted of his friends had come to him, and had at once alluded to the very circumstances which had been pressing so heavily on his mind. 'I was delighted,' continued the elder Duke, 'when I heard that you had determined to go to Gatherum Castle this year.'

'If a man has a big house I suppose he ought to live in it, sometimes.'

'Certainly. It was for such purposes as this now intended that your uncle built it. He never became a public man, and therefore, though he went there, every year I believe, he never really used it.'

'He hated it,—in his heart. And so do I. And so does Glencora. I don't see why any man should have his private life interrupted by being made to keep a huge caravansary* open for persons he doesn't care a straw about.'

'You would not like to live alone.'

'Alone,—with my wife and children,—I would certainly, during a portion of the year at least.'

'I doubt whether such a life, even for a month, even for a week, is compatible with your duties. You would hardly find it possible. Could you do without your private secretaries? Would you know enough of what is going on, if you did not discuss matters with others? A man cannot be both private and public at the same time.'

'And therefore one has to be chopped up, like "a reed out of the river",* as the poet said, "and yet not give sweet music afterwards." ' The Duke of St Bungay said nothing in answer to this, as he did not understand the chopping of the reed. 'I'm afraid I've been wrong about this collection of people down at Gatherum,' continued the younger Duke. 'Glencora is impulsive, and has overdone the thing. Just look at that.' And he handed a letter to his friend. The old Duke put on his spectacles and read the letter through,—which ran as follows:

'Private.'

'My Lord Duke,—

'I do not doubt but that your Grace is aware of my position in regard to the public press of the country, and I beg to assure your Grace that my present proposition is made, not on account of the great honour and pleasure which would be conferred upon myself should your Grace accede to it, but because I feel assured that I might so be best enabled to discharge an important duty for the benefit of the public generally.

'Your Grace is about to receive the whole fashionable world of England and many distinguished foreign ambassadors at your ancestral halls, not solely for social delight,—for a man in your Grace's high position is not able to think only of a pleasant life,—but in order that the prestige of your combined Ministry may be so best maintained. That your Grace is thereby doing a duty to your country no man who understands the country can doubt. But it must be the case that the country at large should interest itself in your festivities, and should demand to have accounts of the gala doings of your ducal palace. Your Grace will probably agree with me that these records could be better given by one empowered by yourself to give them, by one who had been present, and who would write in your Grace's interest, than by some interloper who would receive his tale only at second hand.

'It is my purport now to inform your Grace that should I be honoured by an invitation to your Grace's party at Gatherum, I should obey such a call with the greatest alacrity, and would devote my pen and the public organ which is at my disposal to your Grace's service with the readiest good-will.

'I have the honour to be,
    'My Lord Duke,
        'Your Grace's most obedient
            'And very humble servant,

'QUINTUS SLIDE.'*

The old Duke, when he had read the letter, laughed heartily. 'Isn't that a terribly bad sign of the times?' said the younger.

'Well;—hardly that, I think. The man is both a fool and a black-guard; but I don't think we are therefore to suppose that there are many fools and blackguards like him. I wonder what he really has wanted.'

'He has wanted me to ask him to Gatherum.'

'He can hardly have expected that. I don't think he can have been such a fool. He may have thought that there was a possible off chance, and that he would not lose even that for want of asking. Of course you won't have noticed it.'

'I have asked Warburton to write to him, saying that he cannot be received at my house. I have all letters answered unless they seem to have come from insane persons. Would it not shock you if your private arrangements were invaded in that way?'

'He can't invade you.'

'Yes he can. He does. That is an invasion. And whether he is there or not, he can and will write about my house. And though no one else will make himself such a fool as he has done by his letter, nevertheless even that is a sign of what others are doing. You yourself were saying just now that we were going to do something,—something particular, you said.'

'It was your word, and I echoed it. I suppose you are going to have a great many people?'

'I am afraid Glencora has overdone it. I don't know why I should trouble you by saying so, but it makes me uneasy.'

'I can't see why.'

'I fear she has got some idea into her head of astounding the world by display.'

'I think she has got an idea of conquering the world by graciousness and hospitality.'

'It is as bad. It is, indeed, the same thing. Why should she want to conquer what we call the world? She ought to want to entertain my friends because they are my friends; and if from my public position I have more so-called friends than would trouble me in a happier condition of private life, why, then, she must entertain more people. There should be nothing beyond that. The idea of conquering people, as you call it, by feeding them, is to me abominable. If it goes on it will drive me mad. I shall have to give up everything, because I cannot bear the burden.' This he said with more excitement, with stronger passion, than his friend had ever seen in him before; so much so that the old Duke was frightened. 'I ought never to have been where I am,' said the Prime Minister, getting up from his chair and walking about the room.

'Allow me to assure you that in that you are decidedly mistaken,' said his Grace of St Bungay.

'I cannot make even you see the inside of my heart in such a matter as this,' said his Grace of Omnium.

'I think I do. It may be that in saying so I claim for myself greater power than I possess, but I think I do. But let your heart say what it may on the subject, I am sure of this,—that when the Sovereign, by the advice of two outgoing Ministers, and with the unequivocally expressed assent of the House of Commons, calls on a man to serve her and the country, that man cannot be justified in refusing, merely by doubts about his own fitness. If your health is failing you, you may know it, and say so. Or it may be that your honour,—your faith to others,— should forbid you to accept the position. But of your own general fitness you must take the verdict given by such general consent. They have seen clearer than you have done what is required, and know better than you can know how that which is wanted is to be secured.'

'If I am to be here and do nothing, must I remain?'

'A man cannot keep together the Government of a country and do nothing. Do not trouble yourself about this crowd at Gatherum. The Duchess, easily, almost without exertion, will do that which to you, or to me either, would be impossible. Let her have her way, and take no notice of the Quintus Slides.' The Prime Minister smiled, as though this repeated allusion to Mr Slide's letter had brought back his good humour, and said nothing further then as to his difficulties. There were a few words to be spoken as to some future Cabinet meeting, some- thing perhaps to be settled as to some man's work or position, a hint to be given, and a lesson to be learned,—for of these inner Cabinet Councils between these two statesmen there was frequent use; and then the Duke of St Bungay took his leave.

Our Duke, as soon as his friend had left him, rang for his private secretary, and went to work diligently, as though nothing had disturbed him. I do not know that his labours on that occasion were of a very high order. Unless there be some special effort of law-making before the country, some reform bill to be passed, some attempt at education to be made, some fetters to be forged or to be relaxed, a Prime Minister is not driven hard by the work of his portfolio,—as are his colleagues. But many men were in want of many things, and contrived by many means to make their wants known to the Prime Minister. A dean would fain be a bishop, or a judge a chief justice, or a commissioner a chairman, or a secretary a commissioner. Knights would fain be baronets, baronets barons, and barons earls. In one guise or another the wants of gentle- men were made known, and there was work to be done. A ribbon cannot be given away without breaking the hearts of, perhaps, three gentlemen and of their wives and daughters. And then he went down to the House of Lords,—for the last time this Session as far as work was concerned. On the morrow legislative work would be over, and the gentlemen of Parliament would be sent to their country houses, and to their pleasant country joys.

It had been arranged that on the day after the prorogation of Parliament the Duchess of Omnium should go down to Gatherum to prepare for the coming of the people, which was to commence about three days later, taking her ministers, Mrs Finn and Locock, with her; and that her husband with his private secretaries and dispatch boxes was to go for those three days to Matching, a smaller place than Gatherum, but one to which they were much better accustomed. If, as the Duchess thought to be not unlikely, the Duke should prolong his stay for a few days at Matching, she felt confident that she would be able to bear the burden of the Castle on her own shoulders. She had thought it to be very probable that he would prolong his stay at Matching, and if the absence were not too long, this might be well explained to the assembled company. In the Duchess's estimation a Prime Minister would lose nothing by pleading the nature of his business as an excuse for such absence,—or by having such a plea made for him. Of course he must appear at last. But as to that she had no fear. His timidity, and his conscience also, would both be too potent to allow him to shirk the nuisance of Gatherum altogether. He would come, she was sure; but she did not much care how long he deferred his coming. She was, therefore, not a little surprised when he announced to her an alteration in his plans. This he did not many hours after the Duke of St Bungay had left him at the Treasury Chambers. 'I think I shall go down with you at once to Gatherum,' he said.

'What is the meaning of that?' The Duchess was not skilled in hiding her feelings, at any rate from him, and declared to him at once by her voice and eye that the proposed change was not gratifying to her.

'It will be better. I had thought that I would get a quiet day or two at Matching. But as the thing has to be done, it may as well be done at first. A man ought to receive his own guests. I can't say that I look forward to any great pleasure in doing so on this occasion;—but I shall do it.' It was very easy to understand also the tone of his voice. There was in it something of offended dignity, something of future marital intentions,—something also of the weakness of distress.

She did not want him to come at once to Gatherum. A great deal of money was being spent, and the absolute spending was not yet quite perfected. There might still be possibility of interference. The tents were not all pitched. The lamps were not as yet all hung in the conservatories. Waggons would still be coming in and workmen still be going out. He would think less of what had been done if he could be kept from seeing it while it was being done. And the greater crowd which would be gathered there by the end of the first week would carry off the vastness of the preparations. As to money, he had given her almost carte blanche, having at one vacillatory period of his Prime Ministership been talked by her into some agreement with her own plans.

And in regard to money he would say to himself that he ought not to interfere with any whim of hers on that score, unless he thought it right to crush the whim on some other score. Half what he possessed had been hers, and even if during this year he were to spend more than his income,—if he were to double or even treble the expenditure of past years,—he could not consume the additions to his wealth which had accrued and heaped themselves up since his marriage. He had therefore written a line to his banker, and a line to his lawyer, and he had himself seen Locock, and his wife's hands had been loosened. 'I didn't think, your Grace,' said Locock, 'that his Grace would be so very,—very,—very.' 'Very what, Locock?' 'So very free, your Grace.' The Duchess, as she thought of it, declared to herself that her husband was the truest nobleman in all England. She revered, admired, and almost loved him. She knew him to be infinitely better than herself. But she could hardly sympathize with him, and was quite sure that he did not sympathize with her. He was so good about the money! But yet it was necessary that he should be kept in the dark as to the spending of a good deal of it. Now he was going to upset a portion of her plans by coming to Gatherum before he was wanted. She knew him to be obstinate, but it might be possible to turn him back to his old purpose by clever manipulation.

'Of course it would be much nicer for me,' she said.

'That alone would be sufficient.'

'Thanks, dear. But we had arranged for people to come at first whom I thought you would not specially care to meet. Sir Orlando and Mr Rattler will be there with their wives.'

'I have become quite used to Sir Orlando and Mr Rattler.'

'No doubt, and therefore I wanted to spare you something of their company. The Duke, whom you really do like, isn't coming yet. I thought, too, you would have your work to finish off.'

'I fear it is of a kind that won't bear finishing off. However, I have made up my mind, and have already told Locock to send word to the people at Matching to say I shall not be there yet. How long will all this last at Gatherum?'

'Who can say?'

'I should have thought you could. People are not coming, I suppose, for an indefinite time.'

'As one set leaves, one asks others.'

'Haven't you asked enough as yet? I should like to know when we may expect to get away from the place.'

'You needn't stay till the end, you know.'

'But you must.'

'Certainly.'

'And I should wish you to go with me, when we do go to Matching.'

'Oh, Plantagenet,' said the wife, 'what a Darby and Joan* kind of thing you like to have it!'

'Yes, I do. The Darby and Joan kind of thing is what I like.'

'Only Darby is to be in an office all day, and in Parliament all night,— and Joan is to stay at home.'

'Would you wish me not to be in an office, and not to be in Parliament? But don't let us misunderstand each other. You are doing the best you can to further what you think to be my interests.'

'I am,' said the Duchess.

'I love you the better for it, day by day.' This so surprised her, that as she took him by the arm, her eyes were filled with tears. 'I know that you are working for me quite as hard as I work myself, and that you are doing so with the pure ambition of seeing your husband a great man.'

'And myself as a great man's wife.'

'It is the same thing. But I would not have you overdo your work. I would not have you make yourself conspicuous by anything like display. There are ill-natured people who will say things that you do not expect, and to which I should be more sensitive than I ought to be. Spare me such pain as this, if you can.' He still held her hand as he spoke, and she answered him only by nodding her head. 'I will go down with you to Gatherum on Friday.' Then he left her.

CHAPTER 19

VULGARITY

THE Duke and Duchess with their children and personal servants reached Gatherum Castle the day before the first crowd of visitors was expected. It was on a lovely autumn afternoon, and the Duke, who had endeavoured to make himself pleasant during the journey, had suggested that as soon as the heat would allow them they would saunter about the grounds and see what was being done. They could dine late, at half-past eight or nine, so that they might be walking from seven to eight. But the Duchess when she reached the Castle declined to fall in with this arrangement. The journey had been hot and dusty, and she

was a little cross. They reached the place about five, and then she
declared that she would have a cup of tea and lie down; she was too tired
to walk; and the sun, she said, was still scorchingly hot. He then asked
that the children might go with him; but the two little girls were weary
and travel-worn, and the two boys, the elder of whom was home from
Eton* and the younger from some minor Eton, were already out about
the place after their own pleasures. So the Duke started for his walk
alone.

The Duchess certainly did not wish to have to inspect the works in
conjunction with her husband. She knew how much there was that she
ought still to do herself, how many things that she herself ought to see.
But she could neither do anything nor see anything to any purpose
under his wing. As to lying down, that she knew to be quite out of the
question. She had already found out that the life which she had adopted
was one of incessant work. But she was neither weak nor idle. She was
quite prepared to work,—if only she might work after her own fashion
and with companions chosen by herself. Had not her husband been so
perverse, she would have travelled down with Mrs Finn, whose coming was now postponed for two days, and Locock would have been
with her. The Duke had given directions which made it necessary that
Locock's coming should be postponed for a day, and this was another
grievance. She was put out a good deal, and began to speculate whether
her husband was doing it on purpose to torment her. Nevertheless, as
soon as she knew that he was out of the way, she went to her work. She
could not go out among the tents and lawns and conservatories, as she
would probably meet him. But she gave orders as to bedchambers, saw
to the adornments of the reception-rooms, had an eye to the banners
and martial trophies suspended in the vast hall, and the busts and
statues which adorned the corners, looked in on the plate which was
being prepared for the great dining-room, and superintended the
moving about of chairs, sofas, and tables generally. 'You may take it as
certain, Mrs Pritchard,' she said to the housekeeper, 'that there will
never be less than forty for the next two months.'

'Forty to sleep, my lady?' To Pritchard the Duchess had for many
years been Lady Glencora, and she perhaps understood that her mistress liked the old appellation.

'Yes, forty to sleep, and forty to eat, and forty to drink. But that's
nothing. Forty to push through twenty-four hours every day! Do you
think you've got everything that you want?'

'It depends, my lady, how long each of 'em stays.'

'One night! No,—say two nights on an average.'

'That makes shifting the beds very often;—doesn't it, my lady?'

'Send up to Puddick's for sheets to-morrow. Why wasn't that thought of before?'

'It was, my lady,—and I think we shall do. We've got the steam-washery put up.'

'Towels!' suggested the Duchess.

'Oh yes, my lady. Puddick's did send a great many things;—a whole waggon load there was come from the station. But the tablecloths ain't, none of 'em, long enough for the big table.' The Duchess's face fell. 'Of course there must be two. On them very long tables, my lady, there always is two.'

'Why didn't you tell me, so that I could have had them made? It's impossible,—impossible that one brain should think of it all. Are you sure you've got enough hands in the kitchen?'

'Well, my lady;—we couldn't do with more; and they ain't an atom of use,—only just in the way,—if you don't know something about 'em. I suppose Mr Millepois will be down soon.' This name, which Mrs Pritchard called Milleypoise, indicated a French cook who was as yet unknown at the Castle.

'He'll be here to-night.'

'I wish he could have been here a day or two sooner, my lady, so as just to see about him.'

'And how should we have got our dinner in town? He won't make any difficulties. The confectioner did come?'

'Yes, my lady; and to tell the truth out at once, he was that drunk last night that——; oh, dear, we didn't know what to do with him.'

'I don't mind that before the affair begins. I don't suppose he'll get tipsy while he has to work for all these people. You've plenty of eggs?'

These questions went on so rapidly that in addition to the asking of them the Duchess was able to go through all the rooms before she dressed for dinner, and in every room she saw something to speak of, noting either perfection or imperfection. In the meantime the Duke had gone out alone. It was still hot, but he had made up his mind that he would enjoy his first holiday out of town by walking about his own grounds, and he would not allow the heat to interrupt him. He went out through the vast hall, and the huge front door, which was so huge and so grand that it was very seldom used. But it was now open by chance, owing to some incident of this festival time, and he passed through it and stood upon the grand terrace, with the well-known and much-lauded portico over head. Up to the terrace, though it was very high, there ran a road, constructed upon arches, so that grand guests could drive almost into the house. The Duke, who was never grand himself, as he stood there looking at the far-stretching view before him, could not remember that he had ever but once before placed himself on that spot. Of what use had been the portico, and the marbles, and the huge pile of stone,—of what use the enormous hall just behind him, cutting the house in two, declaring aloud by its own aspect and proportions that it had been built altogether for show and in no degree for use or comfort? And now as he stood there he could already see that men were at work about the place, that ground had been moved here, and grass laid down there, and a new gravel road constructed in another place. Was it not possible that his friends should be entertained without all these changes in the gardens? Then he perceived the tents, and descending from the terrace and turning to the left towards the end of the house he came upon a new conservatory. The exotics with which it was to be filled were at this moment being brought in on great barrows. He stood for a moment and looked, but said not a word to the men. They gazed at him but evidently did not know him. How should they know him,—him, who was seldom there, and who when there never showed himself about the place? Then he went farther afield from the house and came across more and more men. A great ha-ha* fence had been made, enclosing on three sides a large flat and turfed parallelogram of ground, taken out of the park and open at one end to the gardens, containing, as he thought, about an acre. 'What are you doing this for?' he said to one of the labourers. The man stared at him and at first seemed hardly inclined to make him an answer. 'It be for the quality to shoot their bows and harrows,' he said at last, as he continued the easy task of patting with his spade the completed work. He evidently regarded this stranger as an intruder who was not entitled to ask questions, even if he were permitted to wander about the grounds.

From one place he went on to another, and found changes, and new erections, and some device for throwing away money everywhere. It angered him to think that there was so little of simplicity left in the world that a man could not entertain his friends without such a fuss as this. His mind applied itself frequently to the consideration of the money, not that he grudged the loss of it, but the spending of it in such a cause. And then perhaps there occurred to him an idea that all this should not have been done without a word of consent from himself. Had she come to him with some scheme for changing everything about the place, making him think that the alterations were a matter of taste or of mere personal pleasure, he would probably have given his assent at once, thinking nothing of the money. But all this was sheer display. Then he walked up and saw the flag waving over the Castle, indicating that he, the Lord Lieutenant* of the County, was present there on his own soil. That was right. That was as it should be, because the flag was waving in compliance with an acknowledged ordinance. Of all that properly belonged to his rank and station he could be very proud, and would allow no diminution of that outward respect to which they were entitled. Were they to be trenched on by his fault in his person, the rights of others to their enjoyment would be endangered, and the benefits accruing to his country from established marks of reverence would be imperilled. But here was an assumed and preposterous grandeur that was as much within the reach of some rich swindler or of some prosperous haberdasher as of himself,—having, too, a look of raw newness about it which was very distasteful to him. And then, too, he knew that nothing of all this would have been done unless he had become Prime Minister. Why on earth should a man's grounds be knocked about because he becomes Prime Minister? He walked on arguing this within his own bosom, till he had worked himself almost up to anger. It was clear that he must henceforth take things more into his own hands, or he would be made to be absurd before the world. Indifference he knew he could bear. Harsh criticism he thought he could endure. But to ridicule he was aware that he was pervious. Suppose the papers were to say of him that he built a new conservatory and made an archery ground for the sake of maintaining the Coalition!

When he got back to the house he found his wife alone in the small room in which they intended to dine. After all her labours she was now reclining for the few minutes her husband's absence might allow her, knowing that after dinner there were a score of letters for her to write. 'I don't think,' said she, 'I was ever so tired in my life.'

'It isn't such a very long journey after all.'

'But it's a very big house, and I've been, I think, into every room since I have been here, and I've moved most of the furniture in the drawing-rooms with my own hand, and I've counted the pounds of butter, and inspected the sheets and tablecloths.'

'Was that necessary, Glencora?'

'If I had gone to bed instead, the world, I suppose, would have gone on, and Sir Orlando Drought would still have led the House of Commons;—but things should be looked after, I suppose.'

'There are people to do it. You are like Martha,* troubling yourself with many things.'

'I always felt that Martha was very ill-used. If there were no Marthas there would never be anything fit to eat. But it's odd how sure a wife is to be scolded. If I did nothing at all, that wouldn't please a busy, hard-working man like you.'

'I don't know that I have scolded,—not as yet.'

'Are you going to begin?'

'Not to scold, my dear. Looking back, can you remember that I ever scolded you?'

'I can remember a great many times when you ought.'

'But to tell you the truth, I don't like all that you have done here. I cannot see that it was necessary.'

'People make changes in their gardens without necessity sometimes.'

'But these changes are made because of your guests. Had they been made to gratify your own taste, I would have said nothing,—although even in that case I think you might have told me what you proposed to do.'

'What;—when you are so burdened with work that you do not know how to turn?'

'I am never so burdened that I cannot turn to you. But, as you know, that is not what I complain of. If it were done for yourself, though it were the wildest vagary, I would learn to like it. But it distresses me to think that what might have been good enough for our friends before should be thought to be insufficient because of the office I hold. There is a—a—a—I was almost going to say vulgarity about it which distresses me.'

'Vulgarity!' she exclaimed, jumping up from her sofa.

'I retract the word. I would not for the world say anything that should annoy you;—but pray, pray do not go on with it.' Then again he left her.

Vulgarity! There was no other word in the language so hard to bear as that. He had, indeed, been careful to say that he did not accuse her of vulgarity,—but nevertheless the accusation had been made. Could you call your friend a liar more plainly than by saying to him that you would not say that he lied? They dined together, the two boys, also, dining with them, but very little was said at dinner. The horrid word was clinging to the lady's ears, and the remembrance of having uttered the word was heavy on the man's conscience. He had told himself very plainly that the thing was vulgar, but he had not meant to use the word. When uttered it came even upon himself as a surprise. But it had been uttered; and, let what apology there may be made, a word uttered

cannot be retracted. As he looked across the table at his wife, he saw
that the word had been taken in deep dudgeon.

She escaped, to the writing of her letters she said, almost before the
meal was done. 'Vulgarity!' She uttered the word aloud to herself, as
she sat herself down in the little room upstairs which she had assigned
to herself for her own use. But though she was very angry with him,
she did not, even in her own mind, contradict him. Perhaps it was
vulgar. But why shouldn't she be vulgar, if she could most surely get
what she wanted by vulgarity? What was the meaning of the word
vulgarity? Of course she was prepared to do things,—was daily doing
things,—which would have been odious to her had not her husband
been a public man. She submitted, without unwillingness, to constant
contact with disagreeable people. She lavished her smiles,—so she
now said to herself,—on butchers and tinkers. What she said, what
she read, what she wrote, what she did, whither she went, to whom
she was kind and to whom unkind,—was it not all said and done and
arranged with reference to his and her own popularity? When a man
wants to be Prime Minister he has to submit to vulgarity, and must
give up his ambition if the task be too disagreeable to him. The
Duchess thought that that had been understood, at any rate ever since
the days of Coriolanus.* 'The old Duke kept out of it,' she said to
herself, 'and chose to live in the other way. He had his choice. He
wants it to be done. And when I do it for him because he can't do it for
himself, he calls it by an ugly name!' Then it occurred to her that
the world tells lies every day,—telling on the whole much more lies
than truth,—but that the world has wisely agreed that the world
shall not be accused of lying. One doesn't venture to express open
disbelief even of one's wife; and with the world at large a word spoken,
whether lie or not, is presumed to be true, of course,—because
spoken. Jones has said it, and therefore Smith,—who has known the
lie to be a lie,—has asserted his assured belief, lying again. But in this
way the world is able to live pleasantly. How was she to live pleasantly
if her husband accused her of vulgarity? Of course it was all vulgar,
but why should he tell her so? She did not do it from any pleasure that
she got from it.

The letters remained long unwritten, and then there came a moment
in which she resolved that they should not be written. The work was
very hard, and what good would come from it? Why should she make
her hands dirty, so that even her husband accused her of vulgarity?
Would it not be better to give it all up, and be a great woman, *une
grande dame*,* of another kind,—difficult of access, sparing of her

favours, aristocratic to the back-bone,—a very Duchess of duchesses?
The role would be one very easy to play. It required rank, money, and
a little manner,—and these she possessed. The old Duke had done it
with ease, without the slightest trouble to himself, and had been treated
almost like a god because he had secluded himself. She could make the
change even yet,—and as her husband told her that she was vulgar, she
thought she would make it.

But at last, before she had abandoned her desk and paper, there had
come to her another thought. Nothing to her was so distasteful as failure. She had known that there would be difficulties, and had assured
herself that she would be firm and brave in overcoming them. Was not
this accusation of vulgarity simply one of the difficulties which she had
to overcome? Was her courage already gone from her? Was she so weak
that a single word should knock her over,—and a word evidently
repented of as soon as uttered? Vulgar! Well;—let her be vulgar as long
as she gained her object. There had been no penalty of everlasting punishment against vulgarity. And then a higher idea touched her, not
without effect,—an idea which she could not analyse, but which was
hardly on that account the less effective. She did believe thoroughly in
her husband, to the extent of thinking him the fittest man in all the
country to be its Prime Minister. His fame was dear to her. Her nature
was loyal; and though she might, perhaps, in her younger days have
been able to lean upon him with a more loving heart had he been other
than he was, brighter, more gay, given to pleasures, and fond of trifles,
still, she could recognize merits with which her sympathy was imperfect. It was good that he should be England's Prime Minister, and
therefore she would do all she could to keep him in that place. The
vulgarity was a necessary essential. He might not acknowledge this,—
might even, if the choice were left to him, refuse to be Prime Minister
on such terms. But she need not, therefore, give way. Having in this
way thought it all out, she took up her pen and completed the batch of
letters before she allowed herself to go to bed.

CHAPTER 20

SIR ORLANDO'S POLICY

WHEN the guests began to arrive our friend the Duchess had apparently got through her little difficulties, for she received them with that
open, genial hospitality which is so delightful as coming evidently from

the heart. There had not been another word between her and her husband as to the manner in which the thing was to be done, and she had determined that the offensive word should pass altogether out of her memory. The first comer was Mrs Finn,—who came indeed rather as an assistant hostess than as a mere guest, and to her the Duchess uttered a few half-playful hints as to her troubles. 'Considering the time, haven't we done marvels? Because it does look nice,—doesn't it? There are no dirt heaps about, and it's all as green as though it had been there since the Conquest. He doesn't like it because it looks new. And we've got forty-five bedrooms made up. The servants are all turned out over the stables somewhere,—quite comfortable, I assure you. Indeed they like it. And by knocking down the ends of two passages we've brought everything together. And the rooms are all numbered, just like an inn. It was the only way. And I keep one book myself, and Locock has another. I have everybody's room, and where it is, and how long the tenant is to be allowed to occupy it. And here's the way everybody is to take everybody down to dinner for the next fortnight. Of course that must be altered, but it is easier when we have a sort of settled basis. And I have some private notes as to who should flirt with whom.'

'You'd better not let that lie about.'

'Nobody could understand a word of it if they had it. A. B. always means X. Y. Z. And this is the code of the Gatherum Archery Ground. I never drew a bow in my life,—not a real bow in the flesh, that is, my dear,—and yet I've made 'em all out, and had them printed. The way to make a thing go down is to give it some special importance. And I've gone through the bill of fare for the first week with Millepois, who is a perfect gentleman,—perfect.' Then she gave a little sigh as she remembered that word from her husband, which had so wounded her. 'I used to think that Plantagenet worked hard when he was doing his decimal coinage; but I don't think he ever stuck to it as I have done.'

'What does the Duke say to it all?'

'Ah; well, upon the whole he behaves like an angel. He behaves so well that half my time I think I'll shut it all up and have done with it,—for his sake. And then, the other half, I'm determined to go on with it,—also for his sake.'

'He has not been displeased?'

'Ask no questions, my dear, and you'll hear no stories. You haven't been married twice without knowing that women can't have everything smooth. He only said one word. It was rather hard to bear, but it has passed away.'

That afternoon there was quite a crowd. Among the first comers were Mr and Mrs Roby, and Mr and Mrs Rattler. And there were Sir Orlando and Lady Drought, Lord Ramsden, and Sir Timothy Beeswax. These gentlemen with their wives represented, for the time, the Ministry of which the Duke was the head, and had been asked in order that their fealty and submission might be thus riveted. There were also there Mr and Mrs Boffin, with Lord Thrift and his daughter Angelica, who had belonged to former ministries,—one on the Liberal and the other on the Conservative side,—and who were now among the Duke's guests, in order that they and others might see how wide the Duke wished to open his hands. And there was our friend Ferdinand Lopez, who had certainly made the best use of his opportunities in securing for himself so great a social advantage as an invitation to Gatherum Castle. How could any father, who was simply a barrister, refuse to receive as his son-in-law a man who had been a guest at the Duke of Omnium's country house? And then there were certain people from the neighbourhood;—Frank Gresham* of Greshambury, with his wife and daughter, the master of the hounds in those parts, a rich squire of old blood, and head of the family to which one of the aspirant Prime Ministers of the day belonged. And Lord Chiltern,* another master of fox hounds, two counties off,—and also an old friend of ours,—had been asked to meet him, and had brought his wife. And there was Lady Rosina De Courcy,* an old maid, the sister of the present Earl De Courcy, who lived not far off and had been accustomed to come to Gatherum Castle on state occasions for the last thirty years,—the only relic in those parts of a family which had lived there for many years in great pride of place; for the elder brother, the Earl, was a ruined man, and her younger brothers were living with their wives abroad, and her sisters had married, rather lowly in the world, and her mother now was dead, and Lady Rosina lived alone in a little cottage outside the old park palings, and still held fast within her bosom all the old pride of the De Courcys. And then there were Captain Gunner and Major Pountney, two middle-aged young men, presumably belonging to the army, whom the Duchess had lately enlisted among her followers as being useful in their way. They could eat their dinners without being shy, dance on occasions, though very unwillingly, talk a little, and run on messages;—and they knew the peerage by heart, and could tell the details of every unfortunate marriage for the last twenty years. Each thought himself, especially since this last promotion, to be indispensably necessary to the formation of London society, and was comfortable in a conviction that he had thoroughly succeeded in life by acquiring the privilege of sitting down to dinner three times a week with peers and peeresses.

The list of guests has by no means been made as complete here as it was to be found in the county newspapers, and in the 'Morning Post' of the time, but enough of names has been given to show of what nature was the party. 'The Duchess has got rather a rough lot to begin with,' said the Major to the Captain.

'Oh, yes. I knew that. She wanted me to be useful, so of course I came. I shall stay here this week, and then be back in September.' Up to this moment Captain Gunner had not received any invitation for September, but then there was no reason why he should not do so.

'I've been getting up that archery code with her,' said Pountney, 'and I was pledged to come down and set it going. That little Gresham girl isn't a bad-looking thing.'

'Rather flabby,' said Captain Gunner.

'Very nice colour. She'll have a lot of money, you know.'

'There's a brother,' said the Captain.

'Oh, yes; there's a brother, who will have the Greshambury property, but she's to have her mother's money. There's a very odd story* about all that, you know.' Then the Major told the story, and told every particular of it wrongly. 'A man might do worse than look there,' said the Major. A man might have done worse, because Miss Gresham was a very nice girl; but of course the Major was all wrong about the money.

'Well;—now you've tried it, what do you think about it?' This question was put by Sir Timothy to Sir Orlando as they sat in a corner of the archery ground, under the shelter of a tent, looking on while Major Pountney taught Mrs Boffin how to fix an arrow to her bowstring. It was quite understood that Sir Timothy was inimical to the Coalition though he still belonged to it, and that he would assist in breaking it up if only there were a fair chance of his belonging to the party which would remain in power. Sir Timothy had been badly treated, and did not forget it. Now Sir Orlando had also of late shown some symptoms of a disturbed ambition. He was the leader of the House of Commons, and it had become an almost recognized law of the Constitution that the leader of the House of Commons should be the First Minister of the Crown. It was at least understood by many that such was Sir Orlando's reading of the laws of the Constitution.

'We've got along, you know,' said Sir Orlando.

'Yes;—yes. We've got along. Can you imagine any possible concatenation of circumstances in which we should not get along?

There's always too much good sense in the House for an absolute collapse. But are you contented?'

'I won't say I'm not,' said the cautious baronet. 'I didn't look for very great things from a Coalition, and I didn't look for very great things from the Duke.'

'It seems to me that the one achievement to which we've all looked has been the reaching the end of the Session in safety. We've done that certainly.'

'It is a great thing to do, Sir Timothy. Of course the main work of Parliament is to raise supplies;*—and, when that has been done with ease, when all the money wanted has been voted without a break-down, of course Ministers are very glad to get rid of the Parliament. It is as much a matter of course that a Minister should dislike Parliament now as that a Stuart King* should have done so two hundred and fifty years ago. To get a session over and done with is an achievement and a delight.'

'No Ministry can go on long on that *far niente** principle, and no minister who accedes to it will remain long in any ministry.' Sir Timothy in saying this might be alluding to the Duke, or the reference might be to Sir Orlando himself. 'Of course I'm not in the Cabinet, and am not entitled to say a word; but I think that if I were in the Cabinet, and if I were anxious,—which I confess I'm not,—for a continuation of the present state of things, I should endeavour to obtain from the Duke some idea of his policy for the next Session.' Sir Orlando was a man of certain parts. He could speak volubly,—and yet slowly,—so that reporters and others could hear him. He was patient, both in the House and in his office, and had the great gift of doing what he was told by men who understood things better than he did himself. He never went very far astray in his official business, because he always obeyed the clerks and followed precedents. He had been a useful man,—and would still have remained so had he not been lifted a little too high. Had he been only one in the ruck on the Treasury Bench he would have been useful to the end; but special honour and special place had been assigned to him, and therefore he desired still bigger things. The Duke's mediocrity of talent and of energy and of general governing power had been so often mentioned of late in Sir Orlando's hearing, that Sir Orlando had gradually come to think that he was the Duke's equal in the Cabinet, and that perhaps it behoved him to lead the Duke. At the commencement of their joint operations he had held the Duke in some awe, and perhaps something of that feeling in reference to the Duke personally still restrained him. The Dukes of Omnium had always been big people. But still it might be his duty to say a word to the Duke. Sir Orlando assured himself that if ever convinced of the propriety of doing so, he could say a word even to the Duke of Omnium. 'I am confident that we should not go on quite as we are at present,' said Sir Timothy as he closed the conversation.

'Where did they pick him up?' said the Major to the Captain, pointing with his head to Ferdinand Lopez, who was shooting with Angelica Thrift and Mr Boffin and one of the Duke's private secretaries.

'The Duchess found him somewhere. He's one of those fabulously rich fellows out of the city who make a hundred thousand pounds at a blow. They say his people were grandees of Spain.'

'Does anybody know him?' asked the Major.

'Everybody soon will know him,' answered the Captain. 'I think I heard that he's going to stand for some place in the Duke's interest. He don't look the sort of fellow I like; but he's got money and he comes here, and he's good looking,—and therefore he'll be a success.' In answer to this the Major only grunted. The Major was a year or two older than the Captain, and therefore less willing even than his friend to admit the claims of new comers to social honours.

Just at this moment the Duchess walked across the ground up to the shooters, accompanied by Mrs Finn and Lady Chiltern. She had not been seen in the gardens before that day, and of course a little concourse was made round her. The Major and the Captain, who had been driven away by the success of Ferdinand Lopez, returned with their sweetest smiles. Mr Boffin put down his treatise on the nature of Franchises,* which he was studying in order that he might lead an opposition against the Ministry next Session, and even Sir Timothy Beeswax, who had done his work with Sir Orlando, joined the throng.

'Now I do hope,' said the Duchess, 'that you are all shooting by the new code. That is, and is to be, the Gatherum Archery Code, and I shall break my heart if anybody rebels.'

'There are one or two men,' said Major Pountney very gravely, 'who won't take the trouble to understand it.'

'Mr Lopez,' said the Duchess, pointing with her finger at our friend, 'are you that rebel?'

'I fear I did suggest——' began Mr Lopez.

'I will have no suggestions,—nothing but obedience. Here are Sir Timothy Beeswax and Mr Boffin, and Sir Orlando Drought is not far off; and here is Mr Rattler, than whom no authority on such a subject can be better. Ask them whether in other matters suggestions are wanted.'

'Of course not,' said Major Pountney.

'Now, Mr Lopez, will you or will you not be guided by a strict and close interpretation of the Gatherum Code? Because, if not, I'm afraid we shall feel constrained to accept your resignation.'

'I won't resign, and I will obey,' said Lopez.

'A good ministerial reply,' said the Duchess. 'I don't doubt but that in time you'll ascend to high office and become a pillar of the Gatherum constitution. How does he shoot, Miss Thrift?'

'He will shoot very well indeed, Duchess, if he goes on and practises,' said Angelica, whose life for the last seven years had been devoted to archery. Major Pountney retired far away into the park, a full quarter of a mile off, and smoked a cigar under a tree. Was it for this that he had absolutely given up a month to drawing out this code of rules, going backwards and forwards two or three times to the printers in his desire to carry out the Duchess's wishes? 'Women are so d—— ungrateful!' he said aloud in his solitude, as he turned himself on the hard ground. 'And some men are so d—— lucky!' This fellow, Lopez, had absolutely been allowed to make a good score off his own intractable disobedience.

The Duchess's little joke about the Ministers generally, and the advantages of submission on their part to their chief, was thought by some who heard it not to have been made in good taste. The joke was just such a joke as the Duchess would be sure to make,—meaning very little but still not altogether pointless. It was levelled rather at her husband than at her husband's colleagues who were present, and was so understood by those who really knew her,—as did Mrs Finn, and Mr Warburton, the private secretary. But Sir Orlando and Sir Timothy and Mr Rattler, who were all within hearing, thought that the Duchess had intended to allude to the servile nature of their position; and Mr Boffin, who heard it, rejoiced within himself, comforting himself with the reflection that his withers were unwrung,* and thinking with what pleasure he might carry the anecdote into the farthest corners of the clubs. Poor Duchess! 'Tis pitiful to think that after such Herculean labours she should injure the cause by one slight unconsidered word, more, perhaps, than she had advanced it by all her energy.

During this time the Duke was at the Castle, but he showed himself seldom to his guests,—so acting, as the reader will I hope understand, from no sense of the importance of his own personal presence, but influenced by a conviction that a public man should not waste his time. He breakfasted in his own room, because he could thus eat his breakfast in ten minutes. He read all the papers in solitude, because he was thus enabled to give his mind to their contents. Life had always been too serious to him to be wasted. Every afternoon he walked for the sake of exercise, and would have accepted any companion if any companion had especially offered himself. But he went off by some side-door, finding the side-door to be convenient, and therefore when seen by others was supposed to desire to remain unseen. 'I had no idea there was so much pride about the Duke,' Mr Boffin said to his old colleague, Sir Orlando. 'Is it pride?' asked Sir Orlando. 'It may be shyness,' said the wise Boffin. 'The two things are so alike you can never tell the difference. But the man who is cursed by either should hardly be a Prime Minister.'

It was on the day after this that Sir Orlando thought that the moment had come in which it was his duty to say that salutary word to the Duke which it was clearly necessary that some colleague should say, and which no colleague could have so good a right to say as he who was the Leader of the House of Commons. He understood clearly that though they were gathered together then at Gatherum Castle for festive purposes, yet that no time was unfit for the discussion of State matters. Does not all the world know that when in autumn the Bismarcks* of the world, or they who are bigger than Bismarcks, meet at this or that delicious haunt of salubrity, the affairs of the world are then settled in little conclaves, with greater ease, rapidity, and certainty than in large parliaments or the dull chambers of public offices? Emperor meets Emperor, and King meets King, and as they wander among rural glades in fraternal intimacy, wars are arranged, and swelling territories are enjoyed in anticipation. Sir Orlando hitherto had known all this, but had hardly as yet enjoyed it. He had been long in office, but these sweet confidences can of their very nature belong only to a very few. But now the time had manifestly come.

It was Sunday afternoon, and Sir Orlando caught the Duke in the very act of leaving the house for his walk. There was no archery, and many of the inmates of the Castle were asleep. There had been a question as to the propriety of Sabbath archery, in discussing which reference had been made to Laud's book of sports,* and the growing idea that the National Gallery* should be opened on the Lord's-day. But the Duchess would not have the archery. 'We are just the people who shouldn't prejudge the question,' said the Duchess. The Duchess with various ladies, with the Pountneys and Gunners, and other obedient male followers, had been to church. None of the Ministers had of course been able to leave the swollen pouches which are always sent out from London on Saturday night, probably,—we cannot but think,—as arranged excuses for such defalcation, and had passed their mornings comfortably dozing over new novels. The Duke, always right in his purpose but generally wrong in his practice, had stayed at home working all the morning, thereby scandalizing the strict, and had gone to church alone in the afternoon, thereby offending the social. The church was close to the house, and he had gone back to change his coat and hat, and to get his stick. But as he was stealing out of the little side-gate, Sir Orlando was down upon him. 'If your Grace is going for a walk, and will admit of company, I shall be delighted to attend you,' said Sir Orlando. The Duke professed himself to be well pleased, but in truth was pleased. He would be glad to increase his personal intimacy with his colleagues if it might be done pleasantly.

They had gone nearly a mile across the park, watching the stately movements of the herds of deer, and talking of this and that trifle, before Sir Orlando could bring about an opportunity for uttering his word. At last he did it somewhat abruptly. 'I think upon the whole we did pretty well this Session,' he said, standing still under an old oak-tree.

'Pretty well,' re-echoed the Duke.

'And I suppose we have not much to be afraid of next Session?'

'I am afraid of nothing,' said the Duke.

'But——;' then Sir Orlando hesitated. The Duke, however, said not a word to help him on. Sir Orlando thought that the Duke looked more ducal than he had ever seen him look before. Sir Orlando remembered the old Duke, and suddenly found that the uncle and nephew were very like each other. But it does not become the leader of the House of Commons to be afraid of any one. 'Don't you think,' continued Sir Orlando, 'we should try and arrange among ourselves something of a policy? I am not quite sure that a ministry without a distinct course of action before it can long enjoy the confidence of the country. Take the last half century. There have been various policies, commanding more or less of general assent; free trade——.' Here Sir Orlando gave a kindly wave of his hand, showing that on behalf of his companion he was willing to place at the head of the list a policy which had not always commanded his own assent;—'continued reform in Parliament, to which I have, with my whole heart, given my poor assistance.' The Duke remembered how the bathers' clothes were stolen,* and that Sir Orlando had been one of the most nimble-fingered of the thieves. 'No popery, Irish grievances, the ballot, retrenchment, efficiency of the public service, all have had their time.'

'Things to be done offer themselves, I suppose, because they are in themselves desirable; not because it is desirable to have something to do.'

'Just so;—no doubt. But still, if you will think of it, no ministry can endure without a policy. During the latter part of the last Session it was understood that we had to get ourselves in harness together, and nothing more was expected from us; but I think we should be prepared with a distinct policy for the coming year. I fear that nothing can be done in Ireland.'

'Mr Finn has ideas——'

'Ah, yes;—well, your Grace. Mr Finn is a very clever young man certainly; but I don't think we can support ourselves by his plan of Irish reform.' Sir Orlando had been a little carried away by his own eloquence and the Duke's tameness, and had interrupted the Duke. The Duke again looked ducal, but on this occasion Sir Orlando did not observe his countenance. 'For myself, I think, I am in favour of increased armaments. I have been applying my mind to the subject, and I think I see that the people of this country do not object to a slightly rising scale of estimates in that direction. Of course there is the county suffrage——'

'I will think of what you have been saying,' said the Duke.

'As to the county suffrage——'

'I will think it over,' said the Duke. 'You see that oak. That is the largest tree we have here at Gatherum; and I doubt whether there be a larger one in this part of England.' The Duke's voice and words were not uncourteous, but there was something in them which hindered Sir Orlando from referring again on that occasion to county suffrages or increased armaments.

VOLUME II

CHAPTER 21

THE DUCHESS'S NEW SWAN

WHEN the party had been about a week collected at Gatherum Castle, Ferdinand Lopez had manifestly become the favourite of the Duchess for the time, and had, at her instance, promised to remain there for some further days. He had hardly spoken to the Duke since he had been in the house,—but then but few of that motley assembly did talk much with the Duke. Gunner and Pountney had gone away,—the Captain having declared his dislike of the upstart Portuguese to be so strong that he could not stay in the same house with him any longer, and the Major, who was of stronger mind, having resolved that he would put the intruder down. 'It is horrible to think what power money has in these days,' said the Captain. The Captain had shaken the dust of Gatherum altogether from his feet,* but the Major had so arranged that a bed was to be found for him again in October,—for another happy week; but he was not to return till bidden by the Duchess. 'You won't forget;—now will you, Duchess?' he said, imploring her to remember him as he took his leave. 'I did take a deal of trouble about the code;—didn't I?' 'They don't seem to me to care for the code,' said the Duchess, 'but, nevertheless, I'll remember.'

'Who, in the name of all that's wonderful, was that I saw you with in the garden?' the Duchess said to her husband one afternoon.

'It was Lady Rosina De Courcy, I suppose!'

'Heaven and earth!—what a companion for you to choose.'

'Why not?—why shouldn't I talk to Lady Rosina De Courcy?'

'I'm not jealous a bit, if you mean that. I don't think Lady Rosina will steal your heart from me. But why you should pick her out of all the people here, when there are so many would think their fortunes made if you would only take a turn with them, I cannot imagine.'

'But I don't want to make anyone's fortune,' said the Duke: 'and certainly not in that way.'

'What could you be saying to her?'

'She was talking about her family. I rather like Lady Rosina. She is living all alone, it seems, and almost in poverty. Perhaps there is nothing so sad in the world as the female scions of a noble but impoverished stock.'

'Nothing so dull, certainly.'

'People are not dull to me, if they are real. I pity that poor lady. She is proud of her blood and yet not ashamed of her poverty.'

'Whatever might come of her blood, she has been all her life willing enough to get rid of her poverty. It isn't above three years since she was trying her best to marry that brewer at Silverbridge. I wish you could give your time a little to some of the other people.'

'To go and shoot arrows?'

'No;—I don't want you to shoot arrows. You might act the part of host without shooting. Can't you walk about with anybody except Lady Rosina De Courcy?'

'I was walking about with Sir Orlando Drought last Sunday, and I very much prefer Lady Rosina.'

'There has been no quarrel?' asked the Duchess sharply.

'Oh dear no.'

'Of course he's an empty-headed idiot. Everybody has always known that. And he's put above his place in the House. But it wouldn't do to quarrel with him now.'

'I don't think I am a quarrelsome man, Cora. I don't remember at this moment that I have ever quarrelled with anybody to your knowledge. But I may perhaps be permitted to——'

'Snub a man, you mean. Well: I wouldn't even snub Sir Orlando very much, if I were you; though I can understand that it might be both pleasant and easy.'

'I wish you wouldn't put slang phrases into my mouth, Cora. If I think that a man intrudes upon me, I am of course bound to let him know my opinion.'

'Sir Orlando has—intruded!'

'By no means. He is in a position which justifies his saying many things to me which another might not say. But then, again, he is a man whose opinion does not go far with me, and I have not the knack of seeming to agree with a man while I let his words pass idly by me.'

'That is quite true, Plantagenet.'

'And, therefore, I was uncomfortable with Sir Orlando, while I was able to sympathize with Lady Rosina.'

'What do you think of Ferdinand Lopez?' asked the Duchess, with studied abruptness.

'Think of Mr Lopez! I haven't thought of him at all. Why should I think of him?'

'I want you to think of him. I think he's a very pleasant fellow, and I'm sure he's a rising man.'

'You might think the latter, and perhaps feel sure of the former.'

'Very well. Then, to oblige you, I'll think the latter and feel sure of the former. I suppose it's true that Mr Grey* is going on this mission to Persia?' Mr Grey was the Duke's intimate friend, and was at this time member for the neighbouring borough of Silverbridge.

'I think he will go. I've no doubt about it. He is to go after Christmas.'

'And will give up his seat?'

The Duke did not answer her immediately. It had only just been decided,—decided by his friend himself,—that the seat should be given up when the journey to Persia was undertaken. Mr Grey, somewhat in opposition to the Duke's advice, had resolved that he could not be in Persia and do his duty in the House of Commons at the same time. But this resolution had only now been made known to the Duke, and he was rather puzzled to think how the Duchess had been able to be so quick upon him. He had, indeed, kept the matter back from the Duchess, feeling that she would have something to say about it, which might possibly be unpleasant, as soon as the tidings should reach her. 'Yes,' he said, 'I think he will give up his seat. That is his purpose, though I think it is unnecessary.'

'Let Mr Lopez have it.'

'Mr Lopez!'

'Yes;—he is a clever man, a rising man, a man that is sure to do well, and who will be of use to you. Just take the trouble to talk to him. It is assistance of that kind that you want. You Ministers go on shuffling the old cards till they are so worn out and dirty that one can hardly tell the pips on them.'

'I am one of the dirty old cards myself,' said the Duke.

'That's nonsense, you know. A man who is at the head of affairs as you are can't be included among the pack I am speaking of. What you want is new blood, or new wood, or new metal, or whatever you may choose to call it. Take my advice and try this man. He isn't a pauper. It isn't money that he wants.'

'Cora, your geese are all swans.'

'That's not fair. I have never brought to you a goose yet. My swans have been swans. Who was it brought you and your pet swan of all, Mr Grey, together? I won't name any names, but it is your swans have been geese.'

'It is not for me to return a member for Silverbridge.' When he said this, she gave him a look which almost upset even his gravity, a look which was almost the same as asking him whether he would not—'tell that to the marines.'* 'You don't quite understand these things, Cora,' he continued. 'The influence which owners of property may have in boroughs is decreasing every day, and there arises the question whether a conscientious man will any longer use such influence.'

'I don't think you'd like to see a man from Silverbridge opposing you in the House.'

'I may have to bear worse even than that.'

'Well;—there it is. The man is here and you have the opportunity of knowing him. Of course I have not hinted at the matter to him. If there were any Palliser wanted the borough I wouldn't say a word. What more patriotic thing can a patron do with his borough than to select a man who is unknown to him, not related to him, a perfect stranger, merely for his worth?'

'But I do not know what may be the worth of Mr Lopez.'

'I will guarantee that,' said the Duchess. Whereupon the Duke laughed, and then left her.

The Duchess had spoken with absolute truth when she told her husband that she had not said a word to Mr Lopez about Silverbridge, but it was not long before she did say a word. On that same day she found herself alone with him in the garden,—or so much alone as to be able to speak with him privately. He had certainly made the best use of his time since he had been at the Castle, having secured the good-will of many of the ladies, and the displeasure of most of the men. 'You have never been in Parliament, I think,' said the Duchess.

'I have never even tried to get there.'

'Perhaps you dislike the idea of that kind of life.'

'No, indeed,' he said. 'So far from it, that I regard it as the highest kind of life there is in England. A seat in Parliament gives a man a status in this country which it has never done elsewhere.'

'Then why don't you try it?'

'Because I've got into another groove. I've become essentially a city man,—one of those who take up the trade of making money generally.'

'And does that content you?'

'No, Duchess;—certainly not. Instead of contenting me it disgusts me. Not but that I like the money,—only it is so insufficient a use of one's life. I suppose I shall try to get into Parliament some day. Seats in Parliament don't grow like blackberries on bushes.'

'Pretty nearly,' said the Duchess.

'Not in my part of the country. These good things seem to be appointed to fall in the way of some men, and not of others. If there were a general election going on to-morrow, I should not know how to look for a seat.'

'They are to be found sometimes even without a general election,' said the Duchess.

'Are you alluding to anything now?'

'Well;—yes, I am. But I'm very discreet, and do not like to do more than allude. I fancy that Mr Grey, the member for Silverbridge, is going to Persia. Mr Grey is a Member of Parliament. Members of Parliament ought to be in London and not in Persia. It is generally supposed that no man in England is more prone to do what he ought to do than Mr Grey. Therefore, Mr Grey will cease to be Member for Silverbridge. That's logic, isn't it?'

'Has your Grace any logic equally strong to prove that I can follow him in the borough?'

'No;—or if I have, the logic that I should use in that matter must for the present be kept to myself.' She certainly had a little syllogism in her head as to the Duke ruling the borough, the Duke's wife ruling the Duke, and therefore the Duke's wife ruling the borough; but she did not think it prudent to utter this on the present occasion. 'I think it much better that men in Parliament should be unmarried,' said the Duchess.

'But I am going to be married,' said he.

'Going to be married, are you?'

'I have no right to say so, because the lady's father has rejected me.' Then he told her the whole story, and so told it as to secure her entire sympathy. In telling it he never said that he was a rich man, he never boasted that that search after wealth of which he had spoken, had been successful; but he gave her to understand that there was no objection to him at all on the score of money. 'You may have heard of the family,' he said.

'I have heard of the Whartons of course, and know that there is a baronet,—but I know nothing more of them. He is not a man of large property, I think.'

'My Miss Wharton,—the one I would fain call mine,—is the daughter of a London barrister. He I believe is rich.'

'Then she will be an heiress.'

'I suppose so;—but that consideration has had no weight with me. I have always regarded myself as the architect of my own fortune, and have no wish to owe my material comfort to a wife.'

'Sheer love!' suggested the Duchess.

'Yes, I think so. It's very ridiculous; is it not?'

'And why does the rich barrister object?'

'The rich barrister, Duchess, is an out and out old Tory, who thinks that his daughter ought to marry no one but an English Tory. I am not exactly that.'

'A man does not hamper his daughter in these days by politics, when she is falling in love.'

'There are other cognate reasons. He does not like a foreigner. Now I am an Englishman, but I have a foreign name. He does not think that a name so grandly Saxon as Wharton should be changed to one so meanly Latin as Lopez.'

'The lady does not object to the Latinity?'

'I fancy not.'

'Or to the bearer of it?'

'Ah;—there I must not boast. But in simple truth there is only the father's ill-will between us.'

'With plenty of money on both sides?' asked the Duchess. Lopez shrugged his shoulders. A shrug at such a time may mean anything, but the Duchess took this shrug as signifying that the question was so surely settled as to admit of no difficulty. 'Then,' said the Duchess, 'the old gentleman may as well give way at once. Of course his daughter will be too many for him.' In this way the Duchess of Omnium became the fast friend of Ferdinand Lopez.

CHAPTER 22

ST JAMES'S PARK

TOWARDS the end of September Everett Wharton and Ferdinand Lopez were in town together, and as no one else was in town,—so at least they both professed to say,—they saw a good deal of each other. Lopez, as we know, had spent a portion of the preceding month at Gatherum Castle, and had made good use of his time, but Everett Wharton had been less fortunate. He had been a little cross with his father, and perhaps a little cross with all the Whartons generally, who did not, he thought, make quite enough of him. In the event of 'anything happening' to that ne'er-do-well nephew, he himself would be the heir; and he reflected not unfrequently that something very probably might happen to the nephew. He did not often see this particular cousin, but he always heard of him as being drunk, overwhelmed with debt and difficulty, and altogether in that position of life in which it is probable that something will 'happen'. There was always of course the danger that the young man might marry and have a child;—but in the meantime surely he, Everett Wharton, should have been as much thought of on the banks of the Wye as Arthur Fletcher. He had been asked down to Wharton Hall,—but he had been asked in a way which he had not thought to be flattering and had declined to go. Then there had been a plan for joining Arthur Fletcher in a certain shooting, but that had failed in consequence of a few words between himself and Arthur respecting Lopez. Arthur had wanted him to say that Lopez was an unpardonable intruder,—but he had taken the part of Lopez, and therefore, when the time came round, he had nothing to do with the shooting. He had stayed in town till the middle of August, and had then started by himself across the continent with some keen intention of studying German politics; but he had found perhaps that German politics do not manifest themselves in the autumn, or that a foreign country cannot be well studied in solitude,—and he had returned.

Late in the summer, just before his father and sister had left town, he had had some words with the old barrister. There had been a few bills to be paid, and Everett's allowance had been insufficient. It often was insufficient, and then ready money for his German tour was absolutely necessary. Mr Wharton might probably have said less about the money had not his son accompanied his petition by a further allusion to Parliament. 'There are some fellows at last really getting themselves together at the Progress, and of course it will be necessary to know who will be ready to come forward at the next general election.'

'I think I know one who won't,' said the father, 'judging from the manner in which he seems at present to manage his own money affairs.' There was more severity in this than the old man had intended, for he had often thought within his own bosom whether it would not be well that he should encourage his son to stand for some seat. And the money that he had now been asked to advance had not been very much,—not more, in truth, than he expected to be called upon to pay in addition to the modest sum which he professed to allow his son. He was a rich man, who was not in truth made unhappy by parting with his money. But there had been, he thought, an impudence in the conjoint attack which it was his duty to punish. Therefore he had given his son very little encouragement.

'Of course, sir, if you tell me that you are not inclined to pay anything beyond the allowance you make me, there is an end of it.'

'I rather think that you have just asked me to pay a considerable sum beyond your allowance, and that I have consented.' Everett argued the matter no further, but he permitted his mind to entertain an idea that he was ill-used by his father. The time would come when he would probably be heir not only to his father's money, but also to the Wharton title and the Wharton property,—when his position in the country would really be, as he frequently told himself, quite considerable. Was it possible that he should refrain from blaming his father for not allowing him to obtain, early in life, that parliamentary education which would fit him to be an ornament to the House of Commons, and a safeguard to his country in future years?

Now he and Lopez were at the Progress together, and they were almost the only men in the club. Lopez was quite contented with his own present sojourn in London. He had not only been at Gatherum Castle but was going there again. And then he had brilliant hopes before him,—so brilliant that they began, he thought, to assume the shape of certainties. He had corresponded with the Duchess, and he had gathered from her somewhat dubious words that the Duke would probably accede to her wishes in the matter of Silverbridge. The vacancy had not yet been declared. Mr Grey was deterred, no doubt by certain high State purposes, from applying for the stewardship of the Chiltern Hundreds,* and thereby releasing himself from his seat in Parliament, and enabling himself to perform, with a clear conscience, duties in a distant part of the world which he did not feel to be compatible with that seat. The seekers after seats were, no doubt, already on the track; but the Duchess had thought that as far as the Duke's good word went, it might possibly be given in favour of Mr Lopez. The happy aspirant had taken this to be almost as good as a promise. There were also certain pecuniary speculations on foot, which could not be kept quite quiet even in September, as to which he did not like to trust entirely to the unaided energy of Mr Sextus Parker, or to the boasted alliance of Mr Mills Happerton. Sextus Parker's whole heart and soul were now in the matter, but Mr Mills Happerton, an undoubted partner in Hunky and Sons, had blown a little coldly on the affair. But in spite of this Ferdinand Lopez was happy. Was it probable that Mr Wharton should continue his opposition to a marriage which would make his daughter the wife of a member of Parliament and of a special friend of the Duchess of Omnium?

He had said a word about his own prospects in reference to the marriage, but Everett had been at first far too full of his own affairs to attend much to a matter which was comparatively so trifling.

'Upon my word,' he said, 'I am beginning to feel angry with the governor, which is a kind of thing I don't like at all.'

'I can understand that when he's angry with you, you shouldn't like it.'

'I don't mind that half so much. He'll come round. However unjust he may be now, at the moment, he's the last man in the world to do an injustice in his will. I have thorough confidence in him. But I find myself driven into hostility to him by a conviction that he won't let me take any real step in life, till my life has been half frittered away.'

'You're thinking of Parliament.'

'Of course I am. I don't say you ain't an Englishman, but you are not quite enough of an Englishman to understand what Parliament is to us.'

'I hope to be,—some of these days,' said Lopez.

'Perhaps you may. I won't say but what you may get yourself educated to it when you've been married a dozen years to an English wife, and have half-a-dozen English children of your own. But, in the meantime, look at my position. I am twenty-eight years old.'

'I am four years your senior.'

'It does not matter a straw to you,' continued Everett. 'But a few years are everything with me. I have a right to suppose that I may be able to represent the county,—say in twenty years. I shall probably then be the head of the family and a rich man. Consider what a parliamentary education would be to me! And then it is just the life for which I have laid myself out, and in which I could make myself useful. You don't sympathize with me, but you might understand me.'

'I do both. I think of going into the House myself.'

'You!'

'Yes, I do.'

'You must have changed your ideas very much then within the last month or two.'

'I have changed my ideas. My one chief object in life is, as you know, to marry your sister; and if I were a Member of Parliament I think that some difficulties would be cleared away.'

'But there won't be an election for the next three years at any rate,' said Everett Wharton, staring at his friend. 'You don't mean to keep Emily waiting for a dissolution?'

'There are occasional vacancies,' said Lopez.

'Is there a chance of anything of that kind falling in your way?'

'I think there is. I can't quite tell you all the particulars because other people are concerned, but I don't think it improbable that I may be in the House before——; well, say in three months' time.'

'In three months' time!' exclaimed Everett, whose mouth was watering at the prospects of his friend. 'That is what comes from going to stay with the Prime Minister, I suppose.' Lopez shrugged his shoulders. 'Upon my word I can't understand you,' continued the other. 'It was only the other day you were arguing in this very room as to the absurdity of a parliamentary career,—pitching into me, by George, like the very mischief, because I had said something in its favour,—and now you are going in for it yourself in some sort of mysterious way that a fellow can't understand.' It was quite clear that Everett Wharton thought himself ill-used by his friend's success.

'There is no mystery;—only I can't tell people's names.'

'What is the borough?'

'I cannot tell you that at present.'

'Are you sure there will be a vacancy?'

'I think I am sure.'

'And that you will be invited to stand?'

'I am not sure of that.'

'Of course anybody can stand whether invited or not.'

'If I come forward for this place I shall do so on the very best interest. Don't mention it. I tell you because I already regard my connection with you as being so close as to call upon me to tell you anything of that kind.'

'And yet you do not tell me the details.'

'I tell you all that I can in honour tell.'

Everett Wharton certainly felt aggrieved by his friend's news, and plainly showed that he did so. It was so hard that if a stray seat in Parliament were going a-begging, it should be thrown in the way of this man who didn't care for it, and couldn't use it to any good purpose, instead of in his own way! Why should any one want Ferdinand Lopez to be in Parliament? Ferdinand Lopez had paid no attention to the great political questions of the Commonwealth. He knew nothing of Labour and Capital, of Unions, Strikes, and Lock-outs.* But because he was rich, and, by being rich, had made his way among great people, he was to have a seat in Parliament! As for the wealth, it might be at his own command also,—if only his father could be got to see the matter in a proper light. And as for the friendship of great people,—Prime Ministers, Duchesses, and such like,—Everett Wharton was quite confident that he was at any rate as well qualified to shine among them as Ferdinand Lopez. He was of too good a nature to be stirred to injustice against his friend by the soreness of this feeling. He did not wish to rob his friend of his wealth, of his Duchesses, or of his embryo seat in Parliament. But for the moment there came upon him a doubt whether Ferdinand was so very clever, or so peculiarly gentlemanlike or in any way very remarkable, and almost a conviction that he was very far from being good-looking.

They dined together, and quite late in the evening they strolled out into St James's Park. There was nobody in London, and there was nothing for either of them to do, and therefore they agreed to walk round the park, dark and gloomy as they knew the park would be. Lopez had seen and had quite understood the bitterness of spirit by which Everett had been oppressed, and with that peculiarly imperturbable good humour which made a part of his character bore it all, even with tenderness. He was a man, as are many of his race, who could bear contradictions, unjust suspicions, and social ill-treatment without a shadow of resentment, but who, if he had a purpose, could carry it out without a shadow of a scruple. Everett Wharton had on this occasion made himself very unpleasant, and Lopez had borne with him as an angel would hardly have done; but should Wharton ever stand in his friend's way, his friend would sacrifice him without compunction. As it was, Lopez bore with him, simply noting in his own mind that Everett Wharton was a greater ass than he had taken him to be. It was Wharton's idea that they should walk round the park, and Lopez for a time had discouraged the suggestion. 'It is a wretchedly dark place at night, and you don't know whom you may meet there.'

'You don't mean to say that you are afraid to walk round St James's Park with me, because it's dark!' said Wharton.

'I certainly should be afraid by myself, but I don't know that I am afraid with you. But what's the good?'

'It's better than sitting here doing nothing, without a soul to speak to. I've already smoked half-a-dozen cigars, till I'm so muddled I don't know what I'm about. It's so hot one can't walk in the day, and this is just the time for exercise.' Lopez yielded, being willing to yield in almost anything at present to the brother of Emily Wharton; and, though the thing seemed to him to be very foolish, they entered the park by St James's Palace, and started to walk round it, turning to the right and going in front of Buckingham Palace. As they went on Wharton still continued his accusation against his father and said also some sharp things against Lopez himself, till his companion began to think that the wine he had drunk had been as bad as the cigars. 'I can't understand your wanting to go into Parliament,' he said. 'What do you know about it?'

'If I get there I can learn like anybody else, I suppose.'

'Half of those who go there don't learn. They are, as it were, born to it, and they do very well to support this party or that.'

'And why shouldn't I support this party,—or that?'

'I don't suppose you know which party you would support,—except that you'd vote for the Duke, if, as I suppose, you are to get in under the Duke's influence. If I went into the House I should go with a fixed and settled purpose of my own.'

'I'm not there yet,' said Lopez, willing to drop the subject.

'It will be a great expense to you, and will stand altogether in the way of your profession. As far as Emily is concerned, I should think my father would be dead against it.'

'Then he would be unreasonable.'

'Not at all, if he thought you would injure your professional prospects. It is a d—— piece of folly; that's the long and the short of it.'

This certainly was very uncivil, and it almost made Lopez angry. But he had made up his mind that his friend was a little the worse for the wine he had drunk, and therefore he did not resent even this. 'Never mind politics and Parliament now,' he said, 'but let us get home. I am beginning to be sick of this. It's so awfully dark, and whenever I do hear a step, I think somebody is coming to rob us. Let us get on a bit.'

'What the deuce are you afraid of?' said Everett. They had then come up the greater part of the length of the Birdcage Walk, and the lights at Storey's Gate* were just visible, but the road on which they were then walking was very dark. The trees were black over their heads, and not a step was heard near them. At this time it was just midnight. Now, certainly, among the faults which might be justly attributed to Lopez, personal cowardice could not be reckoned. On this evening he had twice spoken of being afraid, but the fear had simply been that which ordinary caution indicates; and his object had been that of hindering Wharton in the first place from coming into the park, and then of getting him out of it as quickly as possible.

'Come along,' said Lopez.

'By George, you are in a blue funk,' said the other. 'I can hear your teeth chattering.' Lopez, who was beginning to be angry, walked on and said nothing. It was too absurd, he thought, for real anger, but he kept a little in front of Wharton, intending to show that he was displeased. 'You had better run away at once,' said Wharton.

'Upon my word, I shall begin to think you're tipsy,' said Lopez.

'Tipsy!' said the other. 'How dare you say such a thing to me? You never in your life saw me in the least altered by any thing I had drunk.'

Lopez knew that at any rate this was untrue. 'I've seen you as drunk as Cloe* before now,' said he.

'That's a lie,' said Everett Wharton.

'Come, Wharton,' said the other, 'do not disgrace yourself by conduct such as that. Something has put you out, and you do not know what you are saying. I can hardly imagine that you should wish to insult me.'

'It was you who insulted me. You said I was drunk. When you said it you knew it was untrue.'

Lopez walked on a little way in silence, thinking over this most absurd quarrel. Then he turned round and spoke. 'This is all the greatest nonsense I ever heard in the world. I'll go on and go to bed, and to-morrow morning you'll think better of it. But pray remember that under no circumstances should you call a man a liar, unless on cool consideration you are determined to quarrel with him for lying, and determined also to see the quarrel out.'

'I am quite ready to see this quarrel out.'

'Good night,' said Lopez, starting off at a quick pace. They were then close to the turn in the park, and Lopez went on till he had nearly reached the park front of the new offices.* As he had walked he had listened to the footfall of his friend, and after a while had perceived, or had thought that he had perceived, that the sound was discontinued. It seemed to him that Wharton had altogether lost his senses;—the insult to himself had been so determined and so absolutely groundless! He had striven his best to conquer the man's ill-humour by good-natured forbearance, and had only suggested that Wharton was perhaps tipsy in order to give him some excuse. But if his companion were really drunk, as he now began to think, could it be right to leave him unprotected in the park? The man's manner had been strange the whole evening, but there had been no sign of the effect of wine till after they had left the club. But Lopez had heard of men who had been apparently sober, becoming drunk as soon as they got out into the air. It might have been so in this case, though Wharton's voice and gait had not been those of a drunken man. At any rate, he would turn back and look after him; and as he did turn back, he resolved that whatever Wharton might say to him on this night he would not notice. He was too wise to raise a further impediment to his marriage by quarrelling with Emily's brother.

As soon as he paused he was sure that he heard footsteps behind him which were not those of Everett Wharton. Indeed, he was sure that he heard the footsteps of more than one person. He stood still for a moment to listen, and then he distinctly heard a rush and a scuffle. He ran back to the spot at which he had left his friend, and at first thought that he perceived a mob of people in the dusk. But as he got nearer, he saw that there were a man and two women. Wharton was on the ground, on his back, and the man was apparently kneeling on his neck and head while the women were rifling his pockets.* Lopez, hardly knowing how he was acting, was upon them in a moment, flying in the first place at the man, who had jumped up to meet him as he came. He received at once a heavy blow on his head from some weapon, which, however, his hat so far stopped as to save him from being felled or stunned, and then he felt another blow from behind on the ear, which he afterwards conceived to have been given him by one of the women. But before he could well look about him, or well know how the whole thing had happened, the man and the two women had taken to their legs, and Wharton was standing on his feet leaning against the iron railings.

The whole thing had occupied a very short space of time, and yet the effects were very grave. At the first moment Lopez looked round and endeavoured to listen, hoping that some assistance might be near,— some policeman, or, if not that, some wanderer by night who might be honest enough to help him. But he could hear or see no one. In this condition of things it was not possible for him to pursue the ruffians, as he could not leave his friend leaning against the park rails. It was at once manifest to him that Wharton had been much hurt, or at any rate incapacitated for immediate exertion, by the blows he had received;— and as he put his hand up to his own head, from which in the scuffle his hat had fallen, he was not certain that he was not severely hurt himself. Lopez could see that Wharton was very pale, that his cravat had been almost wrenched from his neck by pressure, that his waistcoat was torn open and the front of his shirt soiled,—and he could see also that a fragment of the watch-chain was hanging loose, showing that the watch was gone. 'Are you hurt much?' he said, coming close up and taking a tender hold of his friend's arm. Wharton smiled and shook his head, but spoke not a word. He was in truth more shaken, stunned, and bewildered than actually injured. The ruffian's fist had been at his throat, twisting his cravat, and for half a minute he had felt that he was choked. As he had struggled while one woman pulled at his watch and the other searched for his purse,—struggling, alas! unsuccessfully,— the man had endeavoured to quiet him by kneeling on his chest, strangling him with his own necktie, and pressing hard on his gullet. It is a treatment which, after a few seconds of vigorous practice, is apt to leave the patient for a while disconcerted and unwilling to speak. 'Say a word if you can,' whispered Lopez, looking into the other man's face with anxious eyes.

At the moment there came across Wharton's mind a remembrance that he had behaved very badly to his friend, and some sort of vague misty doubt whether all this evil had not befallen him because of his misconduct. But he knew at the same time that Lopez was not responsible for the evil, and dismayed as he had been, still he recalled enough of the nature of the struggle in which he had been engaged, to be aware that Lopez had befriended him gallantly. He could not even yet speak; but he saw the blood trickling down his friend's temple and forehead, and lifting up his hand, touched the spot with his fingers. Lopez also put his hand up, and drew it away covered with blood. 'Oh,' said he, 'that does not signify in the least. I got a knock, I know, and I am afraid I have lost my hat, but I'm not hurt.'

'Oh, dear!' The word was uttered with a low sigh. Then there was a pause, during which Lopez supported the sufferer. 'I thought that it was all over with me at one moment.'

'You will be better now.'

'Oh, yes. My watch is gone!'

'I fear it is,' said Lopez.

'And my purse,' said Wharton, collecting his strength together sufficiently to search for his treasures. 'I had eight £5 notes* in it.'

'Never mind your money or your watch if your bones are not broken.'

'It's a bore all the same to lose every shilling that one has.' Then they walked very slowly away towards the steps at the Duke of York's column, Wharton regaining his strength as he went, but still able to progress but leisurely. Lopez had not found his hat, and, being covered with blood, was, as far as appearances went, in a worse plight than the other. At the foot of the steps they met a policeman, to whom they told their story, and who, as a matter of course, was filled with an immediate desire to arrest them both. To the policeman's mind it was most distressing that a bloody-faced man without a hat, with a companion almost too weak to walk, should not be conveyed to a police-station. But after ten minutes' parley, during which Wharton sat on the bottom step and Lopez explained all the circumstances, he consented to get them a cab, to take their address, and then to go alone to the station and make his report. That the thieves had got off with their plunder was only too manifest. Lopez took the injured man home to the house in Manchester Square, and then returned in the same cab, hatless, to his own lodgings.

As he returned he applied his mind to think how he could turn the events of the evening to his own use. He did not believe that Everett Wharton was severely hurt. Indeed there might be a question whether in the morning his own injury would not be the most severe. But the immediate effect on the flustered and despoiled unfortunate one had been great enough to justify Lopez in taking strong steps if strong steps could in any way benefit himself. Would it be best to publish this affair on the housetops, or to bury it in the shade, as nearly as it might be buried? He had determined in his own mind that his friend certainly had been tipsy. In no other way could his conduct be understood. And a row with a tipsy man at midnight in the park is not, at first sight, creditable. But it could be made to have a better appearance if told by himself, than if published from other quarters. The old housekeeper at Manchester Square must know something about it, and would, of course, tell what she knew, and the loss of the money and the watch must in all probability be made known. Before he had reached his own door he had quite made up his mind that he himself would tell the story after his own fashion.

And he told it, before he went to bed that night. He washed the blood from his face and head, and cut away a part of the clotted hair, and then wrote a letter to old Mr Wharton at Wharton Hall. And between three and four o'clock in the morning he went out and posted his letter in the nearest pillar, so that it might go down by the day mail and certainly be preceded by no other written tidings. The letter which he sent was as follows:—

'DEAR MR WHARTON,

'I regret to have to send to you an account of a rather serious accident which has happened to Everett. I am now writing at 3 a.m., having just taken him home, and it occurred at about midnight. You may be quite sure that there is no danger or I should have advertised you by telegram.

'There is nothing doing in town, and therefore, as the night was fine, we, very foolishly, agreed to walk round St James's Park late after dinner. It is a kind of thing that nobody does;—but we did it. When we had nearly got round I was in a hurry, whereas Everett was for strolling slowly, and so I went on before him. But I was hardly two hundred yards in front of him before he was attacked by three persons, a man and two women. The man I presume came upon him from behind, but he has not sufficiently collected his thoughts to remember exactly what occurred. I heard the scuffle and of course turned back,—and was luckily in time to get up before he was seriously hurt. I think the man would otherwise have strangled him. I am sorry to say that he lost both his watch and his purse.

'He undoubtedly has been very much shaken, and altogether "knocked out of time," as people say. Excuse the phrase, because I think it will best explain what I want you to understand. The man's hand at his throat must have stopped his breathing for some seconds. He certainly has received no permanent injury, but I should not wonder if he should be unwell for some days. I tell you all exactly as it occurred, as it strikes me that you may like to run up to town for a day just to look at him. But you need not do so on the score of any danger. Of course he will see a doctor to-morrow. There did not seem to be any necessity for calling one up to-night. We did give notice to the police as we were coming home, but I fear the ruffians had ample time for escape. He was too weak, and I was too fully employed with him, to think of pursuing them at the time.

'Of course he is at Manchester Square,

'Most faithfully yours,

'FERDINAND LOPEZ.'

He did not say a word about Emily, but he knew that Emily would see the letter and would perceive that he had been the means of preserving her brother; and, in regard to the old barrister himself, Lopez thought that the old man could not but feel grateful for his conduct. He had in truth behaved very well to Everett. He had received a heavy blow on the head in young Wharton's defence,—of which he was determined to make good use, though he had thought it expedient to say nothing about the blow in the letter. Surely it would all help. Surely the paternal mind would be softened towards him when the father should be made to understand how great had been the service to the son. That Everett would make little of what had been done for him he did not in the least fear. Everett Wharton was sometimes silly but was never ungenerous.

In spite of his night's work Lopez was in Manchester Square before nine the following morning, and on the side of his brow he bore a great patch of black plaster. 'My head is very thick,' he said laughing, when Everett asked after his wound. 'But it would have gone badly with me if the ruffian had struck an inch lower. I suppose my hat saved me, though I remember very little. Yes, old fellow, I have written to your father, and I think he will come up. It was better that it should be so.'

'There is nothing the matter with me,' said Everett.

'One didn't quite know last night whether there was or no. At any rate his coming won't hurt you. It's always well to have your banker near you, when your funds are low.'

Then after a pause Everett made his apology,—'I know I made a great ass of myself last night.'

'Don't think about it.'

'I used a word I shouldn't have used, and I beg your pardon.'

'Not another word, Everett. Between you and me things can't go wrong. We love each other too well.'

CHAPTER 23

SURRENDER

THE letter given in the previous chapter was received at Wharton Hall late in the evening of the day on which it was written, and was discussed among all the Whartons that night. Of course there was no doubt as to the father's going up to town on the morrow. The letter was just such a letter as would surely make a man run to his son's bedside. Had the son written himself it would have been different; but the fact that the letter had come from another man seemed to be evidence that the poor sufferer could not write. Perhaps the urgency with which Lopez had sent off his dispatch, getting his account of the fray ready for the very early day mail, though the fray had not taken place till midnight, did not impress them sufficiently when they accepted this as evidence of Everett's dangerous condition. At this conference at Wharton very little was said about Lopez, but there was a general feeling that he had behaved well. 'It was very odd that they should have parted in the park,' said Sir Alured. 'But very lucky that they should not have parted sooner,' said John Fletcher. If a grain of suspicion against Lopez might have been set afloat in their minds by Sir Alured's suggestion, it was altogether dissipated by John Fletcher's reply;—for everybody there knew that John Fletcher carried common sense for the two families. Of course they all hated Ferdinand Lopez, but nothing could be extracted from the incident, as far as its details were yet known to them, which could be turned to his injury.

While they sat together discussing the matter in the drawing-room Emily Wharton hardly said a word. She uttered a little shriek when the account of the affair was first read to her, and then listened with silent attention to what was said around her. When there had seemed for a moment to be a doubt,—or rather a question, for there had been no doubt,—whether her father should go at once to London, she had spoken just a word. 'Of course you will go, papa.' After that, she said nothing till she came to him in his own room. 'Of course I will go with you to-morrow, papa.'

'I don't think that will be necessary.'

'Oh, yes. Think how wretched I should be.'

'I would telegraph to you immediately.'

'And I shouldn't believe the telegraph. Don't you know how it always is? Besides we have been more than the usual time. We were to go to town in ten days, and you would not think of returning to fetch me. Of course I will go with you. I have already begun to pack my things, and Jane is now at it.' Her father, not knowing how to oppose her, yielded, and Emily before she went to bed had made the ladies of the house aware that she also intended to start the next morning at eight o'clock.

During the first part of the journey very little was said between Mr Wharton and Emily. There were other persons in the carriage, and she, though she had determined in some vague way that she would speak some words to her father before she reached their own house, had still wanted time to resolve what those words should be. But before she had reached Gloucester she had made up her mind, and going on from Gloucester she found herself for a time alone with her father. She was sitting opposite to him, and after conversing for a while she touched his knee with her hand. 'Papa,' she said, 'I suppose I must now have to meet Mr Lopez in Manchester Square?'

'Why should you have to meet Mr Lopez in Manchester Square?'

'Of course he will come there to see Everett. After what has occurred you can hardly forbid him the house. He has saved Everett's life.'

'I don't know that he has done anything of the kind,' said Mr Wharton, who was vacillating between different opinions. He did in his heart believe that the Portuguese whom he so hated had saved his son from the thieves, and he also had almost come to the conviction that he must give his daughter to the man,—but at the same time he could not as yet bring himself to abandon his opposition to the marriage.

'Perhaps you think the story is not true.'

'I don't doubt the story in the least. Of course one man sticks to another in such an affair, and I have no doubt that Mr Lopez behaved as any English gentleman would.'

'Any English gentleman, papa, would have to come afterwards and see the friend he had saved. Don't you think so?'

'Oh, yes;—he might call.'

'And Mr Lopez will have an additional reason for calling,—and I know he will come. Don't you think he will come?'

'I don't want to think anything about it,' said the father.

'But I want you to think about it, papa. Papa, I know you are not indifferent to my happiness.'

'I hope you know it.'

'I do know it. I am quite sure of it. And therefore I don't think you ought to be afraid to talk to me about what must concern my happiness so greatly. As far as my own self and my own will are concerned I consider myself given away to Mr Lopez already. Nothing but his marrying some other woman,—or his death,—would make me think of myself otherwise than as belonging to him. I am not a bit ashamed of owning my love—to you; nor to him, if the opportunity were allowed me. I don't think there should be concealment about anything so important between people who are dear to each other. I have told you that I will do whatever you bid me about him. If you say that I shall not speak to him or see him, I will not speak to him or see him—willingly. You certainly need not be afraid that I should marry him without your leave.'

'I am not in the least afraid of it.'

'But I think you should think over what you are doing. And I am quite sure of this,—that you must tell me what I am to do in regard to receiving Mr Lopez in Manchester Square.' Mr Wharton listened attentively to what his daughter said to him, shaking his head from time to time as though almost equally distracted by her passive obedience and by her passionate protestations of love; but he said nothing. When she had completed her supplication he threw himself back in his seat and after a while took his book. It may be doubted whether he read much, for the question as to his girl's happiness was quite as near his heart as she could wish it to be.

It was late in the afternoon before they reached Manchester Square, and they were both happy to find that they were not troubled by Mr Lopez at the first moment. Everett was at home and in bed, and had not indeed as yet recovered from the effect of the man's knuckles at his windpipe; but he was well enough to assure his father and sister that they need not have disturbed themselves or hurried their return from Herefordshire on his account. 'To tell the truth,' said he, 'Ferdinand Lopez was hurt worse than I was.'

'He said nothing of being hurt himself,' said Mr Wharton.

'How was he hurt?' asked Emily in the quietest, stillest voice.

'The fact is,' said Everett, beginning to tell the whole story after his own fashion, 'if he hadn't been at hand then, there would have been an end of me. We had separated, you know,——'

'What could make two men separate from each other in the darkness of St James's Park?'

'Well,—to tell the truth we had quarrelled. I had made an ass of myself. You need not go into that any further, except that you should know that it was all my fault. Of course it wasn't a real quarrel,'—when he said this Emily, who was sitting close to his bed-head, pressed his arm under the clothes with her hand,—'but I had said something rough, and he had gone on just to put an end to it.'

'It was uncommonly foolish,' said the old Wharton. 'It was very foolish going round the park at all at that time of night.'

'No doubt, sir;—but it was my doing. And if he had not gone with me, I should have gone alone.' Here there was another pressure. 'I was a little low in spirits, and wanted the walk.'

'But how is he hurt?' asked the father.

'The man who was kneeling on me and squeezing the life out of me jumped up when he heard Lopez coming, and struck him over the head with a bludgeon. I heard the blow, though I was pretty well done for at the time myself. I don't think they hit me, but they got something round my neck, and I was half strangled before I knew what they were doing. Poor Lopez bled horribly, but he says he is none the worse for it.' Here there was another little pressure under the bed-clothes; for Emily felt that her brother was pleading for her in every word that he said.

About ten on the following morning Lopez came and asked for Mr Wharton. He was shown into the study, where he found the old man, and at once began to give his account of the whole concern in an easy, unconcerned manner. He had the large black patch on the side of his head, which had been so put on as almost to become him. But it was so conspicuous as to force a question concerning it from Mr Wharton. 'I am afraid you got rather a sharp knock yourself, Mr Lopez?'

'I did get a knock, certainly;—but the odd part of it is that I knew nothing about it till I found the blood in my eyes after they had decamped. But I lost my hat, and there is a rather long cut just above the temple. It hasn't done me the slightest harm. The worst of it was that they got off with Everett's watch and money.'

'Had he much money?'

'Forty pounds!' And Lopez shook his head, thereby signifying that forty pounds at the present moment was more than Everett Wharton could afford to lose. Upon the whole he carried himself very well, ingratiating himself with the father, raising no question about the daughter, and saying as little as possible about himself. He asked

whether he could go up and see his friend, and of course was allowed to
do so. A minute before he entered the room Emily left it. They did not
see each other. At any rate he did not see her. But there was a feeling
with both of them that the other was close,—and there was something
present to them, almost amounting to conviction, that the accident of
the park robbery would be good for them.

'He certainly did save Everett's life,' Emily said to her father the
next day.

'Whether he did or not, he did his best,' said Mr Wharton.

'When one's dearest relation is concerned,' said Emily, 'and when
his life has been saved, one feels that one has to be grateful even if it has
been an accident. I hope he knows, at any rate, that I am grateful.'

The old man had not been a week in London before he knew that he
had absolutely lost the game. Mrs Roby came back to her house round
the corner, ostensibly with the object of assisting her relatives in nursing Everett,—a purpose for which she certainly was not needed; but, as
the matter progressed, Mr Wharton was not without suspicion that her
return had been arranged by Ferdinand Lopez. She took upon herself,
at any rate, to be loud in the praise of the man who had saved the life of
her 'darling nephew,'—and to see that others also should be loud in his
praise. In a little time all London had heard of the affair, and it had
been discussed out of London. Down at Gatherum Castle the matter
had been known, or partly known,—but the telling of it had always
been to the great honour and glory of the hero. Major Pountney had
almost broken his heart over it, and Captain Gunner, writing to his
friend from the Curragh, had asserted his knowledge that it was all a
'got-up thing' between the two men. The 'Breakfast Table' and the
'Evening Pulpit' had been loud in praise of Lopez; but the 'People's
Banner,' under the management of Mr Quintus Slide, had naturally
thrown much suspicion on the incident when it became known to the
Editor that Ferdinand Lopez had been entertained by the Duke and
Duchess of Omnium. 'We have always felt some slight doubts as to the
details of the affair said to have happened about a fortnight ago, just at
midnight, in St James's Park. We should be glad to know whether the
policemen have succeeded in tracing any of the stolen property, or
whether any real attempt to trace it has been made.' This was one of the
paragraphs, and it was hinted still more plainly afterwards that Everett
Wharton, being short of money, had arranged the plan with the view of
opening his father's purse. But the general effect was certainly serviceable to Lopez. Emily Wharton did believe him to be a hero. Everett was
beyond measure grateful to him,—not only for having saved him from

the thieves, but also for having told nothing of his previous folly. Mrs Roby always alluded to the matter as if, for all coming ages, every Wharton ought to acknowledge that gratitude to a Lopez was the very first duty of life. The old man felt the absurdity of much of this, but still it affected him. When Lopez came he could not be rough to the man who had done a service to his son. And then he found himself compelled to do something. He must either take his daughter away, or he must yield. But his power of taking his daughter away seemed to be less than it had been. There was an air of quiet, unmerited suffering about her, which quelled him. And so he yielded.

It was after this fashion. Whether affected by the violence of the attack made upon him, or from other cause, Everett had been unwell after the affair, and had kept his room for a fortnight. During this time Lopez came to see him daily, and daily Emily Wharton had to take herself out of the man's way, and hide herself from the man's sight. This she did with much tact and with lady-like quietness, but not without an air of martyrdom, which cut her father to the quick. 'My dear,' he said to her one evening, as she was preparing to leave the drawing-room on hearing his knock, 'stop and see him if you like it.'

'Papa!'

'I don't want to make you wretched. If I could have died first, and got out of the way, perhaps it would have been better.'

'Papa, you will kill me if you speak in that way! If there is anything to say to him, do you say it.' And then she escaped.

Well! It was an added bitterness, but no doubt it was his duty. If he did intend to consent to the marriage, it certainly was for him to signify that consent to the man. It would not be sufficient that he should get out of the way and leave his girl to act for herself as though she had no friend in the world. The surrender which he had made to his daughter had come from a sudden impulse at the moment, but it could not now be withdrawn. So he stood out on the staircase, and when Lopez came up on his way to Everett's bedroom, he took him by the arm and led him into the drawing-room. 'Mr Lopez,' he said, 'you know that I have not been willing to welcome you into my house as a son-in-law. There are reasons on my mind,—perhaps prejudices,—which are strong against it. They are as strong now as ever. But she wishes it, and I have the utmost reliance on her constancy.'

'So have I,' said Lopez.

'Stop a moment, if you please, sir. In such a position a father's thought is only as to his daughter's happiness and prosperity. It is not his own that he should consider. I hear you well spoken of in the outer world, and I do not know that I have a right to demand of my daughter that she should tear you from her affections, because—because you are not just such as I would have her husband to be. You have my permission to see her.' Then, before Lopez could say a word, he left the room, and took his hat and hurried away to his club.

As he went he was aware that he had made no terms at all;—but then he was inclined to think that no terms should be made. There seemed to be a general understanding that Lopez was doing well in the world,—in a profession of the working of which Mr Wharton himself knew absolutely nothing. He had a large fortune at his own bestowal,—intended for his daughter,—which would have been forthcoming at the moment and paid down on the nail, had she married Arthur Fletcher. The very way in which the money should be invested and tied up and made to be safe and comfortable to the Fletcher-cum-Wharton interests generally, had been fully settled among them. But now this other man, this stranger, this Portuguese, had entered in upon the inheritance. But the stranger, the Portuguese, must wait. Mr Wharton knew himself to be an old man. She was his child, and he would not wrong her. But she should have her money closely settled upon herself on his death,—and on her children, should she then have any. It should be done by his will. He would say nothing about money to Lopez, and if Lopez should, as was probable, ask after his daughter's fortune, he would answer to this effect. Thus he almost resolved that he would give his daughter to the man without any inquiry as to the man's means. The thing had to be done, and he would take no further trouble about it. The comfort of his life was gone. His home would no longer be a home to him. His daughter could not now be his companion. The sooner that death came to him the better, but till death should come he must console himself as well as he could by playing whist at the Eldon. It was after this fashion that Mr Wharton thought of the coming marriage between his daughter and her lover.

'I have your father's consent to marry your sister,' said Ferdinand immediately on entering Everett's room.

'I knew it must come soon,' said the invalid.

'I cannot say that it has been given in the most gracious manner,—but it has been given very clearly. I have his express permission to see her. Those were his last words.'

Then there was a sending of notes between the sick-room and the sick man's sister's room. Everett wrote and Ferdinand wrote, and Emily wrote,—short lines each of them,—a few words scrawled. The last from Emily was as follows:—'Let him go into the drawing-room.

E.W.' And so Ferdinand went down, to meet his love,—to encounter her for the first time as her recognized future husband and engaged lover. Passionate, declared, and thorough as was her love for this man, the familiar intercourse between them had hitherto been very limited. There had been little,—we may perhaps say none,—of that dalliance between them which is so delightful to the man and so wondrous to the girl till custom has staled the edge of it. He had never sat with his arm round her waist. He had rarely held even her hand in his for a happy recognized pause of a few seconds. He had never kissed even her brow. And there she was now, standing before him, all his own, absolutely given to him, with the fullest assurance of love on her part, and with the declared consent of her father. Even he had been a little confused as he opened the door,—even he, as he paused to close it behind him, had had to think how he would address her, and perhaps had thought in vain. But he had not a moment for any thought after entering the room. Whether it was his doing or hers he hardly knew; but she was in his arms, and her lips were pressed to his, and his arm was tight round her waist, holding her close to his breast. It seemed as though all that was wanting had been understood in a moment, and as though they had lived together and loved for the last twelve months with the fullest mutual confidence. And she was the first to speak:—

'Ferdinand, I am so happy! Are you happy?'

'My love; my darling!'

'You have never doubted me, I know,—since you first knew it.'

'Doubted you, my girl!'

'That I would be firm! And now papa has been good to me, and how quickly one's sorrow is over. I am yours, my love, for ever and ever. You knew it before, but I like to tell you. I will be true to you in everything! Oh, my love!'

He had but little to say to her, but we know that for 'lovers lacking matter, the cleanliest shift is to kiss.'* In such moments silence charms, and almost any words are unsuitable except those soft, bird-like murmurings of love which, sweet as they are to the ear, can hardly be so written as to be sweet to the reader.

CHAPTER 24

THE MARRIAGE

THE engagement was made in October, and the marriage took place in the latter part of November. When Lopez pressed for an early day,—which he did very strongly,—Emily raised no difficulties in the way of his wishes. The father, foolishly enough, would at first have postponed it, and made himself so unpleasant to Lopez by his manner of doing this, that the bride was driven to take her lover's part. As the thing was to be done, what was to be gained by the delay? It could not be made a joy to him; nor, looking at the matter as he looked at it, could he make a joy even of her presence during the few intervening weeks. Lopez proposed to take his bride into Italy for the winter months, and to stay there at any rate through December and January, alleging that he must be back in town by the beginning of February;—and this was taken as a fair plea for hastening the marriage.

When the matter was settled, he went back to Gatherum Castle, as he had arranged to do with the Duchess, and managed to interest her Grace in all his proceedings. She promised that she would call on his bride in town, and even went so far as to send her a costly wedding present. 'You are sure she has got money?' said the Duchess.

'I am not sure of anything,' said Lopez,—'except this, that I do not mean to ask a single question about it. If he says nothing to me about money, I certainly shall say nothing to him. My feeling is this, Duchess; I am not marrying Miss Wharton for her money. The money, if there be any, has had nothing to do with it. But of course it will be a pleasure added if it be there.' The Duchess complimented him, and told him that this was exactly as it should be.

But there was some delay as to the seat for Silverbridge. Mr Grey's departure for Persia had been postponed,—the Duchess thought only for a month or six weeks. The Duke, however, was of opinion that Mr Grey should not vacate his seat till the day of his going was at any rate fixed. The Duke, moreover, had not made any promise of supporting his wife's favourite. 'Don't set your heart upon it too much, Mr Lopez,' the Duchess had said; 'but you may be sure I will not forget you.' Then it had been settled between them that the marriage should not be postponed, or the proposed trip to Italy abandoned, because of the probable vacancy at Silverbridge. Should the vacancy occur during his absence, and should the Duke consent, he could return at once. All this occurred in the last week or two before his marriage.

There were various little incidents which did not tend to make the happiness of Emily Wharton complete. She wrote to her cousin Mary Wharton, and also to Lady Wharton;—and her father wrote to Sir Alured; but the folk at Wharton Hall did not give in their adherence. Old Mrs Fletcher was still there, but John Fletcher had gone home to Longbarns. The obduracy of the Whartons might probably be owing to these two accidents. Mrs Fletcher declared aloud, as soon as the tidings reached her, that she never wished to see or hear anything more of Emily Wharton. 'She must be a girl,' said Mrs Fletcher, 'of an ingrained vulgar taste.' Sir Alured, whose letter from Mr Wharton had been very short, replied as shortly to his cousin. 'Dear Abel,—We all hope that Emily will be happy, though of course we regret the marriage.' The father, though he had not himself written triumphantly, or even hopefully,—as fathers are wont to write when their daughters are given away in marriage,—was wounded by the curtness and unkindness of the baronet's reply, and at the moment declared to himself that he would never go to Herefordshire any more. But on the following day there came a worse blow than Sir Alured's single line. Emily, not in the least doubting but that her request would be received with the usual ready assent, had asked Mary Wharton to be one of her bridesmaids. It must be supposed that the answer to this was written, if not under the dictation, at any rate under the inspiration, of Mrs Fletcher. It was as follows:—

'DEAR EMILY,

'Of course we all wish you to be very happy in your marriage, but equally of course we are all disappointed. We had taught ourselves to think that you would have bound yourself closer with us down here, instead of separating yourself entirely from us.

'Under all the circumstances mamma thinks it would not be wise for me to go up to London as one of your bridesmaids.

'Your affectionate Cousin,
'MARY WHARTON.'

This letter made poor Emily very angry for a day or two. 'It is as unreasonable as it is ill-natured,' she said to her brother.

'What else could you expect from a stiffnecked, prejudiced set of provincial ignoramuses?'

'What Mary says is not true. She did not think I was going to bind myself closer with them, as she calls it. I have been quite open with her, and have always told her that I could not be Arthur Fletcher's wife.'

'Why on earth should you marry to please them?'

'Because they don't know Ferdinand and are determined to insult him. It is an insult never to mention even his name. And to refuse to come to my marriage! The world is wide and there is room for us and them; but it makes me unhappy,—very unhappy,—that I should have to break with them.' And then the tears came into her eyes. It was intended, no doubt, to be a complete breach, for not a single wedding present was sent from Wharton Hall to the bride. But from Longbarns,—from John Fletcher himself,—there did come an elaborate coffee-pot, which, in spite of its inutility and ugliness, was very valuable to Emily.

But there was one other of her old Herefordshire friends who received the tidings of her marriage without quarrelling with her. She herself had written to her old lover.

'MY DEAR ARTHUR,

'There has been so much true friendship and affection between us that I do not like that you should hear from any one but myself the news that I am going to be married to Mr Lopez. We are to be married on the 28th of November,—this day month.

'Yours affectionately,
'EMILY WHARTON'

To this she received a very short reply;—

'DEAR EMILY,

'I am as I always have been.

'Yours,
'A. F.'

He sent her no present, nor did he say a word beyond this; but in her anger against the Herefordshire people she never included Arthur Fletcher. She pored over the little note a score of times, and wept over it, and treasured it up among her inmost treasures, and told herself that it was a thousand pities. She could talk, and did talk, to Ferdinand about the Whartons, and about old Mrs Fletcher, and described to him the arrogance and the stiffness and the ignorance of the Herefordshire squirearchy generally; but she never spoke to him of Arthur Fletcher,—except in that one narrative of her past life, in which, girl-like, she told her lover of the one other lover who had loved her.

But these things of course gave a certain melancholy to the occasion which perhaps was increased by the season of the year,—by the

November fogs, and by the emptiness and general sadness of the town. And added to this was the melancholy of old Mr Wharton himself. After he had given his consent to the marriage he admitted a certain amount of intimacy with his son-in-law, asking him to dinner, and discussing with him matters of general interest,—but never, in truth, opening his heart to him. Indeed, how can any man open his heart to one whom he dislikes? At best he can only pretend to open his heart, and even this Mr Wharton would not do. And very soon after the engagement Lopez left London and went to the Duke's place in the country. His objects in doing this and his aspirations in regard to a seat in Parliament were all made known to his future wife,—but he said not a word on the subject to her father; and she, acting under his instructions, was equally reticent. 'He will get to know me in time,' he said to her, 'and his manner will be softened towards me. But till that time shall come, I can hardly expect him to take a real interest in my welfare.'

When Lopez left London not a word had been said between him and his father-in-law as to money. Mr Wharton was content with such silence, not wishing to make any promise as to immediate income from himself, pretending to look at the matter as though he should say that, as his daughter had made for herself her own bed, she must lie on it, such as it might be. And this silence certainly suited Ferdinand Lopez at the time. To tell the truth of him—though he was not absolutely penniless, he was altogether propertyless. He had been speculating in money without capital, and though he had now and again been successful, he had also now and again failed. He had contrived that his name should be mentioned here and there with the names of well-known wealthy commercial men, and had for the last twelve months made up a somewhat intimate alliance with that very sound commercial man, Mr Mills Happerton. But his dealings with Mr Sextus Parker were in truth much more confidential than those with Mr Mills Happerton, and at the present moment poor Sexty Parker was alternately between triumph and despair as things went this way or that.

It was not, therefore, surprising that Ferdinand Lopez should volunteer no statements to the old lawyer about money, and that he should make no inquiries. He was quite confident that Mr Wharton had the wealth which was supposed to belong to him, and was willing to trust his power of obtaining a fair portion of it as soon as he should in truth be Mr Wharton's son-in-law. Situated as he was, of course, he must run some risk. And then, too, he had spoken of himself with a grain of truth when he had told the Duchess that he was not marrying for money.

Ferdinand Lopez was not an honest man or a good man. He was a self-seeking, intriguing adventurer, who did not know honesty from dishonesty when he saw them together. But he had at any rate this good about him, that he did love the girl whom he was about to marry. He was willing to cheat all the world,—so that he might succeed, and make a fortune, and become a big and a rich man; but he did not wish to cheat her. It was his ambition now to carry her up with him, and he thought how he might best teach her to assist him in doing so,—how he might win her to help him in his cheating, especially in regard to her own father. For to himself, to his own thinking, that which we call cheating was not dishonesty. To this thinking there was something bold, grand, picturesque, and almost beautiful in the battle which such a one as himself must wage with the world before he could make his way up in it. He would not pick a pocket, or turn a false card, or, as he thought, forge a name. That which he did, and desired to do, took with him the name of speculation. When he persuaded poor Sexty Parker to hazard his all, knowing well that he induced the unfortunate man to believe what was false, and to trust what was utterly untrustworthy, he did not himself think that he was going beyond the lines of fair enterprise. Now, in his marriage, he had in truth joined himself to real wealth. Could he only command at once that which he thought ought to be his wife's share of the lawyer's money, he did not doubt but that he could make a rapid fortune. It would not do for him to seem to be desirous of the money a day before the time;—but, when the time should come, would not his wife help him in his great career? But before she could do so she must be made to understand something of the nature of that career, and of the need of such aid.

Of course there arose the question where they should live. But he was ready with an immediate answer to this question. He had been to look at a flat,—a set of rooms,—in the Belgrave Mansions, in Pimlico, or Belgravia* you ought more probably to call it. He proposed to take them furnished till they could look about at their leisure and get a house that should suit them. Would she like a flat? She would have liked a cellar with him, and so she told him. Then they went to look at the flat, and old Mr Wharton condescended to go with them. Though his heart was not in the business, still he thought that he was bound to look after his daughter's comfort. 'They are very handsome rooms,' said Mr Wharton, looking round upon the rather gorgeous furniture.

'Oh, Ferdinand, are they not too grand?' said Emily.

'Perhaps they are a little more than we quite want just at present,' he said. 'But I'll tell you, sir, just how it has happened. A man I know wanted to let them for one year, just as they are, and offered them to me for £450,*—if I could pay the money in advance, at the moment. And so I paid it.'

'You have taken them, then?' said Mr Wharton.

'Is it all settled?' said Emily, almost with disappointment.

'I have paid the money, and I have so far taken them. But it is by no means settled. You have only to say you don't like them, and you shall never be asked to put your foot in them again.'

'But I do like them,' she whispered to him.

'The truth is, sir, that there is not the slightest difficulty in parting with them. So that when the chance came in my way I thought it best to secure the thing. It had all to be done, so to say, in an hour. My friend,—as far as he was a friend, for I don't know much about him,—wanted the money and wanted to be off. So here they are, and Emily can do as she likes.' Of course the rooms were regarded from that moment as the home for the next twelve months of Mr and Mrs Ferdinand Lopez.

And then they were married. The marriage was by no means a gay affair, the chief management of it falling into the hands of Mrs Dick Roby. Mrs Dick indeed provided not only the breakfast,—or saw rather that it was provided, for of course Mr Wharton paid the bill,— but the four bridesmaids also, and all the company. They were married in the church in Vere Street,* then went back to the house in Manchester Square, and within a couple of hours were on their road to Dover. Through it all not a word was said about money. At the last moment,—when he was free from fear as to any questions about his own affairs,—Lopez had hoped that the old man would say something. 'You will find so many thousand pounds at your bankers;'—or, 'You may look to me for so many hundreds a year.' But there was not a word. The girl had come to him without the assurance of a single shilling. In his great endeavour to get her he had been successful. As he thought of this in the carriage, he pressed his arm close round her waist. If the worst were to come to the worst, he would fight the world for her. But if this old man should be stubborn, close-fisted, and absolutely resolved to bestow all his money upon his son because of this marriage,—ah!— how should he be able to bear such a wrong as that?

Half-a-dozen times during that journey to Dover, he resolved to think nothing further about it, at any rate for a fortnight; and yet, before he reached Dover, he had said a word to her. 'I wonder what your father means to do about money? He never told you?'

'Not a word.'

'It is very odd that he should never have said anything.'

'Does it matter, dear?'

'Not in the least. But of course I have to talk about everything to you;—and it is odd.'

CHAPTER 25

THE BEGINNING OF THE HONEYMOON

ON the morning of his marriage, before he went to the altar, Lopez made one or two resolutions as to his future conduct. The first was that he would give himself a fortnight from his marriage day in which he would not even think of money. He had made certain arrangements, in the course of which he had caused Sextus Parker to stare with surprise and to sweat with dismay, but which nevertheless were successfully concluded. Bills were drawn to run over to February, and ready money to a moderate extent was forthcoming, and fiscal tranquillity was insured for a certain short period. The confidence which Sextus Parker had once felt in his friend's own resources was somewhat on the decline, but he still believed in his friend's skill and genius, and, after due inquiry, he believed entirely in his friend's father-in-law. Sextus Parker still thought that things would come round. Ferdinand,—he always now called his friend by his Christian name,—Ferdinand was beautifully, seraphically confident. And Sexty, who had been in a manner magnetized by Ferdinand, was confident too—at certain periods of the day. He was very confident when he had had his two or three glasses of sherry at luncheon, and he was often delightfully confident with his cigar and brandy-and-water at night. But there were periods in the morning in which he would shake with fear and sweat with dismay.

But Lopez himself, having with his friend's assistance arranged his affairs comfortably for a month or two, had, as a first resolution, promised himself a fortnight's freedom from all carking cares. His second resolution had been that at the end of the fortnight he would commence his operations on Mr Wharton. Up to the last moment he had hoped,—had almost expected,—that a sum of money would have been paid to him. Even a couple of thousand pounds for the time would have been of great use to him;—but no tender of any kind had been made. Not a word had been said. Things could not of course go on in that way. He was not going to play the coward with his father-in-law. Then he bethought himself how he would act if his father-in-law were sternly to refuse to do anything for him, and he assured himself that in such circumstances he would make himself very disagreeable to his father-in-law. And then his third resolution had reference to his wife. She must be instructed in his ways. She must learn to look at the world with his eyes. She must be taught the great importance of money,—not in a griping, hard-fisted, prosaic spirit; but that she might participate in that feeling of his own which had in it so much that was grand, so much that was delightful, so much that was picturesque. He would never ask her to be parsimonious,—never even to be economical. He would take a glory in seeing her well dressed and well attended, with her own carriage and her own jewels. But she must learn that the enjoyment of these things must be built upon a conviction that the most important pursuit in the world was the acquiring of money. And she must be made to understand, first of all, that she had a right to at any rate a half of her father's fortune. He had perceived that she had much influence with her father, and she must be taught to use this influence unscrupulously on her husband's behalf.

We have already seen that under the pressure of his thoughts he did break his first resolution within an hour or two of his marriage. It is easy for a man to say that he will banish care, so that he may enjoy to the full the delights of the moment. But this is a power which none but a savage possesses,—or perhaps an Irishman. We have learned the lesson from the divines, the philosophers, and the poets. Post equitem sedet atra cura.* Thus was Ferdinand Lopez mounted high on his horse,—for he had triumphed greatly in his marriage, and really felt that the world could give him no delight so great as to have her beside him, and her as his own. But the inky devil sat close upon his shoulders. Where would he be at the end of three months if Mr Wharton would do nothing for him,—and if a certain venture in guano,* to which he had tempted Sexty Parker, should not turn out the right way? He believed in the guano and he believed in Mr Wharton, but it is a terrible thing to have one's whole position in the world hanging upon either an unwilling father-in-law or a probable rise in the value of manure! And then how would he reconcile himself to her if both father-in-law and guano should go against him, and how should he endure her misery?

The inky devil had forced him to ask the question even before they had reached Dover. 'Does it matter?' she had asked. Then for the time he had repudiated his solicitude, and had declared that no question of money was of much consequence to him,—thereby making his future task with her so much the more difficult. After that he said nothing to her on the subject on that their wedding day,—but he could not prevent himself from thinking of it. Had he gone to the depth of ruin without a wife, what would it have mattered? For years past he had been at the same kind of work,—but while he was unmarried there had been a charm in the very danger. And as a single man he had succeeded, being sometimes utterly impecunious, but still with capacity of living. Now he had laden himself with a burden of which the very intensity of his love immensely increased the weight. As for not thinking of it, that was impossible. Of course she must help him. Of course she must be taught how imperative it was that she should help him at once. 'Is there anything troubles you?' she said, as she sat leaning against him after their dinner in the hotel at Dover.

'What should trouble me on such a day as this?'

'If there is anything, tell it me. I do not mean to say now, at this moment,—unless you wish it. Whatever may be your troubles, it shall be my greatest happiness, as it is my first duty, to lessen them if I can.'

The promise was very well. It all went in the right direction. It showed him that she was at any rate prepared to take a part in the joint work of their life. But, nevertheless, she should be spared for the moment. 'When there is trouble, you shall be told everything,' he said, pressing his lips to her brow, 'but there is nothing that need trouble you yet.' He smiled as he said this, but there was something in the tone of his voice which told her that there would be trouble.

When he was in Paris he received a letter from Parker, to whom he had been obliged to intrust a running address, but from whom he had enforced a promise that there should be no letter-writing unless under very pressing circumstances. The circumstances had not been pressing. The letter contained only one paragraph of any importance, and that was due to what Lopez tried to regard as fidgety cowardice on the part of his ally. 'Please to bear in mind that I can't and won't arrange for the bills for £1500* due 3rd February.' That was the paragraph. Who had asked him to arrange for these bills? And yet Lopez was well aware that he intended poor Sexty should 'arrange' for them, in the event of his failure to make arrangements with Mr Wharton.

At last he was quite unable to let the fortnight pass by without beginning the lessons which his wife had to learn. As for that first intention as to driving his cares out of his own mind for that time, he had long since abandoned even the attempt. It was necessary to him that a considerable sum of money should be extracted from the father-in-law, at any rate before the end of January, and a week or even a day might be of importance. They had hurried on southwards from Paris, and before the end of the first week had passed over the Simplon, and were at a pleasant inn on the shores of Como. Everything in their travels had been as yet delightful to Emily. This man, of whom she knew in truth so little, had certain good gifts,—gifts of intellect, gifts of temper, gifts of voice and manner and outward appearance,—which had hitherto satisfied her. A husband who is also an eager lover must be delightful to a young bride. And hitherto no lover could have been more tender than Lopez. Every word and every act, every look and every touch, had been loving. Had she known the world better she might have felt, perhaps, that something was expected where so much was given. Perhaps a rougher manner, with some little touch of marital self-assertion, might be a safer commencement of married life,—safer to the wife as coming from her husband. Arthur Fletcher by this time would have asked her to bring him his slippers, taking infinite pride in having his little behests obeyed by so sweet a servitor. That also would have been pleasant to her had her heart in the first instance followed his image; but now also the idolatry of Ferdinand Lopez had been very pleasant.

But the moment for the first lesson had come. 'Your father has not written to you since you started?' he said.

'Not a line. He has not known our address. He is never very good at letter-writing. I did write to him from Paris, and I scribbled a few words to Everett yesterday.'

'It is very odd that he should never have written to me.'

'Did you expect him to write?'

'To tell you the truth, I rather did. Not that I should have dreamed of his corresponding with me had he spoken to me on a certain subject. But as, on that subject, he never opened his mouth to me, I almost thought he would write.'

'Do you mean about money?' she asked in a very low voice.

'Well;—yes; I do mean about money. Things hitherto have gone so very strangely between us. Sit down, dear, till we have a real domestic talk.'

'Tell me everything,' she said, as she nestled herself close to his side.

'You know how it was at first between him and me. He objected to me violently,—I mean openly, to my face. But he based his objection solely on my nationality,—nationality and blood. As to my condition in the world, fortune, or income, he never asked a word. That was strange.'

'I suppose he thought he knew.'

'He could not have thought he knew, dearest. But it was not for me to force the subject upon him. You can see that.'

'I am sure whatever you did was right, Ferdinand.'

'He is indisputably a rich man,—one who might be supposed to be able and willing to give an only daughter a considerable fortune. Now I certainly had never thought of marrying for money.' Here she rubbed her face upon his arm. 'I felt that it was not for me to speak of money. If he chose to be reticent, I could be so equally. Had he asked me, I should have told him that I had no fortune, but was making a large though precarious income. It would then be for him to declare what he intended to do. That would, I think, have been preferable. As it is we are all in doubt. In my position a knowledge of what your father intends to do would be most valuable to me.'

'Should you not ask him?'

'I believe there has always been a perfect confidence between you and him?'

'Certainly,—as to all our ways of living. But he never said a word to me about money in his life.'

'And yet, my darling, money is most important.'

'Of course it is. I know that, Ferdinand.'

'Would you mind asking?' She did not answer him at once, but sat thinking. And he also paused before he went on with his lesson. But, in order that the lesson should be efficacious, it would be as well that he should tell her as much as he could even at this first lecture. 'To tell you the truth, this is quite essential to me at present,—very much more than I had thought it would be when we fixed the day for our marriage.' Her mind within her recoiled at this, though she was very careful that he should not feel any such motion in her body. 'My business is precarious.'

'What is your business, Ferdinand?' Poor girl! That she should have been allowed to marry a man, and then have to ask him such a question!

'It is generally commercial. I buy and sell on speculation. The world, which is shy of new words, has not yet given it a name. I am a good deal at present in the South American trade.' She listened, but received no glimmering of an idea from his words. 'When we were engaged everything was as bright as roses with me.'

'Why did you not tell me this before,—so that we might have been more prudent?'

'Such prudence would have been horrid to me. But the fact is that I should not now have spoken to you at all, but that since we left England I have had letters from a sort of partner of mine. In our business things will go astray sometimes. It would be of great service to me if I could learn what are your father's intentions.'

'You want him to give you some money at once.'

'It would not be unusual, dear,—when there is money to be given. But I want you specially to ask him what he himself would propose to do. He knows already that I have taken a home for you and paid for it, and he knows——. But it does not signify going into that.'

'Tell me everything.'

'He is aware that there are many expenses. Of course if he were a poor man there would not be a word about it. I can with absolute truth declare that had he been penniless it would have made no difference to my suit to you. But it would possibly have made some difference as to our after plans. He is a thorough man of the world, and he must know all that. I am sure he must feel that something is due to you,—and to me as your husband. But he is odd-tempered, and, as I have not spoken to him, he chooses to be silent to me. Now, my darling, you and I cannot afford to wait and see who can be silent the longest.'

'What do you want me to do?'

'To write to him.'

'And ask him for money?'

'Not exactly in that way. I think you should say that we should be glad to know what he intends to do, also saying that a certain sum of money would at present be of use to me.'

'Would it not be better from you? I only ask, Ferdinand. I never have even spoken to him about money, and of course he would know that you had dictated what I said.'

'No doubt he would. It is natural that I should do so. I hope the time may come when I may write quite freely to your father myself, but hitherto he has hardly been courteous to me. I would rather that you should write,—if you do not mind it. Write your own letter, and show it me. If there is anything too much or anything too little I will tell you.'

And so the first lesson was taught. The poor young wife did not at all like the lesson. Even within her own bosom she found no fault with her husband. But she began to understand that the life before her was not to be a life of roses. The first word spoken to her in the train, before it reached Dover, had explained something of this to her. She had felt at once that there would be trouble about money. And now, though she did not at all understand what might be the nature of those troubles, though she had derived no information whatever from her husband's hints about the South American trade, though she was as ignorant as ever of his affairs, yet she felt that the troubles would come soon. But never for a moment did it seem to her that he had been unjust in bringing her into troubled waters. They had loved each other, and therefore, whatever might be the troubles, it was right that they should marry each other. There was not a spark of anger against him in her bosom;—but she was unhappy.

He demanded from her the writing of the letter almost immediately after the conversation which has been given above, and of course the letter was written,—written and recopied, for the paragraph about money was, of course, at last of his wording. And she could not make the remainder of the letter pleasant. The feeling that she was making a demand for money on her father ran through it all. But the reader need only see the passage in which Ferdinand Lopez made his demand,— through her hand.

'Ferdinand has been speaking to me about my fortune.' It had gone much against the grain with her to write these words, 'my fortune.' 'But I have no fortune,' she said. He insisted however, explaining to her that she was entitled to use these words by her father's undoubted wealth. And so, with an aching heart, she wrote them. 'Ferdinand has been speaking to me about my fortune. Of course I told him that I knew nothing, and that as he had never spoken to me about money before our marriage, I had never asked about it. He says that it would be of great service to him to know what are your intentions; and also that he hopes that you may find it convenient to allow him to draw upon you for some portion of it at present. He says that £3000* would be of great use to him in his business.' That was the paragraph, and the work of writing it was so distasteful to her that she could hardly bring herself to form the letters. It seemed as though she were seizing the advantage of the first moment of her freedom to take a violent liberty with her father.

'It is altogether his own fault, my pet,' he said to her. 'I have the greatest respect in the world for your father, but he has allowed himself to fall into the habit of keeping all his affairs secret from his children; and, of course as they go out into the world, this secrecy must in some degree be invaded. There is precisely the same thing going on between him and Everett; only Everett is a great deal rougher to him than you are likely to be. He never will let Everett know whether he is to regard himself as a rich man or a poor man.'

'He gives him an allowance.'

'Because he cannot help himself. To you he does not do even as much as that, because he can help himself. I have chosen to leave it to him and he has done nothing. But this is not quite fair, and he must be told so. I don't think he could be told in more dutiful language.'

Emily did not like the idea of telling her father anything which he might not like to hear; but her husband's behests were to her in these, her early married days, quite imperative.

CHAPTER 26

THE END OF THE HONEYMOON

MRS LOPEZ had begged her father to address his reply to her at Florence, where,—as she explained to him,—they expected to find themselves within a fortnight from the date of her writing. They had reached the lake about the end of November, when the weather had still been fine, but they intended to pass the winter months of December and January within the warmth of the cities. That intervening fortnight was to her a period of painful anticipation. She feared to see her father's handwriting, feeling almost sure that he would be bitterly angry with her. During that time her husband frequently spoke to her about the letter,—about her own letter and her father's expected reply. It was necessary that she should learn her lesson, and she could only do so by having the subject of money made familiar to her ears. It was not a part of his plan to tell her anything of the means by which he hoped to make himself a wealthy man. The less she knew of that the better. But the fact that her father absolutely owed to him a large amount of money as her fortune could not be made too clear to her. He was very desirous to do this in such a manner as not to make her think that he was accusing her,—or that he would accuse her if the money was not forthcoming. But she must learn the fact, and must be imbued with the conviction that her husband would be the most ill-treated of men unless the money were forthcoming. 'I am a little nervous about it too,' said he, alluding to the expected letter;—'not so much as to the money itself, though that is important; but as to his conduct. If he chooses simply to ignore us after our marriage he will be behaving very badly.' She had no answer to make to this. She could not defend her father, because by doing so she would offend her husband. And yet her whole life-long trust in her father could not allow her to think it possible that he should behave ill to them.

On their arrival at Florence he went at once to the post-office, but there was as yet no letter. The fortnight, however, which had been named had only just run itself out. They went on from day to day inspecting buildings, looking at pictures, making for themselves a taste in marble and bronze, visiting the lovely villages which cluster on the hills round the city,—doing precisely in this respect as do all young married couples who devote a part of their honeymoon to Florence;— but in all their little journeyings and in all their work of pleasure the inky devil sat not only behind him but behind her also. The heavy care of life was already beginning to work furrows on her face. She would already sit, knitting her brow, as she thought of coming troubles. Would not her father certainly refuse? And would not her husband then begin to be less loving and less gracious to herself?

Every day for a week he called at the post-office when he went out with her, and still the letter did not come. 'It can hardly be possible,' he said at last to her, 'that he should decline to answer his own daughter's letter.'

'Perhaps he is ill,' she replied.

'If there were anything of that kind Everett would tell us.'

'Perhaps he has gone back to Herefordshire?'

'Of course his letter would go after him. I own it is very singular to me that he should not write. It looks as though he were determined to cast you off from him altogether because you have married against his wishes.'

'Not that, Ferdinand;—do not say that!'

'Well; we shall see.'

And on the next day they did see. He went to the post-office before breakfast, and on this day he returned with a letter in his hand. She was sitting waiting for him with a book in her lap, and saw the letter at once. 'Is it from papa?' she said. He nodded his head as he handed it to her. 'Open it and read it, Ferdinand. I have got to be so nervous about it, that I cannot do it. It seems to be so important.'

'Yes;—it is important,' he said with a grim smile, and then he opened the letter. She watched his face closely as he read it, and at first she could tell nothing from it. Then, in that moment, it first occurred to her that he had a wonderful command of his features. All this, how- ever, lasted but half a minute. Then he chucked the letter, lightly, in among the tea-cups, and coming to her took her closely in his arms and almost hurt her by the violence of his repeated kisses.

'Has he written kindly?' she said, as soon as she could find her breath to speak.

'By George, he's a brick after all. I own I did not think it. My darling, how much I owe you for all the trouble I have given you.'

'Oh, Ferdinand! If he has been good to you I shall be so happy.'

'He has been awfully good. Ha, ha, ha!' And then he began walking about the room as he laughed in an unnatural way. 'Upon my word it is a pity we didn't say four thousand, or five. Think of his taking me just at my word. It's a great deal better than I expected; that's all that I can say. And at the present moment it is of the utmost importance to me.'

All this did not take above a minute or two, but during that minute or two she had been so bewildered by his manner as almost to fancy that the expressions of his delight had been ironical. He had been so unlike himself as she had known him that she almost doubted the reality of his joy. But when she took the letter and read it, she found that his joy was true enough. The letter was very short, and was as follows:—

'MY DEAR EMILY,

'What you have said under your husband's instruction about money, I find upon consideration to be fair enough. I think he should have spoken to me before his marriage; but then again perhaps I ought to have spoken to him. As it is, I am willing to give him the sum he requires, and I will pay £3000 to his account, if he would tell me where he would have it lodged. Then I shall think I have done my duty by him. What I shall do with the remainder of any money that I may have, I do not think he is entitled to ask.

'Everett is well again, and as idle as ever. Your aunt Roby is making a fool of herself at Harrogate. I have heard nothing from Herefordshire. Everything is very quiet and lonely here.

'Your affectionate father,
'A. WHARTON.'

As he had dined at the Eldon every day since his daughter had left him, and had played on an average a dozen rubbers of whist daily, he was not justified in complaining of the loneliness of London.

The letter seemed to Emily herself to be very cold, and had not her husband rejoiced over it so warmly she would have considered it to be unsatisfactory. No doubt the £3000 would be given; but that, as far as she could understand her father's words, was to be the whole of her fortune. She had never known anything of her father's affairs or of his intentions, but she had certainly supposed that her fortune would be very much more than this. She had learned in some indirect way that a large sum of money would have gone with her hand to Arthur Fletcher, could she have brought herself to marry that suitor favoured by her family. And now, having learned, as she had learned, that money was of vital importance to her husband, she was dismayed at what seemed to her to be parental parsimony. But he was overjoyed,—so much so that for a while he lost that restraint over himself which was habitual to him. He ate his breakfast in a state of exultation, and talked,—not alluding specially to this £3000,—as though he had the command of almost unlimited means. He ordered a carriage and drove her out, and bought presents for her,—things as to which they had both before decided that they should not be bought because of the expense. 'Pray don't spend your money for me,' she said to him. 'It is nice to have you giving me things, but it would be nicer to me even than that to think that I could save you expense.'

But he was not in a mood to be denied. 'You don't understand,' he said. 'I don't want to be saved from little extravagances of this sort. Owing to circumstances your father's money was at this moment of importance to me;—but he has answered to the whip and the money is there, and that trouble is over. We can enjoy ourselves now. Other troubles will spring up, no doubt, before long.'

She did not quite like being told that her father 'had answered to the whip,'—but she was willing to believe that it was a phrase common among men to which it would be prudish to make objection. There was, also, something in her husband's elation which was distasteful to her. Could it be that reverses of fortune with reference to moderate sums of money, such as this which was now coming into his hands, would always affect him in the same way? Was it not almost unmanly, or at any rate was it not undignified? And yet she tried to make the best of it, and lent herself to his holiday mood as well as she was able. 'Shall I write and thank papa?' she said that evening.

'I have been thinking of that,' he said. 'You can write if you like, and of course you will. But I also will write, and had better do so a post or two before you. As he has come round I suppose I ought to show myself civil. What he says about the rest of his money is of course absurd. I shall ask him nothing about it, but no doubt after a bit he will make permanent arrangements.' Everything in the business wounded her more or less. She now perceived that he regarded this £3000 only as the first instalment of what he might get, and that his joy was due simply to this temporary success. And then he called her father absurd to her face. For a moment she thought that she would defend her father; but she could not as yet bring herself to question her husband's words even on such a subject as that.

He did write to Mr Wharton, but in doing so he altogether laid aside that flighty manner which for a while had annoyed her. He thoroughly understood that the wording of the letter might be very important to him, and he took much trouble with it. It must be now the great work of his life to ingratiate himself with this old man, so that, at any rate at the old man's death, he might possess at least half of the old man's money. He must take care that there should be no division between his wife and her father of such a nature as to make the father think that his son ought to enjoy any special privilege of primogeniture or of male inheritance. And if it could be so managed that the daughter should, before the old man's death, become his favourite child, that also would be well. He was therefore very careful about the letter, which was as follows:—

'My Dear Mr Wharton,

'I cannot let your letter to Emily pass without thanking you myself for the very liberal response made by you to what was of course a request from myself. Let me in the first place assure you that had you, before our marriage, made any inquiry about my money affairs, I would have told you everything with accuracy; but as you did not do so I thought that I should seem to intrude upon you, if I introduced the subject. It is too long for a letter, but whenever you may like to allude to it, you will find that I will be quite open with you.

'I am engaged in business which often requires the use of a considerable amount of capital. It has so happened that even since we were married the immediate use of a sum of money became essential to me to save me from sacrificing a cargo of guano which will be of greatly increased value in three months' time, but which otherwise must have gone for what it would now fetch. Your kindness will see me through that difficulty.

'Of course there is something precarious in such a business as mine;—but I am endeavouring to make it less so from day to day, and hope very shortly to bring it into that humdrum groove which best befits a married man. Should I ask further assistance from you in doing this, perhaps you will not refuse it if I can succeed in making the matter clear to you. As it is I thank you sincerely for what you have done. I will ask you to pay the £3000 you have so kindly promised to my account at Messrs Hunky and Sons, Lombard Street. They are not regular bankers, but I have an account there.

'We are wandering about and enjoying ourselves mightily in the properly romantic manner. Emily sometimes seems to think that she would like to give up business, and London, and all sublunary troubles, in order that she might settle herself for life under an Italian sky.

But the idea does not generally remain with her very long. Already she is beginning to show symptoms of home sickness in regard to Manchester Square.

'Yours always most faithfully,

'FERDINAND LOPEZ.'

To this letter Lopez received no reply;—nor did he expect one. Between Emily and her father a few letters passed, not very long; nor, as regarded those from Mr Wharton, were they very interesting. In none of them, however, was there any mention of money. But early in January, Lopez received a more pressing,—we might almost say an agonizing letter from his friend Parker. The gist of the letter was to make Lopez understand that Parker must at once sell certain interests in a coming cargo of guano,—at whatever sacrifice,—unless he could be certified as to that money which must be paid in February, and which he, Parker, must pay, should Ferdinand Lopez be at that moment unable to meet his bond. The answer sent to Parker shall be given to the reader.

'MY DEAR OLD AWFULLY SILLY, AND ABSURDLY IMPATIENT FRIEND,

'You are always like a toad under a harrow, and that without the slightest cause. I have money lying at Hunky's more than double enough for the bills. Why can't you trust a man? If you won't trust me in saying so, you can go to Mills Happerton and ask him. But, remember, I shall be very much annoyed if you do so,—and that such an inquiry cannot but be injurious to me. If, however, you won't believe me, you can go and ask. At any rate don't meddle with the guano. We should lose over £1000 each of us, if you were to do so. By George, a man should neither marry, nor leave London for a day, if he has to do with a fellow so nervous as you are. As it is I think I shall be back a week or two before my time is properly up, lest you and one or two others should think that I have levanted* altogether.

'I have no hesitation in saying that more fortunes are lost in business by trembling cowardice than by any amount of imprudence or extravagance. My hair stands on end when you talk of parting with guano in December because there are bills which have to be met in February. Pluck up your heart, man, and look around, and see what is done by men with good courage.

'Yours always,

'FERDINAND LOPEZ.'

These were the only communications between our married couple and their friends at home with which I need trouble my readers. Nor need I tell any further tales of their honeymoon. If the time was not one of complete and unalloyed joy to Emily,—and we must fear that it was not,—it is to be remembered that but very little complete and unalloyed joy is allowed to sojourners in this vale of tears, even though they have been but two months married. In the first week in February they appeared in the Belgrave mansion, and Emily Lopez took possession of her new home with a heart as full of love for her husband as it had been when she walked out of the church in Vere Street, though it may be that some of her sweetest illusions had already been dispelled.

CHAPTER 27

THE DUKE'S MISERY

WE must go back for a while to Gatherum Castle and see the guests whom the Duchess had collected there for her Christmas festivities. The hospitality of the Duke's house had been maintained almost throughout the autumn. Just at the end of October they went to Matching, for what the Duchess called a quiet month,—which, however, at the Duke's urgent request, became six weeks. But even here the house was full at the time, though from deficiency of bedrooms the guests were very much less numerous. But at Matching the Duchess had been uneasy and almost cross. Mrs Finn had gone with her husband to Ireland, and she had taught herself to fancy that she could not live without Mrs Finn. And her husband had insisted upon having round him politicians of his own sort, men who really preferred work to archery, or even to hunting, and who discussed the evils of direct taxation absolutely in the drawing-room. The Duchess was assured that the country could not be governed by the support of such men as these, and was very glad to get back to Gatherum,—whither also came Phineas Finn with his wife, and the St Bungay people, and Barrington Erle, and Mr Monk, the Chancellor of the Exchequer, with Lord and Lady Cantrip, and Lord and Lady Drummond,—Lord Drummond being the only representative of the other or coalesced party. And Major Pountney was there, having been urgent with the Duchess,—and having fully explained to his friend Captain Gunner that he had acceded to the wishes of his hostess only on the assurance of her Grace that the house would not be again troubled by the presence of Ferdinand Lopez.

Such assurances were common between the two friends, but were inno-cent, as, of course, neither believed the other. And Lady Rosina was again there,—with many others. The melancholy poverty of Lady Rosina had captivated the Duke. 'She shall come and live here, if you like,' the Duchess had said in answer to a request from her husband on his new friend's behalf,—'I've no doubt she will be willing.' The place was not crowded as it had been before; but still about thirty guests sat down to dinner daily, and Locock, Millepois, and Mrs Pritchard were all kept hard at work. Nor was our Duchess idle. She was always making up the party,—meaning the coalition,—doing something to strengthen the buttresses, writing little letters to little people, who, little as they were, might become big by amalgamation. 'One has always to be binding one's fagot,' she said to Mrs Finn, having read her Æsop* not altogether in vain. 'Where should we have been without you?' she had whispered to Sir Orlando Drought when that gentleman was leaving Gatherum at the termination of his second visit. She had particularly disliked Sir Orlando, and was aware that her husband had on this occasion been hardly as gracious as he should have been, in true policy, to so powerful a colleague. Her husband had been peculiarly shy of Sir Orlando since the day on which they had walked together in the park,—and, consequently, the Duchess had whispered to him. 'Don't bind your fagot too conspicuously,' Mrs Finn had said to her. Then the Duchess had fallen to a seat almost exhausted by labour, mingled with regrets, and by the doubts which from time to time pervaded even her audacious spirit. 'I'm not a god,' she said, 'or a Pitt,* or an Italian with a long name beginning with M.,* that I should be able to do these things without ever making a mistake. And yet they must be done. And as for him,—he does not help me in the least. He wanders about among the clouds of the multiplication table, and thinks that a majority will drop into his mouth because he does not shut it. Can you tie the fagot any better?' 'I think I would leave it untied,' said Mrs Finn. 'You would not do anything of the kind. You'd be just as fussy as I am.' And thus the game was carried on at Gatherum Castle from week to week.

'But you won't leave him?' This was said to Phineas Finn by his wife a day or two before Christmas, and the question was intended to ask whether Phineas thought of giving up his place.

'Not if I can help it.'

'You like the work.'

'That has but little to do with the question, unfortunately. I certainly like having something to do. I like earning money.'

'I don't know why you like that especially,' said the wife laughing.

'I do at any rate,—and, in a certain sense, I like authority. But in serving with the Duke I find a lack of that sympathy which one should have with one's chief. He would never say a word to me unless I spoke to him. And when I do speak, though he is studiously civil,—much too courteous,—I know that he is bored. He has nothing to say to me about the country. When he has anything to communicate, he prefers to write a minute for Warburton, who then writes to Morton,—and so it reaches me.'

'Doesn't it do as well?'

'It may do with me. There are reasons which bind me to him, which will not bind other men. Men don't talk to me about it, because they know that I am bound to him through you. But I am aware of the feeling which exists. You can't be really loyal to a king if you never see him,—if he be always locked up in some almost divine recess.'

'A king may make himself too common, Phineas.'

'No doubt. A king has to know where to draw the line. But the Duke draws no intentional line at all. He is not by nature gregarious or communicative, and is therefore hardly fitted to be the head of a ministry.'

'It will break her heart if anything goes wrong.'

'She ought to remember that Ministries seldom live very long,' said Phineas. 'But she'll recover even if she does break her heart. She is too full of vitality to be much repressed by any calamity. Have you heard what is to be done about Silverbridge?'

'The Duchess wants to get it for this man, Ferdinand Lopez.'

'But it has not been promised yet?'

'The seat is not vacant,' said Mrs Finn, 'and I don't know when it will be vacant. I think there is a hitch about it,—and I think the Duchess is going to be made very angry.'

Throughout the autumn the Duke had been an unhappy man. While the absolute work of the Session had lasted he had found something to console him; but now, though he was surrounded by private secretaries, and though dispatch-boxes went and came twice a day, though there were dozens of letters as to which he had to give some instruction,—yet, there was in truth nothing for him to do. It seemed to him that all the real work of Government had been filched from him by his colleagues, and that he was stuck up in pretended authority,—a kind of wooden Prime Minister, from whom no real ministration was demanded. His first fear had been that he was himself unfit;—but now he was uneasy, fearing that others thought him to be unfit. There was Mr Monk with his budget, and Lord Drummond with his three or four dozen half-rebellious colonies, and Sir Orlando Drought with the House to lead and a ship to build, and Phineas Finn with his scheme of municipal Home Rule for Ireland, and Lord Ramsden with a codified Statute Book,—all full of work, all with something special to be done. But for him,—he had to arrange who should attend the Queen, what ribbons* should be given away, and what middle-aged young man should move the address. He sighed as he thought of those happy days in which he used to fear that his mind and body would both give way under the pressure of decimal coinage.

But Phineas Finn had read the Duke's character rightly in saying that he was neither gregarious nor communicative, and therefore but little fitted to rule Englishmen. He had thought that it was so himself, and now from day to day he was becoming more assured of his own deficiency. He could not throw himself into cordial relations with the Sir Orlando Droughts, or even the Mr Monks. But, though he had never wished to be put into his present high office, now that he was there he dreaded the sense of failure which would follow his descent from it. It is this feeling rather than genuine ambition, rather than the love of power or patronage or pay, which induces men to cling to place. The absence of real work, and the quantity of mock work, both alike made the life wearisome to him; but he could not endure the idea that it should be written in history that he had allowed himself to be made a *fainéant* Prime Minister, and then had failed even in that. History would forget what he had done as a working Minister in recording the feebleness of the Ministry which would bear his name.

The one man with whom he could talk freely, and from whom he could take advice, was now with him, here at his Castle. He was shy at first even with the Duke of St Bungay, but that shyness he could generally overcome, after a few words. But though he was always sure of his old friend's sympathy and of his old friend's wisdom, yet he doubted his old friend's capacity to understand himself. The young Duke felt the old Duke to be thicker-skinned than himself and therefore unable to appreciate the thorns which so sorely worried his own flesh. 'They talk to me about a policy,' said the host. They were closeted at this time in the Prime Minister's own sanctum, and there yet remained an hour before they need dress for dinner.

'Who talks about a policy?'

'Sir Orlando Drought especially.' For the Duke of Omnium had never forgotten the arrogance of that advice given in the park.

'Sir Orlando is of course entitled to speak, though I do not know that he is likely to say anything very well worth the hearing. What is his special policy?'

'If he had any, of course, I would hear him. It is not that he wants any special thing to be done, but he thinks that I should get up some special thing in order that Parliament may be satisfied.'

'If you wanted to create a majority that might be true. Just listen to him and have done with it.'

'I cannot go on in that way. I cannot submit to what amounts to complaint from the gentlemen who are acting with me. Nor would they submit long to my silence. I am beginning to feel that I have been wrong.'

'I don't think you have been wrong at all.'

'A man is wrong if he attempts to carry a weight too great for his strength.'

'A certain nervous sensitiveness, from which you should free yourself as from a disease, is your only source of weakness. Think about your business as a shoemaker thinks of his. Do your best, and then let your customers judge for themselves. Caveat emptor.* A man should never endeavour to price himself, but should accept the price which others put on him,—only being careful that he should learn what that price is. Your policy should be to keep your government together by a strong majority. After all, the making of new laws is too often but an unfortunate necessity laid on us by the impatience of the people. A lengthened period of quiet and therefore good government with a minimum of new laws would be the greatest benefit the country could receive. When I recommended you to comply with the Queen's behest I did so because I thought that you might inaugurate such a period more certainly than any other one man.' This old Duke was quite content with a state of things such as he described. He had been a Cabinet Minister for more than half his life. He liked being a Cabinet Minister. He thought it well for the country generally that his party should be in power,—and if not his party in its entirety, then as much of his party as might be possible. He did not expect to be written of as a Pitt or a Somers;* but he thought that memoirs would speak of him as a useful nobleman,—and he was contented. He was not only not ambitious himself, but the effervescence and general turbulence of ambition in other men was distasteful to him. Loyalty was second nature to him, and the power of submitting to defeat without either shame or sorrow had become perfect with him by long practice. He would have made his brother Duke such as he was himself,—had not his brother Duke been so lamentably thin-skinned.

'I suppose we must try it for another Session?' said the Duke of Omnium with a lachrymose voice.

'Of course we must,—and for others after that, I both hope and trust,' said the Duke of St Bungay, getting up. 'If I don't go up-stairs I shall be late, and then her Grace will look at me with unforgiving eyes.'

On the following day after lunch the Prime Minister took a walk with Lady Rosina De Courcy. He had fallen into a habit of walking with Lady Rosina almost every day of his life, till the people in the Castle began to believe that Lady Rosina was the mistress of some deep policy of her own. For there were many there who did in truth think that statecraft could never be absent from a minister's mind, day or night. But in truth Lady Rosina chiefly made herself agreeable to the Prime Minister by never making the most distant allusion to public affairs. It might be doubted whether she even knew that the man who paid her so much honour was the Head of the British Government as well as the Duke of Omnium. She was a tall, thin, shrivelled-up old woman,—not very old, fifty perhaps, but looking at least ten years more,—very melancholy, and sometimes very cross. She had been notably religious, but that was gradually wearing off as she advanced in years. The rigid strictness of Sabbatarian* practice requires the full energy of middle life. She had been left entirely alone in the world, with a very small income, and not many friends who were in any way interested in her existence. But she knew herself to be Lady Rosina De Courcy, and felt that the possession of that name ought to be more to her than money and friends, or even than brothers and sisters. 'The weather is not frightening you,' said the Duke. Snow had fallen, and the paths, even where they had been swept, were wet and sloppy.

'Weather never frightens me, your Grace. I always have thick boots,—I am very particular about that;—and cork soles.'

'Cork soles are admirable.'

'I think I owe my life to cork soles,' said Lady Rosina enthusiastically. 'There is a man named Sprout in Silverbridge who makes them. Did your Grace ever try him for boots?'

'I don't think I ever did,' said the Prime Minister.

'Then you had better. He's very good and very cheap too. Those London tradesmen never think they can charge you enough. I find I can wear Sprout's boots the whole winter through and then have them resoled. I don't suppose you ever think of such things?'

'I like to have my feet dry.'

'I have got to calculate what they cost.' They then passed Major Pountney, who was coming and going between the stables and the house, and who took off his hat and who saluted the host and his companion with perhaps more flowing courtesy than was necessary. 'I never have found out what that gentleman's name is yet,' said Lady Rosina.

'Pountney, I think. I believe they call him Major Pountney.'

'Oh, Pountney! There are Pountneys in Leicestershire. Perhaps he is one of them.'

'I don't know where he comes from,' said the Duke,—'nor, to tell the truth, where he goes to.' Lady Rosina looked up at him with an interested air. 'He seems to be one of those idle men who get into people's houses heaven knows why, and never do anything.'

'I suppose you asked him?' said Lady Rosina.

'The Duchess did, I dare say.'

'How odd it would be if she were to suppose that you had asked him.'

'The Duchess, no doubt, knows all about it.' Then there was a little pause. 'She is obliged to have all sorts of people,' said the Duke apologetically.

'I suppose so,—when you have so many coming and going. I am sorry to say that my time is up to-morrow, so that I shall make way for somebody else.'

'I hope you won't think of going, Lady Rosina,—unless you are engaged elsewhere. We are delighted to have you.'

'The Duchess has been very kind, but——'

'The Duchess I fear is almost too much engaged to see as much of her guests individually as she ought to do. To me your being here is a great pleasure.'

'You are too good to me,—much too good. But I shall have stayed out my time, and I think, Duke, I will go to-morrow. I am very methodical, you know, and always act by rule. I have walked my two miles now, and I will go in. If you do want boots with cork soles mind you go to Sprout's. Dear me; there is that Major Pountney again. That is four times he has been up and down that path since we have been walking here.'

Lady Rosina went in, and the Duke turned back, thinking of his friend and perhaps thinking of the cork soles of which she had to be so careful and which was so important to her comfort. It could not be that he fancied Lady Rosina to be clever, nor can we imagine that her conversation satisfied any of those wants to which he and all of us are subject. But nevertheless he liked Lady Rosina, and was never bored by her. She was natural, and she wanted nothing from him. When she talked about cork soles she meant cork soles. And then she did not tread on any of his numerous corns. As he walked on he determined that he would induce his wife to persuade Lady Rosina to stay a little longer at the Castle. In meditating upon this he made another turn in the grounds, and again came upon Major Pountney as that gentleman was returning from the stables. 'A very cold afternoon,' he said, feeling it to be ungracious to pass one of his own guests in his own grounds without a word of salutation.

'Very cold indeed, your Grace,—very cold.' The Duke had intended to pass on, but the Major managed to stop him by standing in the pathway. The Major did not in the least know his man. He had heard that the Duke was shy, and therefore thought that he was timid. He had not hitherto been spoken to by the Duke,—a condition of things which he attributed to the Duke's shyness and timidity. But, with much thought on the subject, he had resolved that he would have a few words with his host, and had therefore passed backwards and forwards between the house and the stables rather frequently. 'Very cold, indeed, but yet we've had beautiful weather. I don't know when I have enjoyed myself so much altogether as I have at Gatherum Castle.' The Duke bowed, and made a little but a vain effort to get on. 'A splendid pile!' said the Major, stretching his hand gracefully towards the building.

'It is a big house,' said the Duke.

'A noble mansion;—perhaps the noblest mansion in the three kingdoms,' said Major Pountney. 'I have seen a great many of the best country residences in England, but nothing that at all equals Gatherum.' Then the Duke made a little effort at progression, but was still stopped by the daring Major. 'By-the-by, your Grace, if your Grace has a few minutes to spare,—just a half a minute,—I wish you would allow me to say something.' The Duke assumed a look of disturbance, but he bowed and walked on, allowing the Major to walk by his side. 'I have the greatest possible desire, my Lord Duke, to enter public life.'

'I thought you were already in the army,' said the Duke.

'So I am;—was on Sir Bartholomew Bone's staff in Canada for two years, and have seen as much of what I call home service as any man going. One of my chief objects is to take up the army.'

'I seems that you have taken it up.'

'I mean in Parliament, your Grace. I am very fairly off as regards private means, and would stand all the racket of the expense of a contest myself,—if there were one. But the difficulty is to get a seat, and, of course, if it can be privately managed, it is very comfortable.' The Duke looked at him again,—this time without bowing. But the Major, who was not observant, rushed on to his destruction. 'We all know that Silverbridge will soon be vacant. Let me assure your Grace that if it might be consistent with your Grace's plans in other respects to turn your kind countenance towards me, you would find that you have a supporter than whom none would be more staunch, and perhaps I may say one, who in the House would not be the least useful!' That portion of the Major's speech which referred to the Duke's kind countenance had been learned by heart, and was thrown trippingly off the tongue with a kind of twang. The Major had perceived that he had not been at once interrupted when he began to open the budget of his political aspirations, and had allowed himself to indulge in pleasing auguries. 'Nothing ask and nothing have,' had been adopted as the motto of his life, and more than once he had expressed to Captain Gunner his conviction that,—'By George, if you've only cheek enough, there is nothing you cannot get.' On this emergency the Major certainly was not deficient in cheek. 'If I might be allowed to consider myself your Grace's candidate, I should indeed be a happy man,' said the Major.

'I think, sir,' said the Duke, 'that your proposition is the most unbecoming and the most impertinent that ever was addressed to me.' The Major's mouth fell, and he stared with all his eyes as he looked up into the Duke's face. 'Good afternoon,' said the Duke, turning quickly round and walking away. The Major stood for a while transfixed to the place, and cold as was the weather, was bathed in perspiration. A keen sense of having 'put his foot into it' almost crushed him for a time. Then he assured himself that, after all, the Duke 'could not eat him,' and with that consolatory reflection he crept back to the house and up to his own room.

To put the man down had of course been an easy task to the Duke, but he was not satisfied with that. To the Major it seemed that the Duke had passed on with easy indifference,—but in truth he was very far from being easy. The man's insolent request had wounded him at many points. It was grievous to him that he should have as a guest in his own house a man whom he had been forced to insult. It was grievous to him that he himself should not have been held in personal respect high enough to protect him from such an insult. It was grievous to him that he should be openly addressed,—addressed by an absolute stranger,—as a borough-mongering lord, who would not scruple to give away a seat in Parliament as seats were given away in former days. And it was specially grievous to him that all these misfortunes should have come upon him as a part of the results of his wife's manner of exercising his hospitality. If this was to be Prime Minister he certainly would not be Prime Minister much longer! Had any aspirant to political life ever dared so to address Lord Brock, or Lord de Terrier, or Mr Mildmay, the old Premiers whom he remembered? He thought not. They had managed differently. They had been able to defend themselves from such attacks by personal dignity. And would it have been possible that any man should have dared so to speak to his uncle, the late Duke? He thought not. As he shut himself up in his own room he grieved inwardly with a deep grief. After a while he walked off to his wife's room, still perturbed in spirit. The perturbation had indeed increased from minute to minute. He would rather give up politics altogether and shut himself up in absolute seclusion than find himself subject to the insolence of any Pountney that might address him. With his wife he found Mrs Finn. Now for this lady personally he entertained what for him was a warm regard. In various matters of much importance he and she had been brought together, and she had, to his thinking, invariably behaved well. And an intimacy had been established which had enabled him to be at ease with her,—so that her presence was often a comfort to him. But at the present moment he had not wished to find any one with his wife, and felt that she was in his way. 'Perhaps I am disturbing you,' he said in a tone of voice that was solemn and almost funereal.

'Not at all,' said the Duchess, who was in high spirits. 'I want to get your promise now about Silverbridge. Don't mind her. Of course she knows everything.' To be told that anybody knew everything was another shock to him. 'I have just got a letter from Mr Lopez.' Could it be right that his wife should be corresponding on such a subject with a person so little known as this Mr Lopez? 'May I tell him that he shall have your interest when the seat is vacant?'

'Certainly not,' said the Duke, with a scowl that was terrible even to his wife. 'I wished to speak to you, but I wished to speak to you alone.'

'I beg a thousand pardons,' said Mrs Finn, preparing to go.

'Don't stir, Marie,' said the Duchess, 'he is going to be cross.'

'If Mrs Finn will allow me, with every feeling of the most perfect respect and sincerest regard, to ask her to leave me with you for a few minutes, I shall be obliged. And if, with her usual hearty kindness, she will pardon my abruptness——' Then he could not go on, his emotion being too great; but he put out his hand, and taking hers raised it to his lips and kissed it. The moment had become too solemn for any further hesitation as to the lady's going. The Duchess for a moment was struck dumb, and Mrs Finn, of course, left the room.

'In the name of heaven, Plantagenet, what is the matter?'

'Who is Major Pountney?'

'Who is Major Pountney! How on earth should I know? He is—— Major Pountney. He is about everywhere.'

'Do not let him be asked into any house of mine again. But that is a trifle.'

'Anything about Major Pountney must, I should think, be a trifle. Have tidings come that the heavens are going to fall? Nothing short of that could make you so solemn.'

'In the first place, Glencora, let me ask you not to speak to me again about the seat for Silverbridge. I am not at present prepared to argue the matter with you, but I have resolved that I will know nothing about the election. As soon as the seat is vacant, if it should be vacated, I shall take care that my determination be known in Silverbridge.'

'Why should you abandon your privileges in that way? It is sheer weakness.'

'The interference of any peer is unconstitutional.'

'There is Braxon,' said the Duchess energetically, 'where the Marquis of Crumber returns the member regularly, in spite of all their Reform bills; and Bamford, and Cobblersborough;—and look at Lord Lumley with a whole county in his pocket, not to speak of two boroughs! What nonsense, Plantagenet! Anything is constitutional, or anything is unconstitutional, just as you choose to look at it.' It was clear that the Duchess had really studied the subject carefully.

'Very well, my dear, let it be nonsense. I only beg to assure you that it is my intention, and I request you to act accordingly. And there is another thing I have to say to you. I shall be sorry to interfere in any way with the pleasure which you may derive from society, but as long as I am burdened with the office which has been imposed upon me, I will not again entertain any guests in my own house.'

'Plantagenet!'

'You cannot turn the people out who are here now; but I beg that they may be allowed to go as the time comes, and that their places may not be filled by further invitations.'

'But further invitations have gone out ever so long ago, and have been accepted. You must be ill, my dear.'

'Ill at ease,—yes. At any rate let none others be sent out.' Then he remembered a kindly purpose which he had formed early in the day, and fell back upon that. 'I should, however, be glad if you would ask Lady

Rosina De Courcy to remain here.' The Duchess stared at him, really thinking now that something was amiss with him. 'The whole thing is a failure and I will have no more of it. It is degrading me.' Then without allowing her a moment in which to answer him, he marched back to his own room.

But even here his spirit was not as yet at rest. That Major must not go unpunished. Though he hated all fuss and noise he must do something. So he wrote as follows to the Major:—

'The Duke of Omnium trusts that Major Pountney will not find it inconvenient to leave Gatherum Castle shortly. Should Major Pountney wish to remain at the Castle over the night, the Duke of Omnium hopes that he will not object to be served with his dinner and with his breakfast in his own room. A carriage and horses will be ready for Major Pountney's use, to take him to Silverbridge, as soon as Major Pountney may express to the servants his wish to that effect.

'*Gatherum Castle,——December, 18—.'*

This note the Duke sent by the hands of his own servant, having said enough to the man as to the carriage and the possible dinner in the Major's bedroom, to make the man understand almost exactly what had occurred. A note from the Major was brought to the Duke while he was dressing. The Duke having glanced at the note threw it into the fire; and the Major that evening ate his dinner at the Palliser Arms Inn at Silverbridge.

CHAPTER 28

THE DUCHESS IS MUCH TROUBLED

It is hardly possible that one man should turn another out of his house without many people knowing it; and when the one person is a Prime Minister and the other such a Major as Major Pountney, the affair is apt to be talked about very widely. The Duke of course never opened his mouth on the subject, except in answer to questions from the Duchess; but all the servants knew it. 'Pritchard tells me that you have sent that wretched man out of the house with a flea in his ear,' said the Duchess.

'I sent him out of the house, certainly.'

'He was hardly worth your anger.'

'He is not at all worth my anger;—but I could not sit down to dinner with a man who had insulted me.'

'What did he say, Plantagenet? I know it was something about Silverbridge.' To this question the Duke gave no answer, but in respect to Silverbridge he was stern as adamant. Two days after the departure of the Major it was known in Silverbridge generally that in the event of there being an election the Duke's agent would not as usual suggest a nominee. There was a paragraph on the subject in the County paper, and another in the London 'Evening Pulpit.' The Duke of Omnium,— that he might show his respect to the law, not only as to the letter of the law, but as to the spirit also,—had made it known to his tenantry in and round Silverbridge generally that he would in no way influence their choice of candidate in the event of an election. But these newspapers did not say a word about Major Pountney.

The clubs of course knew all about it, and no man at any club ever knew more than Captain Gunner. Soon after Christmas he met his friend the Major on the steps of the new military club, The Active Service,* which was declared by many men in the army to have left all the other military clubs 'absolutely nowhere.' 'Halloa, Punt!' he said, 'you seem to have made a mess of it at last down at the Duchess's.'

'I wonder what you know about it.'

'You had to come away pretty quick, I take it.'

'Of course I came away pretty quick.' So much as that the Major was aware must be known. There were details which he could deny safely, as it would be impossible that they should be supported by evidence, but there were matters which must be admitted. 'I'll bet a fiver that beyond that you know nothing about it.'

'The Duke ordered you off, I take it.'

'After a fashion he did. There are circumstances in which a man cannot help himself.' This was diplomatical, because it left the Captain to suppose that the Duke was the man who could not help himself.

'Of course I was not there,' said Gunner, 'and I can't absolutely know, but I suppose you had been interfering with the Duchess about Silverbridge. Glencora will bear a great deal,—but since she has taken up politics, by George, you had better not touch her there.' At last it came to be believed that the Major had been turned out by the order of the Duchess, because he had ventured to put himself forward as an opponent to Ferdinand Lopez, and the Major felt himself really grateful to his friend the Captain for this arrangement of the story. And there came at last to be mixed up with the story some half-understood innuendo that the Major's jealousy against Lopez had been of a double nature,—in reference both to the Duchess and the borough,—so that he escaped from much of that disgrace which naturally attaches itself to a man who has been kicked out of another man's house. There was a mystery;—and when there is a mystery a man should never be condemned. Where there is a woman in the case a man cannot be expected to tell the truth. As for calling out or in any way punishing the Prime Minister, that of course was out of the question. And so it went on till at last the Major was almost proud of what he had done, and talked about it willingly with mysterious hints, in which practice made him perfect.

But with the Duchess the affair was very serious, so much so that she was driven to call in advice,—not only from her constant friend, Mrs Finn, but afterwards from Barrington Erle, from Phineas Finn, and lastly even from the Duke of St Bungay, to whom she was hardly willing to subject herself, the Duke being the special friend of her husband. But the matter became so important to her that she was unable to trifle with it. At Gatherum the expulsion of Major Pountney soon became a forgotten affair. When the Duchess learned the truth she quite approved of the expulsion, only hinting to Barrington Erle that the act of kicking out should have been more absolutely practical. And the loss of Silverbridge, though it hurt her sorely, could be endured. She must write to her friend Ferdinand Lopez, when the time should come, excusing herself as best she might, and must lose the exquisite delight of making a Member of Parliament out of her own hand. The newspapers, however, had taken that matter up in the proper spirit, and political capital might to some extent be made of it. The loss of Silverbridge, though it bruised, broke no bones. But the Duke had again expressed himself with unusual sternness respecting her ducal hospitalities, and had reiterated the declaration of his intention to live out the remainder of his period of office in republican simplicity. 'We have tried it and it has failed, and let there be an end of it,' he said to her. Simple and direct disobedience to such an order was as little in her way as simple or direct obedience. She knew her husband well, and knew how he could be managed and how he could not be managed. When he declared that there should be an 'end of it,'—meaning an end of the very system by which she hoped to perpetuate his power,—she did not dare to argue with him. And yet he was so wrong! The trial had been no failure. The thing had been done and well done, and had succeeded. Was failure to be presumed because one impertinent puppy had found his way into the house? And then to abandon the system at once, whether it had failed or whether it had succeeded, would be to call the attention of all the world to an acknowledged failure,—to a failure so disreputable that its acknowledgement must lead to the loss of everything! It was known now,—so argued the Duchess to herself,—that she had devoted herself to the work of cementing and consolidating the Coalition by the graceful hospitality which the wealth of herself and her husband enabled her to dispense. She had made herself a Prime Ministress by the manner in which she opened her saloons, her banqueting halls, and her gardens. It had never been done before, and now it had been well done. There had been no failure. And yet everything was to be broken down because his nerves had received a shock!

'Let it die out,' Mrs Finn had said. 'The people will come here and will go away, and then, when you are up in London, you will soon fall into your old ways.' But this did not suit the new ambition of the Duchess. She had so fed her mind with daring hopes that she could not bear that 'it should die out.' She had arranged a course of things in her own mind by which she should come to be known as the great Prime Minister's wife; and she had, perhaps unconsciously, applied the epithet more to herself than to her husband. She, too, wished to be written of in memoirs, and to make a niche for herself in history. And now she was told that she was to let it 'die out!'

'I suppose he is a little bilious,' Barrington Erle had said. 'Don't you think he'll forget all about it when he gets up to London?' The Duchess was sure that her husband would not forget anything. He never did forget anything. 'I want him to be told,' said the Duchess, 'that everybody thinks that he is doing very well. I don't mean about politics exactly, but as to keeping the party together. Don't you think that we have succeeded?' Barrington Erle thought upon the whole they had succeeded; but suggested at the same time that there were seeds of weakness. 'Sir Orlando and Sir Timothy Beeswax are not sound, you know,' said Barrington Erle. 'He can't make them sounder by shutting himself up like a hermit,' said the Duchess. Barrington Erle, who had peculiar privileges of his own, promised that if he could by any means make an occasion, he would let the Duke know that their side of the Coalition was more than contented with the way in which he did his work.

'You don't think we've made a mess of it?' she said to Phineas, asking him a question. 'I don't think that the Duke has made a mess of it,—or you,' said Phineas, who had come to love the Duchess because his wife loved her. 'But it won't go on for ever, Duchess.' 'You know what I've done,' said the Duchess, who took it for granted that Mr Finn knew all that his wife knew. 'Has it answered?' Phineas was silent for a moment. 'Of course you will tell me the truth. You won't be so bad as to flatter me now that I am so much in earnest.' 'I almost think,' said Phineas, 'that the time has gone by for what one may call drawing-room influences. They used to be very great. Old Lord Brock used them extensively, though by no means as your Grace has done. But the spirit of the world has changed since then.' 'The spirit of the world never changes,' said the Duchess, in her soreness.

But her strongest dependence was on the old Duke. The party at the Castle was almost broken up when she consulted him. She had been so far true to her husband as not to ask another guest to the house since his command;—but they who had been asked before came and went as had been arranged. Then, when the place was nearly empty, and when Locock and Millepois and Pritchard were wondering among themselves at this general collapse, she asked her husband's leave to invite their old friend again for a day or two. 'I do so want to see him, and I think he'll come,' said the Duchess. The Duke gave his permission with a ready smile,—not because the proposed visitor was his own confidential friend, but because it suited his spirit to grant such a request as to anyone after the order that he had given. Had she named Major Pountney, I think he would have smiled and acceded.

The Duke came, and to him she poured out her whole soul. 'It has been for him and for his honour that I have done it;—that men and women might know how really gracious he is, and how good. Of course, there has been money spent, but he can afford it without hurting the children. It has been so necessary that with a Coalition people should know each other! There was some little absurd row here. A man who was a mere nobody, one of the travelling butterfly men that fill up spaces and talk to girls, got hold of him and was impertinent. He is so thin-skinned that he could not shake the creature into the dust as you would have done. It annoyed him,—that, and, I think, seeing so many strange faces,—so that he came to me and declared, that as long as he remained in office he would not have another person in the house, either here or in London. He meant it literally, and he meant me to understand it literally. I had to get special leave before I could ask so dear an old friend as your Grace.'

'I don't think he would object to me,' said the Duke, laughing.

'Of course not. He was only too glad to think you would come. But he took the request as being quite the proper thing. It will kill me if this is to be carried out. After all that I have done, I could show myself nowhere. And it will be so injurious to him! Could you not tell him, Duke? No one else in the world can tell him but you. Nothing unfair has been attempted. No job has been done. I have endeavoured to make his house pleasant to people, in order that they might look upon him with grace and favour. Is that wrong? Is that unbecoming a wife?'

The old Duke patted her on the head as though she were a little girl, and was more comforting to her than her other counsellors. He would say nothing to her husband now;—but they must both be up in London at the meeting of Parliament, and then he would tell his friend that, in his opinion, no sudden change should be made. 'This husband of yours is a very peculiar man,' he said, smiling. 'His honesty is not like the honesty of other men. It is more downright;—more absolutely honest; less capable of bearing even the shadow which the stain from another's dishonesty might throw upon it. Give him credit for all that, and remember that you cannot find everything combined in the same person. He is very practical in some things, but the question is, whether he is not too scrupulous to be practical in all things.' At the close of the interview the Duchess kissed him and promised to be guided by him. The occurrences of the last few weeks had softened the Duchess much.

CHAPTER 29

THE TWO CANDIDATES FOR SILVERBRIDGE

On his arrival in London Ferdinand Lopez found a letter waiting for him from the Duchess. This came into his hand immediately on his reaching the rooms in Belgrave Mansions, and was of course the first object of his care. 'That contains my fate,' he said to his wife, putting his hand down upon the letter. He had talked to her much of the chance that had come in his way, and had shown himself to be very ambitious of the honour offered to him. She of course had sympathized with him, and was willing to think all good things both of the Duchess and of the Duke, if they would between them put her husband into Parliament. He paused a moment, still holding the letter under his hand. 'You would hardly think that I should be such a coward that I don't like to open it,' he said.

'You've got to do it.'

'Unless I make you do it for me,' he said, holding out the letter to her. 'You will have to learn how weak I am. When I am really anxious I become like a child.'

'I do not think you are ever weak,' she said, caressing him. 'If there were a thing to be done you would do it at once. But I'll open it if you like.'

Then he tore off the envelope with an air of comic importance and stood for a few minutes while he read it.

'What I first perceive is that there has been a row about it,' he said.

'A row about it! What sort of a row?'

'My dear friend the Duchess has not quite hit it off with my less dear friend the Duke.'

'She does not say so?'

'Oh dear no! My friend the Duchess is much too discreet for that;—but I can see that it has been so.'

'Are you to be the new member? If that is arranged I don't care a bit about the Duke and Duchess.'

'These things do not settle themselves quite so easily as that. I am not to have the seat at any rate without fighting for it. There's the letter.'

The Duchess's letter to her new adherent shall be given, but it must first be understood that many different ideas had passed through the writer's mind between the writing of the letter and the order given by the Prime Minister to his wife concerning the borough. She of course became aware at once that Mr Lopez must be informed that she could not do for him what she had suggested that she would do. But there was no necessity of writing at the instant. Mr Grey had not yet vacated the seat, and Mr Lopez was away on his travels. The month of January was passed in comparative quiet at the Castle, and during that time it became known at Silverbridge that the election would be open. The Duke would not even make a suggestion, and would neither express, nor feel, resentment should a member be returned altogether hostile to his Ministry. By degrees the Duchess accustomed herself to this condition of affairs, and as the consternation caused by her husband's very imperious conduct wore off, she began to ask herself whether even yet she need quite give up the game. She could not make a Member of Parliament altogether out of her own hand, as she had once fondly hoped she might do; but still she might do something. She would in nothing disobey her husband, but if Mr Lopez were to stand for Silverbridge, it could not but be known in the borough that Mr Lopez was her friend. Therefore she wrote the following letter:—

'*Gatherum,* ——*January, 18*—.

'MY DEAR MR LOPEZ,

'I remember that you said that you would be home at this time, and therefore I write to you about the borough. Things are changed since you went away, and, I fear, not changed for your advantage.

'We understand that Mr Grey will apply for the Chiltern Hundreds at the end of March, and that the election will take place in April. No candidate will appear as favoured from hence. We used to run a favourite, and our favourite would sometimes win,—would sometimes even have a walk over; but those good times are gone. All the good times are going, I think. There is no reason that I know why you should not stand as well as any one else. You can be early in the field;—because it is only now known that there will be no Gatherum interest. And I fancy it had already leaked out that you would have been the favourite if there had been a favourite;—which might be beneficial.

'I need hardly say that I do not wish my name to be mentioned in the matter.

'Sincerely yours,
'GLENCORA OMNIUM.

'Sprugeon, the ironmonger, would, I do not doubt, be proud to nominate you.'

'I don't understand much about it,' said Emily.

'I dare say not. It is not meant that any novice should understand much about it. Of course you will not mention her Grace's letter.'

'Certainly not.'

'She intends to do the very best she can for me. I have no doubt that some understrapper from the Castle has had some communication with Mr Sprugeon. The fact is that the Duke won't be seen in it, but that the Duchess does not mean that the borough shall quite slip through their fingers.'

'Shall you try it?'

'If I do I must send an agent down to see Mr Sprugeon on the sly, and the sooner I do so the better. I wonder what your father will say about it?'

'He is an old Conservative.'

'But would he not like his son-in-law to be in Parliament?'

'I don't know that he would care about it very much. He seems always to laugh at people who want to get into Parliament. But if you have set your heart upon it, Ferdinand——'

'I have not set my heart on spending a great deal of money. When I first thought of Silverbridge the expense would have been almost nothing. It would have been a walk over, as the Duchess calls it. But now there will certainly be a contest.'

'Give it up if you cannot afford it.'

'Nothing venture nothing have. You don't think your father would help me in doing it? It would add almost as much to your position as to mine.' Emily shook her head. She had always heard her father ridicule the folly of men who spent more than they could afford in the vanity of writing two letters after their name, and she now explained that it had always been so with him. 'You would not mind asking him,' he said.

'I will ask him if you wish it, certainly.' Ever since their marriage he had been teaching her,—intentionally teaching her,—that it would be the duty of both of them to get all they could from her father. She had learned the lesson, but it had been very distasteful to her. It had not induced her to think ill of her husband. She was too much engrossed with him, too much in love with him for that. But she was beginning to feel that the world in general was hard and greedy and uncomfortable. If it was proper that a father should give his daughter money when she was married, why did not her father do so without waiting to be asked? And yet, if he were unwilling to do so, would it not be better to leave him to his pleasure in the matter? But now she began to perceive that her father was to be regarded as a milch cow, and that she was to be the dairymaid. Her husband at times would become terribly anxious on the subject. On receiving the promise of £3000 he had been elated, but since that he had continually talked of what more her father ought to do for them.

'Perhaps I had better take the bull by the horns,' he said, 'and do it myself. Then I shall find out whether he really has our interest at heart, or whether he looks on you as a stranger because you've gone away from him.'

'I don't think he will look upon me as a stranger.'

'We'll see,' said Lopez.

It was not long before he made the experiment. He had called himself a coward as to the opening of the Duchess's letter, but he had in truth always courage for perils of this nature. On the day of their arrival they dined with Mr Wharton in Manchester Square, and certainly the old man had received his daughter with great delight. He had been courteous also to Lopez, and Emily, amidst the pleasure of his welcome, had forgotten some of her troubles. The three were alone together, and when Emily had asked after her brother, Mr Wharton had laughed and said that Everett was an ass. 'You have not quarrelled with him?' she said. He ridiculed the idea of any quarrel, but again said that Everett was an ass.

After dinner Mr Wharton and Lopez were left together, as the old man, whether alone or in company, always sat for an hour sipping port wine after the manner of his forefathers. Lopez had already determined that he would not let the opportunity escape him, and began his attack at once. 'I have been invited, sir,' he said with his sweetest smile, 'to stand for Silverbridge.'

'You too!' said Mr Wharton. But, though there was a certain amount of satire in the exclamation, it had been good-humoured satire.

'Yes, sir. We all get bit sooner or later, I suppose.'

'I never was bit.'

'Your sagacity and philosophy have been the wonder of the world, sir. There can be no doubt that in my profession a seat in the House would be of the greatest possible advantage to me. It enables a man to do a great many things which he could not touch without it.'

'It may be so. I don't know anything about it.'

'And then it is a great honour.'

'That depends on how you get it, and how you use it;—very much also on whether you are fit for it.'

'I shall get it honestly if I do get it. I hope I may use it well. And as for my fitness, I must leave that to be ascertained when I am there. I am sorry to say there will probably be a contest.'

'I suppose so. A seat in Parliament without a contest does not drop into every young man's mouth.'

'It very nearly dropped into mine.' Then he told his father-in-law almost all the particulars of the offer which had been made him, and of the manner in which the seat was now suggested to him. He somewhat hesitated in the use of the name of the Duchess, leaving an impression on Mr Wharton that the offer had in truth come from the Duke. 'Should there be a contest, would you help me?'

'In what way? I could not canvass at Silverbridge, if you mean that.'

'I was not thinking of giving you personal trouble.'

'I don't know a soul in the place. I shouldn't know that there was such a place except that it returns a member of Parliament.'

'I meant with money, sir.'

'To pay the election bills!* No; certainly not. Why should I?'

'For Emily's sake.'

'I don't think it would do Emily any good, or you either. It would certainly do me none. It is a kind of luxury that a man should not attempt unless he can afford it easily.'

'A luxury!'

'Yes, a luxury; just as much as a four-in-hand coach, or a yacht. Men go into Parliament because it gives them fashion, position, and power.'

'I should go to serve my country.'

'Success in your profession I thought you said was your object. Of course you must do as you please. If you ask me for advice, I advise you not to try it. But certainly I will not help you with money. That ass Everett is quarrelling with me at this moment because I won't give him money to go and stand somewhere.'

'Not at Silverbridge!'

'I'm sure I can't say. But don't let me do him an injury. To give him his due, he is more reasonable than you, and only wants a promise from me that I will pay his electioneering bills for him at the next general election. I have refused him,—though for reasons which I need not mention I think him better fitted for Parliament than you. I must certainly also refuse you. I cannot imagine any circumstances which would induce me to pay a shilling towards getting you into Parliament. If you won't drink any more wine, we'll join Emily upstairs.'

This had been very plain speaking, and by no means comfortable to Lopez. What of personal discourtesy there had been in the lawyer's words,—and they had not certainly been flattering,—he could throw off from him as meaning nothing. As he could not afford to quarrel with his father-in-law, he thought it probable that he might have to bear a good deal of incivility from the old man. He was quite prepared to bear it as long as he could see a chance of a reward;—though, should there be no such chance, he would be ready to avenge it. But there had been a decision in the present refusal which made him quite sure that it would be vain to repeat his request. 'I shall find out, sir,' he said, 'whether it may probably be a costly affair, and if so I shall give it up. You are rather hard upon me as to my motives.'

'I only repeated what you told me yourself.'

'I am quite sure of my own intentions, and know that I need not be ashamed of them.'

'Not if you have plenty of money. It all depends on that. If you have plenty of money, and your fancy goes that way, it is all very well. Come, we'll go upstairs.'

The next day he saw Everett Wharton, who welcomed him back with warm affection. 'He'll do nothing for me;—nothing at all. I am almost beginning to doubt whether he'll ever speak to me again.'

'Nonsense!'

'I tell you everything, you know,' said Everett. 'In January I lost a little money at whist. They got plunging at the club, and I was in it. I had to tell him, of course. He keeps me so short that I can't stand any blow without going to him like a school-boy.'

'Was it much?'

'No;—to him no more than half-a-crown to you. I had to ask him for a hundred and fifty.'

'He refused it!'

'No;—he didn't do that. Had it been ten times as much, if I owed the money, he would pay it. But he blew me up, and talked about gambling,—and—and——'

'I should have taken that as a matter of course.'

'But I'm not a gambler. A man now and then may fall into a thing of that kind, and if he's decently well off and don't do it often, he can bear it.'

'I thought your quarrel had been altogether about Parliament.'

'Oh no! He has been always the same about that. He told me that I was going head foremost to the dogs, and I couldn't stand that. I shouldn't be surprised if he hasn't lost more at cards than I have during the last two years.' Lopez made an offer to act as go-between, to effect a reconciliation; but Everett declined the offer. 'It would be making too much of an absurdity,' he said. 'When he wants to see me, I suppose he'll send for me.'

Lopez did dispatch an agent down to Mr Sprugeon at Silverbridge, and the agent found that Mr Sprugeon was a very discreet man. Mr Sprugeon at first knew little or nothing,—seemed hardly to be aware that there was a member of Parliament for Silverbridge, and declared himself to be indifferent as to the parliamentary character of the borough. But at last he melted a little, and by degrees, over a glass of hot brandy and water with the agent at the Palliser Arms, confessed to a shade of an opinion that the return of Mr Lopez for the borough would not be disagreeable to some person or persons who did not live quite a hundred miles away. The instructions given by Lopez to his agent were of the most cautious kind. The agent was merely to feel the ground, make a few inquiries, and do nothing. His client did not intend to stand unless he could see the way to almost certain success with very little outlay. But the agent, perhaps liking the job, did a little outstep his employer's orders. Mr Sprugeon, when the frost of his first modesty had been thawed, introduced the agent to Mr Sprout, the maker of cork soles, and Mr Sprugeon and Mr Sprout between them had soon decided that Mr Ferdinand Lopez should be run for the borough as the 'Castle' candidate. 'The Duke won't interfere,' said Sprugeon; 'and, of course, the Duke's man of business can't do anything openly;—but the Duke's people will know.' Then Mr Sprout told the agent that there was already another candidate in the field, and in a whisper communicated the gentleman's name. When the agent got back to

London, he gave Lopez to understand that he must certainly put himself forward. The borough expected him. Sprugeon and Sprout considered themselves pledged to bring him forward and support him,—on behalf of the Castle. Sprugeon was quite sure that the Castle influence was predominant. The Duke's name had never been mentioned at Silverbridge,—hardly even that of the Duchess. Since the Duke's declaration 'The Castle' had taken the part which the old Duke used to play. The agent was quite sure that no one could get in for Silverbridge without having the Castle on his side. No doubt the Duke's declaration had had the ill effect of bringing up a competitor, and thus of causing expense. That could not now be helped. The agent was of opinion that the Duke had had no alternative. The agent hinted that times were changing, and that though dukes were still dukes, and could still exercise ducal influences, they were driven by these changes to act in an altered form. The proclamation had been especially necessary because the Duke was Prime Minister. The agent did not think that Mr Lopez should be in the least angry with the Duke. Everything would be done that the Castle could do, and Lopez would be no doubt returned,—though, unfortunately, not without some expense. How much would it cost? Any accurate answer to such a question would be impossible, but probably about £600. It might be £800;—could not possibly be above £1000.* Lopez winced as he heard these sums named, but he did not decline the contest.

Then the name of the opposition candidate was whispered to Lopez. It was Arthur Fletcher! Lopez started, and asked some questions as to Mr Fletcher's interest in the neighbourhood. The Fletchers were connected with the De Courcys, and as soon as the declaration of the Duke had been made known, the De Courcy interest had aroused itself, and had invited that rising young barrister, Arthur Fletcher, to stand for the borough on strictly conservative views. Arthur Fletcher had acceded, and a printed declaration of his purpose and political principles had been just published. 'I have beaten him once,' said Lopez to himself, 'and I think I can beat him again.'

CHAPTER 30

'YES;—A LIE!'

'So you went to Happerton after all,' said Lopez to his ally, Mr Sextus Parker. 'You couldn't believe me when I told you the money was all right! What a cur you are!'

'That's right;—abuse me.'

'Well, it was horrid. Didn't I tell you that it must necessarily injure me with the house? How are two fellows to get on together unless they can put some trust in each other? Even if I did run you into a difficulty, do you really think I'm ruffian enough to tell you that the money was there if it were untrue?'

Sexty looked like a cur and felt like a cur, as he was being thus abused. He was not angry with his friend for calling him bad names, but only anxious to excuse himself. 'I was out of sorts,' he said, 'and so d——d hippish. I didn't know what I was about.'

'Brandy and soda!' suggested Lopez.

'Perhaps a little of that;—though, by Jove, it isn't often I do that kind of thing. I don't know a fellow who works harder for his wife and children than I do. But when one sees such things all round one,—a fellow utterly smashed here who had a string of hunters yesterday, and another fellow buying a house in Piccadilly and pulling it down because it isn't big enough, who was contented with a little box at Hornsey last summer, one doesn't quite know how to keep one's legs.'

'If you want to learn a lesson look at the two men, and see where the difference lies. The one has had some heart about him, and the other has been a coward.'

Parker scratched his head, balanced himself on the hind legs of his stool, and tacitly acknowledged the truth of all that his enterprising friend said to him. 'Has old Wharton come down well?' at last he asked.

'I have never said a word to old Wharton about money,' Lopez replied,—'except as to the cost of this election I was telling you of.'

'And he wouldn't do anything in that?'

'He doesn't approve of the thing itself. I don't doubt but that the old gentleman and I shall understand each other before long.'

'You've got the length of his foot.'

'But I don't mean to drive him. I can get along without that. He's an old man, and he can't take his money along with him when he goes the great journey.'

'There's a brother, Lopez,—isn't there?'

'Yes,—there's a brother; but Wharton has enough for two; and if he were to put either out of his will it wouldn't be my wife. Old men don't like parting with their money, and he's like other old men. If it were not so I shouldn't bother myself coming into the city at all.'

'Has he enough for that, Lopez?'

'I suppose he's worth a quarter of a million.'

'By Jove! And where did he get it?'

'Perseverance, sir. Put by a shilling a day, and let it have its natural increase, and see what it will come to at the end of fifty years. I suppose old Wharton has been putting by two or three thousand out of his professional income, at any rate for the last thirty years, and never for a moment forgetting its natural increase. That's one way to make a fortune.'

'It ain't rapid enough for you and me, Lopez.'

'No. That was the old-fashioned way, and the most sure. But, as you say, it is not rapid enough; and it robs a man of the power of enjoying his money when he has made it. But it's a very good thing to be closely connected with a man who has already done that kind of thing. There's no doubt about the money when it is there. It does not take to itself wings and fly away.'

'But the man who has it sticks to it uncommon hard.'

'Of course he does;—but he can't take it away with him.'

'He can leave it to hospitals, Lopez. That's the devil!'

'Sexty, my boy, I see you have taken an outlook into human life which does you credit. Yes, he can leave it to hospitals. But why does he leave it to hospitals?'

'Something of being afraid about his soul, I suppose.'

'No; I don't believe in that. Such a man as this, who has been hard-fisted all his life, and who has had his eyes thoroughly open, who has made his own money in the sharp intercourse of man to man, and who keeps it to the last gasp,—he doesn't believe that he'll do his soul any good by giving it to hospitals when he can't keep it himself any longer. His mind has freed itself from those cobwebs long since. He gives his money to hospitals because the last pleasure of which he is capable is that of spiting his relations. And it is a great pleasure to an old man, when his relations have been disgusted with him for being old and loving his money. I rather think I should do it myself.'

'I'd give myself a chance of going to heaven, I think,' said Parker.

'Don't you know that men will rob and cheat on their death-beds, and say their prayers all the time? Old Wharton won't leave his money to hospitals if he's well handled by those about him.'

'And you'll handle him well;—eh, Lopez?'

'I won't quarrel with him, or tell him that he's a curmudgeon because he doesn't do all that I want him. He's over seventy, and he can't carry his money with him.'

All this left so vivid an impression of the wisdom of his friend on the mind of Sextus Parker, that in spite of the harrowing fears by which he had been tormented on more than one occasion already, he allowed himself to be persuaded into certain fiscal arrangements, by which Lopez would find himself put at ease with reference to money at any rate for the next four months. He had at once told himself that this election would cost him £1000. When various sums were mentioned in reference to such an affair, safety alone could be found in taking the outside sum;—perhaps might generally be more surely found by adding fifty per cent to that. He knew that he was wrong about the election, but he assured himself that he had had no alternative. The misfortune had been that the Duke should have made his proclamation about the borough immediately after the offer made by the Duchess. He had been almost forced to send the agent down to inquire;—and the agent, when making his inquiries, had compromised him. He must go on with it now. Perhaps some idea of the pleasantness of increased intimacy with the Duchess of Omnium encouraged him in this way of thinking. The Duchess was up in town in February, and Lopez left a card in Carlton Terrace. On the very next day the card of the Duchess was left for Mrs Lopez at the Belgrave Mansions.

Lopez went into the city every day, leaving home at about eleven o'clock, and not returning much before dinner. The young wife at first found that she hardly knew what to do with her time. Her aunt, Mrs Roby, was distasteful to her. She had already learned from her husband that he had but little respect for Mrs Roby. 'You remember the sapphire brooch,' he had said once. 'That was part of the price I had to pay for being allowed to approach you.' He was sitting at the time with his arm round her waist, looking out on beautiful scenery and talking of his old difficulties. She could not find it in her heart to be angry with him, but the idea brought to her mind was disagreeable to her. And she was thoroughly angry with Mrs Roby. Of course in these days Mrs Roby came to see her, and of course when she was up in Manchester Square, she went to the house round the corner,—but there was no close intimacy between the aunt and the niece. And many of her father's friends,—whom she regarded as the Herefordshire set,—were very cold to her. She had not made herself a glory to Herefordshire, and,—as all these people said,—had broken the heart of the best Herefordshire young man of the day. This made a great falling-off in her acquaintance, which was the more felt as she had never been, as a girl, devoted to a large circle of dearest female friends. She whom she had loved best had been Mary Wharton, and Mary Wharton had refused to be her bridesmaid almost without an expression of regret. She saw her father occasionally. Once he came and dined with them at their rooms, on which occasion Lopez struggled hard to make up a well-sounding party. There were Roby from the Admiralty, and the Happertons, and Sir Timothy Beeswax, with whom Lopez had become acquainted at Gatherum, and old Lord Mongrober. But the barrister, who had dined out a good deal in his time, perceived the effort. Who, that ever with difficulty scraped his dinner guests together, was able afterwards to obliterate the signs of the struggle? It was, however, a first attempt, and Lopez, whose courage was good, thought that he might do better before long. If he could get into the House and make his mark there people then would dine with him fast enough. But while this was going on Emily's life was rather dull. He had provided her with a brougham, and everything around her was even luxurious, but there came upon her gradually a feeling that by her marriage she had divided herself from her own people. She did not for a moment allow this feeling to interfere with her loyalty to him. Had she not known that this division would surely take place? Had she not married him because she loved him better than her own people? So she sat herself down to read Dante,—for they had studied Italian together during their honeymoon, and she had found that he knew the language well. And she was busy with her needle. And she already began to anticipate the happiness which would come to her when a child of his should be lying in her arms.

She was of course much interested about the election. Nothing could as yet be done, because as yet there was no vacancy; but still the subject was discussed daily between them. 'Who do you think is going to stand against me?' he said one day with a smile. 'A very old friend of yours.' She knew at once who the man was, and the blood came to her face. 'I think he might as well have left it alone, you know,' he said.

'Did he know?' she asked in a whisper.

'Know;—of course he knew. He is doing it on purpose. But I beat him once, old girl, didn't I? And I'll beat him again.' She liked him to call her old girl. She loved the perfect intimacy with which he treated her. But there was something which grated against her feelings in this allusion by him to the other man who had loved her. Of course she had told him the whole story. She had conceived it to be her duty to do so. But then the thing should have been over. It was necessary, perhaps, that he should tell her who was his opponent. It was impossible that she should not know when the fight came. But she did not like to hear him boast that he had beaten Arthur Fletcher once, and that he would beat him again. By doing so he likened the sweet fragrance of her love to the dirty turmoil of an electioneering contest.

He did not understand,—how should he?—that though she had never loved Arthur Fletcher, had never been able to bring herself to love him when all her friends had wished it, her feelings to him were nevertheless those of affectionate friendship;—that she regarded him as being perfect in his way, a thorough gentleman, a man who would not for worlds tell a lie, as most generous among the generous, most noble among the noble. When the other Whartons had thrown her off, he had not been cold to her. That very day, as soon as her husband had left her, she looked again at that little note. 'I am as I always have been!' And she remembered that farewell down by the banks of the Wye. 'You will always have one,—one besides him,—who will love you best in the world.' They were dangerous words for her to remember; but in recalling them to her memory she had often assured herself that they should not be dangerous to her. She was too sure of her own heart to be afraid of danger. She had loved the one man and had not loved the other;—but yet, now, when her husband talked of beating this man again, she could not but remember the words.

She did not think,—or rather had not thought,—that Arthur Fletcher would willingly stand against her husband. It had occurred to her at once that he must first have become a candidate without knowing who would be his opponent. But Ferdinand had assured her as a matter of fact that Fletcher had known all about it. 'I suppose in politics men are different,' she said to herself. Her husband had evidently supposed that Arthur Fletcher had proposed himself as a candidate for Silverbridge, with the express object of doing an injury to the man who had carried off his love. And she repeated to herself her husband's words, 'He is doing it on purpose.' She did not like to differ from her husband, but she could hardly bring herself to believe that revenge of this kind should have recommended itself to Arthur Fletcher.

Some little time after this, when she had been settled in London about a month, a letter was brought her, and she at once recognized Arthur Fletcher's writing. She was alone at the time, and it occurred to her at first that perhaps she ought not to open any communication from him without showing it to her husband. But then it seemed that such a hesitation would imply a doubt of the man, and almost a doubt of herself. Why should she fear what any man might write to her? So she opened the letter, and read it,—with infinite pleasure. It was as follows:—

'MY DEAR MRS LOPEZ,

'I think it best to make an explanation to you as to a certain coincidence which might possibly be misunderstood unless explained.

I find that your husband and I are to be opponents at Silverbridge. I wish to say that I had pledged myself to the borough before I had heard his name as connected with it. I have very old associations with the neighbourhood, and was invited to stand by friends who had known me all my life as soon as it was understood that there would be an open contest. I cannot retire now without breaking faith with my party, nor do I know that there is any reason why I should do so. I should not, however, have come forward had I known that Mr Lopez was to stand. I think you had better tell him so, and tell him also, with my compliments, that I hope we may fight our political battle with mutual good-fellowship and good-feeling.

'Yours very sincerely,
'ARTHUR FLETCHER.'

Emily was very much pleased by this letter, and yet she wept over it. She felt that she understood accurately all the motives that were at work within the man's breast when he was writing it. As to its truth,—of course the letter was gospel to her. Oh,—if the man could become her husband's friend how sweet it would be! Of course she wished, thoroughly wished, that her husband should succeed at Silverbridge. But she could understand that such a contest as this might be carried on without personal animosity. The letter was so like Arthur Fletcher,—so good, so noble, so generous, so true! The moment her husband came in she showed it to him with delight. 'I was sure,' she said as he was reading the letter, 'that he had not known you were to stand.'

'He knew it as well as I did,' he replied, and as he spoke there came a dark scowl across his brow. 'His writing to you is a piece of infernal impudence.'

'Oh, Ferdinand!'

'You don't understand, but I do. He deserves to be horsewhipped for daring to write to you, and if I can come across him he shall have it.'

'Oh,—for heaven's sake!'

'A man who was your rejected lover,—who has been trying to marry you for the last two years, presuming to commence a correspondence with you without your husband's sanction!'

'He meant you to see it. He says I am to tell you.'

'Psha! That is simple cowardice. He meant you not to tell me; and then when you had answered him without telling me, he would have had the whip-hand of you.'

'Oh, Ferdinand, what evil thoughts you have!'

'You are a child, my dear, and must allow me to dictate to you what you ought to think in such a matter as this. I tell you he knew all about my candidature, and that what he has said here to the contrary is a mere lie,—yes, a lie.' He repeated the word because he saw that she shrank at hearing it; but he did not understand why she shrank,—that the idea of such an accusation against Arthur Fletcher was intolerable to her. 'I have never heard of such a thing,' he continued. 'Do you suppose it is common for men who have been thrown over to write to the ladies who have rejected them immediately after their marriage?'

'Do not the circumstances justify it?'

'No;—they make it infinitely worse. He should have felt himself to be debarred from writing to you, both as being my wife and as being the wife of the man whom he intends to oppose at Silverbridge.'

This he said with so much anger that he frightened her. 'It is not my fault,' she said.

'No; it is not your fault. But you should regard it as a great fault committed by him.'

'What am I to do?'

'Give me the letter. You, of course, can do nothing.'

'You will not quarrel with him?'

'Certainly I will. I have quarrelled with him already. Do you think I will allow any man to insult my wife without quarrelling with him? What I shall do I cannot as yet say, and whatever I may do, you had better not know. I never thought much of these Herefordshire swells who believe themselves to be the very cream of the earth, and now I think less of them than ever.'

He was then silent, and slowly she took herself out of the room, and went away to dress. All this was very terrible. He had never been rough to her before, and she could not at all understand why he had been so rough to her now. Surely it was impossible that he should be jealous because her old lover had written to her such a letter as that which she had shown him! And then she was almost stunned by the opinions he had expressed about Fletcher, opinions which she knew,—was sure that she knew,—to be absolutely erroneous. A liar! Oh, heavens! And then the letter itself was so ingenuous and so honest! Anxious as she was to do all that her husband bade her, she could not be guided by him in this matter. And then she remembered his words: 'You must allow me to dictate to you what you ought to think.' Could it be that marriage meant as much as that,—that a husband was to claim to dictate to his wife what opinions she was to form about this and that person,—about a person she had known so well, whom he had never known? Surely she

could only think in accordance with her own experience and her own
intelligence! She was certain that Arthur Fletcher was no liar. Not even
her own husband could make her think that.

CHAPTER 31

'YES;—WITH A HORSEWHIP IN MY HAND'

EMILY LOPEZ, when she crept out of her own room and joined her
husband just before dinner, was hardly able to speak to him, so thoroughly was she dismayed, and troubled, and horrified, by the manner
in which he had taken Arthur Fletcher's letter. While she had been
alone she had thought it all over, anxious if possible to bring herself
into sympathy with her husband; but the more she thought of it the
more evident did it become to her that he was altogether wrong. He was
so wrong that it seemed to her that she would be a hypocrite if she pretended to agree with him. There were half-a-dozen accusations conveyed against Mr Fletcher by her husband's view of the matter. He was
a liar, giving a false account of his candidature;—and he was a coward;
and an enemy to her, who had laid a plot by which he had hoped to
make her act fraudulently towards her own husband, who had endeavoured to creep into a correspondence with her, and so to compromise
her! All this, which her husband's mind had so easily conceived, was
not only impossible to her, but so horrible that she could not refrain
from disgust at her husband's conception. The letter had been left with
him, but she remembered every word of it. She was sure that it was an
honest letter, meaning no more than had been said,—simply intending
to explain to her that he would not willingly have stood in the way of a
friend whom he had loved, by interfering with her husband's prospects.
And yet she was told that she was to think as her husband bade her
think! She could not think so. She could not say that she thought so. If
her husband would not credit her judgement, let the matter be referred
to her father. Ferdinand would at any rate acknowledge that her father
could understand such a matter even if she could not.

During dinner he said nothing on the subject, nor did she. They
were attended by a page in buttons whom he had hired to wait upon
her, and the meal passed off almost in silence. She looked up at him
frequently and saw that his brow was still black. As soon as they were
alone she spoke to him, having studied during dinner what words she
would first say: 'Are you going down to the club to-night?' He had told

her that the matter of this election had been taken up at the Progress, and that possibly he might have to meet two or three persons there on this evening. There had been a proposition that the club should bear a part of the expenditure, and he was very solicitous that such an arrangement should be made.

'No,' said he, 'I shall not go out to-night. I am not sufficiently light-hearted.'

'What makes you heavy-hearted, Ferdinand?'

'I should have thought you would have known.'

'I suppose I do know,—but I don't know why it should. I don't know why you should be displeased. At any rate, I have done nothing wrong.'

'No;—not as to the letter. But it astonishes me that you should be so—so bound to this man that——'

'Bound to him, Ferdinand!'

'No;—you are bound to me. But that you have so much regard for him as not to see that he has grossly insulted you.'

'I have a regard for him.'

'And you dare to tell me so?'

'Dare! What should I be if I had any feeling which I did not dare to tell you? There is no harm in regarding a man with friendly feelings whom I have known since I was a child, and whom all my family have loved.'

'Your family wanted you to marry him!'

'They did. But I have married you, because I loved you. But I need not think badly of an old friend, because I did not love him. Why should you be angry with him? What can you have to be afraid of?' Then she came and sat on his knee and caressed him.

'It is he that shall be afraid of me,' said Lopez. 'Let him give the borough up if he means what he says.'

'Who could ask him to do that?'

'Not you,—certainly.'

'Oh, no.'

'I can ask him.'

'Could you, Ferdinand?'

'Yes;—with a horsewhip in my hand.'

'Indeed, indeed you do not know him. Will you do this;—will you tell my father everything, and leave it to him to say whether Mr Fletcher has behaved badly to you?'

'Certainly not. I will not have any interference from your father between you and me. If I had listened to your father, you would not have been here now. Your father is not as yet a friend of mine. When he comes to know what I can do for myself, and that I can rise higher than these Herefordshire people, then perhaps he may become my friend. But I will consult him in nothing so peculiar to myself as my own wife. And you must understand that in coming to me all obligation from you to him became extinct. Of course he is your father; but in such a matter as this he has no more say to you than any stranger.' After that he hardly spoke to her; but sat for an hour with a book in his hand, and then rose and said that he would go down to the club. 'There is so much villainy about,' he said, 'that a man if he means to do anything must keep himself on the watch.'

When she was alone she at once burst into tears; but she soon dried her eyes, and putting down her work, settled herself to think of it all. What did it mean? Why was he thus changed to her? Could it be that he was the same Ferdinand to whom she had given herself without a doubt as to his personal merit? Every word that he had spoken since she had shown him the letter from Arthur Fletcher had been injurious to her, and offensive. It almost seemed as though he had determined to show himself to be a tyrant to her, and had only put off playing the part till the first convenient opportunity after their honeymoon. But through all this, her ideas were loyal to him. She would obey him in all things where obedience was possible, and would love him better than all the world. Oh yes;—for was he not her husband? Were he to prove himself the worst of men she would still love him. It had been for better or for worse; and as she had repeated the words to herself, she had sworn that if the worst should come, she would still be true.

But she could not bring herself to say that Arthur Fletcher had behaved badly. She could not lie. She knew well that his conduct had been noble and generous. Then unconsciously and involuntarily,—or rather in opposition to her own will and inward efforts,—her mind would draw comparisons between her husband and Arthur Fletcher. There was some peculiar gift, or grace, or acquirement belonging without dispute to the one, and which the other lacked. What was it? She had heard her father say when talking of gentlemen,—of that race of gentlemen with whom it had been his lot to live,—that you could not make a silk purse out of a sow's ear. The use of the proverb had offended her much, for she had known well whom he had then regarded as a silk purse and whom as a sow's ear. But now she perceived that there had been truth in all this, though she was as anxious as ever to think well of her husband, and to endow him with all possible virtues. She had once ventured to form a doctrine for herself, to preach to herself a sermon of her own, and to tell herself that this gift of gentle blood and of gentle nurture, of which her father thought so much, and to which something of divinity was attributed down in Herefordshire, was after all but a weak, spiritless quality. It could exist without intellect, without heart, and with very moderate culture. It was compatible with many littlenesses and with many vices. As for that love of honest, courageous truth which her father was wont to attribute to it, she regarded his theory as based upon legends, as in earlier years was the theory of the courage, and constancy, and loyalty of the knights of those days. The beau ideal of a man which she then pictured to herself was graced, first with intelligence, then with affection, and lastly with ambition. She knew no reason why such a hero as her fancy created should be born of lords and ladies rather than of working mechanics, should be English rather than Spanish or French. The man could not be her hero without education, without attributes to be attained no doubt more easily by the rich than by the poor; but, with that granted, with those attained, she did not see why she, or why the world, should go back beyond the man's own self. Such had been her theories as to men and their attributes, and acting on that, she had given herself and all her happiness into the keeping of Ferdinand Lopez. Now, there was gradually coming upon her a change in her convictions,—a change that was most unwelcome, that she strove to reject,—one which she would not acknowledge that she had adopted even while adopting it. But now,—ay, from the very hour of her marriage,—she had commenced to learn what it was that her father had meant when he spoke of the pleasure of living with gentlemen. Arthur Fletcher certainly was a gentleman. He would not have entertained the suspicion which her husband had expressed. He could not have failed to believe such assertions as had been made. He could never have suggested to his own wife that another man had endeavoured to entrap her into a secret correspondence. She seemed to hear the tones of Arthur Fletcher's voice, as those of her husband still rang in her ear when he bade her remember that she was now removed from her father's control. Every now and then the tears would come to her eyes, and she would sit pondering, listless, low in heart. Then she would suddenly rouse herself with a shake, and take up her book with a resolve that she would read steadily, would assure herself as she did so that her husband should still be her hero. The intelligence at any rate was there, and, in spite of his roughness, the affection which she craved. And the ambition, too, was there. But, alas, alas! why should such vile suspicions have fouled his mind?

He was late that night, but when he came he kissed her brow as she lay in bed, and she knew that his temper was again smooth. She feigned to be sleepy, though not asleep, as she just put her hand up to his cheek. She did not wish to speak to him again that night, but she was glad to know that in the morning he would smile on her. 'Be early at breakfast,' he said to her as he left her the next morning, 'for I'm going down to Silverbridge to-day.'

Then she started up. 'To-day!'

'Yes;—by the 11.20. There is plenty of time, only don't be unusually late.'

Of course she was something more than usually early, and when she came out she found him reading his paper. 'It's all settled now,' he said. 'Grey has applied for the Hundreds, and Mr Rattler is to move for the new writ* to-morrow. It has come rather sudden at last, as these things always do after long delays. But they say the suddenness is rather in my favour.'

'When will the election take place?'

'I suppose in about a fortnight;—perhaps a little longer.'

'And must you be at Silverbridge all that time?'

'Oh dear no. I shall stay there to-night, and perhaps to-morrow night. Of course I shall telegraph you directly I find how it is to be. I shall see the principal inhabitants, and probably make a speech or two.'

'I do so wish I could hear you.'

'You'd find it awfully dull work, my girl. And I shall find it awfully dull too. I do not imagine that Mr Sprugeon and Mr Sprout will be pleasant companions. Well; I shall stay there a day or two and settle when I am to go down for the absolute canvass.* I shall have to go with my hat in my hand to every blessed inhabitant in that dirty little town, and ask them all to be kind enough to drop in a paper for the most humble of their servants, Ferdinand Lopez.'

'I suppose all candidates have to do the same.'

'Oh yes;—your friend, Master Fletcher, will have to do it.' She winced at this. Arthur Fletcher was her friend, but at the present moment he ought not so to have spoken of him. 'And from all I hear, he is just the sort of fellow that will like the doing of it. It is odious to me to ask a fellow that I despise for anything.'

'Why should you despise them?'

'Low, ignorant, greasy cads, who have no idea of the real meaning of political privileges;—men who would all sell their votes for thirty shillings each, if that game had not been made a little too hot!'

'If they are like that I would not represent them.'

'Oh yes, you would;—when you came to understand the world. It's a fine thing to be in Parliament, and that is the way to get in. However, on this visit I shall only see the great men of the town,—the Sprouts and Sprugeons.'

'Shall you go to Castle Gatherum?'

'Oh, heavens, no! I may go anywhere now rather than there. The Duke is supposed to be in absolute ignorance of the very names of the candidates, or whether there are candidates. I don't suppose that the word Silverbridge will be even whispered in his ear till the thing is over.'

'But you are to get in by his friendship.'

'Or by hers;—at least I hope so. I have no doubt that the Sprouts and the Sprugeons have been given to understand by the Lococks and the Pritchards what are the Duchess's wishes, and that it has also been intimated in some subtle way that the Duke is willing to oblige the Duchess. There are ever so many ways, you know, of killing a cat.'

'And the expense?' suggested Emily.

'Oh,—ah; the expense. When you come to talk of the expense things are not so pleasant. I never saw such a set of meaningless asses in my life as those men at the club. They talk and talk, but there is not one of them who knows how to do anything. Now at the club over the way* they do arrange matters. It's a common cause, and I don't see what right they have to expect that one man should bear all the expense. I've a deuced good mind to leave them in the lurch.'

'Don't do it, Ferdinand, if you can't afford it.'

'I shall go on with it now. I can't help feeling that I've been a little let in among them. When the Duchess first promised me it was to be a simple walk over. Now that they've got their candidate, they go back from that and open the thing to any comer. I can't tell you what I think of Fletcher for taking advantage of such a chance. And then the political committee of the club coolly say that they've got no money. It isn't honest, you know.'

'I don't understand all that,' said Emily sadly. Every word that he said about Fletcher cut her to the heart;—not because it grieved her that Fletcher should be abused, but that her husband should condescend to abuse him. She escaped from further conflict at the moment by proclaiming her ignorance of the whole matter; but she knew enough of it to be well aware that Arthur Fletcher had as good a right to stand as her husband, and that her husband lowered himself by personal animosity to the man. Then Lopez took his departure. 'Oh, Ferdinand,' she said, 'I do so hope you may be successful.'

'I don't think he can have a chance. From what people say, he must be a fool to try. That is, if the Castle is true to me. I shall know more about it when I come back.'

That afternoon she dined with her father, and there met Mrs Roby. It was of course known that Lopez had gone down to Silverbridge, and Emily learned in Manchester Square that Everett had gone with him. 'From all I hear, they're two fools for their pains,' said the lawyer.

'Why, papa?'

'The Duke has given the thing up.'

'But still his interest remains.'

'No such thing! If there is an honest man in England it is the Duke of Omnium, and when he says a thing he means it. Left to themselves, the people of a little town like Silverbridge are sure to return a Conservative. They are half of them small farmers, and of course will go that way if not made to go the other. If the club mean to pay the cost——'

'The club will pay nothing, papa.'

'Then I can only hope that Lopez is doing well in his business!' After that, nothing further was said about the election, but she perceived that her father was altogether opposed to the idea of her husband being in Parliament, and that his sympathies and even his wishes were on the other side. When Mrs Roby suggested that it would be a very nice thing for them all to have Ferdinand in Parliament,—she always called him Ferdinand now,—Mr Wharton railed at her. 'Why should it be a nice thing? I wonder whether you have any idea of a meaning in your head when you say that. Do you suppose that a man gets £1000* a year by going into Parliament?'

'Laws, Mr Wharton; how uncivil you are! Of course I know that members of Parliament ain't paid.'

'Where's the niceness then? If a man has his time at his command and has studied the art of legislation it may be nice, because he will be doing his duty;—or if he wants to get into the government ruck like your brother-in-law, it may be nice;—or if he be an idle man with a large fortune it may be nice to have some place to go. But why it should be nice for Ferdinand Lopez I cannot understand. Everett has some idea in his head when he talks about Parliament,—though I cannot say that I agree with him.' It may easily be understood that after this Emily would say nothing further in Manchester Square as to her husband's prospects at Silverbridge.

Lopez was at Silverbridge for a couple of days, and then returned, as his wife thought, by no means confident of success. He remained in town nearly a week, and during that time he managed to see the Duchess. He had written to her saying that he would do himself the honour of calling on her, and when he came was admitted. But the account he gave to his wife of the visit did not express much satisfaction. It was quite late in the evening before he told her whither he had been. He had intended to keep the matter to himself, and at last spoke of it,—guided by the feeling which induces all men to tell their secrets to their wives,—because it was a comfort to him to talk to some one who would not openly contradict him. 'She's a sly creature after all,' he said.

'I had always thought that she was too open rather than sly,' said his wife.

'People always try to get a character just opposite to what they deserve. When I hear that a man is always to be believed, I know that he is the most dangerous liar going. She hummed and hawed and would not say a word about the borough. She went so far as to tell me that I wasn't to say a word about it to her.'

'Wasn't that best if her husband wished her not to talk of it?'

'It is all humbug and falsehood to the very bottom. She knows that I am spending money about it, and she ought to be on the square with me. She ought to tell me what she can do and what she can't. When I asked her whether Sprugeon might be trusted, she said that she really wished I wouldn't say anything more to her about it. I call that dishonest and sly. I shouldn't at all wonder but that Fletcher has been with the Duke. If I find that out, won't I expose them both?'

CHAPTER 32

'WHAT BUSINESS IS IT OF YOURS?'

THINGS had not gone altogether smoothly with the Duchess herself since the breaking up of the party at Gatherum Castle,—nor perhaps quite smoothly with the Duke. It was now March. The House was again sitting, and they were both in London,—but till they came to town they had remained at the Castle, and that huge mansion had not been found to be more comfortable by either of them as it became empty. For a time the Duchess had been cowed by her husband's stern decision; but as he again became gentle to her,—almost seeming by his manner to apologize for his unwonted roughness,—she plucked up her spirit and declared to herself that she would not give up the battle. All that she did,—was it not for his sake? And why should she not have her ambition in life as well as he his? And had she not succeeded in all that she had done? Could it be right that she should be asked to abandon everything, to own herself to have been defeated, to be shown to have failed before all the world, because such a one as Major Pountney had made a fool of himself? She attributed it all to Major Pountney;—very wrongly. When a man's mind is veering towards some decision, some conclusion which he has been perhaps slow in reaching, it is probably a little thing which at last fixes his mind and clenches his thoughts. The Duke had been gradually teaching himself to hate the crowd around him and to reprobate his wife's strategy, before he had known that there was a Major Pountney under his roof. Others had offended him, and first and foremost among them his own colleague, Sir Orlando. The Duchess hardly read his character aright, and certainly did not understand his present motives, when she thought that all might be forgotten as soon as the disagreeable savour of the Major should have passed away.

But in nothing, as she thought, had her husband been so silly as in his abandonment of Silverbridge. When she heard that the day was fixed for declaring the vacancy, she ventured to ask him a question. His manner to her lately had been more than urbane, more than affectionate;—it had almost been that of a lover. He had petted her and caressed her when they met, and once even said that nothing should really trouble him as long as he had her with him. Such a speech as that never in his life had he made before to her! So she plucked up her courage and asked her question,—not exactly on that occasion, but soon afterwards. 'May not I say a word to Sprugeon about the election?'

'Not a word!' And he looked at her as he had looked on that day when he had told her of the Major's sins. She tossed her head and pouted her lips and walked on without speaking. If it was to be so, then indeed would she have failed. And, therefore, though in his general manner he was loving to her, things were not going smooth with her.

And things were not going smooth with him because there had reached him a most troublous dispatch from Sir Orlando Drought only two days before the Cabinet meeting at which the points to be made in the Queen's speech* were to be decided. It had been already agreed that a proposition should be made to Parliament by the Government, for an extension of the county suffrage, with some slight redistribution of seats. The towns with less than 20,000 inhabitants were to take in some increased portion of the country parishes around. But there was not enough of a policy in this to satisfy Sir Orlando, nor was the conduct of the bill through the House to be placed in his hands. That was to be intrusted to Mr Monk, and Mr Monk would be, if not nominally the leader, yet the chief man of the Government in the House of Commons. This was displeasing to Sir Orlando, and he had, therefore, demanded from the Prime Minister more of a 'policy'. Sir Orlando's present idea of a policy was the building of four bigger ships of war* than had ever been built before,—with larger guns, and more men, and thicker iron plates, and, above all, with a greater expenditure of money. He had even gone so far as to say, though not in his semi-official letter to the Prime Minister, that he thought that 'The Salvation of the Empire' should be the cry of the Coalition party. 'After all,' he said, 'what the people care about is the Salvation of the Empire!' Sir Orlando was at the head of the Admiralty; and if glory was to be achieved by the four ships, it would rest first on the head of Sir Orlando.

Now the Duke thought that the Empire was safe, and had been throughout his political life averse to increasing the army and navy estimates. He regarded the four ships as altogether unnecessary,—and when reminded that he might in this way consolidate the Coalition, said that he would rather do without the Coalition and the four ships than have to do with both of them together,—an opinion which was thought by some to be almost traitorous to the party as now organized. The secrets of Cabinets are not to be disclosed lightly, but it came to be understood,—as what is done at Cabinet meetings generally does come to be understood,—that there was something like disagreement. The Prime Minister, the Duke of St Bungay, and Mr Monk were altogether against the four ships. Sir Orlando was supported by Lord Drummond and another of his old friends. At the advice of the elder Duke, a paragraph was hatched, in which it was declared that her Majesty, 'having regard to the safety of the nation and the possible, though happily not probable, chances of war, thought that the present strength of the navy should be considered.' 'It will give him scope for a new gun-boat on an altered principle,' said the Duke of St Bungay. But the Prime Minister, could he have had his own way, would have given Sir Orlando no scope whatever. He would have let the Coalition have gone to the dogs and have fallen himself into infinite political ruin, but that he did not dare that men should hereafter say of him that this attempt at government had failed because he was stubborn, imperious, and self-confident. He had known when he took his present place that he must yield to others; but he had not known how terrible it is to have to yield when a principle is in question,—how great is the suffering when a man finds himself compelled to do that which he thinks should not be done!

Therefore, though he had been strangely loving to his wife, the time had not gone smoothly with him.

In direct disobedience to her husband the Duchess did speak a word to Mr Sprugeon. When at the Castle she was frequently driven through Silverbridge, and on one occasion had her carriage stopped at the ironmonger's door. Out came Mr Sprugeon, and there were at first half-a-dozen standing by who could hear what she said. Millepois, the cook, wanted to have some new kind of iron plate erected in the kitchen. Of course she had provided herself beforehand with her excuse. As a rule, when the cook wanted anything done, he did not send word to the tradesman by the Duchess. But on this occasion the Duchess was personally most anxious. She wanted to see how the iron plate would work. It was to be a particular kind of iron plate. Then, having watched her opportunity, she said her word, 'I suppose we shall be safe with Mr Lopez.' When Mr Sprugeon was about to reply, she shook her head and went on about the iron plate. This would be quite enough to let Mr Sprugeon understand that she was still anxious about the borough. Mr Sprugeon was an intelligent man, and possessed of discretion to a certain extent. As soon as he saw the little frown and the shake of the head, he understood it all. He and the Duchess had a secret together. Would not everything about the Castle in which a morsel of iron was employed want renewing? And would not the Duchess take care that it should all be renewed by Sprugeon? But then he must be active, and his activity would be of no avail unless others helped him. So he whispered a word to Sprout, and it soon became known that the Castle interest was all alive.

But unfortunately the Duke was also on the alert. The Duke had been very much in earnest when he made up his mind that the old custom should be abandoned at Silverbridge and had endeavoured to impress that determination of his upon his wife. The Duke knew more about his property and was better acquainted with its details than his wife or others believed. He heard that in spite of all his orders the Castle interest was being maintained, and a word was said to him which seemed to imply that this was his wife's doings. It was then about the middle of February, and arrangements were in process for the removal of the family to London. The Duke had already been up to London for the meeting of Parliament, and had now come back to Gatherum, purporting to return to London with his wife. Then it was that it was hinted to him that her Grace was still anxious as to the election,—and had manifested her anxiety. The rumour hurt him, though he did not in the least believe it. It showed to him, as he thought, not that his wife had been false to him,—as in truth she had been,—but that even her name could not be kept free from slander. And when he spoke to her on the subject, he did so rather with the view of proving to her how necessary it was that she should keep herself altogether aloof from such matters, than with any wish to make further inquiry. But he elicited the whole truth. 'It is so hard to kill an old-established evil,' he said.

'What evil have you failed to kill now?'

'Those people at Silverbridge still say that I want to return a member for them.'

'Oh; that's the evil! You know I think instead of killing an evil, you have murdered an excellent institution.' This at any rate was very imprudent on the part of the Duchess. After that disobedient word spoken to Mr Sprugeon, she should have been more on her guard.

'As to that, Glencora, I must judge for myself.'

'Oh yes,—you have been jury, and judge, and executioner.'

'I have done as I thought right to do. I am sorry that I should fail to carry you with me in such a matter, but even failing in that I must do my duty. You will at any rate agree with me that when I say the thing should be done, it should be done.'

'If you wanted to destroy the house, and cut down all the trees, and turn the place into a wilderness, I suppose you would only have to speak. Of course I know it would be wrong that I should have an opinion. As "man" you are of course to have your own way.' She was in one of her most aggravating moods. Though he might compel her to obey, he could not compel her to hold her tongue.

'Glencora, I don't think you know how much you add to my troubles, or you would not speak to me like that.'

'What am I to say? It seems to me that any more suicidal thing than throwing away the borough never was done. Who will thank you? What additional support will you get? How will it increase your power? It's like King Lear throwing off his clothes in the storm because his daughters turned him out. And you didn't do it because you thought it right.'

'Yes, I did,' he said, scowling.

'You did it because Major Pountney disgusted you. You kicked him out. Why wouldn't that satisfy you without sacrificing the borough? It isn't what I think or say about it, but that everybody is thinking and saying the same thing.'

'I choose that it shall be so.'

'Very well.'

'And I don't choose that your name shall be mixed up in it. They say in Silverbridge that you are canvassing for Mr Lopez.'

'Who says so?'

'I presume it's not true.'

'Who says so, Plantagenet?'

'It matters not who has said so, if it be untrue. I presume it to be false.'

'Of course it is false.' Then the Duchess remembered her word to Mr Sprugeon, and the cowardice of the lie was heavy on her. I doubt whether she would have been so shocked by the idea of a falsehood as to have been kept back from it had she before resolved that it would save her; but she was not in her practice a false woman, her courage being too high for falsehood. It now seemed to her that by this lie she was owning herself to be quelled and brought into absolute sub-jection by her husband. So she burst out into the truth. 'Now I think of it I did say a word to Mr Sprugeon. I told him that—that I hoped Mr Lopez would be returned. I don't know whether you call that canvassing.'

'I desired you not to speak to Mr Sprugeon,' he thundered forth.

'That's all very well, Plantagenet, but if you desire me to hold my tongue altogether, what am I to do?'

'What business is this of yours?'

'I suppose I may have my political sympathies as well as another. Really you are becoming so autocratic that I shall have to go in for women's rights.'

'You mean me to understand then that you intend to put yourself in opposition to me.'

'What a fuss you make about it all!' she said. 'Nothing that one can do is right! You make me wish that I was a milkmaid or a farmer's wife.' So saying she bounced out of the room, leaving the Duke sick at heart, low in spirit, and doubtful whether he were right or wrong in his attempts to manage his wife. Surely he must be right in feeling that in his high office a clearer conduct and cleaner way of walking was expected from him than from other men! Noblesse oblige! To his uncle the privilege of returning a member to Parliament had been a thing of course; and when the Radical newspapers of the day abused his uncle, his uncle took that abuse as a thing of course. The old Duke acted after his kind, and did not care what others said of him. And he himself, when he first came to his dukedom, was not as he was now. Duties, though they were heavy enough, were lighter then. Serious matters were less serious. There was this and that matter of public policy on which he was intent, but, thinking humbly of himself, he had not yet learned to conceive that he must fit his public conduct in all things to a straight rule of patriotic justice. Now it was different with him, and though the change was painful, he felt it to be imperative. He would fain have been as other men, but he could not. But in this change it was so needful to him that he should carry with him the full sympathies of one person;—that she who was the nearest to him of all should act with him! And now she had not only disobeyed him, but had told him, as some grocer's wife might tell her husband, that he was 'making a fuss about it all!'

And then, as he thought of the scene which has been described, he could not quite approve of himself. He knew that he was too self-conscious,—that he was thinking too much about his own conduct and the conduct of others to him. The phrase had been odious to him, but still he could not acquit himself of 'making a fuss.' Of one thing only was he sure,—that a grievous calamity had befallen him when circumstances compelled him to become the Queen's Prime Minister.

He said nothing further to his wife till they were in London together, and then he was tempted to caress her again, to be loving to her, and to show her that he had forgiven her. But she was brusque to him, as though she did not wish to be forgiven. 'Cora,' he said, 'do not separate yourself from me.'

'Separate myself! What on earth do you mean? I have not dreamed of such a thing.' The Duchess answered him as though he had alluded to some actual separation.

'I do not mean that. God forbid that a misfortune such as that should ever happen! Do not disjoin yourself from me in all these troubles.'

'What am I to do when you scold me? You must know pretty well by this time that I don't like being scolded. "I desired you not to speak to Mr Sprugeon!"' As she repeated his words she imitated his manner and voice closely. 'I shouldn't dream of addressing the children with such magnificence of anger. "What business is it of yours?" No woman likes that sort of thing, and I'm not sure that I am acquainted with any woman who likes it much less than—Glencora, Duchess of Omnium.' As she said these last words in a low whisper, she curtseyed down to the ground.

'You know how anxious I am,' he began, 'that you should share everything with me,—even in politics. But in all things there must at last be one voice that shall be the ruling voice.'

'And that is to be yours,—of course.'

'In such a matter as this it must be.'

'And, therefore, I like to do a little business of my own behind your back. It's human nature, and you've got to put up with it. I wish you had a better wife. I dare say there are many who would be better. There's the Duchess of St Bungay who never troubles her husband about politics, but only scolds him because the wind blows from the east. It is just possible there might be worse.'

'Oh, Glencora!'

'You had better make the best you can of your bargain and not expect too much from her. And don't ride over her with a very high horse. And let her have her own way a little if you really believe that she has your interest at heart.'

After this he was quite aware that she had got the better of him altogether. On that occasion he smiled and kissed her, and went his way. But he was by no means satisfied. That he should be thwarted by her, ate into his very heart;—and it was a wretched thing to him that he could not make her understand his feeling in that respect. If it were to go on he must throw up everything. Ruat cælum, fiat*—proper subordination from his wife in regard to public matters! No wife had a fuller allowance of privilege, or more complete power in her hands, as to things fit for women's management. But it was intolerable to him that she should seek to interfere with him in matters of a public nature. And she was constantly doing so. She had always this or that aspirant for office on hand;—this or that job to be carried, though the jobs were not perhaps much in themselves;—this or that affair to be managed by her own political allies, such as Barrington Erle and Phineas Finn. And in his heart he suspected her of a design of managing the Government in her own way, with her own particular friend, Mrs Finn, for her Prime Minister. If he could in no other way put an end to such evils as these, he must put an end to his own political life. Ruat cælum fiat justitia. Now 'justitia' to him was not compatible with feminine interference in his own special work.

It may therefore be understood that things were not going very smoothly with the Duke and Duchess; and it may also be understood why the Duchess had had very little to say to Mr Lopez about the election. She was aware that she owed something to Mr Lopez, whom she had certainly encouraged to stand for the borough, and she had therefore sent her card to his wife and was prepared to invite them both to her parties;—but just at present she was a little tired of Ferdinand Lopez, and perhaps unjustly disposed to couple him with the unfortunate wretch, Major Pountney.

CHAPTER 33

SHOWING THAT A MAN SHOULD NOT HOWL

ARTHUR FLETCHER, in his letter to Mrs Lopez, had told her that when he found out who was to be his antagonist at Silverbridge, it was too late for him to give up the contest. He was, he said, bound in faith to continue it by what had passed between himself and others. But in truth he had not reached his conclusion without some persuasion from others. He had been at Longbarns with his brother when he first heard that Lopez intended to stand, and he at once signified his desire to give way. The information reached him from Mr Frank Gresham, of Greshambury, a gentleman connected with the De Courcys who was now supposed to represent the De Courcy interest in the county, and who had first suggested to Arthur that he should come forward. It was held at Longbarns that Arthur was bound in honour to Mr Gresham and to Mr Gresham's friends, and to this opinion he had yielded.

Since Emily Wharton's marriage her name had never been mentioned at Longbarns in Arthur's presence. When he was away,—and of course his life was chiefly passed in London,—old Mrs Fletcher was free enough in her abuse of the silly creature who had allowed herself to be taken out of her own rank by a Portuguese Jew. But she had been made to understand by her elder son, the lord of Longbarns, that not a word was to be said when Arthur was there. 'I think he ought to be taught to forget her,' Mrs Fletcher had said. But John in his own quiet but imperious way, had declared that there were some men to whom such lessons could not be taught, and that Arthur was one of them. 'Is he never to get a wife, then?' Mrs Fletcher had asked. John wouldn't pretend to answer that question, but was quite sure that his brother would not be tempted into other matrimonial arrangements by anything that could be said against Emily Lopez. When Mrs Fletcher declared her extreme anger that Arthur was a fool for his trouble, John did not contradict her, but declared that the folly was of a nature to require tender treatment.

Matters were in this condition at Longbarns when Arthur communicated to his brother the contents of Mr Gresham's letter, and expressed his own purpose of giving up Silverbridge. 'I don't quite see that,' said John.

'No;—and it is impossible that you should be expected to see it. I don't quite know how to talk about it even to you, though I think you are about the softest-hearted fellow out.'

'I don't acknowledge the soft heart;—but go on.'

'I don't want to interfere with that man. I have a sort of feeling that as he has got her he might as well have the seat too.'

'The seat, as you call it, is not there for his gratification or for yours. The seat is there in order that the people of Silverbridge may be represented in Parliament.'

'Let them get somebody else. I don't want to put myself in opposition to him, and I certainly do not want to oppose her.'

'They can't change their candidate in that way at a day's notice. You would be throwing Gresham over, and, if you ask me, I think that is a thing you have no right to do. This objection of yours is sentimental, and there is nothing of which a man should be so much in dread as sentimentalism. It is not your fault that you oppose Mr Lopez. You were in the field first, and you must go on with it.' John Fletcher, when he spoke in this way, was, at Longbarns, always supposed to be right; and on the present occasion he, as usual, prevailed. Then Arthur Fletcher wrote his letter to the lady. He would not have liked to have had it known that the composition and copying of that little note had cost him an hour. He had wished that she should understand his feelings, and yet it was necessary that he should address her in words that should be perfectly free from affection or emotion. He must let her know that, though he wrote to her, the letter was for her husband as well as for herself, and he must do this in a manner which would not imply any fear that his writing to her would be taken amiss. The letter when completed was at any rate simple and true; and yet, as we know, it was taken very much amiss.

Arthur Fletcher had by no means recovered from the blow he had received that day when Emily had told him everything down by the river side; but then, it must be said of him, that he had no intention of recovery. He was as a man who, having taken a burden on his back, declares to himself that he will, for certain reasons, carry it throughout his life. The man knows that with the burden he cannot walk as men walk who are unencumbered, but for those reasons of his he has chosen to lade himself, and having done so he abandons regret and submits to his circumstances. So had it been with him. He would make no attempt to throw off the load. It was now far back in his life, as much at least as three years, since he had first assured himself of his desire to make Emily Wharton the companion of his life. From that day she had been the pivot on which his whole existence had moved. She had refused his offers more than once, but had done so with so much tender kindness, that, though he had found himself to be wounded and bruised, he had never abandoned his object. Her father and all his own friends encouraged him. He was continually told that her coldness was due to the simple fact that she had not yet learned to give her heart away. And so he had persevered, being ever thoroughly intent on his purpose, till he was told by herself that her love was given to this other man.

Then he knew that it behoved him to set some altered course of life before him. He could not shoot his rival or knock him over the head, nor could he carry off his girl, as used to be done in rougher times. There was nothing now for a man in such a catastrophe as this but submission. But he might submit and shake off his burden, or submit and carry it hopelessly. He told himself that he would do the latter. She had been his goddess, and he would not now worship at another shrine. And then ideas came into his head,—not hopes, or purposes, or a belief even in any possibility,—but vague ideas, mere castles in the air, that a time might come in which it might be in his power to serve her, and to prove to her beyond doubting what had been the nature of his love. Like others of his family, he thought ill of Lopez, believing the man to be an adventurer, one who would too probably fall into misfortune, however high he might now seem to hold his head. He was certainly a man not standing on the solid basis of land, or of Three per Cents,*— those solidities to which such as the Whartons and Fletchers are wont to trust. No doubt, should there be such fall, the man's wife would have other help than that of her rejected lover. She had a father, brother, and cousins, who would also be there to aid her. The idea was, therefore, but a castle in the air. And yet it was dear to him. At any rate he resolved that he would live for it, and that the woman should still be his goddess, though she was the wife of another man, and might now perhaps never even be seen by him. Then there came upon him, immediately almost after their marriage, the necessity of writing to her. The task was one which, of course, he did not perform lightly.

He never said a word of this to anybody else;—but his brother understood it all, and in a somewhat silent fashion fully sympathized with him. John could not talk to him about love, or mark passages of poetry for him to read, or deal with him at all romantically; but he could take care that his brother had the best horses to ride, and the warmest corner out shooting, and that everything in the house should be done for his brother's comfort. As the squire looked and spoke at Longbarns, others looked and spoke,—so that everybody knew that Mr Arthur was to be contradicted in nothing. Had he, just at this period, ordered a tree in the park cut down, it would, I think, have been cut down, without reference to the master! But, perhaps, John's power was most felt in the way in which he repressed the expressions of his mother's high indignation. 'Mean slut!' she once said, speaking of Emily in her eldest son's hearing. For the girl, to her thinking, had been mean and had been a slut. She had not known,—so Mrs Fletcher thought,—what birth and blood required of her.

'Mother,' John Fletcher had said, 'you would break Arthur's heart if he heard you speak in that way, and I am sure you would drive him from Longbarns. Keep it to yourself.' The old woman had shaken her head angrily, but she had endeavoured to do as she had been bid.

'Isn't your brother riding that horse a little rashly?' Reginald Cotgrave said to John Fletcher in the hunting field one day.

'I didn't observe,' said John; 'but whatever horse he's on, he always rides rashly.' Arthur was mounted on a long, raking thorough-bred black animal, which he had bought himself about a month ago, and which, having been run at steeplechases, rushed at every fence as though he were going to swallow it. His brother had begged him to put some rough-rider up till the horse could be got to go quietly, but Arthur had persevered. And during the whole of this day the squire had been in a tremor, lest there should be some accident.

'He used to have a little more judgement, I think,' said Cotgrave. 'He went at that double just now as hard as the brute could tear. If the horse hadn't done it all, where would he have been?'

'In the further ditch, I suppose. But you see the horse did it all.'

This was all very well as an answer to Reginald Cotgrave,—to whom it was not necessary that Fletcher should explain the circumstances. But the squire had known as well as Cotgrave that his brother had been riding rashly, and he had understood the reason why. 'I don't think a man ought to break his neck,' he said, 'because he can't get everything that he wishes.' The two brothers were standing then together before the fire in the squire's own room, having just come in from hunting.

'Who is going to break his neck?'

'They tell me that you tried to to-day.'

'Because I was riding a pulling horse. I'll back him to be the biggest leaper and the quickest horse in Herefordshire.'

'I dare say,—though for the matter of that the chances are very much against it. But a man shouldn't ride so as to have those things said of him.'

'What is a fellow to do if he can't hold a horse?'

'Get off him.'

'That's nonsense, John!'

'No, it's not. You know what I mean very well. If I were to lose half my property to-morrow, don't you think it would cut me up a good deal?'

'It would me, I know.'

'But what would you think of me if I howled about it?'

'Do I howl?' asked Arthur angrily.

'Every man howls who is driven out of his ordinary course by any trouble. A man howls if he goes about frowning always.'

'Do I frown?'

'Or laughing.'

'Do I laugh?'

'Or galloping over the country like a mad devil who wants to get rid of his debts by breaking his neck. Æqam memento——.* You remember all that, don't you?'

'I remember it; but it isn't so easy to do it.'

'Try. There are other things to be done in life except getting married. You are going into Parliament.'

'I don't know that.'

'Gresham tells me there isn't a doubt about it. Think of that. Fix your mind upon it. Don't take it only as an accident, but as the thing you're to live for. If you'll do that,—if you'll so manage that there shall be something to be done in Parliament which only you can do, you won't ride a runaway horse as you did that brute to-day.' Arthur looked up into his brother's face almost weeping. 'We expect much of you, you know. I'm not a man to do anything except be a good steward for the family property, and keep the old house from falling down. You're a clever fellow,—so that between us, if we both do our duty, the Fletchers may still thrive in the land. My house shall be your house, and my wife your wife, and my children your children. And then the honour you win shall be my honour. Hold up your head,—and sell that beast.' Arthur Fletcher squeezed his brother's hand and went away to dress.

CHAPTER 34

THE SILVERBRIDGE ELECTION

ABOUT a month after this affair with the runaway horse Arthur Fletcher went to Greshambury, preparatory to his final sojourn at Silverbridge, for the week previous to his election. Greshambury, the seat of Francis Gresham, Esq., who was a great man in these parts, was about twenty miles from Silverbridge, and the tedious work of canvassing the electors could not therefore be done from thence;—but he spent a couple of pleasant days with his old friend, and learned what was being said and what was being done in and about the borough. Mr Gresham was a man, not as yet quite forty years of age, very popular, with a large family, of great wealth, and master of the county hounds. His father had been an embarrassed man, with a large estate; but this Gresham had married a lady with immense wealth, and had prospered in the world. He was not an active politician. He did not himself care for Parliament, or for the good things which political power can give; and was on this account averse to the Coalition. He thought that Sir Orlando Drought and the others were touching pitch* and had defiled themselves. But he was conscious that in so thinking he was one of but a small minority; and, bad as the world around him certainly was, terrible as had been the fall of the glory of old England, he was nevertheless content to live without loud grumbling as long as the farmers paid him their rent, and the labourers in his part of the country did not strike for wages, and the land when sold would fetch thirty years' purchase. He had not therefore been careful to ascertain that Arthur Fletcher would pledge himself to oppose the Coalition before he proffered his assistance in this matter of the borough. It would not be easy to find such a candidate, or perhaps possible to bring him in when found. The Fletchers had always been good Conservatives, and were proper people to be in Parliament. A Conservative in Parliament is, of course, obliged to promote a great many things which he does not really approve. Mr Gresham quite understood that. You can't have tests and qualifications, rotten boroughs and the divine right of kings,* back again. But as the glorious institutions of the country are made to perish, one after the other, it is better that they should receive the coup de grâce tenderly from loving hands than be roughly throttled by Radicals. Mr Gresham would thank his stars that he could still preserve foxes down in his own country, instead of doing any of this dirty work,—for let the best be made of such work, still it was dirty,—and was willing, now as always, to give his assistance, and if necessary to spend a little money, to put a Fletcher into Parliament and to keep a Lopez out.

There was to be a third candidate. That was the first news that Fletcher heard. 'It will do us all the good in the world,' said Mr Gresham. 'The Rads* in the borough are not satisfied with Mr Lopez. They say they don't know him. As long as a certain set could make it be believed that he was the Duke's nominee they were content to accept him;—even though he was not proposed directly by the Duke's people in the usual way. But the Duke has made himself understood at last. You have seen the Duke's letter?' Arthur had not seen the Duke's letter, which had only been published in the 'Silverbridge Gazette' of that week, and he now read it, sitting in Mr Gresham's magistrate's-room, as a certain chamber in the house had been called since the days of the present squire's great-grandfather.

The Duke's letter was addressed to his recognized man of business in those parts, and was as follows:—

'*Carlton Terrace*, — *March, 187*—.

'MY DEAR MR MORETON.' (Mr Moreton was the successor of one Mr Fothergill, who had reigned supreme in those parts under the old Duke.)

'I am afraid that my wishes with regard to the borough and the forthcoming election there of a member of Parliament are not yet clearly understood, although I endeavoured to declare them when I was at Gatherum Castle. I trust that no elector will vote for this or that gentleman with an idea that the return of any special candidate will please me. The ballot will of course prevent me or any other man from knowing how an elector may vote;—but I beg to assure the electors generally that should they think fit to return a member pledged to oppose the Government of which I form a part, it would not in any way change my cordial feelings towards the town. I may perhaps be allowed to add that, in my opinion, no elector can do his duty except by voting for the candidate whom he thinks best qualified to serve the country. In regard to the gentlemen who are now before the constituency, I have no feeling for one rather than for the other; and had I any such feeling I should not wish it to actuate the vote of a single elector. I should be glad if this letter could be published so as to be brought under the eyes of the electors generally.

'Yours faithfully,

'OMNIUM.'

When the Duke said that he feared that his wishes were not understood, and spoke of the inefficacy of his former declaration, he was alluding of course to the Duchess and to Mr Sprugeon. Mr Sprugeon guessed that it might be so, and, still wishing to have the Duchess for his good friend, was at once assiduous in explaining to his friends in the borough that even this letter did not mean anything. A Prime Minister was bound to say that kind of thing! But the borough, if it wished to please the Duke, must return Lopez in spite of the Duke's letter. Such was Mr Sprugeon's doctrine. But he did not carry Mr Sprout with him. Mr Sprout at once saw his opportunity, and suggested to Mr Du Boung, the local brewer, that he should come forward. Du Boung was a man rapidly growing into provincial eminence, and jumped at the offer. Consequently there were three candidates. Du Boung came forward as a Conservative prepared to give a cautious, but very cautious, support to the Coalition. Mr Du Boung, in his printed address, said very sweet things of the Duke generally. The borough was blessed by the vicinity of the Duke. But, looking at the present perhaps unprecedented crisis in affairs, Mr Du Boung was prepared to give no more than a very cautious support to the Duke's Government. Arthur Fletcher read Mr Du Boung's address immediately after the Duke's letter.

'The more the merrier,' said Arthur.

'Just so. Du Boung will not rob you of a vote, but he will cut the ground altogether from under the other man's feet. You see that as far as the actual political programme goes there isn't much to choose between any of you. You are all Government men.'

'With a difference.'

'One man in these days is so like another,' continued Gresham sarcastically, 'that it requires good eyes to see the shades of the colours.'

'Then you'd better support Du Boung,' said Arthur.

'I think you've just a turn in your favour. Besides, I couldn't really carry a vote myself. As for Du Boung, I'd sooner have him than a foreign cad like Lopez.' Then Arthur Fletcher frowned and Mr Gresham became confused, remembering the catastrophe about the young lady whose story he had heard. 'Du Boung used to be plain English as Bung before he got rich and made his name beautiful,' continued Gresham, 'but I suppose Mr Lopez does come of foreign extraction.'

'I don't know what he comes from,' said Arthur moodily. 'They tell me he's a gentleman. However, as we are to have a contest, I hope he mayn't win.'

'Of course you do. And he shan't win. Nor shall the great Du Boung. You shall win, and become Prime Minister, and make me a peer. Would you like papa to be Lord Greshambury?' he said to a little girl, who then rushed into the room.

'No, I wouldn't. I'd like papa to give me the pony which the man wants to sell out in the yard.'

'She's quite right, Fletcher,' said the squire. 'I'm much more likely to be able to buy them ponies as simple Frank Gresham than I should be if I had a lord's coronet to pay for.'

This was on a Saturday, and on the following Monday Mr Gresham drove the candidate over to Silverbridge and started him on his work of canvassing. Mr Du Boung had been busy ever since Mr Sprout's brilliant suggestion had been made, and Lopez had been in the field even before him. Each one of the candidates called at the house of every elector in the borough,—and every man in the borough was an elector. When they had been at work for four or five days each candidate assured the borough that he had already received promises of votes sufficient to insure his success, and each candidate was as anxious as ever,—nay, was more rabidly anxious than ever,—to secure the promise of a single vote. Hints were made by honest citizens of the pleasure they would have in supporting this or that gentleman,—for the honest citizens assured one gentleman after the other of the satisfaction they had in seeing so all-sufficient a candidate in the borough,—if the smallest pecuniary help were given them, even a day's pay, so that their poor children might not be injured by their going to the poll. But the candidates and their agents were stern in their replies to such temptations. 'That's a dodge of that rascal Sprout,' said Sprugeon to Mr Lopez. 'That's one of Sprout's men. If he could get half-a-crown* from you it would be all up with us.' But though Sprugeon called Sprout a rascal, he laid the same bait both for Du Boung and for Fletcher;—but laid it in vain. Everybody said that it was a very clean election. 'A brewer standing, and devil a glass of beer!' said one old elector who had remembered better things when the borough never heard of a contest.

On the third day of his canvass Arthur Fletcher with his gang of agents and followers behind him met Lopez with his gang in the street. It was probable that they would so meet, and Fletcher had resolved what he would do when such a meeting took place. He walked up to Lopez, and with a kindly smile offered his hand. The two men, though they had never been intimate, had known each other, and Fletcher was determined to show that he would not quarrel with a man because that man had been his favoured rival. In comparison with that other matter this affair of the candidature was of course trivial. But Lopez who had, as the reader may remember, made some threat about a horsewhip, had come to a resolution of a very different nature. He put his arms a-kimbo, resting his hands on his hips, and altogether declined the proffered civility. 'You had better walk on,' he said, and then stood, scowling, on the spot till the other should pass by. Fletcher looked at him for a moment, then bowed and passed on. At least a dozen men saw what had taken place, and were aware that Mr Lopez had expressed his determination to quarrel personally with Mr Fletcher, in opposition to

Mr Fletcher's expressed wish for amity. And before they had gone to bed that night all the dozen knew the reason why. Of course there was some one then at Silverbridge clever enough to find out that Arthur Fletcher had been in love with Miss Wharton, but that Miss Wharton had lately been married to Mr Lopez. No doubt the incident added a pleasurable emotion to the excitement caused by the election at Silverbridge generally. A personal quarrel is attractive everywhere. The expectation of such an occurrence will bring together the whole House of Commons. And of course this quarrel was very attractive in Silverbridge. There were some Fletcherites and Lopezites in the quarrel; as there were also Du Boungites, who maintained that when gentlemen could not canvass without quarrelling in the streets they were manifestly unfit to represent such a borough as Silverbridge in Parliament;—and that therefore Mr Du Boung should be returned.

Mr Gresham was in the town that day, though not till after the occurrence, and Fletcher could not avoid speaking of it. 'The man must be a cur,' said Gresham.

'It would make no difference in the world to me,' said Arthur, struggling hard to prevent signs of emotion from showing themselves in his face, 'were it not that he has married a lady whom I have long known and whom I greatly esteem.' He felt that he could hardly avoid all mention of the marriage, and yet was determined that he would say no word that his brother would call 'howling.'

'There has been no previous quarrel, or offence?' asked Gresham.

'None in the least.' When Arthur so spoke he forgot altogether the letter he had written; nor, had he then remembered it, would he have thought it possible that that letter should have given offence. He had been the sufferer, not Lopez. This man had robbed him of his happiness; and, though it would have been foolish in him to make a quarrel for a grievance such as that, there might have been some excuse had he done so. It had taken him some time to perceive that greatly as this man had injured him, there had been no injustice done to him, and that therefore there should be no complaint made by him. But that this other man should complain was to him unintelligible.

'He is not worth your notice,' said Mr Gresham. 'He is simply not a gentleman, and does not know how to behave himself. I am very sorry for the young lady;—that's all.' At this allusion to Emily Arthur felt that his face became red with the rising blood; and he felt also that his friend should not have spoken thus openly,—thus irreverently,—on so sacred a subject. But at the moment he said nothing further. As far as his canvass was concerned it had been successful, and he was beginning to feel sure that he would be the new member. He endeavoured therefore to drown his sorrow in this coming triumph.

But Lopez had been by no means gratified with his canvass or with the conduct of the borough generally. He had already begun to feel that the Duchess and Mr Sprugeon and the borough had thrown him over shamefully. Immediately on his arrival in Silverbridge a local attorney had with the blandest possible smile asked him for a cheque for £500.* Of course there must be money spent at once, and of course the money must come out of the candidate's pocket. He had known all this beforehand, and yet the demand for the money had come upon him as an injury. He gave the cheque, but showed clearly by his manner that he resented the application. This did not tend to bind to him more closely the services of those who were present when the demand was made. And then, as he began his canvass, he found that he could not conjure at all with the name of the Duke, or even with that of the Duchess; and was told on the second day by Mr Sprugeon himself that he had better fight the battle 'on his own hook.' Now his own hook in Silverbridge was certainly not a strong hook. Mr Sprugeon was still of the opinion that a good deal might be done by judicious manipulation, and went so far as to suggest that another cheque for £500 in the hands of Mr Wise, the lawyer, would be effective. But Lopez did not give the other cheque, and Sprugeon whispered to him that the Duke had been too many for the Duchess. Still he had persevered, and a set of understrappers around him, who would make nothing out of the election without his candidature, assured him from time to time that he would even yet come out all right at the ballot. With such a hope still existing he had not scrupled to affirm in his speeches that the success of his canvass had been complete. But, on the morning of the day on which he met Fletcher in the street, Mr Du Boung had called upon him accompanied by two of the Du Boung agents and by Mr Sprugeon himself,—and had suggested that he, Lopez, should withdraw from the contest, so that Du Boung might be returned, and that the 'Liberal interests' of the borough might not be sacrificed.

This was a heavy blow, and one which Ferdinand Lopez was not the man to bear with equanimity. From the moment in which the Duchess had mentioned the borough to him, he had regarded the thing as certain. After a while he had understood that his return must be accompanied by more trouble and greater expense than he had at first anticipated;—but still he had thought that it was all but sure. He had altogether misunderstood the nature of the influence exercised by the Duchess, and the nature also of the Duke's resolution. Mr Sprugeon had of course wished to have a candidate, and had allured him. Perhaps he had in some degree been ill-treated by the borough. But he was a man, whom the feeling of injustice to himself would drive almost to frenzy, though he never measured the amount of his own injustice to others. When the proposition was made to him, he scowled at them all, and declared that he would fight the borough to the last. 'Then you'll let Mr Fletcher in to a certainty,' said Mr Sprout. Now there was an idea in the borough that, although all the candidates were ready to support the Duke's government, Mr Du Boung and Mr Lopez were the two Liberals. Mr Du Boung was sitting in the room when the appeal was made, and declared that he feared that such would be the result. 'I'll tell you what I'll do,' said Lopez; 'I'll toss up which of us retires.' Mr Sprout, on behalf of Mr Du Boung, protested against that proposition. Mr Du Boung, who was a gentleman of great local influence, was in possession of four-fifths of the Liberal interests of the borough. Even were he to retire, Mr Lopez could not get in. Mr Sprout declared that this was known to all the borough at large. He, Sprout, was sorry that a gentleman like Mr Lopez should have been brought down there under false ideas. He had all through told Mr Sprugeon that the Duke had been in earnest, but Mr Sprugeon had not comprehended the position. It had been a pity. But anybody who understood the borough could see with one eye that Mr Lopez had not a chance. If Mr Lopez would retire Mr Du Boung would no doubt be returned. If Mr Lopez went to the poll, Mr Fletcher would probably be the new member. This was the picture as it was painted by Mr Sprout,—who had, even then, heard something of the loves of the two candidates, and who had thought that Lopez would be glad to injure Arthur Fletcher's chances of success. So far he was not wrong;—but the sense of injury done to himself oppressed Lopez so much that he could not guide himself by reason. The idea of retiring was very painful to him, and he did not believe these men. He thought it to be quite possible that they were there to facilitate the return of Arthur Fletcher. He had never even heard of Du Boung till he had come to Silverbridge two or three days ago. He still could not believe that Du Boung would be returned. He thought over it all for a moment, and then he gave his answer. 'I've been brought down here to fight, and I'll fight it to the last,' he said. 'Then you'll hand over the borough to Mr Fletcher,' said Sprout, getting up and ushering Mr Du Boung out of the room.

It was after that, but on the same day, that Lopez and Fletcher met each other in the street. The affair did not take a minute, and then they parted, each on his own way. In the course of that evening Mr Sprugeon told his candidate that he, Sprugeon, could not concern himself any further in that election. He was very sorry for what had occurred;— very sorry indeed. It was no doubt a pity that the Duke had been so firm. 'But,'—and Mr Sprugeon shrugged his shoulders as he spoke,— 'when a nobleman like the Duke chooses to have a way of his own, he must have it.' Mr Sprugeon went on to declare that any further candidature would be a waste of money, waste of time, and waste of energy, and then signified his intention of retiring, as far as this election went, into private life. When asked, he acknowledged that they who had been acting with him had come to the same resolve. Mr Lopez had in fact come there as the Duke's nominee, and as the Duke had no nominee, Mr Lopez was in fact 'nowhere.'

'I don't suppose that any man was ever so treated before, since members were first returned to Parliament,' said Lopez.

'Well, sir;—yes, sir; it is a little hard. But, you see, sir, her Grace meant the best. Her Grace did mean the best, no doubt. It may be, sir, there was a little misunderstanding;—a little misunderstanding at the Castle, sir.' Then Mr Sprugeon retired, and Lopez understood that he was to see nothing more of the ironmonger.

Of course there was nothing for him now but to retire;—to shake the dust off his feet and get out of Silverbridge as quickly as he could. But his friends had all deserted him and he did not know how to retire. He had paid £500, and he had a strong opinion that a portion at least of the money should be returned to him. He had a keen sense of ill-usage, and at the same time a feeling that he ought not to run out of the borough like a whipt dog, without showing his face to any one. But his strongest sensation at this moment was one of hatred against Arthur Fletcher. He was sure that Arthur Fletcher would be the new member. He did not put the least trust in Mr Du Boung. He had taught himself really to think that Fletcher had insulted him by writing to his wife, and that a further insult had been offered to him by that meeting in the street. He had told his wife that he would ask Fletcher to give up the borough, and that he would make that request with a horsewhip in his hand. It was too late now to say anything of the borough, but it might not be too late for the horsewhip. He had a great desire to make good that threat as far as the horsewhip was concerned,—having an idea that he would thus lower Fletcher in his wife's eyes. It was not that he was jealous,— not jealous according to the ordinary meaning of the word. His wife's love to himself had been too recently given and too warmly maintained for such a feeling as that. But there was a rancorous hatred in his heart against the man, and a conviction that his wife at any rate esteemed the man whom he hated. And then would he not make his retreat from the borough with more honour if before he left he could horsewhip his successful antagonist? We, who know the feeling of Englishmen generally better than Mr Lopez did, would say—certainly not. We would think that such an incident would by no means redound to the credit of Mr Lopez. And he himself, probably, at cooler moments, would have seen the folly of such an idea. But anger about the borough had driven him mad, and now in his wretchedness the suggestion had for him a certain charm. The man had outraged all propriety by writing to his wife. Of course he would be justified in horsewhipping him. But there were difficulties. A man is not horsewhipped simply because you wish to horsewhip him.

In the evening, as he was sitting alone, he got a note from Mr Sprugeon. 'Mr Sprugeon's compliments. Doesn't Mr Lopez think an address to the electors should appear in to-morrow's "Gazette,"—very short and easy;—something like the following.' Then Mr Sprugeon added a very 'short and easy letter' to the electors of the borough of Silverbridge, in which Mr Lopez was supposed to tell them that although his canvass promised him every success, he felt that he owed it to the borough to retire, lest he should injure the borough by splitting the Liberal interest with their much respected fellow-townsman, Mr Du Boung. In the course of the evening he did copy that letter, and sent it out to the newspaper office. He must retire, and it was better for him that he should retire after some recognized fashion. But he wrote another letter also, and sent it over to the opposition hotel. The other letter was as follows:—

'SIR,—

'Before this election began you were guilty of gross impertinence in writing a letter to my wife,—to her extreme annoyance and to my most justifiable anger. Any gentleman would think that the treatment you had already received at her hands would have served to save her from such insult, but there are men who will never take a lesson without a beating. And now, since you have been here, you have presumed to offer to shake hands with me in the street, though you ought to have known that I should not choose to meet you on friendly terms after what has taken place. I now write to tell you that I shall carry a horsewhip while I am here, and that if I meet you in the streets again before I leave the town I shall use it.

                                                    'FERDINAND LOPEZ.

'Mr Arthur Fletcher.'

This letter he sent at once to his enemy, and then sat late into the night thinking of the threat and of the manner in which he would follow it up. If he could only get one fair blow at Fletcher his purpose, he thought, would be achieved. In any matter of horsewhipping the truth hardly ever gets itself correctly known. The man who has given the first blow is generally supposed to have thrashed the other. What might follow, though it might be inconvenient, must be borne. The man had insulted him by writing to his wife, and the sympathies of the world, he thought, would be with him. To give him his due, it must be owned that he had no personal fear as to the encounter.

That night Arthur Fletcher had gone over to Greshambury, and on the following morning he returned with Mr Gresham. 'For heaven's sake look at that!' he said, handing the letter to his friend.

'Did you ever write to his wife?' asked Gresham, when he read it.

'Yes;—I did. All this is dreadful to me;—dreadful. Well;—you know how it used to be with me. I need not go into all that; need I?'

'Don't say a word more than you think necessary.'

'When you asked me to stand for the place I had not heard that he thought of being a candidate. I wrote and told her so, and told her also that had I known it before I would not have come here.'

'I don't quite see that,' said Gresham.

'Perhaps not;—perhaps I was a fool. But we needn't go into that. At any rate there was no insult to him. I wrote in the simplest language.'

'Looking at it all round I think you had better not have written.'

'You wouldn't say so if you saw the letter. I'm sure you wouldn't. I had known her all my life. My brother is married to her cousin. Oh heavens! we had been all but engaged. I would have done anything for her. Was it not natural that I should tell her? As far as the language was concerned the letter was one to be read at Charing Cross.'

'He says that she was annoyed and insulted.'

'Impossible! It was a letter that any man might have written to any woman.'

'Well;—you have got to take care of yourself at any rate. What will you do?'

'What ought I to do?'

'Go to the police.' Mr Gresham had himself once, when young, thrashed a man who had offended him,* and had then thought himself much aggrieved because the police had been called in. But that had been twenty years ago, and Mr Gresham's opinions had been matured and, perhaps, corrected by age.

'No; I won't do that,' said Arthur Fletcher.

'That's what you ought to do.'

'I couldn't do that.'

'Then take no notice of the letter, and carry a fairly big stick. It should be big enough to hurt him a good deal, but not to do him any serious damage.' At that moment an agent came in with news of the man's retirement from the contest. 'Has he left the town?' asked Gresham. No;—he had not left the town, nor had he been seen by any one that morning. 'You had better let me go out and get the stick, before you show yourself,' said Gresham. And so the stick was selected.

As the two walked down the street together, almost the first thing they saw was Lopez standing at his hotel door with a cutting whip in his hand. He was at that moment quite alone, but on the opposite side of the street there was a policeman,—one of the borough constables,—very slowly making his way along the pavement. His movement, indeed, was so slow that any one watching him would have come to the conclusion that that particular part of the High Street had some attraction for him at that special moment. Alas, alas! How age will alter the spirit of a man! Twenty years since Frank Gresham would have thought any one to be a mean miscreant who would have interposed a policeman between him and his foe. But it is to be feared that while selecting that stick he had said a word which was causing the constable to loiter on the pavement!

But Gresham turned no eye to the policeman as he walked on with his friend, and Fletcher did not see the man. 'What an ass he is!' said Fletcher,—as he got the handle of the stick well into his hand. Then Lopez advanced to them with his whip raised; but as he did so the policeman came across the street quickly, but very quietly, and stood right before him. The man was so thoroughly in the way of the aggrieved wretch that it was out of the question that he should touch Fletcher with his whip.

'Do you usually walk about attended by a policeman?' said Lopez, with all the scorn which he knew how to throw into his voice.

'I didn't know that the man was here,' said Fletcher.

'You may tell that to the marines. All the borough shall know what a coward you are.' Then he turned round and addressed the street, but still under the shadow, as it were, of the policeman's helmet. 'This man who presumes to offer himself as a candidate to represent Silverbridge in Parliament has insulted my wife. And now, because he fears that I shall horsewhip him, he goes about the street under the care of a policeman.'

'This is intolerable,' said Fletcher, turning to his friend.

'Mr Lopez,' said Gresham. 'I am sorry to say that I must give you in charge;—unless you will undertake to leave the town without interfering further with Mr Fletcher either by word or deed.'

'I will undertake nothing,' said Lopez. 'The man has insulted my wife, and is a coward.'

About two o'clock on the afternoon of that day Mr Lopez appeared before the Silverbridge bench of magistrates, and was there sworn to keep the peace to Mr Fletcher for the next six months. After that he was allowed to leave the town, and was back in London, with his wife in Belgrave Mansions, to dinner that evening.

On the day but one after this the ballot was taken, and at eight o'clock on the evening of that day Arthur Fletcher was declared to be duly elected. But Mr Du Boung ran him very hard.

The numbers were—

FLETCHER	.	.	.	315
DU BOUNG	.	.	.	308

Mr Du Boung's friends during these last two days had not hesitated to make what use they could on behalf of their own candidate of the Lopez and Fletcher quarrel. If Mr Fletcher had insulted the other man's wife, surely he could not be a proper member for Silverbridge. And then the row was declared to have been altogether discreditable. Two strangers had come into this peaceful town and had absolutely quarrelled with sticks and whips in the street, calling each other opprobrious names. Would it not be better that they should elect their own respectable townsman? All this was nearly effective. But, in spite of all, Arthur Fletcher was at last returned.

CHAPTER 35

LOPEZ BACK IN LONDON

LOPEZ, as he returned to town, recovered something of his senses, though he still fancied that Arthur Fletcher had done him a positive injury by writing to his wife. But something of that madness left him which had come from his deep sense of injury, both as to the letter and as to the borough, and he began to feel that he had been wrong about the horsewhip. He was very low in spirits on this return journey. The money which he had spent had been material to him, and the loss of it for the moment left him nearly bare. While he had had before his eyes the hope of being a member of Parliament he had been able to buoy himself up. The position itself would have gone very far with Sexty Parker, and would, he thought, have had some effect even with his father-in-law. But now he was returning a beaten man. Who is there that has not felt that fall from high hope to utter despair which comes from some single failure? As he thought of this he was conscious that his anger had led him into great imprudence at Silverbridge. He had not been circumspect, as it specially behoved a man to be surrounded by such difficulties as his. All his life he had been schooling his temper so as to keep it under control,—sometimes with great difficulty, but always with a consciousness that in his life everything might depend on it. Now he had, alas, allowed it to get the better of him. No doubt he had been insulted;—but, nevertheless, he had been wrong to speak of a horsewhip.

His one great object must now be to conciliate his father-in-law, and he had certainly increased his difficulty in doing this by his squabble down at Silverbridge. Of course the whole thing would be reported in the London papers, and of course the story would be told against him, as the respectabilities of the town had been opposed to him. But he knew himself to be clever, and he still hoped that he might overcome these difficulties. Then it occurred to him that in doing this he must take care to have his wife entirely on his side. He did not doubt her love; he did not in the least doubt her rectitude;— but there was the lamentable fact that she thought well of Arthur Fletcher. It might be that he had been a little too imperious with his wife. It suited his disposition to be imperious within his own household;—to be imperious out of it, if that were possible;—but he was conscious of having had a fall at Silverbridge, and he must for a while take in some sail.

He had telegraphed to her, acquainting her with his defeat, and telling her to expect his return. 'Oh, Ferdinand,' she said, 'I am so unhappy about this. It has made me so wretched!'

'Better luck next time,' he said with his sweetest smile. 'It is no good groaning over spilt milk. They haven't treated me really well,— have they?'

'I suppose not,—though I do not quite understand it all.'

He was burning to abuse Arthur Fletcher, but he abstained. He would abstain at any rate for the present moment. 'Dukes and duchesses are no doubt very grand people,' he said, 'but it is a pity they should not know how to behave honestly, as they expect others to behave to them.

The Duchess has thrown me over in the most infernal way. I really can't understand it. When I think of it I am lost in wonder. The truth, I suppose, is, that there has been some quarrel between him and her.'

'Who will get in?'

'Oh, Du Boung, no doubt.' He did not think so, but he could not bring himself to declare the success of his enemy to her. 'The people there know him. Your old friend is as much a stranger there as I am. By-the-way he and I had a little row in the place.'

'A row, Ferdinand!'

'You needn't look like that, my pet. I haven't killed him. But he came up to speak to me in the street, and I told him what I thought about his writing to you.' On hearing this Emily looked very wretched. 'I could not restrain myself from doing that. Come;—you must admit that he shouldn't have written.'

'He meant it in kindness.'

'Then he shouldn't have meant it. Just think of it. Suppose that I had been making up to any girl,—which by-the-way I never did but to one in my life,'—then he put his arm round her waist and kissed her, 'and she were to have married someone else. What would have been said of me if I had begun to correspond with her immediately? Don't suppose I am blaming you, dear.'

'Certainly I do not suppose that,' said Emily.

'But you must admit that it was rather strong.' He paused, but she said nothing. 'Only I suppose you can bring yourself to admit nothing against him. However, so it was. There was a row, and a policeman came up, and they made me give a promise that I didn't mean to shoot him or anything of that kind.' As she heard this she turned pale, but said nothing. 'Of course I didn't want to shoot him. I wished him to know what I thought about it, and I told him. I hate to trouble you with all this, but I couldn't bear that you shouldn't know it all.'

'It is very sad!'

'Sad enough! I have had plenty to bear, I can tell you. Everybody seemed to turn away from me there. Everybody deserted me.' As he said this he could perceive that he must obtain her sympathy by recounting his own miseries and not Arthur Fletcher's sins. 'I was all alone and hardly knew how to hold up my head against so much wretchedness. And then I found myself called upon to pay an enormous sum for my expenses.'

'Oh, Ferdinand!'

'Think of their demanding £500!'

'Did you pay it?'

'Yes, indeed. I had no alternative. Of course they took care to come for that before they talked of my resigning. I believe it was all planned beforehand. The whole thing seems to me to have been a swindle from beginning to end. By heaven, I'm almost inclined to think that the Duchess knew all about it herself!'

'About the £500!'

'Perhaps not the exact sum, but the way in which the thing was to be done. In these days one doesn't know whom to trust. Men, and women too, have become so dishonest that nobody is safe anywhere. It has been awfully hard upon me,—awfully hard. I don't suppose that there was ever a moment in my life when the loss of £500 would have been so much to me as it is now. The question is, what will your father do for us?' Emily could not but remember her husband's intense desire to obtain money from her father not yet three months since, as though all the world depended on his getting it,—and his subsequent elation, as though all his sorrows were over for ever, because the money had been promised. And now,—almost immediately,—he was again in the same position. She endeavoured to judge him kindly, but a feeling of insecurity in reference to his affairs struck her at once and made her heart cold. Everything had been achieved, then, by a gift of £3000,—surely a small sum to effect such a result with a man living as her husband lived. And now the whole £3000 was gone;—surely a large sum to have vanished in so short a time! Something of the uncertainty of business she could understand, but a business must be perilously uncertain if subject to such vicissitudes as these! But as ideas of this nature crowded themselves into her mind she told herself again and again that she had taken him for better and for worse. If the worse were already coming, she would still be true to her promise. 'You had better tell papa everything.'

'Had it not better come from you?'

'No, Ferdinand. Of course I will do as you bid me. I will do anything that I can do. But you had better tell him. His nature is such that he will respect you more if it come from yourself. And then it is so necessary that he should know all;—all.' She put whatever emphasis she knew how to use upon this word.

'You could tell him—all, as well as I.'

'You would not bring yourself to tell it to me, nor could I understand it. He will understand everything, and if he thinks that you have told him everything, he will at any rate respect you.'

He sat silent for a while meditating, feeling always and most acutely that he had been ill-used,—never thinking for an instant that he had ill-used others. '£3000, you know, was no fortune for your father to give you!' She had no answer to make, but she groaned in spirit as she heard the accusation. 'Don't you feel that yourself?'

'I know nothing about money, Ferdinand. If you had told me to speak to him about it before we were married I would have done so.'

'He ought to have spoken to me. It is marvellous how close-fisted an old man can be. He can't take it with him.' Then he sat for half an hour in moody silence, during which she was busy with her needle. After that he jumped up, with a manner altogether altered,—gay, only that the attempt was too visible to deceive even her,—and shook himself, as though he were ridding himself of his trouble. 'You are right, old girl. You are always right,—almost. I will go to your father to-morrow, and tell him everything. It isn't so very much that I want him to do. Things will all come right again. I'm ashamed that you should have seen me in this way;—but I have been disappointed about the election, and troubled about that Mr Fletcher. You shall not see me give way again like this. Give me a kiss, old girl.'

She kissed him, but she could not even pretend to recover herself as he had done. 'Had we not better give up the brougham?' she said.

'Certainly not. For heaven's sake do not speak in that way! You do not understand things.'

'No; certainly I do not.'

'It isn't that I haven't the means of living, but that in my business money is so often required for instant use. And situated as I am at present an addition to my capital would enable me to do so much!' She certainly did not understand it, but she had sufficient knowledge of the world and sufficient common sense to be aware that their present rate of expenditure ought to be a matter of importance to a man who felt the loss of £500 as he felt that loss at Silverbridge.

On the next morning Lopez was at Mr Wharton's chambers early,—so early that the lawyer had not yet reached them. He had resolved,—not that he would tell everything, for such men never even intend to tell everything,—but that he would tell a good deal. He must, if possible, affect the mind of the old man in two ways. He must ingratiate himself;—and at the same time make it understood that Emily's comfort in life would depend very much on her father's generosity. The first must be first accomplished, if possible,—and then the second, as to which he could certainly produce at any rate belief. He had not married a rich man's daughter without an intention of getting the rich man's money! Mr Wharton would understand that. If the worst came to the worst, Mr Wharton must of course maintain his daughter,—and his daughter's husband! But things had not come to the worst as yet, and he did not intend on the present occasion to present that view of his affairs to his father-in-law.

Mr Wharton when he entered his chambers found Lopez seated there. He was himself at this moment very unhappy. He had renewed his quarrel with Everett,—or Everett rather had renewed the quarrel with him. There had been words between them about money lost at cards. Hard words had been used, and Everett had told his father that if either of them were a gambler it was not he. Mr Wharton had resented this bitterly and had driven his son from his presence,—and now the quarrel made him very wretched. He certainly was sorry that he had called his son a gambler, but his son had been, as he thought, inexcusable in the retort which he had made. He was a man to whom his friends gave credit for much sternness;—but still he was one who certainly had no happiness in the world independent of his children. His daughter had left him, not as he thought under happy auspices,—and he was now, at this moment, soft-hearted and tender in his regards as to her. What was there in the world for him but his children? And now he felt himself to be alone and destitute. He was already tired of whist at the Eldon. That which had been a delight to him once or twice a week, became almost loathsome when it was renewed from day to day;—and not the less when his son told him that he also was a gambler. 'So you have come back from Silverbridge?' he said.

'Yes, sir; I have come back, not exactly triumphant. A man should not expect to win always.' Lopez had resolved to pluck up his spirit and carry himself like a man.

'You seem to have got into some scrape down there, besides losing your election.'

'Oh; you have seen that in the papers already. I have come to tell you of it. As Emily is concerned in it you ought to know.'

'Emily concerned! How is she concerned?'

Then Lopez told the whole story,—after his own fashion, and yet with no palpable lie. Fletcher had written to her a letter which he had thought to be very offensive. On hearing this, Mr Wharton looked very grave, and asked for the letter. Lopez said that he had destroyed it, not thinking that such a document should be preserved. Then he went on to explain that it had had reference to the election, and that he had thought it to be highly improper that Fletcher should write to his wife on that or on any other subject. 'It depends very much on the letter,' said the old man.

'But on any subject,—after what has passed.'

'They were very old friends.'

'Of course I will not argue with you, Mr Wharton; but I own that it angered me. It angered me very much,—very much indeed. I took it to be an insult to her, and when he accosted me in the street down at Silverbridge I told him so. I may not have been very wise, but I did it on her behalf. Surely you can understand that such a letter might make a man angry.'

'What did he say?'

'That he would do anything for her sake,—even retire from Silverbridge if his friends would let him.' Mr Wharton scratched his head, and Lopez saw that he was perplexed. 'Should he have offered to do anything for her sake, after what had passed?'

'I know the man so well,' said Mr Wharton, 'that I cannot and do not believe him to have harboured an improper thought in reference to my child.'

'Perhaps it was an indiscretion only.'

'Perhaps so. I cannot say. And then they took you before the magistrates?'

'Yes;—in my anger I had threatened him. Then there was a policeman and a row. And I had to swear that I would not hurt him. Of course I have no wish to hurt him.'

'I suppose it ruined your chance at Silverbridge?'

'I suppose it did.' This was a lie, as Lopez had retired before the row took place. 'What I care for most now is that you should not think that I have misbehaved myself.'

The story had been told very well, and Mr Wharton was almost disposed to sympathize with his son-in-law. That Arthur Fletcher had meant nothing that could be regarded as offensive to his daughter he was quite sure;—but it might be that in making an offer intended to be generous he had used language which the condition of the persons concerned made indiscreet. 'I suppose,' he said, 'that you spent a lot of money at Silverbridge?' This gave Lopez the opening that he wanted, and he described the manner in which the £500 had been extracted from him. 'You can't play that game for nothing,' said Mr Wharton.

'And just at present I could very ill afford it. I should not have done it had I not felt it a pity to neglect such a chance of rising in the world. After all, a seat in the British House of Commons is an honour.'

'Yes;—yes;—yes.'

'And the Duchess, when she spoke to me about it, was so certain.'

'I will pay the £500,' said Mr Wharton.

'Oh, sir, that is generous!' Then he got up and took the old man's hands. 'Some day, when you are at liberty, I hope that you will allow me to explain to you the exact state of my affairs. When I wrote to you from Como I told you that I would wish to do so. You do not object?'

'No,' said the lawyer,—but with infinite hesitation in his voice. 'No; I don't object. But I do not know how I could serve them. I shall be busy just now, but I will give you the cheque. And if you and Emily have nothing better to do, come and dine to-morrow.' Lopez with real tears in his eyes took the cheque, and promised to come on the morrow. 'And in the meantime I wish you would see Everett.' Of course he promised that he would see Everett.

Again he was exalted, on this occasion not so much by the acquisition of the money as by the growing conviction that his father-in-law was a cow capable of being milked. And the quarrel between Everett and his father might clearly be useful to him. He might either serve the old man by reducing Everett to proper submission, or he might manage to creep into the empty space which his son's defection would make in the father's heart and the father's life. He might at any rate make himself necessary to the old man, and become such a part of the household in Manchester Square as to be indispensable. Then the old man would every day become older and more in want of assistance. He thought that he saw the way to worm himself into confidence, and, soon into possession. The old man was not a man of iron as he had feared, but quite human, and if properly managed, soft and malleable.

He saw Sexty Parker in the city that day, and used his cheque for £500 in some triumphant way, partly cajoling and partly bullying his poor victim. To Sexty also he had to tell his own story about the row down at Silverbridge. He had threatened to thrash the fellow in the street, and the fellow had not dared to come out of his house without a policeman. Yes;—he had lost his election. The swindling of those fellows at Silverbridge had been too much for him. But he flattered himself that he had got the better of Master Fletcher. That was the tone in which he told the story to his friend in the city.

Then, before dinner, he found Everett at the club. Everett Wharton was to be found there now almost every day. His excuse to himself lay in the political character of the institution. The club intended to do great things,—to find Liberal candidates for all the boroughs and counties in England which were not hitherto furnished, and then to supply the candidates with money. Such was the great purpose of the Progress. It had not as yet sent out many candidates or collected much money. As yet it was, politically, almost quiescent. And therefore Everett Wharton, whose sense of duty took him there, spent his afternoons either in the whist-room or at the billiard-table.

The story of the Silverbridge row had to be told again, and was told nearly with the same incidents as had been narrated to the father. He could of course abuse Arthur Fletcher more roundly, and be more confident in his assertion that Fletcher had insulted his wife. But he came as quickly as he could to the task which he had on hand. 'What's all this between you and your father?'

'Simply this. I sometimes play a game of whist, and therefore he called me a gambler. Then I reminded him that he also sometimes played a game of whist, and I asked him what deduction was to be drawn.'

'He is awfully angry with you.'

'Of course I was a fool. My father has the whip hand of me, because he has money and I have none, and it was simply kicking against the pricks* to speak as I did. And then too there isn't a fellow in London has a higher respect for his father than I have, nor yet a warmer affection. But it is hard to be driven in that way. Gambler is a nasty word.'

'Yes, it is; very nasty. But I suppose a man does gamble when he loses so much money that he has to ask his father to pay it for him.'

'If he does so often, he gambles. I never asked him for money to pay what I had lost before in my life.'

'I wonder you told him.'

'I never lie to him, and he ought to know that. But he is just the man to be harder to his own son than to anybody else in the world. What does he want me to do now?'

'I don't know that he wants you to do anything,' said Lopez.

'Did he send you to me?'

'Well;—no; I can't say that he did. I told him I should see you as a matter of course, and he said something rough,—about your being an ass.'

'I dare say he did.'

'But if you ask me,' said Lopez, 'I think he would take it kindly of you if you were to go and see him. Come and dine to-day, just as if nothing had happened.'

'I could not do that,—unless he asked me.'

'I can't say that he asked you, Everett. I would say so, in spite of its being a lie, if I didn't fear that your father might say something unkind, so that the lie would be detected by both of you.'

'And yet you ask me to go and dine there!'

'Yes, I do. It's only going away if he does cut up rough. And if he takes it well,—why then,—the whole thing is done.'

'If he wants me, he can ask me.'

'You talk about it, my boy, just as if a father were the same as anybody else. If I had a father with a lot of money, by George he should knock me about with his stick if he liked, and I would be just the same next day.'

'Unfortunately I am of a stiffer nature,' said Everett, taking some pride to himself for his stiffness, and being perhaps as little 'stiff' as any young man of his day.

That evening, after dinner at Manchester Square, the conversation between the father-in-law and the son-in-law turned almost exclusively on the son and brother-in-law. Little or nothing was said about the election, and the name of Arthur Fletcher was not mentioned. But out of his full heart the father spoke. He was wretched about Everett. Did Everett mean to cut him? 'He wants you to withdraw some name you called him,' said Lopez.

'Withdraw some name,—as he might ask some hot-headed fellow to do, of his own age, like himself; some fellow that he had quarrelled with! Does he expect his father to send him a written apology? He had been gambling, and I told him that he was a gambler. Is that too much for a father to say?' Lopez shrugged his shoulders, and declared that it was a pity. 'He will break my heart if he goes on like this,' said the old man.

'I asked him to come and dine to-day, but he didn't seem to like it.'

'Like it! No. He likes nothing but that infernal club.'

When the evening was over Lopez felt that he had done a good stroke of work. He had not exactly made up his mind to keep the father and son apart. That was not a part of his strategy,—at any rate as yet. But he did intend to make himself necessary to the old man,—to become the old man's son, and if possible the favourite son. And now he thought that he had already done much towards the achievement of his object.

CHAPTER 36

THE JOLLY BLACKBIRD

THERE was great triumph at Longbarns when the news of Arthur's victory reached the place;—and when he arrived there himself with his friend Mr Gresham, he was received as a conquering hero. But of course the tidings of 'the row' had gone before him, and it was necessary that both he and Mr Gresham should tell the story;—nor could it be told privately. Sir Alured Wharton was there, and Mrs Fletcher.

The old lady had heard of the row, and of course required to be told all the particulars. This was not pleasant to the hero, as in talking of the man it was impossible for them not to talk of the man's wife. 'What a terrible misfortune for poor Mr Wharton,' said the old lady, nodding her head at Sir Alured. Sir Alured sighed and said nothing. Certainly a terrible misfortune, and one which affected more or less the whole family of Whartons!

'Do you mean to say that he was going to attack Arthur with a whip?' asked John Fletcher.

'I only know that he was standing there with a whip in his hand,' said Mr Gresham.

'I think he would have had the worst of that.'

'You would have laughed,' said Arthur, 'to see me walking majestically along the High Street with a cudgel which Gresham had just bought for me as being of the proper medium size. I don't doubt he meant to have a fight. And then you should have seen the policeman sloping over and putting himself in the way. I never quite understood where that policeman came from.'

'They are very well off for policemen in Silverbridge,' said Gresham. 'They've always got them going about.'

'He must be mad,' said John.

'Poor unfortunate young woman!' said Mrs Fletcher, holding up both her hands. 'I must say that I cannot but blame Mr Wharton. If he had been firm, it never would have come to that. I wonder whether he ever sees him.'

'Of course he does,' said John. 'Why shouldn't he see him? You'd see him if he'd married a daughter of yours.'

'Never!' exclaimed the old woman. 'If I had had a child so lost to all respect as that, I do not say that I would not have seen her. Human nature might have prevailed. But I would never willingly have put myself into contact with one who had so degraded me and mine.'

'I shall be very anxious to know what Mr Wharton does about his money,' said John.

Arthur allowed himself but a couple of days among his friends, and then hurried up to London to take his seat. When there he was astonished to find how many questions were asked him about 'the row,' and how much was known about it,—and at the same time how little was really known. Everybody had heard that there had been a row, and everybody knew that there had been a lady in the case. But there seemed to be a general idea that the lady had been in some way misused, and that Arthur Fletcher had come forward like a Paladin* to protect her. A letter had been written, and the husband, ogre-like, had intercepted the letter. The lady was the most unfortunate of human beings,—or would have been but for that consolation which she must have in the constancy of her old lover. As to all these matters the stories varied; but everybody agreed on one point. All the world knew that Arthur Fletcher had gone to Silverbridge, had stood for the borough, and had taken the seat away from his rival,—because that rival had robbed him of his bride. How the robbery had been effected the world could not quite say. The world was still of the opinion that the lady was violently attached to the man she had not married. But Captain Gunner explained it all clearly to Major Pountney by asserting that the poor girl had been coerced into the marriage by her father. And thus Arthur Fletcher found himself almost as much a hero in London as at Longbarns.

Fletcher had not been above a week in town, and had become heartily sick of the rumours which in various shapes made their way round to his own ears, when he received an invitation from Mr Wharton to go and dine with him at a tavern called the Jolly Blackbird. The invitation surprised him,—that he should be asked by such a man to dine at such a place,—but he accepted it as a matter of course. He was indeed much interested in a Bill for the drainage of common lands which was to be discussed in the House that night; there was a good deal of common land round Silverbridge, and he had some idea of making his first speech,—but he calculated that he might get his dinner and yet be back in time for the debate. So he went to the Jolly Blackbird,*—a very quaint, old-fashioned law dining-house in the neighbourhood of Portugal Street, which had managed not to get itself pulled down a dozen years ago on behalf of the Law Courts* which are to bless some coming generation. Arthur had never been there before and was surprised at the black wainscoting, the black tables, the old-fashioned grate, the two candles on the table, and the silent waiter. 'I wanted to see you, Arthur,' said the old man pressing his hand in a melancholy way, 'but I couldn't ask you to Manchester Square. They come in sometimes in the evening, and it might have been unpleasant. At your young men's clubs they let strangers dine. We haven't anything of that kind at the Eldon. You'll find they'll give you a very good bit of fish here, and a fairish steak.' Arthur declared that he thought it a capital place,—the best fun in the world. 'And they've a very good bottle of claret;—better than we get at the Eldon, I think. I don't know that I can say much for their champagne. We'll try it. You young fellows always drink champagne.'

'I hardly ever touch it,' said Arthur. 'Sherry and claret are my wines.'

'Very well;—very well. I did want to see you, my boy. Things haven't turned out just as we wished;—have they?'

'Not exactly, sir.'

'No indeed. You know the old saying, "God disposes it all." I have to make the best of it,—and so no doubt do you.'

'There's no doubt about it, sir,' said Arthur, speaking in a low but almost angry voice. They were not in a room by themselves, but in a recess which separated them from the room. 'I don't know that I want to talk about it, but to me it is one of those things for which there is no remedy. When a man loses his leg, he hobbles on, and sometimes has a good time of it at last;—but there he is, without a leg.'

'It wasn't my fault, Arthur.'

'There has been no fault but my own. I went in for the running and got distanced. That's simply all about it, and there's no more to be said.'

'You ain't surprised that I should wish to see you.'

'I'm ever so much obliged. I think it's very kind of you.'

'I can't go in for a new life as you can. I can't take up politics and Parliament. It's too late for me.'

'I'm going to. There's a Bill coming on this very night that I'm interested about. You mustn't be angry if I rush off a little before ten. We are going to lend money to the parishes on the security of the rates for draining bits of common land. Then we shall sell the land and endow the unions so as to lessen the poor rates, and increase the cereal products of the country. We think we can bring 300,000 acres under the plough in three years, which now produce almost nothing, and in five years would pay all the expenses. Putting the value of the land at £25 an acre, which is low, we shall have created property to the value of seven millions and a half.* That's something, you know.'

'Oh, yes,' said Mr Wharton, who felt himself quite unable to follow with any interest the aspirations of the young legislator.

'Of course it's complicated,' continued Arthur, 'but when you come to look into it it comes out clear enough. It is one of the instances of the omnipotence of capital. Parliament can do such a thing, not because it has any creative power of its own, but because it has the command of unlimited capital.' Mr Wharton looked at him, sighing inwardly as he reflected that unrequited love should have brought a clear-headed young barrister into mists so thick and labyrinths so mazy as these. 'A very good beefsteak indeed,' said Arthur. 'I don't know when I ate a better one. Thank you, no;—I'll stick to the claret.' Mr Wharton had offered him Madeira. 'Claret and brown meat always go well together. Pancake! I don't object to a pancake. A pancake's a very good thing. Now would you believe it, sir; they can't make a pancake at the House.'

'And yet they sometimes fall very flat too,' said the lawyer, making a real lawyer's joke.

'It's all in the mixing, sir,' said Arthur, carrying it on. 'We've mixture enough just at present, but it isn't of the proper sort;—too much of the flour, and not enough of the egg.'

But Mr Wharton still had something to say, though he hardly knew how to say it. 'You must come and see us in the Square after a bit.'

'Oh;—of course.'

'I wouldn't ask you to dine there to-day, because I thought we should be less melancholy here;—but you mustn't cut us altogether. You haven't seen Everett since you've been in town?'

'No, sir. I believe he lives a good deal,—a good deal with— Mr Lopez. There was a little row down at Silverbridge. Of course it will wear off, but just at present his lines and my lines don't converge.'

'I'm very unhappy about him, Arthur.'

'There's nothing the matter!'

'My girl has married that man. I've nothing to say against him;—but of course it wasn't to my taste; and I feel it as a separation. And now Everett has quarrelled with me.'

'Quarrelled with you!'

Then the father told the story as well as he knew how. His son had lost some money, and he had called him a gambler;—and consequently his son would not come near him. 'It is bad to lose them both, Arthur.'

'That is so unlike Everett.'

'It seems to me that everybody has changed,—except myself. Who would have dreamed that she would have married that man? Not that I have anything to say against him except that he was not of our sort. He has been very good about Everett, and is very good about him. But Everett will not come to me unless I—withdraw the word;—say that I was wrong to call him a gambler. That is a proposition that no son should make to a father.'

'It is very unlike Everett,' repeated the other. 'Has he written to that effect?'

'He has not written a word.'

'Why don't you see him yourself, and have it out with him?'

'Am I to go to that club after him?' said the father.

'Write to him and bid him come to you. I'll give up my seat if he don't come to you. Everett was always a quaint fellow, a little idle, you know,—mooning about after ideas——

'He's no fool, you know,' said the father.

'Not at all;—only vague. But he's the last man in the world to have nasty vulgar ideas of his own importance as distinguished from yours.'

'Lopez says——'

'I wouldn't quite trust Lopez.'

'He isn't a bad fellow in his way, Arthur. Of course he is not what I would have liked for a son-in-law. I needn't tell you that. But he is kind and gentle-mannered, and has always been attached to Everett. You know he saved Everett's life at the risk of his own.' Arthur could not but smile as he perceived how the old man was being won round by the son-in-law, whom he had treated so violently before the man had become his son-in-law. 'By the way, what was all that about a letter you wrote to him?'

'Emily,—I mean Mrs Lopez,—will tell you if you ask her.'

'I don't want to ask her. I don't want to appear to set the wife against the husband. I am sure, my boy, you would write nothing that could affront her.'

'I think not, Mr Wharton. If I know myself well at all, or my own nature, it is not probable that I should affront your daughter.'

'No; no; no. I know that, my dear boy. I was always sure of that. Take some more wine.'

'No more, thank you. I must be off because I'm so anxious about this Bill.'

'I couldn't ask Emily about this letter. Now that they are married I have to make the best of it,—for her sake. I couldn't bring myself to say anything to her which might seem to accuse him.'

'I thought it right, sir, to explain to her that were I not in the hands of other people, I would not do anything to interfere with her happiness by opposing her husband. My language was most guarded.'

'He destroyed the letter.'

'I have a copy of it, if it comes to that,' said Arthur.

'It will be best, perhaps, to say nothing further about it. Well;— good-night, my boy, if you must go.' Then Fletcher went off to the House, wondering as he went at the change which had apparently come over the character of his old friend. Mr Wharton had always been a strong man, and now he seemed to be as weak as water. As to Everett, Fletcher was sure that there was something wrong, but he could not see his way to interfere himself. For the present he was divided from the family. Nevertheless he told himself again and again that that division should not be permanent. Of all the world she must always be to him the dearest.

CHAPTER 37

THE HORNS

THE first months of the Session went on very much as the last Session had gone. The ministry did nothing brilliant. As far as the outer world could see, they seemed to be firm enough. There was no opposing party in the House strong enough to get a vote against them on any subject. Outsiders, who only studied politics in the columns of their newspapers, imagined the Coalition to be very strong. But they who were inside, members themselves, and the club quidnuncs* who were always rubbing their shoulders against members, knew better. The opposition to the Coalition was within the Coalition itself. Sir Orlando Drought had not been allowed to build his four ships, and was consequently eager in his fears that the country would be invaded by the combined forces of Germany and France, that India would be sold by those powers to Russia, that Canada would be annexed to the States, that a great independent Roman Catholic hierarchy would be established in Ireland, and that Malta and Gibraltar would be taken away from us;— all which evils would be averted by the building of four big ships. A wet blanket of so terrible a size was in itself pernicious to the Cabinet, and heartrending to the poor Duke. But Sir Orlando could do worse even than this. As he was not to build his four ships neither should Mr Monk be allowed to readjust the county suffrage. When the skeleton of Mr Monk's scheme was discussed in the Cabinet, Sir Orlando would not agree to it. The gentlemen, he said, who had joined the present Government with him, would never consent to a measure which would be so utterly destructive of the county interest. If Mr Monk insisted on his measure in its proposed form, he must, with very great regret, place his resignation in the Duke's hands, and he believed that his friends would find themselves compelled to follow the same course. Then our Duke consulted the old Duke. The old Duke's advice was the same as ever. The Queen's Government was the main object. The present ministry enjoyed the support of the country, and he considered it the duty of the First Lord of the Treasury to remain at his post. The country was in no hurry, and the question of suffrages in the counties might be well delayed. Then he added a little counsel which might be called quite private, as it was certainly intended for no other ears than those of his younger friend. 'Give Sir Orlando rope enough and he'll hang himself. His own party are becoming tired of him. If you quarrel with him this Session, Drummond, and Ramsden, and Beeswax, would go out with him, and the Government would be broken up; but next Session you may get rid of him safely.'

'I wish it were broken up,' said the Prime Minister.

'You have your duty to do by the country and by the Queen, and you mustn't regard your own wishes. Next Session, let Monk be ready with his Bill again,—the same measure exactly. Let Sir Orlando resign then if he will. Should he do so I doubt whether anyone would go with him. Drummond does not like him much better than you and I do.' The poor Prime Minister was forced to obey. The old Duke was his only trusted counsellor, and he found himself constrained by his conscience to do as that counsellor counselled him. When, however, Sir Orlando, in his place as Leader of the House, in answer to some question from a hot and disappointed Radical, averred that the whole of her Majesty's Government had been quite in unison on this question of the county suffrage, he was hardly able to restrain himself. 'If there be differences of opinion they must be kept in the background,' said the Duke of St Bungay. 'Nothing can justify a direct falsehood,' said the Duke of Omnium. Thus it came to pass that the only real measure which the Government had in hand was one by which Phineas Finn hoped so to increase the power of Irish municipalities as to make the Home Rulers believe that a certain amount of Home Rule was being conceded to them. It was not a great measure, and poor Phineas himself hardly believed in it. And thus the Duke's ministry came to be called the Faineants.

But the Duchess, though she had been much snubbed, still persevered. Now and again she would declare herself to be broken-hearted, and would say that things might go their own way, that she would send in her resignation, that she would retire into private life and milk cows, that she would shake hands with no more parliamentary cads and 'caddesses',—a word which her Grace condescended to coin for her own use; that she would spend the next three years in travelling about the world; and lastly that, let there come of it whatever might, Sir Orlando Drought should never again be invited into any house of which she was the mistress. This last threat, which was perhaps the most indiscreet of them all, she absolutely made good,—thereby adding very greatly to her husband's difficulties.

But by the middle of June the parties at the house in Carlton Terrace were as frequent and as large as ever. Indeed it was all party with her. The Duchess possessed a pretty little villa down at Richmond, on the river, called The Horns, and gave parties there when there were none in London. She had picnics, and flower parties, and tea parties, and afternoons, and evenings, on the lawn,—till half London was always on its way to Richmond or back again. How she worked! And yet from day to day she swore that the world was ungrateful, and that she would work no more! I think that the world was ungrateful. Everybody went. She was so far successful that nobody thought of despising her parties. It was quite the thing to go to the Duchess's, whether at Richmond or in London. But people abused her and laughed at her. They said that she intrigued to get political support for her husband,—and, worse than that, they said that she failed. She did not fail altogether. The world was not taken captive as she had intended. Young members of Parliament did not become hotly enthusiastic in support of her and her husband as she had hoped that they would do. She had not become an institution of granite as her dreams had fondly told her might be possible;—for there had been moments in which she had almost thought that she could rule England by giving dinner and supper parties, by ices and champagne. But in a dull, phlegmatic way, they who ate the ices and drank the champagne were true to her. There was a feeling abroad that 'Glencora' was a 'good sort of fellow' and ought to be supported. And when the ridicule became too strong, or the abuse too sharp, men would take up the cudgels for her, and fight her battles;—a little too openly, perhaps, as they would do it under her eyes, and in her hearing, and would tell her what they had done, mistaking on such occasions her good humour for sympathy. There was just enough of success to prevent that abandonment of her project which she so often threatened, but not enough to make her triumphant. She was too clever not to see that she was ridiculed. She knew that men called her Glencora among themselves. She was herself quite alive to the fact that she herself was wanting in dignity, and that with all the means at her disposal, with all her courage and all her talent, she did not quite play the part of the really great lady. But she did not fail to tell herself that labour continued would at last be successful, and she was strong to bear the buffets of the ill-natured. She did not think that she brought first-class materials to her work, but she believed,—a belief as erroneous as, alas, it is common,—that first-rate results might be achieved by second-rate means. 'We had such a battle about your Grace last night,' Captain Gunner said to her.

'And were you my knight?'

'Indeed I was. I never heard such nonsense.'

'What were they saying?'

'Oh, the old story;—that you were like Martha,* busying yourself about many things.'

'Why shouldn't I busy myself about many things? It is a pity, Captain Gunner, that some of you men have not something to busy yourselves about.' All this was unpleasant. She could on such an occasion make up her mind to drop any Captain Gunner who had ventured to take too much upon himself; but she felt that in the efforts which she had made after popularity, she had submitted herself to unpleasant familiarities;—and though persistent in her course, she was still angry with herself.

When she had begun her campaign as the Prime Minister's wife, one of her difficulties had been with regard to money. An abnormal expenditure became necessary, for which her husband's express sanction must be obtained, and steps taken in which his personal assistance would be necessary;—but this had been done, and there was now no further impediment in that direction. It seemed to be understood that she was to spend what money she pleased. There had been various contests between them, but in every contest she had gained something. He had been majestically indignant with her in reference to the candidature at Silverbridge,—but, as is usual with many of us, had been unable to maintain his anger about two things at the same time. Or, rather, in the majesty of his anger about her interference, he had disdained to descend to the smaller faults of her extravagance. He had seemed to concede everything else to her, on condition that he should be allowed to be imperious in reference to the borough. In that matter she had given way, never having opened her mouth about it after that one unfortunate word to Mr Sprugeon. But, having done so, she was entitled to squander her thousands without remorse,—and she squandered them. 'It is your five-and-twenty thousand pounds,* my dear,' she once said to Mrs Finn, who often took upon herself to question the prudence of all this expenditure. This referred to a certain sum of money which had been left by the old Duke to Madame Goesler, as she was then called,—a legacy which that lady had repudiated. The money had, in truth, been given away to a relation of the Duke's by the joint consent of the lady and the Duke himself, but the Duchess was pleased to refer to it occasionally as a still existing property.

'My five-and-twenty thousand pounds, as you call it, would not go very far.'

'What's the use of money if you don't spend it? The Duke would go on collecting it and buying more property, which always means more trouble,—not because he is avaricious, but because for the time that comes easier than spending. Supposing he had married a woman without a shilling, he would still have been a rich man. As it is, my property was more even than his own. If we can do any good by spending the money, why shouldn't it be spent?'

'If you can do any good!'

'It all comes round to that. It isn't because I like always to live in a windmill! I have come to hate it. At this moment I would give worlds to be down at Matching with no one but the children, and to go about in a straw hat and a muslin gown. I have a fancy that I could sit under a tree and read a sermon, and think it the sweetest recreation. But I've made the attempt to do all this, and it is so mean to fail!'

'But where is to be the end of it?'

'There shall be no end as long as he is Prime Minister. He is the first man in England. Some people would say the first in Europe,—or in the world. A Prince should entertain like a Prince.'

'He need not be always entertaining.'

· 'Hospitality should run from a man with his wealth and his position, like water from a fountain. As his hand is known to be full, so it should be known to be open. When the delight of his friends is in question, he should know nothing of cost. Pearls should drop from him as from a fairy. But I don't think you understand me.'

'Not when the pearls are to be picked up by Captain Gunners, Lady Glen.'

'I can't make the men any better,—nor yet the women. They are poor mean creatures. The world is made up of such. I don't know that Captain Gunner is worse than Sir Orlando Drought or Sir Timothy Beeswax. People seen by the mind are exactly different to things seen by the eye. They grow smaller and smaller as you come nearer down to them, whereas things become bigger. I remember when I used to think that members of the Cabinet were almost gods, and now they seem to be no bigger than the shoeblacks,—only less picturesque. He told me the other day of the time when he gave up going into power for the sake of taking me abroad. Ah me! how much was happening then,—and how much has happened since that! We didn't know you then.'

'He has been a good husband to you.'

'And I have been a good wife to him! I have never had him for an hour out of my heart since that, or ever for a moment forgotten his interest. I can't live with him because he shuts himself up reading blue books, and is always at his office or in the House;—but I would if I could. Am I not doing it all for him? You don't think that the Captain Gunnners are particularly pleasant to me! Think of your life and of mine. You have had lovers.'

'One in my life,—when I was entitled to have one.'

'Well; I am the Duchess of Omnium, and I am the wife of the Prime Minister, and I had a larger property of my own than any other young woman that ever was born; and I am myself too,—Glencora M'Cluskie that was, and I've made for myself a character that I'm not ashamed of. But I'd be the curate's wife to-morrow, and make puddings, if I could only have my own husband and my own children with me. What's the use of it all? I like you better than anybody else, but you do nothing but scold me.' Still the parties went on, and the Duchess laboured hard among her guests, and wore her jewels, and stood on her feet all the night, night after night, being civil to one person, bright to a second, confidential to a third, and sarcastic to an unfortunate fourth;—and in the morning she would work hard with her lists, seeing who had come to her and who had stayed away, and arranging who should be asked and who should be omitted.

In the meantime the Duke altogether avoided those things. At first he had been content to show himself, and escape as soon as possible;— but now he was never seen at all in his own house, except at certain heavy dinners. To Richmond he never went at all, and in his own house in town very rarely even passed through the door that led into the reception rooms. He had not time for ordinary society. So said the Duchess. And many, perhaps the majority of those who frequented the house, really believed that his official duties were too onerous to leave him time for conversation. But in truth the hours went heavily with him as he sat alone in his study, sighing for some sweet parliamentary task, and regretting the days in which he was privileged to sit in the House of Commons till two o'clock in the morning, in the hope that he might get a clause or two passed in his Bill for decimal coinage.

It was at The Horns at an afternoon party, given there in the gardens by the Duchess, early in July, that Arthur Fletcher first saw Emily after her marriage, and Lopez after the occurrence in Silverbridge. As it happened he came out upon the lawn close after them, and found them speaking to the Duchess as they passed on. She had put herself out of the way to be civil to Mr and Mrs Lopez, feeling that she had in some degree injured him in reference to the election, and had therefore invited both him and his wife on more than one occasion. Arthur Fletcher was

there as a young man well known in the world, and as a supporter of the
Duke's Government. The Duchess had taken up Arthur Fletcher,—as
she was wont to take up new men, and had personally become tired of
Lopez. Of course she had heard of the election, and had been told that
Lopez had behaved badly. Of Mr Lopez she did not know enough to
care anything, one way or the other;—but she still encouraged him
because she had caused him disappointment. She had now detained
them a minute on the terrace before the windows while she said a word,
and Arthur Fletcher became one of the little party before he knew
whom he was meeting. 'I am delighted,' she said, 'that you two
Silverbridge heroes should meet together here as friends.' It was almost
incumbent on her to say something, though it would have been better
for her not to have alluded to their heroism. Mrs Lopez put out her
hand, and Arthur Fletcher of course took it. Then the two men bowed
slightly to each other, raising their hats. Arthur paused a moment with
them, as they passed on from the Duchess, thinking that he would say
something in a friendly tone. But he was silenced by the frown on the
husband's face, and was almost constrained to go away without a word.
It was very difficult for him even to be silent, as her greeting had been
kind. But yet it was impossible for him to ignore the displeasure displayed in the man's countenance. So he touched his hat, and asking her
to remember him affectionately to her father, turned off the path and
went away.

'Why did you shake hands with that man?' said Lopez. It was the
first time since their marriage that his voice had been that of an angry
man and an offended husband.

'Why not, Ferdinand? He and I are very old friends, and we have not
quarrelled.'

'You must take up your husband's friendships and your husband's
quarrels. Did I not tell you that he had insulted you?'

'He never insulted me.'

'Emily, you must allow me to be the judge of that. He insulted you,
and then he behaved like a poltroon down at Silverbridge, and I will
not have you know him any more. When I say so I suppose that will be
enough.' He waited for a reply, but she said nothing. 'I ask you to tell
me that you will obey me in this.'

'Of course he will not come to my house, nor should I think of going
to his, if you disapproved.'

'Going to his house! He is unmarried.'

'Supposing he had a wife! Ferdinand, perhaps it will be better that
you and I should not talk about him.'

'By G——,' said Lopez, 'there shall be no subject on which I will be afraid to talk to my own wife. I insist on your assuring me that you will never speak to him again.'

He had taken her along one of the upper walks because it was desolate, and he could there speak to her, as he thought, without being heard. She had, almost unconsciously, made a faint attempt to lead him down upon the lawn, no doubt feeling averse to private conversation at the moment; but he had persevered, and had resented the little effort. The idea in his mind that she was unwilling to hear him abuse Arthur Fletcher, unwilling to renounce the man, anxious to escape his order for such renunciation, added fuel to his jealousy. It was not enough for him that she had rejected this man and had accepted him. The man had been her lover, and she should be made to denounce the man. It might be necessary for him to control his feelings before old Wharton;—but he knew enough of his wife to be sure that she would not speak evil of him or betray him to her father. Her loyalty to him, which he could understand though not appreciate, enabled him to be a tyrant to her. So now he repeated his order to her, pausing in the path, with a voice unintentionally loud, and frowning down upon her as he spoke. 'You must tell me, Emily, that you will never speak to him again.'

She was silent, looking up into his face, not with tremulous eyes, but with infinite woe written in them, had he been able to read the writing. She knew that he was disgracing himself, and yet he was the man whom she loved! 'If you bid me not to speak to him, I will not,—but he must know the reason why.'

'He shall know nothing from you. You do not mean to say that you would write to him.'

'Papa must tell him.'

'I will not have it so. In this matter, Emily, I will be the master,—as it is fit that I should be. I will not have you talk to your father about Mr Fletcher.'

'Why not, Ferdinand?'

'Because I have so decided. He is an old family friend. I can understand that, and do not therefore wish to interfere between him and your father. But he has taken upon himself to write an insolent letter to you as my wife, and to interfere in my affairs. As to what should be done between you and him, I must be the judge and not your father.'

'And must I not speak to papa about it?'

'No!'

'Ferdinand, you make too little, I think, of the associations and affections of a whole life.'

'I will hear nothing about affection,' he said angrily.

'You cannot mean that—that—you doubt me?'

'Certainly not. I think too much of myself and too little of him.' It did not occur to him to tell her that he thought too well of her for that. 'But the man who has offended me must be held to have offended you also.'

'You might say the same if it were my father.'

He paused at this, but only for a moment. 'Certainly I might. It is not probable, but no doubt I might do so. If your father were to quarrel with me, you would not, I suppose, hesitate between us?'

'Nothing on earth could divide me from you.'

'Nor me from you. In this very matter I am only taking your part, if you did but know it.' They had now passed on, and had met other persons, having made their way through a little shrubbery on to a further lawn; and she had hoped, as they were surrounded by people, that he would allow the matter to drop. She had been unable as yet to make up her mind as to what she would say if he pressed her hard. But if it could be passed by,—if nothing more were demanded from her,—she would endeavour to forget it all, saying to herself that it had come from sudden passion. But he was too resolute for such a termination as that, and too keenly alive to the expediency of making her thoroughly subject to him. So he turned her round and took her back through the shrubbery, and in the middle of it stopped her again and renewed his demand.

'Promise me that you will not speak again to Mr Fletcher.'

'Then I must tell papa.'

'No;—you shall tell him nothing.'

'Ferdinand, if you exact a promise from me that I will not speak to Mr Fletcher, or bow to him should circumstances bring us together as they did just now, I must explain to my father why I have done so.'

'You will wilfully disobey me?'

'In that I must.' He glared at her, almost as though he were going to strike her, but she bore his look without flinching. 'I have left all my old friends, Ferdinand, and have given my heart and soul to you. No woman did so with a truer love or more devoted intention of doing her duty to her husband. Your affairs shall be my affairs.'

'Well; yes; rather.'

She was endeavouring to assure him of her truth, but could understand the sneer which was conveyed in his acknowledgement. 'But you cannot, nor can I for your sake, abolish the things which have been.'

'I wish to abolish nothing that has been. I speak of the future.'

'Between our family and that of Mr Fletcher there has been old friendship which is still very dear to my father,—the memory of which is still very dear to me. At your request I am willing to put all that aside from me. There is no reason why I should ever see any of the Fletchers again. Our lives will be apart. Should we meet our greeting would be very slight. The separation can be effected without words. But if you demand an absolute promise,—I must tell my father.'

'We will go home at once,' he said instantly, and aloud. And home they went, back to London, without exchanging a word on the journey. He was absolutely black with rage, and she was content to remain silent. The promise was not given, nor, indeed, was it exacted under the conditions which the wife had imposed upon it. He was most desirous to make her subject to his will in all things, and quite prepared to exercise tyranny over her to any extent,—so that her father should know nothing of it. He could not afford to quarrel with Mr Wharton. 'You had better go to bed,' he said, when he got her back to town;—and she went, if not to bed, at any rate into her own room.

CHAPTER 38

SIR ORLANDO RETIRES

'HE is a horrid man. He came here and quarrelled with the other man in my house, or rather down at Richmond, and made a fool of himself, and then quarrelled with his wife and took her away. What fools, what asses, what horrors men are! How impossible it is to be civil and gracious without getting into a mess. I am tempted to say that I will never know anybody any more.' Such was the complaint made by the Duchess to Mrs Finn a few days after the Richmond party, and from this it was evident that the latter affair had not passed without notice.

'Did he make a noise about it?' asked Mrs Finn.

'There was not a row, but there was enough of a quarrel to be visible and audible. He walked about and talked loud to the poor woman. Of course it was my own fault. But the man was clever and I liked him, and people told me that he was of the right sort.'

'The Duke heard of it?'

'No;—and I hope he won't. It would be such a triumph for him, after all the fuss at Silverbridge. But he never hears of anything. If two men fought a duel in his own dining-room he would be the last man in London to know it.'

'Then say nothing about it, and don't ask the men any more.'

'You may be sure I won't ask the man with the wife any more. The other man is in Parliament and can't be thrown over so easily—and it wasn't his fault. But I'm getting so sick of it all! I'm told that Sir Orlando has complained to Plantagenet that he isn't asked to the dinners.'

'Impossible!'

'Don't you mention it, but he has. Warburton has told me so.' Warburton was one of the Duke's private secretaries.

'What did the Duke say?'

'I don't quite know. Warburton is one of my familiars, but I didn't like to ask him for more than he chose to tell me. Warburton suggested that I should invite Sir Orlando at once; but there I was obdurate. Of course if Plantagenet tells me I'll ask the man to come every day of the week;—but it is one of those things that I shall need to be told directly. My idea is, you know, that they had better get rid of Sir Orlando,—and that if Sir Orlando chooses to kick over the traces, he may be turned loose without any danger. One has little birds that give one all manner of information, and one little bird has told me that Sir Orlando and Mr Roby don't speak. Mr Roby is not very much himself, but he is a good straw to show which way the wind blows. Plantagenet certainly sent no message about Sir Orlando, and I'm afraid the gentleman must look for his dinners elsewhere.'

The Duke had in truth expressed himself very plainly to Mr Warburton; but with so much indiscreet fretfulness that the discreet private secretary had not told it even to the Duchess. 'This kind of thing argues a want of cordiality that may be fatal to us,' Sir Orlando had said somewhat grandiloquently to the Duke, and the Duke had made—almost no reply. 'I suppose I may ask my own guests in my own house,' he had said afterwards to Mr Warburton, 'though in public life I am everybody's slave.' Mr Warburton, anxious of course to maintain the unity of the party, had told the Duchess so much as would, he thought, induce her to give way; but he had not repeated the Duke's own observations, which were, Mr Warburton thought, hostile to the interests of the party. The Duchess had only smiled and made a little grimace, with which the private secretary was already well acquainted. And Sir Orlando received no invitation.

In those days Sir Orlando was unhappy and irritable, doubtful of further success as regarded the Coalition, but quite resolved to pull the house down about the ears of the inhabitants rather than to leave it with gentle resignation. To him it seemed to be impossible that the Coalition should exist without him. He too had had moments of high-vaulting ambition, in which he had almost felt himself to be the great man required by the country, the one ruler who could gather together in his grasp the reins of government and drive the State coach single-handed safe through its difficulties for the next half-dozen years. There are men who cannot conceive of themselves that anything should be difficult for them, and again others who cannot bring themselves so to trust themselves as to think that they can ever achieve anything great. Samples of each sort from time to time rise high in political life, carried thither apparently by Epicurean concourse of atoms;* and it often happens that the more confident samples are by no means the most capable. The concourse of atoms had carried Sir Orlando so high that he could not but think himself intended for something higher. But the Duke, who had really been wafted to the very top, had always doubted himself, believing himself capable of doing some one thing by dint of industry, but with no further confidence in his own powers. Sir Orlando had perceived something of his leader's weakness, and had thought that he might profit by it. He was not only a distinguished member of the Cabinet, but even the recognized Leader of the House of Commons. He looked out the facts and found that for five-and-twenty years out of the last thirty the Leader of the House of Commons had been the Head of the Government. He felt that he would be mean not to stretch out his hand and take the prize destined for him. The Duke was a poor timid man who had very little to say for himself. Then came the little episode about the dinners. It had become very evident to all the world that the Duchess of Omnium had cut Sir Orlando Drought,—that the Prime Minister's wife, who was great in hospitality, would not admit the First Lord of the Admiralty into her house. The doings at Gatherum Castle, and in Carlton Terrace, and at the Horns were watched much too closely by the world at large to allow such omissions to be otherwise than conspicuous. Since the commencement of the Session there had been a series of articles in the 'People's Banner' violently abusive of the Prime Minister, and in one or two of these the indecency of these exclusions had been exposed with great strength of language. And the Editor of the 'People's Banner' had discovered that Sir Orlando Drought was the one man in Parliament fit to rule the nation. Till Parliament should discover this fact, or at least acknowledge it,—the discovery having been happily made by the 'People's Banner,'—the Editor of the 'People's Banner' thought there could be no hope for the country. Sir Orlando of course saw all these articles, and his very heart believed that a man had at length sprung up among them fit to conduct a newspaper. The Duke also unfortunately saw the 'People's Banner.' In his old happy days two papers a day, one in the morning and the other before dinner, sufficed to tell him all that he wanted to know. Now he felt it necessary to see almost every rag that was published. And he would skim through them all till he found the lines in which he himself was maligned, and then, with sore heart and irritated nerves, would pause over every contumelious word. He would have bitten his tongue out rather than have spoken of the tortures he endured, but he was tortured and did endure. He knew the cause of the bitter personal attacks made on him,—of the abuse with which he was loaded, and of the ridicule, infinitely more painful to him, with which his wife's social splendour was bespattered. He remembered well the attempt which Mr Quintus Slide had made to obtain an entrance into his house, and his own scornful rejection of that gentleman's overtures. He knew,—no man knew better,—the real value of that able Editor's opinion. And yet every word of it was gall and wormwood to him. In every paragraph there was a scourge which hit him on the raw and opened wounds which he could show to no kind surgeon, for which he could find solace in no friendly treatment. Not even to his wife could he condescend to say that Mr Quintus Slide had hurt him.

Then Sir Orlando had come himself. Sir Orlando explained himself gracefully. He of course could understand that no gentleman had a right to complain because he was not asked to another gentleman's house. But the affairs of the country were above private considerations; and he, actuated by public feelings, would condescend to do that which under other circumstances would be impossible. The public press, which was ever vigilant, had suggested that there was some official estrangement, because he, Sir Orlando, had not been included in the list of guests invited by his Grace. Did not his Grace think that there might be seeds of,—he would not quite say decay for the Coalition, in such a state of things? The Duke paused a moment, and then said that he thought there were no such seeds. Sir Orlando bowed haughtily and withdrew,—swearing at the moment that the Coalition should be made to fall into a thousand shivers. This had all taken place a fortnight before the party at the Horns from which poor Mrs Lopez had been withdrawn so hastily.

But Sir Orlando, when he commenced the proceedings consequent on this resolution, did not find all that support which he had expected. Unfortunately there had been an uncomfortable word or two between him and Mr Roby, the political Secretary at the Admiralty. Mr Roby had never quite seconded Sir Orlando's ardour in that matter of the four ships, and Sir Orlando in his pride of place had ventured to snub Mr Roby. Now Mr Roby could bear a snubbing perhaps as well as any other official subordinate,—but he was one who would study the question and assure himself that it was, or that it was not, worth his while to bear it. He, too, had discussed with his friends the condition of the Coalition, and had come to conclusions rather adverse to Sir Orlando than otherwise. When, therefore, the First Secretary sounded him as to the expediency of some step in the direction of a firmer political combination than that at present existing,—by which of course was meant the dethronement of the present Prime Minister,—Mr Roby had snubbed him! Then there had been slight official criminations and recriminations, till a state of things had come to pass which almost justified the statement made by the Duchess to Mrs Finn.

The Coalition had many component parts, some coalescing without difficulty, but with no special cordiality. Such was the condition of things between the very conservative Lord-Lieutenant of Ireland and his somewhat radical Chief Secretary, Mr Finn,—between probably the larger number of those who were contented with the duties of their own offices and the pleasures and profits arising therefrom. Some by this time hardly coalesced at all, as was the case with Sir Gregory Grogram and Sir Timothy Beeswax, the Attorney-General and Solicitor-General;—and was especially the case with the Prime Minister and Sir Orlando Drought. But in one or two happy cases the Coalition was sincere and loyal,—and in no case was this more so than with regard to Mr Rattler and Mr Roby. Mr Rattler and Mr Roby had throughout their long parliamentary lives belonged to opposite parties, and had been accustomed to regard each other with mutual jealousy and almost with mutual hatred. But now they had come to see how equal, how alike, and how sympathetic were their tastes, and how well each might help the other. As long as Mr Rattler could keep his old place at the Treasury,—and his ambition never stirred him to aught higher,— he was quite contented that his old rival should be happy at the Admiralty. And that old rival, when he looked about him and felt his present comfort, when he remembered how short-lived had been the good things which had hitherto come in his way, and how little probable it was that long-lived good things should be his when the Coalition was broken up, manfully determined that loyalty to the present Head of Government was his duty. He had sat for too many years on the same bench with Sir Orlando to believe much in his power of governing the country. Therefore, when Sir Orlando dropped his hint Mr Roby did not take it.

'I wonder whether it's true that Sir Orlando complained to the Duke that he was not asked to dinner?' said Mr Roby to Mr Rattler.

'I should hardly think so. I can't fancy that he would have the pluck,' said Mr Rattler. 'The Duke isn't the easiest man in the world to speak to about such a thing as that.'

'It would be a monstrous thing for a man to do! But Drought's head is quite turned. You can see that.'

'We never thought much about him, you know, on our side.'

'It was what your side thought about him,' rejoined Roby, 'that put him where he is now.'

'It was the fate of accidents, Roby, which puts so many of us in our places, and arranges our work for us, and makes us little men or big men. There are other men besides Drought who have been tossed up in a blanket till they don't know whether their heads or their heels are highest.'

'I quite believe in the Duke,' said Mr Roby, almost alarmed by the suggestion which his new friend had seemed to make.

'So do I, Roby. He has not the obduracy of Lord Brock, nor the ineffable manner of Mr Mildmay, nor the brilliant intellect of Mr Gresham.'

'Nor the picturesque imagination of Mr Daubeny,' said Mr Roby, feeling himself bound to support the character of his late chief.

'Nor his audacity,' said Mr Rattler. 'But he has the peculiar gift of his own, and gifts fitted for the peculiar combination of circumstances, if he will only be content to use them. He is a just, unambitious, intelligent man, in whom after a while the country would come to have implicit confidence. But he is thin-skinned and ungenial.'

'I have got into his boat,' said Roby enthusiastically, 'and he will find that I shall be true to him.'

'There is no better boat to be in at present,' said the slightly sarcastic Rattler. 'As to the Drought pinnace, it will be more difficult to get it afloat than the four ships themselves. To tell the truth honestly, Roby, we have to rid ourselves of Sir Orlando. I have a great regard for the man.'

'I can't say I ever liked him,' said Roby.

'I don't talk about liking,—but he has achieved success, and is to be regarded. Now he has lost his head, and he is bound to get a fall. The question is,—who shall fall with him?'

'I do not feel myself at all bound to sacrifice myself.'

'I don't know who does. Sir Timothy Beeswax, I suppose, will resent the injury done to him. But I can hardly think that a strong government can be formed by Sir Orlando Drought and Sir Timothy Beeswax. Any secession is a weakness,—of course; but I think he may survive it.' And so Mr Rattler and Mr Roby made up their minds that the First Lord of the Admiralty might be thrown overboard without much danger to the Queen's ship.

Sir Orlando, however, was quite in earnest. The man had spirit enough to feel that no alternative was left to him after he had condescended to suggest that he should be asked to dinner and had been refused. He tried Mr Roby, and found that Mr Roby was a mean fellow, wedded, as he told himself, to his salary. Then he sounded Lord Drummond, urging various reasons. The country was not safe without more ships. Mr Monk was altogether wrong about revenue. Mr Finn's ideas about Ireland were revolutionary. But Lord Drummond thought that, upon the whole, the present Ministry served the country well, and considered himself bound to adhere to it. 'He cannot bear the idea of being out of power,' said Sir Orlando to himself. He next said a word to Sir Timothy; but Sir Timothy was not the man to be led by the nose by Sir Orlando. Sir Timothy had his grievances and meant to have his revenge, but he knew how to choose his own time. 'The Duke's not a bad fellow,' said Sir Timothy,—'perhaps a little weak, but well-meaning. I think we ought to stand by him a little longer. As for Finn's Irish Bill, I haven't troubled myself about it.' Then Sir Orlando declared to himself that Sir Timothy was a coward, and resolved that he would act alone.

About the middle of July he went to the Duke at the Treasury, was closeted with him, and in a very long narration of his own differences, difficulties, opinions, and grievances, explained to the Duke that his conscience called upon him to resign. The Duke listened and bowed his head, and with one or two very gently-uttered words expressed his regret. Then Sir Orlando, in another long speech, laid bare his bosom to the Chief whom he was leaving, declaring the inexpressible sorrow with which he had found himself called upon to take a step which he feared might be prejudicial to the political status of a man whom he honoured so much as he did the Duke of Omnium. Then the Duke bowed again, but said nothing. The man had been guilty of the impropriety of questioning the way in which the Duke's private hospitality was exercised, and the Duke could not bring himself to be genially civil to such an offender. Sir Orlando went on to say that he would of course explain his views in the Cabinet, but that he had thought it right to make them known to the Duke as soon as they were formed. 'The best friends must part, Duke,' he said as he took his leave. 'I hope not, Sir Orlando; I hope not,' said the Duke. But Sir Orlando had been too

full of himself and of the words he was to speak, and of the thing he was
about to do, to understand either the Duke's words or his silence.

And so Sir Orlando resigned, and thus supplied the only morsel of
political interest which the Session produced. 'Take no more notice of
him than if your footman was going,' had been the advice of the old
Duke. Of course there was a Cabinet meeting on the occasion, but even
there the commotion was very slight, as every member knew before
entering the room what it was that Sir Orlando intended to do. Lord
Drummond said that the step was one to be much lamented. 'Very
much indeed,' said the Duke of St Bungay. His words themselves were
false and hypocritical, but the tone of his voice took away all the deceit.
'I am afraid,' said the Prime Minister, 'from what Sir Orlando has said
to me privately, that we cannot hope that he will change his mind.'
'That I certainly cannot do,' said Sir Orlando, with all the dignified
courage of a modern martyr.

On the next morning the papers were full of the political fact, and
were blessed with a subject on which they could exercise their pro-
phetical sagacity. The remarks made were generally favourable to the
Government. Three or four of the morning papers were of opinion that
though Sir Orlando had been a strong man, and a good public servant,
the Ministry might exist without him. But the 'People's Banner' was
able to expound to the people at large, that the only grain of salt by
which the Ministry had been kept from putrefaction had been now cast
out, and that mortification, death, and corruption, must ensue. It was
one of Mr Quintus Slide's greatest efforts.

CHAPTER 39

'GET ROUND HIM'

FERDINAND LOPEZ maintained his anger against his wife for more
than a week after the scene at Richmond, feeding it with reflections on
what he called her disobedience. Nor was it a make-believe anger. She
had declared her intention to act in opposition to his expressed orders.
He felt that his present condition was prejudicial to his interests, and
that he must take his wife back into favour, in order that he might make
progress with her father, but could hardly bring himself to swallow
his wrath. He thought that it was her duty to obey him in everything,—
and that disobedience on a matter touching her old lover was an abominable offence, to be visited with severest marital displeasure, and with

a succession of scowls that should make her miserable for a month at least. Nor on her behalf would he have hesitated, though the misery might have continued for three months. But then the old man was the main hope of his life, and must be made its mainstay. Brilliant prospects were before him. He had used to think that Mr Wharton was a hale man, with some terribly vexatious term of life before him. But now, now that he was seen more closely, he appeared to be very old. He would sit half bent in the arm-chair in Stone Buildings, and look as though he were near a hundred. And from day to day he seemed to lean more upon his son-in-law, whose visits to him were continued, and always well taken. The constant subject of discourse between them was Everett Wharton, who had not yet seen his father since the misfortune of their quarrel. Everett had declared to Lopez a dozen times that he would go to his father if his father wished it, and Lopez as often reported to the father that Everett would not go to him unless the father expressed such a wish. And so they had been kept apart. Lopez did not suppose that the old man would disinherit his son altogether,—did not, perhaps, wish it. But he thought that the condition of the old man's mind would affect the partition of his property, and that the old man would surely make some new will in the present state of his affairs. The old man always asked after his daughter begging that she would come to him, and at last it was necessary that an evening should be fixed. 'We shall be delighted to come to-day or to-morrow,' Lopez said.

'We had better say to-morrow. There would be nothing to eat to-day. The house isn't now what it used to be.' It was therefore expedient that Lopez should drop his anger when he got home, and prepare his wife to dine in Manchester Square in a proper frame of mind.

Her misery had been extreme;—very much more bitter than he had imagined. It was not only that his displeasure made her life for the time wearisome, and robbed the only society she had of all its charms. It was not only that her heart was wounded by his anger. Those evils might have been short-lived. But she had seen,—she could not fail to see,— that his conduct was unworthy of her and of her deep love. Though she struggled hard against the feeling, she could not but despise the meanness of his jealousy. She knew thoroughly well that there had been no grain of offence in that letter from Arthur Fletcher,—and she knew that no man, no true man, would have taken offence at it. She tried to quench her judgement, and to silence the verdict which her intellect gave against him, but her intellect was too strong even for her heart. She was beginning to learn that the god of her idolatry was but a little human creature, and that she should not have worshipped at so poor a shrine. But nevertheless the love should be continued, and, if possible, the worship, though the idol had been already found to have feet of clay.* He was her husband, and she would be true to him. As morning after morning he left her, still with that harsh, unmanly frown upon his face, she would look up at him with entreating eyes, and when he returned would receive him with her fondest smile.

At length he, too, smiled. He came to her after that interview with Mr Wharton and told her, speaking with the soft yet incisive voice which she used to love so well, that they were to dine in the Square on the following day. 'Let there be an end of all this,' he said, taking her in his arms and kissing her. Of course she did not tell him that 'all this' had sprung from his ill-humour and not from hers. 'I own I have been angry,' he continued. 'I will say nothing more about it now; but that man did vex me.'

'I have been so sorry that you should have been vexed.'

'Well;—let it pass away. I don't think your father is looking very well.'

'He is not ill?'

'Oh no. He feels the loss of your society. He is so much alone. You must be more with him.'

'Has he not seen Everett yet?'

'No. Everett is not behaving altogether well.' Emily was made unhappy by this and showed it. 'He is the best fellow in the world. I may safely say there is no other man whom I regard so warmly as I do your brother. But he takes wrong ideas into his head, and nothing will knock them out. I wonder what your father has done about his will.'

'I have not an idea. Nothing you may be sure will make him unjust to Everett.'

'Ah!—You don't happen to know whether he ever made a will?'

'Not at all. He would be sure to say nothing about it to me,—or to anybody.'

'That is the kind of secrecy which I think is wrong. It leads to so much uncertainty. You wouldn't like to ask him?'

'No;—certainly.'

'It is astonishing to me how afraid you are of your father. He hasn't any land, has he?'

'Land!'

'Real estate. You know what I mean. He couldn't well have landed property without your knowing it.' She shook her head. 'It might make an immense difference to us, you know.'

'Why so?'

'If he were to die without a will, any land,—houses and that kind of property,—would go to Everett. I never knew a man who told his children so little. I want to make you understand these things. You and I will be badly off if he doesn't do something for us.'

'You don't think he is really ill?'

'No;—not ill. Men above seventy are apt to die, you know.'

'Oh, Ferdinand,—what a way to talk of it!'

'Well, my love, the thing is so seriously matter-of-fact, that it is better to look at it in a matter-of-fact way. I don't want your father to die.'

'I hope not. I hope not.'

'But I should be very glad to learn what he means to do while he lives. I want to get you into sympathy with me on this matter;—but it is so difficult.'

'Indeed I sympathize with you.'

'The truth is that he has taken an aversion to Everett.'

'God forbid!'

'I am doing all I can to prevent it. But if he does throw Everett over we ought to have the advantage of it. There is no harm in saying as much as that. Think what it would be if he should take it into his head to leave his money to hospitals. My G——; fancy what my condition would be if I were to hear of such a will as that! If he destroyed an old will, partly because he didn't like our marriage, and partly in anger against Everett, and then died without making another, the property would be divided,—unless he had bought land. You see how many dangers there are. Oh dear! I can look forward and see myself mad,—or else see myself so proudly triumphant!' All this horrified her, but he did not see her horror. He knew that she disliked it, but thought that she disliked the trouble, and that she dreaded her father. 'Now I do think that you could help me a little,' he continued.

'What can I do?'

'Get round him when he's a little down in the mouth. That is the way in which old men are conquered.' How utterly ignorant he was of the very nature of her mind and disposition! To be told by her husband that she was to 'get round' her father! 'You should see him every day. He would be delighted if you would go to him at his chambers. Or you could take care to be in the Square when he comes home. I don't know whether we had not better leave this and go and live near him. Would you mind that?'

'I would do anything you suggest as to living anywhere.'

'But you won't do anything I suggest as to your father.'

'As to being with him, if I thought he wished it,—though I had to walk my feet off, I would go to him.'

'There's no need of hurting your feet. There's the brougham.'

'I do so wish, Ferdinand, you would discontinue the brougham. I don't at all want it. I don't at all dislike cabs. And I was only joking about walking. I walk very well.'

'Certainly not. You fail altogether to understand my ideas about things. If things were going bad with us, I would infinitely prefer getting a pair of horses for you to putting down the one you have.' She certainly did not understand his ideas. 'Whatever we do we must hold our heads up. I think he is coming round to cotton to me. He is very close, but I can see that he likes my going to him. Of course, as he grows older from day to day, he'll constantly want some one to lean on more than heretofore.'

'I would go and stay with him if he wanted me.'

'I have thought of that too. Now that would be a saving,—without any fall. And if we were both there we could hardly fail to know what he was doing. You could offer that, couldn't you? You could say as much as that?'

'I could ask him if he wished it.'

'Just so. Say that it occurs to you that he is lonely by himself, and that we will both go to the Square at a moment's notice if he thinks it will make him comfortable. I feel sure that that will be the best step to take. I have already had an offer for these rooms, and could get rid of the things we have bought to advantage.'

This, too, was terrible to her, and at the same time altogether unintelligible. She had been invited to buy little treasures to make their home comfortable, and had already learned to take that delight in her belongings which is one of the greatest pleasures of a young married woman's life. A girl in her old home, before she is given up to a husband, has many sources of interest, and probably from day to day sees many people. And the man just married goes out to his work, and occupies his time, and has his thickly-peopled world around him. But the bride, when the bridal honours of the honeymoon are over, when the sweet care of the first cradle has not yet come to her, is apt to be lonely and to be driven to the contemplation of the pretty things with which her husband and her friends have surrounded her. It had certainly been so with this young bride, whose husband left her in the morning and only returned for their late dinner. And now she was told that her household gods had had a price put upon them and that they were to be sold. She had intended to suggest that she would pay her father a visit, and her husband immediately proposed that they should quarter themselves permanently on the old man! She was ready to give up her brougham, though she liked the comfort of it well enough; but to that he would not consent because the possession of it gave him an air of wealth; but without a moment's hesitation he could catch at the idea of throwing upon her father the burden of maintaining both her and himself! She understood the meaning of this. She could read his mind so far. She endeavoured not to read the book too closely,—but there it was, opened to her wider day by day, and she knew that the lessons which it taught were vulgar and damnable.

And yet she had to hide from him her own perception of himself! She had to sympathize with his desires and yet to abstain from doing that which his desires demanded from her. Alas, poor girl! She soon knew that her marriage had been a mistake. There was probably no one moment in which she made the confession to herself. But the conviction was there, in her mind, as though the confession had been made. Then there would come upon her unbidden, unwelcome reminiscences of Arthur Fletcher,—thoughts that she would struggle to banish, accusing herself of some heinous crime because the thoughts would come back to her. She remembered his light wavy hair, which she had loved as one loves the beauty of a dog, which had seemed to her young imagination, to her in the ignorance of her early years, to lack something of a dreamed-of manliness. She remembered his eager, boyish, honest entreaties to herself, which to her had been without that dignity of a superior being which a husband should possess. She became aware that she had thought the less of him because he had thought the more of her. She had worshipped this other man because he had assumed superiority and had told her that he was big enough to be her master. But now,—now that it was all too late,—the veil had fallen from her eyes. She could now see the difference between manliness and 'deportment.' Ah,—that she should ever have been so blind, she who had given herself credit for seeing so much clearer than they who were her elders! And now, though at last she did see clearly, she could not have the consolation of telling any one what she had seen. She must bear it all in silence, and live with it, and still love this god of clay that she had chosen. And, above all, she must never allow herself even to think of that other man with the wavy light hair,—that man who was rising in the world, of whom all people said all good things,* who was showing himself to be a man by the work he did, and whose true tenderness she could never doubt.

Her father was left to her. She could still love her father. It might be that it would be best for him that she should go back to her old home, and take care of his old age. If he should wish it, she would make no difficulty of parting with the things around her. Of what concern were the prettinesses of life to one whose inner soul was hampered with such ugliness? It might be better that they should live in Manchester Square,—if her father wished it. It was clear to her now that her husband was in urgent want of money, though of his affairs, even of his way of making money, she knew nothing. As that was the case, of course she would consent to any practicable retrenchment which he would propose. And then she thought of other coming joys and coming troubles,—of how in future years she might have to teach a girl falsely to believe that her father was a good man, and to train a boy to honest purposes whatever parental lessons might come from the other side.

But the mistake she had made was acknowledged. The man who could enjoin her to 'get round' her father could never have been worthy of the love she had given him.

CHAPTER 40

'COME AND TRY IT'

THE husband was almost jovial when he came home just in time to take his young wife to dine with their father. 'I've had such a day in the city,' he said, laughing. 'I wish I could introduce you to my friend, Mr Sextus Parker.'

'Cannot you do so?'

'Well, no; not exactly. Of course you'd like him because he is such a wonderful character, but he'd hardly do for your drawing-room. He's the vulgarest little creature you ever put your eyes on; and yet in a certain way he's my partner.'

'Then I suppose you trust him?'

'Indeed I don't;—but I make him useful. Poor little Sexty! I do trust him to a degree, because he believes in me and thinks he can do best by sticking to me. The old saying of "honour among thieves" isn't without a dash of truth in it. When two men are in a boat together, they must be true to each other, else neither will get to the shore.'

'You don't attribute high motives to your friend.'

'I'm afraid there are not very many high motives in the world, my girl, especially in the city;—nor yet at Westminster. It can hardly be from high motives when a lot of men, thinking differently on every possible subject, come together for the sake of pay and power. I don't know whether, after all, Sextus Parker mayn't have as high motives as the Duke of Omnium. I don't suppose any one ever had lower motives than the Duchess when she chiselled me about Silverbridge. Never mind;—it'll all be one a hundred years hence. Get ready, for I want you to be with your father a little before dinner.'

Then, when they were in the brougham together, he began a course of very plain instructions. 'Look here, dear; you had better get him to talk to you before dinner. I dare say Mrs Roby will be there, and I will get her on one side. At any rate you can manage it because we shall be early, and I'll take up a book while you are talking to him.'

'What do you wish me to say to him, Ferdinand?'

'I have been thinking of your own proposal, and I am quite sure that we had better join him in the Square. The thing is, I am in a little mess about the rooms, and can't stay on without paying very dearly for them.'

'I thought you had paid for them.'

'Well;—yes; in one sense I had; but you don't understand about business. You had better not interrupt me now, as I have got a good deal to say before we get to the Square. It will suit me to give up the rooms. I don't like them, and they are very dear. As you yourself said, it will be a capital thing for us to go and stay with your father.'

'I meant only for a visit.'

'It will be for a visit,—and we'll make it a long visit.' It was odd that the man should have been so devoid of right feeling himself as not to have known that the ideas which he expressed were revolting! 'You can sound him. Begin by saying that you are afraid he is desolate. He told me himself that he was desolate, and you can refer to that. Then tell him that we are both of us prepared to do anything that we can to relieve him. Put your arm over him, and kiss him, and all that sort of thing.' She shrunk from him into the corner of the brougham, and yet he did not perceive it. 'Then say that you think he would be happier if we were to join him here for a time. You can make him understand that there would be no difficulty about the apartments. But don't say it all in a set speech, as though it were prepared,—though of course you can let him know that you have suggested it to me and that I am willing. Be sure to let him understand that the idea began with you.'

'But it did not.'

'You proposed to go and stay with him. Tell him just that. And you should explain to him that he can dine at the club just as much as he likes. When you were alone with him here of course he had to come home; but he needn't do that now unless he chooses. Of course the brougham would be my affair. And if he should say anything about sharing the house expenses, you can tell him that I would do anything he might propose.' Her father to share the household expenses in his own house, and with his own children! 'You say as much as you can of all this before dinner, so that when we are sitting below he may suggest it if he pleases. It would suit me to get in there next week if possible.'

And so the lesson had been given. She had said little or nothing in reply, and he had only finished as they entered the Square. She had hardly a minute allowed her to think how far she might follow, and in what she must ignore, her husband's instructions. If she might use her own judgement, she would tell her father at once that a residence for a time beneath his roof would be a service to them pecuniarily. But this she might not do. She understood that her duty to her husband did forbid her to proclaim his poverty in opposition to his wishes. She would tell nothing that he did not wish her to tell,—but then no duty could require her to say what was false. She would make the suggestion about their change of residence, and would make it with proper affection;—but as regarded themselves she would simply say that it would suit their views to give up their rooms if it suited him.

Mr Wharton was all alone when they entered the drawing-room,—but, as Lopez had surmised, had asked his sister-in-law round the corner to come to dinner. 'Roby always likes an excuse to get to his club,' said the old man, 'and Harriet likes an excuse to go anywhere.' It was not long before Lopez began to play his part by seating himself close to the open window and looking out into the Square; and Emily when she found herself close to her father, with her hand in his, could hardly divest herself of a feeling that she also was playing her part. 'I see so very little of you,' said the old man plaintively.

'I'd come up oftener if I thought you'd like it.'

'It isn't liking, my dear. Of course you have to live with your husband. Isn't this sad about Everett?'

'Very sad. But Everett hasn't lived here for ever so long.'

'I don't know why he shouldn't. He was a fool to go away when he did. Does he go to you?'

'Yes;—sometimes.'

'And what does he say?'

'I'm sure he would be with you at once if you would ask him.'

'I have asked him. I've sent word by Lopez over and over again. If he means that I am to write to him and say that I'm sorry for offending him, I won't. Don't talk of him any more. It makes me so angry that I sometimes feel inclined to do things which I know I should repent when dying.'

'Not anything to injure Everett, papa!'

'I wonder whether he ever thinks that I am an old man and all alone, and that his brother-in-law is daily with me. But he's a fool, and thinks of nothing. I know it is very sad being here night after night by myself.' Mr Wharton forgot, no doubt, at the moment, that he passed the majority of his evenings at the Eldon,—though, had he been reminded of it, he might have declared with perfect truth that the delights of his club were not satisfactory.

'Papa,' said Emily, 'would you like us to come and live here?'

'What,—you and Lopez;—here, in the Square?'

'Yes;—for a time. He is thinking of giving up the place in Belgrave Mansions.'

'I thought he had them for—for ever so many months.'

'He does not like them, and they are expensive, and he can give them up. If you would wish it, we would come here,—for a time.' He turned round and looked at her almost suspiciously; and she,—she blushed as she remembered how accurately she was obeying her husband's orders. 'It would be such a joy to me to be near you again.'

There was something in her voice which instantly reassured him. 'Well——;' he said; 'come and try it if it will suit him. The house is big enough. It will ease his pocket and be a comfort to me. Come and try it.'

It astonished her that the thing should be done so easily. Here was all that her husband had proposed to arrange by deep diplomacy settled in three words. And yet she felt ashamed of herself,—as though she had taken her father in. That terrible behest to 'get round him' still grated on her ears. Had she got round him? Had she cheated him into this? 'Papa,' she said, 'do not do this unless you feel sure that you will like it.'

'How is anybody to feel sure of anything, my dear?'

'But if you doubt, do not do it.'

'I feel sure of one thing, that it will be a great saving to your husband, and I am nearly sure that that ought not to be a matter of indifference to him. There is plenty of room here, and it will at any rate be a comfort to me to see you sometimes.' Just at this moment Mrs Roby came in, and the old man began to tell his news aloud. 'Emily has not gone away for long. She's coming back like a bad shilling.'

'Not to live in the Square?' said Mrs Roby, looking round at Lopez.

'Why not? There's room here for them, and it will be just as well to save expense. When will you come, my dear?'

'Whenever the house may be ready, papa.'

'It's ready now. You ought to know that. I am not going to refurnish the rooms for you, or anything of that kind. Lopez can come in and hang up his hat whenever it pleases him.'

During this time Lopez had hardly known how to speak or what to say. He had been very anxious that his wife should pave the way, as he would have called it. He had been urgent with her to break the ice to her father. But it had not occurred to him that the matter would be settled without any reference to himself. Of course he had heard every word that had been spoken, and was aware that his own poverty had been suggested as the cause for such a proceeding. It was a great thing for him in every way. He would live for nothing, and would also have almost unlimited power of being with Mr Wharton as old age grew on him. This ready compliance with his wishes was a benefit far too precious to be lost. But yet he felt that his own dignity required some reference to himself. It was distasteful to him that his father-in-law should regard him,—or, at any rate, that he should speak of him,—as a pauper, unable to provide a home for his own wife. 'Emily's notion in suggesting it, sir,' he said, 'has been her care for your comfort.' The barrister turned round and looked at him, and Lopez did not quite like the look. 'It was she thought of it first, and she certainly had no other idea than that. When she mentioned it to me, I was delighted to agree.'

Emily heard it all and blushed. It was not absolutely untrue in words,—this assertion of her husband's,—but altogether false in spirit. And yet she could not contradict him. 'I don't see why it should not do very well indeed,' said Mrs Roby.

'I hope it may,' said the barrister. 'Come, Emily, I must take you down to dinner to-day. You are not at home yet, you know. As you are to come, the sooner the better.'

During dinner not a word was said on the subject. Lopez exerted himself to be pleasant, and told all that he had heard as to the difficulties of the Cabinet. Sir Orlando had resigned, and the general opinion was that the Coalition was going to pieces. Had Mr Wharton seen the last article in the 'People's Banner' about the Duke? Lopez was strongly of the opinion that Mr Wharton ought to see that article. 'I never had the "People's Banner" within my fingers in my life,' said the barrister angrily, 'and I certainly never will.'

'Ah, sir; this is an exception. You should see this. When Slide really means to cut a fellow up, he can do it. There's no one like him. And the Duke has deserved it. He's a poor, vacillating creature, led by the Duchess; and she,—according to all that one hears,—she isn't much better than she should be.'

'I thought the Duchess was a great friend of yours,' said Mr Wharton.

'I don't care much for such friendship. She threw me over most shamefully.'

'And therefore, of course, you are justified in taking away her character. I never saw the Duchess of Omnium in my life, and should probably be very uncomfortable if I found myself in her society; but I believe her to be a good sort of woman in her way.' Emily sat perfectly silent, knowing that her husband had been rebuked, but feeling that he had deserved it. He, however, was not abashed; but changed the conversation, dashing into city rumours, and legal reforms. The old man from time to time said sharp little things, showing that his intellect was not senile, all of which his son-in-law bore imperturbably. It was not that he liked it, or was indifferent, but that he knew that he could not get the good things which Mr Wharton could do for him without making some kind of payment. He must take the sharp words of the old man,—and take all that he could get besides.

When the two men were alone together after dinner, Mr Wharton used a different tone. 'If you are to come,' he said, 'you might as well do it as soon as possible.'

'A day or two will be enough for us.'

'There are one or two things you should understand. I shall be very happy to see your friends at any time, but I shall like to know when they are coming before they come.'

'Of course, sir.'

'I dine out a good deal.'

'At the club,' suggested Lopez.

'Well;—at the club or elsewhere. It doesn't matter. There will always be dinner here for you and Emily, just as though I were at home. I say this, so that there need be no questionings or doubts about it hereafter. And don't let there ever be any question of money between us.'

'Certainly not.'

'Everett has an allowance, and this will be tantamount to an allowance to Emily. You have also had £3500. I hope it has been well expended;—except the £500 at that election, which has, of course, been thrown away.'

'The other was brought into the business.'

'I don't know what the business is. But you and Emily must understand that the money has been given as her fortune.'

'Oh, quite so;—part of it, you mean.'

'I mean just what I say.'

'I call it part of it, because, as you observed just now, our living here will be the same as though you made Emily an allowance.'

'Ah;—well; you can look at it in that light if you please. John has the key of the cellar. He's a man I can trust. As a rule I have port and sherry at table every day. If you like claret I will get some a little cheaper than what I use when friends are here.'

'What wine I have is quite indifferent to me.'

'I like it good, and I have it good. I always breakfast at 9.30. You can have yours earlier if you please. I don't know that there's anything else to be said. I hope we shall get into the way of understanding each other, and being mutually comfortable. Shall we go upstairs to Emily and Mrs Roby?' And so it was determined that Emily was to come back to her old house about eight months after her marriage.

Mr Wharton himself sat late into the night, all alone, thinking about it. What he had done, he had done in a morose way, and he was aware that it was so. He had not beamed with smiles, and opened his arms lovingly, and, bidding God bless his dearest children, told them that if they would only come and sit round his hearth, he should be the happiest old man in London. He had said little or nothing of his own affection even for his daughter, but had spoken of the matter as one of which the pecuniary aspect alone was important. He had found out that the saving so effected would be material to Lopez, and had resolved that there should be no shirking of the truth in what he was prepared to do. He had been almost asked to take the young married couple in, and feed them,—so that they might live free of expense. He was willing to do it,—but was not willing that there should be any soft-worded, high-toned false pretension. He almost read Lopez to the bottom,—not, however, giving the man credit for dishonesty so deep or cleverness so great as he possessed. But as regarded Emily, he was also actuated by a personal desire to have her back again as an element of happiness to himself. He had pined for her since he had been left alone, hardly knowing what it was that he had wanted. And now as he thought of it all, he was angry with himself that he had not been more loving and softer in his manner to her. She at any rate was honest. No doubt of that crossed his mind. And now he had been bitter to her,—bitter in his manner,—simply because he had not wished to appear to have been taken in by her husband. Thinking of all this, he got up, and went to his desk, and wrote her a note, which she would receive on the following morning after her husband had left her. It was very short.

'Dearest E.

'I am so overjoyed that you are coming back to me.

'A. W.'

He had judged her quite rightly. The manner in which the thing had been arranged had made her very wretched. There had been no love in it;—nothing apparently but assertions on one side that much was being given, and on the other acknowledgements that much was to be received. She was aware that in this her father had condemned her husband. She also had condemned him;—and felt, alas, that she also had been condemned. But this little letter took away that sting. She could read in her father's note all the action of his mind. He had known that he was bound to acquit her, and he had done so with one of the old long-valued expressions of his love.

VOLUME III

CHAPTER 41

THE VALUE OF A THICK SKIN

SIR ORLANDO DROUGHT must have felt bitterly the quiescence with which he sank into obscurity on the second bench on the opposite side of the House. One great occasion he had on which it was his privilege to explain to four or five hundred gentlemen the insuperable reasons which caused him to break away from those right honourable friends to act with whom had been his comfort and his duty, his great joy and his unalloyed satisfaction. Then he occupied the best part of an hour in abusing those friends and all their measures. This no doubt had been a pleasure, as practice had made the manipulation of words easy to him,—and he was able to revel in that absence of responsibility which must be as a fresh perfumed bath to a minister just freed from the trammels of office. But the pleasure was surely followed by much suffering when Mr Monk,—Mr Monk who was to assume his place as Leader of the House,—only took five minutes to answer him, saying that he and his colleagues regretted much the loss of the Right Honourable Baronet's services, but that it would hardly be necessary for him to defend the Ministry on all those points on which it had been attacked, as, were he to do so, he would have to repeat the arguments by which every measure brought forward by the present Ministry had been supported. Then Mr Monk sat down, and the business of the House went on just as if Sir Orlando Drought had not moved his seat at all.

'What makes everybody and everything so dead?' said Sir Orlando to his old friend Mr Boffin as they walked home together from the House that night. They had in former days been staunch friends, sitting night after night close together, united in opposition, and sometimes, for a few halcyon months, in the happier bonds of office. But when Sir Orlando had joined the Coalition, and when the sterner spirit of Mr Boffin had preferred principles to place,—to use the language in which he was wont to speak to himself and to his wife and family of his own abnegation,—there had come a coolness between them. Mr Boffin, who was not a rich man, nor by any means indifferent to the comforts of office, had felt keenly the injury done to him when he was left hopelessly in the cold by the desertion of his old friends. It had come to pass that there had been no salt left in the opposition. Mr Boffin in all his parliamentary experience had known nothing like it. Mr Boffin had been sure that British honour was going to the dogs and that British greatness was at an end. But the secession of Sir Orlando gave a little fillip to his life. At any rate he could walk home with his old friend and talk of the horrors of the present day.

'Well, Drought, if you ask me, you know, I can only speak as I feel. Everything must be dead when men holding different opinions on every subject under the sun come together in order that they may carry on a government as they would a trade business. The work may be done, but it must be done without spirit.'

'But it may be all important that the work should be done,' said the Baronet, apologizing for his past misconduct.

'No doubt;—and I am very far from judging those who make the attempt. It has been made more than once before, and has, I think, always failed. I don't believe in it myself, and I think that the death-like torpor of which you speak is one of its worst consequences.' After that Mr Boffin admitted Sir Orlando back into his heart of hearts.

Then the end of the Session came, very quietly and very early. By the end of July there was nothing left to be done, and the world of London was allowed to go down into the country almost a fortnight before its usual time.

With many men, both in and out of Parliament, it became a question whether all this was for good or evil. The Boffinites had of course much to say for themselves. Everything was torpid. There was no interest in the newspapers,—except when Mr Slide took the tomahawk into his hands. A member of Parliament this Session had not been by half so much bigger than another man as in times of hot political warfare. One of the most moving sources of our national excitement seemed to have vanished from life. We all know what happens to stagnant waters. So said the Boffinites, and so also now said Sir Orlando. But the Government was carried on and the country was prosperous. A few useful measures had been passed by unambitious men, and the Duke of St Bungay declared that he had never known a Session of Parliament more thoroughly satisfactory to the ministers.

But the old Duke in so saying had spoken as it were his public opinion,—giving, truly enough, to a few of his colleagues, such as Lord Drummond, Sir Gregory Grogram and others, the results of his general experience; but in his own bosom and with a private friend he was compelled to confess that there was a cloud in the heavens.

The Prime Minister had become so moody, so irritable, and so unhappy, that the old Duke was forced to doubt whether things could go on much longer as they were. He was wont to talk of these things to his friend Lord Cantrip, who was not a member of the Government, but who had been a colleague of both the Dukes, and whom the old Duke regarded with peculiar confidence. 'I cannot explain it to you,' he said to Lord Cantrip. 'There is nothing that ought to give him a moment's uneasiness. Since he took office there hasn't once been a majority against him in either House on any question that the Government has made its own. I don't remember such a state of things,—so easy for the Prime Minister,—since the days of Lord Liverpool. He had one thorn in his side, our friend who was at the Admiralty, and that thorn like other thorns has worked itself out. Yet at this moment it is impossible to get him to consent to the nomination of a successor to Sir Orlando.' This was said a week before the Session had closed.

'I suppose it is his health,' said Lord Cantrip.

'He's well enough as far as I can see;—though he will be ill unless he can relieve himself from the strain on his nerves.'

'Do you mean by resigning?'

'Not necessarily. The fault is that he takes things too seriously. If he could be got to believe that he might eat, and sleep, and go to bed, and amuse himself like other men, he might be a very good Prime Minister. He is over troubled by his conscience. I have seen a good many Prime Ministers, Cantrip, and I've taught myself to think that they are not very different from other men. One wants in a Prime Minister a good many things, but not very great things. He should be clever but need not be a genius; he should be conscientious but by no means strait-laced; he should be cautious but never timid, bold but never venture-some; he should have a good digestion, genial manners, and, above all, a thick skin. These are the gifts we want, but we can't always get them, and have to do without them. For my own part, I find that though Smith be a very good Minister, the best perhaps to be had at the time, when he breaks down Jones does nearly as well.'

'There will be a Jones, then, if your Smith does break down?'

'No doubt. England wouldn't come to an end because the Duke of Omnium shut himself up at Matching. But I love the man, and, with some few exceptions, am contented with the party. We can't do better, and it cuts me to the heart when I see him suffering, knowing how much I did myself to make him undertake the work.'

'Is he going to Gatherum Castle?'

'No;—to Matching. There is some discomfort about that.'

'I suppose,' said Lord Cantrip,—speaking almost in a whisper, although they were closeted together, 'I suppose the Duchess is a little troublesome.'

'She's the dearest woman in the world,' said the Duke of St Bungay. 'I love her almost as I do my own daughter. And she is most zealous to serve him.'

'I fancy she overdoes it.'

'No doubt.'

'And that he suffers from perceiving it,' said Lord Cantrip.

'But a man hasn't a right to suppose that he shall have no annoyances. The best horse in the world has some fault. He pulls, or he shies, or is slow at his fences, or doesn't like heavy ground. He has no right to expect that his wife shall know everything and do everything without a mistake. And then he has such faults of his own! His skin is so thin. Do you remember dear old Brock? By heavens;—there was a covering, a hide impervious to fire or steel! He wouldn't have gone into tantrums because his wife asked too many people to the house. Nevertheless, I won't give up all hope.'

'A man's skin may be thickened, I suppose.'

'No doubt;—as a blacksmith's arm.'

But the Duke of St Bungay, though he declared that he wouldn't give up hope, was very uneasy on the matter. 'Why won't you let me go?' the other Duke had said to him.

'What;—because such a man as Sir Orlando Drought throws up his office?'

But in truth the Duke of Omnium had not been instigated to ask the question by the resignation of Sir Orlando. At that very moment the 'People's Banner' had been put out of sight at the bottom of a heap of other newspapers behind the Prime Minister's chair, and his present misery had been produced by Mr Quintus Slide. To have a festering wound and to be able to show the wound to no surgeon, is wretchedness indeed! 'It's not Sir Orlando, but a sense of general failure,' said the Prime Minister. Then his old friend had made use of that argument of the ever-recurring majorities to prove that there had been no failure. 'There seems to have come a lethargy upon the country,' said the poor victim. Then the Duke of St Bungay knew that his friend had read that pernicious article in the 'People's Banner,' for the Duke had also read it and remembered that phrase of a 'lethargy on the country,' and understood at once how the poison had rankled.

It was a week before he would consent to ask any man to fill the vacancy made by Sir Orlando. He would not allow suggestions to be made to him and yet would name no one himself. The old Duke, indeed, did make a suggestion, and anything coming from him was of course borne with patience. Barrington Erle, he thought, would do for the Admiralty. But the Prime Minister shook his head. 'In the first place he would refuse, and that would be a great blow to me.'

'I could sound him,' said the old Duke. But the Prime Minister again shook his head and turned the subject. With all his timidity he was becoming autocratic and peevishly imperious. Then he went to Lord Cantrip, and when Lord Cantrip, with all the kindness which he could throw into his words, stated the reasons which induced him at present to decline office, he was again in despair. At last he asked Phineas Finn to move to the Admiralty, and, when our old friend somewhat reluctantly obeyed, of course he had the same difficulty in filling the office Finn had held. Other changes and other complications became necessary, and Mr Quintus Slide, who hated Phineas Finn even worse than the poor Duke, found ample scope for his patriotic indignation.

This all took place in the closing week of the Session, filling our poor Prime Minister with trouble and dismay, just when other people were complaining that there was nothing to think of and nothing to do. Men do not really like leaving London before the grouse calls them,—the grouse or rather the fashion of the grouse. And some ladies were very angry at being separated so soon from their swains in the city. The tradesmen too were displeased,—so that there were voices to re-echo the abuse of the 'People's Banner.' The Duchess had done her best to prolong the Session by another week, telling her husband of the evil consequences above suggested, but he had thrown wide his arms and asked her with affected dismay whether he was to keep Parliament sitting in order that more ribbons might be sold! 'There is nothing to be done,' said the Duke almost angrily.

'Then you should make something to be done,' said the Duchess, mimicking him.

CHAPTER 42

RETRIBUTION

THE Duchess had been at work with her husband for the last two months in the hope of renewing her autumnal festivities, but had been lamentably unsuccessful. The Duke had declared that there should be no more rural crowds, no repetition of what he called London turned loose on his own grounds. He could not forget the necessity which had been imposed upon him of turning Major Pountney out of his house, or the change that had been made in his gardens, or his wife's attempt to conquer him at Silverbridge. 'Do you mean,' she said, 'that we are to have nobody?' He replied that he thought it would be best to go to Matching. 'And live a Darby and Joan life?' said the Duchess.

'I said nothing of Darby and Joan. Whatever may be my feelings I hardly think that you are fitted for that kind of thing. Matching is not so big as Gatherum, but it is not a cottage. Of course you can ask your own friends.'

'I don't know what you mean by my own friends. I endeavour always to ask yours.'

'I don't know that Major Pountney, and Captain Gunner, and Mr Lopez were ever among the number of my friends.'

'I suppose you mean Lady Rosina?' said the Duchess. 'I shall be happy to have her at Matching if you wish it.'

'I should like to see Lady Rosina De Courcy at Matching very much.'

'And is there to be nobody else? I'm afraid I should find it rather dull while you two were opening your hearts to each other.' Here he looked at her angrily. 'Can you think of anybody besides Lady Rosina?'

'I suppose you will wish to have Mrs Finn?'

'What an arrangement! Lady Rosina for you to flirt with, and Mrs Finn for me to grumble to.'

'That is an odious word,' said the Prime Minister.

'What;—flirting? I don't see anything bad about the word. The thing is dangerous. But you are quite at liberty if you don't go beyond Lady Rosina. I should like to know whether you would wish anybody else to come?' Of course he made no becoming answer to this question, and of course no becoming answer was expected. He knew that she was trying to provoke him because he would not let her do this year as she had done last. The house, he had no doubt, would be full to overflowing when he got there. He could not help that. But as compared with Gatherum Castle the house at Matching was small, and his domestic authority sufficed at any rate for shutting up Gatherum for the time.

I do not know whether at times her sufferings were not as acute as his own. He, at any rate, was Prime Minister, and it seemed to her that she was to be reduced to nothing. At the beginning of it all he had, with unwonted tenderness, asked her for her sympathy in his undertaking, and, according to her powers, she had given it to him with her whole heart. She had thought that she had seen a way by which she might assist him in his great employment, and she had worked at it like a slave. Every day she told herself that she did not, herself, love the Captain Gunners and Major Pountneys, nor the Sir Orlandos, nor, indeed, the Lady Rosinas. She had not followed the bent of her own inclination when she had descended to sheets and towels, and busied herself to establish an archery-ground. She had not shot an arrow during the whole season, nor had she cared who had won and who had lost. It had not been for her own personal delight that she had kept open house for forty persons throughout four months of the year, in doing which he had never taken an ounce of the labour off her shoulders by any single word or deed! It had all been done for his sake,—that his reign might be long and triumphant, that the world might say that his hospitality was noble and full, that his name might be in men's mouths, and that he might prosper as a British Minister. Such, at least, were the assertions which she made to herself, when she thought of her own grievances and her own troubles. And now she was angry with her husband. It was very well for him to ask for her sympathy, but he had none to give her in return! He could not pity her failures,—even though he had himself caused them! If he had a grain of intelligence about him he must, she thought, understand well enough how sore it must be for her to descend from her princely entertainments to solitude at Matching, and thus to own before all the world that she was beaten. Then when she asked him for advice, when she was really anxious to know how far she might go in filling her house without offending him, he told her to ask Lady Rosina De Courcy! If he chose to be ridiculous he might. She would ask Lady Rosina De Courcy. In her active anger she did write to Lady Rosina De Courcy a formal letter, in which she said that the Duke hoped to have the pleasure of her ladyship's company at Matching Park on the 1st of August. It was an absurd letter, somewhat long, written very much in the Duke's name, with overwhelming expressions of affection, instigated in the writer's mind partly by the fun of supposition that such a man as her husband should flirt with such a woman as Lady Rosina. There was something too of anger in what she wrote, some touch of revenge. She sent off this invitation, and she sent no other. Lady Rosina took it all in good part, and replied saying that she should have the greatest pleasure in going to Matching. She had declared to herself that she would ask none but those he had named, and in accordance with her resolution she sent out no other written invitation.

He had also told her to ask Mrs Finn. Now this had become almost a matter of course. There had grown up from accidental circumstances so strong a bond between these two women, that it was taken for granted by both their husbands that they should be nearly always within reach of one another. And the two husbands were also on kindly, if not affectionate, terms with each other. The nature of the Duke's character was such that, with a most loving heart, he was hardly capable of that opening out of himself to another which is necessary for positive friendship. There was a stiff reserve about him, of which he was himself only too conscious, which almost prohibited friendship. But he liked Mr Finn both as a man and a member of his party, and was always satisfied to have him as a guest. The Duchess, therefore, had taken it for granted that Mrs Finn would come to her,—and that Mr Finn would come also during any time that he might be able to escape from Ireland. But, when the invitation was verbally conveyed, Mr Finn had gone to the Admiralty, and had already made arrangements for going to sea, as a gallant sailor should. 'We are going away in the "Black Watch" for a couple of months,' said Mrs Finn. Now the 'Black Watch' was the Admiralty yacht.

'Heavens and earth!' ejaculated the Duchess.

'It is always done. The First Lord would have his epaulets stripped if he didn't go to sea in August.'

'And must you go with him?'

'I have promised.'

'I think it very unkind,—very hard upon me. Of course you knew that I should want you.'

'But if my husband wants me too?'

'Bother your husband! I wish with all my heart I had never helped to make up the match.'

'It would have been made up just the same, Lady Glen.'

'You know that I cannot get on without you. And he ought to know it too. There isn't another person in the world that I can really say a thing to.'

'Why don't you have Mrs Grey?'

'She's going to Persia with her husband. And then she is not wicked enough. She always lectured me, and she does it still. What do you think is going to happen?'

'Nothing terrible, I hope,' said Mrs Finn, mindful of her husband's new honours at the Admiralty, and hoping that the Duke might not have repeated his threat of resigning.

'We are going to Matching.'

'So I supposed.'

'And whom do you think we are going to have?'

'Not Major Pountney?'

'No;—not at my asking.'

'Nor Mr Lopez?'

'Nor yet Mr Lopez. Guess again.'

'I suppose there will be a dozen to guess.'

'No,' shrieked the Duchess. 'There will only be one. I have asked one,—at his special desire,—and as you won't come I shall ask nobody else. When I pressed him to name a second he named you. I'll obey him to the letter. Now, my dear, who do you think is the chosen one,—the one person who is to solace the perturbed spirit of the Prime Minister for the three months of the autumn?'

'Mr Warburton, I should say.'

'Oh, Mr Warburton! No doubt Mr Warburton will come as part of his luggage, and possibly half-a-dozen Treasury clerks. He declares, however, that there is nothing to do, and therefore Mr Warburton's strength alone may suffice to help him to do it. There is to be one unnecessary guest,—unnecessary, that is, for official purpose; though,—oh,—so much needed for his social happiness. Guess once more.'

'Knowing the spirit of mischief that is in you,—perhaps it is Lady Rosina.'

'Of course it is Lady Rosina,' said the Duchess, clapping her hands together. 'And I should like to know what you mean by a spirit of mischief! I asked him, and he himself said that he particularly wished to have Lady Rosina at Matching. Now, I'm not a jealous woman,—am I?'

'Not of Lady Rosina.'

'I don't think they'll do any harm together, but it is particular, you know. However, she is to come. And nobody else is to come. I did count upon you.' Then Mrs Finn counselled her very seriously as to the bad taste of such a joke, explaining to her that the Duke had certainly not intended that her invitations should be confined to Lady Rosina. But it was not all joke with the Duchess. She had been driven almost to despair, and was very angry with her husband. He had brought the thing upon himself, and must now make the best of it. She would ask nobody else. She declared that there was nobody whom she could ask with propriety. She was tired of asking. Let her ask whom she would, he was dissatisfied. The only two people he cared to see were Lady Rosina and the old Duke. She had asked Lady Rosina for his sake. Let him ask his old friend himself if he pleased.

The Duke and Duchess with all the family went down together, and Mr Warburton went with them. The Duchess had said not a word more to her husband about his guests, nor had he alluded to the subject.

But each was labouring under a conviction that the other was misbehaving, and with that feeling it was impossible that there should be
confidence between them. He busied himself with books and papers,—
always turning over those piles of newspapers to see what evil was said
of himself,—and speaking only now and again to his private Secretary.
She engaged herself with the children or pretended to read a novel.
Her heart was sore within her. She had wished to punish him, but in
truth she was punishing herself.

On the day of their arrival, the father and mother, with Lord
Silverbridge, the eldest son, who was home from Eton, and the private
Secretary dined together. As the Duke sat at table, he began to think
how long it was since such a state of things had happened to him before,
and his heart softened towards her. Instead of being made angry by the
strangeness of her proceeding, he took delight in it, and in the course
of the evening spoke a word to signify his satisfaction. 'I'm afraid it
won't last long,' she said, 'for Lady Rosina comes to-morrow.'

'Oh, indeed.'

'You bid me ask her yourself.'

Then he perceived it all;—how she had taken advantage of his
former answer to her and had acted upon it in a spirit of contradictory
petulance. But he resolved that he would forgive it and endeavour to
bring her back to him. 'I thought we were both joking,' he said good-
humouredly.

'Oh, no! I never suspected you of a joke. At any rate she is coming.'

'She will do neither of us any harm. And Mrs Finn?'

'You have sent her to sea.'

'She may be at sea,—and he too; but it is without my sending. The
First Lord I believe usually does go a cruize. Is there nobody else?'

'Nobody else,—unless you have asked any one.'

'Not a creature. Well;—so much the better. I dare say Lady Rosina
will get on very well.'

'You will have to talk to her,' said the Duchess.

'I will do my best,' said the Duke.

Lady Rosina came and no doubt did think it odd. But she did not say
so, and it really did seem to the Duchess as though all her vengeance
had been blown away by the winds. And she too laughed at the
matter—to herself, and began to feel less cross and less perverse. The
world did not come to an end because she and her husband with Lady
Rosina and her boy and the private Secretary sat down to dinner every
day together. The parish clergyman with the neighbouring squire and
his wife and daughter did come one day,—to the relief of M. Millepois,

who had begun to feel that the world had collapsed. And every day at a certain hour the Duke and Lady Rosina walked together for an hour and a half in the park. The Duchess would have enjoyed it, instead of suffering, could she only have had her friend, Mrs Finn, to hear her jokes. 'Now, Plantagenet,' she said, 'do tell me one thing. What does she talk about?'

'The troubles of her family generally, I think.'

'That can't last for ever.'

'She wears cork soles to her boots and she thinks a good deal about them.'

'And you listen to her?'

'Why not? I can talk about cork soles as well as anything else. Anything that may do material good to the world at large, or even to yourself privately, is a fit subject for conversation to rational people.'

'I suppose I never was one of them.'

'But I can talk upon anything,' continued the Duke, 'as long as the talker talks in good faith and does not say things that should not be said, or deal with matters that are offensive. I could talk for an hour about bankers' accounts, but I should not expect a stranger to ask me the state of my own. She has almost persuaded me to send to Mr Sprout of Silverbridge and get some cork soles myself.'

'Don't do anything of the kind,' said the Duchess with animation;—as though she had secret knowledge that cork soles were specially fatal to the family of the Pallisers.

'Why not, my dear?'

'He was the man who especially, above all others, threw me over at Silverbridge.' Then again there came upon his brow that angry frown which during the last few days had been dissipated by the innocence of Lady Rosina's conversation. 'Of course I don't mean to ask you to take any interest in the borough again. You have said that you wouldn't, and you are always as good as your word.'

'I hope so.'

'But I certainly would not employ a tradesman just at your elbow who has directly opposed what was generally understood in the town to be your interests.'

'What did Mr Sprout do? This is the first I have heard of it.'

'He got Mr Du Boung to stand against Mr Lopez.'

'I am very glad for the sake of the borough that Mr Lopez did not get in.'

'So am I. But that is nothing to do with it. Mr Sprout knew at any rate what my wishes were, and went directly against them.'

'You were not entitled to have wishes in the matter, Glencora.'

'That's all very well;—but I had, and he knew it. As for the future of course the thing is over. But you have done everything for the borough.'

'You mean that the borough has done much for me.'

'I know what I mean very well;—and I shall take it very ill if a shilling out of the Castle ever goes into Mr Sprout's pocket again.'

It is needless to trouble the reader at length with the sermon which he preached her on the occasion,—showing the utter corruption which must come from the mixing up of politics with trade, or with the scorn which she threw into the few words with which she interrupted him from time to time. 'Whether a man makes good shoes, and at a reasonable price, and charges for them honestly,—that is what you have to consider,' said the Duke impressively.

'I'd rather pay double for bad shoes to a man who did not thwart me.'

'You should not condescend to be thwarted in such a matter. You lower yourself by admitting such a feeling.' And yet he writhed himself under the lashes of Mr Slide!

'I know an enemy when I see him,' said the Duchess, 'and as long as I live I'll treat an enemy as an enemy.'

There was ever so much of it, in the course of which the Duke declared his purpose of sending at once to Mr Sprout for ever so many cork soles, and the Duchess,—most imprudently,—declared her purpose of ruining Mr Sprout. There was something in this threat which grated terribly against the Duke's sense of honour;—that his wife should threaten to ruin a poor tradesman, that she should do so in reference to the political affairs of the borough which he all but owned,—that she should do so in declared opposition to him! Of course he ought to have known that her sin consisted simply in her determination to vex him at the moment. A more good-natured woman did not live;—or one less prone to ruin any one. But any reference to the Silverbridge election brought back upon him the remembrance of the cruel attacks which had been made upon him, and rendered him for the time moody, morose, and wretched. So they again parted ill friends, and hardly spoke when they met at dinner.

The next morning there reached Matching a letter which greatly added to his bitterness of spirit against the world in general and against her in particular. The letter, though marked 'private,' had been opened, as were all his letters, by Mr Warburton, but the private Secretary thought it necessary to show the letter to the Prime Minister. He, when he had read it, told Warburton that it did not signify, and maintained for half an hour an attitude of quiescence. Then he walked forth, having the letter hidden in his hand, and finding his wife alone, gave it her to read. 'See what you have brought upon me,' he said, 'by your interference and disobedience.' The letter was as follows:—

'Manchester Square, August 3, 187—.
'MY LORD DUKE,
    'I consider myself entitled to complain to your Grace of the conduct with which I was treated at the last election at Silverbridge, whereby I was led into very heavy expenditure without the least chance of being returned for the borough. I am aware that I had no direct conversation with your Grace on the subject, and that your Grace can plead that, as between man and man, I had no authority from yourself for supposing that I should receive your Grace's support. But I was distinctly asked by the Duchess to stand, and was assured by her that if I did so I should have all the assistance that your Grace's influence could procure for me;—and it was also explained to me that your Grace's official position made it inexpedient that your Grace on this special occasion should have any personal conference with your own candidate. Under these circumstances I submit to your Grace that I am entitled to complain of the hardship I have suffered.

    'I had not been long in the borough before I found that my position was hopeless. Influential men in the town who had been represented to me as being altogether devoted to your Grace's interests started a third candidate,—a Liberal as myself,—and the natural consequence was that neither of us succeeded, though my return as your Grace's candidate would have been certain had not this been done. That all this was preconcerted there can be no doubt, but, before the mine was sprung on me,—immediately, indeed, on my arrival, if I remember rightly,—an application was made to me for £500, so that the money might be exacted before the truth was known to me. Of course I should not have paid the £500 had I known that your Grace's usual agents in the town,—I may name Mr Sprout especially,—were prepared to act against me. But I did pay the money, and I think your Grace will agree with me that a very opprobrious term might be applied without injustice to the transaction.

    'My Lord Duke, I am a poor man;—ambitious I will own, whether that be a sin or a virtue,—and willing perhaps to incur expenditure which can hardly be justified in pursuit of certain public objects. But I must say, with the most lively respect for your Grace personally, that I do not feel inclined to sit down tamely under such a loss as this. I should not have dreamed of interfering in the election at Silverbridge had not the Duchess exhorted me to do so. I would not even have run the risk of a doubtful contest. But I came forward at the suggestion of the Duchess, backed by her personal assurance that the seat was certain as being in your Grace's hands. It was no doubt understood that your Grace would not yourself interfere, but it was equally well understood that your Grace's influence was for the time deputed to the Duchess. The Duchess herself will, I am sure, confirm my statement that I had her direct authority for regarding myself as your Grace's candidate.

'I can of course bring an action against Mr Wise, the gentleman to whom I paid the money, but I feel that as a gentleman I should not do so without reference to your Grace, as circumstances might possibly be brought out in evidence,—I will not say prejudicial to your Grace,— but which would be unbecoming. I cannot, however, think that your Grace will be willing that a poor man like myself, in his search for an entrance into public life, should be mulcted to so heavy an extent in consequence of an error on the part of the Duchess. Should your Grace be able to assist me in my view of getting into Parliament for any other seat I shall be willing to abide the loss I have incurred. I hardly, how-ever, dare to hope for such assistance. In this case I think your Grace ought to see that I am reimbursed.

'I have the honour to be,
'My Lord Duke,
'Your Grace's very faithful Servant',
'FERDINAND LOPEZ.'

The Duke stood over her in her own room upstairs, with his back to the fireplace and his eyes fixed upon her while she was reading this letter. He gave her ample time, and she did not read it very quickly. Much of it indeed she perused twice, turning very red in the face as she did so. She was thus studious partly because the letter astounded even her, and partly because she wanted time to consider how she would meet his wrath. 'Well,' said he, 'what do you say to that?'

'The man is a blackguard,—of course.'

'He is so;—though I do not know that I wish to hear him called such a name by your lips. Let him be what he may he was your friend.'

'He was my acquaintance.'

'He was the man whom you selected to be your candidate for the borough in opposition to my wishes, and whom you continued to support in direct disobedience to my orders.'

'Surely, Plantagenet, we had all that about disobedience out before.'

'You cannot have such things "out,"—as you call it. Evil-doing will not bury itself out of the way and be done with. Do you feel no shame at having your name mentioned a score of times with reprobation as that man mentions it;—at being written about by such a man as that?'

'Do you want me to roll in the gutter because I mistook him for a gentleman?'

'That was not all,—nor half. In your eagerness to serve such a miserable creature as this you forgot my entreaties, my commands, my position! I explained to you why I, of all men, and you, of all women, as a part of me, should not do this thing; and yet you did it, mistaking such a cur as that for a man! What am I to do? How am I to free myself from the impediments which you make for me? My enemies I can overcome,—but I cannot escape the pitfalls which are made for me by my own wife. I can only retire into private life and hope to console myself with my children and my books.'

There was a reality of tragedy about him which for the moment overcame her. She had no joke ready, no sarcasm, no feminine countergrumble. Little as she agreed with him when he spoke of the necessity of retiring into private life because a man had written to him such a letter as this, incapable as she was of understanding fully the nature of the irritation which tormented him, still she knew that he was suffering, and acknowledged to herself that she had been the cause of the agony. 'I am sorry,' she ejaculated at last. 'What more can I say?'

'What am I to do? What can be said to the man? Warburton read the letter, and gave it me in silence. He could see the terrible difficulty.'

'Tear it in pieces, and then let there be an end of it.'

'I do not feel sure but that he has right on his side. He is, as you say, certainly a blackguard, or he would not make such a claim. He is taking advantage of the mistake made by a good-natured woman through her folly and her vanity;'—as he said this the Duchess gave an absurd little pout, but luckily he did not see it,—'and he knows very well that he is doing so. But still he has a show of justice on his side. There was, I suppose, no chance for him at Silverbridge after I had made myself fully understood. The money was absolutely wasted. It was your persuasion and your continued encouragement that led him on to spend the money.'

'Pay it then. The loss will not hurt you.'

'Ah;—if we could but get out of our difficulties by paying! Suppose that I do pay it. I begin to think that I must pay it;—that after all

I cannot allow such a plea to remain unanswered. But when it is paid;—
what then? Do you think such a payment made by the Queen's Minister
will not be known to all the newspapers, and that I shall escape the
charge of having bribed the man to hold his tongue?'

'It will be no bribe if you pay him because you think you ought.'

'But how shall I excuse it? There are things done which are holy as
the heavens,—which are clear before God as the light of the sun, which
leave no stain on the conscience, and which yet the malignity of man
can invest with the very blackness of hell! I shall know why I pay this
£500. Because she who of all the world is the nearest and dearest
to me,'—she looked up into his face with amazement, as he stood
stretching out both his arms in his energy,—'has in her impetuous
folly committed a grievous blunder, from which she would not allow
her husband to save her, this sum must be paid to the wretched craven.
But I cannot tell the world that. I cannot say abroad that this small
sacrifice of money was the justest means of retrieving the injury which
you have done.'

'Say it abroad. Say it everywhere.'

'No, Glencora.'

'Do you think I would have you spare me if it was my fault? And
how would it hurt me? Will it be new to any one that I have done a foolish thing? Will the newspapers disturb my peace? I sometimes think,
Plantagenet, that I should have been the man, my skin is so thick; and
that you should have been the woman, yours is so tender.'

'But it is not so.'

'Take the advantage, nevertheless, of my toughness. Send him the
£500 without a word,—or make Warburton do so, or Mr Moreton.
Make no secret of it. Then if the papers talk about it——'

'A question might be asked about it in the House.'

'Or if questioned in any way,—say that I did it. Tell the exact truth.
You are always saying that nothing but truth ever serves. Let the truth
serve now. I shall not blench. Your saying it all in the House of Lords
won't wound me half so much as your looking at me as you did just
now.'

'Did I wound you? God knows I would not hurt you willingly.'

'Never mind. Go on. I know you think I have brought it all on myself
by my own wickedness. Pay this man the money, and then if anything
is said about it, explain that it was my fault, and say that you paid the
money because I had done wrong.'

When he came in she had been seated on a sofa, which she constantly
used herself, and he had stood over her, masterful, imperious, and

almost tyrannical. She had felt his tyranny, but had resented it less than usual,—or rather had been less determined in holding her own against him and asserting herself as his equal,—because she confessed to herself that she had injured him. She had, she thought, done but little, but that which she had done had produced this injury. So she had sat and endured the oppression of his standing posture. But now he sat down by her, very close to her, and put his hand upon her shoulder,— almost round her waist.

'Cora,' he said, 'you do not quite understand it.'

'I never understand anything, I think,' she answered.

'Not in this case,—perhaps never,—what it is that a husband feels about his wife. Do you think that I could say a word against you, even to a friend?'

'Why not?'

'I never did. I never could. If my anger were at the hottest I would not confess to a human being that you were not perfect,—except to yourself.'

'Oh, thank you! If you were to scold me vicariously I should feel it less.'

'Do not joke with me now, for I am so much in earnest! And if I could not consent that your conduct should be called in question even by a friend, do you suppose it possible that I could contrive an escape from public censure by laying the blame publicly on you?'

'Stick to the truth;—that's what you always say.'

'I certainly shall stick to the truth. A man and his wife are one.* For what she does he is responsible.'

'They couldn't hang you, you know, because I committed a murder.'

'I should be willing that they should do so. No;—if I pay this money I shall take the consequences. I shall not do it in any way under the rose. But I wish you would remember——'

'Remember what? I know I shall never forget all this trouble about that dirty little town, which I never will enter again as long as I live.'

'I wish you would think that in all that you do you are dealing with my feelings, with my heartstrings, with my reputation. You cannot divide yourself from me; nor, for the value of it all, would I wish that such a division were possible. You say that I am thin-skinned.'

'Certainly you are. What people call a delicate organization,— whereas I am rough and thick and monstrously commonplace.'

'Then should you too be thin-skinned for my sake.'

'I wish I could make you thick-skinned for your own. It's the only way to be decently comfortable in such a coarse, rough-and-tumble world as this is.'

'Let us both do our best,' he said, now putting his arm round her and kissing her. 'I think I shall send the man his money at once. It is the least of two evils. And now let there never be a word more about it between us.'

Then he left her and went back,—not to the study in which he was wont, when at Matching, to work with his private Secretary,—but to a small inner closet of his own, in which many a bitter moment was spent while he thought over that abortive system of decimal coinage by which he had once hoped to make himself one of the great benefactors of his nation, revolving in his mind the troubles which his wife brought upon him, and regretting the golden inanity of the coronet which in the very prime of life had expelled him from the House of Commons. Here he seated himself, and for an hour neither stirred from his seat, nor touched a pen, nor opened a book. He was trying to calculate in his mind what might be the consequences of paying the money to Mr Lopez. But when the calculation slipped from him,—as it did,— then he demanded of himself whether strict high-minded justice did not call upon him to pay the money let the consequences be what they might. And here his mind was truer to him, and he was able to fix himself to a purpose,—though the resolution to which he came was not, perhaps, wise.

When the hour was over he went to his desk, drew a cheque for £500 in favour of Ferdinand Lopez, and then caused his Secretary to send it in the following note:—

'*Matching, August 4, 187—*.

'Sir,—

'The Duke of Omnium has read the letter you have addressed to him, dated the 3rd instant. The Duke of Omnium, feeling that you may have been induced to undertake the late contest at Silverbridge by misrepresentations made to you at Gatherum Castle, directs me to enclose a cheque for £500, that being the sum stated by you to have been expended in carrying on the contest at Silverbridge.

'I am, sir,

'Your obedient servant,

'Arthur Warburton.

'Ferdinand Lopez, Esq.'

CHAPTER 43

KAURI GUM

THE reader will no doubt think that Ferdinand Lopez must have been very hardly driven indeed by circumstances before he would have made such an appeal to the Duke as that given in the last chapter. But it was not want of money only that had brought it about. It may be remembered that the £500 had already been once repaid him by his father-in-law,—that special sum having been given to him for that special purpose. And Lopez, when he wrote to the Duke, assured himself that if, by any miracle, his letter should produce pecuniary results in the shape of a payment from the Duke, he would refund the money so obtained to Mr Wharton. But when he wrote the letter he did not expect to get money,—nor, indeed, did he expect that aid towards another seat, to which he alluded at the close of his letter. He expected probably nothing but to vex the Duke, and to drive the Duke into a correspondence with him.

Though this man had lived nearly all his life in England, he had not quite acquired that knowledge of the way in which things are done which is so general among men of a certain class, and so rare among those beneath them. He had not understood that the Duchess's promise of her assistance at Silverbridge might be taken by him for what it was worth, and that her aid might be used as far as it went,—but, that in the event of its failing him, he was bound in honour to take the result without complaining, whatever that result might be. He felt that a grievous injury had been done to him, and that it behoved him to resent that injury,—even though it were against a woman. He just knew that he could not very well write to the Duchess herself,—though there was sometimes present to his mind a plan for attacking her in public, and telling her what evil she had done him. He had half resolved that he would do so in her own garden at The Horns;—but on that occasion the apparition of Arthur Fletcher had disturbed him, and he had vented his anger in another direction. But still his wrath against the Duke and Duchess remained, and he was wont to indulge it with very violent language as he sat upon one of the chairs in Sexty Parker's office, talking somewhat loudly of his own position, of the things that he would do, and of the injury done him. Sexty Parker sympathized with him to the full,—especially as that first £500, which he had received from Mr Wharton, had gone into Sexty's coffers. At that time Lopez and Sexty were together committed to large speculations in the guano

trade, and Sexty's mind was by no means easy in the early periods of
the day. As he went into town by his train, he would think of his wife
and family and of the terrible things that might happen to them. But
yet, up to this period, money had always been forthcoming from Lopez
when absolutely wanted, and Sexty was quite alive to the fact that he
was living with a freedom of expenditure in his own household that he
had never known before, and that without apparent damage. Whenever,
therefore, at some critical moment, a much-needed sum of money was
produced, Sexty would become lighthearted, triumphant, and very
sympathetic. 'Well;—I never heard such a story,' he had said when
Lopez was insisting on his wrongs. 'That's what the Dukes and
Duchesses call honour among thieves! Well, Ferdy, my boy, if you
stand that you'll stand anything.' In these latter days Sexty had become
very intimate indeed with his partner.

'I don't mean to stand it,' Lopez had replied, and then on the spot
had written the letter which he had dated from Manchester Square.
He had certainly contrived to make that letter as oppressive as possible.
He had been clever enough to put into it words which were sure to
wound the poor Duke and to confound the Duchess. And having written it he was very careful to keep the first draft, so that if occasion came
he might use it again and push his vengeance farther. But he certainly
had not expected such a result as it produced.

When he received the private Secretary's letter with the money he
was sitting opposite to his father-in-law at breakfast, while his wife was
making the tea. Not many of his letters came to Manchester Square.
Sexty Parker's office or his club were more convenient addresses; but
in this case he had thought that Manchester Square would have a
better sound and appearance. When he opened the letter the cheque of
course appeared bearing the Duke's own signature. He had seen that
and the amount before he had read the letter, and as he saw it his
eye travelled quickly across the table to his father-in-law's face.
Mr Wharton might certainly have seen the cheque and even the
amount, probably also the signature, without the slightest suspicion as
to the nature of the payment made. As it was, he was eating his toast,
and had thought nothing about the letter. Lopez, having concealed the
cheque, read the few words which the private Secretary had written,
and then put the document with its contents into his pocket. 'So you
think, sir, of going down to Herefordshire on the 15th,' he said in a
very cheery voice. The cheery voice was still pleasant to the old man,
but the young wife had already come to distrust it. She had learned,
though she was hardly conscious how the lesson had come to her, that

a certain tone of cheeriness indicated, if not deceit, at any rate concealment of something. It grated against her spirit; and when this tone
reached her ears a frown or look of sorrow would cross her brow. And
her husband also had perceived that it was so, and knew at such times
that he was rebuked. He was hardly aware what doings, and especially
what feelings, were imputed to him as faults,—not understanding the
lines which separated right from wrong; but he knew that he was often
condemned by his wife, and he lived in fear that he should also be condemned by his wife's father. Had it been his wife only he thought that
he could soon have quenched her condemnation. He would soon have
made her tired of showing her disapproval. But he had put himself into
the old man's house, where the old man could see not only him but his
treatment of his wife, and the old man's good-will and good opinion
were essential to him. Yet he could not restrain one glance of anger at
her when she saw that look upon her face.

'I suppose I shall,' said the barrister. 'I must go somewhere.
My going need not disturb you.'

'I think we have made up our mind,' said Lopez, 'to take a cottage at
Dovercourt. It is not a very lively place, nor yet fashionable. But it is
very healthy, and I can run up to town easily. Unfortunately my business won't let me be altogether away this autumn.'

'I wish my business would keep me,' said the barrister.

'I did not understand that you had made up your mind to go to
Dovercourt,'* said Emily. He had spoken to Mr Wharton of their joint
action in the matter, and as the place had only once been named by him
to her, she resented what seemed to be a falsehood. She knew that she
was to be taken or left as it suited him. If he had said boldly,—'We'll go
to Dovercourt. That's what I've settled on. That's what will suit me,'
she would have been contented. She quite understood that he meant to
have his own way in such things. But it seemed to her that he wanted
to be a tyrant without having the courage necessary for tyranny.

'I thought you seemed to like it,' he said.

'I don't dislike it at all.'

'Then, as it suits my business, we might as well consider it settled.'
So saying, he left the room and went off to the city. The old man was
still sipping his tea and lingering over his breakfast in a way that was
not usual with him. He was generally anxious to get away to Lincoln's
Inn, and on most mornings had left the house before his son-in-law.
Emily of course remained with him, sitting silent in her place opposite
to the teapot, meditating perhaps on her prospects of happiness at
Dovercourt,—a place of which she had never heard even the name two

days ago, and in which it was hardly possible that she should find even an acquaintance. In former years these autumn months, passed in Herefordshire, had been the delight of her life.

Mr Wharton also had seen the cloud on his daughter's face, and had understood the nature of the little dialogue about Dovercourt. And he was aware,—had been aware since they had both come into his house,—that the young wife's manner and tone to her husband was not that of perfect conjugal sympathy. He had already said to himself more than once that she had made her bed for herself, and must lie upon it. She was the man's wife, and must take her husband as he was. If she suffered under this man's mode and manner of life, he, as her father, could not assist her,—could do nothing for her, unless the man should become absolutely cruel. He had settled that within his own mind already; but yet his heart yearned towards her, and when he thought that she was unhappy he longed to comfort her and tell her that she still had a father. But the time had not come as yet in which he could comfort her by sympathizing with her against her husband. There had never fallen from her lips a syllable of complaint. When she had spoken to him a chance word respecting her husband, it had always carried with it some tone of affection. But still he longed to say to her something which might tell her that his heart was soft towards her. 'Do you like the idea of going to this place?' he said.

'I don't at all know what it will be like. Ferdinand says it will be cheap.'

'Is that of such vital consequence?'

'Ah;—yes; I fear it is.'

This was very sad to him. Lopez had already had from him a considerable sum of money, having not yet been married twelve months, and was now living in London almost free of expense. Before his marriage he had always spoken of himself, and had contrived to be spoken of, as a wealthy man, and now he was obliged to choose some small English seaside place to which to retreat, because thus he might live at a low rate! Had they married as poor people there would have been nothing to regret in this;—there would be nothing that might not be done with entire satisfaction. But, as it was, it told a bad tale for the future! 'Do you understand his money matters, Emily?'

'Not at all, papa.'

'I do not in the least mean to make inquiry. Perhaps I should have asked before;—but if I did make inquiry now it would be of him. But I think a wife should know.'

'I know nothing.'

'What is his business?'

'I have no idea. I used to think he was connected with Mr Mills Happerton and with Messrs Hunky and Sons.'

'Is he not connected with Hunky's house?'

'I think not. He has a partner of the name of Parker, who is,—who is not, I think, quite—quite a gentleman. I never saw him.'

'What does he do with Mr Parker?'

'I believe they buy guano.'

'Ah;—that, I fancy, was only one affair.'

'I'm afraid he lost money, papa, by that election at Silverbridge.'

'I paid that,' said Mr Wharton sternly. Surely he should have told his wife that he had received that money from her family!

'Did you? That was very kind. I am afraid, papa, we are a great burden on you.'

'I should not mind it, my dear, if there were confidence and happiness. What matter would it be to me whether you had your money now or hereafter, so that you might have it in the manner that would be most beneficial to you? I wish he would be open with me, and tell me everything.'

'Shall I let him know that you say so?'

He thought for a minute or two before he answered her. Perhaps the man would be more impressed if the message came to him through his wife. 'If you think that he will not be annoyed with you, you may do so.'

'I don't know why he should,—but if it be right, that must be borne. I am not afraid to say anything to him.'

'Then tell him so. Tell him that it will be better that he should let me know the whole condition of his affairs. God bless you, dear.' Then he stooped over her, and kissed her, and went his way to Stone Buildings.

It was not as he sat at the breakfast table that Ferdinand Lopez made up his mind to pocket the Duke's money and to say nothing about it to Mr Wharton. He had been careful to conceal the cheque, but he had done so with the feeling that the matter was one to be considered in his own mind before he took any step. As he left the house, already considering it, he was inclined to think that the money must be surrendered. Mr Wharton had very generously paid his electioneering expenses, but had not done so simply with the view of making him a present of money. He wished the Duke had not taken him at his word. In handing this cheque over to Mr Wharton, he would be forced to tell the story of his letter to the Duke, and was sure that Mr Wharton would not approve of his having written such a letter. How could any one approve of his having applied for a sum of money which had already been paid to him? How could such a one as Mr Wharton,—an old-fashioned English gentleman,—approve of such an application being made under any circumstances? Mr Wharton would very probably insist on having the cheque sent back to the Duke,—which would be a sorry end to the triumph as at present achieved. And the more he thought of it the more sure he was that it would be imprudent to mention to Mr Wharton his application to the Duke. The old men of the present day were, he said to himself, such fools that they understood nothing. And then the money was very convenient to him. He was intent on obtaining Sexty Parker's consent to a large speculation, and knew that he could not do so without a show of funds. By the time, therefore, that he had reached the city he had resolved that at any rate for the present he would use the money and say nothing about it to Mr Wharton. Was it not spoil got from the enemy by his own courage and cleverness? When he was writing his acknowledgement for the money to Warburton he had taught himself to look upon the sum extracted from the Duke as a matter quite distinct from the payment made to him by his father-in-law.

It was evident on that day to Sexty Parker that his partner was a man of great resources. Though things sometimes looked very bad, yet money always 'turned up.' Some of their buyings and sellings had answered pretty well. Some had been great failures. No great stroke had been made as yet, but then the great stroke was always being expected. Sexty's fears were greatly exaggerated by the feeling that the coffee and guano were not always real coffee and guano. His partner, indeed, was of opinion that in such a trade as this they were following there was no need at all of real coffee and real guano, and explained his theory with considerable eloquence. 'If I buy a ton of coffee and keep it six weeks, why do I buy it and keep it, and why does the seller sell it instead of keeping it? The seller sells it because he thinks he can do best by parting with it now at a certain price. I buy it because I think I can make money by keeping it. It is just the same as though we were to back our opinions. He backs the fall. I back the rise. You needn't have coffee and you needn't have guano to do this. Indeed the possession of the coffee or the guano is only a very clumsy addition to the trouble of your profession. I make it my study to watch the markets;—but I needn't buy everything I see in order to make money by my labour and intelligence.' Sexty Parker before his lunch always thought that his partner was wrong, but after that ceremony he almost daily became a convert to the great doctrine. Coffee and guano still had to be bought because the world was dull and would not learn the tricks of trade as taught by Ferdinand Lopez,—also possibly because somebody might want such articles,—but our enterprising hero looked for a time in which no such dull burden should be imposed on him.

On this day, when the Duke's £500 was turned into the business, Sexty yielded in a large matter which his partner had been pressing upon him for the last week. They bought a cargo of Kauri gum,* coming from New Zealand. Lopez had reasons for thinking that Kauri gum must have a great rise. There was an immense demand for amber, and Kauri gum might be used as a substitute, and in six months' time would be double its present value. This unfortunately was a real cargo. He could not find an individual so enterprising as to venture to deal in a cargo of Kauri gum after his fashion. But the next best thing was done. The real cargo was bought and his name and Sexty's name were on the bills given for the goods. On that day he returned home in high spirits, for he did believe in his own intelligence and good fortune.

CHAPTER 44

MR WHARTON INTENDS TO MAKE A NEW WILL

ON that afternoon, immediately on the husband's return to the house, his wife spoke to him as her father had desired. On that evening Mr Wharton was dining at his club, and therefore there was the whole evening before them; but the thing to be done was disagreeable, and therefore she did it at once,—rushing into the matter almost before he had seated himself in the arm-chair which he had appropriated to his use in the drawing-room. 'Papa was talking about our affairs after you left this morning, and he thinks that it would be so much better if you would tell him all about them.'

'What made him talk of that to-day?' he said, turning at her almost angrily and thinking at once of the Duke's cheque.

'I suppose it is natural that he should be anxious about us, Ferdinand;—and the more natural as he has money to give if he chooses to give it.'

'I have asked him for nothing lately;—though, by George, I intend to ask him and that very roundly. Three thousand pounds isn't much of a sum of money for your father to have given you.'

'And he paid the election bill;—didn't he?'

'He has been complaining of that behind my back,—has he? I didn't ask him for it. He offered it. I wasn't such a fool as to refuse, but he needn't bring that up as a grievance to you.'

'It wasn't brought up as a grievance. I was saying that your standing had been a heavy expenditure——'

'Why did you say so? What made you talk about it at all? Why should you be discussing my affairs behind my back?'

'To my own father! And that too when you are telling me every day that I am to induce him to help you!'

'Not by complaining that I am poor. But how did it all begin?' She had to think for a moment before she could recollect how it did begin. 'There has been something,' he said, 'which you are ashamed to tell me.'

'There is nothing that I am ashamed to tell you. There never has been and never will be anything.' And she stood up as she spoke, with open eyes and extended nostrils. 'Whatever may come, however wretched it may be, I shall not be ashamed of myself.'

'But of me!'

'Why do you say so? Why do you try to make unhappiness between us?'

'You have been talking of—my poverty.'

'My father asked why you should go to Dovercourt,—and whether it was because it would save expense.'

'You want to go somewhere?'

'Not at all. I am contented to stay in London. But I said that I thought the expense had a good deal to do with it. Of course it has.'

'Where do you want to be taken? I suppose Dovercourt is not fashionable.'

'I want nothing.'

'If you are thinking of travelling abroad, I can't spare the time. It isn't an affair of money, and you had no business to say so. I thought of the place because it is quiet and because I can get up and down easily. I am sorry that I ever came to live in this house.'

'Why do you say that, Ferdinand?'

'Because you and your father make cabals behind my back. If there is anything I hate it is that kind of thing.'

'You are very unjust,' she said to him sobbing. 'I have never caballed. I have never done anything against you. Of course papa ought to know.'

'Why ought he to know? Why is your father to have the right of inquiry into all my private affairs?'

'Because you want his assistance. It is only natural. You always tell me to get him to assist you. He spoke most kindly, saying that he would like to know how things are.'

'Then he won't know. As for wanting his assistance, of course I want the fortune which he ought to give you. He is man of the world enough to know that as I am in business capital must be useful to me. I should have thought that you would understand as much as that yourself.'

'I do understand it, I suppose.'

'Then why don't you act as my friend rather than his? Why don't you take my part? It seems to me that you are much more his daughter than my wife.'

'That is most unfair.'

'If you had any pluck you would make him understand that for your sake he ought to say what he means to do, so that I might have the advantage of the fortune which I suppose he means to give you some day. If you had the slightest anxiety to help me you could influence him. Instead of that you talk to him about my poverty. I don't want him to think that I am a pauper. That's not the way to get round a man like your father, who is rich himself and who thinks it a disgrace in other men not to be rich too.'

'I can't tell him in the same breath that you are rich and that you want money.'

'Money is the means by which men make money. If he was confident of my business he'd shell out his cash quick enough! It is because he has been taught to think that I am in a small way. He'll find his mistake some day.'

'You won't speak to him then?'

'I don't say that at all. If I find that it will answer my own purpose I shall speak to him. But it would be very much easier to me if I could get you to be cordial in helping me.'

Emily by this time quite knew what such cordiality meant. He had been so free in his words to her that there could be no mistake. He had instructed her to 'get round' her father. And now again he spoke of her influence over her father. Although her illusions were all melting away,—oh, so quickly vanishing, still she knew that it was her duty to be true to her husband, and to be his wife rather than her father's daughter. But what could she say on his behalf, knowing nothing of his affairs? She had no idea what was his business, what was his income, what amount of money she ought to spend as his wife. As far as she could see,—and her common sense in seeing such things was good,—he had no regular income, and was justified in no expenditure. On her own account she would ask for no information. She was too proud to request that from him which should be given to her without any request. But in her own defence she must tell him that she could use no influence with her father as she knew none of the circumstances by which her father would be guided. 'I cannot help you in the manner you mean,' she said, 'because I know nothing myself.'

'You know that you can trust me to do the best with your money if I could get hold of it, I suppose?' She certainly did not know this, and held her tongue. 'You could assure him of that?'

'I could only tell him to judge for himself.'

'What you mean is that you'd see me d——d before you would open your mouth for me to the old man!'

He had never sworn at her before, and now she burst out into a flood of tears. It was to her a terrible outrage. I do not know that a woman is very much the worse because her husband may forget himself on an occasion and 'rap out an oath at her,' as he would call it when making the best of his own sin. Such an offence is compatible with uniform kindness and most affectionate consideration. I have known ladies who would think little or nothing about it,—who would go no farther than the mildest protest,—'Do remember where you are!' or 'My dear John!'—if no stranger were present. But then a wife should be initiated into it by degrees; and there are different tones of bad language, of which by far the most general is the good-humoured tone. We all of us know men who never damn their servants or inferiors, or strangers, or women,—who in fact keep it all for their bosom friends; and if a little does sometimes flow over in the freedom of domestic life, the wife is apt to remember that she is the bosomest of her husband's friends, and so to pardon the transgression. But here the word had been uttered with all its foulest violence, with virulence and vulgarity. It seemed to the victim to be the sign of a terrible crisis in her early married life,—as though the man who had so spoken to her could never again love her, never again be kind to her, never again be sweetly gentle and like a lover. And as he spoke it he looked at her as though he would like to tear her limbs asunder. She was frightened as well as horrified and astounded. She had not a word to say to him. She did not know in what language to make her complaint of such treatment. She burst into tears, and throwing herself on the sofa, hid her face in her hands. 'You provoke me to be violent,' he said. But still she could not speak to him. 'I come away from the city tired with work and troubled with a thousand things, and you have not a kind word to say to me.' Then there was a pause, during which she still sobbed. 'If your father has anything to say to me, let him say it. I shall not run away. But as to going to him of my own accord with a story as long as my arm about my affairs, I don't mean to do it.' Then he paused a moment again. 'Come, old girl, cheer up! Don't pretend to be broken-hearted because I used a hard word. There are worse things than that to be borne in the world.'

'I—I—I was so startled, Ferdinand.'

'A man can't always remember that he isn't with another man. Don't think anything more about it; but do bear this in mind,—that, situated as we are, your influence with your father may be the making or marring of me.' And so he left the room.

She sat for the next ten minutes thinking of it all. The words which he had spoken were so horrible that she could not get them out of her mind,—could not bring herself to look upon them as a trifle. The darkness of his countenance still dwelt with her,—and that absence of all tenderness, that coarse, un-marital and yet marital roughness, which should not at any rate have come to him so soon. The whole man too was so different from what she had thought him to be. Before their marriage no word as to money had ever reached her ears from his lips. He had talked to her of books,—and especially of poetry. Shakespeare and Molière, Dante and Goethe, had been or had seemed to be dear to him. And he had been full of fine ideas about women, and about men in their intercourse with women. For his sake she had separated herself from all her old friends. For his sake she had hurried into a marriage altogether distasteful to her father. For his sake she had closed her heart against that other lover. Trusting altogether in him she had ventured to think that she had known what was good for her better than all those who had been her counsellors, and had given herself to him utterly. Now she was awake; her dream was over; and the natural language of the man was still ringing in her ears!

They met together at dinner and passed the evening without a further allusion to the scene which had been acted. He sat with a magazine in his hand, every now and then making some remark intended to be pleasant but which grated on her ears as being fictitious. She would answer him,—because it was her duty to do so, and because she would not condescend to sulk; but she could not bring herself even to say to herself that all should be with her as though that horrid word had not been spoken. She sat over her work till ten, answering him when he spoke in a voice which was also fictitious, and then took herself off to her bed that she might weep alone. It would, she knew, be late before he would come to her.

On the next morning there came a message to him as he was dressing. Mr Wharton wished to speak to him. Would he come down before breakfast, or would he call on Mr Wharton in Stone Buildings? He sent down word that he would do the latter at an hour he fixed, and then did not show himself in the breakfast-room till Mr Wharton was gone. 'I've got to go to your father to-day,' he said to his wife, 'and I thought it best not to begin till we come to the regular business. I hope he does not mean to be unreasonable.' To this she made no answer. 'Of course you think the want of reason will be all on my side.'

'I don't know why you should say so.'

'Because I can read your mind. You do think so. You've been in the same boat with your father all your life, and you can't get out of that boat and get into mine. I was wrong to come and live here. Of course it was not the way to withdraw you from his influence.' She had nothing to say that would not anger him, and was therefore silent. 'Well; I must do the best I can by myself, I suppose. Good-bye,' and so he was off.

'I want to know,' said Mr Wharton, on whom was thrown by premeditation on the part of Lopez the task of beginning the conversation,—'I want to know what is the nature of your operations. I have never been quite able to understand it.'

'I do not know that I quite understand it myself,' said Lopez, laughing.

'No man alive,' continued the old barrister almost solemnly, 'has a greater objection to thrust himself into another man's affairs than I have. And as I didn't ask the question before your marriage,—as perhaps I ought to have done,—I should not do so now, were it not that the disposition of some part of the earnings of my life must depend on the condition of your affairs.' Lopez immediately perceived that it behoved him to be very much on the alert. It might be that if he showed himself to be very poor, his father-in-law would see the necessity of assisting him at once; or, it might be, that unless he could show himself to be in prosperous circumstances, his father-in-law would not assist him at all. 'To tell you the plain truth, I am minded to make a new will. I had of course made arrangements as to my property before Emily's marriage. Those arrangements I think I shall now alter. I am greatly distressed with Everett; and from what I see and from a few words which have dropped from Emily, I am not, to tell you the truth, quite happy as to your position. If I understand rightly you are a general merchant, buying and selling goods in the market?'

'That's about it, sir.'

'What capital have you in the business?'

'What capital?'

'Yes;—how much did you put into it at starting?'

Lopez paused a moment. He had got his wife. The marriage could not be undone. Mr Wharton had money enough for them all, and would not certainly discard his daughter. Mr Wharton could place him on a really firm footing, and might not improbably do so if he could be made to feel some confidence in his son-in-law. At this moment there was much doubt with the son-in-law whether he had better not tell the simple truth. 'It has gone in by degrees,' he said. 'Altogether I have about £8000 in it.' In truth he had never been possessed of a shilling.

'Does that include the £3000 you had from me?'

'Yes; it does.'

'Then you have married my girl and started into the world with a business based on £5000, and which had so far miscarried that within a month of two after your marriage you were driven to apply to me for funds!'

'I wanted money for a certain purpose.'

'Have you any partner, Mr Lopez?' This address was felt to be very ominous.

'Yes. I have a partner who is possessed of capital. His name is Parker.'

'Then his capital is your capital.'

'Well;—I can't explain it, but it is not so.'

'What is the name of your firm?'

'We haven't a registered name.'

'Have you a place of business?'

'Parker has a place of business in Little Tankard Yard.'

Mr Wharton turned to a directory and found out Parker's name. 'Mr Parker is a stockbroker.* Are you also a stockbroker?'

'No,—I am not.'

'Then, sir, it seems to me that you are a commercial adventurer.'

'I am not at all ashamed of the name, Mr Wharton. According to your manner of reckoning, half the business in the City of London is done by commercial adventurers. I watch the markets and buy goods,—and sell them at a profit. Mr Parker is a moneyed man, who happens also to be a stockbroker. We can very easily call ourselves merchants, and put up the names of Lopez and Parker over the door.'

'Do you sign bills together?'

'Yes.'

'As Lopez and Parker?'

'No. I sign them and he signs them. I trade also by myself, and so, I believe, does he.'

'One other question, Mr Lopez. On what income have you paid income-tax for the last three years?'

'On £2000* a-year,' said Lopez. This was a direct lie.

'Can you make out any schedule showing your exact assets and liabilities at the present time?'

'Certainly I can.'

'Then do so, and send it to me before I go into Herefordshire. My will as it stands at present would not be to your advantage. But I cannot change it till I know more of your circumstances than I do now.' And so the interview was over.

CHAPTER 45

MRS SEXTY PARKER

THOUGH Mr Wharton and Lopez met every day for the next week, nothing more was said about the schedule. The old man was thinking about it every day, and so also was Lopez. But Mr Wharton had made his demand, and, as he thought, nothing more was to be said on the subject. He could not continue the subject as he would have done with his son. But as day after day passed by he became more and more convinced that his son-in-law's affairs were not in a state which could bear to see the light. He had declared his purpose of altering his will in the man's favour, if the man would satisfy him. And yet nothing was done and nothing was said.

Lopez had come among them and robbed him of his daughter. Since the man had become intimate in his house he had not known an hour's happiness. The man had destroyed all the plans of his life, broken through into his castle, and violated his very hearth. No doubt he himself had vacillated. He was aware of that, and in his present mood was severe enough in judging himself. In his desolation he had tried to take the man to his heart,—had been kind to him, and had even opened his house to him. He had told himself that as the man was the husband of his daughter he had better make the best of it. He had endeavoured to make the best of it, but between him and the man there were such differences that they were poles asunder. And now it became clear to him that the man was, as he had declared to the man's face, no better than an adventurer!

By his will as it at present stood he had left two-thirds of his property to Everett, and one-third to his daughter, with arrangements for settling her share on her children, should she be married and have children at the time of his death. This will had been made many years ago, and he had long since determined to alter it, in order that he might divide his property equally between his children;—but he had postponed the matter, intending to give a large portion of Emily's share to her directly on her marriage with Arthur Fletcher. She had not married Arthur Fletcher;—but still it was necessary that a new will should be made.

When he left town for Herefordshire he had not yet made up his mind how this should be done. He had at one time thought that he would give some considerable sum to Lopez at once, knowing that to a man in business such assistance would be useful. And he had not altogether abandoned that idea, even when he had asked for the schedule. He did not relish the thought of giving his hard-earned money to Lopez, but, still, the man's wife was his daughter, and he must do the best that he could for her. Her taste in marrying the man was inexplicable to him. But that was done;—and now how might he best arrange his affairs so as to serve her interests?

About the middle of August he went to Herefordshire and she to the seaside in Essex,—to the little place which Lopez had selected. Before the end of the month the father-in-law wrote a line to his son-in-law.

'DEAR LOPEZ,' (not without premeditation had he departed from the sternness of that 'Mr Lopez,' which in his anger he had used at his chambers,)—

'When we were discussing your affairs I asked you for a schedule of your assets and liabilities. I can make no new arrangement of my property till I receive this. Should I die leaving my present will as the instrument under which my property would be conveyed to my heirs, Emily's share would go into the hands of trustees for the use of herself and her possible children. I tell you this that you may understand that it is for your own interest to comply with my requisition.

'Yours,
'A. WHARTON.'

Of course questions were asked him as to how the newly married couple were getting on. At Wharton these questions were mild and easily put off. Sir Alured was contented with a slight shake of his head, and Lady Wharton only remarked for the fifth or sixth time that it 'was a pity.' But when they all went to Longbarns, the difficulty became greater. Arthur was not there, and old Mrs Fletcher was in full strength. 'So the Lopezes have come to live with you in Manchester Square?' Mr Wharton acknowledged that it was so with an affirmative grunt. 'I hope he's a pleasant inmate.' There was a scorn in the old woman's voice as she said this, which ought to have provoked any man.

'More so than most men would be,' said Mr Wharton.

'Oh, indeed!'

'He is courteous and forbearing, and does not think that everything around him should be suited to his own peculiar fancies.'

'I am glad you are contented with the marriage, Mr Wharton.'

'Who has said that I am contented with it? No one ought to understand or to share my discontent so cordially as yourself, Mrs Fletcher;—and no one ought to be more chary of speaking of it. You and I had hoped other things, and old people do not like to be disappointed. But I needn't paint the devil blacker than he is.'

'I'm afraid that, as usual, he is rather black.'

'Mother,' said John Fletcher, 'the thing has been done and you might as well let it be. We are all sorry that Emily has not come nearer to us; but she has a right to choose for herself, and I for one wish,—as does my brother also,—that she may be happy in the lot she has chosen.'

'His conduct to Arthur at Silverbridge was so nice!' said the pertinacious old woman.

'Never mind his conduct, mother. What is it to us?'

'That's all very well, John; but according to that nobody is to talk about anybody.'

'I would much prefer at any rate,' said Mr Wharton, 'that you would not talk about Mr Lopez in my hearing.'

'Oh; if that is to be so, let it be so. And now I understand where I am.' Then the old woman shook herself, and endeavoured to look as though Mr Wharton's soreness on the subject were an injury to her as well as robbing her of a useful topic.

'I don't like Lopez, you know,' Mr Wharton said to John Fletcher afterwards. 'How would it be possible that I should like such a man? But there can be no good got by complaints. It is not what your mother suffers, or what even I may suffer,—or worse again, what Arthur may suffer, that makes the sadness of all this. What will be her life? That is the question. And it is too near me, too important to me, for the endurance either of scorn or pity. I was glad you asked your mother to be silent.'

'I can understand it,' said John. 'I do not think that she will trouble you again.'

In the mean time Lopez received Mr Wharton's letter at Dovercourt, and had to consider what answer he should give to it. No answer could be satisfactory,—unless he could impose a false answer on his father-in-law so as to make it credible. The more he thought of it, the more he believed that would be impossible. The cautious old lawyer would not accept unverified statements. A certain sum of money,—by no means illiberal as a present,—he had already extracted from the old man. What he wanted was a further and much larger grant. Though Mr Wharton was old he did not want to have to wait for the death even of an old man. The next two or three years,—probably the very next year,—might be the turning-point of his life. He had married the girl, and ought to have the girl's fortune,—down on the nail! That was his idea; and the old man was robbing him in not acting up to it. As he thought of this he cursed his ill luck. The husbands of other girls had their fortunes conveyed to them immediately on their marriage. What would not £20,000 do for him, if he could get it into his hand? And so he taught himself to regard the old man as a robber and himself as a victim. Who among us is there that does not teach himself the same lesson? And then too how cruelly, how damnably he had been used by the Duchess of Omnium! And now Sexty Parker, whose fortune he was making for him, whose fortune he at any rate intended to make, was troubling him in various ways. 'We're in a boat together,' Sexty had said. 'You've had the use of my money, and by heavens you have it still. I don't see why you should be so stiff. Do you bring your missis to Dovercourt, and I'll take mine, and let 'em know each other.' There was a little argument on the subject, but Sexty Parker had the best of it, and in this way the trip to Dovercourt was arranged.

Lopez was in a very good humour when he took his wife down, and he walked her round the terraces and esplanades of that not sufficiently well-known marine paradise, now bidding her admire the sea and now laughing at the finery of the people, till she became gradually filled with the idea that as he was making himself pleasant, she also ought to do the same. Of course she was not happy. The gilding had so completely and so rapidly been washed off her idol that she could not be very happy. But she also could be good-humoured. 'And now,' said he, smiling, 'I have got something for you to do for me,—something that you will find very disagreeable.'

'What is it? It won't be very bad, I'm sure.'

'It will be very bad, I'm afraid. My excellent but horribly vulgar partner, Mr Sextus Parker, when he found that I was coming here, insisted on bringing his wife and children here also. I want you to know them.'

'Is that all? She must be very bad indeed if I can't put up with that.'

'In one sense she isn't bad at all. I believe her to be an excellent woman, intent on spoiling her children and giving her husband a good dinner every day. But I think you'll find that she is,—well,—not quite what you call a lady.'

'I shan't mind that in the least. I'll help her to spoil the children.'

'You can get a lesson there, you know,' he said, looking into her face. The little joke was one which a young wife might take with pleasure from her husband, but her life had already been too much embittered for any such delight. Yes; the time was coming when that trouble also would be added to her. She dreaded she knew not what, and had often told herself that it would be better that she should be childless.

'Do you like him?' she said.

'Like him. No;—I can't say I like him. He is useful, and in one sense honest.'

'Is he not honest in all senses?'

'That's a large order. To tell you the truth, I don't know any man who is.'

'Everett is honest.'

'He loses money at play which he can't pay without assistance from his father. If his father had refused, where would then have been his honesty? Sexty is as honest as others, I dare say, but I shouldn't like to trust him much farther than I can see him. I shan't go up to town to-morrow, and we'll both look in on them after luncheon.'

In the afternoon the call was made. The Parkers, having children, had dined early, and he was sitting out on a little porch smoking his pipe, drinking whisky and water, and looking at the sea. His eldest girl was standing between his legs, and his wife, with the other three children round her, was sitting on the doorstep. 'I've brought my wife to see you,' said Lopez, holding his hand to Mrs Parker, as she rose from the ground.

'I told her that you'd be coming,' said Sexty, 'and she wanted me to put off my pipe and little drop of drink; but I said that if Mrs Lopez was the lady I took her to be she wouldn't begrudge a hard-working fellow his pipe and glass on a holiday.'

There was a soundness of sense in this which mollified any feeling of disgust which Emily might have felt at the man's vulgarity. 'I think you are quite right, Mr Parker. I should be very sorry if,—if——'

'If I was to put my pipe out. Well, I won't. You'll take a glass of sherry, Lopez? Though I'm drinking spirits myself. I brought down a hamper of sherry wine. Oh, nonsense;—you must take something. That's right, Jane. Let us have the stuff and the glasses, and then they can do as they like.' Lopez lit a cigar, and allowed his host to pour out for him a glass of 'sherry wine,' while Mrs Lopez went into the house with Mrs Parker and the children.

Mrs Parker opened herself out to her new friend immediately. She hoped that they two might see 'a deal of each other,—that is, if you don't think me too pushing.' Sextus, she said, was so much away, coming down to Dovercourt only every other day! And then, within the half hour which was consumed by Lopez with his cigar, the poor woman got upon the general troubles of her life. Did Mrs Lopez think that 'all this speckelation was just the right thing?'

'I don't think that I know anything about it, Mrs Parker.'

'But you ought;—oughtn't you, now? Don't you think that a wife ought to know what it is that her husband is after;—specially if there's children? A good bit of the money was mine, Mrs Lopez; and though I don't begrudge it, not one bit, if any good is to come out of it to him or them, a woman doesn't like what her father has given her should be made ducks and drakes of.'

'But are they making ducks and drakes?'

'When he don't tell me I'm always afeard. And I'll tell you what I know just as well as two and two. When he comes home a little flustered, and then takes more than his regular allowance, he's been at something as don't quite satisfy him. He's never that way when he's done a good day's work at his regular business. He takes to the children then, and has one glass after his dinner, and tells me all about it,— down to the shillings and pence. But it's very seldom he's that way now.'

'You may think it very odd, Mrs Parker, but I don't in the least know what my husband is—in business.'

'And you never ask?'

'I haven't been very long married, you know;—only about ten months.'

'I'd had my fust by that time.'

'Only nine months, I think, indeed.'

'Well; I wasn't very long after that. But I took care to know what it was he was a doing of in the city long before that time. And I did use to know everything, till——' She was going to say, till Lopez had come upon the scene. But she did not wish, at any rate as yet, to be harsh to her new friend.

'I hope it is all right,' said Emily.

'Sometimes he's as though the Bank of England was all his own. And there's been more money come into the house;—that I must say.

And there isn't an open-handeder one than Sexty anywhere. He'd like to see me in a silk gown every day of my life;—and as for the children, there's nothing smart enough for them. Only I'd sooner have a little and safe, than anything ever so fine, and never be sure whether it wasn't going to come to an end.'

'There I agree with you, quite.'

'I don't suppose men feels it as we do; but, oh, Mrs Lopez, give me a little safe, so that I may know that I shan't see my children want. When I thinks what it would be to have them darlings' little bellies empty, and nothing in the cupboard, I get that low that I'm nigh fit for Bedlam.'*

In the mean time the two men outside the porch were discussing their affairs in somewhat the same spirit. At last Lopez showed his friend Wharton's letter, and told him of the expected schedule. 'Schedule be d——d, you know,' said Lopez. 'How am I to put down a rise of 12s. 6d. a ton on Kauri gum in a schedule? But when you come to 2000 tons it's £1250.'*

'He's very old; isn't he?'

'But as strong as a horse.'

'He's got the money?'

'Yes;—he has got it safe enough. There's no doubt about the money.'

'What he talks about is only a will. Now you want the money at once.'

'Of course I do;—and he talks to me as if I were some old fogy with an estate of my own. I must concoct a letter and explain my views; and the more I can make him understand how things really are the better. I don't suppose he wants to see his daughter come to grief.'

'Then the sooner you write it the better,' said Mr Parker.

CHAPTER 46

'HE WANTS TO GET RICH TOO QUICK'

As they strolled home Lopez told his wife that he had accepted an invitation to dine the next day at the Parkers' cottage. In doing this his manner was not quite so gentle as when he had asked her to call on them. He had been a little ruffled by what had been said, and now exhibited his temper. 'I don't suppose it will be very nice,' he said, 'but we may have to put up with worse things than that.'

'I have made no objection.'

'But you don't seem to take to it very cordially.'

'I had thought that I got on very well with Mrs Parker. If you can eat your dinner with them, I'm sure that I can. You do not seem to like him altogether, and I wish you had got a partner more to your taste.'

'Taste, indeed! When you come to this kind of thing it isn't a matter of taste. The fact is that I am in that fellow's hands to an extent I don't like to think of, and don't see my way out of it unless your father will do as he ought to do. You altogether refuse to help me with your father, and you must, therefore, put up with Sexty Parker and his wife. It is quite on the cards that worse things may come even than Sexty Parker.' To this she made no immediate answer, but walked on, increasing her pace, not only unhappy, but also very angry. It was becoming a matter of doubt to her whether she could continue to bear these repeated attacks about her father's money. 'I see how it is,' he continued. 'You think that a husband should bear all the troubles of life, and that a wife should never be made to hear of them.'

'Ferdinand,' she said, 'I declare I did not think that any man could be so unfair to a woman as you are to me.'

'Of course! Because I haven't got thousands a year to spend on you I am unfair.'

'I am content to live in any way that you may direct. If you are poor, I am satisfied to be poor. If you are even ruined, I am content to be ruined.'

'Who is talking about ruin?'

'If you are in want of everything, I also will be in want and will never complain. Whatever our joint lot may bring to us I will endure, and will endeavour to endure with cheerfulness. But I will not ask my father for money, either for you or for myself. He knows what he ought to do. I trust him implicitly.'

'And me not at all.'

'He is, I know, in communication with you about what should be done. I can only say,—tell him everything.'

'My dear, that is a matter in which it may be possible that I understand my own interest best.'

'Very likely. I certainly understand nothing, for I do not even know the nature of your business. How can I tell him that he ought to give you money?'

'You might ask him for your own.'

'I have got nothing. Did I ever tell you that I had?'

'You ought to have known.'

'Do you mean that when you asked me to marry you I should have refused you because I did not know what money papa would give me? Why did you not ask papa?'

'Had I known him then as well as I do now you may be quite sure that I should have done so.'

'Ferdinand, it will be better that we should not speak about my father. I will in all things strive to do as you would have me, but I cannot hear him abused. If you have anything to say, go to Everett.'

'Yes;—when he is such a gambler that your father won't even speak to him. Your father will be found dead in bed some day, and all his money will have been left to some cursed hospital.' They were at their own door when this was said, and she, without further answer, went up to her bedroom.

All these bitter things had been said, not because Lopez had thought that he could further his own views by saying them;—he knew indeed that he was injuring himself by every display of ill-temper;—but she was in his power, and Sexty Parker was rebelling. He thought a good deal that day on the delight he would have in 'kicking that ill-conditioned cur,' if only he could afford to kick him. But his wife was his own, and she must be taught to endure his will, and must be made to know that though she was not to be kicked, yet she was to be tormented and ill-used. And it might be possible that he should so cow her spirit as to bring her to act as he should direct. Still, as he walked alone along the sea-shore, he knew that it would be better for him to control his temper.

On that evening he did write to Mr Wharton,—as follows,—and he dated his letter from Little Tankard Yard, so that Mr Wharton might suppose that that was really his own place of business, and that he was there, at his work:—

'MY DEAR SIR,

'You have asked for a schedule of my affairs, and I have found it quite impossible to give it. As it was with the merchants whom Shakespeare and the other dramatists* described,—so it is with me. My caravels are out at sea, and will not always come home in time. My property at this moment consists of certain shares of cargoes of jute, Kauri gum, guano, and sulphur, worth altogether at the present moment something over £26,000, of which Mr Parker possesses a half;—but then of this property only a portion is paid for,— perhaps something more than a half. For the other half our bills are in the market. But in February next these articles will probably be sold for considerably more than £30,000. If I had £5000 placed to my credit now, I should be worth about £15,000 by the end of next February. I am engaged in sundry other smaller ventures, all returning profits;— but in such a condition of things it is impossible that I should make a schedule.

'I am undoubtedly in the condition of a man trading beyond his capital. I have been tempted by fair offers, and what I think I may call something beyond an average understanding of such matters, to go into ventures beyond my means. I have stretched my arm out too far. In such a position it is not perhaps unnatural that I should ask a wealthy father-in-law to assist me. It is certainly not unnatural that I should wish him to do so.

'I do not think I am a mercenary man. When I married your daughter I raised no question as to her fortune. Being embarked in trade I no doubt thought that her means—whatever they might be—would be joined to my own. I know that a sum of £20,000,* with my experience in the use of money, would give us a noble income. But I would not condescend to ask a question which might lead to a supposition that I was marrying her for her money and not because I loved her.

'You now know, I think, all that I can tell you. If there be any other questions I would willingly answer them. It is certainly the case that Emily's fortune, whatever you may choose to give her, would be of infinitely greater use to me now,—and consequently to her,—than at a future date which I sincerely pray may be very long deferred.

'Believe me to be, your affectionate son-in-law,

'FERDINAND LOPEZ.

'A. Wharton, Esq.'

This letter he himself took up to town on the following day, and there posted, addressing it to Wharton Hall. He did not expect very great results from it. As he read it over, he was painfully aware that all his trash about caravels and cargoes of sulphur would not go very far with Mr Wharton. But it might go farther than nothing. He was bound not to neglect Mr Wharton's letter to him. When a man is in difficulty about money, even a lie,—even a lie that is sure to be found out to be a lie,— will serve his immediate turn better than silence. There is nothing that the courts hate so much as contempt;—not even perjury. And Lopez felt that Mr Wharton was the judge before whom he was bound to plead.

He returned to Dovercourt on that day, and he and his wife dined with the Parkers. No woman of her age had known better what were the manners of ladies and gentlemen than Emily Wharton. She had thoroughly understood that when in Herefordshire she was surrounded by people of that class, and that when she was with her aunt, Mrs Roby, she was not quite so happily placed. No doubt she had been terribly deceived by her husband,—but the deceit had come from the fact that his manners gave no indication of his character. When she found herself in Mrs Parker's little sitting-room, with Mr Parker making florid speeches to her, she knew that she had fallen among people for whose society she had not been intended. But this was a part, and only a very trifling part, of the punishment which she felt that she deserved. If that, and things like that, were all, she would bear them without a murmur.

'Now I call Dovercourt a dooced nice little place,' said Mr Parker, as he helped her to the 'bit of fish,' which he told her he had brought down with him from London.

'It is very healthy, I should think.'

'Just the thing for the children, ma'am. You've none of your own, Mrs Lopez, but there's a good time coming.* You were up to-day, weren't you, Lopez? Any news?'

'Things seemed to be very quiet in the city.'

'Too quiet, I'm afraid. I hate having 'em quiet. You must come and see me in Little Tankard Yard some of these days, Mrs Lopez. We can give you a glass of cham. and the wing of a chicken;—can't we, Lopez?'

'I don't know. It's more than you ever gave me,' said Lopez, trying to look good-humoured.

'But you ain't a lady.'

'Or me,' said Mrs Parker.

'You're only a wife. If Mrs Lopez will make a day of it we'll treat her well in the city;—won't we, Ferdinand?' A black cloud came across 'Ferdinand's' face, but he said nothing. Emily of a sudden drew herself up unconsciously,—and then at once relaxed her features and smiled. If her husband chose that it should be so, she would make no objection.

'Upon my honour, Sexty, you are very familiar,' said Mrs Parker.

'It's a way we have in the city,' said Sexty. Sexty knew what he was about. His partner called him Sexty, and why shouldn't he call his partner Ferdinand?

'He'll call you Emily before long,' said Lopez.

'When you call my wife Jane, I shall,—and I've no objection in life. I don't see why people ain't to call each other by their Christian names.

Take a glass of champagne, Mrs Lopez. I brought down half-a-dozen to-day so that we might be jolly. Care killed a cat. Whatever we call each other, I'm very glad to see you here, Mrs Lopez, and I hope it's the first of a great many. Here's your health.'

It was all his ordering, and if he bade her dine with a crossing-sweeper she would do it. But she could not but remember that not long since he had told her that his partner was not a person with whom she could fitly associate; and she did not fail to perceive that he must be going down in the world to admit such association for her after he had so spoken. And as she sipped the mixture which Sexty called champagne, she thought of Herefordshire and the banks of the Wye, and—alas, alas,—she thought of Arthur Fletcher. Nevertheless, come what might, she would do her duty, even though it might call upon her to sit at dinner with Mr Parker three days in the week. Lopez was her husband, and would be the father of her child, and she would make herself one with him. It mattered not what people might call him,—or even her. She had acted on her own judgement in marrying him, and had been a fool; and now she would bear the punishment without complaint.

When dinner was over Mrs Parker helped the servant to remove the dinner things from the single sitting-room, and the two men went out to smoke their cigars in the covered porch. Mrs Parker herself took out the whisky and hot water, and sugar and lemons, and then returned to have a little matronly discourse with her guest. 'Does Mr Lopez ever take a drop too much?' she asked.

'Never,' said Mrs Lopez.

'Perhaps it don't affect him as it do Sexty. He ain't a drinker;—certainly not. And he's one that works hard every day of his life. But he's getting fond of it these last twelve months, and though he don't take very much it hurries him and flurries him. If I speaks at night he gets cross;—and in the morning when he gets up, which he always do regular, though it's ever so bad with him, then I haven't the heart to scold him. It's very hard sometimes for a wife to know what to do, Mrs Lopez.'

'Yes, indeed.' Emily could not but think how soon she herself had learned that lesson.

'Of course I'd do anything for Sexty,—the father of my bairns, and has always been a good husband to me. You don't know him, of course, but I do. A right good man at bottom;—but so weak!'

'If he,—if he,—injures his health, shouldn't you talk to him quietly about it?'

'It isn't the drink as is the evil, Mrs Lopez, but that which makes him drink. He's not one as goes a mucker merely for the pleasure. When things are going right he'll sit out in our arbour at home, and smoke pipe after pipe, playing with the children, and one glass of gin and water cold will see him to bed. Tobacco, dry, do agree with him, I think. But when he comes to three or four goes of hot toddy, I know it's not as it should be.'

'You should restrain him, Mrs Parker.'

'Of course I should;—but how? Am I to walk off with the bottle and disgrace him before the servant girl? Or am I to let the children know as their father takes too much? If I was as much as to make one fight of it, it'd be all over Ponders End that he's a drunkard;—which he ain't. Restrain him;—oh, yes! If I could restrain that gambling instead of regular business! That's what I'd like to restrain.'

'Does he gamble?'

'What is it but gambling that he and Mr Lopez is a-doing together? Of course, ma'am, I don't know you, and you are different from me. I ain't foolish enough not to know all that. My father stood in Smithfield* and sold hay, and your father is a gentleman as has been high up in the Courts all his life. But it's your husband is a doing this.'

'Oh, Mrs Parker!'

'He is then. And if he brings Sexty and my little ones to the work-house, what'll be the good then of his guano and his gum?'

'Is it not all in the fair way of commerce?'

'I'm sure I don't know about commerce, Mrs Lopez, because I'm only a woman; but it can't be fair. They goes and buys things that they haven't got the money to pay for, and then waits to see if they'll turn up trumps. Isn't that gambling?'

'I cannot say. I do not know.' She felt now that her husband had been accused, and that part of the accusation had been levelled at herself. There was something in her manner of saying these few words which the poor complaining woman perceived, feeling immediately that she had been inhospitable and perhaps unjust. She put out her hand softly, touching the other woman's arm, and looking up into her guest's face. 'If this is so, it's terrible,' said Emily.

'Perhaps I oughtn't to speak so free.'

'Oh, yes;—for your children, and yourself, and your husband.'

'It's them,—and him. Of course it's not your doing, and Mr Lopez, I'm sure, is a very fine gentleman. And if he gets wrong one way, he'll get himself right in another.' Upon hearing this Emily shook her head. 'Your papa is a rich man, and won't see you and yours come to want. There's nothing more to come to me or Sexty let it be ever so.'

'Why does he do it?'

'Why does who do it?'

'Your husband. Why don't you speak to him as you do to me, and tell him to mind only his proper business?'

'Now you are angry with me.'

'Angry! No;—indeed I am not angry. Every word that you say is good, and true, and just what you ought to say. I am not angry, but I am terrified. I know nothing of my husband's business. I cannot tell you that you should trust to it. He is very clever, but——'

'But what, ma'am?'

'Perhaps I should say that he is ambitious.'

'You mean he wants to get rich too quick, ma'am.'

'I'm afraid so.'

'Then it's just the same with Sexty. He's ambitious too. But what's the good of being ambitious, Mrs Lopez, if you never know whether you're on your head or your heels? And what's the good of being ambitious if you're to get into the workhouse? I know what that means. There's one or two of them sort of men gets into Parliament, and has houses as big as the Queen's palace, while hundreds of them has their wives and children in the gutter. Who ever hears of them? Nobody. It don't become any man to be ambitious who has got a wife and family. If he's a bachelor, why, of course, he can go to the Colonies. There's Mary Jane and the two little ones right down on the sea, with their feet in the salt water. Shall we put on our hats, Mrs Lopez, and go and look after them?' To this proposition Emily assented, and the two ladies went out after the children.

'Mix yourself another glass,' said Sexty to his partner.

'I'd rather not. Don't ask me again. You know I never drink and I don't like being pressed.'

'By George! You are particular.'

'What's the use of teasing a fellow to do a thing he doesn't like?'

'You won't mind me having another?'

'Fifty if you please, so that I'm not forced to join you.'

'Forced! It's liberty 'all here, and you can do as you please. Only when a fellow will take a drop with me, he's better company.'

'Then I'm d—— bad company, and you'd better get somebody else to be jolly with. To tell you the truth, Sexty, I suit you better at business than at this sort of thing. I'm like Shylock, you know.'

'I don't know about Shylock,* but I'm blessed if I think you suit me very well at anything. I'm putting up with a deal of ill-usage, and when I try to be happy with you, you won't drink, and you tell me about Shylock. He was a Jew, wasn't he?'

'That is the general idea.'

'Then you ain't very much like him, for they're a sort of people that always have money about 'em.'

'How do you suppose he made his money to begin with? What an ass you are!'

'That's true, I am. Ever since I began putting my name on the same bit of paper with yours, I've been an ass.'

'You'll have to be one a bit longer yet;—unless you mean to throw up everything. At this present moment you are six or seven thousand pounds richer than you were before you first met me.'

'I wish I could see the money.'

'That's like you. What's the use of money you can see? How are you to make money out of money by looking at it? I like to know that my money is fructifying.'

'I like to know that it's all there,—and I did know it before I ever saw you. I'm blessed if I know it now. Go down and join the ladies, will you? You ain't much of a companion up here.'

Shortly after that Lopez told Mrs Parker that he had already bade adieu to her husband, and then he took his wife to their own lodgings.

CHAPTER 47

AS FOR LOVE!

THE time spent by Mrs Lopez at Dovercourt was by no means one of complete happiness. Her husband did not come down very frequently, alleging that his business kept him in town, and that the journey was too long. When he did come he annoyed her either by moroseness or tyranny, or by an affectation of loving good-humour, which was the more disagreeable alternative of the two. She knew that he had no right to be good-humoured, and she was quite able to appreciate the difference between fictitious love and love that was real. He did not while she was at Dovercourt speak to her again directly about her father's money,—but he gave her to understand that he required from her very close economy. Then again she referred to the brougham which she knew was to be in readiness on her return to London; but he told her that he was the best judge of that. The economy which he demanded was that comfortless heart-rending economy which nips the practiser at every turn, but does not betray itself to the world at large. He would have her save out of her washerwoman and linendraper, and yet have a smart gown and go in a brougham. He begrudged her postage stamps, and stopped the subscription at Mudie's, though he insisted on a front seat in the Dovercourt church, paying half a guinea more for it than he would for a place at the side.* And then before their sojourn at the place had come to an end he left her for awhile absolutely penniless, so that when the butcher and baker called for their money she could not pay them. That was a dreadful calamity to her, and of which she was hardly able to measure the real worth. It had never happened to her before to have to refuse an application for money that was due. In her father's house such a thing, as far as she knew, had never happened. She had sometimes heard that Everett was impecunious, but that had simply indicated an additional call upon her father. When the butcher came the second time she wrote to her husband in an agony. Should she write to her father for a supply? She was sure that her father would not leave them in actual want. Then he sent her a cheque, enclosed in a very angry letter. Apply to her father! Had she not learned as yet that she was not to lean on her father any longer, but simply on him? And was she such a fool as to suppose that a tradesman could not wait a month for his money?

During all this time she had no friend,—no person to whom she could speak,—except Mrs Parker. Mrs Parker was very open and very confidential about the business, really knowing very much more about it than did Mrs Lopez. There was some sympathy and confidence between her and her husband, though they had latterly been much lessened by Sexty's conduct. Mrs Parker talked daily about the business now that her mouth had been opened, and was very clearly of opinion that it was not a good business. 'Sexty don't think it good himself,' she said.

'Then why does he go on with it?'

'Business is a thing, Mrs Lopez, as people can't drop out of just at a moment. A man gets hisself entangled, and must free hisself as best he can. I know he's terribly afeard;—and sometimes he does say such things of your husband!' Emily shrunk almost into herself as she heard this. 'You mustn't be angry, for indeed it's better you should know all.'

'I'm not angry; only very unhappy. Surely Mr Parker could separate himself from Mr Lopez if he pleased?'

'That's what I say to him. Give it up, though it be ever so much as you've to lose by him. Give it up, and begin again. You've always got your experience, and if it's only a crust you can earn, that's sure and safe. But then he declares that he means to pull through yet. I know what men are at when they talk of pulling through, Mrs Lopez. There shouldn't be no need of pulling through. It should all come just of its own accord,—little and little; but safe.' Then, when the days of their marine holiday were coming to an end,—in the first week in October,—the day before the return of the Parkers to Ponders End, she made a strong appeal to her new friend. 'You ain't afraid of him; are you?'

'Of my husband?' said Mrs Lopez. 'I hope not. Why should you ask?'

'Believe me, a woman should never be afraid of 'em. I never would give in to be bullied and made little of by Sexty. I'd do a'most anything to make him comfortable; I'm that soft-hearted. And why not, when he's the father of my children? But I'm not going not to say a thing if I thinks it right, because I'm afeard.'

'I think I could say anything if I thought it right.'

'Then tell him of me and my babes,—as how I can never have a quiet night while this is going on. It isn't that they two men are fond of one another. Nothing of the sort! Now you;—I've got to be downright fond of you, though, of course, you think me common.' Mrs Lopez would not contradict her, but stooped forward and kissed her cheek. 'I'm downright fond of you, I am,' continued Mrs Parker, snuffling and sobbing, 'but they two men are only together because Mr Lopez wants to gamble, and Parker has got a little money to gamble with.' This aspect of the thing was so terrible to Mrs Lopez that she could only weep and hide her face. 'Now, if you would tell him just the truth! Tell him what I say, and that I've been a-saying it! Tell him it's for my children I'm a-speaking, who won't have bread in their very mouths if their father's squeezed dry like a sponge! Sure, if you'd tell him this, he wouldn't go on!' Then she paused a moment, looking up into the other woman's face. 'He'd have some bowels of compassion;—wouldn't he now?'

'I'll try,' said Mrs Lopez.

'I know you're good and kind-hearted, my dear. I saw it in your eyes from the very first. But then men, when they get on at money-making,—or money-losing, which makes 'em worse,—are like tigers clawing one another.* They don't care how many they kills, so that they has the least bit for themselves. There ain't no fear of God in it, nor yet no mercy, nor ere a morsel of heart. It ain't what I call manly,—not that longing after other folks' money. When it's come by hard work, as I tell Sexty,—by the very sweat of his brow,—oh,—it's sweet as sweet. When he'd tell me that he'd made his three pound, or his five pound, or, perhaps, his ten pound in a day, and'd calculate it up, how much it'd come to if he did that every day, and where we could go to, and what we could do for the children, I loved to hear him talk about his money. But now——! why, it's altered the looks of the man altogether. It's just as though he was a-thirsting for blood.'

Thirsting for blood! Yes, indeed. It was the very idea that had occurred to Mrs Lopez herself when her husband had bade her to 'get round her father.' No;—it certainly was not manly. There certainly was neither the fear of God in it, nor mercy. Yes;—she would try. But as for bowels of compassion in Ferdinand Lopez——; she, the young wife, had already seen enough of her husband to think that he was not to be moved by any prayers on that side. Then the two women bade each other farewell. 'Parker has been talking of my going to Manchester Square,' said Mrs Parker, 'but I shan't. What'd I be in Manchester Square? And, besides, there'd better be an end of it. Mr Lopez'd turn Sexty and me out of the house at a moment's notice if it wasn't for the money.'

'It's papa's house,' said Mrs Lopez, not, however, meaning to make an attack upon her husband.

'I suppose so, but I shan't come to trouble no one; and we live ever so far away, at Ponders End,—out of your line altogether, Mrs Lopez. But I've taken to you, and will never think ill of you in any way;—only do as you said you would.'

'I will try,' said Mrs Lopez.

In the meantime Lopez had received from Mr Wharton an answer to his letter about the missing caravels, which did not please him. Here is the letter:—

'MY DEAR LOPEZ,

'I cannot say that your statement is satisfactory, nor can I reconcile it to your assurance to me that you have made a trade income for some years past of £2000 a year. I do not know much of business, but I cannot imagine such a result from such a condition of things as you describe. Have you any books; and, if so, will you allow them to be inspected by any accountant I may name?

'You say that a sum of £20,000 would suit your business better now than when I'm dead. Very likely. But with such an account of the business as that you have given me, I do not know that I feel disposed to confide the savings of my life to assist so very doubtful an enterprise. Of course whatever I may do to your advantage will be done for the sake of Emily and her children, should she have any. As far I can see at

present, I shall best do my duty to her, by leaving what I may have to
leave to her, to trustees, for her benefit and that of her children.

'Yours truly,

'A. WHARTON.'

This, of course, did not tend to mollify the spirit of the man to whom
it was written, or to make him gracious towards his wife. He received
the letter three weeks before the lodgings at Dovercourt were given
up,—but during these three weeks he was very little at the place, and
when there did not mention the letter. On these occasions he said nothing about business, but satisfied himself with giving strict injunctions
as to economy. Then he took her back to town on the day after her
promise to Mrs Parker that she would 'try.' Mrs Parker had told her
that no woman ought to be afraid to speak to her husband, and, if necessary, to speak roundly on such subjects. Mrs Parker was certainly not
a highly educated lady, but she had impressed Emily with an admiration for her practical good sense and proper feeling. The lady who was
a lady had begun to feel that in the troubles of her life she might find a
much less satisfactory companion than the lady who was not a lady.
She would do as Mrs Parker had told her. She would not be afraid.
Of course it was right that she should speak on such a matter. She knew
herself to be an obedient wife. She had borne all her unexpected sorrows without a complaint, with a resolve that she would bear all for his
sake,—not because she loved him, but because she had made herself
his wife. Into whatever calamities he might fall, she would share them.
Though he should bring her utterly into the dirt, she would remain in
the dirt with him. It seemed probable to her that it might be so,—that
they might have to go into the dirt;—and if it were so, she would still
be true to him. She had chosen to marry him, and she would be his true
wife. But, as such, she would not be afraid of him. Mrs Parker had told
her that 'a woman should never be afraid of 'em,' and she believed in
Mrs Parker. In this case, too, it was clearly her duty to speak,—for the
injury being done was terrible, and might too probably become tra-
gical. How could she endure to think of that woman and her children,
should she come to know that the husband of the woman and the father
of the children had been ruined by her husband?

Yes,—she would speak to him. But she did fear. It is all very well
for a woman to tell herself that she will encounter some anticipated
difficulty without fear,—or for a man either. The fear cannot be overcome by will. The thing, however, may be done, whether it be leading
a forlorn hope, or speaking to an angry husband,—in spite of fear.

She would do it; but when the moment for doing it came, her very heart trembled within her. He had been so masterful with her, so persistent in repudiating her interference, so exacting in his demands for obedience, so capable of making her miserable by his moroseness when she failed to comply with his wishes, that she could not go to her task without fear. But she did feel that she ought not to be afraid, or that her fears, at any rate, should not be allowed to restrain her. A wife, she knew, should be prepared to yield, but yet was entitled to be her husband's counsellor. And it was now the case that in this matter she was conversant with circumstances which were unknown to her husband. It was to her that Mrs Parker's appeal had been made, and with a direct request from the poor woman that it should be repeated to her husband's partner.

She found that she could not do it on the journey home from Dovercourt, nor yet on that evening. Mrs Dick Roby, who had come back from a sojourn at Boulogne, was with them in the Square, and brought her dear friend Mrs Leslie with her, and also Lady Eustace. The reader may remember that Mr Wharton had met these ladies at Mrs Dick's house some months before his daughter's marriage, but he certainly had never asked them into his own. On this occasion Emily had given them no invitation, but had been told by her husband that her aunt would probably bring them in with her. 'Mrs Leslie and Lady Eustace!' she exclaimed with a little shudder. 'I suppose your aunt may bring a couple of friends with her to see you, though it is your father's house?' he had replied. She had said no more, not daring to have a fight on that subject at present, while the other matter was pressing on her mind. The evening had passed away pleasantly enough, she thought, to all except herself. Mrs Leslie and Lady Eustace had talked a great deal, and her husband had borne himself quite as though he had been a wealthy man and the owner of the house in Manchester Square. In the course of the evening Dick Roby came in and Major Pountney, who since the late affairs at Silverbridge had become intimate with Lopez. So that there was quite a party; and Emily was astonished to hear her husband declare that he was only watching the opportunity of another vacancy in order that he might get into the House, and expose the miserable duplicity of the Duke of Omnium. And yet this man, within the last month, had taken away her subscription at Mudie's, and told her that she shouldn't wear things that wanted washing! But he was able to say ever so many pretty little things to Lady Eustace, and had given a new fan to Mrs Dick, and talked of taking a box for Mrs Leslie at The Gaiety.*

But on the next morning before breakfast she began. 'Ferdinand,'
she said, 'while I was at Dovercourt I saw a good deal of Mrs Parker.'

'I could not help that. Or rather you might have helped it if you
pleased. It was necessary that you should meet, but I didn't tell you
that you were to see a great deal of her.'

'I liked her very much.'

'Then I must say you've got a very odd taste. Did you like him?'

'No. I did not see very much of him, and I think that the manners of
women are less objectionable than those of men. But I want to tell you
what passed between her and me.'

'If it is about her husband's business she ought to have held her
tongue, and you had better hold yours now.'

This was not a happy beginning, but still she was determined to go
on. 'It was I think more about your business than his.'

'Then it was infernal impudence on her part, and you should not
have listened to her for a moment.'

'You do not want to ruin her and her children!'

'What have I to do with her and her children? I did not marry her,
and I am not their father. He has got to look to that.'

'She thinks you are enticing him into risks which he cannot
afford.'

'Am I doing anything for him that I ain't doing for myself! If there is
money made, will not he share it? If money has to be lost, of course he
must do the same.' Lopez in stating his case omitted to say that whatever capital was now being used belonged to his partner. 'But women
when they get together talk all manner of nonsense. Is it likely that I
shall alter my course of action because you tell me that she tells you
that he tells her that he is losing money? He is a half-hearted fellow
who quails at every turn against him. And when he is crying drunk I
dare say he makes a poor mouth to her.'

'I think, Ferdinand, it is more than that. She says that——'

'To tell the truth, Emily, I don't care a d—— what she says. Now
give me some tea.'

The roughness of this absolutely quelled her. It was not now that she
was afraid of him,—not at this moment, but that she was knocked
down as though by a blow. She had been altogether so unused to such
language that she could not get on with her matter in hand, letting the
bad word pass by her as an unmeaning expletive. She wearily poured
out the cup of tea and sat herself down silent. The man was too strong
for her, and would be so always. She told herself at this moment that
language such as that must always absolutely silence her. Then, within

a few minutes, he desired her, quite cheerfully, to ask her uncle and aunt to dinner the day but one following, and also to ask Lady Eustace and Mrs Leslie. 'I will pick up a couple of men, which will make us all right,' he said.

This was in every way horrible to her. Her father had been back in town, had not been very well, and had been recommended to return to the country. He had consequently removed himself,—not to Herefordshire,—but to Brighton, and was now living at an hotel, almost within an hour of London. Had he been at home he certainly would not have invited Mrs Leslie and Lady Eustace to his house. He had often expressed a feeling of dislike to the former lady in the hearing of his son-in-law, and had ridiculed his sister-in-law for allowing herself to be acquainted with Lady Eustace, whose name had at one time been very common in the mouths of people. Emily also felt that she was hardly entitled to give a dinner party in his house in his absence. And, after all that she had lately heard about her husband's poverty, she could not understand how he should wish to incur the expense. 'You would not ask Mrs Leslie here!' she said.

'Why should we not ask Mrs Leslie?'

'Papa dislikes her.'

'But "papa," as you call him, isn't going to meet her.'

'He has said that he doesn't know what day he may be home. And he does more than dislike her. He disapproves of her.'

'Nonsense! She is your aunt's friend. Because your father once heard some cock-and-bull story about her, and because he has always taken it upon himself to criticize your aunt's friends, I am not to be civil to a person I like.'

'But, Ferdinand, I do not like her myself. She never was in this house till the other night.'

'Look here, my dear. Lady Eustace can be useful to me, and I cannot ask Lady Eustace without asking her friend. You do as I bid you,—or else I shall do it myself.'

She paused for a moment, and then she positively refused. 'I cannot bring myself to ask Mrs Leslie to dine in this house. If she comes to dine with you of course I shall sit at the table, but she will be sure to see that she is not welcome.'

'It seems to me that you are determined to go against me in everything I propose.'

'I don't think you would say that if you knew how miserable you made me.'

'I tell you that that other woman can be very useful to me.'

'In what way useful?'

'Are you jealous, my dear?'

'Certainly not of Lady Eustace,—nor of any woman. But it seems so odd that such a person's services should be required.'

'Will you do as I tell you, and ask them? You can go round and tell your aunt about it. She knows that I mean to ask them. Lady Eustace is a very rich woman, and is disposed to do a little in commerce. Now do you understand?'

'Not in the least,' said Emily.

'Why shouldn't a woman who has money buy coffee as well as buy shares?'

'Does she buy shares?'

'By George, Emily, I think that you're a fool.'

'I dare say I am, Ferdinand. I do not in the least know what it all means. But I do know this, that you ought not, in papa's absence, to ask people to dine here whom he particularly dislikes, and whom he would not wish to have in his house.'

'You think I am to be governed by you in such a matter as that?'

'I do not want to govern you.'

'You think that a wife should dictate to a husband as to the way in which he is to do his work, and the partners he may be allowed to have in his business, and the persons whom he may ask to dinner! Because you have been dictating to me on all these matters. Now, look here, my dear. As to my business, you had better never speak to me about it any more. I have endeavoured to take you into my confidence and to get you to act with me, but you have declined that, and have preferred to stick to your father. As to my partners, whether I may choose to have Sexty Parker or Lady Eustace, I am a better judge than you. And as to asking Mrs Leslie and Lady Eustace or any other persons to dinner, as I am obliged to make even the recreations of life subservient to its work, I must claim permission to have my own way.' She had listened, but when he paused she made no reply. 'Do you mean to do as I bid you and ask these ladies?'

'I cannot do that. I know that it ought not to be done. This is papa's house, and we are living here as his guests.'

'D—— your papa!' he said as he burst out of the room. After a quarter of an hour he put his head into the room and saw her sitting, like a statue, exactly where he had left her. 'I have written the notes both to Lady Eustace and to Mrs Leslie,' he said. 'You can't think it any sin at any rate to ask your aunt.'

'I will see my aunt,' she said.

'And remember I am not going to be your father's guest, as you call it. I mean to pay for the dinner myself, and to send in my own wines. Your father shall have nothing to complain of on that head.'

'Could you not ask them to Richmond, or to some hotel?' she said.

'What; in October! If you think that I am going to live in a house in which I can't invite a friend to dinner, you are mistaken.' And with that he took his departure.

The whole thing had now become so horrible to her that she felt unable any longer to hold up her head. It seemed to her to be sacrilege that these women should come and sit in her father's room; but when she spoke of her father her husband had cursed him with scorn! Lopez was going to send food and wine into the house, which would be gall and wormwood to her father. At one time she thought she would at once write to her father and tell him of it all,—or perhaps telegraph to him; but she could not do so without letting her husband know what she had done, and then he would have justice on his side in calling her disobedient. Were she to do that, then it would indeed be necessary that she should take part against her husband.

She had brought all this misery on herself and on her father because she had been obstinate in thinking that she could with certainty read a lover's character. As for love,—that of course had died away in her heart,—imperceptibly, though, alas, so quickly! It was impossible that she could continue to love a man who from day to day was teaching her mean lessons, and who was ever doing mean things, the meanness of which was so little apparent to himself that he did not scruple to divulge them to her. How could she love a man who would make no sacrifice either to her comfort, her pride, or her conscience? But still she might obey him,—if she could feel sure that obedience to him was a duty. Could it be a duty to sin against her father's wishes, and to assist in profaning his house and abusing his hospitality after this fashion? Then her mind again went back to the troubles of Mrs Parker, and her absolute inefficiency in that matter. It seemed to her that she had given herself over body and soul and mind to some evil genius, and that there was no escape.

'Of course we'll come,' Mrs Roby had said to her when she went round the corner into Berkeley Street early in the day. 'Lopez spoke to me about it before.'

'What will papa say about it, Aunt Harriet?'

'I suppose he and Lopez understand each other.'

'I do not think papa will understand this.'

'I am sure Mr Wharton would not lend his house to his son-in-law, and then object to the man he had lent it to asking a friend to dine with him. And I am sure that Mr Lopez would not consent to occupy a house on those terms. If you don't like it, of course we won't come.'

'Pray don't say that. As these other women are to come, pray do not desert me. But I cannot say I think it is right.' Mrs Dick, however, only laughed at her scruples.

In the course of the evening Emily got letters addressed to herself from Lady Eustace and Mrs Leslie, informing her that they would have very much pleasure in dining with her on the day named. And Lady Eustace went on to say, with much pleasantry, that she always regarded little parties, got up without any ceremony, as being the pleasantest, and that she should come on this occasion without any ceremonial observance. Then Emily was aware that her husband had not only written the notes in her name, but had put into her mouth some studied apology as to the shortness of the invitation. Well! She was the man's wife, and she supposed that he was entitled to put any words that he pleased into her mouth.

CHAPTER 48

'HAS HE ILL-TREATED YOU?'

LOPEZ relieved his wife from all care as to provision for his guests. 'I've been to a shop in Wigmore Street,' he said, 'and everything will be done. They'll send in a cook to make the things hot, and your father won't have to pay even for a crust of bread.'

'Papa doesn't mind paying for anything,' she said in her indignation.

'It is all very pretty for you to say so, but my experience of him goes just the other way. At any rate there will be nothing to be paid for. Stewam and Sugarscraps will send in everything, if you'll only tell the old fogies downstairs not to interfere.' Then she made a little request. Might she ask Everett, who was now in town? 'I've already got Major Pountney and Captain Gunner,' he said. She pleaded that one more would make no difference. 'But that's just what one more always does. It destroys everything, and turns a pretty little dinner into an awkward feed. We won't have him this time. Pountney'll take you, and I'll take her ladyship. Dick will take Mrs Leslie, and Gunner will have Aunt Harriet. Dick will sit opposite to me, and the four ladies will sit at the four corners. We shall be very pleasant, but one more would spoil us.'

She did speak to the 'old fogies' downstairs,—the housekeeper, who had lived with her father since she was a child, and the butler, who had been there still longer, and the cook, who, having been in her place only three years, resigned impetuously within half an hour after the advent of Mr Sugarscraps' head man. The 'fogies' were indignant. The butler expressed his intention of locking himself up in his own peculiar pantry, and the housekeeper took upon herself to tell her young mistress that 'Master wouldn't like it.' Since she had known Mr Wharton such a thing as cooked food being sent into the house from a shop had never been so much as heard of. Emily, who had hitherto been regarded in the house as a rather strong-minded young woman, could only break down and weep. Why, oh why, had she consented to bring herself and her misery into her father's house? She could at any rate have prevented that by explaining to her father the unfitness of such an arrangement.

The 'party' came. There was Major Pountney, very fine, rather loud, very intimate with the host, whom on one occasion he called 'Ferdy, my boy', and very full of abuse of the Duke and Duchess of Omnium. 'And yet she was a good creature when I knew her,' said Lady Eustace. Pountney suggested that the Duchess had not then taken up politics. 'I've got out of her way,' said Lady Eustace, 'since she did that.' And there was Captain Gunner, who defended the Duchess, but who acknowledged that the Duke was the 'most consumedly stuck-up cox-comb' then existing. 'And the most dishonest,' said Lopez, who had told his new friends nothing about the repayment of the election expenses. And Dick was there. He liked these little parties, in which a good deal of wine could be drunk, and at which ladies were not supposed to be very stiff. The Major and the Captain, and Mrs Leslie and Lady Eustace, were such people as he liked,—all within the pale, but having a piquant relish of fastness and impropriety. Dick was wont to declare that he hated the world in buckram.* Aunt Harriet was triumphant in a manner which disgusted Emily, and which she thought to be most disrespectful to her father;—but in truth Aunt Harriett did not now care very much for Mr Wharton, preferring the friendship of Mr Wharton's son-in-law. Mrs Leslie came in gorgeous clothes, which, as she was known to be very poor, and to have attached herself lately with almost more than feminine affection to Lady Eustace, were at any rate open to suspicious cavil. In former days Mrs Leslie had taken upon herself to say bitter things about Mr Lopez, which Emily could now have repeated, to that lady's discomfiture, had such a mode of revenge suited her disposition. With Mrs Leslie there was Lady Eustace, pretty as ever, and sharp and witty, with the old passion for some excitement, the old proneness to pretend to trust everybody, and the old incapacity for trusting anybody. Ferdinand Lopez had lately been at her feet, and had fired her imagination with stories of the grand things to be done in trade. Ladies do it? Yes; why not women as well as men? Any one might do it who had money in his pocket and experience to tell him, or to tell her, what to buy and what to sell. And the experience, luckily, might be vicarious. At the present moment half the jewels worn in London were,—if Ferdinand Lopez knew anything about it,—bought from the proceeds of such commerce. Of course there were misfortunes. But these came from a want of that experience which Ferdinand Lopez possessed, and which he was quite willing to place at the service of one whom he admired so thoroughly as he did Lady Eustace. Lady Eustace had been charmed, had seen her way into a new and most delightful life,—but had not yet put any of her money into the hands of Ferdinand Lopez.

I cannot say that the dinner was good. It may be a doubt whether such tradesmen as Messrs Stewam and Sugarscraps do ever produce good food;—or whether, with all the will in the world to do so, such a result is within their power. It is certain, I think, that the humblest mutton chop is better eating than any ‘Supreme of chicken after martial manner,’ *—as I have seen the dish named in a French bill of fare, translated by a French pastrycook for the benefit of his English customers,—when sent in from Messrs Stewam and Sugarscraps even with their best exertions. Nor can it be said that the wine was good, though Mr Sugarscraps, when he contracted for the whole entertainment, was eager in his assurance that he procured the very best that London could produce. But the outside look of things was handsome, and there were many dishes, and enough of servants to hand them, and the wines, if not good, were various. Probably Pountney and Gunner did not know good wines. Roby did, but was contented on this occasion to drink them bad. And everything went pleasantly, with perhaps a little too much noise;—everything except the hostess, who was allowed by general consent to be sad and silent,—till there came a loud double-rap at the door.

‘There’s papa,’ said Emily, jumping up from her seat.

Mrs Dick looked at Lopez, and saw at a glance that for a moment his courage had failed him. But he recovered himself quickly. ‘Hadn’t you better keep your seat, my dear?’ he said to his wife. ‘The servants will attend to Mr Wharton, and I will go to him presently.’

‘Oh, no,’ said Emily, who by this time was almost at the door.

‘You didn’t expect him,—did you?’ asked Dick Roby.

‘Nobody knew when he was coming. I think he told Emily that he might be here any day.’

'He's the most uncertain man alive,' said Mrs Dick, who was a good deal scared by the arrival, though determined to hold up her head and exhibit no fear.

'I suppose the old gentleman will come in and have some dinner,' whispered Captain Gunner to his neighbour Mrs Leslie.

'Not if he knows I'm here,' replied Mrs Leslie, tittering. 'He thinks that I am,—oh, something a great deal worse than I can tell you.'

'Is he given to be cross?' asked Lady Eustace, also affecting to whisper.

'Never saw him in my life,' answered the Major, 'but I shouldn't wonder if he was. Old gentlemen generally are cross. Gout, and that kind of thing, you know.'

For a minute or two the servants stopped their ministrations, and things were very uncomfortable; but Lopez, as soon as he had recovered himself, directed Mr Sugarscraps' men to proceed with the banquet. 'We can eat our dinner, I suppose, though my father-in-law has come back,' he said. 'I wish my wife was not so fussy, though that is a kind of thing, Lady Eustace, that one must expect from young wives.' The banquet did go on, but the feeling was general that a misfortune had come upon them, and that something dreadful might possibly happen.

Emily, when she rushed out, met her father in the hall, and ran into his arms. 'Oh, papa!' she exclaimed.

'What's all this about?' he asked, and as he spoke he passed on through the hall to his own room at the back of the house. There were of course many evidences on all sides of the party,—the strange servants, the dishes going in and out, the clatter of glasses, and the smell of viands. 'You've got a dinner-party,' he said. 'Had you not better go back to your friends?'

'No, papa.'

'What is the matter, Emily? You are unhappy.'

'Oh, so unhappy!'

'What is it all about? Who are they? Whose doing is it,—yours or his? What makes you unhappy?'

He was now seated in his arm-chair, and she threw herself on her knees at his feet. 'He would have them. You mustn't be angry with me. You won't be angry with me;—will you?'

He put his hand upon her head, and stroked her hair. 'Why should I be angry with you because your husband has asked friends to dinner?' She was so unlike her usual self that he knew not what to make of it. It had not been her nature to kneel and ask for pardon, or to be timid and submissive. 'What is it, Emily, that makes you like this?'

'He shouldn't have had the people.'

'Well;—granted. But it does not signify much. Is your aunt Harriet there?'

'Yes.'

'It can't be very bad, then.'

'Mrs Leslie is there, and Lady Eustace,—and two men I don't like.'

'Is Everett here?'

'No;—he wouldn't have Everett.'

'Oughtn't you to go to them?'

'Don't make me go. I should only cry. I have been crying all day, and the whole of yesterday.' Then she buried her face upon his knees, and sobbed as though she would break her heart.

He couldn't at all understand it. Though he distrusted his son-in-law, and certainly did not love him, he had not as yet learned to hold him in aversion. When the connection was once made he had determined to make the best of it, and had declared to himself that as far as manners went the man was well enough. He had not as yet seen the inside of the man, as it had been the sad fate of the poor wife to see him. It had never occurred to him that his daughter's love had failed her, or that she could already be repenting what she had done. And now, when she was weeping at his feet and deploring the sin of the dinner-party,—which, after all, was a trifling sin,—he could not comprehend the feelings which were actuating her. 'I suppose your aunt Harriet made up the party,' he said.

'He did it.'

'Your husband?'

'Yes;—he did it. He wrote to the women in my name when I refused.' Then Mr Wharton began to perceive that there had been a quarrel. 'I told him Mrs Leslie oughtn't to come here.'

'I don't love Mrs Leslie,—nor, for the matter of that, Lady Eustace. But they won't hurt the house, my dear.'

'And he has had the dinner sent in from a shop.'

'Why couldn't he let Mrs Williams do it?' As he said this, the tone of his voice became for the first time angry.

'Cook has gone away. She wouldn't stand it. And Mrs Williams is very angry. And Barker wouldn't wait at table.'

'What's the meaning of it all?'

'He would have it so. Oh, papa, you don't know what I've undergone. I wish,—I wish we had not come here. It would have been better anywhere else.'

'What would have been better, dear?'

'Everything. Whether we lived or died, it would have been better. Why should I bring my misery to you? Oh, papa, you do not know,— you can never know.'

'But I must know. Is there more than this dinner to disturb you?'

Oh, yes;—more than that. Only I couldn't bear that it should be done in your house.'

'Has he——ill-treated you?'

Then she got up, and stood before him. 'I do not mean to complain. I should have said nothing only that you have found us in this way. For myself I will bear it all, whatever it may be. But, papa, I want you to tell him that we must leave this house.'

'He has got no other home for you.'

'He must find one. I will go anywhere. I don't care where it is. But I won't stay here. I have done it myself, but I won't bring it upon you. I could bear it all if I thought that you would never see me again.'

'Emily!'

'Yes;—if you would never see me again. I know it all, and that would be best.' She was now walking about the room. 'Why should you see it all?'

'See what, my love?'

'See his ruin, and my unhappiness, and my baby. Oh,—oh,—oh!'

'I think so very differently, Emily, that under no circumstances will I have you taken to another home. I cannot understand much of all this as yet, but I suppose I shall come to see it. If Lopez be, as you say, ruined, it is well that I have still enough for us to live on. This is a bad time just now to talk about your husband's affairs.'

'I did not mean to talk about them, papa.'

'What would you like best to do now,—now at once. Can you go down again to your husband's friends?'

'No;—no;—no.'

'As for the dinner, never mind about that. I can't blame him for making use of my house in my absence as far as that goes,—though I wish he could have contented himself with such a dinner as my servants could have prepared for him. I will have some tea here.'

'Let me stay with you, papa, and make it for you.'

'Very well, dear. I do not mean to be ashamed to enter my own dining-room. I shall, therefore, go in and make your apologies.' Thereupon Mr Wharton walked slowly forth, and marched into the dining-room.

'Oh, Mr Wharton,' said Mrs Dick, 'we didn't expect you.'

'Have you dined yet, sir?' asked Lopez.

'I dined early,' said Mr Wharton. 'I should not now have come in to disturb you, but that I have found Mrs Lopez unwell, and she has begged me to ask you to excuse her.'

'I will go to her,' said Lopez, rising.

'It is not necessary,' said Wharton. 'She is not ill, but hardly able to take her place at table.' Then Mrs Dick proposed to go to her dear niece; but Mr Wharton would not allow it, and left the room, having succeeded in persuading them to go on with their dinner. Lopez certainly was not happy during the evening, but he was strong enough to hide his misgivings, and to do his duty as host with seeming cheerfulness.

CHAPTER 49

'WHERE IS GUATEMALA?'

THOUGH his daughter's words to him had been very wild they did almost more to convince Mr Wharton that he should not give his money to his son-in-law than even the letters which had passed between them. To Emily herself he spoke very little as to what had occurred that evening. 'Papa,' she said, 'do not ask me anything more about it. I was very miserable,—because of the dinner.' Nor did he at that time ask her any questions, contenting himself with assuring her that, at any rate at present, and till after her baby should have been born, she must remain at Manchester Square. 'He won't hurt me,' said Mr Wharton, and then added with a smile, 'He won't have to have any more dinner parties while I am here.'

Nor did he make any complaint to Lopez as to what had been done, or even allude to the dinner. But when he had been back about a week he announced to his son-in-law his final determination as to money. 'I had better tell you, Lopez, what I mean to do, so that you may not be left in doubt. I shall not intrust any further sum of money into your hands on behalf of Emily.'

'You can do as you please, sir,—of course.'

'Just so. You have had what to me is a very considerable sum,— though I fear that it did not go for much in your large concerns.'

'It was not very much, Mr Wharton.'

'I dare say not. Opinions on such a matter differ, you know. At any rate, there will be no more. At present I wish Emily to live here, and you, of course, are welcome here also. If things are not going well with you, this will, at any rate, relieve you from immediate expense.

'My calculations, sir, have never descended to that.'

'Mine are more minute. The necessities of my life have caused me to think of these little things. When I am dead there will be provision for Emily made by my will,—the income going to trustees for her benefit, and the capital to her children after her death. I thought it only fair to you that this should be explained.'

'And you will do nothing for me?'

'Nothing;—if that is nothing. I should have thought that your present maintenance and the future support of your wife and children would have been regarded as something.'

'It is nothing;—nothing!'

'Then let it be nothing. Good morning.'

Two days after that Lopez recurred to the subject. 'You were very explicit with me the other day, sir.'

'I meant to be so.'

'And I will be equally so to you now. Both I and your daughter are absolutely ruined unless you reconsider your purpose.'

'If you mean money by reconsideration,—present money to be given to you,—I certainly shall not reconsider it. You may take my solemn assurance that I will give you nothing that can be of any service to you in trade.'

Then, sir,—I must tell you my purpose, and give you my assurance, which is equally solemn. Under those circumstances I must leave England, and try my fortune in Central America. There is an opening for me at Guatemala,* though not a very hopeful one.'

'Guatemala!'

'Yes;—friends of mine have a connection there. I have not broken it to Emily yet, but under these circumstances she will have to go.'

'You will not take her to Guatemala!'

'Not take my wife, sir? Indeed I shall. Do you suppose that I would go away and leave my wife a pensioner on your bounty? Do you think that she would wish to desert her husband? I don't think you know your daughter.'

'I wish you had never known her.'

'That is neither here nor there, sir. If I cannot succeed in this country I must go elsewhere. As I have told you before, £20,000* at the present moment would enable me to surmount all my difficulties, and make me a very wealthy man. But unless I can command some such sum by Christmas everything here must be sacrificed.'

'Never in my life did I hear so base a proposition,' said Mr Wharton.

'Why is it base? I can only tell you the truth.'

'So be it. You will find that I mean what I have said.'

'So do I, Mr Wharton.'

'As to my daughter, she must, of course, do as she thinks fit.'

'She must do as I think fit, Mr Wharton.'

'I will not argue with you. Alas, alas; poor girl!'

'Poor girl, indeed! She is likely to be a poor girl if she is treated in this way by her father. As I understand that you intend to use, or to try to use, authority over her, I shall take steps for removing her at once from your house.' And so the interview was ended.

Lopez had thought the matter over, and had determined to 'brazen it out,' as he himself called it. Nothing further was, he thought, to be got by civility and obedience. Now he must use his power. His idea of going to Guatemala was not an invention of the moment, nor was it devoid of a certain basis of truth. Such a suggestion had been made to him some time since by Mr Mills Happerton. There were mines in Guatemala which wanted, or at some future day might want, a resident director. The proposition had been made to Lopez before his marriage, and Mr Happerton probably had now forgotten all about it;—but the thing was of service now. He broke the matter very suddenly to his wife. 'Has your father been speaking to you of my plans?'

'Not lately;—not that I remember.'

'He could not speak of them without your remembering, I should think. Has he told you that I am going to Guatemala?'

'Guatemala! Where is Guatemala, Ferdinand?'

'You can answer my question though your geography is deficient.'

'He has said nothing about your going anywhere.'

'You will have to go,—as soon after Christmas as you may be fit.'

'But where is Guatemala;—and for how long, Ferdinand?'

'Guatemala is in Central America, and we shall probably settle there for the rest of our lives. I have got nothing to live on here.'

During the next two months this plan of seeking a distant home and a strange country was constantly spoken of in Manchester Square, and did receive corroboration from Mr Happerton himself. Lopez renewed his application and received a letter saying that the thing might probably be arranged if he were in earnest. 'I am quite in earnest,' Lopez said as he showed this letter to Mr Wharton. 'I suppose Emily will be able to start two months after her confinement. They tell me that babies do very well at sea.'

During this time, in spite of his threat, he continued to live with Mr Wharton in Manchester Square, and went every day into the city,—whether to make arrangements and receive instructions as to Guatemala, or to carry on his old business, neither Emily nor her father knew. He never at this time spoke about his affairs to either of them, but daily referred to her future expatriation as a thing that was certain. At last there came up the actual question,—whether she were to go or not. Her father told her that though she was doubtless bound by law to obey her husband, in such a matter as this she might defy the law.* 'I do not think that he can actually force you on board the ship,' her father said.

'But if he tells me that I must go?'

'Stay here with me,' said the father. 'Stay here with your baby. I'll fight it out for you. I'll so manage that you shall have all the world on your side.'

Emily at that moment came to no decision, but on the following day she discussed the matter with Lopez himself. 'Of course you will go with me,' he said, when she asked the question.

'You mean that I must, whether I wish to go or not.'

'Certainly you must. Good G——! where is a wife's place? Am I to go out without my child, and without you, while you are enjoying all the comforts of your father's wealth at home? That is not my idea of life.'

'Ferdinand, I have been thinking about it very much. I must beg you to allow me to remain. I ask it of you as if I were asking my life.'

'Your father has put you up to this.'

'No;—not to this.'

'To what then.'

'My father thinks I should refuse to go.'

'He does; does he?'

'But I shall not refuse. I shall go if you insist upon it. There shall be no contest between us about that.'

'Well; I should hope not.'

'But I do implore you to spare me.'

'That is very selfish, Emily.'

'Yes,'—she said, 'yes, I cannot contradict that. But so is the man selfish who prays the judge to spare his life.'

'But you do not think of me. I must go.'

'I shall not make you happier, Ferdinand.'

'Do you think that it is a fine thing for a man to live in such a country as that all alone?'

'I think it would be better so than with a wife he does not—love.'

'Who says I do not love you?'

'Or with one who does—not—love him.' This she said very slowly, very softly, but looking up into his eyes as she said it.

'Do you tell me that to my face?'

'Yes;—what good can I do now by lying? You have not been to me as I thought you would be.'

'And so, because you have built some castle in the air that has fallen to pieces, you tell your husband to his face that you do not love him, and that you prefer not to live with him. Is that your idea of duty?'

'Why have you been so cruel?'

'Cruel! What have I done? Tell me what cruelty. Have I beat you? Have you been starved? Have I not asked and implored your assistance,—only to be refused? The fact is that your father and you have found out that I am not a rich man, and you want to be rid of me. Is that true or false?'

'It is not true that I want to be rid of you because you are poor.'

'I do not mean to be rid of you. You will have to settle down and do your work as my wife in whatever place it may suit me to live. Your father is a rich man, but you shall not have the advantage of his wealth unless it comes to you, as it ought to come, through my hands. If your father would give me the fortune which ought to be yours there need be no going abroad. He cannot bear to part with his money and therefore we must go. Now you know all about it.' She was then turning to leave him, when he asked her a direct question. 'Am I to understand that you intend to resist my right to take you with me?'

'If you bid me go,—I shall go.'

'It will be better, as you will save both trouble and exposure.'

Of course she told her father what had taken place, but he could only shake his head, and sit groaning over his misery in his chambers. He had explained to her what he was willing to do on her behalf, but she declined his aid. He could not tell her that she was wrong. She was the man's wife, and out of that terrible destiny she could not now escape. The only question with him was whether it would not be best to buy the man,—give him a sum of money to go, and to go alone. Could he have been quit of the man even for £20,000, he would willingly have paid the money. But the man would either not go, or would come back as soon as he got the money. His own life, as he passed it now, with this man in the house with him, was horrible to him. For Lopez, though he had more than once threatened that he would carry his wife to another home, had taken no steps towards getting that other home ready for her.

During all this time Mr Wharton had not seen his son. Everett had gone abroad just as his father returned to London from Brighton, and was still on the continent. He received his allowance punctually, and that was the only intercourse which took place between them. But Emily had written to him, not telling him much of her troubles,— only saying that she believed her husband would take her to Central America early in the spring, and begging him to come home before she went.

Just before Christmas her baby was born, but the poor child did not live a couple of days. She herself at the time was so worn with care, so thin and wan and wretched, that looking in the glass she hardly knew her own face. 'Ferdinand,' she said to him, 'I know he will not live. The Doctor says so.'

'Nothing thrives that I have to do with,' he answered gloomily.

'Will you not look at him?'

'Well; yes. I have looked at him, have I not? I wish to God that where he is going I could go with him.'

'I wish I was;—I wish I was going,' said the poor mother. Then the father went out, and before he had returned to the house the child was dead. 'Oh, Ferdinand, speak one kind word to me now,' she said.

'What kind word can I speak when you have told me that you do not love me? Do you think that I can forget that because,—because he has gone?'

'A woman's love may always be won back again by kindness.'

'Psha! How am I to kiss and make pretty speeches with my mind harassed as it is now?' But he did touch her brow with his lips before he went away.

The infant was buried, and then there was not much show of mourning in the house. The poor mother would sit gloomily alone day after day, telling herself that it was perhaps better that she should have been robbed of her treasure than have gone forth with him into the wide, unknown, harsh world with such a father as she had given him. Then she would look at all the preparations she had made,—the happy work of her fingers when her thoughts of their future use were her sweetest consolation,—and weep till she would herself feel that there never could be an end to her tears.

The second week in January had come and yet nothing further had been settled as to the Guatemala project. Lopez talked about it as though it was certain, and even told his wife that as they would move so soon it would not be now worth while for him to take other lodgings for her. But when she asked as to her own preparations,—the wardrobe necessary for the long voyage and her general outfit,—he told her that three weeks or a fortnight would be enough for all, and that he would give her sufficient notice. 'Upon my word he is very kind to honour my poor house as he does,' said Mr Wharton.

'Papa, we will go at once if you wish it,' said his daughter.

'Nay, Emily; do not turn upon me. I cannot but be sensible to the insult of his daily presence; but even that is better than losing you.'

Then there occurred a ludicrous incident,—or combination of incidents,—which, in spite of their absurdity, drove Mr Wharton almost frantic. First there came to him the bill from Messrs Stewam and Sugarscraps for the dinner. At this time he kept nothing back from his daughter. 'Look at that!' he said. The bill was absolutely made out in his name.

'It is a mistake, papa.'

'Not at all. The dinner was given in my house, and I must pay for it. I would sooner do so than that he should pay it,—even if he had the means.' So he paid Messrs Stewam and Sugarscraps £25. 9s. 6d.,* begging them as he did so never to send another dinner into his house, and observing that he was in the habit of entertaining his friends at less than three guineas a head. 'But Château Yquem and Côte d'Or!' said Mr Sugarscraps. 'Château fiddlesticks!' said Mr Wharton, walking out of the house with his receipt.

Then came the bill for the brougham,—for the brougham from the very day of their return to town after their wedding trip. This he showed to Lopez. Indeed the bill had been made out to Lopez and sent to Mr Wharton with an apologetic note. 'I didn't tell him to send it,' said Lopez.

'But will you pay it?'

'I certainly shall not ask you to pay it.' But Mr Wharton at last did pay it, and he also paid the rent of the rooms in the Belgrave Mansions, and between £30 and £40 for dresses which Emily had got at Lewes and Allenby's* under her husband's orders in the first days of their married life in London.

'Oh, papa, I wish I had not gone there,' she said.

'My dear, anything that you may have had I do not grudge in the least. And even for him, if he would let you remain here, I would pay willingly. I would supply all his wants if he would only—go away.'

CHAPTER 50

MR SLIDE'S REVENGE

'Do you mean to say, my lady, that the Duke paid his electioneering bill down at Silverbridge?'

'I do mean to say so, Mr Slide,' Lady Eustace nodded her head, and Mr Quintus Slide opened his mouth.

'Goodness gracious!' said Mrs Leslie, who was sitting with them. They were in Lady Eustace's drawing-room, and the patriotic editor of the 'People's Banner' was obtaining from a new ally information which might be useful to the country.

'But 'ow do you know, Lady Eustace? You'll pardon the persistency of my inquiries, but when you come to public information accuracy is everything. I never trust myself to mere report. I always travel up to the very fountain 'ead of truth.'

'I know it,' said Lizzie Eustace oracularly.

'Um—m!' The Editor as he ejaculated the sound looked at her ladyship with admiring eyes,—with eyes that were intended to flatter. But Lizzie had been looked at so often in so many ways and was so well accustomed to admiration, that this had no effect on her at all. ''E didn't tell you himself; did 'e, now?'

'Can you tell me the truth as to trusting him with my money?'

'Yes, I can.'

'Shall I be safe if I take the papers which he calls bills of sale?'

'One good turn deserves another, my lady.'

'I don't want to make a secret of it, Mr Slide. Pountney found it out. You know the Major?'

'Yes, I know Major Pountney. He was at Gatherum 'imself, and got a little bit of cold shoulder;—didn't he?'

'I dare say he did. What has that to do with it? You may be sure that Lopez applied to the Duke for his expenses at Silverbridge, and that the Duke sent him the money.'

'There's no doubt about it, Mr Slide,' said Mrs Leslie. 'We got it all from Major Pountney. There was some bet between him and Pountney, and he had to show Pountney the cheque.'

'Pountney saw the money,' said Lady Eustace.

Mr Slide stroked his hand over his mouth and chin as he sat thinking of the tremendous national importance of this communication. The man who had paid the money was the Prime Minister of England,—and was, moreover, Mr Slide's enemy! 'When the right 'and of fellowship has been rejected, I never forgive,' Mr Slide has been heard to say. Even Lady Eustace, who was not particular as to the appearance of people, remarked afterwards to her friend that Mr Slide had looked like the devil as he was stroking his face. 'It's very remarkable,' said Mr Slide; 'very remarkable!'

'You won't tell the Major that we told you,' said her Ladyship.

'Oh dear no. I only wanted to 'ear how it was. And as to embarking your money, my lady, with Ferdinand Lopez,—I wouldn't do it.'

'Not if I get the bills of sale? It's for rum, and they say rum will go up to any price.'

'Don't, Lady Eustace. I can't say any more,—but don't. I never mention names. But don't.'

Then Mr Slide went out in search of Major Pountney, and having found the Major at his club extracted from him all that he knew about the Silverbridge payment. Pountney had really seen the Duke's cheque for £500. 'There was some bet,—eh, Major?' asked Mr Slide.

'No, there wasn't. I know who has been telling you. That's Lizzie Eustace, and just like her mischief. The way of it was this;—Lopez, who was very angry, had boasted that he would bring the Duke down on his marrow-bones. I was laughing at him as we sat at dinner one day afterwards, and he took out the cheque and showed it me. There was the Duke's own signature for £500,—"Omnium," as plain as letters could make it.' Armed with this full information, Mr Slide felt that he had done all that the most punctilious devotion to accuracy could demand of him, and immediately shut himself up in his cage at the 'People's Banner' office and went to work.

This occurred about the first week in January. The Duke was then at Matching with his wife and a very small party. The singular arrangement which had been effected by the Duchess in the early autumn had passed off without any wonderful effects. It had been done by her in pique, and the result had been apparently so absurd that it had at first frightened her. But in the end it answered very well. The Duke took great pleasure in Lady Rosina's company, and enjoyed the comparative solitude which enabled him to work all day without interruption. His wife protested that it was just what she liked, though it must be feared that she soon became weary of it. To Lady Rosina it was of course a Paradise on earth. In September, Phineas Finn and his wife came to them, and in October there were other relaxations and other business. The Prime Minister and his wife visited their Sovereign, and he made some very useful speeches through the country on his old favourite subject of decimal coinage. At Christmas, for a fortnight, they went to

Gatherum Castle and entertained the neighbourhood,—the nobility and squirearchy dining there on one day, and the tenants and other farmers on another. All this went very smoothly, and the Duke did not become outrageously unhappy because the 'People's Banner' made sundry severe remarks on the absence of Cabinet Councils through the autumn.

After Christmas they returned to Matching, and had some of their old friends with them. There was the Duke of St Bungay and the Duchess, and Phineas Finn and his wife, and Lord and Lady Cantrip, Barrington Erle, and one or two others. But at this period there came a great trouble. One morning as the Duke sat in his own room after breakfast he read an article in the 'People's Banner,' of which the following sentences were a part. 'We wish to know by whom were paid the expenses incurred by Mr Ferdinand Lopez during the late contest at Silverbridge. It may be that they were paid by that gentleman himself,—in which case we shall have nothing further to say, not caring at the present moment to inquire whether those expenses were or were not excessive. It may be that they were paid by subscription among his political friends,—and if so, again we shall be satisfied. Or it is possible that funds were supplied by a new political club of which we have lately heard much, and with the action of such body we of course have nothing to do. If an assurance can be given to us by Mr Lopez or his friends that such was the case we shall be satisfied.

'But a report has reached us, and we may say more than a report, which makes it our duty to ask this question. Were those expenses paid out of the private pocket of the present Prime Minister? If so, we maintain that we have discovered a blot in that nobleman's character which it is our duty to the public to expose. We will go farther and say that if it be so,—if these expenses were paid out of the private pocket of the Duke of Omnium, it is not fit that that nobleman should any longer hold the high office which he now fills.

'We know that a peer should not interfere in elections for the House of Commons. We certainly know that a Minister of the Crown should not attempt to purchase parliamentary support. We happen to know also the almost more than public manner,—are we not justified in saying the ostentation?—with which at the last election the Duke repudiated all that influence with the borough which his predecessors, and we believe he himself, had so long exercised. He came forward telling us that he, at least, meant to have clean hands;—that he would not do as his forefathers had done;—that he would not even do as he himself had done in former years. What are we to think of the Duke of

Omnium as a Minister of this country, if, after such assurances, he has out of his own pocket paid the electioneering expenses of a candidate at Silverbridge?' There was much more in the article, but the passages quoted will suffice to give the reader a sufficient idea of the accusation made, and which the Duke read in the retirement of his own chamber.

He read it twice before he allowed himself to think of the matter. The statement made was at any rate true to the letter. He had paid the man's electioneering expenses. That he had done so from the purest motives he knew and the reader knows;—but he could not even explain those motives without exposing his wife. Since the cheque was sent he had never spoken of the occurrence to any human being,—but he had thought of it very often. At the time his private Secretary, with much hesitation, almost with trepidation, had counselled him not to send the money. The Duke was a man with whom it was very easy to work, whose courtesy to all dependent on him was almost exaggerated, who never found fault, and was anxious as far as possible to do everything for himself. The comfort of those around him was always matter of interest to him. Everything he held, he held as it were in trust for the enjoyment of others. But he was a man whom it was very difficult to advise. He did not like advice. He was so thin-skinned that any counsel offered to him took the form of criticism. When cautioned what shoes he should wear,—as had been done by Lady Rosina; or what wine or what horses he should buy, as was done by his butler and coachman, he was thankful, taking no pride to himself for knowledge as to shoes, wine, or horses. But as to his own conduct, private or public, as to any question of politics, as to his opinions and resolutions, he was jealous of interference. Mr Warburton therefore had almost trembled when asking the Duke whether he was quite sure about sending the money to Lopez. 'Quite sure,' the Duke had answered, having at that time made up his mind. Mr Warburton had not dared to express a further doubt and the money had been sent. But from the moment of sending it doubts had repeated themselves in the Prime Minister's mind.

Now he sat with the newspaper in his hand thinking of it. Of course it was open to him to take no notice of the matter,—to go on as though he had not seen the article, and to let the thing die if it would die. But he knew Mr Quintus Slide and his paper well enough to be sure that it would not die. The charge would be repeated in the 'People's Banner' till it was copied into other papers; and then the further question would be asked,—why had the Prime Minister allowed such an accusation to remain unanswered? But if he did notice it, what notice should he take of it? It was true. And surely he had a right to do what he liked with his own money so long as he disobeyed no law. He had bribed no one. He had spent his money with no corrupt purpose. His sense of honour had taught him to think that the man had received injury through his wife's imprudence, and that he therefore was responsible as far as the pecuniary loss was concerned. He was not ashamed of the thing he had done;—but yet he was ashamed that it should be discussed in public.

Why had he allowed himself to be put into a position in which he was subject to such grievous annoyance? Since he had held his office he had not had a happy day, nor,—so he told himself,—had he received from it any slightest gratification, nor could he buoy himself up with the idea that he was doing good service for his country. After a while he walked into the next room and showed the paper to Mr Warburton. 'Perhaps you were right,' he said, 'when you told me not to send that money.'

'It will matter nothing,' said the private Secretary when he had read it,—thinking, however, that it might matter much, but wishing to spare the Duke.

'I was obliged to repay the man as the Duchess had,—had encouraged him. The Duchess had not quite,—quite understood my wishes.' Mr Warburton knew the whole history now, having discussed it all with the Duchess more than once.

'I think your Grace should take no notice of the article.'

No notice was taken of it, but three days afterwards there appeared a short paragraph in large type,—beginning with a question. 'Does the Duke of Omnium intend to answer the question asked by us last Friday? Is it true that he paid the expenses of Mr Lopez when that gentleman stood for Silverbridge? The Duke may be assured that the question shall be repeated till it is answered.' This the Duke also saw and took to his private Secretary.

'I would do nothing at any rate till it be noticed in some other paper,' said the private Secretary. 'The "People's Banner" is known to be scandalous.'

'Of course it is scandalous. And, moreover, I know the motives and the malice of the wretched man who is the editor. But the paper is read, and the foul charge if repeated will become known, and the allegation made is true. I did pay the man's election expenses;—and, moreover, to tell the truth openly as I do not scruple to do to you, I am not prepared to state publicly the reason why I did so. And nothing but that reason could justify me.'

'Then I think your Grace should state it.'

'I cannot do so.'

'The Duke of St Bungay is here. Would it not be well to tell the whole affair to him?'

'I will think of it. I do not know why I should have troubled you.'

'Oh, my lord!'

'Except that there is always some comfort in speaking even of one's trouble. I will think about it. In the meantime you need perhaps not mention it again.'

'Who? I? Oh, certainly not.'

'I did not mean to others,—but to myself. I will turn it in my mind and speak of it when I have decided anything.' And he did think about it,—thinking of it so much that he could hardly get the matter out of his mind day or night. To his wife he did not allude to it at all. Why trouble her with it? She had caused the evil, and he had cautioned her as to the future. She could not help him out of the difficulty she had created. He continued to turn the matter over in his thoughts till he so magnified it, and built it up into such proportions, that he again began to think that he must resign. It was, he thought, true that a man should not remain in office as Prime Minister who in such a matter could not clear his own conduct.

Then there was a third attack in the 'People's Banner,' and after that the matter was noticed in the 'Evening Pulpit.' This notice the Duke of St Bungay saw and mentioned to Mr Warburton. 'Has the Duke spoken to you of some allegations made in the press as to the expenses of the late election at Silverbridge?' The old Duke was at this time, and had been for some months, in a state of nervous anxiety about his friend. He had almost admitted to himself that he had been wrong in recommending a politician so weakly organized to take the office of Prime Minister. He had expected the man to be more manly,—had perhaps expected him to be less conscientiously scrupulous. But now, as the thing had been done, it must be maintained. Who else was there to take the office? Mr Gresham would not. To keep Mr Daubeny out was the very essence of the Duke of St Bungay's life,—the turning-point of his political creed, the one grand duty the idea of which was always present to him. And he had, moreover, a most true and affectionate regard for the man whom he now supported, appreciating the sweetness of his character,—believing still in the Minister's patriotism, intelligence, devotion, and honesty; though he was forced to own to himself that the strength of a man's heart was wanting.

'Yes,' said Warburton, 'he did mention it.'

'Does it trouble him?'

'Perhaps you had better speak to him about it.' Both the old Duke and the private Secretary were as fearful and nervous about the Prime Minister as a mother is for a weakly child. They could hardly tell their opinions to each other, but they understood one another, and between them they coddled their Prime Minister. They were specially nervous as to what might be done by the Prime Minister's wife, nervous as to what was done by every one who came in contact with him. It had been once suggested by the private Secretary that Lady Rosina should be sent for, as she had a soothing effect upon the Prime Minister's spirit.

'Has it irritated him?' asked the Duke.

'Well;—yes, it has;—a little, you know. I think your Grace had better speak to him;—and not perhaps mention my name.' The Duke of St Bungay nodded his head, and said that he would speak to the great man and would not mention any one's name.

And he did speak. 'Has any one said anything to you about it?' asked the Prime Minister.

'I saw it in the "Evening Pulpit" myself. I have not heard it mentioned anywhere.'

'I did pay the man's expenses.'

'You did!'

'Yes,—when the election was over, and, as far as I can remember, some time after it was over. He wrote to me saying that he had incurred such and such expenses, and asking me to repay him. I sent him a cheque for the amount.'

'But why?'

'I was bound in honour to do it.'

'But why?'

There was a short pause before this second question was answered. 'The man had been induced to stand by representations made to him from my house. He had been, I fear, promised certain support which certainly was not given him when the time came.'

'You had not promised it?'

'No;—not I.'

'Was it the Duchess?'

'Upon the whole, my friend, I think I would rather not discuss it further, even with you. It is right that you should know that I did pay the money,—and also why I paid it. It may also be necessary that we should consider whether there may be any further probable result from my doing so. But the money has been paid, by me myself,—and was paid for the reason I have stated.'

'A question might be asked in the House.'

'If so, it must be answered as I have answered you. I certainly shall not shirk any responsibility that may be attached to me.'

'You would not like Warburton to write a line to the newspaper?'

'What;—to the "People's Banner!"'

'It began there, did it? No, not to the "People's Banner," but to the "Evening Pulpit," He could say, you know, that the money was paid by you, and that the payment had been made because your agents had misapprehended your instructions.'

'It would not be true,' said the Prime Minister slowly.

'As far as I can understand that was what occurred,' said the other Duke.

'My instructions were not misapprehended. They were disobeyed. I think that perhaps we had better say no more about it.'

'Do not think that I wish to press you,' said the old man tenderly; 'but I fear that something ought to be done;—I mean for your own comfort.'

'My comfort!' said the Prime Minister. 'That has vanished long ago;—and my peace of mind, and my happiness.'

'There has been nothing done which cannot be explained with perfect truth. There has been no impropriety.'

'I do not know.'

'The money was paid simply from an over-nice sense of honour.'

'It cannot be explained. I cannot explain it even to you, and how then can I do it to all the gaping fools of the country who are ready to trample upon a man simply because he is in some way conspicuous among them?'

After that the old Duke again spoke to Mr Warburton, but Mr Warburton was very loyal to his chief. 'Could one do anything by speaking to the Duchess?' said the old Duke.

'I think not.'

'I suppose it was her Grace who did it all?'

'I cannot say. My own impression is that he had better wait till the Houses meet, and then, if any question is asked, let it be answered. He himself would do it in the House of Lords, or Mr Finn or Barrington Erle, in our House. It would surely be enough to explain that his Grace had been made to believe that the man had received encouragement at Silverbridge from his own agents, which he himself had not intended should be given, and that therefore he had thought it right to pay the money. After such an explanation what more could any one say?'

'You might do it yourself.'

'I never speak.'

'But in such a case as that you might do so; and then there would be no necessity for him to talk to another person on the matter.'

So the affair was left for the present, though the allusions to it in the 'People's Banner' were still continued. Nor did any other of the Prime Minister's colleagues dare to speak to him on the subject. Barrington Erle and Phineas Finn talked of it among themselves, but they did not mention it even to the Duchess. She would have gone to her husband at once; and they were too careful of him to risk such a proceeding. It certainly was the case that among them they coddled the Prime Minister.

CHAPTER 51

CODDLING THE PRIME MINISTER

PARLIAMENT was to meet on the 12th of February, and it was of course necessary that there should be a Cabinet Council before that time. The Prime Minister, about the end of the third week in January, was prepared to name a day for this, and did so, most unwillingly. But he was then ill, and talked both to his friend the old Duke and his private Secretary of having the meeting held without him. 'Impossible!' said the old Duke.

'If I could not go it would have to be possible.'

'We could all come here if it were necessary.'

'Bring fourteen or fifteen ministers out of town because a poor creature such as I am is ill!' But in truth the Duke of St Bungay hardly believed in this illness. The Prime Minister was unhappy rather than ill.

By this time everyone in the House,—and almost everybody in the country who read the newspapers,—had heard of Mr Lopez and his election expenses,—except the Duchess. No one had yet dared to tell her. She saw the newspapers daily, but probably did not read them very attentively. Nevertheless she knew that something was wrong. Mr Warburton hovered about the Prime Minister more tenderly than usual; the Duke of St Bungay was more concerned; the world around her was more mysterious, and her husband more wretched. 'What is it that's going on?' she said one day to Phineas Finn.

'Everything,—in the same dull way as usual.'

'If you don't tell me, I'll never speak to you again. I know there is something wrong.'

'The Duke, I'm afraid, is not quite well.'

'What makes him ill? I know well when he's ill, and when he's well. He's troubled by something.'

'I think he is, Duchess. But as he has not spoken to me I am loath to make guesses. If there be anything, I can only guess at it.'

Then she questioned Mrs Finn, and got an answer, which, if not satisfactory, was at any rate explanatory. 'I think he is uneasy about that Silverbridge affair.'

'What Silverbridge affair?'

'You know that he paid the expenses which that man Lopez says that he incurred.'

'Yes;—I know that.'

'And you know that that other man Slide has found it out, and published it all in the "People's Banner?"'

'No!'

'Yes, indeed. And a whole army of accusations has been brought against him. I have never liked to tell you, and yet I do not think that you should be left in the dark.'

'Everybody deceives me,' said the Duchess angrily.

'Nay;—there has been no deceit.'

'Everybody keeps things from me. I think you will kill me among you. It was my doing. Why do they attack him? I will write to the papers. I encouraged the man after Plantagenet had determined that he should not be assisted,—and, because I had done so, he paid the man his beggarly money. What is there to hurt him in that? Let me bear it. My back is broad enough.'

'The Duke is very sensitive.'

'I hate people to be sensitive. It makes them cowards. A man when he is afraid of being blamed, dares not at last even show himself, and has to be wrapped up in lamb's-wool.'

'Of course men are differently organized.'

'Yes;—but the worst of it is, that when they suffer from this weakness, which you call sensitiveness, they think that they are made of finer material than other people. Men shouldn't be made of Sèvres china, but of good stone earthenware. However, I don't want to abuse him, poor fellow.'

'I don't think you ought.'

'I know what that means. You do want to abuse me. So they've been bullying him about the money he paid to that man Lopez. How did anybody know anything about it?'

'Lopez must have told of it,' said Mrs Finn.

'The worst, my dear, of trying to know a great many people is, that you are sure to get hold of some that are very bad. Now that man is very bad. Yet they say he has married a nice wife.'

'That's often the case, Duchess.'

'And the contrary;—isn't it, my dear? But I shall have it out with Plantagenet. If I have to write letters to all the newspapers myself, I'll put it right.' She certainly coddled her husband less than the others; and, indeed, in her heart of hearts disapproved altogether of the coddling system. But she was wont at this particular time to be somewhat tender to him because she was aware that she herself had been imprudent. Since he had discovered her interference at Silverbridge, and had made her understand its pernicious results, she had been,—not, perhaps, shamefaced, for that word describes a condition to which hardly any series of misfortunes could have reduced the Duchess of Omnium,—but inclined to quiescence by feelings of penitence. She was less disposed than heretofore to attack him with what the world of yesterday calls 'chaff,' or with what the world of to-day calls 'cheek.' She would not admit to herself that she was cowed;—but the greatness of the game and the high interest attached to her husband's position did in some degree dismay her. Nevertheless she executed her purpose of 'having it out with Plantagenet,' 'I have just heard,' she said, having knocked at the door of his own room, and having found him alone,— 'I have just heard, for the first time, that there is a row about the money you paid to Mr Lopez.'

'Who told you?'

'Nobody told me,—in the usual sense of the word. I presumed that something was the matter, and then I got it out from Marie. Why had you not told me?'

'Why should I tell you?'

'But why not? If anything troubled me I should tell you. That is, if it troubled me much.'

'You take it for granted that this does trouble me much.' He was smiling as he said this, but the smile passed very quickly from his face. 'I will not, however, deceive you. It does trouble me.'

'I knew very well that something was wrong.'

'I have not complained.'

'One can see as much as that without words. What is it that you fear? What can the man do to you? What matter is it to you if such a one as that pours out his malice on you? Let it run off like the rain from the housetops. You are too big even to be stung by such a reptile as that.' He looked into her face, admiring the energy with which she spoke to him. 'As for answering him,' she continued to say, 'that may or may not be proper. If it should be done, there are people to do it. But I am speaking of your own inner self. You have a shield against your equals, and a sword to attack them with if necessary. Have you no armour of proof against such a creature as that? Have you nothing inside you to make you feel that he is too contemptible to be regarded?'

'Nothing,' he said.

'Oh, Plantagenet!'

'Cora, there are different natures which have each their own excellencies and their own defects. I will not admit that I am a coward, believing as I do that I could dare to face necessary danger. But I cannot endure to have my character impugned,—even by Mr Slide and Mr Lopez.'

'What matter,—if you are in the right? Why blench if your conscience accuses you of no fault? I would not blench even if it did. What;—is a man to be put in the front of everything, and then to be judged as though he could give all his time to the picking of his steps?'

'Just so! And he must pick them more warily than another.'

'I do not believe it. You see all this with jaundiced eyes. I read somewhere the other day that the great ships have always little worms attached to them, but that the great ships swim on and know nothing of the worms.'

'The worms conquer at last.'

'They shouldn't conquer me! After all, what is it that they say about the money? That you ought not to have paid it?'

'I begin to think that I was wrong to pay it.'

'You certainly were not wrong. I had led the man on. I had been mistaken. I had thought that he was a gentleman. Having led him on at first, before you had spoken to me, I did not like to go back from my word. I did go to the man at Silverbridge who sells the pots, and no doubt the man, when thus encouraged, told it all to Lopez. When Lopez went to the town he did suppose that he would have what the people call the Castle interest.'

'And I had done so much to prevent it!'

'What's the use of going back to that now, unless you want me to put my neck down to be trodden on? I am confessing my own sins as fast as I can.'

'God knows I would not have you trodden on.'

'I am willing,—if it be necessary. Then came the question;—as I had done this evil, how was it to be rectified? Any man with a particle of spirit would have taken his rubs and said nothing about it. But as this man asked for the money, it was right that he should have it. If it is all made public he won't get very well out of it.'

'What does that matter to me?'

'Nor shall I;—only luckily I do not mind it.'

'But I mind it for you.'

'You must throw me to the whale.* Let somebody say in so many words that the Duchess did so and so. It was very wicked no doubt; but they can't kill me,—nor yet dismiss me. And I won't resign. In point of fact I shan't be a penny the worse for it.'

'But I should resign.'

'If all the Ministers of England were to give up as soon as their wives do foolish things, that question about Queen's Government would become very difficult.'

'They may do foolish things, dear; and yet——'

'And yet what?'

'And yet not interfere in politics.'

'That's all you know about it, Plantagenet. Doesn't everybody know that Mrs Daubeny got Dr MacFuzlem made a bishop, and that Mrs Gresham got her husband to make that hazy speech about women's rights, so that nobody should know which way he meant to go? There are others just as bad as me, only I don't think they get blown up so much. You do now as I ask you.'

'I couldn't do it, Cora. Though the stain were but a little spot, and the thing to be avoided political destruction, I could not ride out of the punishment by fixing that stain on my wife. I will not have your name mentioned. A man's wife should be talked about by no one.'

'That's high-foluting, Plantagenet.'

'Glencora, in these matters you must allow me to judge for myself, and I will judge. I will never say that I didn't do it;—but that it was my wife who did.'

'Adam said so,*—because he chose to tell the truth.'

'And Adam has been despised ever since,—not because he ate the apple, but because he imputed the eating of it to a woman. I will not do it. We have had enough of this now.' Then she turned to go away,— but he called her back. 'Kiss me, dear,' he said. Then she stooped over him and kissed him. 'Do not think I am angry with you because the thing vexes me. I am dreaming always of some day when we may go away together with the children, and rest in some pretty spot, and live as other people live.'

'It would be very stupid,' she muttered to herself as she left the room.

He did go up to town for the Cabinet meeting. Whatever may have been done at that august assembly there was certainly no resignation, or the world would have heard it. It is probable, too, that nothing was said about these newspaper articles. Things if left to themselves will generally die at last. The old Duke and Phineas Finn and Barrington Erle were all of the opinion that the best plan for the present was to do nothing. 'Has anything been settled?' the Duchess asked Phineas when he came back.

'Oh yes;—the Queen's Speech. But there isn't very much in it.'

'But about the payment of this money?'

'I haven't heard a word about it,' said Phineas.

'You're just as bad as all the rest, Mr Finn, with your pretended secrecy. A girl with her first sweetheart isn't half so fussy as a young Cabinet Minister.'

'The Cabinet Ministers get used to it sooner, I think,' said Phineas Finn.

Parliament had already met before Mr Slide had quite determined in what way he would carry on the war. He could indeed go on writing pernicious articles about the Prime Minister *ad infinitum*,—from year's end to year's end. It was an occupation in which he took delight, and for which he imagined himself to be peculiarly well suited. But readers will become tired even of abuse if it be not varied. And the very continuation of such attacks would seem to imply that they were not much heeded. Other papers had indeed taken the matter up,—but they had taken it up only to drop it. The subject had not been their own. The little discovery had been due not to their acumen, and did not therefore bear with them the highest interest. It had almost seemed as though nothing would come of it;—for Mr Slide in his wildest ambition could have hardly imagined the vexation and hesitation, the nervousness and serious discussions which his words had occasioned among the great people at Matching. But certainly the thing must not be allowed to pass away as a matter of no moment. Mr Slide had almost worked his mind up to real horror as he thought of it. What! A prime minister, a peer, a great duke,—put a man forward as a candidate for a borough, and, when the man was beaten, pay his expenses! Was this to be done,—to be done and found out and nothing come of it in these days of purity, when a private member of Parliament, some mere nobody, loses his seat because he has given away a few bushels of coals or a score or two of rabbits! Mr Slide's energetic love of public virtue was scandalized as he thought of the probability of such a catastrophe. To his thinking, public virtue consisted in carping at men high placed, in abusing ministers and judges and bishops—and especially in finding out something for which they might be abused. His own public virtue was in this matter very great, for it was he who had ferreted out the secret. For his intelligence and energy in that matter the country owed him much. But the country would pay him nothing, would give him none of the credit he desired, would rob him of this special opportunity of declaring a dozen times that the 'People's Banner' was the surest guardian of the people's liberty,—unless he could succeed in forcing the matter further into public notice. 'How terrible is the apathy of the people at large,' said Mr Slide to himself, 'when they cannot be awakened by such a revelation as this!'

Mr Slide knew very well what ought to be the next step. Proper notice should be given and a question should be asked in Parliament. Some gentleman should declare that he had noticed such and such statements in the public press, and that he thought it right to ask whether such and such payments had been made by the Prime Minister. In his meditations Mr Slide went so far as to arrange the very words which the indignant gentleman should utter, among which words was a graceful allusion to a certain public-spirited newspaper. He did even go so far as to arrange a compliment to the editor,—but in doing so he knew that he was thinking only of that which ought to be, and not of that which would be. The time had not come as yet in which the editor of a newspaper in this country received a tithe of the honour due to him. But the question in any form, with or without a compliment to the 'People's Banner,' would be the thing that was now desirable.

Who was to ask the question? If public spirit were really strong in the country there would be no difficulty on that point. The crime committed had been so horrible that all the great politicians of the country ought to compete for the honour of asking it. What greater service can be trusted to the hands of a great man than that of exposing the sins of the rulers of the nation? So thought Mr Slide. But he knew that he was in advance of the people, and that the matter would not be seen in the proper light by those who ought so to see it. There might be a difficulty in getting any peer to ask the question in the House in which the Prime Minister himself sat, and even in the other House there was now but little of that acrid, indignant opposition upon which, in Mr Slide's opinion, the safety of the nation altogether depends.

When the statement was first made in the 'People's Banner,' Lopez had come to Mr Slide at once and had demanded his authority for making it. Lopez had found the statement to be most injurious to himself. He had been paid his election expenses twice over, making a clear profit of £500 by the transaction; and, though the matter had at one time troubled his conscience, he had already taught himself to regard it as one of those bygones to which a wise man seldom refers. But now Mr Wharton would know that he had been cheated, should this statement reach him. 'Who gave you authority to publish all this?' asked Lopez, who at this time had become intimate with Mr Slide.

'Is it true, Lopez?' asked the editor.

'Whatever was done was done in private,—between me and the Duke.'

'Dukes, my dear fellow, can't be private, and certainly not when they are Prime Ministers.'

'But you've no right to publish these things about me.'

'Is it true? If it's true I have got every right to publish it. If it's not true, I've got the right to ask the question. If you will 'ave to do with Prime Ministers you can't 'ide yourself under a bushel. Tell me this;—is it true? You might as well go 'and in 'and with me in the matter. You can't 'urt yourself. And if you oppose me,—why, I shall oppose you.'

'You can't say anything of me.'

'Well;—I don't know about that. I can generally 'it pretty 'ard if I feel inclined. But I don't want to 'it you. As regards you I can tell the story one way,—or the other, just as you please.' Lopez, seeing it in the same light, at last agreed that the story should be told in a manner not inimical to himself. The present project of his life was to leave his troubles in England,—Sexty Parker being the worst of them,—and get away to Guatemala. In arranging this the good word of Mr Slide might not benefit him, but his ill word might injure him. And then, let him do what he would, the matter must be made public. Should Mr Wharton hear of it,—as of course he would,—it must be brazened out. He could not keep it from Mr Wharton's ears by quarrelling with Quintus Slide.

'It was true,' said Lopez.

'I knew it before just as well as though I had seen it. I ain't often very wrong in these things. You asked him for the money,—and threatened him.'

'I don't know about threatening him.'

' 'E wouldn't have sent it else.'

'I told him that I had been deceived by his people in the borough, and that I had been put to expense through the misrepresentations of the Duchess. I don't think I did ask for the money. But he sent a cheque, and of course I took it.'

Of course;—of course. You couldn't give me a copy of your letter?'

'Never kept a copy.' He had a copy in his breast coat-pocket at that moment, and Slide did not for a moment believe the statement made. But in such discussions one man hardly expects truth from another. Mr Slide certainly never expected truth from any man. 'He sent the cheque almost without a word,' said Lopez.

'He did write a note, I suppose?'

'Just a few words.'

'Could you let me 'ave that note?'

'I destroyed it at once.' This was also in his breast-pocket at the time.

'Did 'e write it 'imself?'

'I think it was his private Secretary, Mr Warburton.'

'You must be sure, you know. Which was it?'

'It was Mr Warburton.'

'Was it civil?'

'Yes, it was. If it had been uncivil I should have sent it back. I'm not the man to take impudence even from a duke.'

'If you'll give me those two letters, Lopez, I'll stick to you through thick and thin. By heavens I will! Think what the "People's Banner" is. You may come to want that kind of thing some of these days.' Lopez remained silent, looking into the other man's eager face. 'I shouldn't publish them, you know; but it would be so much to me to have the evidence in my hands. You might do worse, you know, than make a friend of me.'

'You won't publish them?'

'Certainly not. I shall only refer to them.'

Then Lopez pulled a bundle of papers out of his pocket. 'There they are,' he said.

'Well,' said Slide, when he had read them, 'it is one of the rummest transactions I ever 'eard of. Why did 'e send the money? That's what I want to know. As far as the claim goes, you 'adn't a leg to stand on.'

'Not legally.'

'You 'adn't a leg to stand on any way. But that doesn't much matter. He sent the money, and the sending of the money was corrupt. Who shall I get to ask the question? I suppose young Fletcher wouldn't do it?'

'They're birds of a feather,' said Lopez.

'Birds of a feather do fall out sometimes. Or Sir Orlando Drought? I wonder whether Sir Orlando Drought would do it. If any man ever 'ated another Sir Orlando Drought must 'ate the Duke of Omnium.'

'I don't think he'd let himself down to that kind of thing.'

'Let 'imself down! I don't see any letting down in it. But those men who have been in cabinets do stick to one another even when they are enemies. They think themselves so mighty that they oughtn't to be 'andled like other men. But I'll let 'em know that I'll 'andle them. A Cabinet Minister or a cowboy is the same to Quintus Slide when he has got his pen in 'is 'and.'

On the next morning there came out another article in the 'People's Banner,' in which the writer declared that he had in his own possession the damnatory correspondence between the Prime Minister and the late candidate at Silverbridge. 'The Prime Minister may deny the fact,' said the article. 'We do not think it probable, but it is possible. We wish to be fair and above-board in everything. And therefore we at once inform the noble Duke that the entire correspondence is in our hands.' In saying this Mr Quintus Slide thought that he had quite kept the promise which he made when he said that he would only refer to the letters.

CHAPTER 52

'I CAN SLEEP HERE TO-NIGHT, I SUPPOSE?'

THAT scheme of going to Guatemala had been in the first instance propounded by Lopez with the object of frightening Mr Wharton into terms. There had, indeed, been some previous thoughts on the subject,—some plan projected before his marriage; but it had been resuscitated mainly with the hope that it might be efficacious to extract money. When by degrees the son-in-law began to feel that even this would not be operative on his father-in-law's purse,—when under this threat neither Wharton nor Emily gave way,—and when, with the view of strengthening his threat, he renewed his inquiries as to Guatemala and found that there might still be an opening for him in that direction,— the threat took the shape of a true purpose, and he began to think that he would in real earnest try his fortunes in a new world. From day to day things did not go well with him, and from day to day Sexty Parker became more unendurable. It was impossible for him to keep from his partner this plan of emigration,—but he endeavoured to make Parker believe that the thing, if done at all, was not to be done till all his affairs were settled,—or in other words all his embarrassments cleared by downright money payments, and that Mr Wharton was to make these payments on the condition that he thus expatriated himself. But Mr Wharton had made no such promise. Though the threatened day came nearer and nearer he could not bring himself to purchase a short respite for his daughter by paying money to a scoundrel,—which payment he felt sure would be of no permanent service. During all this time Mr Wharton was very wretched. If he could have freed his daughter from her marriage by half his fortune he would have done it without a second thought. If he could have assuredly purchased the permanent absence of her husband, he would have done it at a large price. But let him pay what he would, he could see his way to no security. From day to day he became more strongly convinced of the rascality of this man who was his son-in-law, and who was still an inmate in his own house. Of course he had accusations enough to make within his own breast against his daughter, who, when the choice was open to her, would not take the altogether fitting husband provided for her, but had declared herself to be broken-hearted for ever since she were allowed to throw herself away upon this wretched creature. But he blamed himself almost as much as he did her. Why had he allowed himself to be so enervated by her prayers at last as to surrender everything,—as he had done? How could he presume to think that he should be allowed to escape, when he had done so little to prevent the misery?

He spoke to Emily about it,—not often indeed, but with great earnestness. 'I have done it myself,' she said, 'and I will bear it.'

'Tell him you cannot go till you know to what home you are going.'

'That is for him to consider. I have begged him to let me remain, and I can say no more. If he chooses to take me, I shall go.'

Then he spoke to her about money. 'Of course I have money,' he said. 'Of course I have enough both for you and Everett. If I could do any good by giving it to him, he should have it.'

'Papa,' she answered, 'I will never again ask you to give him a single penny. That must be altogether between you and him. He is what they call a speculator. Money is not safe with him.'

'I shall have to send it to you when you are in want.'

'When I am—dead there will be no more to be sent. Do not look like that, papa. I know what I have done, and I must bear it. I have thrown away my life. It is just that. If baby had lived it would have been different.' This was about the end of January, and then Mr Wharton heard of the great attack made by Mr Quintus Slide against the Prime Minister, and heard, of course, of the payment alleged to have been made to Ferdinand Lopez by the Duke on the score of the election at Silverbridge. Some persons spoke to him on the subject. One or two friends at the club asked him what he supposed to be the truth in the matter, and Mrs Roby inquired of him on the subject. 'I have asked Lopez,' she said, 'and I am sure from his manner that he did get the money.'

'I don't know anything about it,' said Mr Wharton.

'If he did get it I think he was very clever.' It was well known at this time to Mrs Roby that the Lopez marriage had been a failure, that Lopez was not a rich man, and that Emily, as well as her father, was discontented and unhappy. She had latterly heard of the Guatemala scheme, and had of course expressed her horror. But she sympathized with Lopez rather than with his wife, thinking that if Mr Wharton would only open his pockets wide enough things might still be right. 'It was all the Duchess's fault, you know,' she said to the old man.

'I know nothing about it, and when I want to know I certainly shall not come to you. The misery he has brought upon me is so great that it makes me wish I had never seen any one who knew him.'

'It was Everett who introduced him to your house.'

It was you who introduced him to Everett.'

'There you are wrong,—as you so often are, Mr Wharton. Everett met him first at the club.'

'What's the use of arguing about it? It was at your house that Emily met him. It was you that did it. I wonder you can have the face to mention his name to me.'

'And the man living all the time in your own house!'

Up to this time Mr Wharton had not mentioned to a single person the fact that he had paid his son-in-law's election expenses at Silverbridge. He had given him the cheque without much consideration, with the feeling that by doing so he would in some degree benefit his daughter; and had since regretted the act, finding that no such payment from him could be of any service to Emily. But the thing had been done,—and there had been, so far, an end of it. In no subsequent discussion would Mr Wharton have alluded to it, had not circumstances now as it were driven it back upon his mind. And since the day on which he had paid that money he had been, as he declared to himself, swindled over and over again by his son-in-law. There was the dinner in Manchester Square, and after that the brougham, and the rent, and a score of bills, some of which he had paid and some declined to pay! And yet he had said but little to the man himself of all these injuries. Of what use was it to say anything? Lopez would simply reply that he had asked him to pay nothing. 'What is it all,' Lopez had once said, 'to the fortune I had a right to expect with your daughter?' 'You had no right to expect a shilling,' Wharton had said. Then Lopez had shrugged his shoulders, and there had been an end of it.

But now, if this rumour were true, there had been positive dishonesty. From whichever source the man might have got the money first, if the money had been twice got, the second payment had been fraudulently obtained. Surely if the accusation had been untrue Lopez would have come to him and declared it to be false, knowing what must otherwise be his thoughts. Lately, in the daily worry of his life, he had avoided all conversation with the man. He would not allow his mind to contemplate clearly what was coming. He entertained some irrational undefined hope that something would at last save his daughter from the threatened banishment. It might be, if he held his own hand tight enough, that there would not be money enough even to pay for her passage out. As for her outfit, Lopez would of course order what he wanted and have the bills sent to Manchester Square. Whether or not this was being done neither he nor Emily knew. And thus matters went on without much speech between the two men. But now the old barrister thought that he was bound to speak. He therefore waited on a certain morning till Lopez had come down, having previously desired his daughter to leave the room. 'Lopez,' he asked, 'what is this that the newspapers are saying about your expenses at Silverbridge?'

Lopez had expected the attack and had endeavoured to prepare himself for it. 'I should have thought, sir, that you would not have paid much attention to such statements in a newspaper.'

'When they concern myself, I do. I paid your electioneering expenses.'

'You certainly subscribed £500 towards them, Mr Wharton.'

'I subscribed nothing, sir. There was no question of a subscription,—by which you intend to imply contribution from various sources. You told me that the contest cost you £500 and that sum I handed to you, with the full understanding on your part, as well as on mine, that I was paying for the whole. Was that so?'

'Have it your own way, sir.'

'If you are not more precise, I shall think that you have defrauded me.'

'Defrauded you?'

'Yes, sir;—defrauded me, or the Duke of Omnium. The money is gone, and it matters little which. But if that be so I shall know that either from him or from me you have raised money under false pretences.'

'Of course, Mr Wharton, from you I must bear whatever you may choose to say.'

'Is it true that you have applied to the Duke of Omnium for money on account of your expenses at Silverbridge, and is it true that he has paid you on that score?'

'Mr Wharton, as I have said just now, I am bound to hear and to bear from you anything you may choose to say. Your connection with my wife and your age alike restrain my resentment. But I am not bound to answer your questions when they are accompanied by such language as you have chosen to use, and I refuse to answer further questions on this subject.'

'Of course I know that you have taken the money from the Duke.'

'Then why do you ask me?'

'And of course I know you are as well aware as I am of the nature of the transaction. That you can brazen it out without a blush only proves to me that you have got beyond the reach of shame.'

'Very well, sir.'

'And you have no further explanation to make?'

'What do you expect me to say? Without knowing any of the facts of the case,—except the one, that you contributed £500 to my election expenses,—you take upon yourself to tell me that I am a shameless, fraudulent swindler. And then you ask for a further explanation! In such a position is it likely that I shall explain anything;—that I can be in a humour to be explanatory? Just turn it all over in your mind, and ask yourself the question.'

'I have turned it over in my own mind, and I have asked myself the question, and I do not think it probable that you should wish to explain anything. I shall take steps to let the Duke know that I as your father-in-law had paid the full sum which you had stated that you had spent at Silverbridge.'

'Much the Duke will care about that.'

'And after what has passed I am obliged to say that the sooner you leave this house the better I shall be pleased.'

'Very well, sir. Of course I shall take my wife with me.'

'That must be as she pleases.'

'No, Mr Wharton. That must be as I please. She belongs to me,—not to you or to herself. Under your influence she has forgotten much of what belongs to the duty of a wife, but I do not think that she will so far have forgotten herself as to give me more trouble than to bid her come with me when I desire it.'

'Let that be as it may. I must request that you, sir, will absent yourself. I will not entertain as my guest a man who has acted as you have done in this matter,—even though he be my son-in-law.'

'I can sleep here to-night, I suppose?'

'Or to-morrow if it suits you. As for Emily, she can remain here, if you will allow her to do so.'

'That will not suit me,' said Lopez.

'In that case, as far as I am concerned, I shall do whatever she may ask me to do. Good morning.'

Mr Wharton left the room, but did not leave the house. Before he did so he would see his daughter; and, thinking it probable that Lopez would also choose to see his wife, he prepared to wait in his own room. But, in about ten minutes, Lopez started from the hall door in a cab, and did so without going upstairs. Mr Wharton had reason to believe that his son-in-law was almost destitute of money for immediate purposes. Whatever he might have would at any rate be serviceable to him before he started. Any home for Emily must be expensive; and no home in their present circumstances could be so reputable for her as one under her father's roof. He therefore almost hoped that she might still be left with him till that horrid day should come,—if it ever did come,—in which she would be taken away from him for ever. 'Of course, papa, I shall go if he bids me,' she said, when he told her all that he thought it right to tell her of that morning's interview.

'I hardly know how to advise you,' said the father, meaning in truth to bring himself round to the giving of some advice adverse to her husband's will.

'I want no advice, papa.'

'Want no advice! I never knew a woman who wanted it more.'

'No, papa. I am bound to do as he tells me. I know what I have done. When some poor wretch has got himself into perpetual prison by his misdeeds, no advice can serve him then. So it is with me.'

'You can at any rate escape from your prison.'

'No;—no. I have a feeling of pride which tells me that as I chose to become the wife of my husband,—as I insisted on it in opposition to all my friends,—as I would judge for myself,—I am bound to put up with my choice. If this had come upon me through the authority of others, if I had been constrained to marry him, I think I could have reconciled myself to deserting him. But I did it myself, and I will abide by it. When he bids me go, I shall go.' Poor Mr Wharton went to his chambers, and sat there the whole day without taking a book or a paper into his hands. Could there be no rescue, no protection, no relief! He turned over in his head various plans, but in a vague and useless manner. What if the Duke were to prosecute Lopez for the fraud! What if he could induce Lopez to abandon his wife,—pledging himself by some deed not to return to her,—for, say, twenty or even thirty thousand pounds! What if he himself were to carry his daughter away to the continent, half forcing and half persuading her to make the journey! Surely there might be some means found by which the man might be frightened into compliance. But there he sat,—and did nothing. And in the evening he ate a solitary mutton chop at The Jolly Blackbird, because he could not bear to face even his club, and then returned to his chambers,—to the great disgust of the old woman who had them in charge at nights. And at about midnight he crept away to his own house, a wretched old man.

Lopez when he left Manchester Square did not go in search of a new home for himself and his wife, nor during the whole of the day did he trouble himself on that subject. He spent most of the day at the rooms in Coleman Street of the San Juan Mining Association,* of which Mr Mills Happerton had once been Chairman. There was now another Chairman and other Directors; but Mr Mills Happerton's influence had so far remained with the Company as to enable Lopez to become well known in the Company's offices, and acknowledged as a claimant for the office of resident Manager at San Juan in Guatemala. Now the present project was this,—that Lopez was to start on behalf of the Company early in May, that the Company was to pay his own personal expenses out to Guatemala, and that they should allow him while there a salary of £1000 a year for managing the affairs of the mine. As far as this offer went, the thing was true enough. It was true that Lopez had absolutely secured the place. But he had done so subject to the burden of one very serious stipulation. He was to become the proprietor of 50 shares in the mine, and to pay up £100 each on those shares. It was considered that the man who was to get £1000 a year in Guatemala for managing the affair, should at any rate assist the affair, and show his confidence in the affair to an extent as great as that. Of course the holder of these 50 shares would be as fully entitled as any other share-holder to that 20 per cent which those who promoted the mine prom-ised as the immediate result of the speculation.

At first Lopez had hoped that he might be enabled to defer the actual payment of the £5000 till after he had sailed. When once out in Guatemala as manager, as manager he would doubtless remain. But by degrees he found that the payment must actually be made in advance. Now there was nobody to whom he could apply but Mr Wharton. He was, indeed, forced to declare at the office that the money was to come from Mr Wharton, and had given some excellent but fictitious reason why Mr Wharton could not pay the money till February.

And in spite of all that had come and gone he still did hope that if the need to go were actually there he might even yet get the money from Mr Wharton. Surely Mr Wharton would sooner pay such a sum than be troubled at home with such a son-in-law. Should the worst come to the worst, of course he could raise the money by consenting to leave his wife at home. But this was not part of his plan, if he could avoid it. £5000 would be a very low price at which to sell his wife, and all that he might get from his connection with her. As long as he kept her with him he was in possession at any rate of all that Mr Wharton would do for her. He had not therefore as yet made his final application to his father-in-law for the money, having found it possible to postpone the payment till the middle of February. His quarrel with Mr Wharton this morning he regarded as having little or no effect upon his circumstances. Mr Wharton would not give him the money because he loved him, nor yet from personal respect, nor from any sense of duty as to what he might owe to a son-in-law. It would be simply given as the price by which his absence might be purchased, and his absence would not be the less desirable because of this morning's quarrel.

But, even yet, he was not quite resolved as to going to Guatemala. Sexty Parker had been sucked nearly dry, and was in truth at this moment so violent with indignation and fear and remorse that Lopez did not dare to show himself in Little Tankard Yard; but still there were, even yet, certain hopes in that direction from which greater results might come. If a certain new spirit which had just been concocted from the bark of trees in Central Africa, and which was called Bios, could only be made to go up in the market, everything might be satisfactorily arranged. The hoardings of London were already telling the public that if it wished to get drunk without any of the usual troubles of intoxication it must drink Bios. The public no doubt does read the literature of the hoardings, but then it reads so slowly! This Bios had hardly been twelve months on the boards as yet! But they were now increasing the size of the letters in the advertisements and the jocundity of the pictures,—and the thing might be done. There was, too, another hope,—another hope of instant moneys by which Guatemala might be staved off, as to which further explanation shall be given in a further chapter.

'I suppose I shall find Dixon a decent sort of fellow?' said Lopez to the Secretary of the Association in Coleman Street.

'Rough, you know.'

'But honest?'

'Oh, yes;—he's all that.'

'If he's honest, and what I call loyal, I don't care a straw for anything else. One doesn't expect West-end manners in Guatemala. But I shall have a deal to do with him,—and I hate a fellow that you can't depend on.'

'Mr Happerton used to think a great deal of Dixon.'

'That's all right,' said Lopez. Mr Dixon was the underground manager out at the San Juan mine, and was perhaps as anxious for a loyal and honest colleague as was Mr Lopez. If so, Mr Dixon was very much in the way to be disappointed.

Lopez stayed at the office all the day studying the affairs of the San Juan mine, and then went to the Progress for his dinner. Hitherto he had taken no steps whatever as to getting lodgings for himself or for his wife.

CHAPTER 53

MR HARTLEPOD

WHEN the time came at which Lopez should have left Manchester Square he was still there. Mr Wharton, in discussing the matter with his daughter,—when wishing to persuade her that she might remain in his house even in opposition to her husband,—had not told her that he had actually desired Lopez to leave it. He had then felt sure that the man would go and take his wife with him, but he did not even yet know the obduracy and the cleverness and the impregnability of his son-in-law. When the time came, when he saw his daughter in the morning after the notice had been given, he could not bring himself even yet to say to her that he had issued an order for his banishment. Days went by and Lopez was still there, and the old barrister said no further word on the subject. The two men never met;—or met simply in the hall or passages. Wharton himself studiously avoided such meetings, thus denying himself the commonest uses of his own house. At last Emily told him that her husband had fixed the day for her departure. The next Indian mail-packet* by which they would leave England would start from Southampton on the 2nd of April, and she was to be ready to go on that day. 'How is it to be till then?' the father asked in a low, uncertain voice.

'I suppose I may remain with you.'

'And your husband?'

'He will be here too,—I suppose.'

'Such a misery,—such a destruction of everything no man ever heard of before!' said Mr Wharton. To this she made no reply, but continued working at some necessary preparation for her final departure. 'Emily,' he said. 'I will make any sacrifice to prevent it. What can be done? Short of injuring Everett's interests, I will do anything.'

'I do not know,' she said.

'You must understand something of his affairs.'

'Nothing whatever. He has told me nothing of them. In earlier days,—soon after our marriage,—he bade me get money from you.'

'When you wrote to me for money from Italy?'

'And after that. I have refused to do anything;—to say a word. I told him that it must be between you and him. What else could I say? And now he tells me nothing.'

'I cannot think that he should want you to go with him.' Then there was again a pause. 'Is it because he loves you?'

'Not that, papa.'

'Why then should he burden himself with a companion? His money, whatever he has, would go further without such impediment.'

'Perhaps he thinks, papa, that while I am with him he has a hold upon you.'

'He shall have a stronger hold by leaving you. What is he to gain? If I could only know his price.'

'Ask him, papa.'

'I do not even know how I am to speak to him again.'

Then again there was a pause. 'Papa,' she said after a while, 'I have done it myself. Let me go. You will still have Everett. And it may be that after a time I shall come back to you. He will not kill me, and it may be that I shall not die.'

'By God!' said Mr Wharton, rising from his chair suddenly, 'if there were money to be made by it I believe he would murder you without scruple.' Thus it was that within eighteen months of her marriage the father spoke to his daughter of her husband.

'What am I to take with me?' she said to her husband a few days later.

'You had better ask your father.'

'Why should I ask him, Ferdinand? How should he know?'

'And how should I?'

'I should have thought you would interest yourself about it.'

'Upon my word I have enough to interest me just at present, without thinking of your finery. I suppose you mean what clothes you should have?'

'I was not thinking of myself only.'

'You need think of nothing else. Ask him what he pleases to allow you to spend, and then I will tell you what to get.'

'I will never ask him for anything, Ferdinand.'

'Then you may go without anything. You might as well do it at once, for you will have to do it sooner or later. Or, if you please, go to his tradesmen and say nothing to him about it. They will give you credit. You see how it is, my dear. He has cheated me in a most rascally manner. He has allowed me to marry his daughter, and because I did not make a bargain with him as another man would have done, he denies me the fortune I had a right to expect with you. You know that the Israelites despoiled the Egyptians,* and it was taken as a merit on their part. Your father is an Egyptian to me, and I will despoil him. You can tell him that I say so if you please.'

And so the days went on till the first week of February had passed, and Parliament had met. Both Lopez and his wife were still living in Manchester Square. Not another word had been said as to that notice to quit, nor an allusion made to it. It was supposed to be a settled thing that Lopez was to start with his wife for Guatemala in the first week of April. Mr Wharton had himself felt that difficulty as to his daughter's outfit, and had told her that she might get whatever it pleased her on his credit. 'For yourself, my dear.'

'Papa, I will get nothing till he bids me.'

'But you can't go across the world without anything. What are you to do in such a place as that unless you have the things you want?'

'What do poor people do who have to go? What should I do if you had cast me off because of my disobedience?'

'But I have not cast you off.'

'Tell him that you will give him so much, and then, if he bids me, I will spend it.'

'Let it be so. I will tell him.'

Upon that Mr Wharton did speak to his son-in-law;—coming upon him suddenly one morning in the dining-room. 'Emily will want an outfit if she is to go to this place.'

'Like other people she wants many things that she cannot get.'

'I will tell my tradesmen to furnish her with what she wants, up to,—well,—suppose I say £200. I have spoken to her and she wants your sanction.'

'My sanction for spending your money? She can have that very quickly.'

'You can tell her so;—or I will do so.'

Upon that Mr Wharton was going, but Lopez stopped him. It was now essential that the money for the shares in the San Juan mine should be paid up, and his father-in-law's pocket was still the source from which the enterprising son-in-law hoped to procure it. Lopez had fully made up his mind to demand it, and thought that the time had now come. And he was resolved that he would not ask it as a favour on bended knee. He was beginning to feel his own power, and trusted that he might prevail by other means than begging. 'Mr Wharton,' he said, 'you and I have not been very good friends lately.'

'No, indeed.'

'There was a time,—a very short time,—during which I thought that we might hit it off together, and I did my best. You do not, I fancy, like men of my class.'

'Well;—well! You had better go on if there be anything to say.'

'I have much to say, and I will go on. You are a rich man, and I am your son-in-law.' Mr Wharton put his left hand up to his forehead, brushing the few hairs back from his head, but he said nothing. 'Had I received from you during the last most vital year that assistance which I think I had a right to expect, I also might have been a rich man now. It is no good going back to that.' Then he paused, but still Mr Wharton said nothing. 'Now you know what has come to me and to your daughter. We are to be expatriated.'

'Is that my fault?'

'I think it is, but I mean to say nothing further of that. This Company which is sending me out, and which will probably be the most thriving thing of the kind which has come up within these twenty years, is to pay me a salary of £1000 a year as resident manager at San Juan.'

'So I understand.'

'The salary alone would be a beggarly thing. Guatemala, I take it, is not the cheapest country in the world in which a man can live. But I am to go out as the owner of fifty shares on which £100 each must be paid up, and I am entitled to draw another £1000 a year as dividend on the profit of those shares.'

'That will be twenty per cent.'

'Exactly.'

'And will double your salary.'

'Just so. But there is one little ceremony to be perfected before I can be allowed to enter upon so halcyon a state of existence. The £100 a share must be paid up.' Mr Wharton simply stared at him. 'I must have the £5000 to invest in the undertaking before I can start.'

'Well!'

'Now I have not got £5000 myself, nor any part of it. You do not wish, I suppose, to see either me or your daughter starve. And as for me, I hardly flatter myself when I say that you are very anxious to be rid of me. £5000 is not very much for me to ask of you, as I regard it.'

'Such consummate impudence I never met in my life before!'

'Nor perhaps so much unprevaricating downright truth. At any rate such is the condition of my affairs. If I am to go the money must be paid this week. I have, perhaps foolishly, put off mentioning the matter till I was sure that I could not raise the sum elsewhere. Though I feel my claim on you to be good, Mr Wharton, it is not pleasant to me to make it.'

'You are asking me for £5000 down!'

'Certainly I am.'

'What security am I to have?'

'Security?'

'Yes;—that if I pay it I shall not be troubled again by the meanest scoundrel that it has ever been my misfortune to meet. How am I to know that you will not come back to-morrow? How am I to know that you will go at all? Do you think it probable that I will give you £5000 on your own simple word?'

'Then the scoundrel will stay in England,—and will generally find it convenient to live in Manchester Square.'

'I'll be d——d if he does. Look here, sir. Between you and me there can be a bargain, and nothing but a bargain. I will pay the £5000,—on certain conditions.'

'I didn't doubt at all that you would pay it.'

'I will go with you to the office of this Company, and will pay for the shares if I can receive assurance there that the matter is as you say, and that the shares will not be placed in your power before you have reached Guatemala.'

'You can come to-day, sir, and receive all that assurance.'

'And I must have a written undertaking from you,—a document which my daughter can show if it be necessary,—that you will never claim her society again or trouble her with any application.'

'You mistake me, Mr Wharton. My wife goes with me to Guatemala.'

'Then I will not pay one penny. Why should I? What is your presence or absence to me except as it concerns her? Do you think that I care for your threats of remaining here? The police will set that right.'

'Wherever I go, my wife goes.'

'We'll see to that too. If you want the money, you must leave her. Good morning.'

Mr Wharton as he went to his chambers thought the matter over. He was certainly willing to risk the £5000 demanded if he could rid himself and his daughter of this terrible incubus,* even if it were only for a time. If Lopez would but once go to Guatemala, leaving his wife behind him, it would be comparatively easy to keep them apart should he ever return. The difficulty now was not in him, but in her. The man's conduct had been so outrageous, so barefaced, so cruel, that the lawyer did not doubt but that he could turn the husband out of his house, and keep the wife, even now, were it not that she was determined to obey the man whom she, in opposition to all her friends, had taken as her master. 'I have done it myself and I will bear it,' was all the answer she would make when her father strove to persuade her to separate herself from her husband. 'You have got Everett,' she would say. 'When a girl is married she is divided from her family;—and I am divided.' But she would willingly stay if Lopez would bid her stay. It now seemed that he could not go without the £5000; and, when the pressure came upon him, surely he would go and leave his wife.

In the course of that day Mr Wharton went to the offices of the San Juan mine and asked to see the Director. He was shown up into a half-furnished room, two stories high, in Coleman Street, where he found two clerks sitting upon stools;—and when he asked for the Director was shown into the back room in which sat the Secretary. The Secretary was a dark, plump little man with a greasy face, who had the gift of assuming an air of great importance as he twisted his chair round to face visitors who came to inquire about the San Juan Mining Company. His name was Hartlepod; and if the San Juan mine 'turned out trumps,' as he intended that it should, Mr Hartlepod meant to be a great man in the City. To Mr Hartlepod Mr Wharton, with considerable embarrassment, explained as much of the joint history of himself and Lopez as he found to be absolutely necessary. 'He has only left the office about half-an-hour,' said Mr Hartlepod.

'Of course you understand that he is my son-in-law.'

'He has mentioned your name to us, Mr Wharton, before now.'

'And he is going out to Guatemala?'

'Oh yes;—he's going out. Has he not told you as much himself?'

'Certainly, sir. And he has told me that he is desirous of buying certain shares in the Company before he starts.'

'Probably, Mr Wharton.'

'Indeed I believe he cannot go, unless he buys them.'

'That may be so, Mr Wharton. No doubt he has told you all that himself.'

'The fact is, Mr Hartlepod, I am willing, under certain stipulations, to advance him the money.' Mr Hartlepod bowed. 'I need not trouble you with private affairs between myself and my son-in-law.' Again the Secretary bowed. 'But it seems to be for his interest that he should go.'

'A very great opening indeed, Mr Wharton. I don't see how a man is to have a better opening. A fine salary! His expenses out paid! One of the very best things that has come up for many years! And as for the capital he is to embark in the affair, he is as safe to get twenty per cent on it,—as safe,—as safe as the Bank of England.'

'He'll have the shares?'

'Oh yes;—the scrip will be handed to him at once.'

'And,—and——'

'If you mean about the mine, Mr Wharton, you may take my word that it's all real. It's not one of those sham things that melt away like snow and leave the shareholders nowhere. There's the prospectus, Mr Wharton. Perhaps you have not seen that before. Take it away and cast your eye over it at your leisure.' Mr Wharton put the somewhat lengthy pamphlet into his pocket. 'Look at the list of Directors. We've three members of Parliament, a baronet, and one or two City names that are as good,—as good as the Bank of England. If that prospectus won't make a man confident I don't know what will. Why, Mr Wharton, you don't think that your son-in-law would get those fifty shares at par* unless he was going out as our general local manager. The shares ain't to be had. It's a large concern as far as capital goes. You'll see if you look. About a quarter of a million* paid up. But it's all in a box as one may say. It's among ourselves. The shares ain't in the market. Of course it's not for me to say what should be done between you and your son-in-law. Lopez is a friend of mine, and a man I esteem, and all that. Nevertheless I shouldn't think of advising you to do this or that,— or not to do it. But when you talk of safety, Mr Wharton,—why, Mr Wharton, I don't scruple to tell you as a man who knows what these things are, that this is an opportunity that doesn't come in a man's way perhaps twice in his life.'

Mr Wharton found he had nothing more to say, and went back to Lincoln's Inn. He knew very well that Mr Hartlepod's assurances were not worth much. Mr Hartlepod himself and his belongings, the clerks in his office, the look of the rooms, and the very nature of the praises which he had sung, all of them inspired anything but confidence.

Mr Wharton was a man of the world; and, though he knew nothing of city ways, was quite aware that no man in his senses would lay out £5000 on the mere word of Mr Hartlepod. But still he was inclined to make the payment. If only he could secure the absence of Lopez,—if he could be sure that Lopez would in truth go to Guatemala, and if also he could induce the man to go without his wife, he would risk the money. The money would, of course, be thrown away,—but he would throw it away. Lopez no doubt had declared that he would not go without his wife, even though the money were paid for him. But the money was an alluring sum! As the pressure upon the man became greater, Mr Wharton thought he would probably consent to leave his wife behind him.

In his emergency the barrister went to his attorney and told him everything. The two lawyers were closeted together for an hour, and Mr Wharton's last words to his old friend were as follows:—'I will risk the money, Walker, or rather I will consent absolutely to throw it away,—as it will be thrown away,—if it can be managed that he shall in truth go to this place without his wife.'

CHAPTER 54

LIZZIE

It cannot be supposed that Ferdinand Lopez at this time was a very happy man. He had, at any rate, once loved his wife, and would have loved her still could he have trained her to think as he thought, to share his wishes, and 'to put herself into the same boat with him,'—as he was wont to describe the unison and sympathy which he required from her. To give him his due, he did not know that he was a villain. When he was exhorting her to 'get round her father' he was not aware that he was giving her lessons which must shock a well-conditioned girl. He did not understand that everything that she had discovered of his moral disposition since her marriage was of a nature to disgust her. And, not understanding all this, he conceived that he was grievously wronged by her in that she adhered to her father rather than to him. This made him unhappy, and doubly disappointed him. He had neither got the wife that he had expected nor the fortune. But he still thought that the fortune must come if he would only hold on to the wife which he had got.

And then everything had gone badly with him since his marriage. He was apt, when thinking over his affairs, to attribute all this to the fears and hesitation and parsimony of Sexty Parker. None of his late ventures with Sexty Parker had been successful. And now Sexty was in a bad condition, very violent, drinking hard, declaring himself to be a ruined man, and swearing that if this and that were not done he would have bitter revenge. Sexty still believed in the wealth of his partner's father-in-law, and still had some hope of salvation from that source. Lopez would declare to him, and up to this very time persevered in protesting, that salvation was to be found in Bios. If Sexty would only risk two or three thousand pounds more upon Bios,—or his credit to that amount, failing the immediate money,—things might still be right. 'Bios be d——,' said Sexty, uttering a string of heavy imprecations. On that morning he had been trusting to native produce rather than to the new African spirit. But now as the Guatemala scheme really took form and loomed on Lopez's eyesight as a thing that might be real, he endeavoured to keep out of Sexty's way. But in vain. Sexty too had heard of Guatemala, and in his misery hunted Lopez about the city. 'By G——, I believe you're afraid to come to Little Tankard Yard,' he said one day, having caught his victim under the equestrian statue in front of the Exchange.

'What is the good of my coming when you will do nothing when I am there?'

'I'll tell you what it is, Lopez,—you're not going out of the country about this mining business, if I know it.'

'Who said I was?'

'I'll put a spoke in your wheel there, my man. I'll give a written account of all the dealings between us to the Directors. By G——, they shall know their man.'

'You're an ass, Sexty, and always were. Look here. If I can carry on as though I were going to this place, I can draw £5000 from old Wharton. He has already offered it. He has treated me with a stinginess that I never knew equalled. Had he done what I had a right to expect, you and I would have been rich men now. But at last I have got a hold upon him to £5000. As you and I stand, pretty nearly the whole of that will go to you. But don't you spoil it all by making an ass of yourself.'

Sexty, who was three parts drunk, looked up into his face for a few seconds, and then made his reply. 'I'm d——d if I believe a word of it.' Upon that Lopez affected to laugh, and then made his escape.

All this, as I have said, did not tend to make his life happy. Though he had impudence enough, and callousness of conscience enough, to get his bills paid by Mr Wharton as often as he could, he was not quite easy in his mind while he was doing so. His ambition had never been high, but it had soared higher than that. He had had great hopes. He had lived with some high people. He had dined with lords and ladies. He had been the guest of a Duchess. He had married the daughter of a gentleman. He had nearly been a member of Parliament. He still belonged to what he considered to be a first-rate club. From a great altitude he looked down upon Sexty Parker and men of Sexty's class, because of his social successes, and because he knew how to talk and to look like a gentleman. It was unpleasant to him, therefore, to be driven to the life he was now living. And the idea of going to Guatemala and burying himself in a mine in Central America was not to him a happy idea. In spite of all that he had done he had still some hope that he might avoid that banishment. He had spoken the truth to Sexty Parker in saying that he intended to get the £5000 from Mr Wharton without that terrible personal sacrifice, though he had hardly spoken the truth when he assured his friend that the greater portion of that money would go to him. There were many schemes fluctuating through his brain, and all accompanied by many doubts. If he could get Mr Wharton's money by giving up his wife, should he consent to give her up? In either case should he stay or should he go? Should he run one further great chance with Bios,—and if so, by whose assistance? And if he should at last decide that he would do so by the aid of a certain friend that was yet left to him, should he throw himself at that friend's feet, the friend being a lady, and propose to desert his wife and begin the world again with her? For the lady in question was a lady in possession, as he believed, of very large means. Or should he cut his throat and have done at once with all his troubles, acknowledging to himself that his career had been a failure, and that, therefore, it might be brought with advantage to an end? 'After all,' said he to himself, 'that may be the best way of winding up a bankrupt concern.'

Our old friend Lady Eustace, in these days, lived in a very small house in a very small street bordering upon May Fair; but the street, though very small, and having disagreeable relations with a mews, still had an air of fashion about it. And with her lived the widow, Mrs Leslie, who had introduced her to Mrs Dick Roby and through Mrs Roby to Ferdinand Lopez. Lady Eustace was in the enjoyment of a handsome income, as I hope that some of my readers may remember,— and this income, during the last year or two, she had learned to foster, if not with much discretion, at any rate with great zeal. During her short life she had had many aspirations. Love, poetry, sport, religion, fashion, Bohemianism had all been tried; but in each crisis there had been a certain care for wealth which had saved her from the folly of squandering what she had won by her early energies in the pursuit of her then prevailing passion. She had given her money to no lover, had not lost it on race-courses, or in building churches,—nor even had she materially damaged her resources by servants and equipages. At the present time she was still young, and still pretty,—though her hair and complexion took rather more time than in the days when she won Sir Florian Eustace. She still liked a lover,—or perhaps two,—though she had thoroughly convinced herself that a lover may be bought too dear. She could still ride a horse, though hunting regularly was too expensive for her. She could talk of religion if she could find herself close to a well-got-up clergyman,—being quite indifferent as to the denomination of the religion. But perhaps a wild dash for a time into fast vulgarity was what in her heart of hearts she liked best,—only that it was so difficult to enjoy that pleasure without risk of losing everything. And then, together with these passions, and perhaps above them all, there had lately sprung up in the heart of Lady Eustace a desire to multiply her means by successful speculation. This was the friend with whom Lopez had lately become intimate, and by whose aid he hoped to extricate himself from some of his difficulties.

Poor as he was he had contrived to bribe Mrs Leslie by handsome presents out of Bond Street;*—for, as he still lived in Manchester Square, and was the undoubted son-in-law of Mr Wharton, his credit was not altogether gone. In the giving of these gifts no purport was, of course, named, but Mrs Leslie was probably aware that her good word with her friend was expected. 'I only know what I used to hear from Mrs Roby,' Mrs Leslie had said to her friend. 'He was mixed up with Hunky's people, who roll in money. Old Wharton wouldn't have given him his daughter if he had not been doing well.'

'It's very hard to be sure,' said Lizzie Eustace.

'He looks like a man who'd know how to feather his own nest,' said Mrs Leslie. 'Don't you think he's very handsome?'

'I don't know that he's likely to do the better for that.'

'Well; no; but there are men of whom you are sure, when you look at them, that they'll be successful. I don't suppose he was anything to begin with, but see where he is now!'

'I believe you are in love with him, my dear,' said Lizzie Eustace.

'Not exactly. I don't know that he has given me any provocation. But I don't see why a woman shouldn't be in love with him if she likes. He is a deal nicer than those fair-haired men who haven't got a word to say to you, and yet look as though you ought to jump down their mouths:—like that fellow you were trying to talk to last night;—that Mr Fletcher.

He could just jerk out three words at a time, and yet he was proud as Lucifer. I like a man who if he likes me is neither ashamed nor afraid to say so.'

'There is a romance there, you know. Mr Fletcher was in love with Emily Wharton, and she threw him over for Lopez. They say he has not held up his head since.'

'She was quite right,' said Mrs Leslie. 'But she is one of those stiff-necked creatures who are set up with pride though they have nothing to be proud of. I suppose she had a lot of money. Lopez would never have taken her without.'

When, therefore, Lopez called one day at the little house in the little street he was not an unwelcome visitor. Mrs Leslie was in the drawing-room, but soon left it after his arrival. He had of late been often there, and when he at once introduced the subject on which he was himself intent it was not unexpected. 'Seven thousand five hundred pounds!'* said Lizzie, after listening to the proposition which he had come to make. 'That is a very large sum of money!'

'Yes;—it's a large sum of money. It's a large affair. I'm in it to rather more than that, I believe.'

'How are you to get people to drink it?' she asked after a pause.

'By telling them that they ought to drink it. Advertise it. It has become a certainty now that if you will only advertise sufficiently you may make a fortune by selling anything. Only the interest on the money expended increases in so large a ratio in accordance with the magnitude of the operation! If you spend a few hundreds in advertising you throw them away. A hundred thousand pounds* well laid out makes a certainty of anything.'

'What am I to get to show for my money;—I mean immediately, you know?'

'Registered shares in the Company.'

'The Bios Company?'

'No;—we did propose to call ourselves Parker and Co., limited. I think we shall change the name. They will probably use my name. Lopez and Co., limited.'

'But it's all for Bios?'

'Oh yes;—all for Bios.'

'And it's to come from Central Africa?'

'It will be rectified in London, you know. Some English spirit will perhaps be mixed. But I must not tell you the secrets of the trade till you join us. That Bios is distilled from the bark of the Duffer-tree is a certainty.'

'Have you drank any?'

'I've tasted it.'

'Is it nice?'

'Very nice;—rather sweet, you know, and will be the better for mixing.'

'Gin?' suggested her ladyship.

'Perhaps so,—or whisky. I think I may say that you can't do very much better with your money. You know I would not say this to you were it not true. In such a matter I treat you just as if,—as if you were my sister.'

'I know how good you are,—but seven thousand five hundred! I couldn't raise so much as that just at present.'

'There are to be six shares,' said Lopez, 'making £45,000* capital. Would you consent to take a share jointly with me? That would be three thousand seven hundred and fifty.'*

'But you have a share already,' said Lizzie suspiciously.

'I should then divide that with Mr Parker. We intend to register at any rate as many as nine partners.* Would you object to hold it with me?' Lopez, as he asked the question, looked at her as though he were offering her half his heart.

'No,' said Lizzie slowly, 'I don't suppose I should object to that.'

'I should be doubly eager about the affair if I were in partnership with you.'

'It's such a venture.'

'Nothing venture nothing have.'

'But I've got something as it is, Mr Lopez, and I don't want to lose it all.'

'There's no chance of that if you join us.'

'You think Bios is so sure!'

'Quite safe,' said Lopez.

'You must give me a little more time to think about it,' said Lady Eustace at last, panting with anxiety, struggling with herself, anxious for the excitement which would come to her from dealing in Bios, but still fearing to risk her money.

This had taken place immediately after Mr Wharton's offer of the £5000, in making which he had stipulated that Emily should be left at home. Then a few days went by, and Lopez was pressed for his money at the office of the San Juan mine. Did he or did he not mean to take up the mining shares allotted to him? If he did mean to do so, he must do it at once. He swore by all his gods that of course he meant to take them up. Had not Mr Wharton himself been at the office saying that he intended to pay for them? Was not that sufficient guarantee? They knew well enough that Mr Wharton was a man to whom the raising of £5000 could be a matter of no difficulty. But they did not know, never could know, how impossible it was to get anything done by Mr Wharton. But Mr Wharton had promised to pay for the shares, and when money was concerned his word would surely suffice. Mr Hartlepod, backed by two of the Directors, said that if the thing was to go on at all, the money must really be paid at once. But the conference was ended by allowing the new local manager another fortnight in which to complete the arrangement.

Lopez allowed four days to pass by, during each of which he was closeted for a time with Lady Eustace, and then made an attempt to get at Mr Wharton through his wife. 'Your father has said that he will pay the money for me,' said Lopez.

'If he has said it he certainly will do it.'

'But he has promised it on the condition that you should remain at home. Do you wish to desert your husband?' To this she made no immediate answer. 'Are you already anxious to be rid of me?'

'I should prefer to remain at home,' she said in a very low voice.

'Then you do wish to desert your husband?'

'What is the use of all this, Ferdinand? You do not love me. You did not marry me because I loved you.'

'By heaven I did;—for that and that only.'

'And how have you treated me?'

'What have I done to you?'

'But I do not mean to make accusations, Ferdinand. I should only add to our miseries by that. We should be happier apart.'

'Not I. Nor is that my idea of marriage. Tell your father that you wish to go with me, and then he will let us have the money.'

'I will tell him no lie, Ferdinand. If you bid me go, I will go. Where you find a home I must find one too if it be your pleasure to take me. But I will not ask my father to give you money because it is my pleasure to go. Were I to say so he would not believe me.'

'It is you who have told him to give it me only on the condition of your staying.'

'I have told him nothing. He knows that I do not wish to go. He cannot but know that. But he knows that I mean to go if you require it.'

'And you will do nothing for me?'

'Nothing,—in regard to my father.' He raised his fist with the thought of striking her, and she saw the motion. But his arm fell again to his side. He had not quite come to that yet. 'Surely you will have the charity to tell me whether I am to go, if it be fixed,' she said.

'Have I not told you twenty times?'

'Then it is fixed.'

Yes;—it is fixed. Your father will tell you about your things. He has promised you some beggarly sum,—about as much as a tallow-chandler would give his daughter.'

'Whatever he does for me will be sufficient for me. I am not afraid of my father, Ferdinand.'

'You shall be afraid of me before I have done with you,' said he, leaving the room.

Then as he sat at his club, dining there alone, there came across his mind ideas of what the world would be like to him if he could leave his wife at home and take Lizzie Eustace with him to Guatemala. Guatemala was very distant, and it would matter little there whether the woman he brought with him was his wife or no. It was clear enough to him that his wife desired no more of his company. What were the conventions of the world to him? This other woman had money at her own command. He could not make it his own because he could not marry her, but he fancied that it might be possible to bring her so far under his control as to make the money almost as good as his own. Mr Wharton's money was very hard to reach; and would be as hard to reach,—perhaps harder,—when Mr Wharton was dead, as now, during his life. He had said a good deal to the lady since the interview of which a report has been given. She had declared herself to be afraid of Bios. She did not in the least doubt that great things might be ultimately done with Bios, but she did not quite see the way with her small capital,—thus humbly did she speak of her wealth,—to be one of those who should take the initiative in the matter. Bios evidently required a great deal of advertisement, and Lizzie Eustace had a short-sighted objection to expend what money she had saved on the hoardings of London. Then he opened to her the glories of Guatemala, not contenting himself with describing the certainty of the 20 per cent, but enlarging on the luxurious happiness of life in a country so golden, so green, so gorgeous, and so grand. It had been the very apple of the eye of the old Spaniards. In Guatemala, he said, Cortez and Pizarro had met and embraced. They might have done so for anything Lizzie Eustace knew to the contrary. And here our hero took advantage of his name. Don Diego di Lopez had been the first to raise the banner of freedom in Guatemala when the kings of Spain became tyrants to their American subjects.* All is fair in love and war, and Lizzie amidst the hard business of her life still loved a dash of romance. Yet, he was about to change the scene and try his fortune in that golden, green, and gorgeous country. 'You will take your wife of course,' Lady Eustace had said. Then Lopez had smiled, and shrugging his shoulders had left the room.

It was certainly the fact that she could not eat him. Other men before Lopez have had to pick up what courage they could in their attacks upon women by remembering that fact. She had flirted with him in a very pleasant way, mixing up her prettiness and her percentages in a manner that was peculiar to herself. He did not know her, and he knew that he did not know her;—but still there was the chance. She had thrown his wife more than once in his face, after the fashion of women when they are wooed by married men, since the days of Cleopatra* downwards. But he had taken that simply as encouragement. He had already let her know that his wife was a vixen who troubled his life. Lizzie had given him her sympathy, and had almost given him a tear. 'But I am not a man to be broken-hearted because I have made a mistake,' said Lopez. 'Marriage vows are very well, but they shall never bind me to misery.' 'Marriage vows are not very well. They may be very ill,' Lizzie had replied, remembering certain passages in her own life.

There was no doubt about her money, and certainly she could not eat him. The fortnight allowed him by the San Juan Company had nearly gone by when he called at the little house in the little street, resolved to push his fortune in that direction without fear and without hesitation. Mrs Leslie again took her departure, leaving them together, and Lizzie allowed her friend to go, although the last words that Lopez had spoken had been, as he thought, a fair prelude to the words he intended to speak to-day. 'And what do you think of it?' he said, taking both her hands in his.

'Think of what?'

'Of our Spanish venture.'

'Have you given up Bios, my friend?'

'No; certainly not,' said Lopez, seating himself beside her. 'I have not taken the other half share, but I have kept my old venture in the scheme. I believe in Bios, you know.'

'Ah;—it is so nice to believe.'

'But I believe more firmly in the country to which I am going.'

'You are going then?'

'Yes, my friend;—I am going. The allurements are too strong to be resisted. Think of that climate and of this.' He probably had not heard of the mosquitoes of Central America when he so spoke. 'Remember that an income which gives you comfort here will there produce for you every luxury which wealth can purchase. It is to be a king there, or to be but very common among commoners here.'

'And yet England is a dear old country.'

'Have you found it so? Think of the wrongs which you have endured;—of the injuries which you have suffered.'

'Yes, indeed.' For Lizzie Eustace had gone through hard days in her time.

'I certainly will fly from such a country to those golden shores on which man may be free and unshackled.'

'And your wife?'

'Oh, Lizzie!' It was the first time that he had called her Lizzie, and she was apparently neither shocked nor abashed. Perhaps he thought too much of this, not knowing how many men had called her Lizzie in her time. 'Do not you at least understand that a man or a woman may undergo that tie, and yet be justified in disregarding it altogether?'

'Oh, yes;—if there has been bigamy, or divorce, or anything of that kind.' Now Lizzie had convicted her second husband of bigamy, and had freed herself after that fashion.

'To h—— with their prurient laws,' said Lopez, rising suddenly from his chair. 'I will neither appeal to them nor will I obey them. And I expect from you as little subservience as I myself am prepared to pay. Lizzy Eustace, will you go with me, to that land of the sun,

> Where the rage of the vulture, the love of the turtle
> Now melt into sorrow, now madden to crime?*

Will you dare to escape with me from the cold conventionalities, from the miserable thraldom of this country bound in swaddling cloths? Lizzie Eustace, if you will say the word, I will take you to that land of glorious happiness.'

But Lizzie Eustace had £4000* a year and a balance at her banker's. 'Mr Lopez,' she said.

'What answer have you to make me?'

'Mr Lopez, I think you must be a fool.'

He did at last succeed in getting himself into the street, and at any rate she had not eaten him.

CHAPTER 55

MRS PARKER'S SORROWS

THE end of February had come, and as far as Mrs Lopez knew she was to start for Guatemala in a month's time. And yet there was so much of indecision in her husband's manner, and apparently so little done by him in regard to personal preparation, that she could hardly bring herself to feel certain that she would have to make the journey. From day to day her father would ask her whether she had made her intended purchases, and she would tell him that she had still postponed the work. Then he would say no more, for he himself was hesitating, doubtful what he would do, and still thinking that when at last the time should come, he would buy his daughter's release at any price that might be demanded. Mr Walker, the attorney, had as yet been able to manage nothing. He had seen Lopez more than once, and had also seen Mr Hartlepod. Mr Hartlepod had simply told him that he would be very happy to register the shares on behalf of Lopez as soon as the money was paid. Lopez had been almost insolent in his bearing. 'Did Mr Wharton think,' he asked, 'that he was going to sell his wife for £5,000?' 'I think you will have to raise your offer,' Mr Walker had said to Mr Wharton. That was all very well. Mr Wharton was willing enough to raise his offer. He would have doubled his offer could he thereby have secured the annihilation of Lopez. 'I will raise it if he will go without his wife, and give her a written assurance that he will never trouble her again.' But the arrangement was one which Mr Walker found it very difficult to carry out. So things went on till the end of February had come.

And during all this time Lopez was still resident in Mr Wharton's house. 'Papa,' she said to him one day, 'this is the cruellest thing of all. Why don't you tell him that he must go?'

'Because he would take you with him.'

'It would be better so. I could come to see you.'

'I did tell him to go,—in my passion. I repented of it instantly, because I should have lost you. But what did my telling matter to him? He was very indignant, and yet he is still here.'

'You told him to go?'

'Yes;—but I am glad that he did not obey me. There must be an end to this soon, I suppose.'

'I do not know, papa.'

'Do you think that he will not go?'

'I feel that I know nothing, papa. You must not let him stay here always, you know.'

'And what will become of you when he goes?'

'I must go with him. Why should you be sacrificed also? I will tell him that he must leave the house. I am not afraid of him, papa.'

'Not yet, my dear;—not yet. We will see.'

At this time Lopez declared his purpose one day of dining at the Progress, and Mr Wharton took advantage of the occasion to remain at home with his daughter. Everett was now expected, and there was a probability that he might come on this evening. Mr Wharton therefore returned from his chambers early; but when he reached the house he was told that there was a woman in the dining-room with Mrs Lopez. The servant did not know what woman. She had asked to see Mrs Lopez, and Mrs Lopez had gone down to her.

The woman in the dining-room was Mrs Parker. She had called at the house at about half-past five, and Emily had at once come down when summoned by tidings that a 'lady' wanted to see her. Servants have a way of announcing a woman as a lady, which clearly expresses their own opinion that the person in question is not a lady. So it had been on the present occasion, but Mrs Lopez had at once gone to her visitor. 'Oh, Mrs Parker, I am so glad to see you. I hope you are well.'

'Indeed, then, Mrs Lopez, I am very far from well. No poor woman, who is the mother of five children, was ever farther from being well than I am.'

'Is anything wrong?'

'Wrong, ma'am! Everything is wrong. When is Mr Lopez going to pay my husband all the money he has took from him?'

'Has he taken money?'

'Taken! he has taken everything. He has shorn my husband as bare as a board. We're ruined, Mrs Lopez, and it's your husband has done it. When we were at Dovercourt, I told you how it was going to be. His business has left him, and now there is nothing. What are we to do?' The woman was seated on a chair, leaning forward with her two hands on her knees. The day was wet, the streets were half mud and half snow, and the poor woman, who had made her way through the slush, was soiled and wet. 'I look to you to tell me what me and my children is to do. He's your husband, Mrs Lopez.'

'Yes, Mrs Parker; he is my husband.'

'Why couldn't he let Sexty alone? Why should the like of him be taking the bread out of my children's mouths? What had we ever done to him? You're rich.'

'Indeed I am not, Mrs Parker.'

'Yes, you are. You're living here in a grand house, and your father's made of money. You'll know nothing of want, let the worst come to the worst. What are we to do, Mrs Lopez? I'm the wife of that poor creature, and you're the wife of the man that has ruined him. What are we to do, Mrs Lopez?'

'I do not understand my husband's business, Mrs Parker.'

'You're one with him, ain't you? If anybody had ever come to me and said my husband had robbed him, I'd never have stopped till I knew the truth of it. If any woman had ever said to me that Parker had taken the bread out of her children's mouths, do you think that I'd sit as you are sitting? I tell you that Lopez has robbed us,—has robbed us, and taken everything.'

'What can I say, Mrs Parker;—what can I do?'

'Where is he?'

'He is not here. He is dining at his club.'

'Where is that? I will go there and shame him before them all. Don't you feel no shame? Because you've got things comfortable here, I suppose it's all nothing to you. You don't care, though my children were starving in the gutter,—as they will do.'

'If you knew me, Mrs Parker, you wouldn't speak to me like that.'

'Know you! Of course I know you. You're a lady, and your father's a rich man, and your husband thinks no end of himself. And we're poor people, so it don't matter whether we're robbed and ruined or not. That's about it.'

'If I had anything, I'd give you all that I had.'

'And he's taken to drinking that hard that he's never rightly sober from morning to night.' As she told this story of her husband's disgrace, the poor woman burst into tears. 'Who's to trust him with business now? He's that broken-hearted that he don't know which way to turn,—only to the bottle. And Lopez has done it all,—done it all! I haven't got a father, ma'am, who has got a house over his head for me and my babies. Only think if you was turned out into the street with your babby, as I am like to be.'

'I have no baby,' said the wretched woman through her tears and sobs.

'Haven't you, Mrs Lopez? Oh dear!' exclaimed the soft-hearted woman, reduced at once to pity. 'How was it then?'

'He died, Mrs Parker,—just a few days after he was born.'

'Did he now? Well, well. We all have our troubles, I suppose.'

'I have mine, I know,' said Emily, 'and very, very heavy they are. I cannot tell you what I have had to suffer.'

'Isn't he good to you?'

'I cannot talk about it, Mrs Parker. What you tell me about yourself has added greatly to my sorrows. My husband is talking of going away,—to live out of England.'

'Yes, at a place they call——I forget what they call it, but I heard it.'

'Guatemala,—in America.'

'I know. Sexty told me. He has no business to go anywhere, while he owes Sexty such a lot of money. He has taken everything, and now he's going to Kattymaly!' At this moment Mr Wharton knocked at the door and entered the room. As he did so Mrs Parker got up and curtseyed.

'This is my father, Mrs Parker,' said Emily. 'Papa, this is Mrs Parker. She is the wife of Mr Parker, who was Ferdinand's partner. She has come here with bad news.'

'Very bad news indeed, sir,' said Mrs Parker, curtsying again. Mr Wharton frowned, not as being angry with the woman, but feeling that some further horror was to be told him of his son-in-law. 'I can't help coming, sir,' continued Mrs Parker. 'Where am I to go if I don't come? Mr Lopez, sir, has ruined us root and branch,—root and branch.'

'That at any rate is not my fault,' said Mr Wharton,

'But she is his wife, sir. Where am I to go if not to where he lives? Am I to put up with everything gone, and my poor husband in the right way to go to Bedlam, and not to say a word about it to the grand relations of him who did it all?'

'He is a bad man,' said Mr Wharton. 'I cannot make him otherwise.'

'Will he do nothing for us?'

'I will tell you all I know about him.' Then Mr Wharton did tell her all that he knew, as to the appointment at Guatemala and the amount of salary which was to be attached to it. 'Whether he will do anything for you, I cannot say;—I should think not, unless he be forced. I should advise you to go to the offices of the Company in Coleman Street and try to make some terms there. But I fear,—I fear it will all be useless.'

'Then we may starve.'

'It is not her fault,' said Mr Wharton, pointing to his daughter. 'She has had no hand in it. She knows less of it all than you do.'

'It is my fault,' said Emily, bursting out into self-reproach,—'my fault that I married him.'

'Whether married or single he would have preyed upon Mr Parker to the same extent.'

'Like enough,' said the poor wife. 'He'd prey upon anybody as he could get hold of. And so, Mr Wharton, you think that you can do nothing for me.'

'If your want be immediate I can relieve it,' said the barrister. Mrs Parker did not like the idea of accepting direct charity, but, nevertheless, on going away did take the five sovereigns which Mr Wharton offered to her.

After such an interview as that the dinner between the father and the daughter was not very happy. She was eaten up by remorse. Gradually she had learned how frightful was the thing she had done in giving herself to a man of whom she had known nothing. And it was not only that she had degraded herself by loving such a man, but that she had been persistent in clinging to him though her father and all his friends had told her of the danger which she was running. And now it seemed that she had destroyed her father as well as herself! All that she could do was to be persistent in her prayer that he would let her go. 'I have done it,' she said that night, 'and I could bear it better, if you would let me bear it alone.' But he only kissed her, and sobbed over her, and held her close to his heart with his clinging arms,—in a manner in which he had never held her in their old happy days.

He took himself to his own rooms before Lopez returned, but she of course had to bear her husband's presence. As she had declared to her father more than once, she was not afraid of him. Even though he should strike her,—though he should kill her,—she would not be afraid of him. He had already done worse to her than anything that could follow. 'Mrs Parker has been here to-day,' she said to him that night.

'And what had Mrs Parker to say?'

'That you had ruined her husband.'

'Exactly. When a man speculates and doesn't win of course he throws the blame on some one else. And when he is too much of a cur to come himself, he sends his wife.'

'She says you owe him money.'

'What business have you to listen to what she says? If she comes again, do not see her. Do you understand me?'

'Yes, I understand. She saw papa also. If you owe him money, should it not be paid?'

'My dearest love, everybody who owes anything to anybody should always pay it. That is so self-evident that one would almost suppose that it might be understood without being enunciated. But the virtue of paying debts is incompatible with an absence of money. Now, if you please, we will not say anything more about Mrs Parker. She is not at any rate a fit companion for you.'

'It was you who introduced me to her.'

'Hold your tongue about her,—and let that be an end of it. I little knew what a world of torment I was preparing for myself when I allowed you to come and live in your father's house.'

CHAPTER 56

WHAT THE DUCHESS THOUGHT OF HER HUSBAND

WHEN the Session began it was understood in the political world that a very strong opposition was to be organized against the Government under the guidance of Sir Orlando Drought, and that the great sin to be imputed to the Cabinet was an utter indifference to the safety and honour of Great Britain, as manifested by their neglect of the navy. All the world knew that Sir Orlando had deserted the Coalition because he was not allowed to build new ships, and of course Sir Orlando would make the most of his grievance. With him was joined Mr Boffin, the patriotic Conservative who had never listened to the voice of the seducer, and the staunch remainder of the old Tory party. And with them the more violent of the Radicals were prepared to act, not desirous, indeed, that new ships should be built, or that a Conservative Government should be established,—or, indeed, that anything should be done,—but animated by intense disgust that so mild a politician as the Duke of Omnium should be Prime Minister. The fight began at once, Sir Orlando objecting violently to certain passages in the Queen's Speech. It was all very well to say that the country was at present at peace with all the world; but how was peace to be maintained without a fleet? Then Sir Orlando paid a great many compliments to the Duke, and ended his speech by declaring him to be the most absolutely *fainéant* minister that had disgraced the country since the days of the Duke of Newcastle.* Mr Monk defended the Coalition, and assured the House that the navy was not only the most powerful navy existing, but that it was the most powerful that ever had existed in the possession of this or any other country, and was probably in absolute efficiency superior to the combined navies of all the world. The House was not shocked by statements so absolutely at variance with each other, coming from two gentlemen who had lately been members of the same Government, and who must be supposed to know what they were talking about, but seemed to think that upon the whole Sir Orlando had done his duty. For though there was complete confidence in the navy as a navy, and though a very small minority would have voted for any considerably increased expense, still it was well that there should be an opposition. And how can there be an opposition without some subject for grumbling,—some matter on which a minister may be attacked? No one really thought that the Prussians and French combined would invade our shores and devastate our fields, and plunder London, and carry our daughters away into captivity. The state of the funds showed very plainly that there was no such fear. But a good cry is a very good thing,—and it is always well to rub up the officials of the Admiralty by a little wholesome abuse. Sir Orlando was thought to have done his business well. Of course he did not risk a division upon the address. Had he done so he would have been 'nowhere.' But, as it was, he was proud of his achievement.

The ministers generally would have been indifferent to the very hard words that were said of them, knowing what they were worth, and feeling aware that a ministry which had everything too easy must lose its interest in the country, had it not been that their chief was very sore on the subject. The old Duke's work at this time consisted almost altogether in nursing the younger Duke. It did sometimes occur to his elder Grace that it might be well to let his brother retire, and that a Prime Minister, *malgré lui*,* could not be a successful Prime Minister, or a useful one. But if the Duke of Omnium went the Coalition must go too, and the Coalition had been the offspring of the old statesman. The country was thriving under the Coalition, and there was no real reason why it should not last for the next ten years. He continued, therefore, his system of coddling, and was ready at any moment, or at every moment, to pour, if not comfort, at any rate consolation into the ears of his unhappy friend. In the present emergency, it was the falsehood and general baseness of Sir Orlando which nearly broke the heart of the Prime Minister. 'How is one to live,' he said, 'if one has to do with men of that kind?'

'But you haven't to do with him any longer,' said the Duke of St Bungay.

'When I see a man who is supposed to have earned the name of a statesman, and been high in the councils of his sovereign, induced by personal jealousy to do as he is doing, it makes me feel that an honest man should not place himself where he may have to deal with such persons.'

'According to that the honest men are to desert their country in order that the dishonest men may have everything their own way.' Our Duke could not answer this, and therefore for the moment he yielded. But he was unhappy, saturnine, and generally silent except when closeted with his ancient mentor. And he knew that he was saturnine and silent, and that it behoved him as a leader of men to be genial and communicative,—listening to counsel even if he did not follow it, and at any rate appearing to have confidence in his colleagues.

During this time Mr Slide was not inactive, and in his heart of hearts the Prime Minister was more afraid of Mr Slide's attacks than of those made upon him by Sir Orlando Drought. Now that Parliament was sitting, and the minds of men were stirred to political feeling by the renewed energy of the House, a great deal was being said in many quarters about the last Silverbridge election. The papers had taken the matter up generally, some accusing the Prime Minister and some defending. But the defence was almost as unpalatable to him as the accusation. It was admitted on all sides that the Duke, both as a peer and as a Prime Minister, should have abstained from any interference whatever in the election. And it was also admitted on all sides that he had not so abstained;—if there was any truth at all in the allegation that he had paid money for Mr Lopez. But it was pleaded on his behalf that the Dukes of Omnium had always interfered at Silverbridge, and that no Reform Bill had ever had any effect in reducing their influence in that borough. Frequent allusion was made to the cautious Dod* who, year after year, had reported that the Duke of Omnium exercised considerable influence in the borough. And then the friendly newspapers went on to explain that the Duke had in this instance stayed his hand, and that the money, if paid at all, had been paid because the candidate who was to have been his nominee had been thrown over, when the Duke at the last moment made up his mind that he would abandon the privilege which had hitherto been always exercised by the head of his family, and which had been exercised more than once or twice in his own favour. But Mr Slide, day after day, repeated his question, 'We want to know whether the Prime Minister did or did not pay the election expenses of Mr Lopez at the last Silverbridge election; and if so, why he paid them. We shall continue to ask this question till it has been answered, and when asking it we again say that the actual correspondence on the subject between the Duke and Mr Lopez is in our own hands.' And then, after a while, allusions were made to the Duchess;—for Mr Slide had learned all the facts of the case from Lopez himself. When Mr Slide found how hard it was 'to draw his badger,' as he expressed himself concerning his own oper-ations, he at last openly alluded to the Duchess, running the risk of any punishment that might fall upon him by action for libel or by severe reprehension from his colleagues of the Press. 'We have as yet,' he said, 'received no answers to the questions which we have felt our-selves called upon to ask in reference to the conduct of the Prime Minister at the Silverbridge election. We are of opinion that all inter-ference by peers with the constituencies of the country should be put down by the strong hand of the law as thoroughly and unmercifully as we are putting down ordinary bribery. But when the offending peer is also the Prime Minister of this great country, it becomes doubly the duty of those who watch over the public safety,'—Mr Slide was always speaking of himself as watching over the public safety,—'to animad-vert upon his crime till it has been assoiled, or at any rate repented. From what we now hear we have reason to believe that the crime itself is acknowledged. Had the payment on behalf of Mr Lopez not been made,—as it certainly was made, or the letters in our hand would be impudent forgeries,—the charge would long since have been denied. Silence in such a matter amounts to confession. But we understand that the Duke intends to escape under the plea that he has a second self, powerful as he is to exercise the baneful influence which his territorial wealth unfortunately gives him, but for the actions of which second self he, as a Peer of Parliament and as Prime Minister, is not responsible. In other words we are informed that the privilege belonging to the Palliser family at Silverbridge was exercised, not by the Duke himself, but by the Duchess;—and that the Duke paid the money when he found that the Duchess had promised more than she could perform. We should hardly have thought that even a man so notoriously weak as the Duke of Omnium would have endeavoured to ride out of responsibility by throwing the blame upon his wife; but he will certainly find that the attempt, if made, will fail.

'Against the Duchess herself we wish to say not a word. She is known as exercising a wide if not a discriminate hospitality. We believe her to be a kind-hearted, bustling, ambitious lady, to whom any little faults may be easily forgiven on account of her good-nature and generosity. But we cannot accept her indiscretion as an excuse for a most unconsti-tutional act performed by the Prime Minister of this country.'

Latterly the Duchess had taken in her own copy of the 'People's Banner.' Since she had found that those around her were endeavouring to keep from her what was being said of her husband in regard to the borough, she had been determined to see it all. She therefore read the

article from which two or three paragraphs have just been given,—and
having read it she handed it to her friend Mrs Finn. 'I wonder that you
trouble yourself with such trash,' her friend said to her.

'That is all very well, my dear, from you; but we poor wretches who
are the slaves of the people have to regard what is said of us in the
"People's Banner."'

'It would be much better for you to neglect it.'

'Just as authors are told not to read the criticisms;—but I never
would believe any author who told me that he didn't read what was said
about him. I wonder when the man found out that I was good-natured.
He wouldn't find me good-natured if I could get hold of him.'

'You are not going to allow it to torment you!'

'For my own sake, not a moment. I fancy that if I might be permitted
to have my own way I could answer him very easily. Indeed with these
dregs of the newspapers, these gutter-slanderers, if one would be open
and say all the truth aloud, what would one have to fear? After all, what
is it that I did? I disobeyed my husband because I thought that he was
too scrupulous. Let me say as much, out loud to the public,—saying
also that I am sorry for it, as I am,—and who would be against me?
Who would have a word to say after that? I should be the most popular
woman in England for a month,—and, as regards Plantagenet,
Mr Slide and his articles would all sink into silence. But even though
he were to continue this from day to day for a twelvemonth it would
not hurt me,—but that I know how it scorches him. This mention of
my name will make it more intolerable to him than ever. I doubt that
you know him even yet.'

'I thought that I did.'

'Though in manner he is as dry as a stick, though all his pursuits are
opposite to the very idea of romance, though he passes his days and
nights thinking how he may take a halfpenny in the pound off the taxes
of the people without robbing the revenue, there is a dash of chivalry
about him worthy of the old poets. To him a woman, particularly his
own woman, is a thing so fine and so precious that the winds of heaven
should hardly be allowed to blow upon her.* He cannot bear to think
that people should even talk of his wife. And yet, Heaven knows, poor
fellow, I have given people occasion enough to talk of me. And he has a
much higher chivalry than that of the old poets. They, or their heroes,
watched their women because they did not want to have trouble about
them,—shut them up in castles, kept them in ignorance, and held them
as far as they could out of harm's way.'

'I hardly think they succeeded,' said Mrs Finn.

'But in pure selfishness they tried all they could. But he is too proud to watch. If you and I were hatching treason against him in the dark, and chance had brought him there, he would stop his ears with his fingers. He is all trust, even when he knows that he is being deceived. He is honour complete from head to foot. Ah, it was before you knew me when I tried him the hardest. I never could quite tell you that story, and I won't try it now; but he behaved like a god. I could never tell him what I felt,—but I felt it.'

'You ought to love him.'

'I do;—but what's the use of it? He is a god, but I am not a goddess;— and then, though he is a god, he is a dry, silent, uncongenial and uncomfortable god. It would have suited me much better to have married a sinner. But then the sinner that I would have married was so irredeemable a scapegrace.'

'I do not believe in a woman marrying a bad man in the hope of making him good.'

'Especially not when the woman is naturally inclined to evil herself. It will half kill him when he reads all this about me. He has read it already, and it has already half killed him. For myself I do not mind it in the least, but for his sake I mind it much. It will rob him of his only possible answer to the accusation. The very thing which this wretch in the newspaper says he will say, and that he will be disgraced by saying, is the very thing that he ought to say. And there would be no disgrace in it,—beyond what I might well bear for my little fault, and which I could bear so easily.'

'Shall you speak to him about it?'

'No; I dare not. In this matter it has gone beyond speaking. I suppose he does talk it over with the old Duke; but he will say nothing to me about it,—unless he were to tell me that he had resigned, and that we were to start off and live in Minorca for the next ten years. I was so proud when they made him Prime Minister; but I think that I am beginning to regret it now.' Then there was a pause, and the Duchess went on with her newspapers; but she soon resumed her discourse. Her heart was full, and out of a full heart the mouth speaks.* 'They should have made me Prime Minister, and have let him be Chancellor of the Exchequer. I begin to see the ways of Government now. I could have done all the dirty work. I could have given away garters and ribbons, and made my bargains while giving them. I could select sleek, easy bishops who wouldn't be troublesome. I could give pensions or withhold them, and make the stupid men peers. I could have the big noblemen at my feet, praying to be Lieutenants of Counties.

I could dole out secretaryships and lordships, and never a one without getting something in return. I could brazen out a job and let the "People's Banner" and the Slides make their worst of it. And I think I could make myself popular with my party, and do the high-flowing patriotic talk for the benefit of the Provinces. A man at a regular office has to work. That's what Plantagenet is fit for. He wants always to be doing something that shall be really useful, and a man has to toil at that and really to know things. But a Prime Minister should never go beyond generalities about commerce, agriculture, peace, and general philanthropy. Of course he should have the gift of the gab, and that Plantagenet hasn't got. He never wants to say anything unless he has got something to say. I could do a Mansion House dinner* to a marvel!'

'I don't doubt that you could speak at all times, Lady Glen.'

'Oh, I do so wish that I had the opportunity,' said the Duchess.

Of course the Duke had read the article in the privacy of his own room, and of course the article had nearly maddened him with anger and grief. As the Duchess had said, the article had taken from him the very ground on which his friends had told him that he could stand. He had never consented, and never would consent, to lay the blame publicly on his wife; but he had begun to think that he must take notice of the charge made against him, and depute some one to explain for him in the House of Commons that the injury had been done at Silverbridge by the indiscretion of an agent who had not fulfilled his employer's intentions, and that the Duke had thought it right afterwards to pay the money in consequence of this indiscretion. He had not agreed to this, but had brought himself to think that he must agree to it. But now, of course, the question would follow:—Who was the indiscreet agent? Was the Duchess the person for whose indiscretion he had had to pay £500 to Mr Lopez? And in this matter did he not find himself in accord even with Mr Slide? 'We should hardly have thought that even a man so notoriously weak as the Duke of Omnium would have endeavoured to ride out of responsibility by throwing the blame upon his wife.' He read and reread these words till he knew them by heart. For a few moments it seemed to him to be an evil in the Constitution that the Prime Minister should not have the power of instantly crucifying so foul a slanderer;—and yet it was the very truth of the words that crushed him. He was weak,—he told himself;—notoriously weak, it must be; and it would be most mean in him to ride out of responsibility by throwing blame upon his wife. But what else was he to do? There seemed to him to be but one course,—to get up in the House of Lords and declare that he paid the money because he had thought it right to do so under circumstances which he could not explain, and to declare that it was not his intention to say another word on the subject, or to have another word said on his behalf.

There was a Cabinet Council held that day, but no one ventured to speak to the Prime Minister as to the accusation. Though he considered himself to be weak, his colleagues were all more or less afraid of him. There was a certain silent dignity about the man which saved him from the evils, as it also debarred him from the advantages, of familiarity. He had spoken on the subject to Mr Monk and to Phineas Finn, and, as the reader knows, very often to his old mentor. He had also mentioned it to his friend Lord Cantrip, who was not in the Cabinet. Coming away from the Cabinet he took Mr Monk's arm, and led him away to his own room in the Treasury Chambers. 'Have you happened to see an article in the "People's Banner" this morning?' he asked.

'I never see the "People's Banner,"' said Mr Monk.

'There it is;—just look at that.' Whereupon Mr Monk read the article. 'You understand what people call constitutional practice as well as any one I know. As I told you before, I did pay that man's expenses. Did I do anything unconstitutional?'

'That would depend, Duke, on the circumstances. If you were to back a man up by your wealth in an expensive contest, I think it would be unconstitutional. If you set yourself to work in that way, and cared not what you spent, you might materially influence the elections, and buy parliamentary support for yourself.'

'But in this case the payment was made after the man had failed, and certainly had not been promised either by me or by any one on my behalf.'

'I think it was unfortunate,' said Mr Monk.

'Certainly, certainly; but I am not asking as to that,' said the Duke impatiently. 'The man had been injured by indiscreet persons acting on my behalf and in opposition to my wishes.' He said not a word about the Duchess; but Mr Monk no doubt knew that her Grace had been at any rate one of the indiscreet persons. 'He applied to me for the money, alleging that he had been injured by my agents. That being so,— presuming that my story be correct,—did I act unconstitutionally?'

'I think not,' said Mr Monk, 'and I think that the circumstances, when explained, will bear you harmless.'

'Thank you; thank you. I did not want to trouble you about that just at present.'

CHAPTER 57

THE EXPLANATION

MR MONK had been altogether unable to decipher the Duke's purpose in the question he had asked. About an hour afterwards they walked down to the Houses together, Mr Monk having been kept at his office. 'I hope I was not a little short with you just now,' said the Duke.

'I did not find it out,' said Mr Monk smiling.

'You read what was in the papers, and you may imagine that it is of a nature to irritate a man. I knew that no one could answer my question so correctly as you, and therefore I was a little eager to keep directly to the question. It occurred to me afterwards that I had been—perhaps uncourteous.'

'Not at all, Duke.'

'If I was, your goodness will excuse an irritated man. If a question were asked about this in the House of Commons who would be the best man to answer it? Would you do it?'

Mr Monk considered awhile. 'I think,' he said, 'that Mr Finn would do it with a better grace. Of course I will do it if you wish it. But he has tact in such matters, and it is known that his wife is much regarded by her Grace.'

'I will not have the Duchess's name mentioned,' said the Duke, turning short upon his companion.

'I did not allude to that, but I thought that the intimacy which existed might make it pleasant to you to employ Mr Finn as the exponent of your wishes.'

'I have the greatest confidence in Mr Finn, certainly, and am on most friendly personal terms with him. It shall be so, if I decide on answering any question in your House on a matter so purely personal to myself.'

'I would suggest that you should have the question asked in a friendly way. Get some independent member, such as Mr Beverley or Sir James Deering, to ask it. The matter would then be brought forward in no carping spirit, and you would be enabled, through Mr Finn, to set the matter at rest. You have probably spoken to the Duke about it.'

'I have mentioned it to him.'

'Is not that what he would recommend?'

The old Duke had recommended that the entire truth should be told, and that the Duchess's operations should be made public. Here was our poor Prime Minister's great difficulty. He and his Mentor were at variance. His Mentor was advising that the real naked truth should be told, whereas Telemachus* was intent upon keeping the name of the actual culprit in the background. 'I will think it all over,' said the Prime Minister as the two parted company at Palace Yard.

That evening he spoke to Lord Cantrip on the subject. Though the matter was so odious to him, he could not keep his mind from it for a moment. Had Lord Cantrip seen the article in the 'People's Banner?' Lord Cantrip, like Mr Monk, declared that the paper in question did not constitute part of his usual morning's recreation. 'I won't ask you to read it,' said the Duke;—'but it contains a very bitter attack upon me,—the bitterest that has yet been made. I suppose I ought to notice the matter?'

'If I were you,' said Lord Cantrip, 'I should put myself into the hands of the Duke of St Bungay, and do exactly what he advises. There is no man in England knows so well as he does what should be done in such a case as this.' The Prime Minister frowned and said nothing. 'My dear Duke,' continued Lord Cantrip, 'I can give you no other advice. Who is there that has your personal interest and your honour at heart so entirely as his Grace;—and what man can be a more sagacious or more experienced adviser?'

'I was thinking that you might ask a question about it in our House.'

'I?'

'You would do it for me in a manner that—that would be free from all offence.'

'If I did it at all, I should certainly strive to do that. But it has never occurred to me that you would make such a suggestion. Would you give me a few moment to think about it?' 'I couldn't do it,' Lord Cantrip said afterwards. 'By taking such a step, even at your request, I should certainly express the opinion that the matter was one which Parliament was entitled to expect that you should make an explanation. But my own opinion is that Parliament has no business to meddle in the matter. I do not think that every action of a minister's life should be made matter of inquiry because a newspaper may choose to make allusions to it. At any rate, if any word is said about it, it should, I think, be said in the other House.'

'The Duke of St Bungay thinks that something should be said.'

'I could not myself consent even to appear to desire information on a matter so entirely personal to yourself.' The Duke bowed, and smiled with a cold, glittering, uncomfortable smile which would sometimes cross his face when he was not pleased, and no more was then said on the subject.

Attempts were made to have the question asked in a far different spirit by some hostile member of the House of Commons. Sir Orlando Drought was sounded, and he for a while did give ear to the suggestion. But, as he came to have the matter full before him, he could not do it. The Duke had spurned his advice as a minister, and had refused to sanction a measure which he, as the head of a branch of the Government, had proposed. The Duke had so offended him that he conceived himself bound to regard the Duke as his enemy. But he knew,—and he could not escape from the knowledge,—that England did not contain a more honourable man than the Duke. He was delighted that the Duke should be vexed, and thwarted, and called ill names in the matter. To be gratified at this discomfiture of his enemy was in the nature of parliamentary opposition. Any blow that might weaken his opponent was a blow in his favour. But this was a blow which he could not strike with his own hands. There were things in parliamentary tactics which even Sir Orlando could not do. Arthur Fletcher was also asked to undertake the task. He was the successful candidate, the man who had opposed Lopez, and who was declared by the 'People's Banner' to have emancipated that borough by his noble conduct from the tyranny of the House of Palliser. And it was thought that he might like an opportunity of making himself known in the House. But he was simply indignant when the suggestion was made to him. 'What is it to me,' he said, 'who paid the blackguard's expenses?'

This went on for some weeks after Parliament had met, and for some days even after the article in which direct allusion was made to the Duchess. The Prime Minister could not be got to consent that no notice should be taken of the matter, let the papers or the public say what they would, nor could he be induced to let the matter be handled in the manner proposed by the elder Duke. And during this time he was in such a fever that those about him felt that something must be done. Mr Monk suggested that if everybody held his tongue,—meaning all the Duke's friends,—the thing would wear itself out. But it was apparent to those who were nearest to the minister, to Mr Warburton, for instance, and the Duke of St Bungay, that the man himself would be worn out first. The happy possessor of a thick skin can hardly understand how one not so blessed may be hurt by the thong of a little whip! At last the matter was arranged. At the instigation of Mr Monk, Sir James Deering, who was really the father of the House,* an independent member, but one who generally voted with the Coalition, consented to ask the question in the House of Commons. And Phineas Finn was instructed by the Duke as to the answer that was to be given.

The Duke of Omnium in giving these instructions made a mystery of the matter which he by no means himself intended. But he was so sore that he could not be simple in what he said. 'Mr Finn,' he said, 'you must promise me this,—that the name of the Duchess shall not be mentioned.'

'Certainly not by me, if you tell me that I am not to mention it.'

'No one else can do so. The matter will take the form of a simple question, and though the conduct of a minister may no doubt be made the subject of debate,—and it is not improbable that my conduct may do so in this instance,—it is, I think, impossible that any member should make an allusion to my wife. The privilege or power of returning a member for the borough has undoubtedly been exercised by our family since as well as previous to both the Reform Bills. At the last election I thought it right to abandon that privilege, and notified to those about me my intention. But that which a man has the power of doing he cannot always do without the interference of those around him. There was a misconception, and among my,—my adherents,— there were some who injudiciously advised Mr Lopez to stand on my interest. But he did not get my interest, and was beaten;—and therefore when he asked me for the money which he had spent, I paid it to him. That is all. I think the House can hardly avoid to see that my effort was made to discontinue an unconstitutional proceeding.'

Sir James Deering asked the question. 'He trusted,' he said, 'that the House would not think that the question of which he had given notice and which he was about to ask was instigated by any personal desire on his part to inquire into the conduct of the Prime Minister. He was one who believed that the Duke of Omnium was as little likely as any man in England to offend by unconstitutional practice on his own part. But a great deal had been talked and written lately about the late election at Silverbridge, and there were those who thought,—and he was one of them,—that something should be said to stop the mouths of cavillers. With this object he would ask the Right Honourable Gentleman who led the House, and who was perhaps first in standing among the noble Duke's colleagues in that House, whether the noble Duke was prepared to have any statement on the subject made.'

The House was full to the very corners of the galleries. Of course it was known to everybody that the question was to be asked and to be answered. There were some who thought that the matter was so serious that the Prime Minister could not get over it. Others had heard in the clubs that Lady Glen, as the Duchess was still called, was to be made the scapegoat. Men of all classes were open-mouthed in their denunciation of the meanness of Lopez,—though no one but Mr Wharton knew half his villainy, as he alone knew that the expenses had been paid twice over. In one corner of the reporters' gallery sat Mr Slide, pencil in hand, prepared to revert to his old work on so momentous an occasion. It was a great day for him. He by his own unassisted energy had brought a Prime Minister to book, and had created all this turmoil. It might be his happy lot to be the means of turning that Prime Minister out of office. It was he who had watched over the nation! The Duchess had been most anxious to be present,—but had not ventured to come without asking her husband's leave, which he had most peremptorily refused to give. 'I cannot understand, Glencora, how you can suggest such a thing,' he had said.

'You make so much of everything,' she had replied petulantly; but she had remained at home. The ladies' gallery was, however, quite full. Mrs Finn was there, of course, anxious not only for her friend, but eager to hear how her husband would acquit himself in his task. The wives and daughters of all the ministers were there,—excepting the wife of the Prime Minister. There never had been, in the memory of them all, a matter that was so interesting to them, for it was the only matter they remembered in which a woman's conduct might probably be called in question in the House of Commons. And the seats appropriated to peers were so crammed that above a dozen grey-headed old lords were standing in the passage which divides them from the common strangers. After all it was not, in truth, much of an affair. A very little man indeed had calumniated the conduct of a minister of the Crown, till it had been thought well that the minister should defend himself. No one really believed that the Duke had committed any great offence. At the worst it was no more than indiscretion, which was noticeable only because a Prime Minister should never be indiscreet. Had the taxation of the whole country for the next year been in dispute there would have been no such interest felt. Had the welfare of the Indian Empire occupied the House, the House would have been empty. But the hope that a certain woman's name would have to be mentioned, crammed it from the floor to the ceiling.

The reader need not be told that that name was not mentioned. Our old friend Phineas, on rising to his legs, first apologized for doing so in place of the Chancellor of the Exchequer. But perhaps the House would accept a statement from him, as the noble Duke at the head of the Government had asked him to make it. Then he made his statement. 'Perhaps,' he said, 'no falser accusation than this had ever been brought forward against a minister of the Crown, for it specially

charged his noble friend with resorting to the employment of unconstitutional practices to bolster up his parliamentary support, whereas
it was known by everybody that there would have been no matter for
accusation at all had not the Duke of his own motion abandoned a
recognized privilege, because in his opinion, the exercise of that privilege was opposed to the spirit of the Constitution. Had the noble
Duke simply nominated a candidate, as candidates had been nominated at Silverbridge for centuries past, that candidate would have been
returned with absolute certainty, and there would have been no word
spoken on the subject. It was not, perhaps, for him, who had the
honour of serving under his Grace, and who, as being a part of his
Grace's Government, was for the time one with his Grace, to expati-
ate at length on the nobility of the sacrifice here made. But they all
knew there at what rate was valued a seat in that House. Thank God
that privilege could not now be rated at any money price. It could not
be bought and sold. But this privilege which his noble friend had so
magnanimously resigned from purely patriotic motives, was, he
believed, still in existence, and he would ask those few who were still
in the happy, or perhaps, he had better say in the envied, position of
being able to send their friends to that House, what was their estimation of the conduct of the Duke in this matter? It might be that there
were one or two such present, and who now heard him,—or, perhaps,
one or two who owed their seats to the exercise of such a privilege.
They might marvel at the magnitude of the surrender. They might
even question the sagacity of the man who could abandon so much
without a price. But he hardly thought that even they would regard it
as unconstitutional.

'This was what the Prime Minister had done,—acting not as Prime
Minister, but as an English nobleman, in the management of his own
property and privileges. And now he would come to the gist of the
accusation made; in making which, the thing which the Duke had really
done had been altogether ignored. When the vacancy had been declared
by the acceptance of the Chiltern Hundreds by a gentleman whose
absence from the House they all regretted, the Duke had signified to
his agents his intention of retiring altogether from the exercise of any
privilege or power in the matter. But the Duke was then, as he was also
now, and would, it was to be hoped, long continue to be, Prime Minister
of England. He need hardly remind gentlemen in that House that the
Prime Minister was not in a position to devote his undivided time to
the management of his own property, or even to the interests of the
Borough of Silverbridge. That his Grace had been earnest in his

instructions to his agents, the sequel fully proved; but that earnestness his agents had misinterpreted.'

Then there was heard a voice in the House, 'What agents?' and from another voice, 'Name them.' For there were present some who thought it to be shameful that the excitement of the occasion should be lowered by keeping back all allusion to the Duchess.

'I have not distinguished,' said Phineas, assuming an indignant tone, 'the honourable gentlemen from whom those questions have come, and therefore I have the less compunction in telling them that it is no part of my duty on this occasion to gratify a morbid and an indecent curiosity.' Then there was a cry of 'Order,' and an appeal to the Speaker. Certain gentlemen wished to know whether indecent was parliamentary. The Speaker, with some hesitation, expressed his opinion that the word, as then used, was not open to objection from him. He thought that it was within the scope of a member's rights to charge another member with indecent curiosity. 'If,' said Phineas, rising again to his legs, for he had sat down for a moment, 'the gentleman who called for a name will rise in his place and repeat the demand, I will recall the word indecent and substitute another,—or others. I will tell him that he is one who, regardless of the real conduct of the Prime Minister, either as a man or as a servant of the Crown, is only anxious to inflict an unmanly wound in order that he may be gratified by seeing the pain he inflicts.' Then he paused, but as no further question was asked, he continued his statement. 'A candidate had been brought forward,' he said, 'by those interested in the Duke's affairs. A man whom he would not name, but who he trusted would never succeed in his ambition to occupy a seat in that House, had been brought forward, and certain tradesmen in Silverbridge had been asked to support him as the Duke's nominee. There was no doubt about it. The House perhaps could understand that the local adherents and neighbours of a man so high in rank and wealth as the Duke of Omnium would not gladly see the privileges of their lord diminished. Perhaps, too, it occurred to them that a Prime Minister could not have his eye everywhere. There would always be worthy men in boroughs who liked to exercise some second-hand authority. At any rate it was the case that this candidate was encouraged. Then the Duke had heard it, and had put his foot upon the little mutiny, and had stamped it out at once. He might perhaps here,' he said, 'congratulate the House on the acquisition it had received by the failure of that candidate. So far, at any rate,' he thought, 'it must be admitted that the Duke had been free from blame;—but now he came to the gravamen of the charge.' The gravamen of the charge is so well known to the reader that the simple account which Phineas gave of it need not be repeated. The Duke had paid the money, when asked for it, because he felt that the man had been injured by incorrect misrepresentations made to him. 'I need hardly pause to stigmatize the meanness of that application,' said Phineas, 'but I may perhaps conclude by saying that whether the last act done by the Duke in this matter was or was not indiscreet, I shall probably have the House with me when I say that it savours much more strongly of nobility than of indiscretion.'

When Phineas Finn sat down no one arose to say another word on the subject. It was afterwards felt that it would only have been graceful had Sir Orlando risen and expressed his opinion that the House had heard the statement just made with perfect satisfaction. But he did not do so, and after a short pause the ordinary business of the day was recommenced. Then there was a speedy descent from the galleries, and the ladies trooped out of their cage, and the grey-headed old peers went back to their own chamber, and the members themselves quickly jostled out through the doors, and Mr Monk was left to explain his proposed alteration in the dog tax to a thin House of seventy or eighty members.

The thing was then over, and people were astonished that so great a thing should be over with so little fuss. It really seemed that after Phineas Finn's speech there was nothing more to be said on the matter. Everybody of course knew that the Duchess had been the chief of the agents to whom he had alluded, but they had known as much as that before. It was, however, felt by everybody that the matter had been brought to an end. The game, such as it was, had been played out. Perhaps the only person who heard Mr Finn's speech throughout, and still hoped that the spark could be again fanned into a flame, was Quintus Slide. He went out and wrote another article about the Duchess. If a man was so unable to rule his affairs at home, he was certainly unfit to be Prime Minister. But even Quintus Slide, as he wrote his article, felt that he was hoping against hope. The charge might be referred to hereafter as one that had never been satisfactorily cleared up. That game is always open to the opponents of a minister. After the lapse of a few months an old accusation can be serviceably used, whether at the time it was proved or disproved. Mr Slide published his article; but he felt that for the present the Silverbridge election papers had better be put by among the properties of the 'People's Banner,' and brought out, if necessary, for further use at some future time.

'Mr Finn,' said the Duke, 'I feel indebted to you for the trouble you have taken.'

'It was only a pleasant duty.'

'I am grateful to you for the manner in which it was performed.' This was all the Duke said, and Phineas felt it to be cold. The Duke, in truth, was grateful; but gratitude with him always failed to exhibit itself readily. From the world at large Phineas Finn received great praise for the manner in which he had performed his task.

CHAPTER 58

'QUITE SETTLED'

THE abuse which was now publicly heaped on the name of Ferdinand Lopez hit the man very hard; but not so hard perhaps as his rejection by Lady Eustace. That was an episode in his life of which even he felt ashamed, and of which he was unable to shake the disgrace from his memory. He had no inner appreciation whatsoever of what was really good or what was really bad in a man's conduct. He did not know that he had done evil in applying to the Duke for the money. He had only meant to attack the Duke; and when the money had come it had been regarded as justifiable prey. And when after receiving the Duke's money, he had kept also Mr Wharton's money, he had justified himself again by reminding himself that Mr Wharton certainly owed him much more than that. In a sense he was what is called a gentleman. He knew how to speak, and how to look, how to use a knife and fork, how to dress himself, and how to walk. But he had not the faintest notion of the feelings of a gentleman. He had, however, a very keen conception of the evil of being generally ill spoken of. Even now, though he was making up his mind to leave England for a long term of years, he understood the disadvantage of leaving it under so heavy a cloud;—and he understood also that the cloud might possibly impede his going altogether. Even in Coleman Street they were looking black upon him, and Mr Hartlepod went so far as to say to Lopez himself, that, 'by Jove, he had put his foot in it.' He had endeavoured to be courageous under his burden, and every day walked into the offices of the Mining Company, endeavouring to look as though he had committed no fault of which he had to be ashamed. But after the second day he found that nothing was said to him of the affairs of the Company, and on the fourth day Mr Hartlepod informed him that the time allowed for paying up his shares had passed by, and that another local manager would be appointed. 'The time is not over till to-morrow,' said Lopez angrily. 'I tell you what I am told to tell you,' said Mr Hartlepod. 'You will only waste your time by coming here any more.'

He had not once seen Mr Wharton since the statement made in Parliament, although he had lived in the same house with him. Everett Wharton had come home, and they two had met;—but the meeting had been stormy. 'It seems to me, Lopez, that you are a scoundrel,' Everett said to him one day after having heard the whole story,—or rather many stories,—from his father. This took place not in Manchester Square, but at the club, where Everett had endeavoured to cut his brother-in-law. It need hardly be said that at this time Lopez was not popular at his club. On the next day a meeting of the whole club was to be held that the propriety of expelling him might be discussed. But he had resolved that he would not be cowed, that he would still show himself, and still defend his conduct. He did not know, however, that Everett Wharton had already made known to the Committee of the club all the facts of the double payment.

He had addressed Everett in that solicitude to which a man should never be reduced of seeking to be recognized by at any rate one acquaintance,—and now his brother-in-law had called him a scoundrel in the presence of other men. He raised his arm as though to use the cane in his hands, but he was cowed by the feeling that all there were his adversaries. 'How dare you use that language to me!' he said very weakly.

'It is the language that I must use if you speak to me.'

'I am your brother-in-law, and that restrains me.'

'Unfortunately you are.'

'And am living in your father's house.'

'That, again, is a misfortune which it appears difficult to remedy. You have been told to go, and you won't go.'

'Your ingratitude, sir, is marvellous! Who saved your life when you were attacked in the park, and were too drunk to take care of yourself? Who has stood your friend with your close-fisted old father when you have lost money at play that you could not pay? But you are one of those who would turn away from any benefactor in his misfortune.'

'I must certainly turn away from a man who has disgraced himself as you have done,' said Everett, leaving the room. Lopez threw himself into an easy-chair, and rang the bell loudly for a cup of coffee, and lit a cigar. He had not been turned out of the club as yet, and the servant at any rate was bound to attend to him.

That night he waited up for his father-in-law in Manchester Square. He would certainly go to Guatemala now,—if it were not too late. He would go though he were forced to leave his wife behind him, and thus surrender any further hope for money from Mr Wharton beyond the sum which he would receive as the price of his banishment. It was true that the fortnight allowed to him by the Company was only at an end that day, and that, therefore, the following morning might be taken as the last day named for the payment of the money. No doubt, also, Mr Wharton's bill at a few days' date would be accepted if that gentleman could not at the moment give a cheque for so large a sum as was required. And the appointment had been distinctly promised to him with no other stipulation than that the money required for the shares should be paid. He did not believe in Mr Hartlepod's threat. It was impossible, he thought, that he should be treated in so infamous a manner merely because he had had his election expenses repaid him by the Duke of Omnium! He would, therefore, ask for the money, and—renounce the society of his wife.

As he made this resolve something like real love returned to his heart, and he became for a while sick with regret. He assured himself that he had loved her, and that he could love her still;—but why had she not been true to him? Why had she clung to her father instead of clinging to her husband? Why had she not learned his ways,—as a wife is bound to learn the ways of the man she marries? Why had she not helped him in his devices, fallen into his plans, been regardful of his fortunes, and made herself one with him? There had been present to him at times an idea that if he could take her away with him to that distant country to which he thought to go, and thus remove her from the upas* influence of her father's roof-tree,* she would then fall into his views and become his wife indeed. Then he would again be tender to her, again love her, again endeavour to make the world soft to her. But it was too late now for that. He had failed in everything as far as England was concerned, and it was chiefly by her fault that he had failed. He would consent to leave her;—but, as he thought of it in his solitude, his eyes became moist with regret.

In these days Mr Wharton never came home till about midnight, and then passed rapidly through the hall to his own room,—and in the morning had his breakfast brought to him in the same room, so that he might not even see his son-in-law. His daughter would go to him when at breakfast, and there, together for some half-hour, they would endeavour to look forward to their future fate. But hitherto they had never been able to look forward in accord, as she still persisted in declaring that if her husband bade her to go with him,—she would go. On this night Lopez sat up in the dining-room, and as soon as he heard Mr Wharton's key in the door, he placed himself in the hall. 'I wish to speak to you to-night, sir,' he said. 'Would you object to come in for a few moments?' Then Mr Wharton followed him into the room. 'As we live now,' continued Lopez, 'I have not much opportunity of speaking to you, even on business.'

'Well, sir; you can speak now,—if you have anything to say.'

'The £5000 you promised me must be paid to-morrow. It is the last day.'

'I promised it only on certain conditions. Had you complied with them the money would have been paid before this.'

'Just so. The conditions were very hard, Mr Wharton. It surprises me that such a one as you should think it right to separate a husband from his wife.'

'I think it right, sir, to separate my daughter from such a one as you are. I thought so before, but I think so doubly now. If I can secure your absence in Guatemala by the payment of this money, and if you will give me a document that shall be prepared by Mr Walker and signed by yourself, assuring your wife that you will not hereafter call upon her to live with you, the money shall be paid.'

'All that will take time, Mr Wharton.'

'I will not pay a penny without it. I can meet you at the office in Coleman Street to-morrow, and doubtless they will accept my written assurance to pay the money as soon as those stipulations shall be complied with.'

'That would disgrace me in the office, Mr Wharton.'

'And are you not disgraced there already? Can you tell me that they have not heard of your conduct in Coleman Street, or that hearing it they disregard it?' His son-in-law stood frowning at him, but did not at the moment say a word. 'Nevertheless, I will meet you there if you please, at any time that you may name, and if they do not object to employ such a man as their manager, I shall not object on their behalf.'

'To the last you are hard and cruel to me,' said Lopez;—'but I will meet you at Coleman Street at eleven to-morrow.' Then Mr Wharton left the room, and Lopez was there alone amidst the gloom of the heavy curtains and the dark paper. A London dining-room at night is always dark, cavernous, and unlovely. The very pictures on the walls lack brightness, and the furniture is black and heavy. This room was large, but old-fashioned and very dark. Here Lopez walked up and down after Mr Wharton had left him, trying to think how far Fate and how far he himself were responsible for his present misfortunes. No doubt he had begun the world well. His father had been little better than a travelling pedlar, but had made some money by selling jewellery, and had educated his son. Lopez could on no score impute blame to his father for what had happened to him. And, when he thought of the means at his disposal in his early youth, he felt that he had a right to boast of some success. He had worked hard, and had won his way upwards, and had almost lodged himself securely among those people with whom it had been his ambition to live. Early in life he had found himself among those who were called gentlemen and ladies. He had been able to assume their manners, and had lived with them on equal terms. When thinking of his past life he never forgot to remind himself that he had been a guest at the house of the Duke of Omnium! And yet how was it with him now? He was penniless. He was rejected by his father-in-law. He was feared, and, as he thought, detested by his wife. He was expelled from his club.* He was cut by his old friends. And he had been told very plainly by the Secretary in Coleman Street that his presence there was no longer desired. What should he do with himself if Mr Wharton's money were now refused, and if the appointment in Guatemala were denied to him? And then he thought of poor Sexty Parker and his family. He was not naturally an ill-natured man. Though he could upbraid his wife for alluding to Mrs Parker's misery, declaring that Mrs Parker must take the rubs of the world just as others took them, still the misfortunes which he had brought on her and on her children did add something to the weight of his own misfortunes. If he could not go to Guatemala, what should he do with himself;—where should he go? Thus he walked up and down the room for an hour. Would not a pistol or a razor give him the best solution for all his difficulties?

On the following morning he kept his appointment at the office in Coleman Street, as did Mr Wharton also. The latter was there first by some minutes, and explained to Mr Hartlepod that he had come there to meet his son-in-law. Mr Hartlepod was civil, but very cold. Mr Wharton saw at the first glance that the services of Ferdinand Lopez were no longer in request by the San Juan Mining Company; but he sat down and waited. Now that he was there, however painful the interview would be, he would go through it. At ten minutes past eleven he made up his mind that he would wait till the half-hour,— and then go, with the fixed resolution that he would never willingly spend another shilling on behalf of that wretched man. But at a quarter past eleven the wretched man came,—swaggering into the office, though it had not, hitherto, been his custom to swagger. But misfortune masters all but the great men, and upsets the best-learned lesson of even a long life. 'I hope I have not kept you waiting, Mr Wharton.

Well, Hartlepod, how are you to-day? So this little affair is to be settled at last, and now these shares shall be bought and paid for.' Mr Wharton did not say a word, not even rising from his chair, or greeting his son-in-law by a word. 'I dare say Mr Wharton has already explained himself,' said Lopez.

'I don't know that there is any necessity,' said Mr Hartlepod.

'Well,—I suppose it's simple enough,' continued Lopez. 'Mr Wharton, I believe I am right in saying that you are ready to pay the money at once.'

'Yes;—I am ready to pay the money as soon as I am assured that you are on your route to Guatemala. I will not pay a penny till I know that as a fact.'

Then Mr Hartlepod rose from his seat and spoke. 'Gentlemen,' he said, 'the matter within the last few days has assumed a different complexion.'

'As how?' exclaimed Lopez.

'The Directors have changed their mind as to sending out Mr Lopez as their local manager. The Directors intend to appoint another gentleman. I had already acquainted Mr Lopez with the Directors' intention.'

'Then the matter is settled?' said Mr Wharton.

'Quite settled,' said Mr Hartlepod.

As a matter of course Lopez began to fume and to be furious. What!—after all that had been done did the Directors mean to go back from their word? After he had been induced to abandon his business in his own country, was he to be thrown over in that way? If the Company intended to treat him like that, the Company would very soon hear from him. Thank God there were laws in the land. 'Yesterday was the last day fixed for the payment of the money,' said Mr Hartlepod.

'It is at any rate certain that Mr Lopez is not to go to Guatemala?' asked Mr Wharton.

'Quite certain,' said Mr Hartlepod. Then Mr Wharton rose from his chair and quitted the room.

'By G——, you have ruined me among you,' said Lopez;—'ruined me in the most shameful manner. There is no mercy, no friendship, no kindness, no forbearance anywhere! Why am I to be treated in this manner?'

'If you have any complaint to make,' said Mr Hartlepod, 'you had better write to the Directors. I have nothing to do but my duty.'

'By heavens, the Directors shall hear of it!' said Lopez as he left the office.

Mr Wharton went to his chambers and endeavoured to make up his mind what step he must now take in reference to this dreadful incubus. Of course he could turn the man out of his house, but in so doing it might well be that he would also turn out his own daughter. He believed Lopez to be utterly without means, and a man so destitute would generally be glad to be relieved from the burden of his wife's support. But this man would care nothing for his wife's comfort; nothing even, as Mr Wharton believed, for his wife's life. He would simply use his wife as best he might as a means for obtaining money. There was nothing to be done but to buy him off, by so much money down and by so much at stated intervals as long as he should keep away. Mr Walker must manage it, but it was quite clear to Mr Wharton that the Guatemala scheme was altogether at an end. In the meantime a certain sum must be offered to the man at once, on condition that he would leave the house and do so without taking his wife with him.

So far Mr Wharton had a plan, and a plan that was at least feasible. Wretched as he was, miserable, as he thought of the fate which had befallen his daughter,—there was still a prospect of some relief. But Lopez as he walked out of the office had nothing to which he could look for comfort. He slowly made his way to Little Tankard Yard and there he found Sexty Parker balancing himself on the back legs of his chair, with a small decanter of public-house sherry before him. 'What; you here?' he said.

'Yes;—I have come to say good-bye.'

'Where are you going then? You shan't start to Guatemala if I know it.'

'That's all over, my boy,' said Lopez, smiling.

'What is it you mean?' said Sexty, sitting square on his chair and looking very serious.

'I am not going to Guatemala or anywhere else. I thought I'd just look in to tell you that I'm done for,—that I haven't a hope of a shilling now or hereafter. You told me the other day that I was afraid to come here. You see that as soon as anything is fixed, I come and tell you everything at once.'

'What is fixed?'

'That I am ruined. That there isn't a penny to come from any source.'

'Wharton has got money,' said Sexty.

'And there is money in the Bank of England,—but I cannot get at it.'

'What are you going to do, Lopez?'

'Ah; that's the question. What am I going to do? I can say nothing about that, but I can say, Sexty, that our affairs are at an end. I'm very sorry for it, old boy. We ought to have made fortunes, but we didn't. As far as the work went, I did my best. Good-bye, old fellow. You'll do well some of these days yet, I don't doubt. Don't teach the bairns to curse me. As for Mrs P. I have no hope there, I know.' Then he went, leaving Sexty Parker quite aghast.

CHAPTER 59

'THE FIRST AND THE LAST'

WHEN Mr Wharton was in Coleman Street, having his final interview with Mr Hartlepod, there came a visitor to Mrs Lopez in Manchester Square. Up to this date there had been great doubt with Mr Wharton whether at last the banishment to Guatemala would become a fact. From day to day his mind had changed. It had been an infinite benefit that Lopez should go, if he could be got to go alone, but as great an evil if at last he should take his wife with him. But the father had never dared to express these doubts to her, and she had taught herself to think that absolute banishment with a man whom she certainly no longer loved, was the punishment she had to pay for the evil she had done. It was now March, and the second or third of April had been fixed for her departure. Of course she had endeavoured from time to time to learn all that was to be learned from her husband. Sometimes he would be almost communicative to her; at other times she could hardly get a word from him. But, through it all, he gave her to believe that she would have to go. Nor did her father make any great effort to turn his mind the other way. If it must be so, of what use would be such false kindness on his part? She had therefore gone to work to make her purchases, studying that economy which must henceforth be the great duty of her life, and reminding herself as to everything she bought that it would have to be worn with tears and used in sorrow.

And then she sent a message to Arthur Fletcher. It so happened that Sir Alured Wharton was up in London at this time with his daughter Mary. Sir Alured did not come to Manchester Square. There was nothing that the old baronet could say in the midst of all this misery,—no comfort that he could give. It was well known now to all the Whartons and all the Fletchers that this Lopez, who had married her who was to have been the pearl of the two families, had proved himself to be a scoundrel. The two old Whartons met no doubt at some club, or perhaps in Stone Buildings, and spoke some few bitter words to each other; but Sir Alured did not see the unfortunate young woman who had disgraced herself by so wretched a marriage. But Mary came, and by her a message was sent to Arthur Fletcher. 'Tell him that I am going,' said Emily. 'Tell him not to come; but give him my love. He was always one of my kindest friends.'

'Why,—why,—why did you not take him?' said Mary, moved by the excitement of the moment to suggestions which were quite at variance with the fixed propriety of her general ideas.

'Why should you speak of that?' said the other. 'I never speak of him,—never think of him. But, if you see him, tell him what I say.' Arthur Fletcher was of course in the Square on the following day,—on that very day on which Mr Wharton learned that, whatever might be his daughter's fate, she would not, at any rate, be taken to Guatemala. They two had never met since the day on which they had been brought together for a moment at the Duchess's party at Richmond. It had of course been understood by both of them that they were not to be allowed to see each other. Her husband had made a pretext of an act of friendship on his part to establish a quarrel, and both of them had been bound by that quarrel. When a husband declares that his wife shall not know a man, that edict must be obeyed,—or, if disobeyed, must be subverted by intrigue. In this case there had been no inclination to intrigue on either side. The order had been obeyed, and as far as the wife was concerned, had been only a small part of the terrible punishment which had come upon her as the result of her marriage. But now, when Arthur Fletcher sent up his name, she did not hesitate as to seeing him. No doubt she had thought it probable that she might see him when she gave her message to her cousin.

'I could not let you go without coming to you,' he said.

'It is very good of you. Yes;—I suppose we are going. Guatemala sounds a long way off, Arthur, does it not? But they tell me it is a beautiful country.' She spoke with a cheerful voice, almost as though she liked the idea of her journey; but he looked at her with beseeching, anxious, sorrow-laden eyes. 'After all, what is a journey of a few weeks? Why should I not be as happy in Guatemala as in London? As to friends, I do not know that it will make much difference,—except papa.'

'It seems to me to make a difference,' said he.

'I never see anybody now,—neither your people, nor the Wharton Whartons. Indeed, I see nobody. If it were not for papa I should be glad to go. I am told that it is a charming country. I have not found Manchester Square very charming. I am inclined to think that all the world is very much alike, and that it does not matter very much where one lives,—or, perhaps, what one does. But at any rate I am going, and I am very glad to be able to say good-bye to you before I start.' All this she said rapidly, in a manner unlike herself. She was forcing herself to speak so that she might save herself, if possible, from breaking down in his presence.

'Of course I came when Mary told me.'

'Yes;—she was here. Sir Alured did not come. I don't wonder at that, however. And your mother was in town some time ago,—but I didn't expect her to come. Why should they come? I don't know whether you might not have better stayed away. Of course I am a Pariah* now; but Pariah as I am, I shall be as good as any one else in Guatemala. You have seen Everett since he has been in town, perhaps?'

'Yes;—I have seen him.'

'I hope they won't quarrel with Everett because of what I have done. I have felt that more than all,—that both papa and he have suffered because of it. Do you know, I think people are hard. They might have thrown me off without being unkind to them. It is that that has killed me, Arthur;—that they should have suffered.' He sat looking at her, not knowing how to interrupt her, or what to say. There was much that he meant to say, but he did not know how to begin it, or how to frame his words. 'When I am gone, perhaps it will be all right,' she continued. 'When he told me that I was to go, that was my comfort. I think I have taught myself to think nothing of myself, to bear it all as a necessity, to put up with it, whatever it may be, as men bear thirst in the desert. Thank God, Arthur, I have no baby to suffer with me. Here,—here, it is still very bad. When I think of papa creeping in and out of his house, I sometimes feel that I must kill myself. But our going will put an end to all that. It is much better that we should go. I wish we might start to-morrow.' Then she looked up at him, and saw that the tears were running down his face, and as she looked she heard his sobs. 'Why should you cry, Arthur? He never cries,—nor do I. When baby died I cried,—but very little. Tears are vain, foolish things. It has to be borne, and there is an end of it. When one makes up one's mind to that, one does not cry. There was a poor woman here the other day whose husband he had ruined. She wept and bewailed herself till I pitied her almost more than myself;—but then she had children.'

'Oh, Emily!'

'You mustn't call me by my name, because he would be angry. I have to do, you know, as he tells me. And I do so strive to do it! Through it all I have an idea that if I do my duty it will be better for me. There are things, you know, which a husband may tell you to do, but you cannot do. If he tells me to rob, I am not to rob;—am I? And now I think of it, you ought not to be here. He would be very much displeased. But it has been so pleasant once more to see an old friend.'

'I care nothing for his anger,' said Arthur moodily.

'Ah, but I do. I have to care for it.'

'Leave him! Why don't you leave him?'

'What!'

'You cannot deceive me. You do not try to deceive me. You know that he is altogether unworthy of you.'

'I will hear nothing of the kind, sir.'

'How can I speak otherwise when you yourself tell me of your own misery? Is it possible that I should not know what he is? Would you have me pretend to think well of him?'

'You can hold your tongue, Arthur.'

'No;—I cannot hold my tongue. Have I not held my tongue ever since you married? And if I am to speak at all, must I not speak now?'

'There is nothing to be said that can serve us at all.'

'Then it shall be said without serving. When I bid you leave him, it is not that you may come to me. Though I love you better than all the world put together, I do not mean that.'

'Oh, Arthur! Arthur!'

'But let your father save you. Only tell him that you will stay with him, and he will do it. Though I should never see you again, I could hope to protect you. Of course, I know,—and you know. He is——a scoundrel!'

'I will not hear it,' said she rising from her seat on the sofa with her hands up to her forehead, but still coming nearer to him as she moved.

'Does not your father say the same thing? I will advise nothing that he does not advise. I would not say a word to you that he might not hear. I do love you. I have always loved you. But do you think that I would hurt you with my love?'

'No;—no;—no!'

'No, indeed;—but I would have you feel that those who loved you of old are still anxious for your welfare. You said just now that you had been neglected.'

'I spoke of papa and Everett. For myself,—of course, I have separated myself from everybody.'

'Never from me. You may be ten times his wife, but you cannot separate yourself from me. Getting up in the morning and going to bed at night I still tell myself that you are the one woman that I love. Stay with us, and you shall be honoured,—as that man's wife of course, but still as the dearest friend we have.'

'I cannot stay,' she said. 'He has told me that I am to go, and I am in his hands. When you have a wife, Arthur, you will wish her to do your bidding. I hope she will do it for your sake, without the pain I have in doing it. Good-bye, dear friend.'

She put her hand out and he grasped it, and stood for a moment looking at her. Then he seized her in his arms and kissed her brow and her lips. 'Oh, Emily, why were you not my wife? My darling, my darling!'

She had hardly extricated herself when the door opened, and Lopez stood in the room. 'Mr Fletcher,' he said, very calmly, 'what is the meaning of this?'

'He has come to bid me farewell,' said Emily. 'When going on so long a journey one likes to see one's old friends,—perhaps for the last time.' There was something of indifference to his anger in her tone, and something also of scorn.

Lopez looked from one to the other, affecting an air of great displeasure. 'You know, sir,' he said, 'that you cannot be welcome here.'

'But he has been welcome,' said his wife.

'And I look upon your coming as a base act. You are here with the intention of creating discord between me and my wife.'

'I am here to tell her that she has a friend to trust to if she ever wants a friend,' said Fletcher.

'And you think that such trust as that would be safer than trust in her husband? I cannot turn you out of this house, sir, because it does not belong to me, but I desire you to leave at once the room which is occupied by my wife.' Fletcher paused a moment to say good-bye to the poor woman, while Lopez continued with increased indignation. 'If you do not go at once you will force me to desire her to retire. She shall not remain in the same room with you.'

'Good-bye, Mr Fletcher,' she said, again putting out her hand.

But Lopez struck it up, not violently, so as to hurt her, but still with eager roughness. 'Not in my presence,' he said. 'Go, sir, when I desire you.'

'God bless you, my friend,' said Arthur Fletcher. 'I pray that I might live to see you back in the old country.'

'He was——kissing you,' said Lopez, as soon as the door was shut.

'He was,' said Emily.

'And you tell me so to my face, with such an air as that!'

'What am I to tell you when you ask me? I did not bid him kiss me.'

'But afterwards you took his part as his friend.'

'Why not? I should lie to you if I pretended that I was angry with him for what he did.'

'Perhaps you will tell me that you love him.'

'Of course I love him. There are different kinds of love, Ferdinand. There is that which a woman gives to a man when she would fain mate with him. It is the sweetest love of all, if it would only last. And there is another love,—which is not given, but which is won, perhaps through long years, by old friends. I have none older than Arthur Fletcher, and none who are dearer to me.'

'And you think it right that he should take you in his arms and kiss you?'

'On such an occasion I could not blame him.'

'You were ready enough to receive it, perhaps.'

'Well; I was. He has loved me well, and I shall never see him again. He is very dear to me, and I was parting from him for ever. It was the first and the last, and I did not grudge it to him. You must remember, Ferdinand, that you are taking me across the world from all my friends.'

'Psha,' he said, 'that is all over. You are not going anywhere that I know of,—unless it be out into the streets when your father shuts his door on you.' And so saying he left the room without another word.

CHAPTER 60

THE TENWAY JUNCTION

AND thus the knowledge was conveyed to Mrs Lopez that her fate in life was not to carry her to Guatemala. At the very moment in which she had been summoned to meet Arthur Fletcher she had been busy with her needle preparing that almost endless collection of garments necessary for a journey of many days at sea. And now she was informed, by a chance expression, by a word aside, as it were, that the journey was not to be made. 'That is all over,' he had said,—and then had left her, telling her nothing further. Of course she stayed her needle. Whether the last word had been true or false, she could not work again, at any rate till it had been contradicted. If it were so, what was to be her fate? One thing was certain to her;—that she could not remain under her father's roof. It was impossible that an arrangement so utterly distasteful as the present one, both to her father and to herself, should be continued. But where then should they live,—and of what nature would her life be if she should be separated from her father?

That evening she saw her father, and he corroborated her husband's statement. 'It is all over now,' he said,—'that scheme of his of going to superintend the mines. The mines don't want him, and won't have him. I can't say that I wonder at it.'

'What are we to do, papa?'

'Ah;—that I cannot say. I suppose he will condescend still to honour me with his company. I do not know why he should wish to go to Guatemala or elsewhere. He has everything here that he can want.'

'You know, papa, that that is impossible.'

'I cannot say what with him is possible or impossible. He is bound by none of the ordinary rules of mankind.'

That evening Lopez returned to his dinner in Manchester Square, which was still regularly served for him and his wife, though the servants who attended upon him did so under silent and oft-repeated protest. He said not a word more as to Arthur Fletcher, nor did he seek any ground of quarrel with his wife. But that her continued melancholy and dejection made anything like good-humour impossible, even on his part, he would have been good-humoured. When they were alone she asked him as to their future destiny. 'Papa tells me you are not going,' she began by saying.

'Did I not tell you so this morning?'

'Yes;—you said so. But I did not know you were earnest. Is it all over?'

'All over,—I suppose.'

'I should have thought that you would have told me with more,— more seriousness.'

'I don't know what you would have. I was serious enough. The fact is, that your father has delayed so long the payment of the promised money that the thing has fallen through of necessity. I do not know that I can blame the Company.'

Then there was a pause. 'And now,' she said, 'what do you mean to do?'

'Upon my word I cannot say. I am quite as much in the dark as you can be.'

'That is nonsense, Ferdinand.'

'Thank you! Let it be nonsense if you will. It seems to me that there is a great deal of nonsense going on in the world; but very little of it as true as what I say now.'

'But it is your duty to know. Of course you cannot stay here.'

'Nor you, I suppose,—without me.'

'I am not speaking of myself. If you choose, I can remain here.'

'And—just throw me overboard altogether.'

'If you provide another home for me, I will go to it. However poor it may be I will go to it, if you bid me. But for you,—of course you cannot stay here.'

'Has your father told you to say so to me?'

'No;—but I can say so without his telling me. You are banishing him from his own house. He has put up with it while he thought that you were going to this foreign country; but there must be an end of that now. You must have some scheme of life.'

'Upon my soul I have none.'

'You must have some intentions for the future?'

'None in the least. I have had intentions, and they have failed;— from want of that support which I had a right to expect. I have struggled and I have failed, and now I have got no intentions. What are yours?'

'It is not my duty to have any purpose, as what I do must depend on your commands.' Then again there was a silence, during which he lit a cigar, although he was sitting in the drawing-room. This was a profanation of the room on which even he had never ventured before, but at the present moment she was unable to notice it by any words. 'I must tell papa,' she said after a while, 'what our plans are.'

'You can tell him what you please. I have literally nothing to say to him. If he will settle an adequate income on us, payable of course to me, I will go and live elsewhere. If he turns me out in the street without provision, he must turn you out too. That is all that I have got to say. It will come better from you than from me. I am sorry, of course, that things have gone wrong with me. When I found myself the son-in-law of a very rich man I thought that I might spread my wings a bit. But my rich father-in-law threw me over, and now I am helpless. You are not very cheerful, my dear, and I think I'll go down to the club.'

He went out of the house and did go down to the Progress. The committee which was to be held with the view of judging whether he was or was not a proper person to remain a member of that assemblage had not yet been held, and there was nothing to impede his entrance to the club, or the execution of the command which he gave for tea and buttered toast. But no one spoke to him; nor, though he affected a look of comfort, did he find himself much at his ease. Among the members of the club there was a much divided opinion whether he should be expelled or not. There was a strong party who declared that his conduct socially, morally, and politically, had been so bad that nothing short of expulsion would meet the case. But there were others who said that no act had been proved against him which the club ought to notice. He had, no doubt, shown himself to be a blackguard, a man without a spark of honour or honesty. But then,—as they said who thought his position in the club to be unassailable,—what had the club to do with that? 'If you turn out all the blackguards and all the dishonourable men, where will the club be?' was a question asked with a great deal of vigour by one middle-aged gentleman who was supposed to know the club-world very thoroughly. He had committed no offence which the law could recognize and punish, nor had he sinned against the club rules. 'He is not required to be a man of honour by any regulation of which I am aware,' said the middle-aged gentleman. The general opinion seemed to be that he should be asked to go, and that, if he declined, no one should speak to him. This penalty was already inflicted on him, for on the evening in question no one did speak to him.

He drank his tea and ate his toast and read a magazine, striving to look as comfortable and as much at his ease as men at their clubs generally are. He was not a bad actor, and those who saw him and made reports as to his conduct on the following day declared that he had apparently been quite indifferent to the disagreeable incidents of his position. But his indifference had been mere acting. His careless manner with his wife had been all assumed. Selfish as he was, void as he was of all principle, utterly unmanly and even unconscious of the worth of manliness, still he was alive to the opinions of others. He thought that the world was wrong to condemn him,—that the world did not understand the facts of his case, and that the world generally would have done as he had done in similar circumstances. He did not know that there was such a quality as honesty, nor did he understand what the word meant. But he did know that some men, an unfortunate class, became subject to evil report from others who were more successful, and he was aware that he had become one of those unfortunates. Nor could he see any remedy for his position. It was all blank and black before him. It may be doubted whether he got much instruction or amusement from the pages of the magazine which he turned.

At about twelve o'clock he left the club and took his way homewards. But he did not go straight home. It was a nasty cold March night, with a catching wind, and occasional short showers of something between snow and rain,—as disagreeable a night for a gentleman to walk in as one could well conceive. But he went round by Trafalgar Square, and along the Strand, and up some dirty streets by the small theatres, and so on to Holborn and by Bloomsbury Square up to Tottenham Court Road, and then through some unused street into Portland Place, along the Marylebone Road, and back to Manchester Square by Baker Street. He had more than doubled the distance,—apparently without any object. He had been spoken to frequently by unfortunates of both sexes, but had answered a word to no one. He had trudged on and on with his umbrella over his head, but almost unconscious of the cold and wet. And yet he was a man sedulously attentive to his own personal comfort and health, who had at any rate shown this virtue in his mode of living, that he had never subjected himself to danger by imprudence. But now the working of his mind kept him warm, and, if not dry, at least indifferent to the damp. He had thrown aside with affected nonchalance those questions which his wife had asked him, but still it was necessary that he should answer them. He did not suppose that he could continue to live in Manchester Square in his present condition. Nor, if it was necessary that he should wander forth into the world, could he force his wife to wander with him. If he would consent to leave her, his father-in-law would probably give him something,—some allowance on which he might exist. But then of what sort would be his life?

He did not fail to remind himself over and over again that he had nearly succeeded. He had been the guest of the Prime Minister, and had been the nominee chosen by a Duchess to represent her husband's borough in Parliament. He had been intimate with Mills Happerton who was fast becoming a millionaire. He had married much above himself in every way. He had achieved a certain popularity and was conscious of intellect. But at the present moment two or three sovereigns* in his pocket were the extent of his worldly wealth and his character was utterly ruined. He regarded his fate as does a card-player who day after day holds sixes and sevens when other men have aces and kings. Fate was against him. He saw no reason why he should not have had the aces and kings continually, especially as fate had given him perhaps more than his share of them at first. He had, however, lost rubber after rubber,—not paying his stakes for some of the last rubbers lost,—till the players would play with him no longer. The misfortune might have happened to any man;—but it had happened to him. There was no beginning again. A possible small allowance and some very retired and solitary life, in which there would be no show of honour, no flattery coming to him, was all that was left to him.

He let himself in at the house, and found his wife still awake. 'I am wet to the skin,' he said, 'I made up my mind to walk, and I would do it;—but I am a fool for my pains.' She made him some feeble answer affecting to be half asleep, and merely turned in her bed. 'I must be out early in the morning. Mind you make them dry my things. They never do anything for my telling.'

'You don't want them dried to-night?'

'Not to-night, of course;—but after I am gone to-morrow. They'll leave them there without putting a hand to them, if you don't speak. I must be off before breakfast to-morrow.'

'Where are you going? Do you want anything packed?'

'No; nothing. I shall be back to dinner. But I must go down to Birmingham, to see a friend of Happerton's on business. I will breakfast at the station. As you said to-day, something must be done. If it's to sweep a crossing, I must sweep it.'

As she lay awake while he slept, she thought that those last words were the best she had heard him speak since they were married. There seemed to be some indication of purpose in them. If he would only sweep a crossing as a man should sweep it, she would stand by him, and at any rate do her duty to him, in spite of all that had happened. Alas! she was not old enough to have learned that a dishonest man cannot begin even to sweep a crossing honestly till he have in very truth repented of his former dishonesty. The lazy man may become lazy no longer, but there must have been first a process through his mind whereby laziness has become odious to him. And that process can hardly be the immediate result of misfortune arising from misconduct. Had Lopez found his crossing at Birmingham he would hardly have swept it well.

Early on the following morning he was up, and before he left his room he kissed his wife. 'Good-bye, old girl,' he said, 'don't be down-hearted.'

'If you have anything before you to do, I will not be down-hearted,' she said.

'I shall have something to do before night, I think. Tell your father, when you see him, that I will not trouble him here much longer. But tell him, also, that I have no thanks to give him for his hospitality.'

'I will not tell him that, Ferdinand.'

'He shall know it, though. But I do not mean to be cross to you. Good-bye, love.' Then he stooped over her and kissed her again;—and so he took his leave of her.

It was raining hard, and when he got into the street he looked about for a cab, but there was none to be found. In Baker Street he got an omnibus which took him down to the underground railway, and by that he went to Gower Street. Through the rain he walked up to the

Euston Station, and there he ordered breakfast. Could he have a mutton chop and some tea? And he was very particular that the mutton chop should be well cooked. He was a good-looking man, of fashionable appearance, and the young lady who attended him noticed him and was courteous to him. He condescended even to have a little light conversation with her, and, on the whole, he seemed to enjoy his breakfast. 'Upon my word, I should like to breakfast here every day of my life,' he said. The young lady assured him that, as far as she could see, there was no objection to such an arrangement. 'Only it's a bore, you know, coming out in the rain when there are no cabs,' he said. Then there were various little jokes between them, till the young lady was quite impressed with the gentleman's pleasant affability.

After a while he went back into the hall and took a first-class return ticket, not for Birmingham, but for the Tenway Junction.* It is quite unnecessary to describe the Tenway Junction, as everybody knows it. From this spot, some six or seven miles distant from London, lines diverge east, west, and north, north-east, and north-west, round the metropolis in every direction, and with direct communication with every other line in and out of London. It is a marvellous place, quite unintelligible to the uninitiated, and yet daily used by thousands who only know that when they get there, they are to do what some one tells them. The space occupied by the convergent rails seems to be sufficient for a large farm. And these rails always run one into another with sloping points, and cross passages, and mysterious meandering sidings, till it seems to the thoughtful stranger to be impossible that the best-trained engine should know its own line. Here and there and around there is ever a wilderness of waggons, some loaded, some empty, some smoking with close-packed oxen, and others furlongs in length black with coals, which look as though they had been stranded there by chance, and were never destined to get again into the right path of traffic. Not a minute passes without a train going here or there, some rushing by without noticing Tenway in the least, crashing through like flashes of substantial lightning, and others stopping, disgorging and taking up passengers by the hundreds. Men and women,—especially the men, for the women knowing their ignorance are generally willing to trust to the pundits* of the place,—look doubtful, uneasy, and bewildered. But they all do get properly placed and unplaced, so that the spectator at last acknowledges that over all this apparent chaos there is presiding a great genius of order. From dusky morn to dark night, and indeed almost throughout the night, the air is loaded with a succession of shrieks. The theory goes that each separate shriek,—if there can be any separation where the sound is so nearly continuous,—is a separate notice to separate ears of the coming or going of a separate train. The stranger, as he speculates on these pandemoniac noises, is able to realize the idea that were they discontinued the excitement necessary for the minds of the pundits might be lowered, and that activity might be lessened, and evil results might follow. But he cannot bring himself to credit that theory of individual notices.

At Tenway Junction there are half-a-dozen long platforms, on which men and women and luggage are crowded. On one of these for a while Ferdinand Lopez walked backwards and forwards as though waiting for the coming of some especial train. The crowd is ever so great that a man might be supposed to walk there from morning to night without exciting special notice. But the pundits are very clever, and have much experience in men and women. A well-taught pundit, who has exercised authority for a year or two at such a station as that of Tenway, will know within a minute of the appearance of each stranger what is his purpose there,—whether he be going or has just come, whether he is himself on the way or waiting for others, whether he should be treated with civility or with some curt command,—so that if his purport be honest all necessary assistance may be rendered him. As Lopez was walking up and down, with smiling face and leisurely pace, now reading an advertisement and now watching the contortions of some amazed passenger, a certain pundit asked him his business. He was waiting, he said, for a train from Liverpool, intending, when his friend arrived, to go with him to Dulwich by a train which went round the west of London. It was all feasible, and the pundit told him that the stopping train from Liverpool was due there in six minutes, but that the express from the north would pass first. Lopez thanked the pundit and gave him sixpence,—which made the pundit suspicious. A pundit hopes to be paid when he handles luggage, but has no such expectation when he merely gives information.

The pundit still had his eye on our friend when the shriek and the whirr of the express from the north was heard. Lopez walked quickly up towards the edge of the platform, when the pundit followed him, telling him that this was not his train. Lopez then ran a few yards along the platform, not noticing the man, reaching a spot that was unoccupied;—and there he stood fixed. And as he stood the express flashed by. 'I am fond of seeing them pass like that,' said Lopez to the man who had followed him.

'But you shouldn't do it, sir,' said the suspicious pundit. 'No one isn't allowed to stand near like that. The very hair* of it might take you off your legs when you're not used to it.'

'All right, old fellow,' said Lopez, retreating. The next train was the Liverpool train; and it seemed that our friend's friend had not come, for when the Liverpool passengers had cleared themselves off, he was still walking up and down the platform. 'He'll come by the next,' said Lopez to the pundit, who now followed him about and kept an eye on him.

'There ain't another from Liverpool stopping here till the 2.20,' said the pundit. 'You had better come again if you mean to meet him by that.'

'He has come on part of the way, and will reach this by some other train,' said Lopez.

'There ain't nothing he can come by,' said the pundit. 'Gentlemen can't wait here all day, sir. The horders is against waiting on the platform.'

'All right,' said Lopez, moving away as though to make his exit through the station.

Now Tenway Junction is so big a place, and so scattered, that it is impossible that all the pundits should by any combined activity maintain to the letter that order of which our special pundit had spoken. Lopez, departing from the platform which he had hitherto occupied, was soon to be seen on another, walking up and down, and again waiting. But the old pundit had had his eye on him, and had followed him round. At that moment there came a shriek louder than all the other shrieks, and the morning express down from Euston to Inverness was seen coming round the curve at a thousand miles an hour. Lopez turned round and looked at it, and again walked towards the edge of the platform. But now it was not exactly the edge that he neared, but a descent to a pathway,—an inclined plane leading down to the level of the rails, and made there for certain purposes of traffic. As he did so the pundit called to him, and then made a rush at him,—for our friend's back was turned to the coming train. But Lopez heeded not the call, and the rush was too late. With quick, but still with gentle and apparently unhurried steps, he walked down before the flying engine——and in a moment had been knocked into bloody atoms.

VOLUME IV

CHAPTER 61

THE WIDOW AND HER FRIENDS

THE catastrophe described in the last chapter had taken place during the first week in March. By the end of that month old Mr Wharton had probably reconciled himself to the tragedy, although in fact it had affected him very deeply. In the first days after the news had reached him he seemed to be bowed to the ground. Stone Buildings were neglected, and the Eldon saw nothing of him. Indeed, he barely left the house from which he had been so long banished by the presence of his son-in-law. It seemed to Everett, who now came to live with him and his sister, as though his father were overcome by the horror of the affair. But after awhile he recovered himself, and appeared one morning in court with his wig and gown, and argued a case,—which was now unusual with him,—as though to show the world that a dreadful epi-sode in his life was passed, and should be thought of no more. At this period, three or four weeks after the occurrence,—he rarely spoke to his daughter about Lopez; but to Everett the man's name would be often on his tongue. 'I do not know that there could have been any other deliverance,' he said to his son one day. 'I thought it would have killed me when I first heard it, and it nearly killed her. But, at any rate, now there is peace.'

But the widow seemed to feel it more as time went on. At first she was stunned, and for a while absolutely senseless. It was not till two days after the occurrence that the fact became known to her,—nor known as a certainty to her father and brother. It seemed as though the man had been careful to carry with him no record of identity, the nature of which would permit it to outlive the crash of the train. No card was found, no scrap of paper with his name; and it was discovered at last that when he left the house on the fatal morning he had been careful to dress himself in shirt and socks, with handkerchief and collar that had been newly purchased for his proposed journey and which bore no mark. The fragments of his body set identity at defiance, and even his watch had been crumpled into ashes. Of course the fact became certain with no great delay. The man himself was missing, and was accurately described both by the young lady from the refreshment room, and by the suspicious pundit who had actually seen the thing done. There was first belief that it was so, which was not communicated to Emily,—and then certainty.

There was an inquest held of course,—well, we will say on the body,—and, singularly enough, great difference of opinion as to the manner, though of course none as to the immediate cause of the death. Had it been accidental, or premeditated? The pundit, who in the performance of his duties on the Tenway platforms was so efficient and valuable, gave half-a-dozen opinions in half-a-dozen minutes when subjected to the questions of the Coroner. In his own mind he had not the least doubt in the world as to what had happened. But he was made to believe that he was not to speak his own mind. The gentleman, he said, certainly might have walked down by accident. The gentleman's back was turned, and it was possible that the gentleman did not hear the train. He was quite certain that the gentleman knew of the train; but yet he could not say. The gentleman walked down before the train o' purpose; but perhaps he didn't mean to do himself an injury. There was a deal of this, till the Coroner, putting all his wrath into his brow, told the man that he was a disgrace to the service, and expressed a hope that the Company would no longer employ a man so evidently unfit for his position. But the man was in truth a conscientious and useful railway pundit, with a large family, and evident capabilities for his business. At last a verdict was given,—that the man's name was Ferdinand Lopez, that he had been crushed by an express train on the London and North Western Line, and that there was no evidence to show how his presence on the line had been occasioned. Of course Mr Wharton had employed counsel, and of course the counsel's object had been to avoid a verdict of felo de se.* Appended to the verdict was a recommendation from the jury that the Railway Company should be advised to signalize their express trains more clearly at the Tenway Junction Station.

When these tidings were told to the widow she had already given way to many fears. Lopez had gone, purporting,—as he said,—to be back to dinner. He had not come then, nor on the following morning; nor had he written. Then she remembered all that he had done and said;—how he had kissed her, and left a parting malediction for her father. She did not at first imagine that he had destroyed himself, but that he had gone away, intending to vanish as other men before now have vanished. As she thought of this something almost like love came back upon her heart. Of course he was bad. Even in her sorrow, even when alarmed as to his fate, she could not deny that. But her oath to him had not been to love him only while he was good. She had made herself a part of him, and was she not bound to be true to him, whether good or bad? She implored her father and she implored her brother to be ceaseless in their endeavours to trace him,—sometimes seeming almost to fear that in this respect she could not fully trust them. Then she discerned from their manner a doubt as to her husband's fate. 'Oh, papa, if you think anything, tell me what you think,' she said late on the evening of the second day. He was then nearly sure that the man who had been killed at Tenway was Ferdinand Lopez;—but he was not quite sure, and he would not tell her. But on the following morning, somewhat before noon, having himself gone out early to Euston Square, he came back to his own house,—and then he told her all. For the first hour she did not shed a tear or lose her consciousness of the horror of the thing;—but sat still and silent, gazing at nothing, casting back her mind over the history of her life, and the misery which she had brought on all who belonged to her. Then at last she gave way, fell into tears, hysteric sobbings, convulsions so violent as for a time to take the appearance of epileptic fits, and was at last exhausted and, happily for herself, unconscious.

After that she was ill for many weeks,—so ill that at times both her father and her brother thought that she would die. When the first month or six weeks had passed by she would often speak of her husband, especially to her father, and always speaking of him as though she had brought him to his untimely fate. Nor could she endure at this time that her father should say a word against him, even when she obliged the old man to speak of one whose conduct had been so infamous. It had all been her doing! Had she not married him there would have been no misfortune! She did not say that he had been noble, true, or honest,—but she asserted that all the evils which had come upon him had been produced by herself. 'My dear,' her father said to her one evening, 'it is a matter which we cannot forget, but on which it is well that we should be silent.'

'I shall always know what that silence means,' she replied.

'It will never mean condemnation of you by me,' said he.

'But I have destroyed your life,—and his. I know I ought not to have married him, because you bade me not. And I know that I should have been gentler with him, and more obedient, when I was his wife. I sometimes wish that I were a Catholic, and that I could go into a convent, and bury it all amidst sackcloths and ashes.'

'That would not bury it,' said her father.

'But I should at least be buried. If I were out of sight, you might forget it all.'

She once stirred Everett up to speak more plainly than her father ever dared to do, and then also she herself used language that was very plain. 'My darling,' said her brother once, when she had been trying to make out that her husband had been more sinned against than sinning,*—'he was a bad man. It is better that the truth should be told.'

'And who is a good man?' she said, raising herself in her bed and looking him full in the face with her deep-sunken eyes. 'If there be any truth in our religion, are we not all bad? Who is to tell the shades of difference in badness? He was not a drunkard, or a gambler. Through it all he was true to his wife.' She, poor creature, was of course ignorant of that little scene in the little street near May Fair, in which Lopez had offered to carry Lizzie Eustace away with him to Guatemala. 'He was industrious. His ideas about money were not the same as yours or papa's. How was he worse than others? It happened that his faults were distasteful to you—and so, perhaps, were his virtues.'

'His faults, such as they were, brought all these miseries.'

'He would have been successful now if he had never seen me. But why should we talk of it? We shall never agree. And you, Everett, can never understand all that has passed through my mind during the last two years.'

There were two or three persons who attempted to see her at this period, but she avoided them all. First came Mrs Roby, who, as her nearest neighbour, as her aunt, and as an aunt who had been so nearly allied to her, had almost a right to demand admittance. But she would not see Mrs Roby. She sent down word to say that she was too ill. And when Mrs Roby wrote to her, she got her father to answer the note. 'You had better let it drop,' the old man said at last to his sister-in-law. 'Of course she remembers that it was you who brought them together.'

'But I didn't bring them together, Mr Wharton. How often am I to tell you so? It was Everett who brought Mr Lopez here.'

'The marriage was made up in your house, and it has destroyed me and my child. I will not quarrel with my wife's sister if I can help it, but at present you had better keep apart.' Then he had left her abruptly, and Mrs Roby had not dared either to write or to call again.

At this time Arthur Fletcher saw both Everett and Mr Wharton frequently, but he did not go to the Square, contenting himself with asking whether he might be allowed to do so. 'Not yet, Arthur,' said the old man. 'I am sure she thinks of you as one of her best friends, but she could not see you yet.'

'She would have nothing to fear,' said Arthur. 'We knew each other when we were children, and I should be now only as I was then.'

'Not yet, Arthur;—not yet,' said the barrister.

Then there came a letter, or rather two letters, from Mary Wharton;—one to Mr Wharton and the other to Emily. To tell the truth as to these letters, they contained the combined wisdom and tenderness of Wharton Hall and Longbarns. As soon as the fate of Lopez had been ascertained and thoroughly discussed in Herefordshire, there went forth an edict that Emily had suffered punishment sufficient and was to be forgiven. Old Mrs Fletcher did not come to this at once,— having some deep-seated feeling which she did not dare to express even to her son, though she muttered it to her daughter-in-law, that Arthur would be disgraced for ever were he to marry the widow of such a man as Ferdinand Lopez. But when this question of receiving Emily back into family favour was mooted in the Longbarns Parliament no one alluded to the possibility of such a marriage. There was the fact that she whom they had all loved had been freed by a great tragedy from the husband whom they had all condemned,—and also the knowledge that the poor victim had suffered greatly during the period of her married life. Mrs Fletcher had frowned, and shaken her head, and made a little speech about the duties of women, and the necessarily fatal consequences when those duties are neglected. There were present there, with the old lady, John Fletcher and his wife, Sir Alured and Lady Wharton, and Mary Wharton. Arthur was not in the county, nor could the discussion have been held in his presence. 'I can only say,' said John, getting up and looking away from his mother, 'that she shall always find a home at Longbarns when she chooses to come here, and I hope Sir Alured will say the same as to Wharton Hall.' After all, John Fletcher was king in these parts, and Mrs Fletcher, with many noddings and some sobbing, had to give way to King John. The end of all this was that Mary Wharton wrote her letters. In that to Mr Wharton she asked whether it would not be better that her cousin should change the scene and come at once into the country. Let her come and stay a month at Wharton, then go on to Longbarns. She might be sure that there would be no company in either house. In June the Fletchers would go up to town for a week, and then Emily might return to Wharton Hall. It was a long letter, and Mary gave many reasons why the poor sufferer would be better in the country than in town. The letter to Emily herself was shorter, but full of affection. 'Do, do, do come. You know how we all love you. Let it be as it used to be. You always liked the country. I will devote myself to try and comfort you.'

But Emily could not as yet submit to receive devotion even from her cousin Mary. Through it all, and under it all,—though she would ever defend her husband because he was dead,—she knew that she had disgraced the Whartons and brought a load of sorrow upon the Fletchers, and she was too proud to be forgiven so quickly.

Then she received another tender of affection from a quarter whence she certainly did not expect it. The Duchess of Omnium wrote to her. The Duchess, though she had lately been considerably restrained by the condition of the Duke's mind, and by the effects of her own political and social mistakes, still from time to time made renewed efforts to keep together the Coalition by giving dinners, balls, and garden parties, and by binding to herself the gratitude and worship of young parliamentary aspirants. In carrying out her plans, she had lately showered her courtesies upon Arthur Fletcher, who had been made welcome even by the Duke as the sitting member for Silverbridge. With Arthur she had of course discussed the conduct of Lopez as to the election bills, and had been very loud in condemning him. And from Arthur also she had heard something of the sorrows of Emily Lopez. Arthur had been very desirous that the Duchess, who had received them both at her house, should distinguish between the husband and the wife. Then had come the tragedy, to which the notoriety of the man's conduct of course gave additional interest. It was believed that Lopez had destroyed himself because of the disgrace which had fallen upon him from the Silverbridge affair. And for much of that Silverbridge affair the Duchess herself was responsible. She waited till a couple of months had gone by, and then, in the beginning of May, sent to the widow what was intended to be, and indeed was, a very kind note. The Duchess had heard the sad story with the greatest grief. She hoped that Mrs Lopez would permit her to avail herself of a short acquaintance to express her sincere sympathy. She would not venture to call as yet, but hoped that before long she might be allowed to come to Manchester Square.

This note touched the poor woman to whom it was written, not because she herself was solicitous to be acquainted with the Duchess of Omnium, but because the application seemed to her to contain something like an acquittal, or at any rate a pardon, of her husband. His sin in that measure of the Silverbridge election,—a sin which her father had been loud in denouncing before the wretch had destroyed himself,—had been especially against the Duke of Omnium. And now the Duchess came forward to say that it should be forgiven and forgotten. When she showed the letter to her father, and asked him what she should say in answer to it, he only shook his head. 'It is meant for kindness, papa.'

'Yes;—I think it is. There are people who have no right to be kind to me. If a man stopped me in the street and offered me half-a-crown it might be kindness;—but I don't want the man's half-crown.'

'I don't think it is the same, papa. There is a reason here.'

'Perhaps so, my dear, but I do not see the reason.'

She became very red, but even to him she would not explain her ideas. 'I think I shall answer it.'

'Certainly answer it. Your compliments to the Duchess and thank her for her kind inquiries.'

'But she says she will come here.'

'I should not notice that.'

'Very well, papa. If you think so, of course I will not. Perhaps it would be an inconvenience, if she were really to come.' On the next day she did write a note, not quite so cold as that which her father proposed, but still saying nothing as to the offered visit. She felt, she said, very grateful for the Duchess's kind remembrance of her. The Duchess would perhaps understand that at present her sorrow overwhelmed her.

And there was one other tender of kindness which was more surprising than even that from the Duchess. The reader may perhaps remember that Ferdinand Lopez and Lady Eustace had not parted when they last saw each other on the pleasantest terms. He had been very affectionate, but when he had proposed to devote his whole life to her and to carry her off to Guatemala she had simply told him that he was—a fool. Then he had escaped from her house and had never again seen Lizzie Eustace. She had not thought very much about it. Had he returned to her the next day with some more tempting proposition for making money she would have listened to him,—and had he begged her pardon for what had taken place on the former day she would have merely laughed. She was not more offended than she would have been had he asked her for half her fortune instead of her person and her honour. But, as it was, he had escaped and had never again shown himself in the little street near May Fair. Then she had the tidings of his death, first seeing the account in a very sensational article from the pen of Mr Quintus Slide himself. She was immediately filled with an intense interest which was infinitely increased by the fact that the man had but a few days before declared himself to be her lover. It was bringing her almost as near to the event as though she had seen it! She was, perhaps, entitled to think that she had caused it! Nay;—in one sense she had caused it, for he certainly would not have destroyed himself had she consented to go with him to Guatemala or elsewhere. And she knew his wife. An uninteresting, dowdy creature she had called her. But, nevertheless, they had been in company together more than once. So she presented her compliments, and expressed her sorrow, and hoped that she might be allowed to call. There had been no one for whom she had felt more sincere respect and esteem than for her late friend Mr Ferdinand Lopez. To this note there was an answer written by Mr Wharton himself.

'MADAM,
   'My daughter is too ill to see even her own friends.
               'I am, Madam,
                   'Your obedient servant,
                         'ABEL WHARTON.'

After this, life went on in a very quiet way at Manchester Square for many weeks. Gradually Mrs Lopez recovered her capability of attending to the duties of life. Gradually she became again able to interest herself in her brother's pursuits and in her father's comforts, and the house returned to its old form as it had been before these terrible two years, in which the happiness of the Wharton and Fletcher families had been marred, and scotched, and almost destroyed for ever by the interference of Ferdinand Lopez. But Mrs Lopez never for a moment forgot that she had done the mischief,—and that the black enduring cloud had been created solely by her own perversity and self-will. Though she would still defend her late husband if any attack were made upon his memory, not the less did she feel that hers had been the fault, though the punishment had come upon them all.

CHAPTER 62

PHINEAS FINN HAS A BOOK TO READ

THE sensation created by the man's death was by no means confined to Manchester Square, but was very general in the metropolis, and, indeed, throughout the country. As the catastrophe became the subject of general conversation, many people learned that the Silverbridge affair had not, in truth, had much to do with it. The man had killed himself, as many other men have done before him, because he had run through his money and had no chance left of redeeming himself. But to the world at large, the disgrace brought upon him by the explanation given in Parliament was the apparent cause of his self-immolation, and there were not wanting those who felt and expressed a sympathy for a man who could feel so acutely the effect of his own wrong-doing. No doubt he had done wrong in asking the Duke for the money. But the request, though wrong, might almost be justified. There could be no doubt, these apologists said, that he had been ill-treated between the Duke and the Duchess. No doubt Phineas Finn, who was now described by some opponents as the Duke's creature, had been able to make out a story in the Duke's favour. But all the world knew what was the worth and what was the truth of ministerial explanations! The Coalition was very strong; and even the question in the House, which should have been hostile, had been asked in a friendly spirit. In this way there came to be a party who spoke and wrote of Ferdinand Lopez as though he had been a martyr.

Of course Mr Quintus Slide was in the front rank of these accusers. He may be said to have led the little army which made this matter a pretext for a special attack upon the Ministry. Mr Slide was especially hostile to the Prime Minister, but he was not less hotly the enemy of Phineas Finn. Against Phineas Finn he had old grudges, which, however, age had never cooled. He could, therefore, write with a most powerful pen when discussing the death of that unfortunate man, the late candidate for Silverbridge, crushing his two foes in the single grasp of his journalistic fist. Phineas had certainly said some hard things against Lopez, though he had not mentioned the man's name. He had congratulated the House that it had not been contaminated by the presence of so base a creature, and he had said that he would not pause to stigmatize the meanness of the application for money which Lopez had made. Had Lopez continued to live and to endure the 'slings and arrows of outrageous fortune,'* no one would have ventured to say that these words would have inflicted too severe a punishment. But death wipes out many faults, and a self-inflicted death caused by remorse will, in the minds of many, wash a blackamoor almost white. Thus it came to pass that some heavy weapons were hurled at Phineas Finn, but none so heavy as those hurled by Quintus Slide. Should not this Irish knight, who was so ready with his lance in the defence of the Prime Minister, asked Mr Slide, have remembered the past events of his own rather peculiar life? Had not he, too, been poor, and driven in his poverty to rather questionable straits? Had he not been abject in his petition for office,—and in what degree were such petitions less disgraceful than a request for money which had been hopelessly expended on an impossible object, attempted at the instance of the great Crœsus* who, when asked to pay it, had at once acknowledged the necessity of doing so? Could not Mr Finn remember that he himself had stood in danger of his life before a British jury,* and that, though he had been, no doubt properly, acquitted of the crime imputed to him, circumstances had come out against him during the trial which, if not as criminal, were at any rate almost as disgraceful? Could he not have had some mercy on a broken political adventurer who, in his aspirations for public life, had shown none of that greed by which Mr Phineas Finn had been characterized in all the relations of life? As for the Prime Minister, 'We,' as Mr Quintus Slide always described himself,—'We do not wish to add to the agony which the fate of Mr Lopez must have brought upon him. He has hounded that poor man to his death in revenge for the trifling sum of money which he was called on to pay for him. It may be that the first blame lay not with the Prime Minister himself, but with the Prime Minister's wife. With that we have nothing to do. The whole thing lies in a nutshell. The bare mention of the name of her Grace the Duchess in Parliament would have saved the Duke, at any rate as effectually as he has been saved by the services of his man-of-all-work, Phineas Finn, and would have saved him without driving poor Ferdinand Lopez to insanity. But rather than do this he allowed his servant to make statements about mysterious agents, which we are justified in stigmatizing as untrue, and to throw the whole blame where but least of the blame was due. We all know the result. It was found in those gory shreds and tatters of a poor human being with which the Tenway Railway Station was bespattered.'

Of course such an article had considerable effect. It was apparent at once that there was ample room for an action of libel against the newspaper, on the part of Phineas Finn if not on that of the Duke. But it was equally apparent that Mr Quintus Slide must have been very well aware of this when he wrote the article. Such an action, even if successful, may bring with it to the man punished more of good than of evil. Any pecuniary penalty might be more than recouped by the largeness of the advertisement which such an action would produce. Mr Slide no doubt calculated that he would carry with him a great body of public feeling by the mere fact that he had attacked a Prime Minister and a Duke. If he could only get all the publicans in London to take his paper because of his patriotic and bold conduct, the fortune of the paper would be made. There is no better trade than that of martyrdom, if the would-be martyr knows how far he may judiciously go, and in what direction. All this Mr Quintus Slide was supposed to have considered very well.

And Phineas Finn knew that his enemy had also considered the nature of the matters which he would have been able to drag into Court if there should be a trial. Allusions, very strong allusions, had been made to former periods of Mr Finn's life. And though there was but little, if anything, in the past circumstances of which he was ashamed,— but little, if anything, which he thought would subject him personally to the odium of good men, could they be made accurately known in all their details,—it would, he was well aware, be impossible that such accuracy should be achieved. And the story if told inaccurately would not suit him. And then, there was a reason against any public proceeding much stronger even than this. Whether the telling of the story would or would not suit him, it certainly would not suit others. As has been before remarked, there are former chronicles respecting Phineas Finn, and in them may be found adequate cause for this conviction on his part. To no outsider was this history known better than to Mr Quintus Slide, and therefore Mr Quintus Slide could dare almost to defy the law.

But not the less on this account were there many who told Phineas that he ought to bring the action. Among these none were more eager than his old friend Lord Chiltern, the Master of the Brake hounds, a man who really loved Phineas, who also loved the abstract idea of justice, and who could not endure the thought that a miscreant should go unpunished. Hunting was over for the season in the Brake country, and Lord Chiltern rushed up to London, having this object among others of a very pressing nature on his mind. His saddler had to be seen,—and threatened,—on a certain matter touching the horses' backs. A draught of hounds were being sent down to a friend in Scotland. And there was a Committee of Masters to sit on a moot question concerning a neutral covert in the XXX country, of which Committee he was one. But the desire to punish Slide was almost as strong in his indignant mind as those other matters referring more especially to the profession of his life. 'Phineas,' he said, 'you are bound to do it. If you will allow a fellow like that to say such things of you, why, by heaven, any man may say anything of anybody.'

Now Phineas could hardly explain to Lord Chiltern his objection to the proposed action. A lady was closely concerned, and that lady was Lord Chiltern's sister. 'I certainly shall not,' said Phineas.

'And why?'

'Just because he wishes me to do it. I should be falling into the little pit that he has dug for me.'

'He couldn't hurt you. What have you to be afraid of? Ruat cœlum.'

'There are certain angels, Chiltern, living up in that heaven which you wish me to pull about our ears, as to whom, if all their heart and all their wishes and all their doings could be known, nothing but praise could be spoken; but who would still be dragged with soiled wings through the dirt if this man were empowered to bring witness after witness into court. My wife would be named. For aught I know, your wife.'

'By G——, he'd find himself wrong there.'

'Leave a chimney-sweep alone when you see him, Chiltern. Should he run against you, then remember that it is one of the necessary penalties of clean linen that it is apt to be soiled.'

'I'm d——d if I'd let him off.'

'Yes you would, old fellow. When you come to see clearly what you would gain and what you would lose, you would not meddle with him.'

His wife was at first inclined to think an action should be taken, but she was more easily convinced than Lord Chiltern. 'I had not thought,' she said, 'of poor Lady Laura. But is it not horrible that a man should be able to go on like that, and that there should be no punishment?' In answer to this he only shrugged his shoulders.

But the greatest pressure came upon him from another source. He did not in truth suffer much himself from what was said in the 'People's Banner.' He had become used to the 'People's Banner,' and had found out that in no relation of life was he less pleasantly situated because of the maledictions heaped upon him in the columns of that newspaper. His position in public life did not seem to be weakened by them. His personal friends did not fall off because of them. Those who loved him did not love him less. It had not been so with him always, but now, at last, he was hardened against Mr Quintus Slide. But the poor Duke was by no means equally strong. This attack upon him, this denunciation of his cruelty, this assurance that he had caused the death of Ferdinand Lopez, was very grievous to him. It was not that he really felt himself to be guilty of the man's blood, but that any one should say that he was guilty. It was of no use to point out to him that other newspapers had sufficiently vindicated his conduct in that respect, that it was already publicly known that Lopez had received payment for those election expenses from Mr Wharton before the application had been made to him, and that therefore the man's dishonesty was patent to all the world. It was equally futile to explain to him that the man's last act had been in no degree caused by what had been said in Parliament, but had been the result of his continued failures in life and final absolute ruin. He fretted and fumed and was very wretched,—and at last expressed his opinion that legal steps should be taken to punish the 'People's Banner.' Now it had been already acknowledged, on the dictum of no less a man than Sir Gregory Grogram, the Attorney-General, that the action for libel, if taken at all, must be taken, not on the part of the Prime Minister, but on that of Phineas Finn. Sir Timothy Beeswax had indeed doubted, but it had come to be understood by all the members of the Coalition that Sir Timothy Beeswax always did doubt whatever was said by Sir Gregory Grogram. 'The Duke thinks that something should be done,' said Mr Warburton, the Duke's private Secretary, to Phineas Finn.

'Not by me, I hope,' said Phineas.

'Nobody else can do it. That is to say it must be done in your name. Of course it would be a Government matter, as far as expense goes, and all that.'

'I am sorry the Duke should think so.'

'I don't see that it could hurt you.'

'I am sorry the Duke should think so,' repeated Phineas,—'because nothing can be done in my name. I have made up my mind about it. I think the Duke is wrong in wishing it, and I believe that were any action taken, we should only be playing into the hands of that wretched fellow, Quintus Slide. I have long been conversant with Mr Quintus Slide, and have quite made up my mind that I will never play upon his pipe. And you may tell the Duke that there are other reasons. The man has referred to my past life, and in seeking to justify those remarks he would be enabled to drag before the public circumstances and stories, and perhaps persons, in a manner that I personally should disregard, but which, for the sake of others, I am bound to prevent. You will explain all this to the Duke?'

'I am afraid you will find the Duke very urgent.'

'I must then express my great sorrow that I cannot oblige the Duke. I trust I need hardly say that the Duke has no colleague more devoted to his interest than I am. Were he to wish me to change my office, or to abandon it, or to undertake any political duty within the compass of my small powers he would find me ready to obey his behests. But in this matter others are concerned, and I cannot make my judgement subordinate to his.' The private Secretary looked very serious, and simply said that he would do his best to explain these objections to his Grace.

That the Duke would take his refusal in bad part Phineas felt nearly certain. He had been a little surprised at the coldness of the Minister's manner to him after the statement he had made in the House, and had mentioned the matter to his wife. 'You hardly know him,' she had said, 'as well as I do.'

'Certainly not. You ought to know him very intimately, and I have had but little personal friendship with him. But it was a moment in which the man might, for the moment, have been cordial.'

'It was not a moment for his cordiality. The Duchess says that if you want to get a really genial smile from him you must talk to him about cork soles. I know exactly what she means. He loves to be simple, but he does not know how to show people that he likes it. Lady Rosina found him out by accident.'

'Don't suppose that I am in the least aggrieved,' he had said. And now he spoke again to his wife in the same spirit. 'Warburton clearly thinks that he will be offended, and Warburton, I suppose, knows his mind.'

'I don't see why he should. I have been reading it longer, and I still find it very difficult. Lady Glen has been at the work for the last fifteen years, and sometimes owns that there are passages she has not mastered yet. I fancy Mr Warburton is afraid of him, and is a little given to fancy that everybody should bow down to him. Now if there is anything certain about the Duke it is this,—that he doesn't want any one to bow down to him. He hates all bowing down.'

'I don't think he loves those who oppose him.'

'It is not the opposition he hates, but the cause in the man's mind which may produce it. When Sir Orlando opposed him, and he thought that Sir Orlando's opposition was founded on jealousy, then he despised Sir Orlando. But had he believed in Sir Orlando's belief in the new ships, he would have been capable of pressing Sir Orlando to his bosom, although he might have been forced to oppose Sir Orlando's ships in the Cabinet.'

'He is a Sir Bayard* to you,' said Phineas, laughing.

'Rather a Don Quixote,* whom I take to have been the better man of the two. I'll tell you what he is, Phineas, and how he is better than all the real knights of whom I have ever read in story. He is a man altogether without guile, and entirely devoted to his country. Do not quarrel with him, if you can help it.'

Phineas had not the slightest desire to quarrel with his chief; but he did think it to be not improbable that his chief would quarrel with him. It was notorious to him as a member of the Cabinet,—as a colleague living with other colleagues by whom the Prime Minister was coddled, and especially as the husband of his wife, who lived almost continually with the Prime Minister's wife,—that the Duke was cut to the quick by the accusation that he had hounded Ferdinand Lopez to his death. The Prime Minister had defended himself in the House against the first charge by means of Phineas Finn, and now required Phineas to defend him from the second charge in another way. This he was obliged to refuse to do. And then the Minister's private Secretary looked very grave, and left him with the impression that the Duke would be much annoyed, if not offended. And already there had grown up an idea that the Duke would have on the list of his colleagues none who were personally disagreeable to himself. Though he was by no means a strong Minister in regard to political measures, or the proper dominion of his party, still men were afraid of him. It was not that he would call upon them to resign, but that, if aggrieved, he would resign himself. Sir Orlando Drought had rebelled and had tried a fall with the Prime Minister,—and had greatly failed. Phineas determined that if frowned upon he would resign, but that he certainly would bring no action for libel against the 'People's Banner.'

A week passed after he had seen Warburton before he by chance found himself alone with the Prime Minister. This occurred at the house in Carlton Gardens, at which he was a frequent visitor,—and could hardly have ceased to be so without being noticed, as his wife spent half her time there. It was evident to him then that the occasion was sought for by the Duke. 'Mr Finn,' said the Duke, 'I wanted to have a word or two with you.'

'Certainly,' said Phineas, arresting his steps.

'Warburton spoke to you about that,—that newspaper.'

'Yes, Duke. He seemed to think that there should be an action for libel.'

'I thought so too. It was very bad, you know.'

'Yes;—it was bad. I have known the "People's Banner" for some time, and it is always bad.'

'No doubt;—no doubt. It is bad, very bad. Is it not sad that there should be such dishonesty, and that nothing can be done to stop it? Warburton says that you won't hear of an action in your name.'

'There are reasons, Duke.'

'No doubt;—no doubt. Well;—there's an end of it. I own I think the man should be punished. I am not often vindictive, but I think that he should be punished. However, I suppose it cannot be.'

'I don't see the way.'

'So be it. So be it. It must be entirely for you to judge. Are you not longing to get into the country, Mr Finn?'

'Hardly yet,' said Phineas, surprised. 'It's only June, and we have two months more of it. What is the use of longing yet?'

'Two months more!' said the Duke. 'Two months certainly. But even two months will come to an end. We go down to Matching quietly,— very quietly,—when the time does come. You must promise that you'll come with us. Eh? I make a point of it, Mr Finn.'

Phineas did promise, and thought that he had succeeded in mastering one of the difficult passages in that book.

CHAPTER 63

THE DUCHESS AND HER FRIEND

BUT the Duke, though he was by far too magnanimous to be angry with Phineas Finn because Phineas would not fall into his views respecting the proposed action, was not the less tormented and goaded by what the newspapers said. The assertion that he had hounded Ferdinand Lopez to his death, that by his defence of himself he had brought the man's blood on his head, was made and repeated till those round him did not dare to mention the name of Lopez in his hearing. Even his wife was restrained and became fearful, and in her heart of hearts began almost to wish for that retirement to which he had occasionally alluded as a distant Elysium which he should never be allowed to reach. He was beginning to have the worn look of an old man. His scanty hair was turning grey, and his long thin cheeks longer and thinner. Of what he did when sitting alone in his chamber, either at home or at the Treasury Chamber, she knew less and less from day to day, and she began to think that much of his sorrow arose from the fact that among them they would allow him to do nothing. There was no special subject now which stirred him to eagerness and brought upon herself explanations which were tedious and unintelligible to her, but evidently delightful to him. There were no quints or semi-tenths* now, no aspirations for decimal perfection, no delightfully fatiguing hours spent in the manipulation of the multiplication table. And she could not but observe that the old Duke now spoke to her much less frequently of her husband's political position than had been his habit. Through the first year and a half of the present ministerial arrangement he had been constant in his advice to her, and had always, even when things were difficult, been cheery and full of hope. He still came frequently to the house, but did not often see her. And when he did see her he seemed to avoid all allusion either to the political successes or the political reverses of the Coalition. And even her other special allies seemed to labour under unusual restraint with her. Barrington Erle seldom told her any news. Mr Rattler never had a word for her. Warburton, who had ever been discreet, became almost petrified by discretion. And even Phineas Finn had grown to be solemn, silent and uncommunicative. 'Have you heard who is the new Prime Minister?' she said to Mrs Finn one day.

'Has there been a change?'

'I suppose so. Everything has become so quiet that I cannot imagine that Plantagenet is still in office. Do you know what anybody is doing?'

'The world is going on very smoothly, I take it.'

'I hate smoothness. It always means treachery and danger. I feel sure that there will be a great blow up before long. I smell it in the air. Don't you tremble for your husband?'

'Why should I? He likes being in office because it gives him something to do; but he would never be an idle man. As long as he has a seat in Parliament, I shall be contented.'

'To have been Prime Minister is something after all, and they can't rob him of that,' said the Duchess, recurring again to her own husband. 'I half fancy sometimes that the charm of the thing is growing upon him.'

'Upon the Duke?'

'Yes. He is always talking of the delight he will have in giving it up. He is always Cincinnatus,* going back to his peaches and his ploughs. But I fear he is beginning to feel that the salt would be gone out of his life if he ceased to be the first man in the kingdom. He has never said so, but there is a nervousness about him when I suggest to him the name of this or that man as his successor which alarms me. And I think he is becoming a tyrant with his own men. He spoke the other day of Lord Drummond almost as though he meant to have him whipped. It isn't what one expected from him;—is it?'

'The weight of the load on his mind makes him irritable.'

'Either that, or having no load. If he had really much to do he wouldn't surely have time to think so much of that poor wretch who destroyed himself. Such sensitiveness is simply a disease. One can never punish any fault in the world if the sinner can revenge himself upon us by rushing into eternity. Sometimes I see him shiver and shudder, and then I know that he is thinking of Lopez.'

'I can understand all that, Lady Glen.'

'It isn't as it should be, though you can understand it. I'll bet you a guinea that Sir Timothy Beeswax has to go out before the beginning of next Session.'

'I've no objection. But why Sir Timothy?'

'He mentioned Lopez's name the other day before Plantagenet. I heard him. Plantagenet pulled that long face of his, looking as though he meant to impose silence on the whole world for the next six weeks. But Sir Timothy is brass itself, a sounding cymbal of brass* that nothing can silence. He went on to declare with that loud voice of his that the death of Lopez was a good riddance of bad rubbish. Plantagenet turned away and left the room and shut himself up. He didn't declare to himself that he'd dismiss Sir Timothy, because that's not the way of his mind. But you'll see that Sir Timothy will have to go.'

'That, at any rate, will be a good riddance of bad rubbish,' said Mrs Finn, who did not love Sir Timothy Beeswax.

Soon after that the Duchess made up her mind that she would interrogate the Duke of St Bungay as to the present state of affairs. It was then the end of June, and nearly one of those long and tedious months had gone by of which the Duke spoke so feelingly when he asked Phineas Finn to come down to Matching. Hope had been expressed in more than one quarter that this would be a short Session. Such hopes are much more common in June than in July, and, though rarely verified, serve to keep up the drooping spirits of languid senators. 'I suppose we shall be early out of town, Duke,' she said one day.

'I think so. I don't see what there is to keep us. It often happens that ministers are a great deal better in the country than in London, and I fancy it will be so this year.'

'You never think of the poor girls who haven't got their husbands yet.'

'They should make better use of their time. Besides, they can get their husbands in the country.'

'It's quite true that they never get to the end of their labours. They are not like you members of Parliament who can shut up your portfolios and go and shoot grouse. They have to keep at their work spring and summer, autumn and winter,—year after year! How they must hate the men they persecute!'

'I don't think we can put off going for their sake.'

'Men are always selfish, I know. What do you think of Plantagenet lately?' The question was put very abruptly, without a moment's notice, and there was no avoiding it.

'Think of him!'

'Yes;—what do you think of his condition;—of his happiness, his health, his capacity of endurance? Will he be able to go on much longer? Now, my dear Duke, don't stare at me like that. You know, and I know, that you haven't spoken a word to me for the last two months. And you know, and I know, how many things there are of which we are both thinking in common. You haven't quarrelled with Plantagenet?'

'Quarrelled with him! Good heavens, no.'

'Of course I know you still call him your noble colleague, and your noble friend, and make one of the same team with him and all that. But it used to be so much more than that.'

'It is still more than that;—very much more.'

'It was you who made him Prime Minister.'

'No, no, no;—and again no. He made himself Prime Minister by obtaining the confidence of the House of Commons. There is no other possible way in which a man can become Prime Minister in this country.'

'If I were not very serious at this moment, Duke, I should make an allusion to the——Marines.' No other human being could have said this to the Duke of St Bungay, except the young woman whom he had petted all his life as Lady Glencora. 'But I am very serious,' she continued, 'and I may say not very happy. Of course the big wigs of a party have to settle among themselves who shall be their leader, and when this party was formed they settled, at your advice, that Plantagenet should be the man.'

'My dear Lady Glen, I cannot allow that to pass without contradiction.'

'Do not suppose that I am finding fault, or even that I am ungrateful. No one rejoiced as I rejoiced. No one still feels so much pride in it as I feel. I would have given ten years of my life to make him Prime Minister, and now I would give five to keep him so. It is like it was to be king, when men struggled among themselves who should be king. Whatever he may be, I am ambitious. I love to think that other men should look to him as being above them, and that something of this should come down upon me as his wife. I do not know whether it was not the happiest moment of my life when he told me that the Queen had sent for him.'

'It was not so with him.'

'No, Duke,—no! He and I are very different. He only wants to be useful. At any rate, that was all he did want.'

'He is still the same.'

'A man cannot always be carrying a huge load up a hill without having his back bent.'

'I don't know that the load need be so heavy, Duchess.'

'Ah, but what is the load? It is not going to the Treasury Chambers at eleven or twelve in the morning, and sitting four or five times a week in the House of Lords till seven or eight o'clock. He was never ill when he would remain in the House of Commons till two in the morning, and not have a decent dinner above twice in the week. The load I speak of isn't work.'

'What is it then?' said the Duke, who in truth understood it all nearly as well as the Duchess herself.

'It is hard to explain, but it is very heavy.'

'Responsibility, my dear, will always be very heavy.'

'But it is hardly that;—certainly not that alone. It is the feeling that so many people blame him for so many things, and the doubt in his own mind whether he may not deserve it. And then he becomes fretful, and conscious that such fretfulness is beneath him, and injurious to his honour. He condemns men in his mind, and condemns himself for condescending to condemn them. He spends one quarter of an hour in thinking that as he is Prime Minister he will be Prime Minister down to his fingers' ends, and the next in resolving that he never ought to have been Prime Minister at all.' Here something like a frown passed across the old man's brow, which was, however, no indication of anger. 'Dear Duke,' she said, 'you must not be angry with me. Who is there to whom I can speak but you?'

'Angry, my dear! No, indeed!'

'Because you looked as though you would scold me.' At this he smiled. 'And of course all this tells upon his health.'

'Do you think he is ill?'

'He never says so. There is no special illness. But he is thin and wan and careworn. He does not eat and he does not sleep. Of course I watch him.'

'Does his doctor see him?'

'Never. When I asked him once to say a word to Sir James Thorax,—for he was getting hoarse, you know,—he only shook his head and turned on his heels. When he was in the other House, and speaking every night, he would see Thorax constantly, and do just what he was told. He used to like opening his mouth and having Sir James to look down it. But now he won't let any one touch him.'

'What would you have me do, Lady Glen?'

'I don't know.'

'Do you think that he is so far out of health that he ought to give it up?'

'I don't say that. I don't dare to say it. I don't dare to recommend anything. No consideration of health would tell with him at all. If he were to die to-morrow as the penalty of doing something useful to-night, he wouldn't think twice about it. If you wanted to make him stay where he is, the way to do it would be to tell him that his health was failing him. I don't know that he does want to give up now.'

'The autumn months will do everything for him;—only let him be quiet.'

'You are coming to Matching, Duke?'

'I suppose so,—if you ask me,—for a week or two.'

'You must come. I am quite nervous if you desert us. I think he becomes estranged every day from all the others. I know you won't do a mischief by repeating what I say.'

'I hope not.'

'He seems to me to turn his nose up at everybody. He used to like Mr Monk; but he envies Mr Monk, because Mr Monk is Chancellor of the Exchequer. I asked him whether we shouldn't have Lord Drummond at Matching and he told me angrily that I might ask all the Government if I liked.'

'Drummond contradicted him the other day.'

'I knew there was something. He has got to be like a bear with a sore head, Duke. You should have seen his face the other day, when Mr Rattler made some suggestion to him about the proper way of dividing farms.'*

'I don't think he ever liked Rattler.'

'What of that? Don't I have to smile upon men whom I hate like poison;—and women too, which is worse? Do you think that I love old Lady Ramsden, or Mrs MacPherson? He used to be so fond of Lord Cantrip.'

'I think he likes Lord Cantrip,' said the Duke.

'He asked his lordship to do something, and Lord Cantrip declined.'

'I know all about that,' said the Duke.

'And now he looks gloomy at Lord Cantrip. His friends won't stand that kind of thing, you know, for ever.'

'He is always courteous to Finn,' said the Duke.

'Yes;—just now he is on good terms with Mr Finn. He would never be harsh to Mr Finn, because he knows that Mrs Finn is the one really intimate female friend whom I have in the world. After all, Duke, besides Plantagenet and the children, there are only two persons in the world whom I really love. There are only you and she. She will never desert me;—and you must not desert me either.' Then he put his hand behind her waist, and stooped over and kissed her brow, and swore to her that he would never desert her.

But what was he to do? He knew, without being told by the Duchess, that his colleague and chief was becoming, from day to day, more difficult to manage. He had been right enough in laying it down as a general rule that Prime Ministers are selected for that position by the general confidence of the House of Commons;—but he was aware at the same time that it had hardly been so in the present instance. There had come to be a dead-lock in affairs, during which neither of the two old and well-recognized leaders of parties could command a sufficient following for the carrying on of government. With unusual patience these two gentlemen had now for the greater part of three Sessions sat by, offering but little opposition to the Coalition, but of course biding their time. They, too, called themselves,—perhaps thought themselves,—Cincinnatuses. But their ploughs and peaches did not suffice to them, and they longed again to be in every mouth, and to have, if not their deeds, then even their omissions blazoned in every paragraph. The palate accustomed to Cayenne pepper can hardly be gratified by simple salt. When that dead-lock had come, politicians who were really anxious for the country had been forced to look about for a Premier,—and in the search the old Duke had been the foremost. The Duchess had hardly said more than the truth when she declared that her husband's promotion had been effected by their old friend. But it is sometimes easier to make than to unmake. Perhaps the time had now in truth come, in which it would be better for the country that the usual state of things should again exist. Perhaps,—nay, the Duke now thought that he saw that it was so,—Mr Gresham might again have a Liberal majority at his back if the Duke of Omnium could find some graceful mode of retiring. But who was to tell all this to the Duke of Omnium? There was only one man in all England to whom such a task was possible, and that was the old Duke himself,—who during the last two years had been constantly urgent with his friend not to retire! How often since he had taken office had the conscientious and timid Minister begged of his friend permission to abandon his high office! But that permission had always been refused, and now, for the last three months, the request had not been repeated. The Duchess probably was right in saying that her husband 'didn't want to give it up now.'

But he, the Duke of St Bungay, had brought his friend into the trouble, and it was certainly his duty to extricate him from it. The admonition might come in the rude shape of repeated minorities in the House of Commons. Hitherto the number of votes at the command of the Ministry had not been very much impaired. A few always fall off as time goes on. Aristides* becomes too just, and the mind of man is greedy of novelty. Sir Orlando, also, had taken with him a few, and it may be that two or three had told themselves that there could not be all that smoke raised by the 'People's Banner' without some fire below it. But there was a good working majority,—very much at Mr Monk's command,—and Mr Monk was moved by none of that feeling of rebellion which had urged Sir Orlando on to his destruction. It was difficult to find a cause for resignation. And yet the Duke of St Bungay, who had watched the House of Commons closely for nearly half a century, was aware that the Coalition which he had created had done its work, and was almost convinced that it would not be permitted to remain very much longer in power. He had seen symptoms of impatience in Mr Daubeny, and Mr Gresham had snorted once or twice, as though eager for the battle.

CHAPTER 64

THE NEW K.G.

EARLY in June had died the Marquis of Mount Fidgett. In all England there was no older family than that of the Fichy Fidgetts, whose baronial castle of Fichy Fellows is still kept up, the glory of archaeologists and the charm of tourists. Some people declare it to be the most perfect castle residence in the country. It is admitted to have been completed in the time of Edward VI, and is thought to have been commenced in the days of Edward I. It has always belonged to the Fichy Fidgett family, who with a persistence that is becoming rarer every day, has clung to every acre that it ever owned, and has added acre to acre in every age. The consequence has been that the existing Marquis of Mount Fidgett has always been possessed of great territorial influence, and has been flattered, cajoled, and revered by one Prime Minister after another. Now the late Marquis had been, as was the custom with the Fichy Fidgetts, a man of pleasure. If the truth may be spoken openly, it should be admitted that he had been a man of sin. The duty of keeping together the family property he had performed with a perfect zeal. It had always been acknowledged on behalf of the existing Marquis, that in whatever manner he might spend his money, however base might be the gullies into which his wealth descended, he never spent more than he had to spend. Perhaps there was but little praise in this, as he could hardly have got beyond his enormous income unless he had thrown it away on race-courses and roulette tables. But it had long been remarked of the Mount Fidgett marquises that they were too wise to gamble. The family had not been an honour to the country, but had nevertheless been honoured by the country. The man who had just died had perhaps been as selfish and as sensual a brute as had ever disgraced humanity;—but nevertheless he had been a Knight of the Garter. He had been possessed of considerable parliamentary interest, and the Prime Minister of the day had not dared not to make him a Knight of the Garter. All the Marquises of Mount Fidgett had for many years past been Knights of the Garter. On the last occasion a good deal had been said about it. A feeling had even then begun to prevail that the highest personal honour in the gift of the Crown should not be bestowed upon a man whose whole life was a disgrace, and who did indeed seem to deserve every punishment which human or divine wrath could inflict. He had a large family, but they were all illegitimate. Wives generally he liked, but of his own wife he very soon broke the heart. Of all the companies with which he consorted he was the admitted king, but his subjects could do no man any honour. The Castle of Fichy Fellows was visited by the world at large, but no man or woman with a character to lose went into any house really inhabited by the Marquis. And yet he had become a Knight of the Garter, and was therefore, presumably, one of those noble Englishmen to whom the majesty of the day was willing to confide the honour, and glory, and safety of the Crown. There were many who disliked this. That a base reprobate should become a Marquis and a peer of Parliament was in accordance with the constitution of the country. Marquises and peers are not as a rule reprobates, and the misfortune was one which could not be avoided. He might have ill-used his own wife and other wives' husbands without special remark, had he not been made a Knight of the Garter. The Minister of the day, however, had known the value of the man's support, and, being thick-skinned, had lived through the reproaches uttered without much damage to himself. Now the wicked Marquis was dead, and it was the privilege and the duty of the Duke of Omnium to select another Knight.

There was a good deal said about it at the time. There was a rumour,—no doubt a false rumour,—that the Crown insisted in this instance on dictating a choice to the Duke of Omnium. But even were it so, the Duke could not have been very much aggrieved, as the choice dictated was supposed to be that of himself. The late Duke had been a Knight, and when he had died, it was thought that his successor would succeed also to the ribbon. The new Duke had been at that time in the

Cabinet, and had remained there, but had accepted an office inferior in rank to that which he had formerly filled. The whole history of these things has been written, and may be read by the curious. The Duchess, newly a duchess then and very keen in reference to her husband's rank, had instigated him to demand the ribbon as his right. This he had not only declined to do, but had gone out of the way to say that he thought it should be bestowed elsewhere. It had been bestowed elsewhere, and there had been a very general feeling that he had been passed over because his easy temperament in such matters had been seen and utilized. Now, whether the Crown interfered or not,—a matter on which no one short of a writer of newspaper articles dares to make a suggestion till time shall have made mellow the doings of sovereigns and their ministers,—the suggestion was made. The Duke of St Bungay ventured to say to his friend that no other selection was possible.

'Recommend her Majesty to give it to myself!' said the Prime Minister.

'You will find it to be her Majesty's wish. It has been very common. Sir Robert Walpole had it.'

'I am not Sir Robert Walpole.' The Duke named other examples of Prime Ministers who had been gartered by themselves. But our Prime Minister declared it to be out of the question. No honour of that description should be conferred upon him as long as he held his present position. The old Duke was much in earnest, and there was a great deal said on the subject,—but at last it became clear, not only to him, but to the members of the Cabinet generally, and then to the outside world, that the Prime Minister would not consent to accept the vacant honour.

For nearly a month after this the question subsided. A Minister is not bound to bestow a Garter the day after it becomes vacant. There are other Knights to guard the throne, and one may be spared for a short interval. But during that interval many eyes were turned towards the stall in St George's Chapel. A good thing should be given away like a clap of thunder if envy, hatred, and malice are to be avoided. A broad blue ribbon across the chest is of all decorations the most becoming, or, at any rate, the most desired. And there was, I fear, an impression on the minds of some men that the Duke in such matters was weak and might be persuaded. Then there came to him an application in the form of a letter from the new Marquis of Mount Fidgett,—a man whom he had never seen, and of whom he had never heard. The new Marquis had hitherto resided in Italy, and men only knew of him that he was odious to his uncle. But he had inherited all the Fichy Fidgett estates, and was now possessed of immense wealth and great honour. He ventured, he said, to represent to the Prime Minister that for gen- erations past the Marquises of Mount Fidgett had been honoured by the Garter. His political status in the country was exactly that enjoyed by his late uncle; but he intended that his political career should be very different. He was quite prepared to support the Coalition. 'What is he that he should expect to be made a Knight of the Garter?' said our Duke to the old Duke.

'He is the Marquis of Mount Fidgett, and next to your self, perhaps, the richest peer in Great Britain.'

'Have riches anything to do with it?'

'Something certainly. You would not name a pauper peer.'

'Yes;—if he was a man whose career had been highly honourable to the country. Such a man, of course, could not be a pauper, but I do not think his want of wealth should stand in the way of his being honoured by the Garter.'

'Wealth, rank, and territorial influence have been generally thought to have something to do with it.'

'And character nothing!'

'My dear Duke, I have not said so.'

'Something very much like it, my friend, if you advocate the claim of the Marquis of Mount Fidgett. Did you approve of the selection of the late Marquis?'

'I was in the Cabinet at the time, and will therefore say nothing against it. But I have never heard anything against this man's character.'

'Nor in favour of it. To my thinking he has as much claim, and no more, as that man who just opened the door. He was never seen in the Lower House.'

'Surely that cannot signify.'

'You think, then, that he should have it?'

'You know what I think,' said the elder statesman thoughtfully. 'In my opinion there is no doubt that you would best consult the honour of the country by allowing her Majesty to bestow this act of grace upon a subject who has deserved so well from her Majesty as yourself.'

'It is quite impossible.'

'It seems to me,' said the Duke, not appearing to notice the refusal of his friend, 'that in this peculiar position you should allow yourself to be persuaded to lay aside your own feeling. No man of high character is desirous of securing to himself decorations which he may bestow upon others.'

'Just so.'

'But here the decoration bestowed upon the chief whom we all follow, would confer a wider honour upon many than it could do if given to anyone else.'

'The same may be said of any Prime Minister.'

'Not so. A commoner, without high permanent rank or large fortune, is not lowered in the world's esteem by not being of the Order. You will permit me to say—that a Duke of Omnium has not reached that position which he ought to enjoy unless he be a Knight of the Garter.' It must be borne in mind that the old Duke, who used this argument, had himself worn the ribbon for the last thirty years. 'But if——'

'Well;—well.'

'But if you are,—I must call it obstinate.'

'I am obstinate in that respect.'

'Then,' said the Duke of St Bungay, 'I should recommend her Majesty to give it to the Marquis.'

'Never,' said the Prime Minister, with very unaccustomed energy. 'I will never sanction the payment of such a price for services which should never be bought or sold.'

'It would give no offence.'

'That is not enough, my friend. Here is a man of whom I only know that he has bought a great many marble statues. He has done nothing for his country, and nothing for his sovereign.'

'If you are determined to look at what you call desert alone, I would name Lord Drummond.' The Prime Minister frowned and looked unhappy. It was quite true that Lord Drummond had contradicted him, and that he had felt the injury grievously. 'Lord Drummond has been very true to us.'

'Yes;—true to us! What is that?'

'He is in every respect a man of character, and well looked upon in the country. There would be some enmity and a good deal of envy— which might be avoided by either of the courses I have proposed; but those courses you will not take. I take it for granted that you are anxious to secure the support of those who generally act with Lord Drummond.'

'I don't know that I am.' The old Duke shrugged his shoulders. 'What I mean is, that I do not think that we ought to pay an increased price for their support. His lordship is very well as the Head of an Office; but he is not nearly so great a man as my friend Lord Cantrip.'

'Cantrip would not join us. There is no evil in politics so great as that of seeming to buy the men who will not come without buying. These rewards are fairly given for political support.'

'I had not, in truth, thought of Lord Cantrip.'

'He does not expect it any more than my butler.'

'I only named him as having a claim stronger than any that Lord Drummond can put forward. I have a man in my mind to whom I think such an honour is fairly due. What do you say to Lord Earlybird?' The old Duke opened his mouth and lifted up his hands in unaffected surprise.

The Earl of Earlybird was an old man of a very peculiar character. He had never opened his mouth in the House of Lords, and had never sat in the House of Commons. The political world knew him not at all. He had a house in town, but very rarely lived there. Early Park, in the parish of Bird, had been his residence since he first came to the title forty years ago, and had been the scene of all his labours. He was a nobleman possessed of a moderate fortune, and, as men said of him, of a moderate intellect. He had married early in life and was blessed with a large family. But he had certainly not been an idle man. For nearly half a century he had devoted himself to the improvement of the labouring classes, especially in reference to their abodes and education, and had gradually, without any desire on his own part, worked himself up into public notice. He was not an eloquent man, but he would take the chair at meeting after meeting, and sit with admirable patience for long hours to hear the eloquence of others. He was a man very simple in his tastes, and had brought up his family to follow his habits. He had therefore been able to do munificent things with moderate means, and in the long course of years had failed in hiding his munificence from the public. Lord Earlybird, till after middle life, had not been much considered, but gradually there had grown up a feeling that there were not very many better men in the country. He was a fat, bald-headed old man, who was always pulling his spectacles on and off, nearly blind, very awkward, and altogether indifferent to appearance. Probably he had no more idea of the Garter in his own mind than he had of a Cardinal's hat. But he had grown into fame, and had not escaped the notice of the Prime Minister.

'Do you know anything against Lord Earlybird?' asked the Prime Minister.

'Certainly nothing against him, Duke.'

'Nor anything in his favour?'

'I know him very well,—I think I may say intimately. There isn't a better man breathing.'

'An honour to the peerage!' said the Prime Minister.

'An honour to humanity rather,' said the other, 'as being of all men the least selfish and most philanthropical.'

'What more can be said of a man?'

'But according to my view he is not the sort of person whom one would wish to see made a Knight of the Garter. If he had the ribbon he would never wear it.'

'The honour surely does not consist in its outward sign. I am entitled to wear some kind of coronet, but I do not walk about with it on my head. He is a man of great heart and of many virtues. Surely the country, and her Majesty on behalf of the country, should delight to honour such a man.'

'I really doubt whether you look at the matter in the right light,' said the ancient statesman, who was in truth frightened at what was being proposed. 'You must not be angry with me if I speak plainly.'

'My friend, I do not think that it is within your power to make me angry.'

'Well then,—I will get you for a moment to listen to my view on the matter. There are certain great prizes in the gift of the Crown and of the Ministers of the Crown,—the greatest of which are now traditionally at the disposal of the Prime Minister. These are always given to party friends. I may perhaps agree with you that party support should not be looked to alone. Let us acknowledge that character and services should be taken into account. But the very theory of our Government will be overset by a reversal of the rule which I have attempted to describe. You will offend all your own friends, and only incur the ridicule of your opponents. It is no doubt desirable that the high seats of the country should be filled by men of both parties. I would not wish to see every Lord Lieutenant of a county a Whig.' In his enthusiasm the old Duke went back to his old phraseology. 'But I know that my opponents when their turn comes will appoint their friends to the Lieutenancies, and that so the balance will be maintained. If you or I appoint their friends, they won't appoint ours. Lord Earlybird's proxy* has been in the hands of the Conservative leader of the House of Lords ever since he succeeded his father.' Then the old man paused, but his friend waited to listen whether the lecture were finished before he spoke, and the Duke of St Bungay continued. 'And, moreover, though Lord Earlybird is a very good man,—so much so that many of us may well envy him,—he is not just the man fitted for this destination. A Knight of the Garter should be a man prone to show himself, a public man, one whose work in the country has brought him face to face with his fellows. There is an aptness, a propriety, a fitness in these things which one can understand perhaps better than explain.'

'Those fitnesses and aptnesses change, I think, from day to day. There was a time when a knight should be a fighting man.'

'That has gone by.'

'And the aptness and fitness in accordance with which the sovereign of the day was induced to grace with the Garter such a man as the late Marquis of Mount Fidgett have, I hope, gone by. You will admit that?'

'There is no such man proposed.'

'And other fitnesses and aptnesses will go by, till the time will come when the man to be selected as Lieutenant of a county will be the man whose selection will be most beneficial to the county, and Knights of the Garter will be chosen for their real virtues.'

'I think you are Quixotic. A Prime Minister is of all men bound to follow the traditions of his country, or, when he leaves them, to leave them with very gradual steps.'

'And if he break that law and throw over all that thraldom;—what then?'

'He will lose the confidence which has made him what he is.'

'It is well that I know the penalty. It is hardly heavy enough to enforce strict obedience. As for the matter in dispute, it had better stand over yet for a few days.' When the Prime Minister said this the old Duke knew very well that he intended to have his own way.

And so it was. A week passed by, and then the younger Duke wrote to the elder Duke saying that he had given to the matter all the consideration in his power, and that he had at last resolved to recommend her Majesty to bestow the ribbon on Lord Earlybird. He would not, however, take any step for a few days so that his friend might have an opportunity of making further remonstrance if he pleased. No further remonstrance was made, and Lord Earlybird, much to his own amazement, was nominated to the vacant Garter.

The appointment was one certainly not popular with any of the Prime Minister's friends. With some, such as Lord Drummond, it indicated a determination on the part of the Duke to declare his freedom from all those bonds which had hitherto been binding on the Heads of Government. Had the Duke selected himself certainly no offence would have been given. Had the Marquis of Mount Fidgett been the happy man, excuses would have been made. But it was unpardonable to Lord Drummond that he should have been passed over and that the Garter should have been given to Lord Earlybird. To the poor old Duke the offence was of a different nature. He had intended to use a very strong word when he told his friend that his proposed conduct would be Quixotic. The Duke of Omnium would surely know that the Duke of St Bungay could not support a Quixotic Prime Minister. And yet the younger Duke, the Telemachus of the last two years,—after hearing that word,—had rebelled against his Mentor, and had obstinately adhered to his Quixotism! The greed of power had fallen upon the man,—so said the dear old Duke to himself,—and the man's fall was certain. Alas, alas; had he been allowed to go before the poison had entered his veins, how much less would have been his suffering!

CHAPTER 65

'THERE MUST BE TIME'

At the end of the third week in July, when the Session was still sitting, and when no day had been absolutely as yet fixed for the escape of members, Mr Wharton received a letter from his friend Arthur Fletcher which certainly surprised him very much, and which left him for a day or two unable to decide what answer ought to be given. It will be remembered that Ferdinand Lopez destroyed himself in March, now three months since. The act had been more than a nine days' wonder, having been kept in the memory of many men by the sedulous efforts of Quintus Slide, and by the fact that the name of so great a man as the Prime Minister was concerned in the matter. But gradually the feeling about Ferdinand Lopez had died away, and his fate, though it had out-lived the nominal nine days, had sunk into general oblivion before the end of the ninth week. The Prime Minister had not forgotten the man, nor had Quintus Slide. The name was still common in the columns of the 'People's Banner,' and was never mentioned without being read by the unfortunate Duke. But others had ceased to talk of Ferdinand Lopez.

To the mind, however, of Arthur Fletcher the fact of the man's death was always present. A dreadful incubus had come upon his life, blighting all his prospects, obscuring all his sun by a great cloud, covering up all his hopes, and changing for him all his outlook into the world. It was not only that Emily Wharton should not have become his wife, but that the woman whom he loved with so perfect a love should have been sacrificed to so vile a creature as this man. He never blamed her,—but looked upon his fate as Fate. Then on a sudden he heard that the incubus was removed. The man who had made him and her wretched had by a sudden stroke been taken away and annihilated. There was nothing now between him and her,—but a memory. He could certainly forgive, if she could forget.

Of course he had felt at the first moment that time must pass by. He had become certain that her mad love for the man had perished. He had been made sure that she had repented her own deed in sackcloth and ashes. It had been acknowledged to him by her father that she had been anxious to be separated from her husband, if her husband would consent to such a separation. And then, remembering as he did his last interview with her, having in his mind as he did every circumstance of that caress which he had given her,—down to the very quiver of the fingers he had pressed,—he could not but flatter himself that at last he had touched her heart. But there must be time! The conventions of the world operate on all hearts, especially on the female heart, and teach that new vows, too quickly given, are disgraceful. The world has seemed to decide that a widow should take two years before she can bestow herself on a second man without a touch of scandal. But the two years is to include everything, the courtship of the second as well as the burial of the first,—and not only the courtship, but the preparation of the dresses and the wedding itself. And then this case was different from all the others. Of course there must be time, but surely not here a full period of two years! Why should the life of two young persons be so wasted, if it were the case that they loved each other? There was horror here, remorse, pity, perhaps pardon; but there was no love,—none of that love which is always for a time increased in its fervour by the loss of the loved object; none of that passionate devotion which must at first make the very idea of another man's love intolerable. There had been a great escape,—an escape which could not but be inwardly acknowledged, however little prone the tongue might be to confess it. Of course there must be time;—but how much time? He argued it in his mind daily, and at each daily argument the time considered by him to be appropriate was shortened. Three months had passed and he had not yet seen her. He had resolved that he would not even attempt to see her till her father should consent. But surely a period had passed sufficient to justify him in applying for that permission. And then he bethought himself that it would be best in applying for that permission to tell everything to Mr Wharton. He well knew that he would be telling no secret.

Mr Wharton knew the state of his feelings as well as he knew it himself.
If ever there was a case in which time might be abridged, this was one;
and therefore he wrote his letter,—as follows:—

'3, —— *Court, Temple, 24th July, 187—*.
'MY DEAR MR WHARTON,

'It is a matter of great regret to me that we should see so little of each
other,—especially of regret that I should never now see Emily.

'I may as well rush into the matter at once. Of course this letter will
not be shown to her, and therefore I may write as I would speak if I were
with you. The wretched man whom she married is gone, and my love for
her is the same as it was before she had ever seen him, and as it has always
been from that day to this. I could not address you or even think of her
as yet, did I not know that that marriage had been unfortunate. But it has
not altered her to me in the least. It has been a dreadful trouble to us
all,—to her, to you, to me, and to all connected with us. But it is over,
and I think that it should be looked back upon as a black chasm which we
have bridged and got over, and to which we need never cast back our eyes.

'I have no right to think that, though she might some day love
another man, she would, therefore, love me; but I think that I have a
right to try, and I know that I should have your good-will. It is a question of time, but if I let time go by, someone else may slip in. Who can
tell? I would not be thought to press indecently, but I do feel that here
the ordinary rules which govern men and women are not to be followed. He made her unhappy almost from the first day. She had made
a mistake which you and she and all acknowledged. She has been punished; and so have I,—very severely I can assure you. Wouldn't it be a
good thing to bring all this to an end as soon as possible,—if it can be
brought to an end in the way I want?

'Pray tell me what you think. I would propose that you should ask
her to see me, and then say just as much as you please. Of course I
should not press her at first. You might ask me to dinner, and all that
kind of thing, and so she would get used to me. It is not as though we
had not been very, very old friends. But I know you will do the best. I
have put off writing to you till I sometimes think that I shall go mad
over it if I sit still any longer.

'Your affectionate friend,
'ARTHUR FLETCHER.'

When Mr Wharton got this letter he was very much puzzled. Could
he have had his wish, he too would have left the chasm behind him as

proposed by his young friend, and have never cast an eye back upon the frightful abyss. He would willingly have allowed the whole Lopez incident to be passed over as an episode in their lives, which, if it could not be forgotten, should at any rate never be mentioned. They had all been severely punished, as Fletcher had said, and if the matter could end there he would be well content to bear on his own shoulders all that remained of that punishment, and to let everything begin again. But he knew very well it could not be so with her. Even yet it was impossible to induce Emily to think of her husband without regret. It had been only too manifest during the last year of their married life that she had felt horror rather than love towards him. When there had been a question of his leaving her behind, should he go to Central America, she had always expressed herself more than willing to comply with such an arrangement. She would go with him should he order her to do so, but would infinitely sooner remain in England. And then, too, she had spoken of him while alive with disdain and disgust, and had submitted to hear her father describe him as infamous. Her life had been one long misery, under which she had seemed gradually to be perishing. Now she was relieved, and her health was re-established. A certain amount of unjoyous cheerfulness was returning to her. It was impossible to doubt that she must have known that a great burden had fallen from her back. And yet she would never allow his name to be mentioned without giving some outward sign of affection for his memory. If he was bad, so were others bad. There were many worse than he. Such were the excuses she made for her late husband. Old Mr Wharton, who really thought that in all his experience he had never known anyone worse than his son-in-law, would sometimes become testy, and at last resolved that he would altogether hold his tongue. But he could hardly hold his tongue now.

He, no doubt, had already formed his hopes in regard to Arthur Fletcher. He had trusted that the man whom he had taught himself some years since to regard as his wished-for son-in-law, might be constant and strong enough in his love to forget all that was past, and to be still willing to redeem his daughter from misery. But as days had crept on since the scene at the Tenway Junction, he had become aware that time must do much before such relief would be accepted. It was, however, still possible that the presence of the man might do something. Hitherto, since the deed had been done, no stranger had dined in Manchester Square. She herself had seen no visitor. She had hardly left the house except to go to church, and then had been enveloped in the deepest crape. Once or twice she had allowed herself to be driven out in a carriage, and, when she had done so, her father had always accompanied her. No widow, since the seclusion of widows was first ordained, had been more strict in maintaining the restraints of widowhood as enjoined. How then could he bid her receive a new lover,—or how suggest to her that a lover was possible? And yet he did not like to answer Arthur Fletcher without naming some period for the present mourning,—some time at which he might at least show himself in Manchester Square.

'I have had a letter from Arthur Fletcher,' he said to his daughter a day or two after he had received it. He was sitting after dinner, and Everett was also in the room.

'Is he in Herefordshire?' she asked.

'No;—he is up in town, attending to the House of Commons, I suppose. He had something to say to me, and as we are not in the way of meeting he wrote. He wants to come and see you.'

'Not yet, papa.'

'He talked of coming and dining here.'

'Oh yes; pray let him come.'

'You would not mind that?'

'I would dine early and be out of the way. I should be so glad if you would have somebody sometimes. I shouldn't think then that I was such a—such a restraint to you.'

But this was not what Mr Wharton desired. 'I shouldn't like that, my dear. Of course he would know that you were in the house.'

'Upon my word, I think you might meet an old friend like that,' said Everett.

She looked at her brother, and then at her father, and burst into tears. 'Of course you shall not be pressed if it would be irksome to you,' said her father.

'It is the first plunge that hurts,' said Everett. 'If you could once bring yourself to do it, you would find afterwards that you were more comfortable.'

'Papa,' she said slowly. 'I know what it means. His goodness I shall always remember. You may tell him I say so. But I cannot meet him yet.' Then they pressed her no further. Of course she had understood. Her father could not even ask her to say a word which might give comfort to Arthur as to some long distant time.

He went down to the House of Commons the next day, and saw his young friend there. Then they walked up and down Westminster Hall for nearly an hour, talking over the matter with the most absolute freedom. 'It cannot be for the benefit of anyone,' said Arthur Fletcher, 'that she should immolate herself like an Indian widow,*—and for the sake of such a man as that! Of course I have no right to dictate to you,—hardly, perhaps, to give an opinion.'

'Yes, yes, yes.'

'It does seem to me, then, that you ought to force her out of that kind of thing. Why should she not go down to Herefordshire?'

'In time, Arthur,—in time.'

'But people's lives are running away.'

'My dear fellow, if you were to see her you would know how vain it would be to try to hurry her. There must be time.'

CHAPTER 66

THE END OF THE SESSION

THE Duke of St Bungay had been very much disappointed. He had contradicted with a repetition of noes the assertion of the Duchess that he had been the Warwick* who had placed the Prime Minister's crown on the head of the Duke of Omnium, but no doubt he felt in his heart that he had done so much towards it that his advice respecting the vacant Garter, when given so much weight, should have been followed. He was an old man, and had known the secrets of Cabinet Councils when his younger friend was a little boy. He had given advice to Lord John, and had been one of the first to congratulate Sir Robert Peel when that statesman became a free-trader. He had sat in conclave with THE Duke, and had listened to the bold Liberalism of old Earl Grey,* both in the Lower and the Upper House. He had been always great in council, never giving his advice unasked, nor throwing his pearls before swine,* and cautious at all times to avoid excesses on this side or that. He had never allowed himself a hobby of his own to ride, had never been ambitious, had never sought to be the ostensible leader of men. But he did now think that when, with all his experience, he spoke very much in earnest, some attention should be paid to what he said. When he had described a certain line of conduct as Quixotic he had been very much in earnest. He did not usually indulge in strong language, and Quixotic, when applied to the conduct of a Prime Minister, was, to his ideas, very strong. The thing described as Quixotic had now been done, and the Duke of St Bungay was a disappointed man.

For an hour or two he thought that he must gently secede from all private counsels with the Prime Minister. To resign, or to put impediments in the way of his own chief, did not belong to his character. That line of strategy had come into fashion since he had learnt his political rudiments, and was very odious to him. But in all party compacts there must be inner parties, peculiar bonds, and confidences stricter, stronger and also sweeter than those which bind together the twenty or thirty gentlemen who form a Government. From those closer ties which had hitherto bound him to the Duke of Omnium he thought, for a while, that he must divorce himself. Surely on such a subject as the nomination of a Knight of the Garter his advice might have been taken,—if only because it had come from him! And so he kept himself apart for a day or two, and even in the House of Lords ceased to whisper kindly, cheerful words into the ears of his next neighbour.

But various remembrances crowded in upon him by degrees, compelling him to moderate and at last to abandon his purpose. Among these the first was the memory of the kiss which he had given the Duchess. The woman had told him that she loved him, that he was one of the very few whom she did love,—and the word had gone straight into his old heart. She had bade him not to desert her; and he had not only given her his promise, but he had converted that promise to a sacred pledge by a kiss. He had known well why she had exacted the promise. The turmoil in her husband's mind, the agony which he sometimes endured when people spoke ill of him, the aversion which he had at first genuinely felt to an office for which he hardly thought himself fit, and now the gradual love of power created by the exercise of power, had all been seen by her, and had created that solicitude which had induced her to ask for the promise. The old Duke had known them both well, but had hardly as yet given the Duchess credit for so true a devotion to her husband. It now seemed to him that, though she had failed to love the man, she had given her entire heart to the Prime Minister. He sympathized with her altogether, and, at any rate could not go back from his promise.

And then he remembered, too, that if this man did anything amiss in the high office which he had been made to fill, he who had induced him to fill it was responsible. What right had he, the Duke of St Bungay, to be angry because his friend was not all-wise at all points? Let the Droughts and the Drummonds and the Beeswaxes quarrel among themselves or with their colleagues. He belonged to a different school, in the teachings of which there was less perhaps of excitement and more of long-suffering;—but surely, also, more of nobility. He was, at any rate, too old to change, and he would therefore be true to his friend through evil and through good. Having thought all this out he again whispered some cheery word to the Prime Minister, as they sat listening to the denunciations of Lord Fawn, a Liberal lord, much used to business, but who had not been received into the Coalition. The first whisper and the second whisper the Prime Minister received very coldly. He had fully appreciated the discontinuance of the whispers, and was aware of the cause. He had made a selection on his own unassisted judgement in opposition to his old friend's advice, and this was the result. Let it be so! All his friends were turning away from him and he would have to stand alone. If so, he would stand alone till the pendulum of the House of Commons had told him that it was time for him to retire. But gradually the determined good-humour of the old man prevailed. 'He has a wonderful gift of saying nothing with second-rate dignity,' whispered the repentant friend, speaking of Lord Fawn.

'A very honest man,' said the Prime Minister in return.

'A sort of bastard honesty,—by precept out of stupidity. There is no real conviction in it, begotten by thought.' This little bit of criticism, harsh as it was, had the effect, and the Prime Minister became less miserable than he had been.

But Lord Drummond forgave nothing. He still held his office, but more than once he was seen in private conference with both Sir Orlando and Mr Boffin. He did not attempt to conceal his anger. Lord Earlybird! An old woman! One whom no other man in England would have thought of making a Knight of the Garter! It was not, he said, personal disappointment in himself. There were half-a-dozen peers whom he would willingly have seen so graced without the slightest chagrin. But this must have been done simply to show the Duke's power, and to let the world understand that he owed nothing and would pay nothing to his supporters. It was almost a disgrace, said Lord Drummond, to belong to a Government the Head of which could so commit himself! The Session was nearly at an end, and Lord Drummond thought that no step could be conveniently taken now. But it was quite clear to him that this state of things could not be continued. It was observed that Lord Drummond and the Prime Minister never spoke to each other in the House, and that the Secretary of State for the Colonies,—that being the office which he held,—never rose in his place after Lord Earlybird's nomination, unless to say a word or two as to his own peculiar duties. It was very soon known to all the world that there was war to the knife between Lord Drummond and the Prime Minister.

And, strange to say, there seemed to be some feeling of general discontent on this very trifling subject. When Aristides has been much too just the oyster-shells* become numerous. It was said that the Duke had been guilty of pretentious love of virtue in taking Lord Earlybird out of his own path of life and forcing him to write K.G. after his name. There came out an article, of course in the 'People's Banner,' headed, 'Our Prime Minister's Good Works,' in which poor Lord Earlybird was ridiculed in a very unbecoming manner, and in which it was asserted that the thing was done as a counterpoise to the iniquity displayed in 'hounding Ferdinand Lopez to his death.' Whenever Ferdinand Lopez was mentioned he had always been hounded. And then the article went on to declare that either the Prime Minister had quarrelled with all his colleagues, or else that all his colleagues had quarrelled with the Prime Minister. Mr Slide did not care which it might be, but, whichever it might be, the poor country had to suffer when such a state of things was permitted. It was notorious that neither the Duke of St Bungay nor Lord Drummond would now even speak to their own chief, so thoroughly were they disgusted with his conduct. Indeed it seemed that the only ally the Prime Minister had in his own Cabinet was the Irish adventurer, Mr Phineas Finn. Lord Earlybird never read a word of all this, and was altogether undisturbed as he sat in his chair in Exeter Hall,*—or just at this time of the year more frequently in the provinces. But the Duke of Omnium read it all. After what had passed he did not dare show it to his brother Duke. He did not dare to tell his friend that it was said in the newspapers that they did not speak to each other. But every word from Mr Slide's pen settled on his own memory, and added to his torments. It came to be a fixed idea in the Duke's mind that Mr Slide was a gadfly sent to the earth for the express purpose of worrying him.

And as a matter of course the Prime Minister in his own mind blamed himself for what he had done. It is the chief torment of a person constituted as he was that strong as may be the determination to do a thing, fixed as may be the conviction that that thing ought to be done, no sooner has it been perfected than the objections of others, which before had been inefficacious, become suddenly endowed with truth and force. He did not like being told by Mr Slide that he ought not to have set his Cabinet against him, but when he had in fact done so, then he believed what Mr Slide told him. As soon almost as the irrecoverable letter had been winged on its way to Lord Earlybird, he saw the absurdity of sending it. Who was he that he should venture to set aside all the traditions of office? A Pitt or a Peel or a Palmerston* might have done so, because they had been abnormally strong. They had been Prime Ministers by the work of their own hands, holding their powers against the whole world. But he,—he told himself daily that he was only there by sufferance, because at the moment no one else could be found to take it. In such a condition should he not have been bound by the traditions of office, bound by the advice of one so experienced and so true as the Duke of St Bungay? And for whom had he broken through these traditions and thrown away this advice? For a man who had no power whatever to help him or any other Minister of the Crown;—for one whose every pursuit in life was at variance with the acquisition of such honours as that now thrust upon him! He could see his own obstinacy, and could even hate the pretentious love of virtue which he had himself displayed.

'Have you seen Lord Earlybird with his ribbon?' his wife said to him.

'I do not know Lord Earlybird by sight,' he replied angrily.

'Nor any one else either. But he would have come and shown himself to you, if he had had a spark of gratitude in his composition. As far as I can learn you have sacrificed the Ministry for his sake.'

'I did my duty as best I knew how to do it,' said the Duke, almost with ferocity, 'and it little becomes you to taunt me with any deficiency.'

'Plantagenet!'

'I am driven,' he said, 'almost beyond myself, and it kills me when you take part against me.'

'Take part against you! Surely there was very little in what I said.' And yet, as she spoke, she repented bitterly that she had at the moment allowed herself to relapse into the sort of badinage which had been usual with her before she had understood the extent of his sufferings. 'If I trouble you by what I say, I will certainly hold my tongue.'

'Don't repeat to me what that man says in the newspaper.'

'You shouldn't regard the man, Plantagenet. You shouldn't allow the paper to come into your hands.'

'Am I to be afraid of seeing what men say of me? Never! But you need not repeat it, at any rate if it be false.' She had not seen the article in question or she certainly would not have repeated the accusation which it contained. 'I have quarrelled with no colleague. If such a one as Lord Drummond chooses to think himself injured, am I to stoop to him? Nothing strikes me so much in all this as the ill-nature of the world at large. When they used to bait a bear tied to a stake, every one around would cheer the dogs and help to torment the helpless animal. It is much the same now, only they have a man instead of a bear for their pleasure.'

'I will never help the dogs again,' she said, coming up to him and clinging within the embrace of his arm.

He knew that he had been Quixotic, and he would sit in his chair repeating the word to himself aloud, till he himself began to fear that he would do it in company. But the thing had been done and could not be undone. He had had the bestowal of one Garter, and he had given it to Lord Earlybird! It was,—he told himself, but not correctly,—the only thing that he had done on his own undivided responsibility since he had been Prime Minister.

The last days of July had passed, and it had been at last decided that the Session should close on the 11th of August. Now the 11th of August was thought to be a great deal too near the 12th* to allow of such an arrangement being considered satisfactory. A great many members were very angry at the arrangement. It had been said all through June and into July that it was to be an early Session, and yet things had been so mismanaged that when the end came everything could not be finished without keeping members of Parliament in town up to the 11th of August! In the memory of present legislators there had never been anything so awkward. The fault, if there was a fault, was attributable to Mr Monk. In all probability the delay was unavoidable. A minister cannot control long-winded gentlemen, and when gentlemen are very long-winded there must be delay. No doubt a strong minister can exercise some control, and it is certain that long-winded gentlemen find an unusual scope for their breath when the reigning dynasty is weak. In that way Mr Monk and the Duke may have been responsible, but they were blamed as though they, for their own special amusement, detained gentlemen in town. Indeed the gentlemen were not detained. They grumbled and growled and then fled,—but their grumblings and growlings were heard even after their departure.

'Well;—what do you think of it all?' the Duke said one day to Mr Monk, at the Treasury, affecting an air of cheery good-humour.

'I think,' said Mr Monk, 'that the country is very prosperous. I don't know that I ever remember trade to have been more evenly satisfactory.'

'Ah, yes. That's very well for the country, and ought, I suppose, to satisfy us.'

'It satisfies me,' said Mr Monk.

'And me, in a way. But if you were walking about in a very tight pair of boots, in an agony with your feet, would you be able just then to relish the news that agricultural wages in that parish had gone up sixpence a week?'

'I'd take my boots off, and then try,' said Mr Monk.

'That's just what I'm thinking of doing. If I had my boots off all that prosperity would be so pleasant to me! But you see you can't take your boots off in company. And it may be that you have a walk before you, and that no boots will be worse for your feet even than tight ones.'

'We'll have our boots off soon, Duke,' said Mr Monk, speaking of the recess.

'And when shall we be quit of them altogether? Joking apart, they have to be worn if the country requires it.'

'Certainly, Duke.'

'And it may be that you and I think that upon the whole they may be worn with advantage. What does the country say to that?'

'The country has never said the reverse. We have not had a majority against us this Session on any Government question.'

'But we have had narrowing majorities. What will the House do as to the Lords' amendments on the Bankruptcy Bill?' There was a bill that had gone down from the House of Commons, but had not originated with the Government. It had, however, been fostered by Ministers in the House of Lords, and had been sent back with certain amendments for which the Lord Chancellor had made himself responsible. It was therefore now almost a Government measure. The manipulation of this measure had been one of the causes of the prolonged sitting of the Houses.

'Grogram says they will take the amendments.'

'And if they don't?'

'Why then,' said Mr Monk, 'the Lords must take our rejection.'

'And we shall have been beaten,' said the Duke.

'Undoubtedly.'

'And beaten simply because the House desires to beat us. I am told that Sir Timothy Beeswax intends to speak and vote against the amendments.'

'What,—Sir Timothy on one side, and Sir Gregory on the other?'

'So Lord Ramsden tells me,' said the Duke. 'If it be so what are we to do?'

'Certainly not go out in August,' said Mr Monk.

When the time came for the consideration of the Lords' amendments in the House of Commons,—and it did not come till the 8th of August,—the matter was exactly as the Duke had said. Sir Gregory Grogram, with a great deal of earnestness, supported the Lords' amendment,—as he was in honour bound to do. The amendment had come from his chief, the Lord Chancellor, and had indeed been discussed with Sir Gregory before it had been proposed. He was very much in earnest;—but it was evident from Sir Gregory's earnestness that he expected a violent opposition. Immediately after him rose Sir Timothy. Now Sir Timothy was a pretentious man, who assumed to be not only an advocate but a lawyer. And he assumed also to be a political magnate. He went into the matter at great length. He began by saying that it was not a party question. The Bill, which he had had the honour of supporting before it went from their own House, had been a private Bill. As such it had received a general support from the Government. It had been materially altered in the other House under the auspices of his noble friend on the woolsack, but from those alterations he was obliged to dissent. Then he said some very heavy things against the Lord Chancellor, and increased in acerbity as he described what he called the altered mind of his honourable and learned friend the Attorney-General. He then made some very uncomplimentary allusions to the Prime Minister, whom he accused of being more than ordinarily reserved with his subordinates. The speech was manifestly arranged and delivered with the express view of damaging the Coalition, of which at the time he himself made a part. Men observed that things were very much altered when such a course as that was taken in the House of Commons. But that was the course taken on this occasion by Sir Timothy Beeswax, and was so far taken with success that the Lords' amendments were rejected and the Government was beaten in a thin House, by a large majority,—composed partly of its own men. 'What am I to do?' asked the Prime Minister of the old Duke.

The old Duke's answer was exactly the same as that given by Mr Monk. 'We cannot resign in August.' And then he went on. 'We must wait and see how things go at the beginning of next Session. The chief question is whether Sir Timothy should not be asked to resign.'

Then the Session was at an end, and they who had been staunch to the last got out of town as quick as the trains could carry them.

CHAPTER 67

MRS LOPEZ PREPARES TO MOVE

THE Duchess of Omnium was not the most discreet woman in the world. That was admitted by her best friends, and was the great sin alleged against her by her worst enemies. In her desire to say sharp things, she would say the sharp thing in the wrong place, and in her wish to be good-natured she was apt to run into offences. Just as she was about to leave town, which did not take place for some days after Parliament had risen, she made an indiscreet proposition to her husband. 'Should you mind my asking Mrs Lopez down to Matching? We shall only be a very small party.'

Now the very name of Lopez was terrible to the Duke's ears. Anything which recalled the wretch and that wretched tragedy to the Duke's mind gave him a stab. The Duchess ought to have felt that any communication between her husband and even the man's widow was to be avoided rather than sought. 'Quite out of the question!' said the Duke, drawing himself up.

'Why out of the question?'

'There are a thousand reasons. I could not have it.'

'Then I will say nothing more about it. But there is a romance there,—something quite touching.'

'You don't mean that she has——a lover?'

'Well;—yes.'

'And she lost her husband only the other day,—lost him in so terrible a manner! If that is so, certainly I do not wish to see her again.'

'Ah, that is because you don't know the story.'

'I don't wish to know it.'

'The man who now wants to marry her knew her long before she had seen Lopez, and had offered to her ever so many times. He is a fine fellow, and you know him.'

'I had rather not hear any more about it,' said the Duke, walking away.

There was an end to the Duchess's scheme of getting Emily down to Matching,—a scheme which could hardly have been successful even had the Duke not objected to it. But yet the Duchess would not abandon her project of befriending the widow. She had injured Lopez. She had liked what she had seen of Mrs Lopez. And she was now endeavouring to take Arthur Fletcher by the hand. She called therefore at Manchester Square on the day before she started for Matching, and left a card and a note. This was on the 15th of August, when London was as empty as it ever is. The streets at the West End were deserted. The houses were shut up. The very sweepers of the crossings seemed to have gone out of town. The public offices were manned by one or two unfortunates each, who consoled themselves by reading novels at their desks. Half the cab-drivers had gone apparently to the seaside,—or to bed. The shops were still open, but all the respectable shop-keepers were either in Switzerland or at their marine villas. The travelling world had divided itself into Cookites and Hookites;—those who escaped trouble under the auspices of Mr Cook,* and those who boldly combated the extortions of foreign innkeepers and the anti–Anglican tendencies of foreign railway officials 'on their own hooks.' The Duchess of Omnium was nevertheless in town, and the Duke might still be seen going in at the back entrance of the Treasury Chambers every day at eleven o'clock. Mr Warburton thought it very hard, for he, too, could shoot grouse; but he would have perished rather than have spoken a word.

The Duchess did not ask to see Mrs Lopez, but left her card and a note. She had not liked, she said, to leave town without calling, though she would not seek to be admitted. She hoped that Mrs Lopez was recovering her health, and trusted that on her return to town she might be allowed to renew her acquaintance. The note was very simple, and could not be taken as other than friendly. If she had been simply Mrs Palliser, and her husband had been a junior clerk in the Treasury, such a visit would have been a courtesy; and it was not less so because it was made by the Duchess of Omnium and by the wife of the Prime Minister. But yet among all the poor widow's acquaintances she was the only one who had ventured to call since Lopez had destroyed himself. Mrs Roby had been told not to come. Lady Eustace had been sternly rejected. Even old Mrs Fletcher when she had been up in town had, after a very solemn meeting with Mr Wharton, contented herself with sending her love. It had come to pass that the idea of being immured was growing to be natural to Emily herself. The longer that it was continued the more did it seem to be impossible to her that she should break from her seclusion. But yet she was gratified by the note from the Duchess.

'She means to be civil, papa.'

'Oh yes;—but there are people whose civility I don't want.'

'Certainly. I did not want the civility of that horrid Lady Eustace. But I can understand this. She thinks that she did Ferdinand an injury.'

'When you begin, my dear,—and I hope it will be soon,—to get back to the world, you will find it more comfortable, I think, to find yourself among your own people.'

'I don't want to go back,' she said, sobbing bitterly.

'But I want you to go back. All who know you want you to go back. Only don't begin at that end.'

'You don't suppose, papa, that I wish to go to the Duchess?'

'I wish you to go somewhere. It can't be good for you to remain here. Indeed I shall think it wicked, or at any rate weak, if you continue to seclude yourself.'

'Where shall I go?' she said imploringly.

'To Wharton. I certainly think you ought to go there first.'

'If you would go, papa, and leave me here,—just this once. Next year I will go,—if they ask me.'

'When I may be dead, for aught that any of us know.'

'Do not say that, papa. Of course any one may die.'

'I certainly shall not go without you. You may take that as certain. Is it likely that I should leave you alone in August and September in this great gloomy house? If you stay, I shall stay.' Now this meant a great deal more than it had meant in former years. Since Lopez had died Mr Wharton had not once dined at the Eldon. He came home regularly at six o'clock, sat with his daughter an hour before dinner, and then remained with her all the evening. It seemed as though he were determined to force her out of her solitude by her natural consideration for him. She would implore him to go to his club and have his rubber, but he would never give way. No;—he didn't care for the Eldon, and disliked whist. So he said. Till at last he spoke more plainly. 'You are dull enough here all day, and I will not leave you in the evenings.' There was a pertinacious tenderness in this which she had not expected from the antecedents of his life. When, therefore, he told her that he would not go into the country without her, she felt herself almost constrained to yield.

And she would have yielded at once but for one fear. How could she insure to herself that Arthur Fletcher should not be there? Of course he would be at Longbarns, and how could she prevent his coming over from Longbarns to Wharton? She could hardly bring herself to ask the question of her father. But she felt an insuperable objection to finding herself in Arthur's presence. Of course she loved him. Of course in all the world he was of all the dearest to her. Of course if she could wipe out the past as with a wet towel, if she could put the crape off her mind as well as from her limbs, she would become his wife with the greatest joy. But the very feeling that she loved him was disgraceful to her in her own thoughts. She had allowed his caress while Lopez was still her husband,—the husband who had ill-used her and betrayed her, who had sought to drag her down to his own depth of baseness. But now she could not endure to think that that other man should even touch her. It was forbidden to her, she believed, by all the canons of womanhood even to think of love again. There ought to be nothing left for her but crape and weepers.* She had done it all by her own obstinacy, and she could make no compensation either to her family, or to the world, or to her own feelings, but by drinking the cup of her misery down to the very dregs. Even to think of joy would in her be a treason. On that occasion she did not yield to her father, conquering him as she had conquered him before by the pleading of her looks rather than of her words.

But a day or two afterwards he came to her with arguments of a very different kind. He at any rate must go to Wharton immediately, in reference to a letter of vital importance which he had received from Sir Alured. The reader may perhaps remember that Sir Alured's heir— the heir to the title and property—was a nephew for whom he entertained no affection whatever. This Wharton had been discarded by all the Whartons as a profligate drunkard. Some years ago Sir Alured had endeavoured to reclaim the man, and had spent perhaps more money than he had been justified in doing in the endeavour, seeing that, as present occupier of the property, he was bound to provide for his own daughters, and that at his death every acre must go to this ne'er-do-well. The money had been allowed to flow like water for a twelve-month, and had done no good whatever. There had then been no hope. The man was strong and likely to live,—and after a while married a wife, some woman that he took from the very streets. This had been his last known achievement, and from that moment not even had his name been mentioned at Wharton. Now there came tidings of his death. It was said that he had perished in some attempt to cross some glaciers in Switzerland;—but by degrees it appeared that the glacier itself had been less dangerous than the brandy which he had swallowed whilst on his journey. At any rate he was dead. As to that Sir Alured's letter was certain. And he was equally certain that he had left no son.

These tidings were quite as important to Mr Wharton as to Sir Alured,—more important to Everett Wharton than to either of them, as he would inherit all after the death of those two old men. At this moment he was away yachting with a friend, and even his address was unknown. Letters for him were to be sent to Oban,* and might, or might not, reach him in the course of a month. But in a man of Sir Alured's feelings, this catastrophe produced a great change. The heir to his title and property was one whom he was bound to regard with affection and almost with reverence,—if it were only possible for him to do so. With his late heir it had been impossible. But Everett Wharton he had always liked. Everett had not been quite all that his father and uncle had wished. But his faults had been exactly those which would be cured,—or would almost be made virtues,—by the possession of a title and property. Distaste for a profession and aptitude for Parliament would become a young man who was heir not only to the Wharton estates, but to half his father's money.

Sir Alured in his letter expressed a hope that Everett might be informed instantly. He would have written himself had he known Everett's address. But he did know that his elder cousin was in town, and he besought his elder cousin to come at once,—quite at once,—to Wharton. Emily, he said, would of course accompany her father on such an occasion. Then there were long letters from Mary Wharton, and even from Lady Wharton, to Emily. The Whartons must have been very much moved when Lady Wharton could be induced to write a long letter. The Whartons were very much moved. They were in a state of enthusiasm at these news, amounting almost to fury. It seemed as though they thought that every tenant and labourer on the estate, and every tenant and labourer's wife, would be in an abnormal condition and unfit for the duties of life, till they should have seen Everett as heir of the property. Lady Wharton went so far as to tell Emily which bedroom was being prepared for Everett,—a bedroom very different in honour from any by the occupation of which he had as yet been graced. And there were twenty points as to new wills and new deeds as to which the present baronet wanted the immediate advice of his cousin. There were a score of things which could now be done which were before impossible. Trees could be cut down, and buildings put up; and a little bit of land sold, and a little bit of land bought;—the doing of all which would give new life to Sir Alured. A life interest in an estate is a much pleasanter thing when the heir is a friend who can be walked about the property, than when he is an enemy who must be kept at arm's length. All these delights could now be Sir Alured's,—if the old heir would give him his counsel and the young one his assistance.

This change in affairs occasioned some flutter also in Manchester Square. It could not make much difference personally to old Mr Wharton. He was, in fact, as old as the baronet, and did not pay much regard to his own chance of succession. But the position was one which would suit his son admirably, and he was now on good terms with his son. He had convinced himself that Lopez had done all that he could to separate them, and therefore found himself to be more bound to his son than ever. 'We must go at once,' he said to his daughter, speaking almost as though he had forgotten her misery for the moment.

'I suppose you and Everett ought to be there.'

'Heaven knows where Everett is. I ought to be there, and I suppose that on such an occasion as this you will condescend to go with me.'

'Condescend, papa;—what does that mean?'

'You know I cannot go alone. It is out of the question that I should leave you here.'

'Why, papa?'

'And at such a time the family ought to come together. Of course they will take it very much amiss if you refuse. What will Lady Wharton think if you refuse after her writing such a letter as that? It is my duty to tell you that you ought to go. You cannot think that it is right to throw over every friend that you have in the world.'

There was a great deal more said in which it almost seemed that the father's tenderness had been worn out. His words were much rougher and more imperious than any that he had yet spoken since his daughter had become a widow, but they were also more efficacious, and therefore probably more salutary. After twenty-four hours of this she found that she was obliged to yield, and a telegram was sent to Wharton,—by no means the first telegram that had been sent since the news had arrived,—saying that Emily would accompany her father. They were to occupy themselves for two days further in preparations for their journey.

These preparations to Emily were so sad as almost to break her heart. She had never as yet packed up her widow's weeds. She had never as yet even contemplated the necessity of coming down to dinner in them before other eyes than those of her father and brother. She had as yet made none of those struggles with which widows seek to lessen the deformity of their costume. It was incumbent on her now to get a ribbon or two less ghastly than those weepers which had, for the last five months, hung about her face and shoulders. And then how should she look if he were to be there? It was not to be expected that the Whartons should seclude themselves because of her grief. This very change in the circumstances of the property would be sure, of itself, to bring the Fletchers to Wharton,—and then how should she look at him, how answer him if he spoke to her tenderly? It is very hard for a woman to tell a lie to a man when she loves him. She may speak the words. She may be able to assure him that he is indifferent to her. But when a woman really loves a man, as she loved this man, there is a desire to touch him which quivers at her fingers' ends, a longing to look at him which she cannot keep out of her eyes, an inclination to be near him which affects every motion of her body. She cannot refrain herself from excessive attention to his words. She has a god to worship, and she cannot control her admiration. Of all this Emily herself felt much,—but felt at the same time that she would never pardon herself if she betrayed

her love by a gleam of her eye, by the tone of a word, or the movement
of a finger. What,—should she be known to love again after such a
mistake as hers, after such a catastrophe?

The evening before they started who should bustle into the house
but Everett himself. It was then about six o'clock, and he was going to
leave London by the night mail. That he should be a little given to
bustle on such an occasion may perhaps be forgiven him. He had heard
the news down on the Scotch coast, and had flown up to London,
telegraphing as he did so backwards and forwards to Wharton. Of
course he felt that the destruction of his cousin among the glaciers,—
whether by brandy or ice he did not much care,—had made him for the
nonce one of the important people of the world. The young man who
would not so feel might be the better philosopher, but one might doubt
whether he would be the better young man. He quite agreed with his
father that it was his sister's duty to go to Wharton, and he was now in
a position to speak with authority as to the duties of members of his
family. He could not wait, even for one night, in order that he might
travel with them. Sir Alured was impatient. Sir Alured wanted him in
Herefordshire. Sir Alured had said that on such an occasion he, the
heir, ought to be on the property with the shortest possible delay. His
father smiled;—but with an approving smile. Everett therefore started
by the night mail, leaving his father and sister to follow him on the
morrow.

CHAPTER 68

THE PRIME MINISTER'S POLITICAL CREED

THE Duke, before he went to Matching, twice reminded Phineas Finn
that he was expected there in a day or two. 'The Duchess says that your
wife is coming to-morrow,' the Duke said on the day of his departure.
But Phineas could not go then. His services to his country were required
among the dockyards and ships, and he postponed his visit till the end
of September. Then he started for Matching, having the double pleasure before him of meeting his wife and his noble host and hostess. He
found a small party there, but not so small as the Duchess had once
suggested to him. 'Your wife will be there, of course, Mr Finn. She is
too good to desert me in my troubles. And there will probably be Lady
Rosina De Courcy. Lady Rosina is to the Duke what your wife is to
me. I don't suppose there will be anybody else,—except, perhaps,

Mr Warburton.' But Lady Rosina was not there. In place of Lady Rosina there were the Duke and Duchess of St Bungay, with their daughters, two or three Palliser offshoots, with their wives, and Barrington Erle. There were, too, the Bishop of the diocese with his wife, and three or four others, coming and going, so that the party never seemed to be too small. 'We asked Mr Rattler,' said the Duchess in a whisper to Phineas, 'but he declined, with a string of florid compliments. When Mr Rattler won't come to the Prime Minister's house, you may depend that something is going to happen. It is like pigs carrying straws* in their mouths. Mr Rattler is my pig.' Phineas only laughed and said that he did not believe Rattler to be a better pig than any one else.

It was soon apparent to Phineas that the Duke's manner to him was entirely altered, so much so that he was compelled to acknowledge to himself that he had not hitherto read the Duke's character aright. Hitherto he had never found the Duke pleasant in conversation. Looking back he could hardly remember that he had in truth ever conversed with the Duke. The man had seemed to shut himself up as soon as he had uttered certain words which the circumstances of the moment had demanded. Whether it was arrogance or shyness Phineas had not known. His wife had said that the Duke was shy. Had he been arrogant the effect would have been the same. He was unbending, hard, and lucid only when he spoke on some detail of business, or on some point of policy. But now he smiled, and though hesitating a little at first, very soon fell into the ways of a pleasant country host. 'You shoot,' said the Duke. Phineas did shoot but cared very little about it. 'But you hunt.' Phineas was very fond of riding to hounds. 'I am beginning to think,' said the Duke, 'that I have made a mistake in not caring for such things. When I was very young I gave them up, because it appeared that other men devoted too much time to them. One might as well not eat because some men are gluttons.'

'Only that you would die if you did not eat.'

'Bread, I suppose, would keep me alive, but still one eats meat without being a glutton. I very often regret the want of amusements, and particularly of those which would throw me more among my fellow-creatures. A man is alone when reading, alone when writing, alone when thinking. Even sitting in Parliament he is very much alone, though there be a crowd around him. Now a man can hardly be thoroughly useful unless he knows his fellow-men, and how is he to know them if he shuts himself up? If I had to begin again I think I would cultivate the amusements of the time.'

Not long after this the Duke asked him whether he was going to join the shooting men on that morning. Phineas declared that his hands were too full of business for any amusement before lunch. 'Then,' said the Duke, 'will you walk with me in the afternoon? There is nothing I really like so much as a walk. There are some very pretty points where the river skirts the park. And I will show you the spot on which Sir Guy de Palliser performed the feat for which the king gave him this property. It was a grand time when a man could get half-a-dozen parishes because he tickled the king's fancy.'

'But suppose he didn't tickle the king's fancy?'

'Ah, then indeed, it might go otherwise with him. But I am glad to say that Sir Guy was an accomplished courtier.'

The walk was taken, and the pretty bends of the river were seen; but they were looked at without much earnestness, and Sir Guy's great deed was not again mentioned. The conversation went away to other matters. Of course it was not long before the Prime Minister was deep in discussing the probabilities of the next Session. It was soon apparent to Phineas that the Duke was no longer desirous of resigning, though he spoke very freely of the probable necessity there might be for him to do so. At the present moment he was in his best humour. His feet were on his own property. He could see the prosperity around him. The spot was the one which he loved best in all the world. He liked his present companion, who was one to whom he was entitled to speak with freedom. But there was still present to him the sense of some injury from which he could not free himself. Of course he did not know that he had been haughty to Sir Orlando, to Sir Timothy, and others. But he did know that he had intended to be true, and he thought that they had been treacherous. Twelve months ago there had been a goal before him which he might attain, a winning-post which was still within his reach. There was in store for him the tranquillity of retirement which he would enjoy as soon as a sense of duty would permit him to seize it. But now the prospect of that happiness had gradually vanished from him. That retirement was no longer a winning-post for him. The poison of place and power and dignity had got into his blood. As he looked forward he feared rather than sighed for retirement. 'You think it will go against us,' he said.

Phineas did think so. There was hardly a man high up in the party who did not think so. When one branch of a Coalition has gradually dropped off, the other branch will hardly flourish long. And then the tints of a political Coalition are so neutral and unalluring that men will only endure them when they feel that no more pronounced colours are within their reach. 'After all,' said Phineas, 'the innings has not been a bad one. It has been of service to the country, and has lasted longer than most men expected.'

'If it has been of service to the country, that is everything. It should at least be everything. With the statesman to whom it is not everything there must be something wrong.' The Duke, as he said this, was preaching to himself. He was telling himself that, though he saw the better way, he was allowing himself to walk on in that which was worse.* For it was not only Phineas who could see the change,—or the old Duke, or the Duchess. It was apparent to the man himself, though he could not prevent it. 'I sometimes think,' he said, 'that we whom chance has led to be meddlers in the game of politics sometimes give ourselves hardly time enough to think what we are about.'

'A man may have to work so hard,' said Phineas, 'that he has no time for thinking.'

'Or more probably, may be so eager in party conflict that he will hardly keep his mind cool enough for thought. It seems to me that many men,—men whom you and I know,—embrace the profession of politics not only without political convictions, but without seeing that it is proper that they should entertain them. Chance brings a young man under the guidance of this or that elder man. He has come of a Whig family, as was my case,—or from some old Tory stock; and loyalty keeps him true to the interests which have first pushed him forward into the world. There is no conviction there.'

'Convictions grow.'

'Yes;—the conviction that it is the man's duty to be a staunch Liberal, but not the reason why. Or a man sees his opening on this side or on that,—as is the case with the lawyers. Or he has a body of men at his back ready to support him on this side or on that, as we see with commercial men. Or perhaps he has some vague idea that aristocracy is pleasant, and he becomes a Conservative,—or that democracy is prospering, and he becomes a Liberal. You are a Liberal, Mr Finn.'

'Certainly, Duke.'

'Why?'

'Well;—after what you have said I will not boast of myself. Experience, however, seems to show me that Liberalism is demanded by the country.'

'So, perhaps, at certain epochs, may the Devil and all his works; but you will hardly say that you will carry the Devil's colours because the country may like the Devil. It is not sufficient, I think, to say that

Liberalism is demanded. You should first know what Liberalism means, and then assure yourself that the thing itself is good. I dare say you have done so; but I see some who never make the inquiry.'

'I will not claim to be better than my neighbours,—I mean my real neighbours.'

'I understand; I understand,' said the Duke laughing. 'You prefer some good Samaritan on the opposition benches to Sir Timothy and the Pharisees. It is hard to come wounded out of the fight, and then to see him who should be your friend not only walking by on the other side, but flinging a stone at you as he goes. But I did not mean just now to allude to the details of recent misfortunes, though there is no one to whom I could do so more openly than to you. I was trying yesterday to explain to myself why I have, all my life, sat on what is called the Liberal side of the House to which I have belonged.'

'Did you succeed?'

'I began life with the misfortune of a ready-made political creed. There was a seat in the House for me when I was twenty-one. Nobody took the trouble to ask me my opinions. It was a matter of course that I should be a Liberal. My uncle, whom nothing could ever induce to move in politics himself, took it for granted that I should run straight,—as he would have said. It was a tradition of the family, and was as inseparable from it as any of the titles which he had inherited. The property might be sold or squandered,—but the political creed was fixed as adamant. I don't know that I ever had a wish to rebel, but I think that I took it at first very much as a matter of course.'

'A man seldom inquires very deeply at twenty-one.'

'And if he does it is ten to one but he comes to a wrong conclusion. But since then I have satisfied myself that chance put me into the right course. It has been, I dare say, the same with you as with me. We both went into office early, and the anxiety to do special duties well probably deterred us both from thinking much of the great question. When a man has to be on the alert to keep Ireland quiet, or to prevent peculation in the dockyards, or to raise the revenue while he lowers the taxes, he feels himself to be saved from the necessity of investigating principles. In this way I sometimes think that ministers, or they who have been ministers and who have to watch the ministers from the Opposition benches, have less opportunity of becoming real politicians than the men who sit in Parliament with empty hands and with time at their own disposal. But when a man has been placed by circumstances as I am now, he does begin to think.'

'And yet you have not empty hands.'

'They are not so full, perhaps, as you think. At any rate I cannot content myself with a single branch of the public service as I used to in old days. Do not suppose that I claim to have made any grand political invention, but I think that I have at least labelled my own thoughts. I suppose what we all desire is to improve the condition of the people by whom we are employed, and to advance our country, or at any rate to save it from retrogression.'

'That of course.'

'So much is of course. I give credit to my opponents in Parliament for that desire quite as readily as I do to my colleagues or to myself. The idea that political virtue is all on one side is both mischievous and absurd. We allow ourselves to talk in that way because indignation, scorn, and sometimes, I fear, vituperation, are the fuel with which the necessary heat of debate is maintained.'

'There are some men who are very fond of poking the fire,' said Phineas.

'Well; I won't name any one at present,' said the Duke, 'but I have seen gentlemen of your country very handy with the pokers.' Phineas laughed, knowing that he had been considered by some to have been a little violent when defending the Duke. 'But we put all that aside when we really think, and can give the Conservative credit for philanthropy and patriotism as readily as the Liberal. The Conservative who has had any idea of the meaning of the name which he carries, wishes, I suppose, to maintain the differences and the distances which separate the highly placed from their lower brethren. He thinks that God has divided the world as he finds it divided, and that he may best do his duty by making the inferior man happy and contented in his position, teaching him that the place which he holds is his by God's ordinance.'

'And it is so.'

'Hardly in the sense that I mean. But that is the great Conservative lesson. That lesson seems to me to be hardly compatible with continual improvement in the condition of the lower man. But with the Conservative all such improvement is to be based on the idea of the maintenance of those distances. I as a Duke am to be kept as far apart from the man who drives my horses as was my ancestor from the man who drove his, or who rode after him to the wars,—and that is to go on for ever. There is much to be said for such a scheme. Let the lords be, all of them, men with loving hearts, and clear intellect, and noble instincts, and it is possible that they should use their powers so beneficently as to spread happiness over the earth. It is one of the millenniums which the mind of man can conceive, and seems to be that which the Conservative mind does conceive.'

'But the other men who are not lords don't want that kind of happiness.'

'If such happiness were attainable it might be well to constrain men to accept it. But the lords of this world are fallible men; and though as units they ought to be and perhaps are better than those others who have fewer advantages, they are much more likely as units to go astray in opinion than the bodies of men whom they would seek to govern. We know that power does corrupt,* and that we cannot trust kings to have loving hearts, and clear intellects, and noble instincts. Men as they come to think about it and to look forward, and to look back, will not believe in such a millennium as that.'

'Do they believe in any millennium?'

'I think they do after a fashion, and I think that I do myself. That is my idea of Conservatism. The doctrine of Liberalism is, of course, the reverse. The Liberal, if he have any fixed idea at all, must, I think, have conceived the idea of lessening distances,—of bringing the coachman and the duke nearer together,—nearer and nearer, till a millennium shall be reached by——'

'By equality?' asked Phineas, eagerly interrupting the Prime Minister, and showing his dissent by the tone of his voice.

'I did not use the word, which is open to many objections. In the first place the millennium, which I have perhaps rashly named, is so distant that we need not even think of it as possible. Men's intellects are at present so various that we cannot even realize the idea of equality, and here in England we have been taught to hate the word by the evil effects of those absurd attempts which have been made elsewhere to proclaim it as a fact accomplished by the scratch of a pen or by a chisel on a stone. We have been injured in that, because a good word signifying a grand idea has been driven out of the vocabulary of good men. Equality would be a heaven, if we could attain it. How can we to whom so much has been given dare to think otherwise? How can you look at the bowed back and bent legs and abject face of that poor ploughman, who winter and summer has to drag his rheumatic limbs to his work, while you go a-hunting or sit in pride of place among the foremost few of your country, and say that it all is as it ought to be? You are a Liberal because you know that it is not all as it ought to be, and because you would still march on to some nearer approach to equality; though the thing itself is so great, so glorious, so godlike,—nay so absolutely divine,—that you have been disgusted by the very promise of it, because its perfection is unattainable. Men have asserted a mock equality till the very idea of equality stinks in men's nostrils.'

The Duke in his enthusiasm had thrown off his hat, and was sitting on a wooden seat which they had reached, looking up among the clouds. His left hand was clenched, and from time to time with his right he rubbed the thin hairs on his brow. He had begun in a low voice, with a somewhat slipshod enunciation of his words, but had gradually become clear, resonant, and even eloquent. Phineas knew that there were stories told of certain bursts of words which had come from him in former days in the House of Commons. These had occasionally surprised men and induced them to declare that Planty Pall,—as he was then often called,—was a dark horse. But they had been few and far between, and Phineas had never heard them. Now he gazed at his companion in silence, wondering whether the speaker would go on with his speech. But the face changed on a sudden, and the Duke with an awkward motion snatched up his hat. 'I hope you ain't cold,' he said.

'Not at all,' said Phineas.

'I came here because of that bend of the river. I am always very fond of that bend. We don't go over the river. That is Mr Upjohn's property.'

'The member for the county?'

'Yes; and a very good member he is too, though he doesn't support us;—an old-school Tory, but a great friend of my uncle, who after all had a good deal of the Tory about him. I wonder whether he is at home. I must remind the Duchess to ask him to dinner. You know him of course.'

'Only by just seeing him in the House.'

'You'd like him very much. When in the country he always wears knee-breeches and gaiters, which I think a very comfortable dress.'

'Troublesome, Duke; isn't it?'

'I never tried it, and I shouldn't dare now. Goodness me; it's past five o'clock, and we've got two miles to get home. I haven't looked at a letter, and Warburton will think that I've thrown myself into the river because of Sir Timothy Beeswax.' Then they started to go home at a fast pace.

'I shan't forget, Duke,' said Phineas, 'your definition of Conservatives and Liberals.'

'I don't think I ventured on a definition;—only a few loose ideas which had been troubling me lately. I say, Finn!'

'Your Grace?'

'Don't you go and tell Ramsden and Drummond that I have been preaching equality, or we shall have a pretty mess. I don't know that it would serve me with my dear friend, the Duke.'

'I will be discretion itself.'

'Equality is a dream. But sometimes one likes to dream,—especially as there is no danger that Matching will fly from me in a dream. I doubt whether I could bear the test that has been attempted in other countries.'

'That poor ploughman would hardly get his share, Duke.'

'No;—that's where it is. We can only do a little and a little to bring it nearer to us;—so little that it won't touch Matching in our day. Here is her ladyship and the ponies. I don't think her ladyship would like to lose her ponies by my doctrine.'

The two wives of the two men were in the pony carriage, and the little Lady Glencora,* the Duchess's eldest daughter, was sitting between them. 'Mr Warburton has sent three messengers to demand your presence,' said the Duchess, 'and, as I live by bread, I believe that you and Mr Finn have been amusing yourselves!'

'We have been talking politics,' said the Duke.

'Of course. What other amusement was possible? But what business have you to indulge in idle talk when Mr Warburton wants you in the library? There has come a box,' she said, 'big enough to contain the resignations of all the traitors of the party.' This was strong language, and the Duke frowned;—but there was no one there to hear it but Phineas Finn and his wife, and they, at least, were trustworthy. The Duke suggested that he had better get back to the house as soon as possible. There might be something to be done requiring time before dinner. Mr Warburton might, at any rate, want to smoke a tranquil cigar after his day's work. The Duchess therefore left the carriage, as did Mrs Finn, and the Duke undertook to drive the little girl back to the house. 'He'll surely go against a tree,' said the Duchess. But,—as a fact,—the Duke did take himself and the child home in safety.

'And what do you think about it, Mr Finn?' said her Grace. 'I suppose you and the Duke have been settling what is to be done.'

'We have certainly settled nothing.'

'Then you must have disagreed.'

'That we as certainly have not done. We have in truth not once been out of cloud-land.'

'Ah;—then there is no hope. When once grown-up politicians get into cloud-land it is because the realities of the world have no longer any charm for them.'

The big box did not contain the resignations of any of the objectionable members of the Coalition. Ministers do not often resign in September,—nor would it be expedient that they should do so.

Lord Drummond and Sir Timothy were safe, at any rate, till next February, and might live without any show either of obedience or mutiny. The Duke remained in comparative quiet at Matching. There was not very much to do, except to prepare the work for the next Session. The great work of the coming year was to be the assimilation, or something very near to the assimilation, of the county suffrages with those of the boroughs.* The measure was one which had now been promised by statesmen for the last two years,—promised at first with that half promise which would mean nothing, were it not that such promises always lead to more defined assurances. The Duke of St Bungay, Lord Drummond, and other Ministers had wished to stave it off. Mr Monk was eager for its adoption, and was of course supported by Phineas Finn. The Prime Minister had at first been inclined to be led by the old Duke. There was no doubt to him but that the measure was desirable and would come, but there might well be a question as to the time at which it should be made to come. The old Duke knew that the measure would come,—but believing it to be wholly undesirable, thought that he was doing good work in postponing it from year to year. But Mr Monk had become urgent, and the old Duke had admitted the necessity. There must surely have been a shade of melancholy on that old man's mind as, year after year, he assisted in pulling down institutions which he in truth regarded as the safeguards of the nation;—but which he knew that, as a Liberal, he was bound to assist in destroying! It must have occurred to him, from time to time, that it would be well for him to depart and be at peace before everything was gone.

When he went from Matching Mr Monk took his place, and Phineas Finn, who had gone up to London for a while, returned; and then the three between them, with assistance from Mr Warburton and others, worked out the proposed scheme of the new county franchise, with the new divisions and the new constituencies. But it could hardly have been hearty work, as they all of them felt that whatever might be their first proposition they would be beat upon it in a House of Commons which thought that this Aristides had been long enough at the Treasury.

CHAPTER 69

MRS PARKER'S FATE

LOPEZ had now been dead more than five months, and not a word had been heard by his widow of Mrs Parker and her children. Her own sorrows had been so great that she had hardly thought of those of the poor woman who had come to her but a few days before her husband's death, telling her of the ruin caused by her husband's treachery. But late on the evening before her departure for Herefordshire,—very shortly after Everett had left the house,—there was a ring at the door, and a poorly-clad female asked to see Mrs Lopez. The poorly-clad female was Sexty Parker's wife. The servant, who did not remember her, would not leave her alone in the hall, having an eye to the coats and umbrellas, but called up one of the maids to carry the message. The poor woman understood the insult and resented it in her heart. But Mrs Lopez recognized the name in a moment, and went down to her in the parlour, leaving Mr Wharton upstairs. Mrs Parker, smarting from her present grievance, had bent her mind on complaining at once of the treatment she had received from the servant, but the sight of the widow's weeds quelled her. Emily had never been much given to fine clothes, either as a girl or as a married woman; but it had always been her husband's pleasure that she should be well dressed,—though he had never carried his trouble so far as to pay the bills; and Mrs Parker's remembrance of her friend at Dovercourt had been that of a fine lady in bright apparel. Now a black shade,—something almost like a dark ghost,—glided into the room, and Mrs Parker forgot her recent injury. Emily came forward and offered her hand, and was the first to speak. 'I have had a great sorrow since we met,' she said.

'Yes, indeed, Mrs Lopez. I don't think there is anything left in the world now except sorrow.'

'I hope Mr Parker is well. Will you not sit down, Mrs Parker?'

'Thank you, ma'am. Indeed, then, he is not well at all. How should he be well? Everything,—everything has been taken away from him.' Poor Emily groaned as she heard this. 'I wouldn't say a word against them as is gone, Mrs Lopez, if I could help it. I know it is bad to bear when him who once loved you isn't no more. And perhaps it is all the worse when things didn't go well with him, and it was, maybe, his own fault. I wouldn't do it, Mrs Lopez, if I could help it.'

'Let me hear what you have to say,' said Emily, determined to suffer everything patiently.

'Well;—it is just this. He has left us that bare that there is nothing left. And that they say isn't the worst of all,—though what can be worse than doing that, how is a woman to think? Parker was that soft, and he had that way with him of talking, that he has talked me and mine out of the very linen on our backs.'

'What do you mean by saying that that is not the worst?'

'They've come upon Sexty for a bill for four hundred and fifty,*—something to do with that stuff they call Bios,—and Sexty says it isn't his name at all. But he's been in that state he don't hardly know how to swear to anything. But he's sure he didn't sign it. The bill was brought to him by Lopez, and there was words between them, and he wouldn't have nothing to do with it. How is he to go to law? And it don't make much difference neither, for they can't take much more from him than they have taken.' Emily as she heard all this sat shivering, trying to repress her groans. 'Only,' continued Mrs Parker, 'they hadn't sold the furniture, and I was thinking they might let me stay in the house, and try to do with letting lodgings,—and now they're seizing everything along of this bill. Sexty is like a madman, swearing this and swearing that;—but what can he do, Mrs Lopez? It's as like his hand as two peas; but he was clever at everything was,—was,—you know who I mean, ma'am.' Then Emily covered her face with her hands and burst into violent tears. She had not determined whether she did or did not believe this last accusation made against her husband. She had had hardly time to realize the criminality of the offence imputed. But she did believe that the woman before her had been ruined by her husband's speculations. 'It's very bad, ma'am; isn't it?' said Mrs Parker, crying for company. 'It's bad all round. If you had five children as hadn't bread you'd know how it is that I feel. I've got to go back by the 10.15 to-night, and when I've paid for a third-class ticket I shan't have but twopence* left in the world.'

This utter depth of immediate poverty, this want of bread for the morrow and the next day, Emily could relieve out of her own pocket. And, thinking of this and remembering that her purse was not with her at the moment, she started up with the idea of getting it. But it occurred to her that that would not suffice; that her duty required more of her than that. And yet, by her own power, she could do no more. From month to month, almost from week to week, since her husband's death, her father had been called upon to satisfy claims for money which he would not resist, lest by doing so he should add to her misery. She had felt that she ought to bind herself to the strictest personal economy because of the miserable losses to which she had subjected him by her ill-starred marriage. 'What would you wish me to do?' she said, resuming her seat.

'You are rich,' said Mrs Parker. Emily shook her head. 'They say your papa is rich. I thought you would not like to see me in want like this.'

'Indeed, indeed, it makes me very unhappy.'

'Wouldn't your papa do something? It wasn't Sexty's fault nigh so much as it was his. I wouldn't say it to you if it wasn't for starving. I wouldn't say it to you if it wasn't for the children. I'd lie in the ditch and die if it was only myself, because——because I know what your feelings is. But what wouldn't you do, and what wouldn't you say, if you had five children at home as hadn't a loaf of bread among 'em?' Hereupon Emily got up and left the room, bidding her visitor wait for a few minutes. Presently the offensive butler came in, who had wronged Mrs Parker by watching his master's coats, and brought a tray with meat and wine. Mr Wharton, said the altered man, hoped that Mrs Parker would take a little refreshment, and he would be down himself very soon. Mrs Parker, knowing that strength for her journey home would be necessary to her, remembering that she would have to walk all through the city to the Bishopsgate Street station, did take some refreshment, and permitted herself to drink the glass of sherry that her late enemy had benignantly poured out for her.

Emily had been nearly half an hour with her father before Mr Wharton's heavy step was heard upon the stairs. And when he reached the dining-room door he paused a moment before he ventured to turn the lock. He had not told Emily what he would do, and had hardly as yet made up his own mind. As every fresh call was made upon him, his hatred for the memory of the man who had stepped in and disturbed his whole life, and turned all the mellow satisfaction of his evening into storm and gloom, was of course increased. The scoundrel's name was so odious to him that he could hardly keep himself from shuddering visibly before his daughter even when the servants called her by it. But yet he had determined that he would devote himself to save her from further suffering. It had been her fault, no doubt. But she was expiating it in very sackcloth and ashes, and he would add nothing to the burden on her back. He would pay, and pay, and pay, merely remembering that what he paid must be deducted from her share of his property. He had never intended to make what is called an elder son of Everett, and now there was less necessity than ever that he should do so, as Everett had become an elder son in another direction. He could satisfy almost any demand that might be made without material injury to himself.

But these demands, one after another, scalded him by their frequency, and by the baseness of the man who had occasioned them. His daughter had now repeated to him with sobbings and wailings the whole story as it had been told to her by the woman downstairs. 'Papa,' she had said, 'I don't know how to tell you or how not.' Then he had encouraged her, and had listened without saying a word. He had endeavoured not even to shrink as the charge of forgery was repeated to him by his own child,—the widow of the guilty man. He endeavoured not to remember at the moment that she had claimed this wretch as the chosen one of her maiden heart, in opposition to all his wishes. It hardly occurred to him to disbelieve the accusation. It was so probable! What was there to hinder the man from forgery, if he could only make it believed that his victim had signed the bill when intoxicated? He heard it all;—kissed his daughter, and then went down to the dining-room.

Mrs Parker, when she saw him, got up, and curtsied low, and then sat down again. Old Wharton looked at her from under his bushy eyebrows before he spoke, and then sat opposite her. 'Madam,' he said, 'this is a very sad story that I have heard.' Mrs Parker again rose, and again curtsied, and put her handkerchief to her face. 'It is of no use talking any more about it here.'

'No, sir,' said Mrs Parker.

'I and my daughter leave town early to-morrow morning.'

'Indeed, sir. Mrs Lopez didn't tell me.'

'My clerk will be in London, at No. 12, Stone Buildings, Lincoln's Inn, till I come back. Do you think you can find the place? I have written it there.'

'Yes, sir, I can find it,' said Mrs Parker, just raising herself from her chair at every word she spoke.

'I have written his name, you see. Mr Crumpy.'

'Yes, sir.'

'If you will permit me, I will give you two sovereigns now.'

'Thank you, sir.'

'And if you can make it convenient to call on Mr Crumpy every Thursday morning about twelve, he will pay you two sovereigns* a week till I come back to town. Then I will see about it.'

'God Almighty bless you, sir!'

'And as to the furniture, I will write to my attorney, Mr Walker. You need not trouble yourself by going to him.'

'No, sir.'

'If necessary, he will send to you, and he will see what can be done. Good night, Mrs Parker.' Then he walked across the room with two sovereigns which he dropped into her hand. Mrs Parker, with many sobs, bade him farewell, and Mr Wharton stood in the hall immovable till the front door had been closed behind her. 'I have settled it,' he said to Emily. 'I'll tell you to-morrow, or some day. Don't worry yourself now, but go to bed.' She looked wistfully,—so sadly, up into his face, and then did as he bade her.

But Mr Wharton could not go to bed without further trouble. It was incumbent on him to write full particulars that very night both to Mr Walker and to Mr Crumpy. And the odious letters in the writing became very long;—odious because he had to confess in them over and over again that his daughter, the very apple of his eye, had been the wife of a scoundrel. To Mr Walker he had to tell the whole story of the alleged forgery, and in doing so could not abstain from the use of hard words. 'I don't suppose that it can be proved, but there is every reason to believe that it's true.' And again—'I believe the man to have been as vile a scoundrel as ever was made by the love of money.' Even to Mr Crumpy he could not be reticent. 'She is an object of pity,' he said. 'Her husband was ruined by the infamous speculations of Mr Lopez.' Then he betook himself to bed. Oh, how happy would he be to pay the two pounds weekly,*—even to add to that the amount of the forged bill, if by doing so he might be saved from ever again hearing the name of Lopez.

The amount of the bill was ultimately lost by the bankers who had advanced the money on it. As for Mrs Sexty Parker, from week to week, and from month to month, and at last from year to year, she and her children,—and probably her husband also,—were supported by the weekly pension of two sovereigns which she always received on Thursday morning from the hands of Mr Crumpy himself. In a little time the one excitement of her life was the weekly journey to Mr Crumpy, whom she came to regard as a man appointed by Providence to supply her with 40s. on Thursday morning. As to poor Sexty Parker,—it is to be feared that he never again became a prosperous man.

'You will tell me what you did for that poor woman, papa,' said Emily leaning over her father in the train.

'I have settled it, my dear.'

'You said you'd tell me.'

'Crumpy will pay her two pounds a week till we know more about it.' Emily pressed her father's hand, and that was an end. No one ever did know any more about it, and Crumpy continued to pay the money.

CHAPTER 70

AT WHARTON

WHEN Mr Wharton and his daughter reached Wharton Hall there were at any rate no Fletchers there as yet. Emily, as she was driven from the station to the house, had not dared to ask a question or even to prompt her father to do so. He would probably have told her that on such an occasion there was but little chance that she would find any visitors, and none at all that she would find Arthur Fletcher. But she was too confused and too ill at ease to think of probabilities, and to the last was in trepidation, specially lest she should meet her lover. She found, however, at Wharton Hall none but Whartons, and she found also to her great relief that this change in the heir relieved her of much of the attention which must otherwise have added to her troubles. At the first glance her dress and demeanour struck them so forcibly that they could not avoid showing their feeling. Of course they had expected to see her in black,—had expected to see her in widow's weeds. But, with her, her very face and limbs had so adapted themselves to her crape, that she looked like a monument of bereaved woe. Lady Wharton took the mourner up into her own room, and there made her a little speech. 'We have all wept for you,' she said, 'and grieve for you still. But excessive grief is wicked, especially in the young. We will do our best to make you happy, and hope we shall succeed. All this about dear Everett ought to be a comfort to you.' Emily promised that she would do her best, not, however, taking much immediate comfort from the prospects of dear Everett. Lady Wharton certainly had never in her life spoken of dear Everett, while the wicked cousin was alive. Then Mary Wharton also made her little speech. 'Dear Emily, I will do all that I can. Pray try to believe in me.' But Everett was so much the hero of the hour, that there was not much room for general attention to any one else.

There was very much room for triumph in regard to Everett. It had already been ascertained that the Wharton who was now dead had had a child,—but that the child was a daughter. Oh,—what salvation or destruction there may be to an English gentleman in the sex of an infant! This poor baby was now little better than a beggar brat, unless the relatives who were utterly disregardful of its fate, should choose, in their charity, to make some small allowance for its maintenance. Had it by chance been a boy, Everett Wharton would have been nobody; and the child, rescued from the iniquities of his parents, would have been nursed in the best bedroom of Wharton Hall, and cherished with the warmest kisses, and would have been the centre of all the hopes of all the Whartons. But the Wharton lawyer by use of reckless telegrams had certified himself that the infant was a girl, and Everett was the hero of the day. He found himself to be possessed of a thousand graces, even in his father's eyesight. It seemed to be taken as a mark of his special good fortune that he had not clung to any business. To have been a banker immersed in the making of money, or even a lawyer attached to his circuit and his court, would have lessened his fitness, or at any rate his readiness, for the duties which he would have to perform. He would never be a very rich man, but he would have a command of ready money, and of course he would go into Parliament.

In his new position as,—not quite head of his family, but head expectant,—it seemed to him to be his duty to lecture his sister. It might be well that some one should lecture her with more severity than her father used. Undoubtedly she was succumbing to the wretchedness of her position in a manner that was repugnant to humanity generally. There is no power so useful to a man as that capacity of recovering himself after a fall, which belongs especially to those who possess a healthy mind in a healthy body. It is not rare to see one,—generally a woman,— whom a sorrow gradually kills; and there are those among us, who hardly perhaps envy, but certainly admire, a spirit so delicate as to be snuffed out by a woe. But it is the weakness of the heart rather than the strength of the feeling which has in such cases most often produced the destruction. Some endurance of fibre has been wanting, which power of endurance is a noble attribute. Everett Wharton saw something of this, and being, now, the heir apparent of the family, took his sister to task. 'Emily,' he said, 'you make us all unhappy when we look at you.'

'Do I?' she said. 'I am sorry for that;—but why should you look at me?'

'Because you are one of us. Of course we cannot shake you off. We would not if we could. We have all been very unhappy because,— because of what has happened. But don't you think you ought to make some sacrifice to us,—to our father, I mean, and to Sir Alured and Lady Wharton? When you go on weeping, other people have to weep too. I have an idea that people ought to be happy if it be only for the sake of their neighbours.'

'What am I to do, Everett?'

'Talk to people a little, and smile sometimes. Move about quicker. Don't look when you come into a room as if you were consecrating it to tears. And, if I may venture to say so, drop something of the heaviness of the mourning.'

'Do you mean that I am a hypocrite?'

'No;—I mean nothing of the kind. You know I don't. But you may exert yourself for the benefit of others without being untrue to your own memories. I am sure you know what I mean. Make a struggle and see if you cannot do something.'

She did make a struggle, and she did do something. No one, not well versed in the mysteries of feminine dress, could say very accurately what it was that she had done; but every one felt that something of the weight was reduced. At first, as her brother's words came upon her ear, and as she felt the blows which they inflicted on her, she accused him in her heart of cruelty. They were very hard to bear. There was a moment in which she was almost tempted to turn upon him and tell him that he knew nothing of her sorrows. But she restrained herself, and when she was alone she acknowledged to herself that he had spoken the truth. No one has a right to go about the world as a Niobe,* damping all joys with selfish tears. What did she not owe to her father, who had warned her so often against the evil she had contemplated, and had then, from the first moment after the fault was done, forgiven her the doing of it? She had at any rate learned from her misfortunes the infinite tenderness of his heart, which in the days of their unalloyed prosperity he had never felt the necessity of exposing to her. So she struggled and did do something. She pressed Lady Wharton's hand, and kissed her cousin Mary, and throwing herself into her father's arms when they were alone, whispered to him that she would try. 'What you told me, Everett, was quite right,' she said afterwards to her brother.

'I didn't mean to be savage,' he answered with a smile.

'It was quite right, and I have thought of it, and I will do my best. I will keep it to myself if I can. It is not quite, perhaps, what you think it is, but I will keep it to myself.' She fancied that they did not understand her, and perhaps she was right. It was not only that he had died and left her a young widow;—nor even that his end had been so harsh a tragedy and so foul a disgrace! It was not only that her love had been misbestowed,—not only that she had made so grievous an error in the one great act of her life which she had chosen to perform on her own judgement! Perhaps the most crushing memory of all was that which told her that she, who had through all her youth been regarded as a bright star in the family, had been the one person to bring a reproach upon the name of all these people who were so good to her. How shall a person conscious of disgrace, with a mind capable of feeling the crushing weight of personal disgrace, move and look and speak as though that disgrace had been washed away? But she made the struggle, and did not altogether fail.

As regarded Sir Alured, in spite of this poor widow's crape, he was very happy at this time, and his joy did in some degree communicate itself to the old barrister. Everett was taken round to every tenant and introduced as the heir. Mr Wharton had already declared his purpose of abdicating any possible possession of the property. Should he outlive Sir Alured he must be the baronet; but when that sad event should take place, whether Mr Wharton should then be alive or no, Everett should at once be the possessor of Wharton Hall. Sir Alured, under these circumstances, discussed his own death with extreme satisfaction, and insisted on having it discussed by the others. That he should have gone and left everything at the mercy of the spendthrift had been terrible to his old heart;—but now, the man coming to the property would have £60,000* with which to support and foster Wharton, with which to mend, as it were, the crevices, and stop up the holes of the estate. He seemed to be almost impatient for Everett's ownership, giving many hints as to what should be done when he himself was gone. He must surely have thought that he would return to Wharton as a spirit, and take a ghostly share in the prosperity of the farms. 'You will find John Griffith a very good man,' said the baronet. John Griffith had been a tenant on the estate for the last half-century, and was an older man than his landlord; but the baronet spoke of all this as though he himself were about to leave Wharton for ever in the course of the next week. 'John Griffith has been a good man, and if not always quite ready with his rent, has never been much behind. You won't be hard on John Griffith?'

'I hope I mayn't have the opportunity, sir.'

'Well;—well;—well; that's as may be. But I don't quite know what to say about young John. The farm has gone from father to son, and there's never been a word of a lease.'

'Is there anything wrong about the young man?'

'He's a little given to poaching.'

'Oh dear!'

'I've always got him off for his father's sake. They say he's going to marry Sally Jones. That may take it out of him. I do like the farms to go from father to son, Everett. It's the way that everything should go. Of course there's no right.'

'Nothing of that kind, I suppose,' said Everett, who was in his way a reformer, and had Radical notions with which he would not for worlds have disturbed the baronet at present.

'No;—nothing of that kind. God in his mercy forbid that a landlord in England should ever be robbed after that fashion.' Sir Alured, when he was uttering this prayer, was thinking of what he had heard of an Irish Land Bill,* the details of which, however, had been altogether incomprehensible to him. 'But I have a feeling about it, Everett; and I hope you will share it. It is good that things should go from father to son. I never make a promise; but the tenants know what I think about it, and then the father works for the son. Why should he work for a stranger? Sally Jones is a very good young woman, and perhaps young John will do better.' There was not a field or fence that he did not show to his heir;—hardly a tree which he left without a word. 'That bit of woodland coming in there,—they call it Barnton Spinnies,—doesn't belong to the estate at all.' This he said in a melancholy tone.

'Doesn't it, really?'

'And it comes right in between Lane's farm and Puddock's. They've always let me have the shooting as a compliment. Not that there's ever anything in it. It's only seven acres. But I like the civility.'

'Who does it belong to?'

'It belongs to Benet.'

'What; Corpus Christi?'*

'Yes, yes;—they've changed the name. It used to be Benet in my days. Walker says the College would certainly sell, but you'd have to pay for the land and the wood separately. I don't know that you'd get much out of it; but it's very unsightly,—on the survey map, I mean.'

'We'll buy it, by all means,' said Everett, who was already jingling his £60,000 in his pocket.

'I never had the money, but I think it should be bought.' And Sir Alured rejoiced in the idea that when his ghost should look at the survey map, that hiatus of Barnton Spinnies would not trouble his spectral eyes.

In this way months ran on at Wharton. Our Whartons had come down in the latter half of August, and at the beginning of September Mr Wharton returned to London. Everett, of course, remained, as he was still learning the lesson of which he was in truth becoming a little weary; and at last Emily had also been persuaded to stay in Herefordshire. Her father promised to return, not mentioning any precise time, but giving her to understand that he would come before the winter. He went, and probably found that his taste for the Eldon and for whist had returned to him. In the middle of November old Mrs Fletcher arrived. Emily was not aware of what was being done; but, in truth, the Fletchers and Whartons combined were conspiring with the view of bringing her back to her former self. Mrs Fletcher had not yielded without some difficulty,—for it was a part of this conspiracy that Arthur was to be allowed to marry the widow. But John had prevailed. 'He'll do it any way, mother,' he had said, 'whether you and I like it or not. And why on earth shouldn't he do as he pleases?'

'Think what the man was, John!'

'It's more to the purpose to think what the woman is. Arthur has made up his mind, and if I know him, he's not the man to be talked out of it.' And so the old woman had given in, and had at last consented to go forward as the advanced guard of the Fletchers, and lay siege to the affections of the woman whom she had once so thoroughly discarded from her heart.

'My dear,' she said, when they first met, 'if there has been anything wrong between you and me, let it be among the things that are past. You always used to kiss me. Give me a kiss now.' Of course Emily kissed her; and after that Mrs Fletcher patted her and petted her, and gave her lozenges, which she declared in private to be 'the sovereignest thing on earth' for debilitated nerves. And then it came out by degrees that John Fletcher and his wife and all the little Fletchers were coming to Wharton for the Christmas weeks. Everett had gone, but was also to be back for Christmas, and Mr Wharton's visit was also postponed. It was absolutely necessary that Everett should be at Wharton for the Christmas festivities, and expedient that Everett's father should be there to see them. In this way Emily had no means of escape. Her father wrote telling her of his plans, saying that he would bring her back after Christmas. Everett's heirship had made these Christmas festivities,— which were, however, to be confined to the two families,—quite a necessity. In all this not a word was said about Arthur, nor did she dare to ask whether he was expected. The younger Mrs Fletcher, John's wife, opened her arms to the widow in a manner that almost plainly said that she regarded Emily as her future sister-in-law. John Fletcher talked to her about Longbarns, and the children,—complete Fletcher talk,—as though she were already one of them, never, however, mentioning Arthur's name. The old lady got down a fresh supply of the lozenges from London because those she had by her might perhaps be a little stale. And then there was another sign which after a while became plain to Emily. No one in either family ever mentioned her name. It was not singular that none of them should call her Mrs Lopez, as she was Emily to all of them. But they never so described her even in speaking to the servants. And the servants themselves, as far as possible, avoided the odious word. The thing was to be buried, if not in oblivion, yet in some speechless grave. And it seemed that her father was joined in this attempt. When writing to her he usually made some excuse for writing also to Everett, or, in Everett's absence, to the baronet,—so that the letter for his daughter might be enclosed and addressed simply to 'Emily'.

She understood it all, and though she was moved to continual solitary tears by this ineffable tenderness, yet she rebelled against them. They should never cheat her back into happiness by such wiles as that! It was not fit that she should yield to them. As a woman utterly disgraced it could not become her again to laugh and be joyful, to give and take loving embraces, to sit and smile, perhaps a happy mother, at another man's hearth. For their love she was grateful. For his love she was more than grateful. How constant must be his heart, how grand his nature, how more than manly his strength of character, when he was thus true to her through all the evil she had done! Love him! Yes;—she would pray for him, worship him, fill the remainder of her days with thinking of him, hoping for him, and making his interests her own. Should he ever be married,—and she would pray that he might,—his wife, if possible, should be her friend, his children should be her darlings; and he should always be her hero. But they should not, with all their schemes, cheat her into disgracing him by marrying him.

At last her father came, and it was he who told her that Arthur was expected on the day before Christmas. 'Why did you not tell me before, papa, so that I might have asked you to take me away?'

'Because I thought, my dear, that it was better that you should be constrained to meet him. You would not wish to live all your life in terror of seeing Arthur Fletcher?'

'Not all my life.'

'Take the plunge and it will be over. They have all been very good to you.'

'Too good, papa. I didn't want it.'

'They are our oldest friends. There isn't a young man in England I think so highly of as John Fletcher. When I am gone, where are you to look for friends?'

'I'm not ungrateful, papa.'

'You can't know them all, and yet keep yourself altogether separated from Arthur. Think what it would be to me never to be able to ask him to the house. He is the only one of the family that lives in London, and now it seems that Everett will spend most of his time down here. Of course it is better that you should meet him and have done with it.'

There was no answer to be made to this, but still she was fixed in her resolution that she would never meet him as her lover.

Then came the morning of the day on which he was to arrive, and his coming was for the first time spoken openly of at breakfast. 'How is Arthur to be brought from the station?' asked old Mrs Fletcher.

'I'm going to take the dog-cart,' said Everett. 'Giles will go for the luggage with the pony. He is bringing down a lot of things;—a new saddle, and a gun for me.' It had all been arranged for her, this question and answer, and Emily blushed as she felt that it was so.

'We shall be so glad to see Arthur,' said young Mrs Fletcher to her.

'Of course you will.'

'He has not been down since the Session was over, and he has got to be quite a speaking man now. I do so hope he'll become something some day.'

'I am sure he will,' said Emily.

'Not a judge, however. I hate wigs. Perhaps he might be Lord Chancellor* in time.' Mrs Fletcher was not more ignorant than some other ladies in being unaware of the Lord Chancellor's wig and exact position.

At last he came. The 9 a.m. express for Hereford,—express, at least, for the first two or three hours out of London,—brought passengers for Wharton to their nearest station at 3 p.m., and the distance was not above five miles. Before four o'clock Arthur was standing before the drawing-room fire, with a cup of tea in his hand, surrounded by Fletchers and Whartons, and being made much of as the young family member of Parliament. But Emily was not in the room. She had studied her Bradshaw,* and learned the hours of the trains, and was now in her bedroom. He had looked around the moment he entered the room, but had not dared to ask for her suddenly. He had said one word about her to Everett in the cart, and that had been all. She was in the house, and he must, at any rate, see her before dinner.

Emily, in order that she might not seem to escape abruptly, had retired early to her solitude. But she, too, knew that the meeting could not be long postponed. She sat thinking of it all, and at last heard the wheels of the vehicle before the door. She paused, listening with all her ears, that she might recognize his voice, or possibly his footstep. She stood near the window, behind the curtain, with her hand pressed to her heart. She heard Everett's voice plainly as he gave some directions to the groom, but from Arthur she heard nothing. Yet she was sure that he was come. The very manner of the approach and her brother's word made her certain that there had been no disappointment. She stood thinking for a quarter of an hour, making up her mind how best they might meet. Then suddenly, with slow but certain step, she walked down into the drawing-room.

No one expected her then, or something perhaps might have been done to encourage her coming. It had been thought that she must meet him before dinner, and her absence till then was to be excused. But now she opened the door, and with much dignity of mien walked into the middle of the room. Arthur at that moment was discussing the Duke's chance for the next Session, and Sir Alured was asking with rapture whether the old Conservative party would not come in. Arthur Fletcher heard the step, turned round, and saw the woman he loved. He went at once to meet her, very quickly, and put out both his hands. She gave him hers, of course. There was no excuse for her refusal. He stood for an instant pressing them, looking eagerly into her sad face, and then he spoke. 'God bless you, Emily!' he said. 'God bless you!' He had thought of no words, and at the moment nothing else occurred to him to be said. The colour had covered all his face, and his heart beat so strongly that he was hardly his own master. She let him hold her two hands, perhaps for a minute, and then, bursting into tears, tore herself from him, and, hurrying out of the room, made her way again into her own chamber. 'It will be better so,' said old Mrs Fletcher. 'It will be better so. Do not let any one follow her.'

On that day John Fletcher took her out to dinner, and Arthur did not sit near her. In the evening he came to her as she was working close to his mother, and seated himself on a low chair close to her knees. 'We are all so glad to see you; are we not, mother?'

'Yes, indeed,' said Mrs Fletcher. Then, after a while, the old woman got up to make a rubber at whist with the two old men and her eldest son, leaving Arthur sitting at the widow's knee. She would willingly have escaped, but it was impossible that she should move.

'You need not be afraid of me,' he said, not whispering, but in a voice which no one else could hear. 'Do not seem to avoid me, and I will say nothing to trouble you. I think that you must wish that we should be friends.'

'Oh, yes.'

'Come out, then, to-morrow, when we are walking. In that way we shall get used to each other. You are troubled now, and I will go.' Then he left her, and she felt herself to be bound to him by infinite gratitude.

A week went on and she had become used to his company. A week passed and he had spoken no word to her that a brother might not have spoken. They had walked together when no one else had been within hearing, and yet he had spared her. She had begun to think that he would spare her altogether, and she was certainly grateful. Might it not be that she had misunderstood him, and had misunderstood the meaning of them all? Might it not be that she had troubled herself with false anticipations? Surely it was so; for how could it be that such a man should wish to make such a woman his wife?

'Well, Arthur?' said his brother to him one day.

'I have nothing to say about it,' said Arthur.

'You haven't changed your mind?'

'Never! Upon my word, to me, in that dress, she is more beautiful than ever.'

'I wish you would make her take it off.'

'I dare not ask her yet.'

'You know what they say about widows generally, my boy.'

'That is all very well when one talks about widows in general. It is easy to chaff about women when one hasn't got any woman in one's mind. But as it is now, having her here, loving her as I do,—by heaven! I cannot hurry her. I don't dare to speak to her after that fashion. I shall do it in time, I suppose;—but I must wait till the time comes.'

CHAPTER 71

THE LADIES AT LONGBARNS DOUBT

IT came at last to be decided among them that when old Mr Wharton returned to town,—and he had now been at Wharton longer than he had ever been known to remain there before,—Emily should still remain in Herefordshire, and that at some period not then fixed she should go for a month to Longbarns. There were various reasons which induced her to consent to this change of plans. In the first place she found herself to be infinitely more comfortable in the country than in town. She could go out and move about and bestir herself, whereas in Manchester Square she could only sit and mope at home. Her father had assured her that he thought that it would be better that she should be away from the reminiscences of the house in town. And then when the first week of February was past Arthur would be up in town, and she would be far away from him at Longbarns, whereas in London she would be close within his reach. Many little schemes were laid and struggles made both by herself and the others before at last their plans were settled. Mr Wharton was to return to London in the middle of January. It was quite impossible that he could remain longer away either from Stone Buildings or from the Eldon, and then at the same time, or a day or two following, Mrs Fletcher was to go back to Longbarns. John Fletcher and his wife and children were already gone,—and Arthur also had been at Longbarns. The two brothers and Everett had been backwards and forwards. Emily was anxious to remain at Wharton at any rate till Parliament should have met, so that she might not be at home with Arthur in his own house. But matters would not arrange themselves exactly as she wished. It was at last settled that she should go to Longbarns with Mary Wharton under the charge of John Fletcher in the first week in February. As arrangements were already in progress for the purchase of Barnton Spinnies Sir Alured could not possibly leave his own house. Not to have walked through the wood on the first day that it became part of the Wharton property would to him have been treason to the estate. His experience ought to have told him that there was no chance of a lawyer and a college dealing together with such rapidity; but in the present state of things he could not bear to absent himself. Orders had already been given for the cutting down of certain trees which could not have been touched had the reprobate lived, and it was indispensable that if a tree fell at Wharton he should see the fall. It thus came to pass that there was a week during which Emily would be forced to live under the roof of the Fletchers together with Arthur Fletcher.

The week came and she was absolutely received by Arthur at the door of Longbarns. She had not been at the house since it had first been intimated to the Fletchers that she was disposed to receive with favour the addresses of Ferdinand Lopez. As she remembered this it seemed to her to be an age ago since that man had induced her to believe that of all men she had ever met he was the nearest to a hero. She never spoke of him now, but of course her thoughts of him were never ending,—as also of herself in that she had allowed herself to be so deceived. She would recall to her mind with bitter inward sobbings all those lessons of iniquity which he had striven to teach her, and which had first opened her eyes to his true character,—how sedulously he had endeavoured to persuade her that it was her duty to rob her father on his behalf, how continually he had endeavoured to make her think that appearance in the world was everything, and that, being in truth poor adventurers, it behoved them to cheat the world into thinking them rich and respectable. Every hint that had been so given had been a wound to her, and those wounds were all now remembered.

Though since his death she had never allowed a word to be spoken in her presence against him, she could not but hate his memory. How glorious was that other man in her eyes, as he stood there at the door welcoming her to Longbarns, fair-haired, open-eyed, with bronzed brow and cheek, and surly the honestest face that a loving woman ever loved to gaze on. During the various lessons she had learned in her married life, she had become gradually but surely aware that the face of that other man had been dishonest. She had learned the false meaning of every glance of his eyes, the subtlety of his mouth, the counterfeit manœuvres of his body,—the deceit even of his dress. He had been all a lie from head to foot; and he had thrown her love aside as useless when she also would not be a liar. And here was this man,—spotless in her estimation, compounded of all good qualities, which she could now see and take at their proper value. She hated herself for the simplicity with which she had been cheated by soft words and a false demeanour into so great a sacrifice.

Life at Longbarns was very quiet during the days which she passed there before he left them. She was frequently alone with him, but he, if he still loved her, did not speak of his love. He explained it all one day to his mother. 'If it is to be,' said the old lady, 'I don't see the use of more delay. Of course the marriage ought not to be till March twelvemonths. But if it is understood that it is to be, she might alter her dress by degrees,—and alter her manner of living. Those things should always be done by degrees. I think it had better be settled, Arthur, if it is to be settled.'

'I am afraid, mother.'

'Dear me! I didn't think you were the man ever to be afraid of a woman. What can she say to you?'

'Refuse me.'

'Then you'd better know it at once. But I don't think she'll be fool enough for that.'

'Perhaps you hardly understand her, mother.'

Mrs Fletcher shook her head with a look of considerable annoyance. 'Perhaps not. But, to tell the truth, I don't like young women whom I can't understand. Young women shouldn't be mysterious. I like people of whom I can give a pretty good guess what they'll do. I'm sure I never could have guessed that she would have married that man.'

'If you love me, mother, do not let that be mentioned between us again. When I said that you did not understand her, I did not mean that she was mysterious. I think that before he died, and since his death, she learned of what sort that man was. I will not say that she hates his memory, but she hates herself for what she has done.'

'So she ought,' said Mrs Fletcher.

'She has not yet brought herself to think that her life should be anything but one long period of mourning, not for him, but for her own mistake. You may be quite sure that I am in earnest. It is not because I doubt of myself that I put it off. But I fear that if once she asserts to me her resolution to remain as she is, she will feel herself bound to keep her word.'

'I suppose she is very much the same as other women, after all, my dear,' said Mrs Fletcher, who was almost jealous of the peculiar superiority of sentiment which her son seemed to attribute to this woman.

'Circumstances, mother, make people different,' he replied.

'So you are going without having anything fixed,' his elder brother said to him the day before he started.

'Yes, old fellow. It seems to be rather slack;—doesn't it?'

'I dare say you know best what you're about. But if you have set your mind on it——'

'You may take your oath on that.'

'Then I don't see why one word shouldn't put it all right. There never is any place so good for that kind of thing as a country house.'

'I don't think that with her it will make much difference where the house is, or what the circumstances.'

'She knows what you mean as well as I do.'

'I dare say she does, John. She must have a very bad idea of me if she doesn't. But she may know what I mean and not mean the same thing herself.'

'How are you to know if you don't ask her?'

'You may be sure that I shall ask her as soon as I can hope that my doing so may give her more pleasure than pain. Remember I have had all this out with her father. I have determined that I will wait till twelve months have passed since that wretched man perished.'

On that afternoon before dinner he was alone with her in the library some minutes before they went up to dress for dinner. 'I shall hardly see you to-morrow,' he said, 'as I must leave this at half-past eight. I breakfast at eight. I don't suppose any one will be down except my mother.'

'I am generally as early as that. I will come down and see you start.'

'I am so glad that you have been here, Emily.'

'So am I. Everybody has been so good to me.'

'It has been like old days,—almost.'

'It will never quite be like old days again, I think. But I have been very glad to be here,—and at Wharton. I sometimes almost wish that I were never going back to London again,—only for papa.'

'I like London myself.'

'You! Yes, of course you like London. You have everything in life before you. You have things to do, and much to hope for. It is all beginning for you, Arthur.'

'I am five years older than you are.'

'What does that matter? It seems to me that age does not go by years. It is long since I have felt myself to be an old woman. But you are quite young. Everybody is proud of you, and you ought to be happy.'

'I don't know,' said he. 'It is hard to say what makes a person happy.' He almost made up his mind to speak to her then; but he had made up his mind before to put it off still for a little time, and he would not allow himself to be changed on the spur of the moment. He had thought of it much, and he had almost taught himself to think that it would be better for herself that she should not accept another man's love so soon. 'I shall come and see you in town,' he said.

'You must come and see papa. It seems that Everett is to be a great deal at Wharton. I had better go up to dress now, or I shall be keeping them waiting.' He put out his hand to her, and wished her good-bye, excusing himself by saying that they should not be alone together again before he started.

She saw him go on the next morning,—and then she almost felt herself to be abandoned, almost deserted. It was a fine crisp winter day, dry and fresh, and clear, but with the frost still on the ground. After breakfast she went out to walk by herself in the long shrubbery paths which went round the house, and here she remained for above an hour. She told herself that she was very thankful to him for not having spoken to her on a subject so unfit for her ears as love. She strengthened herself in her determination never again to listen to a man willingly on that subject. She had made herself unfit to have any dealings of that nature. It was not that she could not love. Oh, no! She knew well enough that she did love,—love with all her heart. If it were not that she were so torn to rags that she was not fit to be worn again, she could now have thrown herself into his arms with a whole heaven of joy before her. A woman, she told herself, had no right to a second chance in life, after having made such shipwreck of herself in the first. But the danger of being seduced from her judgement by Arthur Fletcher was all over. He had been near her for the last week and had not spoken a word. He had been in the same house with her for the last ten days and had been with her as a brother might be with his sister. It was not only she who had seen the propriety of this. He also had acknowledged it, and she was—— grateful to him. As she endeavoured in her solitude to express her gratitude in spoken words the tears rolled down her cheeks. She was glad, she told herself, very glad that it was so. How much trouble and pain to both of them would thus be spared! And yet her tears were bitter tears. It was better as it was;—and yet one word of love would have been very sweet. She almost thought that she would have liked to tell him that for his sake, for his dear sake, she would refuse——that which now would never be offered to her. She was quite clear as to the rectitude of her own judgement, clear as ever. And yet her heart was heavy with disappointment.

It was the end of March before she left Herefordshire for London, having spent the greater part of the time at Longbarns. The ladies at that place were moved by many doubts as to what would be the end of all this. Mrs Fletcher the elder at last almost taught herself to believe that there would be no marriage, and having got back to that belief, was again opposed to the idea of a marriage. Anything and everything that Arthur wanted he ought to have. The old lady felt no doubt as to that. When convinced that he did want to have this widow,—this woman whose life had hitherto been so unfortunate,—she had for his sake taken the woman again by the hand, and had assisted in making her one of themselves. But how much better it would be that Arthur should think better of it! It was the maddest constancy,—this clinging to the widow of such a man as Ferdinand Lopez! If there were any doubt, then she would be prepared to do all she could to prevent the marriage. Emily had been forgiven, and the pardon bestowed must of course be continued. But she might be pardoned without being made Mrs Arthur Fletcher. While Emily was still at Longbarns the old lady almost talked over her daughter-in-law to this way of thinking,—till John Fletcher put his foot upon it altogether. 'I don't pretend to say what she may do,' he said.

'Oh, John,' said his mother, 'to hear a man like you talk like that is absurd. She'd jump at him if he looked at her with half an eye.'

'What she may do,' he continued saying, without appearing to listen to his mother, 'I cannot say. But that he will ask her to be his wife is as certain as that I stand here.'

CHAPTER 72

'HE THINKS THAT OUR DAYS ARE NUMBERED'

ALL the details of the new County Suffrage Bill* were settled at Matching during the recess between Mr Monk, Phineas Finn, and a very experienced gentleman from the Treasury, one Mr Prime, who was supposed to know more about such things than any man living, and was consequently called Constitution Charlie. He was an elderly man, over sixty years of age, who remembered the first Reform Bill, and had been engaged in the doctoring of constituencies ever since. The Bill, if passed, would be mainly his Bill, and yet the world would never hear his name as connected with it. Let us hope that he was comfortable at Matching, and that he found his consolation in the smiles of the Duchess. During this time the old Duke was away, and even the Prime Minister was absent for some days. He would fain have busied himself about the Bill himself, but was hardly allowed by his colleagues to have any hand in framing it. The great points of the measure had of course been arranged in the Cabinet,—where, however, Mr Monk's views had been adopted almost without a change. It may not perhaps be too much to assume that one or two members of the Cabinet did not quite understand the full scope of every suggested clause. The effects which clauses will produce, the dangers which may be expected from this or that change, the manner in which this or that proposition will come out in the washing, do not strike even Cabinet Ministers at a glance. A little study in a man's own cabinet, after the reading perhaps of a few leading articles, and perhaps a short conversation with an astute friend or two, will enable a statesman to be strong at a given time for, or even, if necessary, against a measure, who has listened in silence, and has perhaps given his personal assent, to the original suggestion. I doubt whether Lord Drummond, when he sat silent in the Cabinet, had realized those fears which weighed upon him so strongly afterwards, or had then foreseen that the adoption of a nearly similar franchise for the counties and boroughs must inevitably lead to the American system* of numerical representation. But when time had been given him, and he and Sir Timothy had talked it all over, the mind of no man was ever clearer than that of Lord Drummond.

The Prime Minister, with the diligence which belonged to him, had mastered all the details of Mr Monk's Bill before it was discussed in the Cabinet, and yet he found that his assistance was hardly needed in the absolute preparation. Had they allowed him he would have done it all himself. But it was assumed that he would not trouble himself with such work, and he perceived that he was not wanted. Nothing of moment was settled without a reference to him. He required that everything should be explained as it went on, down to the extension of every borough boundary; but he knew that he was not doing it himself, and that Mr Monk and Constitution Charlie had the prize between them.

Nor did he dare to ask Mr Monk what would be the fate of the Bill. To devote all one's time and mind and industry to a measure which one knows will fall to the ground must be sad. Work under such circumstances must be very grievous. But such is often the fate of statesmen. Whether Mr Monk laboured under such a conviction the Prime Minister did not know, though he saw his friend and colleague almost daily. In truth no one dared to tell him exactly what he thought. Even the old Duke had become partially reticent, and taken himself off to his own woods at Long Royston. To Phineas Finn the Prime Minister would sometimes say a word, but would say even that timidly. On any abstract question, such as that which he had discussed when they had been walking together, he could talk freely enough. But on the matter of the day, those affairs which were of infinite importance to himself, and on which one would suppose he would take delight in speaking to a trusted colleague, he could not bring himself to be open. 'It must be a long Bill, I suppose?' he said to Phineas one day.

'I'm afraid so, Duke. It will run, I fear, to over a hundred clauses.'

'It will take you the best part of the Session to get through it?'

'If we can have the second reading* early in March, we hope to send it up to you* in the first week in June. That will give us ample time.'

'Yes;—yes. I suppose so.' But he did not dare to ask Phineas Finn whether he thought that the House of Commons would assent to the second reading. It was known at this time that the Prime Minister was painfully anxious as to the fate of the Ministry. It seemed to be but the other day that everybody connected with the Government was living in fear lest he should resign. His threats in that direction had always been made to his old friend the Duke of St Bungay; but a great man cannot whisper his thoughts without having them carried in the air. In all the clubs it had been declared that that was the rock by which the Coalition would probably be wrecked. The newspapers had repeated the story, and the 'People's Banner' had assured the world that if it were so the Duke of Omnium would thus do for his country the only good service which it was possible that he should render it. That was at the time when Sir Orlando was mutinous and when Lopez had destroyed himself. But now no such threat came from the Duke, and the 'People's Banner' was

already accusing him of clinging to power with pertinacious and unconstitutional tenacity. Had not Sir Orlando deserted him? Was it not well
known that Lord Drummond and Sir Timothy Beeswax were only
restrained from doing so by a mistaken loyalty?

Everybody came up to town, Mr Monk having his Bill in his pocket,
and the Queen's speech was read, promising the County Suffrage Bill.
The address was voted* with a very few words from either side. The
battle was not to be fought then. Indeed, the state of things was so
abnormal that there could hardly be said to be any sides in the House.
A stranger in the gallery, not knowing the condition of affairs, would
have thought that no minister had for many years commanded so large
a majority, as the crowd of members was always on the Government
side of the House; but the opposition which Mr Monk expected would,
he knew, come from those who sat around him, behind him, and even
at his very elbow. About a week after Parliament met the Bill was read
for the first time, and the second reading was appointed for an early day
in March.

The Duke had suggested to Mr Monk the expedience of some further delay, giving as his reason the necessity of getting through certain
routine work, should the rejection of the Bill create the confusion of a
resignation. No one who knew the Duke could ever suspect him of giving a false reason. But it seemed that in this the Prime Minister was
allowing himself to be harassed by fears of the future. Mr Monk
thought that any delay would be injurious and open to suspicion after
what had been said and done, and was urgent in his arguments. The
Duke gave way, but he did so almost sullenly, signifying his acquies-
cence with haughty silence. 'I am sorry,' said Mr Monk, 'to differ from
your Grace, but my opinion in the matter is so strong that I do not dare
to abstain from expressing it.' The Duke bowed again and smiled. He
had intended that the smile should be acquiescent, but it had been as
cold as steel. He knew that he was misbehaving, but was not sufficiently
master of his own manner to be gracious. He told himself on the spot,—
though he was quite wrong in so telling himself,—that he had now
made an enemy also of Mr Monk, and through Mr Monk of Phineas
Finn. And now he felt that he had no friend left in whom to trust,—for
the old Duke had become cold and indifferent. The old Duke, he
thought, was tired of his work and anxious for rest. It was the old Duke
who had brought him into this hornets' nest; had fixed upon his back
the unwilling load; had compelled him to assume the place which now
to lose would be a disgrace,—and the old Duke was now deserting him!
He was sore all over, angry with every one, ungracious even with his

private Secretary and his wife,—and especially miserable because he was thoroughly aware of his own faults. And yet, through it all, there was present to him a desire to fight on to the very last. Let his colleagues do what they might, and say what they might, he would remain Prime Minister of England as long as he was supported by a majority in the House of Commons.

'I do not know any greater step than this,' Phineas said to him pleasantly one day, speaking of their new measure, 'towards that millennium of which we were talking at Matching, if we can only accomplish it.'

'Those moral speculations, Mr Finn,' he said, 'will hardly bear the wear and tear of real life.' The words of the answer, combined with the manner in which they were spoken, were stern and almost uncivil. Phineas, at any rate, had done nothing to offend him. The Duke paused, trying to find some expression by which he might correct the injury he had done; but, not finding any, passed on without further speech. Phineas shrugged his shoulders and went his way, telling himself that he had received one further injunction not to put his trust in princes.*

'We shall be beaten certainly,' said Mr Monk to Phineas not long afterwards.

'What makes you so sure?'

'I smell it in the air. I see it in men's faces.'

'And yet it's a moderate Bill. They'll have to pass something stronger before long if they throw it out now.'

'It's not the Bill that they'll reject, but us. We have served our turn, and we ought to go.'

'The House is tired of the Duke?'

'The Duke is so good a man that I hardly like to admit even that;— but I fear it is so. He is fretful and he makes enemies.'

'I sometimes think that he is ill.'

'He is ill at ease and sick at heart. He cannot hide his chagrin, and then is doubly wretched because he has betrayed it. I do not know that I ever respected and, at the same time, pitied a man more thoroughly.'

'He snubbed me awfully yesterday,' said Phineas, laughing.

'He cannot help himself. He snubs me at every word that he speaks, and yet I believe that he is most anxious to be civil to me. His ministry has been of great service to the country. For myself, I shall never regret having joined it. But I think that to him it has been a continual sorrow.'

The system on which the Duchess had commenced her career as wife of the Prime Minister had now been completely abandoned. In the first place, she had herself become so weary of it that she had been unable to continue the exertion. She had, too, become in some degree ashamed of her failures. The names of Major Pountney and Mr Lopez were not now pleasant to her ears, nor did she look back with satisfaction on the courtesies she had lavished on Sir Orlando or the smiles she had given to Sir Timothy Beeswax. 'I've known a good many vulgar people in my time,' she said one day to Mrs Finn, 'but none ever so vulgar as our ministerial supporters. You don't remember Mr Bott,* my dear. He was before your time;—one of the arithmetical men, and a great friend of Plantagenet's. He was very bad, but there have come up worse since him. Sometimes, I think, I like a little vulgarity for a change; but, upon my honour, when we get rid of all this it will be a pleasure to go back to ladies and gentlemen.' This the Duchess said in her extreme bitterness.

'It seems to me that you have pretty well got rid of "all this" already.'

'But I haven't got anybody else in their place. I have almost made up my mind not to ask any one into the house for the next twelve months. I used to think that nothing would ever knock me up, but now I feel that I'm almost done for. I hardly dare open my mouth to Plantagenet. The Duke of St Bungay has cut me. Mr Monk looks as ominous as an owl; and your husband hasn't a word to say left. Barrington Erle hides his face and passes by when he sees me. Mr Rattler did try to comfort me the other day by saying that everything was at sixes and sevens, and I really took it almost as a compliment to be spoken to. Don't you think Plantagenet is ill?'

'He is careworn.'

'A man may be worn by care till there comes to be nothing left of him. But he never speaks of giving up now. The old Bishop of St Austell talks of resigning, and he has already made up his mind who is to have the see. He used to consult the Duke about all these things, but I don't think he ever consults any one now. He never forgave the Duke about Lord Earlybird. Certainly, if a man wants to quarrel with all his friends, and to double the hatred of all his enemies, he had better become Prime Minister.'

'Are you really sorry that such was his fate, Lady Glen?'

'Ah,—I sometimes ask myself that question, but I never get at an answer. I should have thought him a poltroon if he had declined. It is to be the greatest man in the greatest country in the world. Do ever so little and the men who write history must write about you. And no man has ever tried to be nobler than he till,—till——'

'Make no exception. If he be careworn and ill and weary, his manners cannot be the same as they were, but his purity is the same as ever.'

'I don't know that it would remain so. I believe in him, Marie, more than in any man,—but I believe in none thoroughly. There is a devil creeps in upon them when their hands are strengthened. I do not know what I would have wished. Whenever I do wish, I always wish wrong. Ah, me; when I think of all those people I had down at Gatherum,—of the trouble I took, and of the glorious anticipations in which I revelled, I do feel ashamed of myself. Do you remember when I was determined that that wretch should be member for Silverbridge?'

'You haven't seen her since, Duchess?'

'No; but I mean to see her. I couldn't make her first husband member, and therefore the man who is member is to be her second husband. But I'm almost sick of schemes. Oh, dear, I wish I knew something that was really pleasant to do. I have never really enjoyed anything since I was in love, and I only liked that because it was wicked.'

The Duchess was wrong in saying that the Duke of St Bungay had cut them. The old man still remembered the kiss and still remembered the pledge. But he had found it very difficult to maintain his old relations with his friend. It was his opinion that the Coalition had done all that was wanted from it, and that now had come the time when they might retire gracefully. It is, no doubt, hard for a Prime Minister to find an excuse for going. But if the Duke of Omnium would have been content to acknowledge that he was not the man to alter the County Suffrage, an excuse might have been found that would have been injurious to no one. Mr Monk and Mr Gresham might have joined, and the present Prime Minister might have resigned, explaining that he had done all that he had been appointed to accomplish. He had, however, yielded at once to Mr Monk, and now it was to be feared that the House of Commons would not accept the Bill from his hands. In such a state of things,—especially after that disagreement about Lord Earlybird,—it was difficult for the old Duke to tender his advice. He was at every Cabinet Council; he always came when his presence was required; he was invariably good-humoured;—but it seemed to him that his work was done. He could hardly volunteer to tell his chief and his colleague that he would certainly be beaten in the House of Commons, and that therefore there was little more now to be done than to arrange the circumstances of their retirement. Nevertheless, as the period for the second reading of the Bill came on, he resolved that he would discuss the matter with his friend. He owed it to himself to do so, and he also owed it to the man whom he had certainly placed in his present position. On himself politics had imposed a burden very much lighter than that which they had inflicted on his more energetic and much less practical colleague. Through his long life he had either been in office, or in such a position that men were sure that he would soon return to it. He had taken it, when it had come, willingly, and had always left it without a regret. As a man cuts in and out at a whist table, and enjoys both the game and the rest from the game, so had the Duke of St Bungay been well pleased in either position. He was patriotic, but his patriotism did not disturb his digestion. He had been ambitious,— but moderately ambitious, and his ambition had been gratified. It never occurred to him to be unhappy because he or his party were beaten on a measure. When President of the Council, he could do his duty and enjoy London life. When in opposition, he could linger in Italy till May and devote his leisure to his trees and his bullocks. He was always esteemed, always self-satisfied, and always Duke of St Bungay. But with our Duke it was very different. Patriotism with him was a fever, and the public service an exacting mistress. As long as this had been all he had still been happy. Not trusting much in himself, he had never aspired to great power. But now, now at last, ambition had laid hold of him,—and the feeling, not perhaps uncommon with such men, that personal dishonour would be attached to political failure. What would his future life be if he had so carried himself in his great office as to have shown himself to be unfit to resume it? Hitherto any office had sufficed him in which he might be useful;—but now he must either be Prime Minister, or a silent, obscure, and humbled man!

'DEAR DUKE,
    'I will be with you to-morrow morning at 11 a.m., if you can give me half-an-hour.
                                    'Yours affectionately,
                                                'ST. B.'

    The Prime Minister received this note one afternoon, a day or two before that appointed for the second reading, and meeting his friend within an hour in the House of Lords, confirmed the appointment. 'Shall I not rather come to you?' he said. But the old Duke, who lived in St James's Square, declared that Carlton Terrace would be in his way to Downing Street,* and so the matter was settled. Exactly at eleven the two Ministers met. 'I don't like troubling you,' said the old man, 'when I know that you have so much to think of.'

'On the contrary, I have but little to think of,—and my thoughts must be very much engaged, indeed, when they shall be too full to admit of seeing you.'

'Of course we are all anxious about this Bill.' The Prime Minister smiled. Anxious! Yes, indeed. His anxiety was of such a nature that it kept him awake all night, and never for a moment left his mind free by day. 'And of course we must be prepared as to what shall be done either in the event of success or of failure.'

'You might as well read that,' said the other. 'It only reached me this morning, or I should have told you of it.' The letter was a communication from the Solicitor-General containing his resignation. He had now studied the County Suffrage Bill closely, and regretted to say that he could not give it conscientious support. It was a matter of sincerest sorrow to him that relations so pleasant should be broken, but he must resign his place, unless, indeed, the clauses as to redistribution could be withdrawn. Of course he did not say this as expecting any such concession would be made to his opinion, but merely as indicating the matter on which his objection was so strong as to over-rule all other considerations. All this he explained at great length.

'The pleasantness of the relations must have been on one side,' said the veteran. 'He ought to have gone long since.'

'And Lord Drummond has already as good as said that unless we will abandon the same clauses he must oppose the Bill in the Lords.'

'And resign, of course.'

'He meant that, I presume. Lord Ramsden has not spoken to me.'

'The clauses will not stick in his throat. Nor ought they. If the lawyers have their own way about the law they should be contented.'

'The question is, whether in these circumstances we should postpone the second reading?' asked the Prime Minister.

'Certainly not,' said the other Duke. 'As to the Solicitor-General you will have no difficulty. Sir Timothy was only placed there as a concession to his party. Drummond will no doubt continue to hold his office till we see what is done in the Lower House. If the second reading be lost there,—why then his lordship can go with the rest of us.'

'Rattler says we shall have a majority. He and Roby are quite agreed about it. Between them they must know,' said the Prime Minister, unintentionally pleading for himself.

'They ought to know, if any men do;—but the crisis is exceptional. I suppose you think that if the second reading is lost we should resign?'

'Oh,—certainly.'

'Or, after that, if the Bill is much mutilated in committee? I don't know that I shall personally break my own heart about the Bill. The existing difference in the suffrages is rather in accordance with my prejudices. But the country desires the measure, and I suppose we cannot consent to any such material alteration as these men suggest.' As he spoke he laid his hand on Sir Timothy's letter.

'Mr Monk would not hear of it,' said the Prime Minister.

'Of course not. And you and I in this measure must stick to Mr Monk. My great, indeed my only strong desire in the matter, is to act in strict unison with you.'

'You are always good and true, Duke.'

'For my own part, I shall not in the least regret to find in all this an opportunity of resigning. We have done our work, and if, as I believe, a majority of the House would again support either Gresham or Monk as the head of the entire Liberal party, I think that that arrangement would be for the welfare of the country.'

'Why should it make any difference to you? Why should you not return to the Council?'

'I should not do so;—certainly not at once; probably never. But you,—who are in the very prime of your life——'

The Prime Minister did not smile now. He knit his brows and a dark shadow came across his face. 'I don't think I could do that,' he said. 'Cæsar could hardly have led a legion under Pompey.'*

'It has been done, greatly to the service of the country, and without the slightest loss of honour or character in him who did it.'

'We need hardly talk of that, Duke. You think then that we shall fail;—fail, I mean, in the House of Commons. I do not know that failure in our House should be regarded as fatal.'

'In three cases we should fail. The loss of any material clause in Committee would be as bad as the loss of the Bill.'

'Oh, yes.'

'And then, in spite of Messrs Rattler and Roby,—who have been wrong before and may be wrong now,—we may lose the second reading.'

'And the third chance against us?'

'You would not probably try to carry on the Bill with a very small majority.'

'Not with three or four.'

'Nor, I think, with six or seven. It would be useless. My own belief is that we shall never carry the Bill into Committee.'

'I have always known you to be right, Duke.'

'I think that general opinion has set in that direction, and general opinion is generally right. Having come to that conclusion I thought it best to tell you, in order that we might have our house in order.' The Duke of Omnium, who with all his haughtiness and all his reserve, was the simplest man in the world and the least apt to pretend to be that which he was not, sighed deeply when he heard this. 'For my own part,' continued the elder, 'I feel no regret that it should be so.'

'It is the first large measure that we have tried to carry.'

'We did not come in to carry large measures, my friend. Look back and see how many large measures Pitt carried;—but he took the country safely through its most dangerous crisis.'

'What have we done?'

'Carried on the Queen's Government prosperously for three years. Is that nothing for a minister to do? I have never been a friend of great measures, knowing that when they come fast, one after another, more is broken in the rattle than is repaired by the reform. We have done what Parliament and the country expected us to do, and to my poor judgement we have done it well.'

'I do not feel much self-satisfaction, Duke. Well;—we must see it out, and if it is as you anticipate, I shall be ready. Of course I have prepared myself for it. And if, of late, my mind has been less turned to retirement than it used to be, it has only been because I have become wedded to this measure, and have wished that it should be carried under our auspices.' Then the old Duke took his leave, and the Prime Minister was left alone to consider the announcement that had been made to him.

He had said that he had prepared himself, but, in so saying, he had hardly known himself. Hitherto, though he had been troubled by many doubts, he had still hoped. The report made to him by Mr Rattler, backed as it had been by Mr Roby's assurances, had almost sufficed to give him confidence. But Mr Rattler and Mr Roby combined were as nothing to the Duke of St Bungay. The Prime Minister knew now,—he felt that he knew, that his days were numbered. The resignation of that lingering old bishop was not completed, and the person in whom he believed would not have the see. He had meditated the making of a peer or two, having hitherto been very cautious in that respect, but he would do nothing of the kind if called upon by the House of Commons to resign with an uncompleted measure. But his thoughts soon ran away from the present to the future. What was now to become of himself? How should he use his future life;—he who as yet had not passed his forty-seventh year? He regretted much having made that apparently pretentious speech about Cæsar, though he knew his old friend well enough to be sure that it would never be used against him. Who was he that he should class himself among the big ones of the world? A man may indeed measure small things by great, but the measurer should be careful to declare his own littleness when he illustrates his position by that of the topping ones of the earth. But the thing said had been true. Let the Pompey be who he might, he, the little Cæsar of the day, could never now command another legion.

He had once told Phineas Finn that he regretted that he had abstained from the ordinary amusements of English gentlemen. But he had abstained also from their ordinary occupations,—except so far as politics is one of them. He cared nothing for oxen or for furrows. In regard to his own land he hardly knew whether the farms were large or small. He had been a scholar, and after a certain fitful fashion he had maintained his scholarship, but the literature to which he had been really attached had been that of blue books and newspapers. What was he to do with himself when called upon to resign? And he understood,—or thought that he understood,—his position too well to expect that after a while, with the usual interval, he might return to power. He had been Prime Minister, not as the leading politician on either side, not as the king of a party, but,—so he told himself,—as a stop-gap. There could be nothing for him now till the insipidity of life should gradually fade away into the grave.

After a while he got up and went off to his wife's apartment, the room in which she used to prepare her triumphs and where now she contemplated her disappointments. 'I have had the Duke with me,' he said.

'What;—at last?'

'I do not know that he could have done any good by coming sooner.'

'And what does his Grace say?'

'He thinks that our days are numbered.'

'Psha!—is that all? I could have told him that ever so long ago. It was hardly necessary that he should disturb himself at last to come and tell us such well-ventilated news. There isn't a porter at one of the clubs who doesn't know it.'

'Then there will be the less surprise,—and to those who are concerned perhaps the less mortification.'

'Did he tell you who was to succeed you?' asked the Duchess.

'Not precisely.'

'He ought to have done that, as I am sure he knows. Everybody knows except you, Plantagenet.'

'If you know, you can tell me.'

'Of course I can. It will be Mr Monk.'

'With all my heart, Glencora. Mr Monk is a very good man.'

'I wonder whether he'll do anything for us. Think how destitute we shall be! What if I were to ask him for a place! Would he not give it us?'

'Will it make you unhappy, Cora?'

'What;—your going?'

'Yes;—the change altogether.'

She looked him in the face for a moment before she answered, with a peculiar smile in her eyes to which he was well used,—a smile half ludicrous and half pathetic,—having in it also a dash of sarcasm. 'I can dare to tell the truth,' she said, 'which you can't. I can be honest and straightforward. Yes, it will make me unhappy. And you?'

'Do you think that I cannot be honest too,—at any rate to you? It does fret me. I do not like to think that I shall be without work.'

'Yes;—Othello's occupation will be gone,—for awhile; for awhile.' Then she came up to him and put both her hands on his breast. 'But yet, Othello,* I shall not be all unhappy.'

'Where will be your contentment?'

'In you. It was making you ill. Rough people, whom the tenderness of your nature could not well endure, trod upon you, and worried you with their teeth and wounded you everywhere. I could have turned at them again with my teeth, and given them worry for worry;—but you could not. Now you will be saved from them, and so I shall not be discontented.' All this she said looking up into his face, still with that smile which was half pathetic and half ludicrous.

'Then I will be contented too,' he said as he kissed her.

CHAPTER 73

ONLY THE DUKE OF OMNIUM

THE night of the debate arrived, but before the debate was commenced, Sir Timothy Beeswax got up to make a personal explanation. He thought it right to state to the House how it came to pass that he found himself bound to leave the Ministry at so important a crisis in its existence. Then an observation was made by an honourable member of the Government,—presumably in a whisper, but still loud enough to catch the sharp ears of Sir Timothy, who now sat just below the gangway. It was said afterwards that the gentleman who made the observation,—an

Irish gentleman named Fitzgibbon, conspicuous rather for his loyalty to his party than his steadiness,—had purposely taken the place in which he then sat, that Sir Timothy might hear his whisper. The whisper suggested that falling houses were often left by certain animals. It was certainly a very loud whisper,—but, if gentlemen are to be allowed to whisper at all, it is almost impossible to restrain the volume of the voice. To restrain Mr Fitzgibbon had always been found difficult. Sir Timothy, who did not lack pluck, turned at once upon his assailant, and declared that words had been used with reference to himself which the honourable member did not dare to get upon his legs and repeat. Larry Fitzgibbon, as the gentleman was called, looked him full in the face, but did not move his hat from his head or stir a limb. It was a pleasant little episode in the evening's work, and afforded satisfaction to the House generally. Then Sir Timothy went on with his explanation. The details of this measure, as soon as they were made known to him, appeared to him, he said, to be fraught with the gravest and most pernicious consequences. He was sure that the members of her Majesty's Government, who were hurrying on this measure with what he thought was indecent haste,—ministers are always either indecent in their haste or treacherous in their delay,—had not considered what they were doing, or, if they had considered, were blind as to its results. He then attempted to discuss the details of the measure, but was called to order. A personal explanation could not be allowed to give his an opportunity of anticipating the debate. He contrived, however, before he sat down, to say some very heavy things against his late chief, and especially to congratulate the Duke on the services of the honourable gentleman, the member for Mayo,—meaning thereby Mr Laurence Fitzgibbon.

It would perhaps have been well for everybody if the measure could have been withdrawn and the Ministry could have resigned without the debate,—as everybody was convinced what would be the end of it. Let the second reading go as it might, the Bill could not be carried. There are measures which require the hopeful heartiness of a new Ministry, and the thorough-going energy of a young Parliament,—and this was one of them. The House was as fully agreed that this change was necessary, as it ever is agreed on any subject,—but still the thing could not be done. Even Mr Monk, who was the most earnest of men, felt the general slackness of all around him. The commotion and excitement which would be caused by a change of Ministry might restore its proper tone to the House, but in its present condition it was unfit for the work. Nevertheless Mr Monk made his speech, and put all his arguments into lucid order. He knew it was for nothing, but nevertheless it must be done. For hour after hour he went on—for it was necessary to give every detail of his contemplated proposition. He went through it as sedulously as though he had expected to succeed, and sat down about nine o'clock in the evening. Then Sir Orlando moved the adjournment of the House till the morrow, giving as his reason for doing so the expedience of considering the details he had heard. To this no opposition was made, and the House was adjourned.

On the following day the clubs were all alive with rumours as to the coming debate. It was known that a strong party had been formed under the auspices of Sir Orlando, and that with him Sir Timothy and other politicians were in close council. It was of course necessary that they should impart to many the secrets of their conclave, so that it was known early in the afternoon that it was the intention of the Opposition not to discuss the Bill, but to move that it be read a second time that day six months. The Ministry had hardly expected this, as the Bill was undoubtedly popular both in the House and the country; and if the Opposition should be beaten in such a course, that defeat would tend greatly to strengthen the hands of the Government. But if the foe should succeed in carrying a positive veto on the second reading, it would under all the circumstances be tantamount to a vote of want of confidence. 'I'm afraid they know almost more than we do as to the feeling of members,' said Mr Roby to Mr Rattler.

'There isn't a man in the House whose feeling in the matter I don't know,' said Rattler, 'but I'm not quite so sure of their principles. On our own side, in our old party, there are a score of men who detest the Duke, though they would fain be true to the Government. They have voted with him through thick and thin, and he has not spoken a word to one of them since he became Prime Minister. What are you to do with such a man? How are you to act with him?'

'Lupton wrote to him the other day about something,' answered the other, 'I forget what, and he got a note back from Warburton as cold as ice,—an absolute slap in the face. Fancy treating a man like Lupton in that way,—one of the most popular men in the House, related to half the peerage, and a man who thinks so much of himself! I shouldn't wonder if he were to vote against us;—I shouldn't indeed.'

'It has all been the old Duke's doing,' said Rattler, 'and no doubt it was intended for the best; but the thing has been a failure from the beginning to the end. I knew it would be so. I don't think there has been a single man who has understood what a ministerial Coalition really means except you and I. From the very beginning all your men were averse to it in spirit.'

'Look how they were treated!' said Mr Roby. 'Was it likely that they should be very staunch when Mr Monk became Leader of the House?'

There was a Cabinet Council that day which lasted but a few minutes, and it may easily be presumed that the Ministers decided that they would all resign at once if Sir Orlando should carry his amendment. It is not unlikely that they were agreed to do the same if he should nearly carry it,—leaving probably the Prime Minister to judge what narrow majority would constitute nearness. On this occasion all the gentlemen assembled were jocund in their manner, and apparently well satisfied,—as though they saw before them an end to all their troubles. The Spartan boy* did not even make a grimace when the wolf bit him beneath his frock, and these were all Spartan boys. Even the Prime Minister, who had fortified himself for the occasion, and who never wept in any company but that of his wife and his old friend, was pleasant in his manner and almost affable. 'We shan't make this step towards the millennium just at present,' he said to Phineas Finn as they left the room together,—referring to words which Phineas had spoken on a former occasion, and which then had not been very well taken.

'But we shall have made a step towards the step,' said Phineas, 'and in getting to a millennium even that is something.'

'I suppose we are all too anxious,' said the Duke, 'to see some great effects come from our own little doings. Good-day. We shall know all about it tolerably early. Monk seems to think that it will be an attack on the Ministry and not on the Bill, and that it will be best to get a vote with as little delay as possible.'

'I'll bet an even five-pound note,' said Mr Lupton at the Carlton, 'that the present Ministry is out to-morrow, and another that no one names five members of the next Cabinet.'

'You can help to win your first bet,' said Mr Beauchamp, a very old member, who, like many other Conservatives, had supported the Coalition.

'I shall not do that,' said Lupton, 'though I think I ought. I won't vote against the man in his misfortunes, though, upon my soul, I don't love him very dearly. I shall vote neither way, but I hope that Sir Orlando may succeed.'

'If he do, who is to come in?' said the other. 'I suppose you don't want to serve under Sir Orlando?'

'Nor certainly under the Duke of Omnium. We shall not want a Prime Minister as long as there are as good fish in the sea as have been caught out of it.'

There had lately been formed a new Liberal club,* established on a broader basis than the Progress, and perhaps with a greater amount of aristocratic support. This had come up since the Duke had been Prime Minister. Certain busy men had never been quite contented with the existing state of things, and had thought that the Liberal party, with such assistance as such a club could give it, would be strong enough to rule alone. That the great Liberal party should be impeded in its work and its triumph by such men as Sir Orlando Drought and Sir Timothy Beeswax was odious to the club. All the Pallisers had, from time immemorial, run straight as Liberals, and therefore the club had been unwilling to oppose the Duke personally, though he was the chief of the Coalition. And certain members of the Government, Phineas Finn, for instance, Barrington Erle, and Mr Rattler were on the committee of the club. But the club, as a club, was not averse to a discontinuance of the present state of things. Mr Gresham might again become Prime Minister, if he would condescend so far, or Mr Monk. It might be possible that the great Liberal triumph contemplated by the club might not be achieved by the present House;—but the present House must go shortly, and then, with that assistance from a well-organized club, which had lately been so terribly wanting,—the lack of which had made the Coalition necessary,—no doubt the British constituencies would do their duty, and a Liberal Prime Minister, pure and simple, might reign,—almost for ever. With this great future before it, the club was very lukewarm in its support of the present Bill. 'I shall go down and vote for them of course,' said Mr O'Mahony, 'just for the look of the thing.' In saying this Mr O'Mahony expressed the feeling of the club, and the feeling of the Liberal party generally. There was something due to the Duke, but not enough to make it incumbent on his friends to maintain him in his position as Prime Minister.

It was a great day for Sir Orlando. At half-past four the House was full,—not from any desire to hear Sir Orlando's arguments against the Bill, but because it was felt that a good deal of personal interest would be attached to the debate. If one were asked in these days what gift should a Prime Minister ask first from the fairies, one would name the power of attracting personal friends. Eloquence, if it be too easy, may become almost a curse. Patriotism is suspected, and sometimes sinks almost to pedantry. A Jove-born intellect* is hardly wanted, and clashes with the inferiorities. Industry is exacting. Honesty is unpractical. Truth is easily offended. Dignity will not bend. But the man who can be all things to all men, who has ever a kind word to speak, a pleasant joke to crack, who can forgive all sins, who is ever prepared for friend or foe, but never very bitter to the latter, who forgets not men's names, and is always ready with little words,—he is the man who will be supported at a crisis such as this that was now in the course of passing. It is for him that men will struggle, and talk, and, if needs be, fight, as though the very existence of the country depended on his political security. The present man would receive no such defence;—but still the violent deposition of a Prime Minister is always a memorable occasion.

Sir Orlando made his speech, and, as had been anticipated, it had very little to do with the Bill, and was almost exclusively an attack upon his late chief. He thought, he said, that this was an occasion on which they had better come to a direct issue with as little delay as possible. If he rightly read the feeling of the House, no Bill of this magnitude coming from the present Ministry would be likely to be passed in an efficient condition. The Duke had frittered away his support in that House, and as a Minister had lost that confidence which a majority of the House had once been willing to place in him. We need not follow Sir Orlando through his speech. He alluded to his own services, and declared that he was obliged to withdraw them because the Duke would not trust him with the management of his own office. He had reason to believe that other gentlemen who had attached themselves to the Duke's Ministry had found themselves equally crippled by this passion for autocratic rule. Hereupon a loud chorus of disapprobation came from the Treasury bench, which was fully answered by opposing noises from the other side of the House. Sir Orlando declared that he need only point to the fact that the Ministry had been already shivered by the secession of various gentlemen. 'Only two,' said a voice. Sir Orlando was turning round to contradict the voice when he was greeted by another. 'And those the weakest,' said the other voice, which was indubitably that of Larry Fitzgibbon. 'I will not speak of myself,' said Sir Orlando pompously, 'but I am authorized to tell the House that the noble lord who is now Secretary of State for the Colonies only holds his office till this crisis shall have passed.'

After that there was some sparring of a very bitter kind between Sir Timothy and Phineas Finn, till at last it seemed that the debate was to degenerate into a war of man against man. Phineas, and Erle, and Laurence Fitzgibbon allowed themselves to be lashed into anger, and, as far as words went, had the best of it. But of what use could it be? Every man there had come into the House prepared to vote for or against the Duke of Omnium,—or resolved, like Mr Lupton, not to vote at all; and it was hardly on the cards that a single vote should be turned this way or that by any violence of speaking. 'Let it pass,' said Mr Monk in a whisper to Phineas. 'The fire is not worth the fuel.'

'I know the Duke's faults,' said Phineas, 'but these men know nothing of his virtues, and when I hear them abuse him I cannot stand it.'

Early in the night,—before twelve o'clock,—the House divided, and even at the moment of the division no one quite knew how it would go. There would be many who would of course vote against the amendment as being simply desirous of recording their opinion in favour of the Bill generally. And there were some who thought that Sir Orlando and his followers had been too forward, and too confident of their own standing in the House, in trying so violent a mode of opposition. It would have been better, these men thought, to have insured success by a gradual and persistent opposition to the Bill itself. But they hardly knew how thoroughly men may be alienated by silence and a cold demeanour. Sir Orlando on the division was beaten, but was beaten only by nine. 'He can't go on with his Bill,' said Rattler in one of the lobbies of the House. 'I defy him. The House wouldn't stand it, you know.' 'No minister,' said Roby, 'could carry a measure like that with a majority of nine on a vote of confidence!' The House was of course adjourned, and Mr Monk went at once to Carlton Terrace.

'I wish it had only been three or four,' said the Duke, laughing.

'Why so?'

'Because there would have been less doubt.'

'Is there any at present?'

'Less possibility for doubt, I will say. You would not wish to make the attempt with such a majority?'

'I could not do it, Duke.'

'I quite agree with you. But there will be those who will say that the attempt might be made,—who will accuse me of being faint-hearted because we do not make it.'

'They will be men who understand nothing of the temper of the House.'

'Very likely. But still, I wish the majority had only been two or three. There is little more to be said, I suppose.'

'Very little, your Grace.'

'We had better meet to-morrow at two, and, if possible, I will see her Majesty in the afternoon. Good night, Mr Monk.'

'Good night, Duke.'

'My reign is ended. You are a good deal an older man than I, and yet probably yours has yet to begin.' Mr Monk smiled and shook his head as he left the room, not trusting himself to discuss so large a subject at so late an hour of the night.

Without waiting a moment after his colleague's departure, the Prime Minister,—for he was still Prime Minister,—went into his wife's room, knowing that she was waiting up till she should hear the result of the division, and there he found Mrs Finn with her. 'Is it over?' asked the Duchess.

'Yes;—there has been a division. Mr Monk has just been with me.'

'Well!'

'We have beaten them, of course, as we always do,' said the Duke, attempting to be pleasant. 'You didn't suppose there was anything to fear? Your husband has always bid you keep up your courage;—has he not, Mrs Finn?'

'My husband has lost his senses, I think,' she said. 'He has taken to such storming and raving about his political enemies that I hardly dare to open my mouth.'

'Tell me what has been done, Plantagenet,' ejaculated the Duchess.

'Don't you be as unreasonable as Mrs Finn, Cora. The House has voted against Sir Orlando's amendment by a majority of nine.'

'Only nine!'

'And I shall cease to be Prime Minister to-morrow.'

'You don't mean to say that it's settled?'

'Quite settled. The play has been played, and the curtain has fallen, and the lights are being put out, and the poor weary actors may go home to bed.'

'But on such an amendment surely any majority would have done.'

'No, my dear. I will not name a number, but nine certainly would not do.'

'And it is all over?'

'My Ministry is all over, if you mean that.'

'Then everything is over for me. I shall settle down in the country and build cottages, and mix draughts. You, Marie, will still be going up the tree. If Mr Finn manages well he may come to be Prime Minister some day.'

'He has hardly such ambition, Lady Glen.'

'The ambition will come fast enough;—will it not, Plantagenet? Let him once begin to dream of it as possible, and the desire will soon be strong enough. How should you feel if it were so?'

'It is quite impossible,' said Mrs Finn, gravely.

'I don't see why anything is impossible. Sir Orlando will be Prime Minister now, and Sir Timothy Beeswax Lord Chancellor. After that anybody may hope to be anything. Well,—I suppose we may go to bed. Is your carriage here, my dear?'

'I hope so.'

'Ring the bell, Plantagenet, for somebody to see her down. Come to lunch to-morrow because I shall have so many groans to utter. What beasts, what brutes, what ungrateful wretches men are!—worse than women when they get together in numbers enough to be bold. Why have they deserted you? What have we not done for them. Think of all the new bedroom furniture that we sent to Gatherum merely to keep the party together. There were thousands of yards of linen, and it has all been of no use. Don't you feel like Wolsey,* Plantagenet?'

'Not in the least, my dear. No one will take anything away from me that is my own.'

'For me, I'm almost as much divorced as Catherine, and have had my head cut off as completely as Anne Bullen and the rest of them. Go away, Marie, because I am going to have a cry by myself.'

The Duke himself on that night put Mrs Finn into her carriage; and as he walked with her downstairs he asked her whether she believed the Duchess to be in earnest in her sorrow. 'She so mixes up her mirth and woe together,' said the Duke, 'that I myself sometimes can hardly understand her.'

'I think she does regret it, Duke.'

'She told me but the other day that she would be contented.'

'A few weeks will make her so. As for your Grace, I hope I may congratulate you.'

'Oh yes;—I think so. We none of us like to be beaten when we have taken a thing in hand. There is always a little disappointment at first. But, upon the whole, it is better as it is. I hope it will not make your husband unhappy.'

'Not for his own sake. He will go again into the middle of the scramble and fight on one side or the other. For my own part I think opposition the pleasantest. Good-night, Duke. I am so sorry that I should have troubled you.'

Then he went alone to his own room, and sat there without moving for a couple of hours. Surely it was a great thing to have been Prime Minister of England for three years,—a prize of which nothing now could rob him. He ought not to be unhappy; and yet he knew himself to be wretched and disappointed. It had never occurred to him to be proud of being a duke, or to think of his wealth otherwise than a chance incident of his life, advantageous indeed, but by no means a source of honour. And he had been aware that he had owed his first seat in

Parliament to his birth, and probably also his first introduction to official life. An heir to a dukedom, if he will only work hard, may almost
with certainty find himself received into one or the other regiment in
Downing Street. It had not in his early days been with him as it had
with his friends Mr Monk and Phineas Finn, who had worked their
way from the very ranks. But even a duke cannot become Prime
Minister by favour. Surely he had done something of which he might
be proud. And so he tried to console himself.

But to have done something was nothing to him,—nothing to his
personal happiness,—unless there was also something left for him to
do. How should it be with him now,—how for the future? Would men
ever listen to him again, or allow him again to work in their behoof, as
he used to do in his happy days in the House of Commons? He feared
that it was all over for him, and that for the rest of his days he must
simply be the Duke of Omnium.

CHAPTER 74

'I AM DISGRACED AND SHAMED'

SOON after the commencement of the Session Arthur Fletcher became
a constant visitor in Manchester Square, dining with the old barrister
almost constantly on Sundays, and not infrequently on other days when
the House and his general engagements would permit it. Between him
and Emily's father there was no secret and no misunderstanding.
Mr Wharton quite understood that the young member of Parliament
was earnestly purposed to marry his daughter, and Fletcher was sure of
all the assistance and support which Mr Wharton could give him. The
name of Lopez was very rarely used between them. It had been tacitly
agreed that there was no need that it should be mentioned. The man had
come like a destroying angel between them and their fondest hopes.
Neither could ever be what he would have been had that man never
appeared to destroy their happiness. But the man had gone away, not
without a tragedy that was appalling;—and each thought that, as regarded
him, he and the tragedy might be, if not forgotten at least put aside, if
only that other person in whom they were interested could be taught to
seem to forget him. 'It is not love,' said the father, 'but a feeling of shame.'
Arthur Fletcher shook his head, not quite agreeing with this. It was not
that he feared that she loved the memory of her late husband. Such love
was, he thought, impossible. But there was, he believed, something more

than the feeling which her father described as shame. There was pride also;—a determination in her own bosom not to confess the fault she had made in giving herself to him whom she must now think to have been so much the least worthy of her two suitors. 'Her fortune will not be what I once promised you,' said the old man plaintively.

'I do not remember that I ever asked you as to her fortune,' Arthur replied.

'Certainly not. If you had I should not have told you. But as I named a sum, it is right that I should explain to you that that man succeeded in lessening it by six or seven thousand pounds.'

'If that were all!'

'And I have promised Sir Alured that Everett, as his heir, should have the use of a considerable portion of his share without waiting for my death. It is odd that the one of my children from whom I certainly expected the greater trouble should have fallen so entirely on his feet; and that the other——; well, let us hope for the best. Everett seems to have taken up with Wharton as though it belonged to him already. And Emily——! Well, my dear boy, let us hope that it may come right yet. You are not drinking your wine. Yes,—pass the bottle; I'll have another glass before I go upstairs.'

In this way the time went by till Emily returned to town. The Ministry had just then resigned, but I think that 'this great reactionary success,' as it was called by the writer in the 'People's Banner,' affected one member of the Lower House much less than the return to London of Mrs Lopez. Arthur Fletcher had determined that he would renew his suit as soon as a year should have expired since the tragedy which had made his love a widow,—and that year had now passed away. He had known the day well,—as had she, when she passed the morning weeping in her own room at Wharton. Now he questioned himself whether a year would suffice,—whether both in mercy to her and with the view of realizing his own hopes he should give her some longer time for recovery. But he had told himself that it should be done at the end of a year, and as he had allowed no one to talk him out of his word, so neither would he be untrue to it himself. But it became with him a deep matter of business, a question of great difficulty, how he should arrange the necessary interview,—whether he should plead his case with her at their first meeting, or whether he had better allow her to become accustomed to his presence in the house. His mother had attempted to ridicule him, because he was, as she said, afraid of a woman. He well remembered that he had never been afraid of Emily Wharton when they had been quite young,—little more than a boy and girl together.

Then he had told her of his love over and over again, and had found almost a comfortable luxury in urging her to say a word, which she had never indeed said, but which probably in those days he still hoped that she would say. And occasionally he had feigned to be angry with her, and had tempted her on to little quarrels with a boyish idea that quick reconciliation would perhaps throw her into his arms. But now it seemed to him that an age had passed since those days. His love had certainly not faded. There had never been a moment when that had been on the wing. But now the azure plumage of his love had become grey as the wings of a dove, and the gorgeousness of his dreams had sobered into hopes and fears which were a constant burden to his heart. There was time enough, still time enough for happiness if she would yield;—and time enough for the dull pressure of unsatisfied aspirations should she persist in her refusal.

At last he saw her, almost by accident, and that meeting certainly was not fit for the purpose of his suit. He called at Stone Buildings the day after her arrival, and found her at her father's chambers. She had come there keeping some appointment with him, and certainly had not expected to meet her lover. He was confused and hardly able to say a word to account for his presence, but she greeted him with almost sisterly affection, saying some word of Longbarns and his family, telling him how Everett, to Sir Alured's great delight, had been sworn in as a magistrate for the County, and how at the last hunt meeting John Fletcher had been asked to take the County hounds,* because old Lord Weobly at seventy-five had declared himself to be unable any longer to ride as a master of hounds ought to ride. All these things Arthur had of course heard, such news being too important to be kept long from him; but on none of these subjects had he much to say. He stuttered and stammered, and quickly went away;—not, however, before he had promised to come to dine as usual on the next Sunday, and not without observing that the anniversary of that fatal day of release had done something to lighten the sombre load of mourning which the widow had hitherto worn.

Yes;—he would dine there on the Sunday, but how would it be with him then? Mr Wharton never went out of the house on a Sunday evening, and could hardly be expected to leave his own drawing-room for the sake of giving a lover an opportunity. No;—he must wait till that evening should have passed, and then make the occasion for himself as best he might. The Sunday came and the dinner was eaten, and after dinner there was the single bottle of port and the single bottle of claret. 'How do you think she is looking?' asked the father. 'She was as pale as death before we got her down into the country.'

'Upon my word, sir,' said he, 'I've hardly looked at her. It is not a matter of looks now, as it used to be. It has got beyond that. It is not that I am indifferent to seeing a pretty face, or that I have no longer an opinion of my own about a woman's figure. But there grows up, I think, a longing which almost kills that consideration.'

'To me she is as beautiful as ever,' said the father proudly.

Fletcher did manage, when in the drawing-room, to talk for a while about John and the hounds, and then went away, having resolved that he would come again on the very next day. Surely she would not give an order that he should be denied admittance. She had been too calm, too even, too confident in herself for that. Yes;—he would come and tell her plainly what he had to say. He would tell it with all the solemnity of which he was capable, with a few words, and those the strongest which he could use. Should she refuse him;—as he almost knew that she would at first,—then he would tell her of her father and of the wishes of all their joint friends. 'Nothing,' he would say to her, 'nothing but personal dislike can justify you in refusing to heal so many wounds.' As he fixed on these words he failed to remember how little probable it is that a lover should ever be able to use the phrases he arranges.

On Monday he came, and asked for Mrs Lopez, slurring over the word as best he could. The butler said his mistress was at home. Since the death of the man he had so thoroughly despised, the old servant had never called her Mrs Lopez. Arthur was shown upstairs, and found the lady he sought,—but he found Mrs Roby also. It may be remembered that Mrs Roby, after the tragedy, had been refused admittance into Mr Wharton's house. Since that there had been some correspondence, and a feeling had prevailed that the woman was not to be quarrelled with for ever. 'I did not do it, papa, because of her,' Emily had said with some scorn, and that scorn had procured Mrs Roby's pardon. She was now making a morning call, and suiting her conversation to the black dress of her niece. Arthur was horrified at seeing her. Mrs Roby had always been to him odious, not only as a personal enemy but as a vulgar woman. He, at any rate, attributed to her a great part of the evil that had been done, feeling sure that had there been no house round the corner, Emily Wharton would never have become Mrs Lopez. As it was he was forced to shake hands with her, and forced to listen to the funereal tone in which Mrs Roby asked him if he did not think that Mrs Lopez looked much improved by her sojourn in Herefordshire. He shrank at the sound, and then, in order that it might not be repeated, took occasion to show that he was allowed to call his early playmate by her

Christian name. Mrs Roby, thinking that she ought to check him, remarked that Mrs Lopez's return was a great thing for Mr Wharton. Thereupon Arthur Fletcher seized his hat off the ground, wished them both good-bye, and hurried out of the room. 'What a very odd manner he has taken up since he became a member of Parliament,' said Mrs Roby.

Emily was silent for a moment, and then with an effort,—with intense pain,—she said a word or two which she thought had better be at once spoken. 'He went because he does not like to hear that name.'

'Good gracious!'

'And papa does not like it. Don't say a word about it, aunt; pray don't;—but call me Emily.'

'Are you going to be ashamed of your name?'

'Never mind, aunt. If you think it wrong you must stay away;—but I will not have papa wounded.'

'Oh;—if Mr Wharton wishes it;——of course.' That evening Mrs Roby told Dick Roby, her husband, what an old fool Mr Wharton was.

The next day, quite early, Fletcher was again at the house and was again admitted upstairs. The butler, no doubt, knew well enough why he came, and also knew that the purport of his coming had at any rate the sanction of Mr Wharton. The room was empty when he was shown into it, but she came to him very soon. 'I went away yesterday rather abruptly,' he said. 'I hope you did not think me rude.'

'Oh no.'

'Your aunt was here, and I had something I wished to say but could not say it very well before her.'

'I knew that she had driven you away. You and Aunt Harriet were never great friends.'

'Never;—but I will forgive her everything. I will forgive all the injuries that have been done me if you will now do as I ask you.'

Of course she knew what it was that he was about to ask. When he had left her at Longbarns without saying a word of his love, without giving her any hint whereby she might allow herself to think that he intended to renew his suit, then she had wept because it was so. Though her resolution had been quite firm as to the duty which was incumbent on her of remaining in her desolate condition of almost nameless widowhood, yet she had been unable to refrain from bitter tears because he also had seemed to see that such was her duty. But now again, knowing that the request was coming, feeling once more confident of the constancy of his love, she was urgent with herself as to that heavy duty.

She would be unwomanly, dead to all shame, almost inhuman, were she to allow herself again to indulge in love after all the havoc she had made. She had been little more than a bride when that husband, for whom she had so often been forced to blush, had been driven by the weight of his misfortunes and disgraces to destroy himself! By the marriage she had made she had overwhelmed her whole family with dishonour. She had done it with a persistency of perverse self-will which she herself could not now look back upon without wonder and horror. She, too, should have died as well as he,—only that death had not been within the compass of her powers as of his. How then could she forget it all, and wipe it away from her mind, as she would figures from a slate with a wet towel? How could it be fit that she should again be a bride with such a spectre of a husband haunting her memory? She had known that the request was to be made when he had come so quickly, and had not doubted it for a moment when he took his sudden departure. She had known it well, when just now the servant told her that Mr Fletcher was in the drawing-room below. But she was quite certain of the answer she must make. 'I should be sorry you should ask me anything I cannot do,' she said in a very low voice.

'I will ask you for nothing for which I have not your father's sanction.'

'The time has gone by, Arthur, in which I might well have been guided by my father. There comes a time when personal feelings must be stronger than a father's authority. Papa cannot see me with my own eyes; he cannot understand what I feel. It is simply this,—that he would have me to be other than I am. But I am what I have made myself.'

'You have not heard me as yet. You will hear me?'

'Oh, yes.'

'I have loved you ever since I was a boy.' He paused as though he expected that she would make some answer to this; but of course there was nothing that she could say. 'I have been true to you since we were together almost as children.'

'It is your nature to be true.'

'In this matter, at any rate, I shall never change. I never for a moment had a doubt about my love. There never has been any one else whom I have ventured to compare with you. Then came that great trouble. Emily, you must let me speak freely this once, as so much, to me at least, depends on it.'

'Say what you will, Arthur. Do not wound me more than you can help.'

'God knows how willingly I would heal every wound without a word if it could be done. I don't know whether you ever thought what

I suffered when he came among us and robbed me,—well, I will not say robbed me of your love, because it was not mine—but took away with him that which I had been trying to win.'

'I did not think a man would feel it like that.'

'Why shouldn't a man feel as well as a woman? I had set my heart on having you for my wife. Can any desire be dearer to a man than that? Then he came. Well, dearest; surely I may say that he was not worthy of you.'

'We were neither of us worthy,' she said.

'I need not tell you that we all grieved. It seemed to us down in Herefordshire as though a black cloud had come upon us. We could not speak of you, nor yet could we be altogether silent.'

'Of course you condemned me,—as an outcast.'

'Did I write to you as though you were an outcast? Did I treat you when I saw you as an outcast? When I come to you to-day, is that proof that I think you to be an outcast? I have never deceived you, Emily.'

'Never.'

'Then you will believe me when I say that through it all not one word of reproach or contumely has ever passed my lips in regard to you. That you should have given yourself to one whom I could not think to be worthy of you was, of course, a great sorrow. Had he been a prince of men it would, of course, have been a sorrow to me. How it went with you during your married life I will not ask.'

'I was unhappy. I would tell you everything if I could. I was very unhappy.'

'Then came—the end.' She was now weeping, with her face buried in her handkerchief. 'I would spare you if I knew how, but there are some things which must be said.'

'No;—no. I will bear it all—from you.'

'Well! His success had not lessened my love. Though then I could have no hope,—though you were utterly removed from me,—all that could not change me. There it was,—as though my arm or my leg had been taken from me. It was bad to live without an arm or leg, but there was no help. I went on with my life and tried not to look like a whipped cur;—though John from time to time would tell me that I failed. But now;—now that has again all changed,—what would you have me do now? It may be that after all my limb may be restored to me, that I may be again as other men are, whole, and sound, and happy;—so happy! When it may possibly be within my reach am I not to look for my happiness?' He paused, but she wept on without speaking a word. 'There are those who will say that I should wait till all these signs of woe have been laid aside. But why should I wait? There has come a great blot upon your life, and is it not well that it should be covered as quickly as possible?'

'It can never be covered.'

'You mean that it can never be forgotten. No doubt there are passages in our life which we cannot forget, though we bury them in the deepest silence. All this can never be driven out of your memory,—nor from mine. But it need not therefore blacken all our lives. In such a condition we should not be ruled by what the world thinks.'

'Not at all. I care nothing for what the world thinks. I am below all that. It is what I think: I myself,—of myself.'

'Will you think of no one else? Are any of your thoughts for me,—or for your father?'

'Oh, yes—for my father.'

'I need hardly tell you what he wishes. You must know how you can best give him back the comfort he has lost.'

'But, Arthur, even for him I cannot do everything.'

'There is one question to be asked,' he said, rising from her feet and standing before her;—'but one; and what you do should depend entirely on the answer which you may be able truly to make to that.'

This he said so solemnly that he startled her.

'What question, Arthur?'

'Do you love me?' To this question at the moment she could make no reply. 'Of course I know that you did not love me when you married him.'

'Love is not all of one kind.'

'You know what love I mean. You did not love me then. You could not have loved me,—though, perhaps, I thought I had deserved your love. But love will change, and memory will sometimes bring back old fancies when the world has been stern and hard. When we were very young I think you loved me. Do you remember seven years ago at Longbarns, when they parted us and sent me away, because,—because we were so young? They did not tell us then, but I think you knew. I know that I knew, and went nigh to swear that I would drown myself. You loved me then, Emily.'

'I was a child then.'

'Now you are not a child. Do you love me now,—to-day? If so, give me your hand, and let the past be buried in silence. All this has come, and gone, and has nearly made us old. But there is life before us yet, and if you are to me as I am to you it is better that our lives should be lived together.' Then he stood before her with his hand stretched out.

'I cannot do it,' she said.

'And why?'

'I cannot be other than the wretched thing I have made myself.'

'But do you love me?'

'I cannot analyse my heart. Love you;—yes! I have always loved you. Everything about you is dear to me. I can triumph in your triumphs, rejoice at your joy, weep at your sorrows, be ever anxious that all good things may come to you;—but, Arthur, I cannot be your wife.'

'Not though it would make us all happy,—Fletchers and Whartons all alike?'

'Do you think I have not thought it over? Do you think that I have forgotten your first letter? Knowing your heart, as I do know it, do you imagine that I have spent a day, an hour, for months past, without asking myself what answer I should make to you if the sweet constancy of your nature should bring you again to me? I have trembled when I have heard your voice. My heart has beat at the sound of your footstep as though it would burst! Do you think I have never told myself what I had thrown away? But it is gone, and it is not now within my reach.'

'It is; it is,' he said, throwing himself on his knees, and twining his arms round her.

'No;—no;—no;—never. I am disgraced and shamed. I have lain among the pots till I am foul and blackened. Take your arms away. They shall not be defiled,' she said as she sprang to her feet. 'You shall not have the thing that he has left.'

'Emily,—it is the only thing in the world that I crave.'

'Be a man and conquer your love,—as I will. Get it under your feet and press it to death. Tell yourself that it is shameful and must be abandoned. That you, Arthur Fletcher, should marry the widow of that man,—the woman that he had thrust so far into the mire that she can never again be clean;—you, the chosen one, the bright star among us all;—you, whose wife should be the fairest, the purest, the tenderest of us all, a flower that has yet been hardly breathed on! While I——Arthur,' she said, 'I know my duty better than that. I will not seek an escape from my punishment in that way,—nor will I allow you to destroy yourself. You have my word as a woman that it shall not be so. Now I do not mind your knowing whether I love you or no.' He stood silent before her, not able for the moment to go on with his prayer. 'And now go,' she said. 'God bless you, and give you some day a fair and happy wife. And, Arthur, do not come again to me. If you will let it be so, I shall have a delight in seeing you;—but not if you come as you have come now. And, Arthur, spare me with papa.

Do not let him think that it is all my fault that I cannot do the thing which he wishes.' Then she left the room before he could say another word to her.

But it was all her fault. No;—in that direction he could not spare her. It must be told to her father, though he doubted his own power of describing all that had been said. 'Do not come again to me,' she had said. At the moment he had been left speechless; but if there was one thing fixed in his mind it was the determination to come again. He was sure now, not only of love that might have sufficed,—but of hot, passionate love. She had told him that her heart had beat at his footsteps, and that she had trembled as she listened to his voice;—and yet she expected that he would not come again! But there was a violence of decision about the woman which made him dread that he might still come in vain. She was so warped from herself by the conviction of her great mistake, so prone to take shame to herself for her own error, so keenly alive to the degradation to which she had been submitted, that it might yet be impossible to teach her that, though her husband had been vile and she mistaken, yet she had not been soiled by his baseness.

He went at once to the old barrister's chambers and told him the result of the meeting. 'She is still a fool,' said the father, not understanding at second-hand the depths of his daughter's feeling.

'No, sir,—not that. She feels herself degraded by his degradation. If it be possible we must save her from that.'

'She did degrade herself.'

'Not as she means it. She is not degraded in my eyes.'

'Why should she not take the only means in her power of rescuing herself and rescuing us all from the evil that she did? She owes it you, to me, and to her brother.'

'I would hardly wish her to come to me in payment of such a debt.'

'There is no room left,' said Mr Wharton angrily, 'for soft sentimentality. Well;—she must take her bed as she makes it. It is very hard on me, I know. Considering what she used to be, it is marvellous to me that she should have so little idea left of doing her duty to others.'

Arthur Fletcher found that the barrister was at the moment too angry to hear reason, or to be made to understand anything of the feelings of mixed love and admiration with which he himself was animated at the moment. He was obliged therefore to content himself with assuring the father that he did not intend to give up the pursuit of his daughter.

CHAPTER 75

THE GREAT WHARTON ALLIANCE

WHEN Mr Wharton got home on that day he said not a word to Emily as to Arthur Fletcher. He had resolved to take various courses,—first to tell her roundly that she was neglecting her duty to herself and to her family, and that he would no longer take her part and be her good friend unless she would consent to marry the man whom she had confessed that she loved. But as he thought of this he became aware,—first that he could not carry out such a threat, and then that he would lack even the firmness to make it. There was something in her face, something even in her dress, something in her whole manner to himself, which softened him and reduced him to vassalage directly he saw her. Then he determined to throw himself on her compassion and to implore her to put an end to all this misery by making herself happy. But as he drew near home he found himself unable to do even this. How is a father to beseech his widowed daughter to give herself away in a second marriage? And therefore when he entered the house and found her waiting for him, he said nothing. At first she looked at him wistfully,—anxious to learn by his face whether her lover had been with him. But when he spoke not a word, simply kissing her in his usual quiet way, she became cheerful in manner and communicative. 'Papa,' she said, 'I have had a letter from Mary.'

'Well, my dear.'

'Just a nice chatty letter,—full of Everett, of course.'

'Everett is a great man now.'

'I am sure that you are very glad that he is what he is. Will you see Mary's letter?' Mr Wharton was not specially given to reading young ladies' correspondence, and did not know why this particular letter should be offered to him. 'You don't suspect anything at Wharton, do you?' she asked.

'Suspect anything! No; I don't suspect anything.' But now, having had his curiosity aroused, he took the letter which was offered to him and read it. The letter was as follows:—

'Wharton, Thursday.

'DEAREST EMILY,—

'We all hope that you had a pleasant journey up to London, and that Mr Wharton is quite well. Your brother Everett came over to Longbarns the day after you started and drove me back to Wharton in the dog-cart.

It was such a pleasant journey, though, now I remember, it rained all the way. But Everett has always so much to say that I didn't mind the rain. I think it will end in John taking the hounds. He says he won't, because he does not wish to be the slave of the whole county;—but he says it in that sort of way that we all think he means to do it. Everett tells him that he ought, because he is the only hunting man on this side of the county who can afford to do it without feeling it much; and of course what Everett says will go a long way with him. Sarah,'—Sarah was John Fletcher's wife,—'is rather against it. But if he makes up his mind she'll be sure to turn round. Of course it makes us all very anxious at present to know how it is to end, for the Master of the Hounds always is the leading man in our part of the world. Papa went to the bench at Ross* yesterday and took Everett with him. It was the first time that Everett had sat there. He says I am to tell his father he has not hung anybody as yet.

'They have already begun to cut down, or what they call stub up, Barnton Spinnies. Everett said that it is no good keeping it as a wood, and papa agreed. So it is to go into the home farm, and Griffiths is to pay rent for it. I don't like having it cut down as the boys always used to get nuts there, but Everett says it won't do to keep woods for little boys to get nuts.

'Mary Stocking has been very ill since you went, and I'm afraid she won't last long. When they get to be so very bad with rheumatism I almost think it's wrong to pray for them, because they are in so much pain. We thought at one time that mamma's ointment had done her good, but when we came to inquire, we found she had swallowed it. Wasn't it dreadful? But it didn't seem to do her any harm. Everett says that it wouldn't make any difference which she did.

'Papa is beginning to be afraid that Everett is a Radical. But I'm sure he's not. He says he is as good a Conservative as there is in all Herefordshire, only that he likes to know what is to be conserved. Papa said after dinner yesterday that everything English ought to be maintained. Everett said that according to that we should have kept the Star Chamber. "Of course I would," said papa. Then they went at it, hammer and tongs. Everett had the best of it. At any rate he talked the longest. But I do hope he is not a Radical. No country gentleman ought to be a Radical. Ought he, dear?

'Mrs Fletcher says you are to get the lozenges at Squire's in Oxford Street, and be sure to ask for the Vade mecum lozenges. She is all in a flutter about the hounds. She says she hopes John will do nothing of the kind because of the expense; but we all know that she would like him to have them. The subscription* is not very good, only £1500, and it would cost him ever so much a year. But everybody says that he is very rich and that he ought to do it. If you see Arthur give him our love. Of course a member of Parliament is too busy to write letters. But I don't think Arthur ever was good at writing. Everett says that men never ought to write letters. Give my love to Mr Wharton.

'I am, dearest Emily,
'Your most affectionate Cousin,
'MARY WHARTON.'

'Everett is a fool,' said Mr Wharton as soon as he had read the letter.
'Why is he a fool, papa?'
'Because he will quarrel with Sir Alured about politics before he knows where he is. What business has a young fellow like that to have an opinion either one side or the other, before his betters?'
'But Everett always had strong opinions.'
'It didn't matter as long as he only talked nonsense at a club in London, but now he'll break that old man's heart.'
'But, papa, don't you see anything else?'
'I see that John Fletcher is going to make an ass of himself and spend a thousand a year in keeping up a pack of hounds for other people to ride after.'
'I think I see something else besides that.'
'What do you see?'
'Would it annoy you if Everett were to become engaged to Mary?'
Then Mr Wharton whistled. 'To be sure she does put his name into every line of her letter. No; it wouldn't annoy me. I don't see why he shouldn't marry his second cousin if he likes. Only if he is engaged to her, I think it odd that he shouldn't write and tell us.'
'I'm sure he's not engaged to her as yet. She wouldn't write at all in that way if they were engaged. Everybody would be told at once, and Sir Alured would never be able to keep it a secret. Why should there be a secret? But I'm sure she is very fond of him. Mary would never write about any man in that way unless she were beginning to be attached to him.'
About ten days after this there came two letters from Wharton Hall to Manchester Square, the shortest of which shall be given first. It ran as follows:—

'MY DEAR FATHER,—
'I have proposed to my cousin Mary, and she has accepted me. Everybody here seems to like the idea. I hope it will not displease you.

Of course you and Emily will come down. I will tell you when the day is fixed.

'Your affectionate son,
'EVERETT WHARTON.'

This the old man read as he sat at breakfast with his daughter opposite to him, while Emily was reading a very much longer letter from the same house. 'So it's going to be just as you guessed,' he said.

'I was quite sure of it, papa. Is that from Everett? Is he very happy?'

'Upon my word, I can't say whether he's happy or not. If he had got a new horse he would have written at much greater length about it. It seems, however, to be quite fixed.'

'Oh, yes. This is from Mary. She is happy at any rate. I suppose men never say so much about these things as women.'

'May I see Mary's letter?'

'I don't think it would be quite fair, papa. It's only a girl's rhapsody about the man she loves,—very nice and womanly, but not intended for any one but me. It does not seem that they mean to wait very long.'

'Why should they wait? Is any day fixed?'

'Mary says that Everett talks about the middle of May. Of course you will go down.'

'We must both go.'

'You will at any rate. Don't promise for me just at present. It must make Sir Alured very happy. It is almost the same as finding himself at last with a son of his own. I suppose they will live at Wharton altogether now,—unless Everett gets into Parliament.'

But the reader may see the young lady's letter, though her future father-in-law was not permitted to do so, and will perceive that there was a paragraph at the close of it which perhaps was more conducive to Emily's secrecy than her feelings as to the sacred obligations of female correspondence.

'*Monday, Wharton.*

'DEAREST EMILY,—

'I wonder whether you will be much surprised at the news I have to tell you. You cannot be more so than I am at having to write it. It has all been so very sudden that I almost feel ashamed of myself. Everett has proposed to me, and I have accepted him. There;—now you know it all. Though you never can know how very dearly I love him and how thoroughly I admire him. I do think that he is everything that a man ought to be, and that I am the most fortunate young woman in the world. Only isn't it odd that I should always have to live all my life in the same house, and never change my name,—just like a man, or an old maid? But I don't mind that because I do love him so dearly and because he is so good. He has written to Mr Wharton, I know. I was sitting by him and his letter didn't take him a minute. But he says that long letters about such things only give trouble. I hope you won't think my letter troublesome. He is not sitting by me now but has gone over to Longbarns to help settle about the hounds. John is going to have them after all. I wish it hadn't happened just at this time because all the gentlemen do think so much about it. Of course Everett is one of the committee.

'Papa and mamma are both very, very glad of it. Of course it is nice for them as it will keep Everett and me here. If I had married anybody else,—though I am sure I never should,—she would have been very lonely. And of course papa likes to think that Everett is already one of us. I hope they never will quarrel about politics; but, as Everett says, the world does change as it goes on, and young men and old men never will think quite the same about things. Everett told papa the other day that if he could be put back a century he would be a Radical. Then there were ever so many words. But Everett always laughs, and at last papa comes round.

'I can't tell you, my dear, what a fuss we are in already about it all. Everett wants our marriage early in May, so that we may have two months in Switzerland before London is what he calls turned loose. And papa says that there is no use in delaying, because he gets older every day. Of course that is true of everybody. So that we are all in a flutter about getting things. Mamma did talk of going up to town, but I believe they have things now quite as good at Hereford. Sarah, when she was married, had all her things from London, but they say that there has been a great change since that. I am sure that I think that you may get anything you want at Muddocks and Cramble's. But mamma says I am to have my veil from Howell and James's.*

'Of course you and Mr Wharton will come. I shan't think it any marriage without. Papa and mamma talk of it as quite of course. You know how fond papa is of the bishop. I think he will marry us. I own I should like to be married by a bishop. It would make it so sweet and so solemn. Mr Higgenbottom could of course assist;—but he is such an odd old man, with his snuff and his spectacles always tumbling off, that I shouldn't like to have no one else. I have often thought that if it were only for marrying people we ought to have a nicer rector at Wharton.

'Almost all the tenants have been to wish me joy. They are very fond of Everett already, and now they feel that there will never be any very great change. I do think it is the very best thing that could be done, even if it were not that I am so thoroughly in love with him. I didn't think I should ever be able to own that I was in love with a man; but now I feel quite proud of it. I don't mind telling you because he is your brother, and I think that you will be glad of it.

'He talks very often about you. Of course you know what it is that we all wish. I love Arthur Fletcher almost as much as if he were my brother. He is my sister's brother-in-law, and if he could become my husband's brother-in-law too, I should be so happy. Of course we all know that he wishes it. Write immediately to wish me joy. Perhaps you could go to Howell and James's about the veil. And promise to come to us in May. Sarah says the veil ought to cost about thirty pounds.

'Dearest, dearest Emily,

'I shall so soon be your most affectionate sister,

'MARY WHARTON.'

Emily's answer was full of warm, affectionate congratulations. She had much to say in favour of Everett. She promised to use all her little skill at Howell and James's. She expressed a hope that the overtures to be made in regard to the bishop might be successful. And she made kind remarks even as to Muddocks and Cramble. But she would not promise that she herself would be at Wharton on the happy day. 'Dear Mary,' she said, 'remember what I have suffered, and that I cannot be quite as other people are. I could not stand at your marriage in black clothes,—nor should I have the courage even if I had the will to dress myself in others.' None of the Whartons had come to her wedding. There was no feeling of anger now left as to that. She was quite aware that they had done right to stay away. But the very fact that it had been right that they should stay away would make it wrong that the widow of Ferdinand Lopez should now assist at the marriage of one Wharton to another. This was all that a marriage ought to be; whereas that had been—all that a marriage ought not to be. In answer to the paragraph about Arthur Fletcher Emily Lopez had not a word to say.

Soon after this, early in April, Everett came up to town. Though his bride might be content to get her bridal clothes in Hereford, none but a London tailor could decorate him properly for such an occasion. During these last weeks Arthur Fletcher had not been seen in Manchester Square; nor had his name been mentioned there by Mr Wharton. Of anything that may have passed between them Emily was altogether ignorant. She observed, or thought that she observed, that her father was more silent with her,—perhaps less tender than he had been since the day on which her husband had perished. His manner of life was the same. He almost always dined at home in order that she might not be alone, and made no complaint as to her conduct. But she could see that he was unhappy, and she knew the cause of his grief. 'I think, papa,' she said one day, 'that it would be better that I should go away.' This was on the day before Everett's arrival,—of which, however, he had given no notice.

'Go away! Where would you go to?'

'It does not matter. I do not make you happy.'

'What do you mean? Who says that I am not happy? Why do you talk like that?'

'Do not be angry with me. Nobody says so. I can see it well enough. I know how good you are to me, but I am making your life wretched. I am a wet blanket to you, and yet I cannot help myself. If I could only go somewhere, where I could be of use.'

'I don't know what you mean. This is your proper home.'

'No;—it is not my home. I ought to have forfeited it. I ought to go where I could work and be of some use in the world.'

'You might be of use if you chose, my dear. Your proper career is before you if you would condescend to accept it. It is not for me to persuade you, but I can see and feel the truth. Till you bring yourself to do that, your days will be blighted,—and so will mine. You have made one great mistake in life. Stop a moment. I do not speak often, but I wish you to listen to me now. Such mistakes do generally produce misery and ruin to all who are concerned. With you it chances that it may be otherwise. You can put your foot again upon the firm ground and recover everything. Of course there must be a struggle. One person has to struggle with circumstances, another with his foes, and a third with his own feelings. I can understand that there should be such a struggle with you; but it ought to be made. You ought to be brave enough and strong enough to conquer your regrets, and to begin again. In no other way can you do anything for me or for yourself. To talk of going away is childish nonsense. Whither would you go? I shall not urge you any more, but I would not have you talk to me in that way.' Then he got up and left the room and the house, and went down to his club,—in order that she might think of what he had said in solitude.

And she did think of it;—but still continually with an assurance to herself that her father did not understand her feelings. The career of which he spoke was no doubt open to her, but she could not regard it as that which it was proper that she should fulfil, as he did. When she told her lover that she had lain among the pots till she was black and defiled, she expressed in the strongest language that which was her real conviction. He did not think her to have been defiled,—or at any rate thought that she might again bear the wings of a dove; but she felt it, and therefore knew herself to be unfit. She had said it all to her lover in the strongest words she could find, but she could not repeat them to her father. The next morning, when he came into the parlour where she was already sitting, she looked up at him almost reproachfully. Did he think that a woman was a piece of furniture which you can mend, and revarnish, and fit out with new ornaments, and then send out for use, second-hand indeed, but for all purposes as good as new?

Then, while she was in this frame of mind, Everett came in upon her unawares, and with his almost boisterous happiness succeeded for a while in changing the current of her thoughts. He was of course now uppermost in his own thoughts. The last few months had made so much of him that he might be excused for being unable to sink himself in the presence of others. He was the heir to the baronetcy,—and to the double fortunes of the two old men. And he was going to be married in a manner as every one told him to increase the glory and stability of the family. 'It's all nonsense about your not coming down,' he said. She smiled and shook her head. 'I can only tell you that it will give the greatest offence to every one. If you knew how much they talk about you down there I don't think you would like to hurt them.'

'Of course I would not like to hurt them.'

'And considering that you have no other brother——'

'Oh, Everett!'

'I think more about it, perhaps, than you do. I think you owe it me to come down. You will never probably have another chance of being present at your brother's marriage.' This he said in a tone that was almost lachrymose.

'A wedding, Everett, should be merry.'

'I don't know about that. It is a very serious sort of thing, to my way of thinking. When Mary got your letter it nearly broke her heart. I think I have a right to expect it, and if you don't come I shall feel myself injured. I don't see what is the use of having a family if the members of it do not stick together. What would you think if I were to desert you?'

'Desert you, Everett?'

'Well, yes;—it is something of the kind. I have made my request, and you can comply with it or not as you please.'

'I will go,' she said very slowly. Then she left him and went to her own room to think in what description of garment she could appear at a wedding with the least violence to the conditions of her life.

'I have got her to say she'll come,' he said to his father that evening. 'If you leave her to me, I'll bring her round.'

Soon after that,—within a day or two,—there came out a paragraph in one of the fashionable newspapers of the day, saying that an alliance had been arranged between the heir to the Wharton title and property and the daughter of the present baronet. I think that this had probably originated in the club gossip. I trust it did not spring directly from the activity or ambition of Everett himself.

CHAPTER 76

WHO WILL IT BE?

FOR the first day or two after the resignation of the Ministry the Duchess appeared to take no further notice of the matter. An ungrateful world had repudiated her and her husband, and he had foolishly assisted and given way to the repudiation. All her grand aspirations were at an end. All her triumphs were over. And worse than that; there was present to her a conviction that she never had really triumphed. There never had come the happy moment in which she had felt herself to be dominant over other women. She had toiled and struggled, she had battled and occasionally submitted; and yet there was present to her a feeling that she had stood higher in public estimation as Lady Glencora Palliser,—whose position had been all her own and had not depended on her husband,—than now she had done as the Duchess of Omnium, and wife of the Prime Minister of England. She had meant to be something, she knew not what, greater than had been the wives of other Prime Ministers and other Dukes; and now she felt that in her failure she had been almost ridiculous. And the failure, she thought, had been his,—or hers,—rather than that of circumstances. If he had been less scrupulous and more persistent it might have been different,—or if she had been more discreet. Sometimes she felt her own failing so violently as to acquit him almost entirely. At other times she was almost beside herself with anger because all her losses seemed to have arisen from want of stubbornness on his part. When he had told her that he and his followers had determined to resign because they had beaten their foes by a majority only of nine, she took it into her head that he was in fault. Why should he go while his supporters were more numerous than his opponents? It was useless to bid him think it over again. Though she was far from understanding all the circumstances of the game, she did know that he could not remain after having arranged with his colleagues that he would go. So she became cross and sullen; and while he was going to Windsor and back and setting his house in order, and preparing the way for his successor,—whoever that successor might be,—she was moody and silent, dreaming over some impossible condition of things in accordance with which he might have remained Prime Minister—almost for ever.

On the Sunday after the fatal division,—the division which the Duchess would not allow to have been fatal,—she came across him somewhere in the house. She had hardly spoken to him since he had come into her room that night and told her that all was over. She had said that she was unwell and had kept out of sight; and he had been here and there, between Windsor and the Treasury Chambers, and had been glad to escape from her ill-humour. But she could not endure any longer the annoyance of having to get all her news through Mrs Finn,—second hand, or third hand, and now found herself driven to capitulate. 'Well,' she said, 'how is it all going to be? I suppose you do not know or you would have told me?'

'There is very little to tell.'

'Mr Monk is to be Prime Minister?' she asked.

'I did not say so. But it is not impossible.'

'Has the Queen sent for him?'

'Not as yet. Her Majesty has seen both Mr Gresham and Mr Daubeny as well as myself. It does not seem a very easy thing to make a Ministry just at present.'

'Why should not you go back?'

'I do not think that is on the cards.'

'Why not? Ever so many men have done it, after going out,—and why not you? I remember Mr Mildmay doing it twice.* It is always the thing when the man who has been sent for makes a mess of it, for the old minister to have another chance.'

'But what if the old minister will not take the chance?'

'Then it is the old minister's fault. Why shouldn't you take the chance as well as another? It isn't many days ago since you were quite anxious to remain in. I thought you were going to break your heart because people even talked of your going.'

'I was going to break my heart, as you call it,' he said smiling, 'not because people talked of my ceasing to be minister, but because the feeling of the House of Commons justified people in so saying. I hope you see the difference.'

'No, I don't. And there is no difference. The people we are talking about are the members,—and they have supported you. You could go on if you chose. I'm sure Mr Monk wouldn't leave you.'

'It is just what Mr Monk would do, and ought to do. No one is less likely than Mr Monk to behave badly in such an emergency. The more I see of Mr Monk, the higher I think of him.'

'He has his own game to play as well as others.'

'I think he has no game to play but that of his country. It is no use our discussing it, Cora.'

'Of course I understand nothing, because I'm a woman.'

'You understand a great deal,—but not quite all. You may at any rate understand this,—that our troubles are at an end. You were saying but the other day that the labours of being a Prime Minister's wife had been almost too many for you.'

'I never said so. As long as you didn't give way no labour was too much for me. I would have done anything,—slaved morning and night,—so that we might have succeeded. I hate being beat. I'd sooner be cut to pieces.'

'There is no help for it now, Cora. The Lord Mayor, you know, is only Lord Mayor for one year, and must then go back to private life.'

'But men have been Prime Ministers for ten years at a time. If you have made up your mind, I suppose we may as well give up. I shall always think it your own fault.' He still smiled. 'I shall,' she said.

'Oh, Cora!'

'I can only speak as I feel.'

'I don't think you would speak as you do, if you knew how much your words hurt me. In such a matter as this I should not be justified in allowing your opinions to have weight with me. But your sympathy would be so much to me!'

'When I thought it was making you ill, I wished that you might be spared.'

'My illness would be nothing, but my honour is everything. I, too, have something to bear as well as you, and if you cannot approve of what I do, at any rate be silent.'

'Yes;—I can be silent.' Then he slowly left her. As he went she was almost tempted to yield, and to throw herself into his arms, and to promise that she would be soft to him, and to say that she was sure that all he did was for the best. But she could not bring herself as yet to be good-humoured. If he had only been a little stronger, a little thicker-skinned, made of clay a little coarser, a little other than he was, it might have been so different!

Early on that Sunday afternoon she had herself driven to Mrs Finn's house in Park Lane, instead of waiting for her friend. Latterly she had but seldom done this, finding that her presence at home was much wanted. She had been filled with, perhaps, foolish ideas of the necessity of doing something,—of adding something to the strength of her husband's position,—and had certainly been diligent in her work. But now she might run about like any other woman. 'This is an honour, Duchess,' said Mrs Finn.

'Don't be sarcastic, Marie. We have nothing further to do with the bestowal of honours. Why didn't he make everybody a peer or a baronet while he was about it? Lord Finn! I don't see why he shouldn't have been Lord Finn. I'm sure he deserved it for the way in which he attacked Sir Timothy Beeswax.'

'I don't think he'd like it.'

'They all say so, but I suppose they do like it, or they wouldn't take it. And I'd have made Locock a knight;—Sir James Locock. He'd make a more knightly knight that Sir Timothy. When a man has power he ought to use it. It makes people respect him. Mr Daubeny made a duke, and people think more of that than anything he did. Is Mr Finn going to join the new ministry?'

'If you can tell me, Duchess, who is to be the next minister, I can give a guess.'

'Mr Monk.'

'Then he certainly will.'

'Or Mr Daubeny.'

'Then he certainly won't.'

'Or Mr Gresham.'

'That I could not answer.'

'Or the Duke of Omnium.'

'That would depend upon his Grace. If the Duke came back, Mr Finn's services would be at his disposal, whether in or out of office.'

'Very prettily said, my dear. I never look round this room without thinking of the first time I came here. Do you remember, when I found the old man sitting there?' The old man alluded to was the late Duke.

'I am not likely to forget it, Duchess.'

'How I hated you when I saw you! What a fright I thought you were! I pictured you to myself as a sort of ogre, willing to eat up everybody for the gratification of your own vanity.'

'I was very vain, but there was a little pride with it.'

'And now it has come to pass that I can't very well live without you. How he did love you!'

'His Grace was very good to me.'

'It would have done no great harm, after all, if he had made you Duchess of Omnium.'

'Very great harm to me, Lady Glen. As it is I got a friend that I loved dearly, and a husband that I love dearly too. In the other case I should have had neither. Perhaps I may say, that in that other case my life would not have been brightened by the affection of the present Duchess.'

'One can't tell how it would have gone, but I well remember the state I was in then.' The door was opened and Phineas Finn entered the room. 'What, Mr Finn, are you at home? I thought everybody was crowding down at the clubs, to know who is to be what. We are settled. We are quiet. We have nothing to do to disturb ourselves. But you ought to be in all the flutter of renewed expectation.'

'I am waiting my destiny in calm seclusion. I hope the Duke is well?'

'As well as can be expected. He doesn't walk about his room with a poniard in his hand,—ready for himself or Sir Orlando; nor is he sitting crowned like Bacchus, drinking the health of the new Ministry with Lord Drummond and Sir Timothy. He is probably sipping a cup of coffee over a blue-book in dignified retirement. You should go and see him.'

'I should be unwilling to trouble him when he is so much occupied.'

'That is just what has done him all the harm in the world. Everybody presumes that he has so much to think of that nobody goes near him. Then he is left to boody* over everything by himself till he becomes a sort of political hermit, or ministerial Lama,* whom human eyes are not to look upon. It doesn't matter now; does it?' Visitor after visitor came in, and the Duchess chatted to them all, leaving the impression on everybody that heard her that she at least was not sorry to be relieved from the troubles attending her husband's late position.

She sat there over an hour, and as she was taking her leave she had a few words to whisper to Mrs Finn. 'When this is all over,' she said, 'I mean to call on that Mrs Lopez.'

'I thought you did go there.'

'That was soon after the poor man had killed himself,—when she was going away. Of course I only left a card. But I shall see her now if I can. We want to get her out of her melancholy if possible. I have a sort of feeling, you know, that among us we made the train run over him.'

'I don't think that.'

'He got so horribly abused for what he did at Silverbridge; and I really don't see why he wasn't to have his money. It was I that made him spend it.'

'He was, I fancy, a thoroughly bad man.'

'But a wife doesn't always want to be made a widow even if her husband be bad. I think I owe her something, and I would pay my debt if I knew how. I shall go and see her, and if she will marry this other man we'll take her by the hand. Good-bye, dear. You'd better come to me early to-morrow, as I suppose we shall know something by eleven o'clock.'

In the course of that evening the Duke of St Bungay came to Carlton Terrace and was closeted for some time with the late Prime Minister. He had been engaged during that and the last two previous days in lending his aid to various political manoeuvres and ministerial attempts, from which our Duke had kept himself altogether aloof. He did not go to Windsor, but as each successive competitor journeyed thither and returned, some one either sent for the old Duke or went to seek his counsel. He was the Nestor of the occasion, and strove heartily to compose all quarrels, and so to arrange matters that a wholesome, moderately Liberal Ministry might be again installed for the good of the country and the comfort of all true Whigs. In such moments he almost ascended to the grand heights of patriotism, being always indifferent as to himself. Now he came to his late chief with a new project. Mr Gresham would attempt to form a Ministry if the Duke of Omnium would join him.

'It is impossible!' said the younger politician, folding his hands together and throwing himself back in his chair.

'Listen to me before you answer me with such certainty. There are three or four gentlemen who, after the work of the last three years, bearing in mind the manner in which our defeat has just been accomplished, feel themselves disinclined to join Mr Gresham unless you will do so also. I may specially name Mr Monk and Mr Finn. I might perhaps add myself, were it not that I had hoped that in any event I might at length regard myself as exempt from further service. The old horse should be left to graze out his last days, Ne peccet ad extremum ridendus.* But you can't consider yourself absolved on that score.'

'There are other reasons.'

'But the Queen's service should count before everything. Gresham and Cantrip with their own friends can hardly make a Ministry as things are now unless Mr Monk will join them. I do not think that any other Chancellor of the Exchequer is at present possible.'

'I will beseech Mr Monk not to let any feeling as to me stand in his way. Why should it?'

'It is not only what you may think and he may think,—but what others will think and say. The Coalition will have done all that ought to have been expected from it if our party in it can now join Mr Gresham.'

'By all means. But I could give them no strength. They may be sure at any rate of what little I can do for them out of office.'

'Mr Gresham has made his acceptance of office,—well, I will not say strictly conditional on your joining him. That would hardly be correct. But he has expressed himself quite willing to make the attempt with your aid, and doubtful whether he can succeed without it. He suggests that you should join him as President of the Council.'

'And you?'

'If I were wanted at all I should take the Privy Seal.'

'Certainly not, my friend. If there were any question of my return we would reverse the offices. But I think I may say my mind is fixed. If you wish it I will see Mr Monk, and do all that I can to get him to go with you. But for myself,—I feel that it would be useless.'

At last, at the Duke's pressing request, he agreed to take twenty-four hours before he gave his final answer to the proposition.

CHAPTER 77

THE DUCHESS IN MANCHESTER SQUARE

THE Duke said not a word to his wife as to this new proposition, and when she asked him what tidings their old friend had brought as to the state of affairs, he almost told a fib in his anxiety to escape from her persecution. 'He is in some doubt what he means to do himself,' said the Duke. The Duchess asked many questions, but got no satisfactory reply to any of them. Nor did Mrs Finn learn anything from her husband, whom, however, she did not interrogate very closely. She would be contented to know when the proper time might come for ladies to be informed. The Duke, however, was determined to take his twenty-four hours all alone,—or at any rate not to be driven to his decision by feminine interference.

In the meantime the Duchess went to Manchester Square intent on performing certain good offices on behalf of the poor widow. It may be doubted whether she had clearly made up her mind what it was that she could do, though she was clear that some debt was due by her to Mrs Lopez. And she knew too in what direction assistance might be serviceable, if only it could in this case be given. She had heard that the present member for Silverbridge had been the lady's lover long before Mr Lopez had come upon the scene, and with those feminine wiles of which she was a perfect mistress she had extracted from him a confession that his mind was unaltered. She liked Arthur Fletcher,—as indeed she had for a time liked Ferdinand Lopez,—and felt that her conscience would be easier if she could assist in this good work. She built castles in the air as to the presence of the bride and bridegroom at Matching, thinking how she might thus repair the evil she had done. But her heart misgave her a little as she drew near to the house, and remembered how very slight was her acquaintance and how extremely delicate the mission on which she had come. But she was not the woman to turn back when she had once put her foot to any work; and she was driven up to the door in Manchester Square without any expressed hesitation on her own part. 'Yes,—his mistress was at home,' said the butler, still shrinking at the sound of the name which he hated. The Duchess was then shown upstairs, and was left alone for some minutes in the drawing-room. It was a large handsome apartment, hung round with valuable pictures, and having signs of considerable wealth. Since she had first invited Lopez to stand for Silverbridge she had heard much about him, and had wondered how he had gained possession of such a girl as Emily Wharton. And now, as she looked about, her wonder was increased. She knew enough of such people as the Whartons and the Fletchers to be aware that as a class they are more impregnable, more closely guarded by their feelings and prejudices against strangers than any other. None keep their daughters to themselves with greater care, or are less willing to see their rules of life changed or abolished. And yet this man, half foreigner half Jew,—and as it now appeared, whole pauper,—had stepped in and carried off a prize for which such a one as Arthur Fletcher was contending! The Duchess had never seen Emily but once,—so as to observe her well,—and had then thought her to be a very handsome woman. It had been at the garden party at Richmond, and Lopez had then insisted that his wife should be well dressed. It would perhaps have been impossible in the whole of that assembly to find a more beautiful woman than Mrs Lopez then was,—or one who carried herself with a finer air. Now when she entered the room in her deep mourning it would have been difficult to recognize her. Her face was much thinner, her eyes apparently larger, and her colour faded. And there had come a settled seriousness on her face which seemed to rob her of her youth. Arthur Fletcher had declared that as he saw her now she was more beautiful than ever. But Arthur Fletcher, in looking at her, saw more than her mere features. To his eyes there was a tenderness added by her sorrow which had its own attraction for him. And he was so well versed in every line of her countenance, that he could see there the old loveliness behind the sorrow; the loveliness which would come forth again, as bright as ever, if the sorrow could be removed. But the Duchess, though she remembered the woman's beauty as she might that of any other lady, now saw nothing but a thing of woe wrapped in customary widow's weeds. 'I hope,' she said, 'I am not intruding in coming to you; but I have been anxious to renew our acquaintance for reasons which I am sure you will understand.'

Emily at the moment hardly knew how to address her august visitor. Though her father had lived all his life in what is called good society, he had not consorted much with dukes and duchesses. She herself had indeed on one occasion been for an hour or two the guest of this grand lady, but on that occasion she had hardly been called upon to talk to her. Now she doubted how to name the Duchess, and with some show of hesitation decided at last upon not naming her at all. 'It is very good of you to come,' she said in a faltering voice.

'I told you that I would when I wrote, you know. That is many months ago, but I have not forgotten it. You have been in the country since that I think?'

'Yes. In Herefordshire. Herefordshire is our county.'

'I know all about it,' said the Duchess, smiling. She generally did contrive to learn 'all about' the people whom she chose to take by the hand. 'We have a Herefordshire gentleman sitting for,—I must not say our borough of Silverbridge.' She was anxious to make some allusion to Arthur Fletcher; but it was difficult to travel on that Silverbridge ground, as Lopez had been her chosen candidate when she still wished to claim the borough as an appanage* of the Palliser family. Emily, however, kept her countenance and did not show by any sign that her thoughts were running in that direction. 'And though we don't presume to regard Mr Fletcher,' continued the Duchess, 'as in any way connected with our local interests, he has always supported the Duke, and I hope has become a friend of ours. I think he is a neighbour of yours in the country.'

'Oh, yes. My cousin is married to his brother.'

'I knew there was something of that kind. He told me that there was some close alliance.' The Duchess as she looked at the woman to whom she wanted to be kind did not as yet dare to express a wish that there might at some not very distant time be a closer alliance. She had come there intending to do so; and had still some hope that she might do it before the interview was over. But at any rate she would not do it yet. 'Have I not heard,' she said, 'something of another marriage?'

'My brother is going to marry his cousin, Sir Alured Wharton's daughter.'

'Ah;—I thought it had been one of the Fletchers. It was our member who told me, and spoke as though they were all his very dear friends.'

'They are dear friends,—very.' Poor Emily still didn't know whether to call her Duchess, my Lady, or your Grace,—and yet felt the need of calling her by some special name.

'Exactly. I supposed it was so. They tell me Mr Fletcher will become quite a favourite in the House. At this present moment nobody knows on which side anybody is going to sit to-morrow. It may be that Mr Fletcher will become the dire enemy of all the Duke's friends.'

'I hope not.'

'Of course I'm speaking of political enemies. Political enemies are often the best friends in the world; and I can assure you from my own experience that political friends are often the bitterest enemies. I never hated any people so much as some of our supporters.' The Duchess made a grimace, and Emily could not refrain from smiling. 'Yes, indeed. There's an old saying that misfortune makes strange bedfellows, but political friendship makes stranger alliances than misfortune. Perhaps you never met Sir Timothy Beeswax.'

'Never.'

'Well;—don't. But, as I was saying, there is no knowing who may support whom now. If I were asked who would be Prime Minister to-morrow, I should take half-a-dozen names and shake them in a bag.'

'It is not settled then?'

'Settled! No, indeed. Nothing is settled.' At that moment indeed everything was settled though the Duchess did not know it. 'And so we none of us can tell how Mr Fletcher may stand with us when things are arranged. I suppose he calls himself a Conservative?'

'Oh, yes!'

'All the Whartons I suppose are Conservatives,—and all the Fletchers.'

'Very nearly. Papa calls himself a Tory.'

'A very much better name, to my thinking. We are all Whigs of course. A Palliser who is not a Whig would be held to have disgraced himself for ever. Are not politics odd? A few years ago I only barely knew what the word meant, and that not correctly. Lately I have been so eager about it, that there hardly seems to be anything else worth living for. I suppose it's wrong, but a state of pugnacity seems to me the greatest bliss which we can reach here on earth.'

'I shouldn't like to be always fighting.'

'That's because you haven't known Sir Timothy Beeswax and two or three other gentlemen whom I could name. The day will come, I dare say, when you will care for politics.'

Emily was about to answer, hardly knowing what to say, when the door was opened and Mrs Roby came into the room. The lady was not announced, and Emily had heard no knock at the door. She was forced to go through some ceremony of introduction. 'This is my aunt, Mrs Roby,' she said, 'Aunt Harriet, the Duchess of Omnium.' Mrs Roby was beside herself,—not all with joy. That feeling would come afterwards as she would boast to her friends of her new acquaintance. At present there was the embarrassment of not quite knowing how to behave herself. The Duchess bowed from her seat, and smiled sweetly,—as she had learned to smile since her husband had become Prime Minister. Mrs Roby curtsied, and then remembered that in these days only housemaids ought to curtsy.

'Anything to our Mr Roby?' said the Duchess, continuing her smile,—'ours as was till yesterday at least.' This she said in an absurd wail of mock sorrow.

'My brother-in-law, your Grace,' said Mrs Roby delighted.

'Oh indeed. And what does Mr Roby think about it, I wonder? But I dare say you have found, Mrs Roby, that when a crisis comes,—a real crisis,—the ladies are told nothing. I have.'

'I don't think, your Grace, that Mr Roby ever divulges political secrets.'

'Doesn't he indeed! What a dull man your brother-in-law must be to live with,—that is as a politician! Good-bye, Mrs Lopez. You must come and see me and let me come to you again. I hope, you know,—I hope the time may come when things may once more be bright with you.' These last words she murmured almost in a whisper, as she held the hand of the woman she wished to befriend. Then she bowed to Mrs Roby, and left the room.

'What was it she said to you?' asked Mrs Roby.

'Nothing in particular, Aunt Harriet.'

'She seems to be very friendly. What made her come?'

'She wrote some time ago to say she would call.'

'But why?'

'I cannot tell you. I don't know. Don't ask me, aunt, about things that are passed. You cannot do it without wounding me.'

'I don't want to wound you, Emily, but I really think that that is nonsense. She is a very nice woman;—though I don't think she ought to have said that Mr Roby is dull. Did Mr Wharton know that she was coming?'

'He knew that she said she would come,' replied Emily very sternly, so that Mrs Roby found herself compelled to pass on to some other subject. Mrs Roby had heard the wish expressed that something 'once more might be bright,' and when she got home told her husband that she was sure that Emily Lopez was going to marry Arthur Fletcher. 'And why the d—— shouldn't she?' said Dick. 'And that poor man destroying himself not much more than twelve months ago! I couldn't do it,' said Mrs Roby. 'I don't mean to give you the chance,' said Dick.

The Duchess when she went away suffered under a sense of failure. She had intended to bring about some crisis of female tenderness in which she might have rushed into future hopes and joyous anticipations, and with the freedom which will come from ebullitions of feeling, have told the widow that the peculiar circumstances of her position would not only justify her in marrying this other man but absolutely called upon her to do it. Unfortunately she had failed in her attempt to bring the interview to a condition in which this would have been possible, and while she was still making the attempt that odious aunt had come in. 'I have been on my mission,' she said to Mrs Finn afterwards.

'Have you done any good?'

'I don't think I've done any harm. Women, you know, are so very different! There are some who would delight to have an opportunity of opening their hearts to a Duchess, and who might almost be talked into anything in an ecstasy.'

'Hardly women of the best sort, Lady Glen.'

'Not of the best sort. But then one doesn't come across the very best, very often. But that kind of thing does have an effect; and as I only wanted to do good, I wish she had been one of the sort for the occasion.'

'Was she—offended?'

'Oh dear no. You don't suppose I attacked her with a husband at the first word. Indeed, I didn't attack her at all. She didn't give me an opportunity. Such a Niobe you never saw.'

'Was she weeping?'

'Not actual tears, but her gown, and her cap, and her strings were weeping. Her voice wept, and her hair, and her nose, and her mouth. Don't you know that look of subdued mourning? And yet they say that that man is dying for love. How beautiful it is to see that there is such a thing as constancy left in the world.'

When she got home she found that her husband had just returned from the old Duke's house, where he had met Mr Monk, Mr Gresham, and Lord Cantrip. 'It's all settled at last,' he said cheerfully.

CHAPTER 78

THE NEW MINISTRY

WHEN the ex-Prime Minister was left by himself after the departure of his old friend his first feeling had been one of regret that he had been weak enough to doubt at all. He had long since made up his mind that after all that had passed he could not return to office as a subordinate. That feeling as to the impropriety of Cæsar descending to serve under others which he had been foolish enough to express, had been strong with him from the very commencement of his Ministry. When first asked to take the place which he had filled the reason strong against it had been the conviction that it would probably exclude him from political work during the latter half of his life. The man who has written Q.C. after his name must abandon his practice behind the bar.* As he then was, although he had already been driven by the unhappy circumstance of his peerage from the House of Commons which he loved so well, there were still open to him many fields of political work. But if he should once consent to stand on the top rung of the ladder, he could not, he thought, take a lower place without degradation. Till he should have been placed quite at the top no shifting his place from this higher to that lower office would injure him in his own estimation. The exigencies of the service and not defeat would produce such changes as that. But he could not go down from being Prime Minister and serve under some other chief without acknowledging himself to have been unfit for the place he had filled. Of all that he had quite assured himself. And yet he had allowed the old Duke to talk him into a doubt!

As he sat considering the question he acknowledged that there might have been room for doubt, though in the present emergency there certainly was none. He could imagine circumstances in which the experience of an individual in some special branch of his country's service might be of such paramount importance to the country as to make it incumbent on a man to sacrifice all personal feeling. But it was not so with him. There was nothing now which he could do, which another might not do as well. That blessed task of introducing decimals into all the commercial relations of British life, which had once kept him aloft in the air, floating as upon eagle's wings, had been denied him. If ever done it must be done from the House of Commons; and the people of the country had become deaf to the charms of that great reform. Othello's occupation was, in truth, altogether gone, and there was no reason by which he could justify to himself the step down in the world which the old Duke had proposed to him.

Early on the following morning he left Carlton Terrace on foot and walked as far as Mr Monk's house, which was close to St James's Street. Here at eleven o'clock he found his late Chancellor of the Exchequer in that state of tedious agitation in which a man is kept who does not yet know whether he is or is not to be one of the actors in the play just about to be performed. The Duke had never before been in Mr Monk's very humble abode, and now caused some surprise. Mr Monk knew that he might probably be sent for, but had not expected that any of the ex-Prime Ministers of the day would come to him. People had said that not improbably he himself might be the man,—but he himself had indulged in no such dream. Office had had no great charms for him;—and if there was one man of the late Government who could lay it down without a personal regret, it was Mr Monk. 'I wish you to come with me to the Duke's house in St James's Square,' said the late Prime Minister. 'I think we shall find him at home.'

'Certainly. I will come this moment.' Then there was not a word spoken till the two men were in the street together. 'Of course I am a little anxious,' said Mr Monk. 'Have you anything to tell me before we get there?'

'You of course must return to office, Mr Monk.'

'With your Grace——I certainly will do so.'

'And without, if there be the need. They who are wanted should be forthcoming. But perhaps you will let me postpone what I have to say till we see the Duke. What a charming morning;—is it not? How sweet it would be down in the country.' March had gone out like a lamb, and even in London the early April days were sweet,—to be followed, no doubt, by the usual nipping inclemency of May. 'I never can get over the feeling,' continued the Duke, 'that Parliament should sit for the six winter months, instead of in summer. If we met on the first of October, how glorious it would be to get away for the early spring!'

'Nothing less strong than grouse could break up Parliament,' said Mr Monk; 'and then what would the pheasants and the foxes say?'

'It is giving up almost too much to our amusements. I used to think that I should like to move for a return of the number of hunting and shooting gentlemen in both Houses. I believe it would be a small minority.'

'But their sons shoot, and their daughters hunt, and all their hangers-on would be against it.'

'Custom is against us, Mr Monk; that is it. Here we are. I hope my friend will not be out, looking up young Lords of the Treasury.' The Duke of St Bungay was not in search of cadets for the Government, but he was at this very moment closeted with Mr Gresham, and Mr Gresham's especial friend Lord Cantrip. He had been at this work so long and so constantly that his very servants had their ministerial-crisis manners and felt and enjoyed the importance of the occasion. The two newcomers were soon allowed to enter the august conclave, and the five great senators greeted each other cordially. 'I hope we have not come inopportunely,' said the Duke of Omnium. Mr Gresham assured him almost with hilarity that nothing could be less inopportune;—and then the Duke was sure that Mr Gresham was to be the new Prime Minister, whoever might join him or whoever might refuse to do so. 'I told my friend here,' continued our Duke, laying his hand upon the old man's arm, 'that I would give him his answer to a proposition he made me within twenty-four hours. But I find that I can do so without that delay.'

'I trust your Grace's answer may be favourable to us,' said Mr Gresham,—who indeed did not doubt much that it would be so, seeing that Mr Monk had accompanied him.

'I do not think it will be unfavourable, though I cannot do as my friend has proposed.'

'Any practicable arrangement——' began Mr Gresham, with a frown, however, on his brow.

'The most practicable arrangement, I am sure, will be for you to form your Government, without hampering yourself with a beaten predecessor.'

'Not beaten,' said Lord Cantrip.

'Certainly not,' said the other Duke.

'It is because of your success that I ask your services,' said Mr Gresham.

'I have none to give,—none that I cannot better bestow out of office than in. I must ask you, gentlemen, to believe that I am quite fixed. Coming here with my friend Mr Monk, I did not state my purpose to him; but I begged him to accompany me, fearing lest in my absence he should feel it incumbent on himself to sail in the same boat with his late colleague.'

'I should prefer to do so,' said Mr Monk.

'Of course it is not for me to say what may be Mr Gresham's ideas; but as my friend here suggested to me that, were I to return to office,

Mr Monk would do so also, I cannot be wrong in surmising that his services are desired.' Mr Gresham bowed assent. 'I shall therefore take the liberty of telling Mr Monk that I think he is bound to give his aid in the present emergency. Were I as happily placed as he is in being the possessor of a seat in the House of Commons, I too should hope that I might do something.'

The four gentlemen, with eager pressure, begged the Duke to reconsider his decision. He could take this office and do nothing in it,—there being, as we all know, offices the holders of which are not called upon for work,—or he could take that place which would require him to labour like a galley slave. Would he be Privy Seal? Would he undertake the India Board? But the Duke of Omnium was at last resolute. Of this administration he would not at any rate be a member. Whether Cæsar might or might not at some future time condescend to command a legion, he could not do so when the purple had been but that moment stripped from his shoulders. He soon afterwards left the house with a repeated request to Mr Monk that he would not follow his late chief's example.

'I regret it greatly,' said Mr Gresham when he was gone.

'There is no man,' said Lord Cantrip, 'whom all who know him more thoroughly respect.'

'He has been worried,' said the old Duke, 'and must take time to recover himself. He has but one fault,—he is a little too conscientious, a little too scrupulous.' Mr Monk, of course, did join them, making one or two stipulations as he did so. He required that his friend Phineas Finn should be included in the Government. Mr Gresham yielded, though poor Phineas was not among the most favoured friends of that statesman. And so the Government was formed, and the crisis was again over, and the lists which all the newspapers had been publishing for the last three days were republished in an amended and nearly correct condition. The triumph of the 'People's Banner,' as to the omission of the Duke, was of course complete. The editor had no hesitation in declaring that he, by his own sagacity and persistency, had made certain the exclusion of that very unfit and very pressing candidate for office.

The list was filled up after the usual fashion. For a while the dilettanti politicians of the clubs, and the strong-minded women who take an interest in such things, and the writers in newspapers, had almost doubted whether, in the emergency which had been supposed to be so peculiar, any Government could be formed. There had been,—so they had said,—peculiarities so peculiar that it might be that the much-dreaded deadlock had come at last. A Coalition had been possible and, though antagonistic to British feelings generally, had carried on the Government. But what might succeed the Coalition, nobody had known. The Radicals and Liberals together would be too strong for Mr Daubeny and Sir Orlando. Mr Gresham had no longer a party of his own at his back, and a second Coalition would be generally spurned. In this way there had been much political excitement, and a fair amount of consequent enjoyment. But after a few days the old men had rattled into their old places,—or, generally, old men into new places,—and it was understood that Mr Gresham would again be supported by a majority.

As we grow old it is a matter of interest to watch how the natural gaps are filled in the two ranks of parliamentary workmen by whom the Government is carried on, either in the one interest or the other. Of course there must be gaps. Some men become too old,—though that is rarely the case. A Peel may perish, or even a Palmerston must die. Some men, though long supported by interest, family connection, or the loyalty of colleagues, are weighed down at last by their own incapacity and sink into peerages. Now and again a man cannot bear the bondage of office, and flies into rebellion and independence which would have been more respectable had it not been the result of discontent. Then the gaps must be filled. Whether on this side or on that, the candidates are first looked for among the sons of Earls and Dukes,— and not unnaturally, as the sons of Earls and Dukes may be educated for such work almost from their infancy. A few rise by the slow process of acknowledged fitness,—men who probably at first have not thought of office but are chosen because they are wanted, and whose careers are grudged them, not by their opponents or rivals, but by the Browns and Joneses of the world who cannot bear to see a Smith or a Walker become something so different to themselves. These men have a great weight to carry, and cannot always shake off the burden of their origin and live among begotten statesmen as though they too had been born to the manner. But perhaps the most wonderful ministerial phenomenon,— though now almost too common to be longer called a phenomenon,— is he who rises high in power and place by having made himself thoroughly detested and also,—alas for parliamentary cowardice!— thoroughly feared. Given sufficient audacity, a thick skin, and power to bear for a few years the evil looks and cold shoulders of his comrades, and that is the man most sure to make his way to some high seat. But the skin must be thicker than that of any animal known, and the audacity must be complete. To the man who will once shrink at the idea of being looked at askance for treachery, or hated for his ill condition, the career is impossible. But let him be obdurate, and the bid will come. 'Not because I want him, do I ask for him,' says some groaning chief of a party,—to himself, and also sufficiently aloud for others' ears,—'but because he stings me and goads me, and will drive me to madness as a foe.' Then the pachydermatous* one enters into the other's heaven, probably with the resolution already formed of ousting that unhappy angel. And so it was in the present instance. When Mr Gresham's completed list was published to the world, the world was astonished to find that Sir Timothy was to be Mr Gresham's Attorney-General. Sir Gregory Grogram became Lord Chancellor, and the Liberal chief was content to borrow his senior law adviser from the Conservative side of the late Coalition. It could not be that Mr Gresham was very fond of Sir Timothy;—but Sir Timothy in the late debates had shown himself to be a man of whom a minister might well be afraid.

Immediately on leaving the old Duke's house, the late Premier went home to his wife, and finding that she was out, waited for her return. Now that he had put his own decision beyond his own power he was anxious to let her know how it was to be with them. 'I think it is settled at last,' he said.

'And you are coming back?'

'Certainly not that. I believe I may say that Mr Gresham is Prime Minister.'

'Then he oughtn't to be,' said the Duchess crossly.

'I am sorry that I must differ from you, my dear, because I think he is the fittest man in England for the place.'

'And you?'

'I am a private gentleman who will now be able to devote more of his time to his wife and children than has hitherto been possible with him.'

'How very nice! Do you mean to say that you like it?'

'I am sure that I ought to like it. At the present moment I am thinking more of what you will like.'

'If you ask me, Plantagenet, you know I shall tell the truth.'

'Then tell the truth.'

'After drinking brandy so long I hardly think that 12 s. claret will agree with my stomach. You ask for the truth, and there it is,—very plainly.'

'Plain enough!'

'You asked, you know.'

'And I am glad to have been told, even though that which you tell me is not pleasant hearing. When a man has been drinking too much brandy, it may be well that he should be put on a course of 12 *s.* claret.'

'He won't like it; and then,—it's kill or cure.'

'I don't think you're gone so far, Cora, that we need fear that the remedy will be fatal.'

'I am thinking of you rather than myself. I can make myself generally disagreeable, and get excitement in that way. But what will you do? It's all very well to talk of me and the children, but you can't bring in a Bill for reforming us. You can't make us go by decimals. You can't increase our consumption by lowering our taxation. I wish you had gone back to some Board.' This she said looking up into his face with an anxiety which was half real and half burlesque.

'I had made up my mind to go back to no Board,—for the present. I was thinking that we could spend some months in Italy, Cora.'

'What; for the summer;—so as to be in Rome in July! After that we could utilize the winter by visiting Norway.'

'We might take Norway first.'

'And be eaten up by mosquitoes! I've got to be too old to like travelling.'

'What do you like, dear?'

'Nothing;—except being the Prime Minister's wife; and upon my word there were times when I didn't like that very much. I don't know anything else that I'm fit for. I wonder whether Mr Gresham would let me go to him as housekeeper? Only we should have to lend him Gatherum, or there would be no room for the display of my abilities. Is Mr Monk in?'

'He keeps his old office.'

'And Mr Finn?'

'I believe so; but in what place I don't know.'

'And who else?'

'Our old friend the Duke, and Lord Cantrip, and Mr Wilson,—and Sir Gregory will be Lord Chancellor.'

'Just the old stupid Liberal team. Put their names in a bag and shake them, and you can always get a ministry. Well, Plantagenet;—I'll go anywhere you like to take me. I'll have something for the malaria at Rome, and something for the mosquitoes in Norway, and will make the best of it. But I don't see why you should run away in the middle of the Session. I would stay and pitch into them, all round, like a true ex-minister and independent member of Parliament.' Then as he was leaving her she fired a last shot. 'I hope you made Sir Orlando and Sir Timothy peers before you gave up.'

It was not till two days after this that she read in one of the daily papers that Sir Timothy Beeswax was to be Attorney-General, and then her patience almost deserted her. To tell the truth, her husband had not dared to mention the appointment when he first saw her after hearing it. Her explosion first fell on the head of Phineas Finn, whom she found at home with his wife, deploring the necessity which had fallen upon him of filling the *fainéant* office of Chancellor of the Duchy of Lancaster. 'Mr Finn,' she said, 'I congratulate you on your colleagues.'

'Your Grace is very good. I was at any rate introduced to many of them under the Duke's auspices.'

'And ought, I think, to have seen enough of them to be ashamed of them. Such a regiment to march through Coventry with!'*

'I do not doubt that we shall be good enough men for any enemies we may meet.'

'It cannot be that you should conquer all the world with such a hero among you as Sir Timothy Beeswax. The idea of Sir Timothy coming back again! What do you feel about it?'

'Very indifferent, Duchess. He won't interfere much with me, as I have an Attorney-General of my own.* You see I'm especially safe.'

'I do believe men would do anything,' said the Duchess, turning to Mrs Finn. 'Of course I mean in the way of politics! But I did not think it possible that the Duke of St Bungay should again be in the same Government with Sir Timothy Beeswax.'

CHAPTER 79

THE WHARTON WEDDING

It was at last settled that the Wharton marriage should take place during the second week in June. There were various reasons for the postponement. In the first place Mary Wharton, after a few preliminary inquiries, found herself forced to declare that Messrs Muddocks and Cramble could not send her forth equipped as she ought to be equipped for such a husband in so short a time. 'Perhaps they do it quicker in London,' she said to Everett with a soft regret, remembering the metropolitan glories of her sister's wedding. And then Arthur Fletcher could be present during the Whitsuntide holidays; and the presence of Arthur Fletcher was essential. And it was not only his presence at the altar that was needed;—Parliament was not so exacting but that he might have given that;—but it was considered by the united families to be highly desirable that he should on this occasion remain some days in the country. Emily had promised to attend the wedding, and would of course be at Wharton for at least a week. As soon as Everett had succeeded in wresting a promise from his sister, the tidings were conveyed to Fletcher. It was a great step gained. When in London she was her own mistress; but surrounded as she would be down in Herefordshire by Fletchers and Whartons, she must be stubborn indeed if she should still refuse to be taken back into the flock, and be made once more happy by marrying the man whom she confessed that she loved with her whole heart. The letter to Arthur Fletcher containing the news was from his brother John, and was written in a very business-like fashion. 'We have put off Mary's marriage for a few days, so that you and she should be down here together. If you mean to go on with it, now is your time.' Arthur, in answer to this, merely said he would spend the Whitsuntide holidays at Longbarns.

It is probable that Emily herself had some idea in her own mind of what was being done to entrap her. Her brother's words to her had been so strong, and the occasion of his marriage was itself so sacred to her, that she had not been able to refuse his request. But from the moment that she had made the promise, she felt that she had greatly added to her own difficulties. That she could yield to Arthur never occurred to her. She was certain of her own persistency. Whatever might be the wishes of others, the fitness of things required that Arthur Fletcher's wife should not have been the widow of Ferdinand Lopez,— and required also that the woman who had married Ferdinand Lopez should bear the results of her own folly. Though since his death she had never spoken a syllable against him,—if those passionate words be excepted which Arthur himself had drawn from her,—still she had not refrained from acknowledging the truth to herself. He had been a man disgraced,—and she as his wife, having become his wife in opposition to the wishes of all her friends, was disgraced also. Let them do what they will with her, she would not soil Arthur Fletcher's name with this infamy. Such was still her steadfast resolution; but she knew that it would be, not endangered, but increased in difficulty by this visit to Herefordshire.

And then there were other troubles. 'Papa,' she said, 'I must get a dress for Everett's marriage.'

'Why not?'

'I can't bear, after all that I have cost you, putting you to such useless expense.'

'It is not useless, and such expenses as that I can surely afford without groaning. Do it handsomely and you will please me best.'

Then she went forth and chose her dress,—a grey silk, light enough not to throw quite a gloom on the brightness of the day, and yet dark enough to declare that she was not as other women are. The very act of purchasing this, almost blushing at her own request as she sat at the counter in her widow's weeds, was a pain to her. But she had no one whom she could employ. On such an occasion she could not ask her aunt Harriet to act for her, as her aunt was distrusted and disliked. And then there was the fitting on of the dress,—very grievous to her, as it was the first time since the heavy black mourning came home that she had clothed herself in other garments.

The day before that fixed for the marriage she and her father went down to Herefordshire together, the conversation on the way being all in respect to Everett. Where was he to live? What was he to do? What income would he require till he should inherit the good things which destiny had in store for him? The old man seemed to feel that Providence, having been so very good to his son in killing that other heir, had put rather a heavy burden on himself. 'He'll want a house of his own, of course,' he said, in a somewhat lachrymose tone.

'I suppose he'll spend a good deal of his time at Wharton.'

'He won't be content to live in another man's house altogether, my dear; and Sir Alured can allow him nothing. It means, of course, that I must give him a thousand a year. It seems very natural to him, I dare say, but he might have asked the question before he took a wife to himself.'

'You won't be angry with him, papa!'

'It's no good being angry. No;—I'm not angry. Only it seems that everybody is uncommonly well pleased without thinking who has to pay for the piper.'

On that evening, at Wharton, Emily still wore her mourning dress. No one, indeed, dared to speak to her on the subject, and Mary was even afraid lest she might appear in black on the following day. We all know in what condition is a house on the eve of a marriage,—how the bride feels that all the world is going to be changed, and that therefore everything is for the moment disjointed; and how the rest of the household, including the servants, are led to share the feeling. Everett was of course away. He was over at Longbarns with the Fletchers, and was to be brought to Wharton Church on the following morning. Old Mrs Fletcher was at Wharton Hall,—and the bishop, whose services had been happily secured. He was formally introduced to Mrs Lopez, the use of the name for the occasion being absolutely necessary, and with all the smiling urbanity, which as a bishop he was bound to possess, he was hardly able not to be funereal as he looked at her and remembered her story. Before the evening was over Mrs Fletcher did venture to give a hint. 'We are so glad you have come, my dear.'

'I could not stay when Everett said he wished it.'

'It would have been wrong; yes, my dear,—wrong. It is your duty, and the duty of us all, to subordinate our feelings to those of others. Even sorrow may be selfish.' Poor Emily listened but could make no reply. 'It is sometimes harder for us to be mindful of others in our grief than in our joy. You should remember, dear, that there are some who will never be light-hearted again till they see you smile.'

'Do not say that, Mrs Fletcher.'

'It is quite true;—and right that you should think of it. It will be particularly necessary that you should think of it to-morrow. You will have to wear a light dress, and——'

'I have come provided,' said the widow.

'Try then to make your heart as light as your frock. You will be doing it for Everett's sake, and for your father's, and for Mary's sake——and Arthur's. You will be doing it for the sake of all of us on a day that should be joyous.' She could not make any promise in reply to this homily, but in her heart of hearts she acknowledged that it was true, and declared to herself that she would make the effort required of her.

On the following morning the house was of course in confusion. There was to be a breakfast after the service, and after the breakfast the bride was to be taken away in a carriage and four as far as Hereford on her route to Paris;—but before the great breakfast there was of course a subsidiary breakfast,—or how could a bishop, bride, or bridesmaids have sustained the ceremony? At this meal Emily did not appear, having begged for a cup of tea in her own room. The carriages to take the party to the church, which was but the other side of the park, were ordered at eleven, and at a quarter before eleven she appeared for the first time in her grey silk dress, and without a widow's cap. Everything was very plain, but the alteration was so great that it was impossible not to look at her. Even her father had not seen the change before. Not a word was said, though old Mrs Fletcher's thanks were implied by the graciousness of her smile. As there were four bridesmaids and four other ladies besides the bride herself, in a few minutes she became obscured by the brightness of the others;—and then they were all packed in their carriages and taken to the church. The eyes which she most dreaded did not meet hers till they were all standing round the altar. It was only then that she saw Arthur Fletcher, who was there as her brother's best man, and it was then that he took her hand and held it for half a minute as though he never meant to part with it, hidden behind the widespread glories of the bridesmaids' finery.

The marriage was as sweet and solemn as a kind-hearted bishop could make it, and all the ladies looked particularly well. The veil from London,—with the orange wreath, also metropolitan,—was perfect, and as for the dress, I doubt whether any woman would have known it to be provincial. Everett looked the rising baronet, every inch of him, and the old barrister smiled and seemed, at least, to be well pleased. Then came the breakfast, and the speech-making, in which Arthur Fletcher shone triumphantly. It was a very nice wedding, and Mary Wharton,—as she had been and still was,—felt herself for a moment to be a heroine. But, through it all, there was present to the hearts of most of them a feeling that much more was to be effected, if possible, than this simple and cosy marriage, and that the fate of Mary Wharton was hardly so important to them as that of Emily Lopez.

When the carriage and four was gone there came upon the household the difficulty usual on such occasions of getting through the rest of the day. The bridesmaids retired and repacked their splendours so that they might come out fresh for other second-rate needs, and with the bridesmaids went the widow. Arthur Fletcher remained at Wharton with all the other Fletchers for the night, and was prepared to renew his suit on that very day, if an opportunity were given him; but Emily did not again show herself till a few minutes before dinner, and then she came down with all the appurtenances of mourning which she usually wore. The grey silk had been put on for the marriage ceremony and for that only. 'You should have kept your dress at any rate for the day,' said Mrs Fletcher. She replied that she had changed it for Everett, and that as Everett was gone there was no further need for her to wear clothes unfitted to her position. Arthur would have cared very little for the clothes could he have had his way with the woman who wore them,—could he have had his way even so far as to have found himself alone with her for half an hour. But no such chance was his. She retreated from the party early, and did not show herself on the following morning till after he had started for Longbarns.

All the Fletchers went back,—not, however, with any intention on the part of Arthur to abandon his immediate attempt. The distance between the houses was not so great but that he could drive himself

over at any time. 'I shall go now,' he said to Mr Wharton, 'because I
have promised John to fish with him to-morrow, but I shall come over
on Monday or Tuesday, and stay till I go back to town. I hope she will
at any rate let me speak to her.' The father said he would do his best,
but that that obstinate resumption of her weeds on her brother's very
wedding day had nearly broken his heart.

When the Fletchers were back at Longbarns, the two ladies were
very severe on her. 'It was downright obstinacy,' said the squire's wife,
'and it almost makes me think that it would serve her right to leave her
as she is.'

'It's pride,' said the old lady. 'She won't give way. I said ever so
much to her,-but it's no use. I feel it the more because we have all gone
so much out of the way to be good to her after she made such a fool of
herself. If it goes on much longer, I shall never forgive her again.'

'You'll have to forgive her, mother,' said her eldest son, 'let her sins
be what they may,—or else you'll have to quarrel with Arthur.'

'I do think it's very hard,' said the old lady, taking herself out of the
room. And it was hard. The offence in the first instance had been very
great and the forgiveness very difficult. But Mrs Fletcher had lived
long enough to know that when sons are thoroughly respectable a widowed mother has to do their bidding.

Emily, through the whole wedding day, and the next day, and day
after day, remembered Mrs Fletcher's words. 'There are some who
will never be light-hearted again till they see you smile.' And the old
woman had named her dearest friends and had ended by naming
Arthur Fletcher. She had then acknowledged to herself that it was her
duty to smile in order that others might smile also. But how is one to
smile with a heavy heart? Should one smile and lie? And how long and
to what good purpose can such forced contentment last? She had
marred her whole life. In former days she had been proud of all her
virgin glories,—proud of her intellect, proud of her beauty, proud of
that obeisance which beauty, birth, and intellect combined, exact from
all comers. She had been ambitious as to her future life;—had intended
to be careful not to surrender herself to some empty fool;—had thought
herself well qualified to pick her own steps. And this had come of it!
They told her that she might still make everything right, annul the past
and begin the world again as fresh as ever,—if she would only smile
and study to forget! Do it for the sake of others, they said, and then it
will be done for yourself also. But she could not conquer the past. The
fire and water of repentance, adequate as they may be for eternity, cannot burn out or wash away the remorse of this life. They scorch and

choke;—and unless it be so there is no repentance. So she told herself,—and yet it was her duty to be light-hearted that others around her might not be made miserable by her sorrow! If she could be in truth light-hearted, then would she know herself to be unfeeling and worthless.

On the third day after the marriage Arthur Fletcher came back to Wharton with the declared intention of remaining there till the end of the holidays. She could make no objection to such an arrangement, nor could she hasten her own return to London. That had been fixed before her departure, and was to be made together with her father. She felt that she was being attacked with unfair weapons, and that undue advantage was taken of the sacrifice which she had made for her brother's sake. And yet,—yet how good to her they all were! How wonderful was it that after the thing she had done, after the disgrace she had brought on herself and them, after the destruction of all that pride which had once been hers, they should still wish to have her among them! As for him,—of whom she was always thinking,—of what nature must be his love, when he was willing to take to himself as his wife such a thing as she had made herself! But, thinking of this, she would only tell herself that as he would not protect himself she was bound to be his protector. Yes;—she would protect him, though she could dream of a world of joy that might be hers if she could do as he would ask her.

He caught her at last and forced her to come out with him into the grounds. He could tell his tale better as he walked by her side than sitting restlessly on a chair or moving awkwardly about the room as on such an occasion he would be sure to do. Within four walls she would have some advantage over him. She could sit still and be dignified in her stillness. But in the open air, when they would both be on their legs, she might not be so powerful with him and he perhaps might be stronger with her. She could not refuse him when he asked her to walk with him. And why should she refuse him? Of course he must be allowed to utter his prayer,—and then she must be allowed to make her answer. 'I think the marriage went off very well,' he said.

'Very well. Everett ought to be a happy man.'

'No doubt he will be,—when he settles down to something. Everything will come right for him. With some people things seem to go smooth; don't they? They have not hitherto gone smoothly with you and me, Emily.'

'You are prosperous. You have everything before you that a man can wish, if only you will allow yourself to think so. Your profession is successful, and you are in Parliament, and everyone likes you.'

'It is all nothing.'

'That is the general discontent of the world.'

'It is all nothing,—unless I have you too. Remember that I had said so long before I was successful, when I did not dream of Parliament; before we had heard of the name of the man who came between me and my happiness. I think I am entitled to be believed when I say so. I think I know my own mind. There are many men who would have been changed by the episode of such a marriage.'

'You ought to have been changed by it,—and by its result.'

'It had no such effect. Here I am, after it all, telling you as I used to tell you before, that I have to look to you for my happiness.'

'You should be ashamed to confess it, Arthur.'

'Never;—not to you, nor to all the world. I know what it has been. I know you are not now as you were then. You have been his wife, and are now his widow.'

'That should be enough.'

'But, such as you are, my happiness is in your hands. If it were not so, do you think that all my family as well as yours would join in wishing that you may become my wife? There is nothing to conceal. When you married that man you know what my mother thought of it; and what John thought of it, and his wife. They had wanted you to be my wife; and they want it now,—because they are anxious for my happiness. And your father wishes it, and your brother wishes it,—because they trust me, and I think that I should be a good husband to you.'

'Good!' she exclaimed, hardly knowing what she meant by repeating the word.

'After that you have no right to set yourself up to judge what may be best for my happiness. They who know how to judge are all united. Whatever you may have been, they believe that it will be good for me that you should now be my wife. After that you must talk about me no longer, unless you will talk of my wishes.'

'Do you think that I am not anxious for your happiness?'

'I do not know;—but I shall find out in time. That is what I have to say about myself. And as to you, is it not much the same? I know you love me. Whatever the feeling was that overcame you as to that other man,—it has gone. I cannot now stop to be tender and soft in my words. The thing to be said is too serious to me. And every friend you have wants you to marry the man you love, and to put an end to the desolation which you have brought on yourself. There is not one among us all, Fletchers and Whartons, whose comfort does not more or less depend on your sacrificing the luxury of your own woe.'

'Luxury!'

'Yes; luxury. No man ever had a right to say more positively to a woman that it was her duty to marry him, than I have to you. And I do say it. I say it on behalf of all of us, that it is your duty. I won't talk of my own love now, because you know it. You cannot doubt it. I won't even talk of yours, because I am sure of it. But I say that it is your duty to give up drowning us all in tears, burying us in desolation. You are one of us, and should do as all of us wish you. If, indeed, you could not love me it would be different. There! I have said what I've got to say. You are crying, and I will not take your answer now. I will come to you again to-morrow, and then you shall answer me. But, remember when you do so that the happiness of many people depends on what you say.' Then he left her very suddenly and hurried back to the house by himself.

He had been very rough with her,—had not once attempted to touch her hand or even her arm, had spoken no soft word to her, speaking of his own love as a thing too certain to need further words; and he had declared himself to be so assured of her love that there was no favour for him now to ask, nothing for which he was bound to pray as a lover. All that was past. He had simply declared it to be her duty to marry him, and had told her so with much sternness. He had walked fast, compelling her to accompany him, had frowned at her, and had more than once stamped his foot upon the ground. During the whole interview she had been so near to weeping that she could hardly speak. Once or twice she had almost thought him to be cruel;—but he had forced her to acknowledge to herself that all that he had said was true and unanswerable. Had he pressed her for an answer at the moment she would not have known in what words to couch a refusal. And yet as she made her way alone back to the house she assured herself that she would have refused.

He had given her four-and-twenty hours, and at the end of that time she would be bound to give him her answer,—an answer which must then be final. And as she said this to herself she found that she was admitting a doubt. She hardly knew how not to doubt, knowing, as she did, that all whom she loved were on one side, while on the other was nothing but the stubbornness of her own convictions. But still the conviction was left to her. Over and over again she declared to herself that it was not fit, meaning thereby to assure herself that a higher duty even than that which she owed to her friends, demanded from her that she should be true to her convictions. She met him that day at dinner, but he hardly spoke to her. They sat together in the same room during the evening, but she hardly once heard his voice. It seemed to her that he avoided even looking at her. When they separated for the night he parted from her almost as though they had been strangers. Surely he was angry with her because she was stubborn,—thought evil of her because she would not do as others wished her! She lay awake during the long night thinking of it all. If it might be so! Oh;—if it might be so! If it might be done without utter ruin to her own self-respect as a woman!

In the morning she was down early,—not having anything to say, with no clear purpose as yet before her,—but still with a feeling that perhaps that morning might alter all things for her. He was the latest of the party, not coming in for prayers as did all the others, but taking his seat when the others had half finished their breakfast. As he sat down he gave a general half-uttered greeting to them all, but spoke no special word to any of them. It chanced that his seat was next to hers, but to her he did not address himself at all. Then the meal was over, and the chairs were withdrawn, and the party grouped itself about with vague, uncertain movements, as men and women do before they leave the breakfast table for the work of the day. She meditated her escape, but felt that she could not leave the room before Lady Wharton or Mrs Fletcher,—who had remained at Wharton to keep her mother company for a while. At last they went;—but then, just as she was escaping, he put his hand upon her and reminded her of her appointment. 'I shall be in the hall in a quarter of an hour,' he said. 'Will you meet me there?' Then she bowed her head to him and passed on.

She was there at the time named and found him standing by the hall door, waiting for her. His hat was already on his head and his back was almost turned to her. He opened the door, and, allowing her to pass out first, led the way to the shrubbery. He did not speak to her till he had closed behind her the little iron gate which separated the walk from the garden, and then he turned upon her with one word. 'Well?' he said. She was silent for a moment and then he repeated his eager question: 'Well;—well?'

'I should disgrace you,' she said, not firmly as before, but whispering the words.

He waited for no other assent. The form of the words told him that he had won the day. In a moment his arms were round her, and her veil was off, and his lips were pressed to hers;—and when she could see his countenance the whole form of his face was altered to her. It was bright as it used to be bright in the old days, and he was smiling on her as he used to smile. 'My own,' he said;—'my wife—my own!' And she had no longer the power to deny him. 'Not yet, Arthur; not yet,' was all that she could say.

CHAPTER 80

THE LAST MEETING AT MATCHING

THE ex-Prime Minister did not carry out his purpose of leaving London in the middle of the season and travelling either to Italy or Norway. He was away from London at Whitsuntide longer perhaps than he might have been if still in office, and during this period regarded himself as a man from whose hands all work had been taken,—as one who had been found unfit to carry any longer a burden serviceably; but before June was over he and the Duchess were back in London, and gradually he allowed himself to open his mouth on this or that subject in the House of Lords,—not pitching into everybody all round, as his wife had recommended, but expressing an opinion now and again, generally in support of his friends, with the dignity which should belong to a retired Prime Minister. The Duchess too recovered much of her good temper,—as far at least as the outward show went. One or two who knew her, especially Mrs Finn, were aware that her hatred and her ideas of revenge were not laid aside; but she went on from day to day anathematizing her special enemies and abstained from reproaching her husband for his pusillanimity. Then came the question as to the autumn. 'Let's have everybody down at Gatherum, just as we had before,' said the Duchess.

The proposition almost took away the Duke's breath. 'Why do you want a crowd, like that?'

'Just to show them that we are not beaten because we are turned out.'

'But, inasmuch as we were turned out, we were beaten. And what has a gathering of people at my private house to do with a political manoeuvre? Do you especially want to go to Gatherum?'

'I hate the place. You know I do.'

'Then why should you propose to go there?' He hardly yet knew his wife well enough to understand that the suggestion had been a joke. 'If you don't wish to go abroad——'

'I hate going abroad.'

'Then we'll remain at Matching. You don't hate Matching.'

'Ah dear! There are memories there too. But you like it.'

'My books are there.'

'Blue books,' said the Duchess.

'And there is plenty of room if you wish to have friends.'

'I suppose we must have somebody. You can't live without your Mentor.'

'You can ask whom you please,' he said almost fretfully.

'Lady Rosina, of course,' suggested the Duchess. Then he turned to the papers before him and wouldn't say another word. The matter ended in a party much as usual being collected at Matching about the middle of October,—Telemachus having spent the early part of the autumn with Mentor at Long Royston. There might perhaps be a dozen guests in the house, and among them of course were Phineas Finn and his wife. And Mr Grey was there, having come back from his eastern mission,—whose unfortunate abandonment of his seat at Silverbridge had caused so many troubles,—and Mrs Grey, who in days now long passed* had been almost as necessary to Lady Glencora, as was now her later friend Mrs Finn,—and the Cantrips, and for a short time the St Bungays. But Lady Rosina De Courcy on this occasion was not present. There were few there whom my patient readers have not seen at Matching before; but among those few was Arthur Fletcher.

'So it is to be,' said the Duchess to the member for Silverbridge one morning. She had by this time become intimate with 'her member,' as she would sometimes call him in joke, and had concerned herself much as to his matrimonial prospects.

'Yes, Duchess, it is to be,—unless some unforeseen circumstance should arise.'

'What circumstance?'

'Ladies and gentlemen sometimes do change their minds;—but in this case I do not think it likely.'

'And why ain't you being married now, Mr Fletcher?'

'We have agreed to postpone it till next year;—so that we may be quite sure of our own minds.'

'I know you are laughing at me; but nevertheless I am very glad that it is settled. Pray tell her from me that I shall call again as soon as ever she is Mrs Fletcher, though I don't think she repaid either of the last two visits I made her.'

'You must make excuses for her, Duchess.'

'Of course. I know. After all she is a most fortunate woman. And as for you,—I regard you as a hero among lovers.'

'I'm getting used to it,' she said one day to Mrs Finn.

'Of course you'll get used to it. We get used to anything that chance sends us in a marvellously short time.'

'What I mean is that I can go to bed, and sleep, and get up and eat my meals without missing the sound of the trumpets so much as I did at first. I remember hearing of people who lived in a mill, and couldn't sleep when the mill stopped. It was like that with me when our mill stopped at first. I had got myself so used to the excitement of it, that I could hardly live without it.'

'You might have all the excitement still, if you pleased. You need not be dead to politics because your husband is not Prime Minister.'

'No; never again,—unless he should come back. If any one had told me ten years ago that I should have taken an interest in this or that man being in the Government, I should have laughed him to scorn. It did not seem possible to me then that I should care what became of such men as Sir Timothy Beeswax and Mr Roby. But I did get to be anxious about it when Plantagenet was shifted from one office to another.'

'Of course you did. Do you think I am not anxious about Phineas?'

'But when he became Prime Minister, I gave myself up to it altogether. I shall never forget what I felt when he came to me and told me that perhaps it might be so;—but told me also that he would escape from it if it were possible. I was the Lady Macbeth of the occasion all over;—whereas he was so scrupulous, so burdened with conscience! As for me I would have taken it by any means. Then it was that the old Duke played the part of the three witches to a nicety. Well, there hasn't been any absolute murder, and I haven't quite gone mad.'

'Nor need you be afraid, though all the woods of Gatherum should come to Matching.'*

'God forbid! I will never see anything of Gatherum again. What annoys me most is, and always was, that he wouldn't understand what I felt about it;—how proud I was that he should be Prime Minister, how anxious that he should be great and noble in his office;—how I worked for him, and not at all for any pleasure of my own.'

'I think he did feel it.'

'No;—not as I did. At last he liked the power,—or rather feared the disgrace of losing it. But he had no idea of the personal grandeur of the place. He never understood that to be Prime Minister in England is as much as to be an Emperor in France, and much more than being President in America. Oh, how I did labour for him,—and how he did scold me for it with those quiet little stinging words of his! I was vulgar!'

'Is that a quiet word?'

'Yes;—as he used it;—and indiscreet, and ignorant, and stupid. I bore it all, though sometimes I was dying with vexation. Now it's all over, and here we are as humdrum as any one else. And the Beeswaxes, and the Robys, and the Droughts, and the Pountneys, and the Lopezes, have all passed over the scene! Do you remember that Pountney affair, and how he turned the poor man out of the house?'

'It served him right.'

'It would have served them all right to be turned out,—only they were there for a purpose. I did like it in a way, and it makes me sad to think that the feeling can never come again. Even if they should have him back again, it would be a very lame affair to me then. I can never again rouse myself to the effort of preparing food and lodging for half the Parliament and their wives. I shall never again think that I can help to rule England by coaxing unpleasant men. It is done and gone, and can never come back again.'

Not long after this the Duke took Mr Monk, who had come down to Matching for a few days, out to the very spot on which he had sat when he indulged himself in lecturing Phineas Finn on Conservatism and Liberalism generally, and then asked the Chancellor of the Exchequer what he thought of the present state of public affairs. He himself had supported Mr Gresham's government, and did not belong to it because he could not at present reconcile himself to filling any office. Mr Monk did not scruple to say that in his opinion the present legitimate division of parties was preferable to the Coalition which had existed for three years. 'In such an arrangement,' said Mr Monk, 'there must always be a certain amount of distrust and such a feeling is fatal to any great work.'

'I think I distrusted no one till separation came,—and when it did come it was not caused by me.'

'I am not blaming any one now,' said the other; 'but men who have been brought up with opinions altogether different, even with different instincts as to politics, who from their mother's milk have been nourished on codes of thought altogether opposed to each other, cannot work together with confidence even though they may desire the same thing. The very ideas which are sweet as honey to the one are bitter as gall to the other.'

'You think, then, that we made a great mistake?'

'I will not say that,' said Mr Monk. 'There was a difficulty at the time, and that difficulty was overcome. The Government was carried on, and was on the whole respected. History will give you credit for patriotism, patience, and courage. No man could have done it better than you did;—probably no other man of the day so well.'

'But it was not a great part to play?' The Duke in his nervousness, as he said this, could not avoid the use of that questioning tone which requires an answer.

'Great enough to satisfy the heart of a man who has fortified himself against the evil side of ambition. After all, what is it that the Prime Minister of such a country as this should chiefly regard? Is it not the prosperity of the country? It is not often that we want great measures, or new arrangements that shall be vital to the country. Politicians now look for grievances, not because the grievances are heavy, but trusting that the honour of abolishing them may be great. It is the old story of the needy knife-grinder* who, if left to himself, would have no grievance of which to complain.'

'But there are grievances,' said the Duke. 'Look at monetary denominations. Look at our weights and measures.'

'Well; yes. I will not say that everything has as yet been reduced to divine order. But when we took office three years ago we certainly did not intend to settle those difficulties.'

'No, indeed,' said the Duke, sadly.

'But we did do all that we meant to do. For my own part, there is only one thing in it that I regret, and one only which you should regret also till you have resolved to remedy it.'

'What thing is that?'

'Your own retirement from official life. If the country is to lose your services for the long course of years during which you will probably sit in Parliament, then I shall think that the country has lost more than it has gained by the Coalition.'

The Duke sat for a while silent, looking at the view, and, before answering Mr Monk,—while arranging his answer,—once or twice in a half-absent way, called his companion's attention to the scene before him. But, during this time he was going through an act of painful repentance. He was condemning himself for a word or two that had been ill-spoken by himself, and which, since the moment of its utterance, he had never ceased to remember with shame. He told himself now, after his own secret fashion, that he must do penance for these words by the humiliation of a direct contradiction of them. He must declare that Cæsar would at some future time be prepared to serve under Pompey. Then he made his answer. 'Mr Monk,' he said, 'I should be false if I were to deny that it pleases me to hear you say so. I have thought much of all that for the last two or three months. You may probably have seen that I am not a man endowed with that fortitude which enables many to bear vexations with an easy spirit. I am given to fretting, and I am inclined to think that a popular minister in a free country should be so constituted as to be free from that infirmity. I shall certainly never desire to be at the head of a Government again. For a few years I would prefer to remain out of office. But I will endeavour to look forward to a time when I may again perhaps be of some humble use.'

APPENDIX

THE CHRONOLOGY AND POLITICAL CONTEXTS
OF THE PALLISER NOVELS

(i) The internal chronology of the series

TROLLOPE'S Palliser series is rightly seen as one of the greatest English examples of the *roman fleuve*, or group of novels written as an extended narrative sequence. But Trollope did not conceive or plan these books as a sequence. Rather, they became a series gradually, one following another as opportunity and inspiration suggested.

Nor were they written and published consecutively. Trollope published six novels with other topics between *Can You Forgive Her?* (1864–5) and *Phineas Finn, the Irish Member* (1867–9), and five between that and *The Eustace Diamonds* (1871–3). Though this was immediately followed by *Phineas Redux* (1873–4), he produced three novels of other kinds between that book and *The Prime Minister* (1875–6), and two more before starting work on the last novel in the series, *The Duke's Children*, in 1876. In retrospect, he clearly came to think of them as linked. He referred in his *Autobiography* to 'a series of semi-political tales' (not including *Can You Forgive Her?*), and, in a letter written to Henry Howard in 1881, to a 'series of novels' (not including *The Eustace Diamonds*) about 'the family of the Pallisers'. But the books were never published as a named sequence in his lifetime.

As a consequence, though each individual novel is chronologically coherent, the time scheme of the sequence as a whole is a muddle. Trollope introduced Plantagenet Palliser, as a minor character of 'about five-and-twenty years of age', in the 'Barsetshire' novel, *The Small House at Allington* (1862–4). The action here takes place over a period of two years explicitly identified as being in the 1860s ('186—'). Palliser meets and becomes engaged to Lady Glencora in the summer of the second year. Since Trollope began writing the book in 1862, and uses the past tense, it would be reasonable to assume that the years in question were 1860 and 1861.

This sense of immediate, or very recent, contemporaneity would have pleased readers who liked their novels to be modern in setting. The starting date does not, however, allow time for the rest of Palliser's career. By Chapter 72 of *The Prime Minister*, he is 46. Twenty-one years seems a reasonable period in which a man might marry, have four children (the eldest now in his mid- or late teens), serve in Parliament in opposition (twice) and government (three times), rise to Cabinet rank, and spend three years as prime minister. Unfortunately, twenty-one years from 1861 takes us to 1882: eight years after the composition of the novel, and six years after publication. Uneasily aware of this difficulty, Trollope covered his tracks with some contradictory information. In Chapter 62 of *The Prime Minister*, supposedly a year before Palliser's forty-sixth birthday, we are told that Lady Glencora has known him for 'fifteen years'. Since she first met him in *The Small House at Allington* in 1861, this takes us to 1876, makes him 40, and reduces the extent to which the action has been allowed to slip into the future. But it makes his crowded political career improbably rapid and allows too few years for the time schemes of the intervening novels.

In Chapter 20 of *Phineas Redux* we are, for once, given an entirely explicit date, when the unhappy Laura Kennedy heads her letter from Dresden, 'Feb. 8, 1870'. On this basis, there have been nine years since the Palliser engagement of 1861, during which time the events of *Can You Forgive Her?* (three years), *Phineas Finn* (five years), *The Eustace Diamonds* (four years), and the first year of the plot of *Phineas Redux* itself are all supposed to have taken place. There may be an overlap between *Phineas Finn* and *The Eustace Diamonds*. But, on the other hand, there have also been intervals between the novels, in which the Tory administrations of, first, De Terrier and Daubeny and, then, Daubeny by himself are supposed to have taken place. Allowing a mere year for each of these governments would cancel out some of the overlap and give us eleven or twelve years of sequential action in a nine-year time span.

The internal chronology of each individual novel is, by contrast, clear enough. The story told in *Can You Forgive Her?*, for example, occupies three years, from the June of the first year to the April of the last, and these periods can sometimes be linked to an external time scheme by references to contemporary phenomena. Thus, in the first year of *Can You Forgive Her?*, Lady Glencora appears to have been reading Lucy Atkinson's *Recollections of the Tartar Steppes* (1863). But Trollope is not consistent about such details. Though Lucy Atkinson's book was in print while Trollope was writing his novel, it would not have been available to his characters two or three years before.

The use of the perpetual calendar to assign dates such as 'Monday, June 5' to a particular year is also untrustworthy. There are five of these in *The Eustace Diamonds* and four of them confirm the years in which the action seems principally to be set: 1865 and 1866. The fifth does not: 'Wednesday, the 5th of November' (Chapter 37), though supposed to occur in 1865, occurred in 1862. In *Phineas Redux*, in the year for which he gives us the explicit date of 1870 (Chapter 20), Trollope also supplies a 'Wednesday, 19th May' (Chapter 54) which belongs to 1869. Even if one overlooks such local slips, the time scheme of the series as a whole remains elusive.

The problem is that Trollope's realism does not allow for the convenient vagueness employed by (for example) Dickens. His account of the manners, morals, and preoccupations of English society is precise in ways which involve the identification of decades ('186—'), and occasionally even a particular year. A better parallel than Dickens might be the famous 'double time scheme' of Shakespeare's play *Othello*. Here, two different clocks seem to be running simultaneously. According to one, the principal action of the play takes place in less than forty-eight hours. According to the other, it involves months of life in Cyprus, without which there would have been no opportunity for the alleged affair between Desdemona and Cassio. Audiences unconsciously accept both time schemes, enjoying the tragic intensity of the rapid action while also requiring the verisimilitude of the slow one.

Trollope, similarly, has two clocks running in the Palliser series, one of which takes us through the 1860s and 1870s in twenty years, the other of which requires at least twenty-three years to cover the same ground. More precisely, he turns the clock back at the beginning of *Phineas Finn* to give himself (in one time scheme at least) the extra years which he now knows he needs, but had neglected to provide in *The Small House at Allington*. There, and in *Can You Forgive Her?*, the Prime Minister is a Whig, Lord Brock, who resembles Palmerston. But at the beginning of *Phineas Finn* there is a Tory administration, led by De Terrier and Daubeny. This sounds like the Conservative government of 1858–9, led by Derby and Disraeli. As such, it gives the impression that the action of *The Small House at Allington* and *Can You Forgive Her?* had somehow taken place, not during Palmerston's second premiership (1859–65), but during the first one (1855–8), thus providing the extra years required for what Trollope, at this stage, was beginning to think of as a Palliser series.

With the stated starting date of 1861 for Palliser's story, a three-year plot in *Can You Forgive Her?*, and a year for the Tory government of De Terrier and Daubeny, the action of *Phineas Finn* would be set in the five years 1866–71. This is too late, both for the period of composition (1866–7), and for the Reform Bill debates with which it is concerned. With a new, implicit starting date for the series in the late 1850s, *Phineas Finn* can take place between 1863 and 1867. We thereby get, more or less correctly, to that date of 'Feb. 8, 1870' in the second year of the plot of *Phineas Redux*, and from there can trace our way without much trouble to the mid- and late 1870s for *The Prime Minister* and *The Duke's Children*. The past tense of that final novel was not, strictly speaking, appropriate during the process of composition (May to October 1876). It had, however, become so by the time of its delayed publication in 1879–80.

This remains a double time scheme, rather than the substitution of one time scheme for another. The new dating is present only by implication, and Trollope did not change the chronological references in later editions of his earlier novels. He did not, of course, expect his original readers to go back and check them either. If the impression can be given that the Palliser narrative has somehow resumed, at the beginning of *Phineas Finn*, in 1863 rather than 1866, then so much the better. The contradictory accounts, in *The Prime Minister*, of the time that has passed since Palliser first met Glencora could, in this sense, be taken as a graceful acknowledgement of a sleight of hand.

Critics who believe that Trollope was a slipshod writer will see this duplicity as a confirmation of their views. Most readers will find it a satisfactory rectification of a mistake made before he had decided to turn Palliser's story into a *roman fleuve*. But, however ingeniously he handles it, the double time scheme does present problems for a comparison between the political narrative of the Palliser series and the real political history of the age. Which year, after all, is one comparing with which? The best answer may be to accept the implicit rewinding of the clock at the beginning of *Phineas Finn* and to assume that the action of the series runs from 1859 (in *Can You Forgive Her?*) to 1879 (in *The Duke's Children*). The resulting chronology is not flawless. There is only just enough time for Phineas Finn's first marriage and spell in Ireland as a Poor Law inspector, and Palliser is still a few years short of 46 at the end of *The Prime Minister*. But the actions of the successive stories can, on this basis, occur sequentially, and can do so while providing the necessary gaps for four periods of Tory government. Trollope was a realistic novelist, not a historian, and what he offers is broadly correct rather than minutely precise. When, in Chapter 45 of *Phineas Redux*, he remarks that the events of *The Eustace Diamonds* took place 'but a year or two since', he is indicating the degree of exactitude which we can, at the margins, reasonably expect.

(ii) The external chronology of the Palliser series

These assumptions suggest the chronology overleaf. Broad parallels here between fictitious and real events, especially in the middle of the series, have led some critics to stress the topicality of the Palliser novels. When Phineas becomes Under-Secretary for the Colonies, for example, in the third year of *Phineas Finn* (1865, in this time scheme), he works on Canadian issues. This is just what his real equivalent would have been doing in the mid-1860s. The American Civil War and the British North America Act made Canada the main foreign policy issue of the period. More substantially, the Second Reform Bill would be both the central concern of British political life in 1866–7 and the key political topic of *Phineas Finn*. Though the internal chronology of the series requires the fictitious Reform Bill debates to be set back slightly into the years 1864–5, Trollope was writing this novel as the real political events unfolded, and presenting a version of them in his story.

At times Trollope is so anxious to locate his fictions in a realistic contemporary setting that he contradicts his own previous novels. Thus, in Chapter 5 of *Phineas Redux*, we are told that the Second Reform Bill has been passed by a Tory government (as, in reality, it was), despite the fact that in *Phineas Finn* it had just been carried by the Whigs. Trollope masks this discrepancy by stressing the 'household suffrage' quality of the Tory Reform Bill, making it possible for readers to believe that the Tory measure had somehow augmented a Whig Bill, rather than defeating and replacing it. Here the wish for topicality and verisimilitude takes precedence over the need for consistency between one novel and another. The incidental detail, too, is often current or very recent. Noting that *Phineas Finn* 'is casually sown with topical references to events of 1865–7', John Sutherland argues that the context is

Year	Internal time-scheme 1	Internal time-scheme 2	
1846–52			
1852			
1852–5			
1855			
1856			
1857		*The Small House at Allington*	
1858			
1859		*Can You Forgive Her?*	
1860	*The Small House at Allington*		
1861			
1862	*Can You Forgive Her?*		
1863		*Phineas Finn (1863–7)*	*The Eustace Diamonds (1863–6)*
1864			
1865			
1866			
1867			
1868			
1869		*Phineas Redux*	
1870			
1871			
1872			
1873		*The Prime Minister*	
1874			
1875			
1876			
1877			
1878		*The Duke's Children*	
1879			

Fictional political events	Real political events	Year
	Whig government (Russell)	1846–52
	Tory government (Derby)	1852
	Aberdeen coalition	1852–5
Whig government (Brock)	Whig government (Palmerston)	1855
		1856
		1857
	Tory government (Derby & Disraeli)	1858
		1859
	Whig/Liberal government (Palmerston then Russell)	1860
1861: Palliser: Chancellor of the Exchequer		1861
Tory government (De Terrier & Daubeny)		1862
Whig/Liberal government (Mildmay then Gresham) Palliser: Chancellor of the Exchequer		1863
1864: First attempt at Whig Reform Bill fails		1864
1865 (Aug.) Second attempt at Whig Reform Bill amended but passed		1865
	Whig Reform Bill fails	1866
	Tory government (Derby & Disraeli) 1867: Tory Reform Bill passed	1867
Tory government (Daubeny)		1868
	Liberal government (Gladstone) Church of Ireland disestablished	1869
1870: Tory bill to disestablish Church of England fails. 1870: Palliser becomes Duke of Omnium.		1870
Liberal government (Gresham) Omnium: Lord Privy Seal, then President of the Board of Trade		1871
Tory government (Daubeny)	1872: Secret ballot introduced	1872
Coalition (Omnium) Omnium: Prime Minister		1873
		1874
	Tory government (Disraeli)	1875
Liberal government (Gresham)		1876
Tory government (Drummond & Beeswax)		1877
		1878
Liberal government (Monk) Omnium: Lord President of the Council		1879

'recognizably contemporary', and that, 'there is no more misleading remark about the novel than Lord David Cecil's . . . that "if we were wafted suddenly back to 1840, we should find . . . the world of *Phineas Finn*" '.

'1840' is an overstatement. But there remains some truth in A. O. J. Cockshut's less extreme claim that, in the political novels, 'Trollope the recorder of tradition looks back'. Despite the topical allusions to political events of the 1860s and 1870s, in other words, the underlying political culture of the Palliser novels belongs to the 1850s. The most obvious symptom of this is instability. In Trollope's fictional world there are no fewer than ten governments between 1859 and 1879 (Whig, Tory, Whig/Liberal, Tory, Liberal, Tory, Coalition, Liberal, Tory, and then Liberal again). In reality there were four. Rather than reflecting the new politics of the 1860s and 1870s, Trollope is remembering a previous decade in which there had been five governments between 1852 and 1859.

The political instability of the 1850s had several causes. One was the fact that party discipline had not yet taken its familiar, modern form. Another was the Tory split over the repeal of the Corn Laws in 1846. Anxious to bring food into the country at the time of the Irish Famine, Peel had led the party of Church, Crown, and Land into an abolition of agricultural protection. The Tories divided into Peelites and Protectionists. As a result, the Whigs became the natural party of government, though only because they could find support from other parliamentary groups (Peelites, Radicals, and Irish members) in ways in which the Protectionist Tories could not.

This meant that politics in the 1850s was an unstable process of temporary agreements and awkward alliances. At its most extreme, it led to the creation of the only true coalition ministry between 1783 and 1895: Lord Aberdeen's Peelite and Whig government of 1852–5. The coalition led by the Duke of Omnium in *The Prime Minister* (in the fictional years 1873–5) is, of course, a version of this episode from the politics of the early 1850s, not an image of events twenty years later. When the Aberdeen coalition fell, there was a brief Whig ministry, followed by an even briefer Tory one. Tired of such uncertainty, Whigs, Peelites, and Radicals met in Willis's Rooms in June 1859 to create what would come to be known as the Liberal Party. Thereafter British politics settled back into a more or less stable, two-party system.

With hindsight not available to Trollope, it is easy now to see the ways in which political culture changed in the 1860s. Parliamentary parties were evolving into national parties, with proper membership organizations. Governments ceased to be hybrid. Party leaders who had previously needed merely to command the confidence of a majority in the House, became figures who required a wide, popular appeal, and sought it on the stump and in the press. This would be the age of Gladstone and Disraeli, star performers who led alternating but relatively long-lasting administrations. Trollope, whose view of politics had been formed in the 1850s, was slow to recognize these developments. In *The Duke's Children* he remarks, correctly, that 'There had of late been a great Conservative reaction in the country'

(Chapter 21). But, in the novel, the resulting Tory government lasts scarcely twelve months. In reality, the Tory administration formed in 1874 would stay in power for more than six years.

Trollope's politicians are also of the old school. Daubeny is not a bad portrait of Disraeli. But Disraeli had been his inimitable self since the 1840s, and Gresham performs aspects of Gladstone's parliamentary role without ever being intended to resemble him as a person. Gladstone started as a Tory, became a Peelite, allied himself with the Whigs, and ended up as a rather radical Liberal. Gresham is simply a Whig, out of the same drawer as the men who led that party in the 1840s and 1850s: Russell and Palmerston. The most conspicuous example of Trollope's 'looking back' is the Duke of St Bungay. Important throughout the Palliser series, he is a fixture in successive Whig cabinets and an indispensable source of shrewd political advice. By common consent he is based on the third Marquis of Lansdowne who died in February 1863, six months before Trollope began to write *Can You Forgive Her?*. Inspired, probably, by a reading of Lansdowne's obituaries, Trollope took a figure from the first half of the century and transferred him, without apology or alteration, into the second.

The political terminology of the Palliser series also belongs more naturally to the 1850s than to the decades in which the novels are set. This is not to say that the vocabulary of politics was suddenly clarified after 1860, or that discussion did not continue about the precise meaning of 'Whig', 'Liberal', 'Tory', 'Conservative', and 'Radical'. As late as 1874 there was a concerted attempt to revive the word 'Whig'. But, in practice, there had been a gradual simplification of the language of politics. By the 1870s there were Liberals and Conservatives, and what those two parties stood for was relatively clear. Tory Protectionists and Ultra Tories had been absorbed into a Disraelian Conservative Party. Whigs, Peelites, and most Radicals had become Gladstonian Liberals.

Back in the 1850s party identity had been more complex, and Trollope's novels reflect that uncertainty. Phineas Finn, without changing his stance, can be referred to by different people as a Whig, a Liberal, and a Radical in the space of a few pages. Trollope can mock the Tories, in Chapter 4 of *The Eustace Diamonds*, and then concede that his target is not mainstream Conservatism but 'ultra-Toryism'. In *The Prime Minister*, Du Boung stands as 'a Conservative' in the Silverbridge election but is 'in possession of four-fifths of the Liberal interests of the borough' and, in that capacity, loses (by 7 votes) to another Conservative. The Duke of St Bungay, in *Can You Forgive Her?*, can observe that he has 'voted for every Liberal measure that has come seriously before Parliament', but 'not been able to get beyond Whiggery yet', while declaring that 'there is nothing' he wants 'so much as to become a Radical'.

If this was confusing at the time, it is even more confusing for modern readers. So it is perhaps worthwhile to try, briefly, to give some meaning to these terms. The Tories, tainted with Jacobitism in the first half of the eighteenth century, returned to respectability at the end of it as the party of monarchy, rather than a particular dynasty of monarchs. In this capacity, they ran the war against the French Revolutionary regicides, an experience which reinforced their belief in tradition, rather than innovation, in constitutional matters. After the Whig First Reform Act of 1832, 'Ultra Tories' argued for repeal of the Act and a return to what Trollope called 'tests and qualifications, rotten boroughs and the divine right of kings' (*The Prime Minister*, Chapter 34). But Sir Robert Peel's *Tamworth Manifesto* in 1835 reinvented Conservativism (as it began to call itself in the 1830s) by accepting the enlarged franchise and committing the party to 'the firm maintenance of established rights, the correction of proved abuses and the redress of real grievances'. The split over the repeal of the Corn Laws in 1846 then broke the party into 'Protectionists' and 'Peelites' and condemned it to opposition, or brief spells of minority government, until 1874. Though the Tories dropped their commitment to agricultural protection, they remained the party of Church, Crown, and the landed interest, seeing the Crown, in an ideal conception, as the protector of the people from the oppressive power of the aristocracy.

The Whigs, by contrast, saw the aristocracy as the protector of the people from oppression by the Crown. Tracing their origins to the Glorious Revolution of the 1680s (and, more fancifully, to the imposition of Magna Carta on King John by the barons in 1215), they had been the 'country' rather than 'court' party in the eighteenth century, and the allies of religious Dissenters against the Church of England. The Whigs split over the French Revolution, when Burke and the Portland Whigs sided with the Tories. This left Charles James Fox the leader of a much-reduced party, committed to peace with France, toleration for Dissenters, abolition of the slave trade, and parliamentary reform: a programme summed up in the slogan 'Civil and Religious Liberty'. The Whigs returned to power in 1830 and enacted their policy of parliamentary reform in the First Reform Bill. By now they were the party of commerce and industry, as well as of Dissent and the liberal aristocracy, and their slogan was 'Peace, retrenchment, and reform'. They supported religious toleration, lower taxes, a free press, and a more humane legal code. Macaulay, in 1834, called them 'the *Centre Gauche*': the centre left.

The term 'Liberal' began to be used, interchangeably with 'Whig', in the 1830s, sometimes merely to describe Whig supporters who did not come from grandly aristocratic backgrounds. But it could also be used to distinguish Whigs who were willing to make further extensions of the franchise from those who had taken a 'Finality' view of the First Reform Bill. In the 1860s, 'Liberal' would replace 'Whig' as the usual name for the party.

'Radical' is the most slippery of these terms, in part because the Radical Members of Parliament were not a party but a miscellany of small groups with diverse views. These included the Manchester School free-traders, the Utilitarian 'Philosophical Radicals', and O'Connell's Irish party. Confusingly, the term was also used of the most 'advanced' members of the Whig party. These 'moderate Radicals' were less restrained than the Liberal Whigs in their attacks on church privileges and military expenditure, and more enthusiastic about further parliamentary reform, usually including the secret ballot. But the difference was relative. In his own eyes, Plantagenet Palliser is not a Radical (*Can You Forgive Her?*, Chapter 23). In the eyes of a Tory like the young Lord Silverbridge (*The Duke's Children*, Chapter 4), he looks rather like one.

In practice, the difference between Tories, Whigs, and Liberals in the politics of the 1850s is perhaps best indicated by the order of priorities in Peel's phrase from the *Tamworth Manifesto*: 'the firm maintenance of established rights, the correction of proved abuses and the redress of real grievances'. There is a great deal of common ground here. But Tories could be said to have seen the first of these things as the most important, Whigs the second, and Liberals the third. Radicals, while sharing the Liberal concern for the redress of grievances, would have reduced the list to two by showing little or no enthusiasm for the 'maintenance of established rights'. By the 1870s, the Radicals had been almost entirely absorbed into the Gladstonian Liberal party, and the party's centre of gravity had shifted somewhat as a result.

Despite the quality of mild archaism which clings to Trollope's account of British political culture in general, there are particular events in the Palliser novels which belong, undeniably, to the 1860s. Most conspicuously, in *Phineas Finn* and *Phineas Redux* he gives his version of the debates in 1866–7 about the Second Reform Bill. When Trollope does present immediately contemporary issues, however, he deliberately distorts them. In reality, Russell and Gladstone introduced a Reform Bill in 1866 which was attacked, from the right wing of their own party, by Robert Lowe. Denounced as an 'Adullamite' (he might, alternatively, have been termed an 'Ultra Whig'), Lowe opposed any alteration of the First Reform Act. With Tory support, Lowe defeated the Bill and the government fell. A year later, in 1867, Disraeli astonishingly 'stole the Whigs' clothes' by introducing a successful Reform Bill of his own.

In Trollope's novel, Mildmay and Gresham introduce a Reform Bill which is opposed, not from the right of their party, but from the left. A Radical, Turnbull, opposes the measure because it does not include provision for a secret ballot. Though Tories could, in reality, support a Whig attack on Whig policy from the right, they cannot, in these new (fictional) circumstances, support an attack from the left. So the Bill is not rejected, and passes into law. So far so good, especially for Whig readers eager to find imaginative compensation for a painful defeat. But Trollope has not yet managed to represent the most dramatic feature of the Reform Bill debates: Disraeli's 'stealing the Whigs' clothes'. In *Phineas Redux*, therefore, he invents another political issue to allow Daubeny to do this. Here, the Tories seek to steal the support which the Whigs had traditionally received from Dissenters by introducing a (wholly fictitious) Bill to disestablish the Church of England. Faced with a choice between opposing a measure which their Nonconformist supporters desire, and allowing the Tories to take the credit for its success, the Whigs fall back on a casuistical 'men not measures' argument. In due course they may themselves introduce such a bill. In the short term, they can vote with right-wing Tory rebels to defeat disestablishment, just as Tories had (in reality) voted with right-wing Whigs to defeat reform.

Trollope is not reproducing the political life of his time, in other words, but creating a credible alternative to it, and these episodes demonstrate the necessary limits of that process. What happens in the major political action of the novels must not be what actually happened, or the books (and their characters) would not be fiction. The outcome of the fictional events, however, must be the same as the outcome of the actual events, or Trollope's parallel universe would begin to diverge from the real world. There has, in fact, been a Second Reform Act, so Gresham's Bill can pass (subject to some correction, at the beginning of *Phineas Redux*, to get the details right). But we are not living in a world in which the Church of England has been disestablished, so Daubeny's Bill must fail. The trick is to achieve the best possible balance between the real and unreal.

Fundamentally, Trollope is creating his credible alternative to the real political world, not for its own sake, but as an environment in which human relationships can be dramatized and discussed. The novels of the Barsetshire series are about people living in a clerical environment, not about religion. The novels of the Palliser series, similarly, are about people living in a political environment, not about politics. Their correspondence to the political events of the 1860s and 1870s needs to be sufficiently correct to make the setting in which the characters exist believable, without being perfect. To achieve this Trollope refracts, rather than reflects, the political circumstances of his time, and does so with a combination of mild archaism and deliberate distortion. In Chapter 17 of *Phineas Redux*, he suggests that his readers need to have 'duly studied the history of the age'. But this is a joke. What such study will reveal, he tells us, is that 'the Duke did make an offer to Madame Goesler'. In novels story, not history, is what really matters.

Nicholas Shrimpton

EXPLANATORY NOTES

THESE notes are built on foundations laid by previous annotators: R. W. Chapman (Oxford, 1952), Jennifer Uglow (Oxford World's Classics, 1983), and David Skilton (Penguin, 1994). The present editor gratefully acknowledges his debt to their work and to Richard Mullen, with James Munsen, for their *Penguin Companion to Trollope* (1996) and R. C. Terry for his *Oxford Reader's Companion to Trollope* (1999). References to the Bible are to the King James Version; definitions are derived from the *Oxford English Dictionary* (*OED*); references to Shakespeare are to the text of *The Complete Works*, ed. Stanley Wells and Gary Taylor (Oxford, 1988); references to Trollope's *Autobiography* are to the Oxford World's Classics edition, ed. Michael Sadleir and Frederick Page (Oxford, 1999); references to Trollope's letters are to *The Letters of Anthony Trollope*, ed. N. John Hall, 2 vols. (Stanford, Calif.: Stanford University Press, 1983); references to Trollope's notes on his copies of Shakespeare and other Jacobean dramatists (now in the Folger Shakespeare Library, Washington DC) are taken from the transcriptions in Elizabeth R. Epperly, *Anthony Trollope's Notes on the Old Drama* (Victoria, British Columbia: English Literary Studies, University of Victoria, 1988); references to *The Times* newspaper are to *The Times Digital Archive 1785–1985*. Conversions of Victorian money are necessarily approximate but are based on the National Register of Archives online currency converter, using 1870 as the base date (http://www.nationalarchives.gov.uk/currency).

VOLUME I

8 *Johnson*: Dr Johnson's *Dictionary of the English Language* (1755) defines 'gentleman' as 'a man of ancestry' and observes that 'All other derivations seem to be whimsical'. It does, however, go on to note that the word can sometimes mean not just 'A man of birth' but also 'A man raised above the vulgar by his character or post'.

9 *At the time with which we are now concerned*: the action of *The Prime Minister* appears to take place between 1873 and 1876 (see Appendix).

German University: in Chapter 3 Lopez will identify this as 'Bohn' (Bonn). By the late 1850s, when Lopez would have been a student, German universities had established a formidable reputation for scholarship. Lucius Mason in *Orley Farm* (1861–2) similarly attends a German university rather than Oxford or Cambridge and combines intellectual sophistication with an inability to integrate comfortably into English upper-class life.

10 *park nag*: a horse suitable for use in the fashionable gatherings of riders and carriages in London's Hyde Park.

garran: a small and inferior kind of horse (*OED*).

brougham: a one-horse closed carriage.

10 *Leighton*: Leighton Buzzard is a market town in Bedfordshire, 40 miles north-west of London. Trollope himself kept horses there, in the spring of 1873, hunting with Baron Meyer de Rothschild's deer hounds and the Whaddon Chase fox hounds. Not liking the latter, he returned to hunting in Essex the following winter.

11 *Metropolitan railway*: the first branch of the London Underground, or Metropolitan Railway, was opened in 1863. The Metropolitan District Railway from South Kensington to Mansion House (later known as the District Line), on which Lopez travels from Westminster, was added in 1871.

Little Tankard Yard: probably a version of Tokenhouse Yard, off Lothbury behind the Bank of England.

12 *bill for three months*: a loan, repayable in three months' time, for which a second signatory, or guarantor, is needed before the lender will release the money. The sum involved, £750, is about £35,000 in modern money.

Accommodation bill: a bill not linked to a commercial transaction but simply a means of borrowing money; since no security was provided, the interest rate would be high.

13 *Ponders End*: suburb in Enfield, 10 miles north of the City of London, which grew rapidly after the arrival of the railway in 1849.

14 *the Progress*: fictitious club; a less grand alternative to the Reform Club (founded in 1832 for Whig supporters of the First Reform Bill). Though chiefly social, it has a political committee with funds which can be used to subsidize the election expenses of members who stand as Liberal candidates. It is on the north side of Pall Mall (see note to p. 237).

the T—— and the G——: the Travellers' Club (1819) and the Garrick Club (1831), neither of them political. Blackballing is the electoral process by which club members can prevent the admission of candidates they consider unsuitable.

15 *corn laws . . . income tax*: Sir Robert Peel repealed the Corn Laws (a protectionist measure for British agriculture) in 1846. Income tax, first used during the Napoleonic Wars, was dropped in 1816 but reintroduced in 1842 at sevenpence in the pound on incomes over £150, rising briefly to one shilling and fourpence after the Crimean War. In the 1870s governments changed the rate almost every year, in a range between sixpence and twopence in the pound.

16 *grey hairs with sorrow to the grave*: Genesis 42: 38: 'then shall ye bring down my gray hairs with sorrow to the grave'.

the schools: the examinations required for an Honours Degree. At this date most Oxford undergraduates were reading for the less demanding Pass Degree.

17 *communism*: Everett Wharton's (theoretical) views at this stage are those of an extreme Radical and include a knowledge of communism, though probably not in its Marxist form: the first volume of *Das Kapital* (1867)

was initially available only in German and the first British Marxist party, the Democratic Federation, would not be founded until 1881. The Paris Commune of 1871 had, however, recently provoked discussion in the British press of communist ideas, including those of Robert Owen, Proudhon, and Louis Blanc.

£400 a year: about £19,000 in modern money.

18 *Pope*: the quotation is from the second epistle of Alexander Pope's poem *An Essay on Man* (1733–4), 2. 2.

19 *court my Morpheus*: go to sleep (Morpheus is the Greek god of dreams).

20 *old military club*: the United Service Club in Pall Mall, founded in 1815 and described as 'old' because long waiting lists for membership led to the subsequent creation of a Junior United Service Club and the Army and Navy Club (1837). Closed in 1976, the building is now that of the Institute of Directors.

22 *Equity Courts*: Equity is the branch of English law evolved in the Court of Chancery to provide relief for wrongs which the common law could not remedy, especially in the field of trusts. Until the Judicature Act of 1873 there were two systems of law: the common law courts and the six Equity or Chancery courts in which the Lord Chancellor was the highest judge. After that date a Supreme Court of Judicature began to administer both systems, with Equity matters assigned to the Chancery Division of the High Court.

stuff gown: a barrister who is a junior counsel wears a woollen or 'stuff' gown. A senior or Queen's Counsel ('QC') wears a silk gown.

bencher at his Inn: a bencher is a member of the governing body of one of the Inns of Court (Gray's Inn, Lincoln's Inn, and the Middle and Inner Temple) to which English barristers are required to belong. Wharton is a member of Lincoln's Inn.

cob: a short-legged, stout variety of horse, usually ridden by heavy persons (*OED*).

the Eldon: a fictitious club for lawyers named after John Scott, first Earl of Eldon (1751–1838), Lord Chancellor in Tory governments, 1801–6 and 1807–27. Remembered as a reactionary, for his opposition to the emancipation of slaves, the enfranchisement of Roman Catholics, and the First Reform Bill, he did play an important part in making Equity law more modern and coherent.

23 *Manchester Square*: laid out in 1776, Manchester Square is a quadrangle of substantial terrace houses in Marylebone. Sir Richard Wallace began to rebuild the north side of the square in 1872 as Hertford House, the home of the Wallace Collection.

24 *Stone Buildings*: one of the buildings of Lincoln's Inn, designed by Sir Robert Taylor in 1774, with a south wing added in 1845.

Mr Mudie's . . . ticket: Charles Mudie's circulating library (1842–1937) was until the 1880s the chief source of new novels for Victorian readers. It attached a bright yellow label to the covers of its books.

24 *Berkeley Street*: the real Berkeley Street is not 'close round the corner' from Manchester Square but runs between Piccadilly and Berkeley Square in Mayfair. This may be a version of Baker Street.

27 *Portuguese*: Sephardic Jews who had been forced to leave Spain and Portugal in the 1490s (such as the Disraeli, Pinero, and Sassoon families) had since settled in England. But Britain also had close links with contemporary Portuguese society, partly through the Port wine trade, partly because Portugal had been Britain's only ally on the Continent for a large part of the Napoleonic Wars.

28 *Bohn*: Bonn University was founded in 1818 by the King of Prussia. Between 1857 and 1861, when Lopez was supposedly a student there, he would have been taught by the great classical scholar Friedrich Ritschl (1806–76). Trollope's mother, writing about Bonn in her *Belgium and Western Germany in 1833*, 2 vols. (John Murray, 1834) observed that 'Everything connected with the University is upon a noble scale: the schools, the library, the academic walks . . . a noble and beautiful seat of learning' (i. 145).

Admirable Crichton: the treatises of Sir Thomas Urquhart (1611–60), collected in 1774 and 1834, included an account of the 'Admirable' James Crichton (1560–82), a Scot noted for his ability to conduct scientific debates with European scholars in their own languages. The phrase became proverbial.

foreign loans: Lopez appears to be lying here. He is a commodity trader, not a bond dealer, but the raising of loans for foreign governments and capital projects (a field in which firms such as Rothschilds and Baring Brothers were prominent) sounds more respectable. See his denial of interest in 'Spanish bonds' on p. 19 and his statement that he is 'in the South American trade' (that is, dealing in guano and coffee) on p. 192. Wharton is not wrong to reply that foreign loans can be risky: the Turkish government defaulted in November 1874, two months after Trollope finished writing this novel.

29 *even to the Bench*: Roman Catholics were enfranchised (subject to property qualifications) in 1829. Jews acquired the right to vote by the Reform Bill of 1832 but were unable to sit in Parliament because of the requirement to make an oath of loyalty 'by the true faith of a Christian'. Though Lionel de Rothschild was elected MP for the City of London in 1847 he could not take his seat until 1858, when the House of Commons oath was modified. The Lords followed in 1866, in which year religious oaths for public offices were removed. The first Jewish barrister was called in 1833. The first Jewish judge, Trollope's friend Sir George Jessell, was appointed 'to the Bench' as Master of the Rolls in 1873. In chapter 78 of *The Way We Live Now* (1874–5) Georgiana Longstaffe remarks that 'One of the greatest judges in the land is a Jew'; Phineas Finn notes that 'You have a Jew among your English judges' (p. 92).

30 *£60,000*: about £2,750,000 in modern money.

31 *Nimrod*: fictitious club for sporting men named after 'Nimrod the mighty hunter' (Genesis 10: 9).

37 *Bell's Life*: *Bell's Life in London* was a popular sporting paper founded by John Bell (1745–1831) who also published the *Morning Post* and the Sunday *Bell's Weekly Messenger*.

41 *Chronicles of her early life*: Trollope is referring to his own previous novels. Lady Glencora M'Cluskie is first described in chapter 55 of *The Small House at Allington* (1862–4). The early years of her marriage to Plantagenet Palliser are covered in *Can You Forgive Her?* (1864–5), and their subsequent life together in *Phineas Finn* (1867–9), *The Eustace Diamonds* (1871–3), and *Phineas Redux* (1873–4), where Plantagenet inherits his uncle's title and becomes Duke of Omnium.

Mr Gresham and Mr Daubeny: Daubeny resembles the Tory politician Benjamin Disraeli (1804–81; Lord Beaconsfield from 1876). Gresham is a Whig leader who has been compared with the Peelite-turned-Liberal William Ewart Gladstone (1809–98) though the similarity is a very partial one (see Appendix).

Windsor: since the Prime Minister is technically the Queen's chief minister, he or she must call on her at whichever of her residences she happens to be occupying (in this case, Windsor Castle) to seek her agreement to a resignation or assumption of the office. Unlike an American President, a British Prime Minister is not directly elected.

boxes: the despatch boxes containing the confidential working papers of cabinet ministers.

42 *special piece of work for the nation*: as Chancellor of the Exchequer and (in *Phineas Redux*) as President of the Board of Trade, Plantagenet Palliser had been preoccupied with an attempt to replace the duodecimal system of British currency (twelve pence to a shilling) with decimal currency. Though the introduction, in 1849, of the florin (a two-shilling coin of which there were ten to the pound), and John Bowring's book *The Decimal System* (1854) had prompted interest in the topic, the currency would not be decimalized until 1971.

43 *Lord Fawn*: Viscount Frederick Fawn has a peerage but not much money, and appears as a timid junior minister in Whig governments in *Phineas Finn*, *The Eustace Diamonds*, and *Phineas Redux*. After a series of unfortunate courtships, he is last seen with a 'pretty' wife 'who liked mild flirtations with mild young men' in chapter 42 of *The Duke's Children*.

44 *Duke of St Bungay*: probably based on the third Marquis of Lansdowne (1780–1863), a key figure in the Whig party in the first half of the nineteenth century. St Bungay is similarly, if anachronistically, an indispensable member of Whig shadow cabinets and cabinets (as Lord President of the Council) throughout the Palliser series (see Appendix and note to p. 496).

domestic circumstance: After Lady Glencora had come close to running away with Burgo Fitzgerald, in chapter 50 of *Can You Forgive Her?*,

Plantagenet Palliser had refused the post of Chancellor of the Exchequer in order to take her on an extended foreign holiday and rebuild their marriage.

45 *Lady Macbeth*: the quotation is from Shakespeare's *Macbeth*, 1. v. 18–19. This is the first of a series of allusions to the play which help to establish Glencora's role as a stimulus to an insufficiently ambitious or ruthless husband.

46 *her own property was separated from his*: before the third of the successive Married Women's Property Acts (1870, 1874, 1882) a woman who wished, or whose family wished, to keep her possessions separate from her husband's would put them into trust, as a 'separate estate' in equity law, before the marriage. Unless this was done, a wife's money became her husband's property under the common-law doctrine of coverture.

Mrs Finn: Marie Goesler first appears in *Phineas Finn*. English by birth (the daughter of a 'small country attorney'), she has been brought up abroad and is the wealthy widow of Max Goesler, a Viennese banker. Widely assumed to be Jewish, she becomes a close friend of the 'old' Duke of Omnium (Plantagenet Palliser's uncle) and, after his death, of Lady Glencora. She marries Phineas Finn in *Phineas Redux*. The character may have been partly based on Lady Waldegrave (Frances Braham, 1821–79): the daughter of a Jewish singer, she was courted by the Duke of Newcastle and married (as her fourth husband) Chichester Fortescue, a possible model for Phineas Finn.

49 *Apollinaris water*: a German mineral water which was becoming popular in the 1870s. Since a friend of Trollope, the publisher George Smith, had acquired the English distribution rights, this may be an instance of 'product placement'.

50 *Cantrip . . . Mildmay . . . Monk*: Lord Cantrip is a Whig peer who serves as Colonial Secretary in *Phineas Finn*. William Mildmay is Whig Prime Minister in *Phineas Finn*; he may in part have been based on Lord John Russell (1792–1878, Prime Minister 1846–52 and 1865–6). Joshua Monk is a Liberal, or Radical Whig, who serves as a mentor to Phineas Finn; he is President of the Board of Trade in *Phineas Finn*, Chancellor of the Exchequer in *The Prime Minister*, and eventually becomes Prime Minister himself in *The Duke's Children*.

51 *Mistress of the Robes*: an official member of the Royal Household who attends the Queen at all state functions and is the only lady of the court who comes into office with the government (unlike the ladies of the bedchamber, the women of the bedchamber, and the maids-of-honour). The actual Mistresses of the Robes in the 1870s were, successively, the Duchess of Sutherland (Liberal) and the Duchess of Wellington (Tory).

52 *Grogram . . . Beeswax*: Sir Gregory Grogram is a Whig lawyer who had previously been Attorney-General in Gresham's government in *Phineas Redux*; grogram is a coarse fabric of silk, mohair, and wool stiffened with gum. Sir Timothy Beeswax is a Tory lawyer who has been

Solicitor-General in Daubeny's government, retains that office under Omnium, and (surprisingly) becomes Attorney-General in Gresham's administration. He returns to his Tory roots as Leader of the House for the Drummond government in *The Duke's Children*, where he is discussed at length in chapter 21.

Drought: Sir Orlando Drought is a Tory politician first seen as a Secretary of State and 'one of Mr Daubeny's leading lieutenants' in *Phineas Redux*. In *The Way We Live Now* (1874–5) he is 'quite a leading Conservative'. He has been Colonial Secretary under Daubeny; the suggestion here that he might be demoted to Postmaster General is a joke at the expense of the ministry in which Trollope himself had been a civil servant. Drought is still an MP in *The Duke's Children*, though it is not clear whether he holds ministerial rank in the Drummond and Beeswax government. (See note to p. 54).

fainéant: (French) idle, lazy, ineffective.

54 *the Council*: the Privy Council is the body, nominally consisting of several hundred senior politicians of all parties but in practice of three or four members of the current cabinet, 'by and with' whose advice the Sovereign acts on matters not dealt with by Parliament. The Lord President of the Council is one of the Great Officers of State, third in precedence after the Prime Minister and the Lord Chancellor.

Eight men . . . certain places: cabinets in the mid-nineteenth century consisted of between twelve and twenty ministers. Trollope identifies only six members of Omnium's coalition cabinet: the Prime Minister (Omnium, Whig), the Lord Chancellor (Lord Ramsden, Tory), the Lord President of the Council (Duke of St Bungay, Whig), the Chancellor of the Exchequer (Mr Monk, Whig-Liberal), the Colonial Secretary (Lord Drummond, Tory), and the First Lord of the Admiralty who is also Leader of the House of Commons (Sir Orlando Drought, Tory). The Foreign Secretary, Home Secretary, Lord Privy Seal, and the ministers for War, the India Office, and the Board of Trade are not mentioned in the novel. The Chief Secretary for Ireland (Phineas Finn, Whig-Liberal) and the Postmaster General (Barrington Erle, Whig) hold posts which would normally have been in the cabinet but do not seem to be so here. Also outside the cabinet, Trollope identifies the Lord Lieutenant of Ireland (the Marquis of Tyrone, 'very conservative'), the two Law Officers (Grogram, Whig, and Beeswax, Tory), and Under-Secretaries at the Exchequer (Rattler, Whig) and the Admiralty (Roby, Tory). The most troublesome appointment is Drought's role as Leader of the House of Commons: this coalition government is, confusingly, led by a Whig in the Lords (Omnium) but a Tory in the Commons. Monk begins to supplant Drought as Leader of the House by Chapter 32 and formally replaces him when he resigns from the government in Chapter 41. Finn then succeeds Drought as First Lord of the Admiralty, thus entering the cabinet.

55 *Lord Brock*: Whig Prime Minister in *Framley Parsonage* (1860–1), *The Small House at Allington* and *Can You Forgive Her?* who in some respects

resembles Lord Palmerston (1784–1865; Prime Minister 1855–8, 1859–65). Trollope would publish an admiring memoir, *Lord Palmerston*, in 1882.

55 *Noblesse oblige*: (French) nobility, or high birth, carries obligations to behave well.

assume a virtue: Shakespeare, *Hamlet*, III. iv. 151: 'Assume a virtue if you have it not' (Hamlet to his mother).

seals: the Great Seal (kept by the Lord Chancellor), the Privy Seal, and the Privy Signet were required to authenticate government grants and decrees until the Great Seal Act (1884) simplified the process of establishing the authority of official documents.

56 *Carlton and Reform Clubs*: the Carlton Club was and is the leading Tory club. The Reform Club was its Whig equivalent.

57 *Patronage Secretary*: the Patronage Secretary was a junior minister in the Treasury, responsible for correspondence connected with appointments. Like the modern Parliamentary Secretary to the Treasury, the post tended to be combined with that of Chief Whip. Rattler and Roby were, respectively, the Whig and Tory Whips in *Phineas Finn*. The question here is who will be Chief Whip in a coalition (in the event it will be Rattler who is appointed to the Treasury).

58 *education questions*: this list is a version of some of the issues addressed by Gladstone's Liberal government of 1868–74: the Education Act of 1870, Gladstone's persistent attempts to reduce income tax (which fell from sixpence in the pound to twopence in 1875), the wish to align county franchise with that in the boroughs (unsuccessfully proposed in 1872 and repeatedly reintroduced as a private bill by Sir George Trevelyan), and the disestablishment of the Irish (not English) Church in 1869.

special bench: the seat used by the Leader of the Opposition.

Wilson: Legge Wilson is a Whig MP who appears in *Phineas Finn*, *The Eustace Diamonds*, *Phineas Redux*, and *The Way We Live Now*. A safe pair of hands rather than a star politician, he is, at different times, Secretary at War, Chancellor of the Exchequer, and Secretary of State for India.

61 *Chief Secretary*: the Lord Lieutenant governed Ireland as the Queen's representative, overseeing law and order and the administration of justice. The Chief Secretary had parliamentary responsibility for Irish policy. The Chief Secretary for Ireland had routinely been a member of Liberal cabinets since 1859, so Omnium's insistence that it is a non-cabinet post is one of the ways in which his government resembles the Aberdeen coalition of 1852–5 rather than the politics of the 1870s.

64 *English people of that name*: the Lopes family of Maristow, Devon ('descended from an ancient and opulent Jamaica family', *Burke's Peerage and Baronetage*, 1906) had been baronets since 1805; wealthy landowners, their title is now Baron Roborough. The first baronet, Sir Manasseh Masseh Lopes (1755–1831), converted from Judaism in 1802 and became MP for New Romney. He is chiefly remembered for his part in a series of

electoral scandals: he was convicted of bribery both at Grampound in Cornwall and at Barnstaple in Devon. After his release from jail in 1823, he sat for his pocket borough of Westbury, resigning it to Sir Robert Peel in 1829 when the latter lost his University of Oxford seat. Trollope's own experience as an (innocent) candidate at a corrupt election, at Beverley in 1868, may have caused him to remember the name. See also note to p. 371.

68 *Lady Monogram*: Sir Damask and his wife had previously appeared in *The Way We Live Now*.

69 *Lady Eustace*: Lizzie Eustace had been the scandalous heroine of *The Eustace Diamonds* and appeared in *Phineas Redux*.

72 *Madame Cliquot's*: Veuve Cliquot is a famous brand of champagne. At '110s.' (a dozen), Dick Roby has paid (in modern money) about £30 a bottle for it.

before the war: the Franco-Prussian War (1870–1) had interrupted the wine trade.

73 *Argus*: in Greek myth, Argos Panoptes was the herdsman that Hera set to watch Io when Zeus fell in love with her. He supposedly had eyes all over his body.

74 *queer story*: see *Can You Forgive Her?* and note to p. 44.

75 *Leoville*: Châteaux Léoville-Las-Cases and Léoville-Barton are vineyards in St-Julien, both included among the 15 Deuxièmes Crus (Second Growths) in the Bordeaux Classification of 1855. Having agreed to dignify a bourgeois dinner party with his aristocratic presence, in return it would seem for good wine, Lord Mongrober may have expected a Premier Cru claret: Lafite, Latour, or Margaux.

consols: consols, or Consolidated Funds, were a bond issued by the British government which paid an annual interest of 3 per cent.

78 *Carlton Terrace*: correctly given as Carlton House Terrace in Chapter 14 (but as 'Carlton Gardens' in *Phineas Redux*, chapter 31), Omnium's London house is in one of the two terraces overlooking St James's Park designed by John Nash and built 1827–32.

Gatherum Castle . . . Matching: Omnium's two country houses. Gatherum Castle, near Silverbridge in Barsetshire, is an uncomfortably large mansion built in the early nineteenth century by Palliser's uncle, the 'old Duke'; the formal ducal seat, it is used only for entertaining (see *Framley Parsonage* and *Doctor Thorne* as well as the other Palliser novels). Matching Priory in Yorkshire is a smaller country house much preferred by Palliser and Lady Glencora (and mentioned in all the Palliser novels).

81 *Pas si mal*: (French) not so bad.

Lady Macbeth: see the banquet scene, Shakespeare's *Macbeth* (Act III Scene iv) where Macbeth is thrown into confusion by the ghost of his most recent victim, Banquo. Duncan was the King of Scotland murdered by the Macbeths in Act II.

81 *Augean stables*: in Greek myth Herakles (Latin, Hercules) killed his wife and children in a fit of madness and, as a penance, was required to undertake twelve apparently impossible labours. One was to clean, in a single day, the stables of Augeas, King of Elis, where thousands of oxen had not been mucked out for thirty years. He achieved it by diverting the river Alphaeus through the premises.

Home Rulers: Isaac Butt (1813–79), previously Tory MP for Youghal, founded the Home Government Association of Ireland in 1870 and was elected MP for Limerick in 1871. Renamed the Home Rule League in 1873, it won fifty-nine seats in the Commons in 1874 and secured sixty-one votes on a motion for Home Rule. Charles Stewart Parnell (1846–91) would not enter the House of Commons until 1875; he replaced Butt as leader of the League in 1880. Gladstone would (unsuccessfully) introduce his first Home Rule Bill in 1886. In chapter 4 of his *Autobiography*, Trollope described the Irish Home Rule movement as a 'nuisance'.

82 *Catholic education and Papal interference*: long-standing issues with Irish implications. Catholic education had been controversial since the Maynooth grant of 1846, when Peel proposed a permanent endowment for the Roman Catholic seminary in Kildare; Gladstone failed to pass his Irish University Bill (affiliating the denominational colleges into a single university) in 1873. The suspicion that the Pope wished to interfere in British public life reached a climax during the 'papal aggression' scare of 1850–1, after the re-establishment of the Roman Catholic hierarchy in England and Wales, but resurfaced in 1870 with the declaration of Papal Infallibility by the Vatican Council. In 1874 Gladstone's pamphlets on Vaticanism claimed that this was inconsistent with civil allegiance and Newman's 'Letter to the Duke of Norfolk' denied it.

Broune . . . Booker: Nicholas Broune, editor of the *Morning Breakfast Table*, and Mr Booker had previously appeared in *The Way We Live Now*. In his manuscript 'advance Lay-Out' for that novel (reproduced in Michael Sadleir, *Trollope: A Commentary* (1927), 427), Trollope identifies (in Sadleir's transcriptions) Broune with 'Morrish' and Booker with 'Alfred Shand'. Mowbray Morris (1819–74) was manager of the *Times* 1847–73, also acting as the foreign, literary, and dramatic editor. He wrote to Trollope on 17 April 1871 to decline his offer of travel articles about Australia (which would appear, instead, in the *Daily Telegraph*); see *Letters*, ii. 544–5. Alexander Shand (1832–1907) was a literary journalist whom Trollope nominated for membership of the Athenaeum Club in February 1871; he would review Trollope's novels for the *Edinburgh* in 1877.

Orpheus: poet (in Greek legend Orpheus was a pre-Homeric poet).

the somewhat wooden novelist: possibly a joking reference by Trollope to himself; in the *Autobiography* (pp. 231–2) he refers to the 'woodenness' of novelists who have lost their original inspiration and remarks that these 'are reflections which . . . are applicable to myself' (see Adam Roberts, 'Trollope in *The Prime Minister*', *Notes & Queries*, 237 (June 1992), 183–4).

83 *Japan*: closed to the outside world since the 1630s, Japan was forcibly reopened in 1853 by an American fleet under Commodore Perry. Significant modernization did not, however, begin until the Meiji restoration in 1868. In the 1870s British firms were involved in the construction of the Japanese railway and telegraph systems, and in the supply of modern ships for its navy.

84 *out-Heroded Herod*: Shakespeare, *Hamlet*, III. ii. 12 (Hamlet's instruction to the Players not to rant or 'tear a passion to tatters').

bread and the games: Juvenal, *Satires*, 10. 80: 'panem et circenses'. Bread and circuses (or food and public entertainments) are what are required, in Juvenal's cynical view, to keep the population happy under the imperial rule of the early second century AD.

wreath of roses: Nero, Roman emperor AD 54–68, was said to have caused the fire of Rome in AD 64, and supposedly fiddled (that is, played his lyre) while it burnt. On his dress and habits see Suetonius, *De Vita Caesarum* ('Lives of the Caesars').

85 *Pandemonium*: Hell, the home of 'all the devils' (Greek).

Barrington Erle: Whig politician seen previously in *Phineas Finn*, *The Eustace Diamonds*, and *Phineas Redux*.

87 *casual-ward . . . bread and skilly*: a casual ward provided temporary accommodation, in a workhouse, for travelling labourers or those without regular employment. Skilly, or oatmeal gruel, was the food provided there.

your "rights": though the campaign for votes for women was only in its early stages in the 1870s, the Women's Rights movement had achieved the Custody of Infants Act (1839), the Matrimonial Causes Act (1857), and the first Married Women's Property Act (1870). John Stuart Mill's *The Subjection of Women* was published in 1869. The 1870 Education Act provided elementary education for girls, as well as boys, and for the first time made women eligible for appointment to public office as members of School Boards.

88 *blue-books*: official reports of Parliament and the Privy Council were issued in dark blue paper covers.

89 *staunch economists*: the Manchester School supporters of free trade and laissez-faire economics, a group of Radical MPs led by Richard Cobden (1804–65) and John Bright (1811–89).

philosophical Radicals: the Philosopical Radicals were followers of Jeremy Bentham (1748–1832), the Utilitarian philosopher. Their Benthamite causes included the extension of the franchise, the mitigation of the criminal law, the improvement of prisons, the abolition of transportation and imprisonment for debt, and the reform of the Poor Laws. They were a small group of intellectual MPs, including, at different times, George Grote (1794–1871), Sir William Molesworth (1810–55), John Stuart Mill (1806–73), and John Roebuck (1801–79) whose call for an inquiry into the conduct of the Crimean War helped to bring down the Aberdeen coalition.

90 *Mr Turnbull*: Radical MP for Staleybridge who had previously appeared in *Phineas Finn* and *Phineas Redux*. Trollope published a letter in the *Daily Telegraph* on 1 April 1869 (see *Letters*, i. 468) denying that the character was based on John Bright (1811–89).

the Phoenix: the Lord Lieutenant of Ireland had an official residence in Phoenix Park, Dublin.

91 *Brooks's club*: Whig club in St James's Street. Founded as a non-political club in 1764, it moved into elegant premises designed by Henry Holland in 1778. Palmerston was a member.

Orangeman: Protestant Irish loyalist, usually a member of the Orange Order, formed in 1795 to uphold the Protestant ascendancy in Ireland. The name derives from William of Orange (King William III) who defeated his predecessor, the deposed Catholic King James II, at the battle of the Boyne (1690).

92 *Heptarchy*: the seven kingdoms of Anglo-Saxon England from the fifth to the early ninth century AD, when Wessex became dominant and formed them into a single entity.

Pope in Italy: the French Catholic Church asserted its autonomy, and the freedom of the French crown from the Pope, by the Four Gallican Articles of 1682. The Pope's temporal power in the former Papal States of Italy had been ended in September 1870.

93 *seat on the bench of judges*: the post appears to be that of Lord Chief Justice, to which one or other of the two government law officers had usually been appointed.

94 *Brewers' Licences . . . Burton*: the licensing of public houses was introduced in 1751 to discourage the drinking of gin. The Beer House Act of 1830 sought to reinforce this by issuing cheaper and simpler licences for premises serving only beer. At the same time the duty on beer was replaced with a tax on malt and hops. Forty thousand beer houses opened in the next decade. Since public sobriety did not improve, the Wine and Beer House Act of 1869 brought beer houses back under normal licensing controls. A Licensing Bill in 1871 to impose further restrictions was fiercely opposed by the brewers and failed; a more moderate Act passed in 1872 but made the Liberal Party unpopular. Burton-upon-Trent became the centre of the brewing industry in the 1840s when the development of the railways enabled its pale ales to be widely distributed.

95 *coy her love*: cover up her love with an affected shyness or reserve. An archaic, transitive use of the verb 'coy' which Trollope probably picked up from his reading of Jacobean drama: *OED* cites Massinger's *A New Way to Pay Old Debts* (1625–6), 'When he comes to woo you, see you do not coy it'.

97 *Brabantio*: Shakespeare's *Othello*, 1. ii. 69–72. Brabantio (or Brabanzio) is Desdemona's father and does not wish her to marry a Moor.

100 *baronets*: the order was created in 1611.

Ballot: Tory governments had unexpectedly repealed the Corn Laws in 1846 and accepted the Liberal introduction of the secret ballot in 1872, contrary to the party's previous policies.

102 *glory was departing from their house*: 1 Samuel 4: 21: 'The glory is departed from Israel'.

103 *Hyperion to a Satyr*: Shakespeare, *Hamlet*, 1. ii. 140: Hamlet comparing his father (as the Titan who was the predecessor of the sun god, Apollo) with his usurping brother Claudius (as a lustful creature, half man, half goat).

105 *fly a kite*: take a risk.

106 *gone rather deep into . . . American mines*: invested in American mining companies.

113 *a few years ago*: duelling to settle legal disputes (judicial combat) was abolished in 1818. Private duelling on matters of honour continued: in 1840 Lord Cardigan wounded Captain Tuckett, was tried by the House of Lords, and was acquitted. An Anti-Duelling Association was formed in 1843 and, with support from Prince Albert, gradually made the practice unacceptable. But in *Phineas Finn* (set in the mid-1860s) the hero and Lord Chiltern go to Blankenberg, in Belgium, to fight over Violet Effingham.

115 *vestigia nulla retrorsum*: (Latin) 'none of the footprints lead back'. Horace, *Epistles*, 1. 1. 75, telling Aesop's story of the fox who declines to visit the sick lion on the grounds that there are footprints leading into his lair, but none suggesting that any visitor has ever made the return journey,

116 *'If she be not fair for me . . . be!'*: a slight misquotation of a poem, 'The Author's Resolution in a Sonnet' ('Shall I, wasting in despair') from *Fidelia* (1615) by George Wither (1588–1667): 'If she think not well of me, | What care I how fair she be?'

119 *Unions*: though the Tolpuddle Martyrs, in 1833, had been farm workers (who joined a Friendly Society), trade unionism developed relatively late on the land. Agricultural trade unions could be found in only three counties in the 1860s, Herefordshire being one of them. The Trade Union Act (1871) provided a clear legal status for unions; Joseph Arch founded the National Agricultural Labourers Union the following year. Initially a success, its membership plunged from 86,000 to 10,000 between 1874 and 1886, probably because of the 'great depression' of those years which chiefly affected farming.

122 *old plays*: John Fletcher's confident allusion to 'the old plays' reflects Trollope's enthusiasm for Elizabethan and Jacobean drama. He read more than 270 of them between 1866 and 1882 and may even have taken the name 'John Fletcher' from the author of the play by which this novel seems to have been most immediately influenced: *Women Pleased* (see Introduction).

131 *six months' vacation*: in the nineteenth century Parliament usually sat only from early February to the end of July.

132 *gilded Treasury log*: in Aesop's fable the frogs ask for a king and are sent a gold-painted log. When they complain that it does nothing, they are sent a stork instead. The stork eats them. 'Treasury' because the Prime Minister is the First Lord of the Treasury.

133 *blue ribbon*: the symbol of the Order of the Garter is a garter of dark blue ribbon, edged with gold.

caravansary: Middle Eastern inn or hotel where entire caravans or convoys of travellers can be accommodated.

"a reed out of the river": a free quotation (indicated more correctly as a paraphrase, without quotation marks, in the manuscript, as David Skilton notes) from Elizabeth Barrett Browning's poem, 'A Musical Instrument' ('What was he doing, the great god Pan'), first published in the *Cornhill* (July 1860). A mythical account of the origin of music and poetry, the poem symbolically suggests the painful separation of the artist from society. Pan cuts a reed and makes it into a panpipe. This is 'The only way, since gods began | To make sweet music, they could succeed'. But the reed 'grows nevermore again | As a reed with the reeds in the river'. In Omnium's account, the politician suffers the alienation of the artist, without the compensating capacity to create beauty.

134 *QUINTUS SLIDE*: a journalist who edits the *People's Banner* from an office in Quartpot Alley (probably a version of Wine Office Court, off Fleet Street). He had previously appeared in *Phineas Finn* (where his paper is a Radical journal) and *Phineas Redux* (where he has switched his support to the Conservatives). The paper's combination of scurrilous gossip and indignant political denunciation reflects the tone of the new popular journalism emerging in the 1860s.

139 *Darby and Joan*: a proverbial old married couple, familiar from popular poems and ballads.

140 *Eton*: leading English public school, in Berkshire, founded by Henry VI in 1440.

142 *ha-ha*: boundary formed by a fence hidden, below eye level, in a ditch (or sometimes just a ditch) so that the view is not interrupted.

143 *Lord Lieutenant*: the monarch's representative in each county, who combines formal duties with responsibilities for the local magistrates and militia. The powers of the post, previously very extensive, had been somewhat reduced in 1871.

Martha: Luke 10: 40–2. When Jesus is teaching in Martha's house, her sister Mary sits and listens while Martha, busy 'serving' those present, is 'careful and troubled about many things'.

145 *Coriolanus*: in Plutarch's *Parallel Lives* (written in the early second century AD to compare Greek and Roman statesmen) and Shakespeare's play *Coriolanus*, this fifth-century BC Roman military leader is unable to make the populist gestures required for the democratic process of election as consul, and is exiled. Trollope's note on *Coriolanus*, made on

27 June 1871, states, 'The conception of the character of Coriolanus is magnificently grand ... Coriolanus, because of the greatness of the great Roman's character, is a very great play' (see Introduction).

une grande dame: (French) a great lady.

148 *Frank Gresham*: previously seen in *Dr Thorne*, *Framley Parsonage*, and *The Last Chronicle of Barset*, the squire of Greshambury in Barsetshire and a relative of the Whig leader Mr Gresham. Given this relationship, it is odd that the Barsetshire Greshams should be Tories. Though Frank Gresham's mother, Lady Arabella De Courcy, is from a Whig family, he continues to support the Conservative party.

Lord Chiltern: first seen in *Phineas Finn* and present in all the subsequent Palliser novels, he is the son of the Earl of Brentford and brother of Lady Laura Kennedy. He marries his childhood sweetheart, the heiress Violet Effingham, after fighting a duel with Phineas Finn over her. An irascible, red-faced man but a model Master of Fox Hounds.

Lady Rosina De Courcy: daughter of the Whig Earl De Courcy, of Courcy Castle in Barsetshire. She appears in several of the Barsetshire novels (*Barchester Towers*, *Dr Thorne*, *Small House at Allington*) as an intensely religious spinster, much influenced by Mrs Proudie. Here she has mellowed into an inoffensive old lady, one of the few likeable members of an otherwise unpleasant family.

149 *very odd story*: in *Doctor Thorne*, Frank Gresham is in love with Mary Thorne, the illegitimate daughter of the doctor's dead brother Henry. Very fortunately, she turns out to be the sole heir of her uncle on her mother's side, the immensely wealthy railway contractor, Roger Scatcherd.

150 *raise supplies*: technically all that a parliament is required to do is pass the Finance Bills which authorize government expenditure. The modern assumption that governments must constantly introduce legislation of other kinds was only gradually establishing itself in the nineteenth century.

a Stuart king: Charles I's battles with Parliament began immediately after his accession in 1625. He dissolved it in 1629 and ruled without it until 1640.

far niente: (Italian) to do nothing.

151 *Franchises*: after the first reform of the franchise, in the Reform Bill of 1832, there was constant discussion of how it might be further extended, including plans for so-called 'fancy franchises'.

152 *withers were unwrung*: Shakespeare, *Hamlet*, III. ii. 221–2: 'Let the galled jade wince, our withers are unwrung'.

153 *Bismarcks*: Otto von Bismarck (1815–98), the so-called 'Iron Chancellor' who united the states of Germany into a single country under Prussian leadership. After his defeat of Austria (1866) and France (1871), Germany became the greatest power in continental Europe. He met Napoleon III,

to arrange French support for his war with Austria, at the spa town of Biarritz (a 'delicious haunt of salubrity') in October 1865.

153 *Laud's book of sports*: the *Book of Sports* was an anti-Puritan document originally issued in 1618 as a royal proclamation by King James I to encourage sports, such as archery, vaulting, and morris dancing on Sundays. It became known as 'Laud's book' because it was republished under Charles I in 1633, when William Laud (1573–1645) was Archbishop of Canterbury. John Fletcher's play *Women Pleased* (*c*.1619), which appears to have influenced this novel (see Introduction), contains a scene (IV. i) in which Bomby, a shoemaker who performs as the hobby-horse in the morris, is persuaded not to abandon the role because of his wife's Puritanism.

National Gallery: on 14 May 1874 Sir Charles Dilke asked a parliamentary question about the opening of museums and picture galleries on Sundays; P. A. Taylor introduced a motion to permit this on 19 May (see *Hansard*, 219, cols. 266, 482). The opposition came from Sabbatarians who believed that the Lord's Day should be kept holy.

154 *bathers' clothes were stolen*: on 28 February 1845, shortly before the debates over the repeal of the Corn Laws (and actually in a discussion of another matter, though this was soon forgotten), Disraeli had accused his own party leader, Sir Robert Peel, of stealing the policies of their Whig opponents: 'The right hon. Gentleman caught the Whigs bathing, and walked away with their clothes'. The joke was revived against Disraeli when he, in turn, stole the Whigs' policy of an extension of the franchise at the time of the Second Reform Bill in 1866–7. Here, as at the beginning of *Phineas Redux*, Trollope is referring to the real Tory Reform Act of 1867 and not to the fictitious Whig one which he had invented in *Phineas Finn* (see Appendix).

VOLUME II

157 *shaken the dust . . . from his feet*: Matthew 10: 14: 'And whosoever shall not receive you, nor hear your words, when ye depart out of that house or city, shake off the dust of your feet'.

159 *Mr Grey*: John Grey is a Cambridgeshire country gentleman of academic tastes who marries Alice Vavasor, the controversial heroine of *Can You Forgive Her?*, and becomes a Whig MP. Persia (modern Iran) was important to Britain because of its border with India. The Shah, Nasir ud-Din, made a state visit to Britain in June 1873 (which may, as John Sutherland has suggested, be reflected in the fictitious state visit by the Emperor of China in *The Way We Live Now*).

160 *'tell that to the marines'*: a phrase meaning 'I don't believe it'.

164 *Chiltern Hundreds*: an elected MP cannot resign but must instead apply for the stewardship of the Chiltern Hundreds, a nominal office of profit under the Crown which is incompatible with membership of the House of Commons.

166 *Lock-outs*: further evidence of Everett Wharton's radical interests (see note to p. 17); the repetition increases the irony of his later role as a country squire.

168 *Storey's Gate*: Wharton and Lopez enter St James's Park from the north (Marlborough Road, by St James's Palace), and walk along its west and south sides until they are in sight of Storey's Gate at its south-east corner.

drunk as Cloe: slang phrase meaning 'very drunk', sometimes linked to the poems addressed to 'Cloe' by Matthew Prior (1664–1721) though it does not occur there.

169 *new offices*: Sir George Gilbert Scott's Government Offices, on a site between Whitehall, Downing Street, St James's Park, and Great George Street, were eventually built, after the long dispute about their design known as 'the Battle of the Styles', in 1868–71 (though the Colonial Office section, on the Whitehall side, would not be completed until 1875). Now the Foreign Office, they originally also housed the Home Office, Colonial Office, and India Office.

170 *rifling his pockets*: Trollope had written an article on 'The Uncontrolled Ruffianism of London', published in *St Paul's Magazine* in January 1868.

171 *eight £5 notes*: about £1,800 in modern money.

181 *'lovers . . . the cleanliest shift is to kiss'*: Shakespeare, *As You Like It*, IV. i. 65–7: 'for lovers, lacking—God warr'nt us—matter, the cleanliest shift is to kiss.'

186 *Pimlico, or Belgravia*: Belgravia is a London district between Buckingham Palace and Sloane Street developed from the 1820s by the builder Thomas Cubitt as an estate of large stuccoed houses. Nineteenth-century residents included Lord John Russell, the Duchess of Kent (Queen Victoria's mother), Sidney Herbert, and the Duke of Connaught. Pimlico is a less grand district, immediately south of Belgravia, also developed by Thomas Cubitt from the mid-1830s. The difference between them is suggested in *The Small House at Allington* (chapter 40), when Adolphus Crosbie marries Lady Alexandrina De Courcy: 'Crosbie himself had wished to go to one of the new Pimlico squares down near Vauxhall Bridge . . . but to this Lady Alexandrina had objected strongly . . . if they could have crept on to the hem of the skirt of Belgravia,—the bride would have been delighted. And at first she was very nearly being taken in . . . Her geographical knowledge of Pimlico had not been perfect . . . But a friend had kindly intervened. "For heaven's sake, my dear, don't let him take you anywhere beyond Eccleston Square!"' Mr and Mrs Lopez will live to the north of Eccleston Square but not by a very wide margin: in Grosvenor Gardens where the Belgrave Mansions Company built the district's first block of mansion flats in the late 1860s; 'red brick instead of all stone . . . with shops below. It contained first-class flats, which in imitation of "the Parisian mode of life" were let furnished, the earliest such in London. A restaurant within saved residents from having to cook' (Simon Bradley

and Nikolaus Pevsner, *The Buildings of England, London 6: Westminster* (New Haven: Yale University Press, 2005), 753).

187 *£450*: the rent is about £20,000 a year in modern money.

the church in Vere Street: St Peter, Vere Street, Emily's parish church in Marylebone. Designed by James Gibbs and built in 1721–4.

189 *Post equitem sedet atra cura*: Horace, *Odes*, 3.1.40: 'Black care sits behind the horseman'.

guano: the dried droppings of seabirds, a fertilizer thirty times more concentrated than farmyard manure, imported between 1840 and 1941 from islands off the coast of Peru. The Gibbs family made an immense fortune from it, which they used to build both their house at Tyntesfield in Somerset and (with a gift in 1873 of £50,000, or £2.5 million in modern money) the chapel of Keble College, Oxford.

190 *£1500*: about £69,000 in modern money.

194 *£3000*: about £138,000 in modern money.

200 *levanted*: absconded, slipped away after losing a bet.

202 *Æsop*: a Greek writer of fables, said by Herodotus to have lived in the sixth century BC, whose stories survived in Latin versions by Phaedrus. In the fable of 'The Bundle of Sticks' an old man shows his quarrelling sons that 'unity is strength' by demonstrating that sticks bound into a faggot will not break, though each single stick is weak.

a Pitt: two generations of the Pitt family had served with distinction as Prime Minister: William Pitt the Elder, first Earl of Chatham (1708–78) in 1756–61 (successfully conducting the Seven Years War) and 1766–8, and his son William Pitt the Younger (1759–1806) in 1783–1801 and 1804–6, during the French Revolution and some of the most difficult phases of the Napoleonic Wars.

Italian with a long name beginning with M.: David Skilton suggests the contemporary names of Marco Minghetti (1818–86, Prime Minister of Italy 1863–4 and 1873–6) and Giuseppe Mazzini (1805–72). But it seems more likely that Glencora is referring to Niccolò Machiavelli (1469–1527) whose book *The Prince* (written in 1513) is perhaps the most famous work of political theory ever written. Machiavelli had been depicted in George Eliot's recent novel *Romola* (1863).

204 *ribbons*: honours or Orders of Knighthood. The most ancient of these are the Garter (see note to p. 133 above), the Thistle (1703), the Bath (revived 1725), and St Patrick (1783). Others, such as the Order of St Michael and St George (1818) and the Star of India (1861), were founded in the nineteenth century.

205 *Caveat emptor*: (Latin) let the buyer beware.

Somers: John Somers, first Baron Evesham (1651–1716), lawyer and Whig politician who helped to frame the Declaration of Right in 1689 and became William III's chief minister.

206 *Sabbatarian*: see notes to p. 153.

213 *The Active Service*: probably a version of the Naval and Military Club in Piccadilly, founded in 1864.

221 *election bills*: agents required funds to fight an election, officially for posters, circulars, and meetings, unofficially for bribes.

224 *£600 ... £800 ... £1000*: in modern money about £28,000 ... £37,000 ... £46,000.

236 *to move for the new writ*: a writ (or written instruction) must be issued by the Clerk of the Crown to the returning officer of a parliamentary constituency before a by-election can be held. The chief whip of the party to which the previous member belonged will put a motion to the House that the Speaker should provide a warrant authorizing this.

absolute canvass: the final phase of soliciting votes at an election, by the candidate himself rather than his agents.

237 *the club over the way*: either the Reform Club (a better funded Whig club) or more probably the Tory Carlton Club which was also on the south side of Pall Mall until its premises were bombed in 1940 and it moved to St James's Street.

238 *£1000*: about £46,000 in modern money.

240 *Queen's speech*: at the beginning of each parliamentary session, the monarch delivers from the throne in the House of Lords a summary account of the legislation which the government will attempt to introduce.

241 *four bigger ships of war*: the Royal Navy had shrunk between 1860 and 1870 (from fifty-seven capital ships to fourty-four) and naval technology was at a point of fundamental change. The building of wooden ships and then putting armour onto them had been abandoned in 1866; the retention of sails on steamships was discredited by the HMS *Captain* disaster in 1870. HMS *Devastation*, built in 1873, was the prototype of the modern metal, entirely steam-driven warship. Though the Navy did not increase in size between 1870 and 1880, there was a case (not made as such by Drought) for the replacement of the existing fleet. Omnium's opposition to this expenditure is the traditional Whig policy of 'retrenchment'.

246 *Ruat cælum, fiat—*: 'Ruat caelum, fiat justitia' ('Though heaven fall, let justice be done'). Latin tag sometimes attributed to Ferdinand I (1373–1416), King of Aragon, surnamed 'The Just'.

249 *Three per Cents*: see note to p. 75.

251 *Æquam memento*: Horace, *Odes*, 2. 3. 1–2: 'Æquam memento rebus in arduis | Servare mentem, non secus in bonis' ('Remember to keep a steady mind when things are hard, and no less in good times').

252 *pitch*: Ecclesiasticus 13: 1: 'He that toucheth pitch shall be defiled therewith'.

tests and qualifications, rotten boroughs and the divine right of kings: Trollope's summary of an extreme Tory position. The divine right of kings had been dismissed by the Glorious Revolution of 1688–9. The Corporation Act of 1661 and the Test Act of 1673, which excluded non-Anglicans from local government and offices under the Crown, had been repealed in 1828.

Rotten boroughs (parliamentary constituencies controlled by a single wealthy individual) were abolished by the Reform Act of 1832. An old-fashioned Ultra-Tory like Francis Gresham feels nostalgic about all of them.

252 *Rads*: Radicals (here meaning radical Whigs, or Liberals).

255 *half-a-crown*: coin worth two shillings and sixpence (one-eighth of a pound); worth about £6 in modern money.

257 *£500*: about £23,000 in modern money. Trollope spent £400 (about £19,000 in modern money) as a candidate in the Beverley election in 1868.

261 *who had offended him*: see Chapter 21 of *Doctor Thorne*, where Mr Moffat is horse-whipped outside his club in Pall Mall after he has jilted Frank Gresham's sister.

271 *kicking against the pricks*: Acts 9: 5: 'And he [Saul] said, Who art thou, Lord? And the Lord said, I am Jesus whom thou persecutest: it is hard for thee to kick against the pricks'.

273 *Paladin*: a knightly hero, originally one of the Twelve Peers of Charlemagne's court.

274 *Jolly Blackbird*: a version of the Magpie and Stump pub (now the George) in Portugal Street near Lincoln's Inn, previously visited by Dickens's Pickwick. Is Wharton conscious of discussing his Portuguese son-in-law in Portugal Street?

Law Courts: an architectural competition was held in 1866–7 for a new Royal Courts of Justice to be built on a site between the Strand and Lincoln's Inn. After a long delay, during which some demolition took place, the foundation stone for G. E. Street's building was laid in 1874. The courts would not be opened until 1882.

275 *£25 . . . seven millions and a half*: £25 would be about £1,150 in modern money; £7.5 m would be £343 m.

278 *quidnuncs*: gossips, people who are constantly asking 'What now?' (Latin).

281 *Martha*: see note to p. 143.

your five-and-twenty thousand pounds: when the 'old' Duke of Omnium dies, in *Phineas Redux*, he leaves Marie Goesler (who had previously refused his proposal of marriage) a legacy of 'twenty thousand pounds and all his jewels'. She will accept nothing except one small diamond ring (chapter 26). Since Plantagenet Palliser will not allow this repudiation of the legacy, she instead gives what has by chapter 69 become 'five-and-twenty thousand pounds' to his cousin Adelaide Palliser so that she can marry Gerard Maule. Lady Glencora continues to speak of it to Marie Goesler (now Mrs Finn) as 'your' money because there is a portion of the Omnium fortune which would have had to be given away to provide a dowry, had the legacy not been substituted for it. £25,000 in modern money would be about £1,150,000: this suggests the scale of Lady Glencora's political hospitality.

289 *Epicurean concourse of atoms*: the Greek philosopher Epicurus (341–270 BC) wrote on physics as well as ethics, giving an account of the natural world derived from Democritus: the universe is not divinely guided but composed of atoms which move randomly about in space to form ephemeral groups or bodies. The theory was best known from the Latin poem *De Rerum Natura* by Lucretius (*c*.99–*c*.55 BC).

296 *feet of clay*: Daniel 2: 32–3: 'This image's head was of fine gold . . . his feet part of iron and part of clay'.

299 *of whom all people said all good things*: Terence, *Andria*, 96–7: 'omnes omnia bona dicere et laudere fortunas meas | qui gnatum haberem tali ingenio praeditum' ('All people said all good things, and praised my good fortune in having a son blessed with such a character'). A favourite Latin tag for Trollope, also used in *The Bertrams, The Eustace Diamonds, Framley Parsonage, He Knew He Was Right, Phineas Finn*, and *Sir Harry Hotspur of Humblethwaite* (see David Skilton, 'Schoolboy Latin and the Mid-Victorian Novelist', *Browning Institute Studies*, 16 (1988), 39–55).

VOLUME III

325 *A man and his wife are one*: the legal doctrine of 'unity of personality' whereby, in the case of a civil (not criminal) wrong committed by a married woman, her husband would be joined as a party to the action and be responsible for the payment of damages.

329 *Dovercourt*: probably a version of Margate, a popular seaside resort in Kent.

333 *Kauri gum*: a resin exuded from the New Zealand Kauri or Cowrie Pine, mostly used to make varnish rather than as a substitute for amber; see Trollope's *Australia and New Zealand* (1873).

339 *stockbroker*: the London Stock Exchange had two classes of member, brokers (agents for the public, on commission) and jobbers (who traded with other members), though until 1908 it was possible to combine the roles. Both were supervised by the Committee of Proprietors and admitted either after the payment of a substantial entrance fee or after apprenticeship as a clerk. Lopez has worked in a 'London . . . stockbroker's office' (p. 9), possibly 'Hunky and Sons' (p. 70), but not become a member; he is a sole trader or speculative investor. Parker has the air of a man who has worked his way up from clerk to member. Business on the Exchange doubled 1862–72, partly because of the London practice of fixed periods for settlement (payment not being required before the end of twenty days), partly because of its openness, both to new enterprises for trading, and to new members who increased from 864 in 1850 to over 2,000 in 1878.

£2000: about £92,000 in modern money.

346 *Bedlam*: the familiar name for the Bethlehem Royal Hospital, London's chief mental hospital since 1377, rebuilt in Lambeth in 1815.

12s. 6d. . . . £1250: about £29 and £58,000 in modern money.

348 *Shakespeare and the other dramatists*: though the ships referred to in *The Merchant of Venice* are 'argosies', rather than caravels (the Portuguese caravela, used by the navigators of the fifteenth and sixteenth centuries), Lopez is allusively associating himself with the Christian merchant venturers of Shakespeare's play. Antonio tells his friend Bassanio (who, like Lopez, is seeking to improve his fortunes by marrying an heiress) that 'Thou know'st that all my fortunes are at sea, | Neither have I money nor commodity | To raise a present sum' (I. i. 177–9); news will arrive at the beginning of Act III that Antonio's ships and their cargoes have all been sunk. Trollope read Dyce's edition of Shakespeare on his voyage to Australia in 1871, though his note on *The Merchant of Venice* ('There is no better reading') would not be made until 18 June 1875. The reference to 'other dramatists' reflects Trollope's extensive reading of 'old plays' in the 1860s and 1870s (see Introduction). Some of these, such as Jonson, Chapman, and Marston's collaborative *Eastward Ho* (1605; read 7 June 1873), also involve merchant venturers.

349 *£26,000 . . . £30,000 . . . £5000 . . . £15,000 . . . £20,000*: in modern money, about £1,190,000 . . . £1,375,000 . . . £229,000 . . . £686,000 . . . £915,000. In round numbers, Lopez is hoping for a total dowry (in modern money) of about one and a quarter million pounds (this £20,000 plus the £3,000 he was given initially and the £500 for his election expenses). Since Emily's actual fortune is more than twice that, he could be said to be making a rather modest estimate of what he might ask for.

350 *there's a good time coming*: phrase from the popular poem 'The Good Time Coming' by Charles Mackay (1814–89), published in *Voices from the Crowd* (1846). When set to music by Henry Russell, the song sold 400,000 copies. Trollope knew Mackay, hoped to place stories with him when he was editor of the *London Review*, and corresponded with him about the criticism of his *Life of Cicero* (see *Letters*, i. 121, ii. 911).

352 *Smithfield*: London's meat market, established in 1638. As well as carcasses, live cattle and horses were sold there (creating a demand for Mrs Parker's father's hay) until 1855, when the live trade moved to Islington. A new market building, modelled on the Crystal Palace and with underground railway links, had opened at Smithfield in 1868.

353 *Shylock*: a second reference within the same chapter to Shakespeare's *The Merchant of Venice* (see note to p. 348). Lopez now compares himself, not with the Christian merchant venturer Antonio, but with the Jewish usurer Shylock who tells Bassanio that 'I will buy with you, sell with you, talk with you, and so following, but I will not eat, drink with you, nor pray with you' (I. iii. 29–32). Trollope's note on the play, made on 18 June 1875, would note 'the grand stage incidents of Shylock'.

355 *a place at the side*: pew rents were often charged for the better seats in parish churches in the nineteenth century; Lopez advertises his respectability (and Anglicanism) by choosing the most conspicuous and expensive location in the church. In modern money 'half a guinea' would be about £25.

356 *like tigers clawing one another*: an echo of John Fletcher's play *Women Pleased* (*c*.1620) where Lopez declares, 'H'as light legs, else I had so Ferret-claw'd him' (III. iv. 94); see Introduction.

359 *The Gaiety*: theatre in the Strand, opened in December 1868 on the site of the Strand Music Hall. It specialized in burlesques, farces, and operettas: *Thespis*, the first Gilbert and Sullivan collaboration, opened here in 1871. Trollope's novel *Ralph the Heir* was adapted by Charles Reade, without permission and to Trollope's intense annoyance, into the play *Shilly-Shally* which ran at the Gaiety in April 1872 (see *Letters*, ii. 558–9, 561–3, 1012–13, 1015).

365 *buckram*: a coarse cloth stiffened with gum, hence a stiff, over-formal manner; lawyer's bags were traditionally made from buckram.

366 *after martial manner*: properly (French) 'Suprêmes de volaille à la maréchale': chicken breasts fried in egg and breadcrumbs and served in a sauce of truffles, veal stock, and lemon juice (Auguste Escoffier, *Ma Cuisine*).

371 *Guatemala*: a country in Central America, part of the Spanish Empire until 1821, then of the Central American Confederation; an independent republic since 1839. It does, in fact, have mineral deposits (of gold, silver, and zinc) but the lack of roads and railways made extracting them difficult, so mining was slow to develop: Melmotte's proposed 'South Central Pacific and Mexican Railway' in *The Way We Live Now* might in theory have helped with this, had the company not been fraudulent. The first full geological survey was made in 1868. Away from the coast the climate is healthy and the capital, Guatemala la Nueva, was known in the late nineteenth century as 'the Paris of Central America'. The characters in Trollope's novel see it as no such thing, possibly because of the ways in which the country had been in the news in the early 1870s. There had been an unsuccessful revolution in March 1872, followed by a brief war with San Salvador and Honduras. This led to a suspension of interest payments on the government's debts: a London investment company, the Foreign and Colonial Government Trust (one of whose directors was a Mr Lopes), reported to its investors on this problem in July 1872 (see *The Times*, 4 July 1872). Then, in May 1874 (about two months before Trollope wrote this section of the novel), there was 'the Guatemalan outrage': Colonel Gonzalez, military commandant of the Port of San José, inflicted 200 lashes on the British Vice-Consul, John Magee. Though the Guatemalan government was quick to apologize, *The Times* leader on 26 May 1874 remarked that 'Strange deeds are done, indeed, in these Central American republics, in the population of which the heat of Spanish blood is often mingled with the savagery of the aboriginal race'. Trollope visited the West Indies and Central America on Post Office business, in 1858–9, spending most of his time in Jamaica, Cuba, Trinidad, Grenada, British Guiana, Panama, and Costa Rica, and published an account of the trip as *The West Indies and the Spanish Main* (1859).

£*20,000*: about £915,000 in modern money.

373 *defy the law*: in English law a husband had traditionally been able to make his wife live with him ('consortium'). In 1852 the courts ruled that a husband could not use habeas corpus to force an absent wife to return to him, though they upheld his right to confine her in the first instance. A married woman's right to her personal liberty would not be fully established until the case of Regina v. Jackson in 1891.

376 *£25 9s. 6d.* about £1,200 in modern money.

Lewes and Allenby's: properly Lewis and Allenby, silk mercers, drapers, and suppliers of silk dresses, with large premises on the corner of Regent Street and Conduit Street. Holders of a royal warrant as silk manufacturers to the Queen since the 1840s, they helped to supply the trousseaux of her daughters the Princess Royal and Princess Alice in 1858 and 1862. The company failed to survive the First World War and was wound up in 1919. Emily's dresses cost between £1,500 and £2,000 in modern money.

389 *You must throw me to the whale*: when a ship was threatened by a whale, sailors supposedly threw a tub overboard to distract it. Hence a decoy or diversion.

Adam said so: Genesis 3: 12: 'And the man said, The woman whom thou gavest to be with me, she gave me of the tree, and I did eat.'

400 *the San Juan Mining Association*: there is in fact a town called San Juan in Guatemala, in the Alto Cuchumatanes mountains, close to the western border with Mexico. Coleman Street runs between Gresham Street and London Wall in the City. Lopez's proposed salary of £1,000 a year would be £46,000, and the cost of the shares he must buy £230,000, in modern money.

402 *Indian mail-packet*: the steamship service to the West Indies.

404 *despoiled the Egyptians*: see Exodus 3: 20–2: 'I will stretch out my hand, and smite Egypt . . . and after that he will let you go . . . ye shall spoil the Egyptians', and 12: 35–6: 'And the children of Israel did according to the word of Moses; and they borrowed of the Egyptians jewels of silver, and jewels of gold, and raiment . . . And they spoiled the Egyptians.'

407 *incubus*: literally a demon that descends upon people in their sleep, figuratively an oppressive burden or trouble.

408 *scrip . . . par*: 'scrip' is technically the document indicating ownership which a company or broker provides prior to the delivery of the actual share certificates; in practice it is used simply to mean 'shares'. 'Par' is the nominal price on a share certificate; the market price from day to day will usually be either more or less than this, and a stock is 'at par' when the two are equal, or in parity.

a quarter of a million: about £11,425,000 in modern money.

412 *Bond Steet*: street in Mayfair noted for shops selling luxury items.

413 *'Seven thousand five hundred pounds!'*: about £343,000 in modern money.

A hundred thousand pounds: about £4,570,000 in modern money.

414 *£45,000*: about £2,057,000 in modern money.

three thousand seven hundred and fifty: about £172,000 in modern money.

nine partners: the Companies Acts of 1856 and 1862 required limited liability and joint stock companies to have a minimum of seven shareholders.

416 *Cortez and Pizarro . . . American subjects*: Guatemala was conquered by Cortés's lieutenant, Pedro de Alvarado (1495–1541) in 1522–4. Hernan Cortés (1485–1547) was the Spanish conqueror of Mexico in 1518–28. Francisco Pizarro (1478–1541) served in Central America in the early part of his career but is remembered for his conquest of Peru and Chile after 1531. Improbably, given his Portuguese rather than Spanish background, Lopez claims a Guatemalan ancestor who supposedly contributed to the achievement (1810–21) of South and Central American independence from Spain in the same way as Simón Bolívar (1783–1830) in Venezuela and Bernardo O'Higgins (1778–1842) in Chile.

417 *Cleopatra*: see Shakespeare's *Antony and Cleopatra*, where Cleopatra (*c.*69–31 BC), Queen of Egypt, is courted by Mark Antony who has a wife, Fulvia, in Rome.

418 *'Where the rage . . . madden to crime?'*: lines 3–4 of the First Canto of Byron's narrative poem *The Bride of Abydos* (1813). Given Lizzie Eustace's enthusiasm for Byron and her tendency to confine her reading to the opening sections of poems (see *The Eustace Diamonds*, chapter 21), Lopez's quotation is skilfully chosen.

£4000: about £183,000 in modern money.

424 *Duke of Newcastle*: Thomas Pelham-Holles, first Duke of Newcastle (1693–1768). Prime Minister 1754–6, resigning after Admiral Byng's failure to defend Minorca from the French (Byng was executed 'pour encourager les autres'). In 1757–62 he was nominally Prime Minister though actually the junior partner in a coalition with Pitt. Honest but ineffectual, he was associated with a long catalogue of government delay and incompetence.

425 *malgré lui*: (French) despite himself.

426 *Dod*: *Dod's Parliamentary Companion*. an annual reference book providing information about members of the Houses of Parliament, first published by Charles Dod in 1865 to replace *The Parliamentary Pocket Companion* founded in 1832.

428 *to blow upon her*: Shakespeare, *Hamlet*, I. ii. 140–2: 'so loving to my mother | That he might not beteem the winds of heaven | Visit her face too roughly' (Hamlet on his father).

429 *out of a full heart the mouth speaks*: Matthew 12: 34: 'out of the abundance of the heart the mouth speaketh'.

430 *Mansion House dinner*: the Mansion House is the official residence of the Lord Mayor of London. Formal dinners are held there each year at

which government ministers make speeches on major matters of policy, especially those which affect business and the City.

433 *Mentor . . . Telemachus*: in Homer's *Odyssey* Odysseus leaves his old friend Mentor in charge of his household in Ithaca, when he leaves for Troy. Mentor acts as an adviser to Odysseus' son Telemachus.

434 *father of the House*: the Member whose continuous service in the House of Commons is the longest.

442 *upas*: the Upas tree (*Antiaris toxicaria*) of Java contains a deadly poison but, contrary to legend, does not in fact kill those who sleep beneath its branches.

roof-tree: the main beam or ridge-pole of a roof; figuratively the entire house.

444 *He was expelled from his club*: premature this, since he returns to the Progress Club in Chapter 60 and we are told on p. 454 that 'The committee which was to be held with the view of judging whether he was or was not a proper person to remain a member . . . had not yet been held'. Lopez may be pessimistically anticipating its conclusions.

449 *Pariah*: a social outcast (literally a member of a low Hindu caste).

456 *two or three sovereigns*: about £137 in modern money.

458 *Tenway Junction*: Willesden Junction in Acton, 5 miles north-west of central London. A complex intersection of mainline and suburban railway lines, begun in 1839. The London and North Western Railway opened a new West Coast Main Line station there in 1866, and the suburban North London Railway built its High Level station in 1869.

pundits: (Hindi) learned men, literally those versed in Sanskrit and Hindu religious doctrine. Here used in a jocular way of well-informed porters or railway officials.

459 *hair*: air (the pundit is a Cockney who sounds his aspirates).

VOLUME IV

462 *felo de se*: suicide (Anglo-Latin: cruelty or harm to the self).

464 *more sinned against than sinning*: Shakespeare, *King Lear*, III. ii. 57–8: 'I am a man | More sinned against than sinning' (Lear in the storm).

469 *'slings and arrows of outrageous fortune'*: Shakespeare, *Hamlet*, III. i. 60.

470 *Cræsus*: King of Lydia (560–546 BC) proverbial for his wealth.

British jury: see *Phineas Redux* chapters 61–7, where Phineas is tried by jury for the murder of Mr Bonteen.

474 *Sir Bayard*: Pierre du Terrail, Seigneur de Bayard (1475–1524), French soldier famous for his chivalry: 'le bon chevalier, sans peur et sans reproche' ('the good knight, fearless and blameless'). He fought in the Italian wars of Charles VIII and Louis XII.

Don Quixote: the hero of the comic novel *Don Quixote de la Mancha* (1605) by Miguel de Cervantes (1547–1616). He is so obsessed with chivalric romance that he fails to see the reality of the modern world around him.

476 *quints or semi-tenths*: a particular difficulty in Plantagenet Palliser's attempt to design a decimal currency was to find an equivalent for the smallest unit in the duodecimal system: the farthing (a quarter of a penny). Since non-decimal fractions would no longer be allowed, its replacement would need to be either smaller, one fifth of a penny, hence 'quint' (Latin, quintus), or larger: half a penny, or half of a 'tenth' (since there would be ten pennies to a shilling). See note to p. 42 and *The Eustace Diamonds*, chapter 47.

477 *Cincinnatus*: a Roman farmer of the fifth century BC who (according to legend) was called from the plough to save the army from defeat by the Aequi. He was made dictator, conquered the enemy, but then returned to his farm.

478 *sounding cymbal of brass*: 1 Corinthians 13: 1: 'Though I speak with the tongues of men and of angels, and have not charity, I am become as sounding brass, or a tinkling cymbal'.

481 *dividing farms*: possibly a detail of the Irish Land Bill (see note to p. 529).

483 *Aristides*: Athenian statesman of the fifth century BC, known as 'The Just'. After a disagreement with Themistocles, he was ostracized (sent into exile, after a popular vote in which citizens wrote the name of the unwanted politician on *ostraca*: potsherds or fragments of broken pottery). According to Plutarch, an illiterate voter asked Aristides to write his own name on his potsherd. When asked what injury Aristides had done him, the voter replied, 'None, but it vexes me to hear him everywhere called the Just'. The allusion is repeated at p. 499 (where Trollope is guilty of the customary mistranslation of 'ostraca' as 'oyster-shells') and p. 519. Juliet McMaster notes that Themistocles, like Sir Orlando Drought, was an advocate of naval rearmament (*Trollope's Palliser Novels* (London: Macmillan, 1978), 119).

489 *Lord Earlybird's proxy*: the accepting of proxy votes in the House of Lords was discontinued in 1868.

496 *Indian widow*: on the death of her husband a Brahmin, or high-caste, Hindu widow would proclaim herself 'suttee' ('a virtuous wife') and throw herself into the funeral pyre. The British prohibited the custom in 1829, though preventing it remained difficult.

Warwick: Richard Neville, Earl of Warwick (1428–71), known as 'the king-maker', supporter first of the Yorkists and then of the Lancastrians in the Wars of the Roses.

Lord John . . . Sir Robert Peel . . . THE Duke . . . Earl Grey: Lord John Russell (1792–1878; Whig Prime Minister 1846–52, 1865–6), Sir Robert Peel (1788–1850; Tory Prime Minister 1834–5, 1841–6), the Duke of Wellington (1769–1852; Tory Prime Minister 1828–30), Earl Grey

(1764–1845; Whig Prime Minister 1830–4). In so far as the Duke of St Bungay is a version of Lord Lansdowne (1780–1863), these associations with great politicians of a previous generation are appropriate. But for an active cabinet minister in the mid-1870s they are simply impossible: to have 'listened to the bold Liberalism of old Earl Grey, both in the Lower and the Upper House' would have required membership of the House of Commons before 1808 (when Charles Grey succeeded to his title and moved to the Lords). This was true of Lansdowne (b. 1780) but would make Trollope's St Bungay more than ninety years old, not 'between seventy and eighty' as he is said to be on p. 53. (See note to p. 43 and Appendix.)

496 *pearls before swine*: Matthew 7: 6: 'Give not that which is holy unto the dogs, neither cast ye your pearls before swine, lest they trample them under their feet, and turn again and rend you.'

499 *oyster-shells*: see note to p. 483.

Exeter Hall: building in the Strand (constructed 1829–31, demolished 1907) used for the meetings of philanthropic and religious organizations, including the Bible Society, the Ragged School Union, the anti-slavery movement, the Temperance Society, and Charles Spurgeon, the charismatic Baptist preacher.

Pitt . . . Peel . . . Palmerston: William Pitt (1759–1806), Sir Robert Peel (1788–1850), Lord Palmerston (1784–1865), all prime ministers noted for their strength of mind and personality.

501 *12th*: the season for shooting grouse opens on 12 August.

505 *Mr Cook*: Thomas Cook (1808–92) founded his pioneering travel agency in the 1840s, moving to London and arranging the first overseas trips in the 1860s. In a variation of the popular phrase 'by hook or by crook', travellers were said to make their arrangements either 'by Cook or off their own hook'.

507 *crape and weepers*: widows' mourning dresses were made from crape (crêpe) (a black silk, or imitation silk, fabric); 'weepers' were broad white cuffs worn on their sleeves.

Oban: seaport on the west coast of Scotland. 'Yachting' at this date meant an extensive cruise on a large sailing boat with cabins and a professional crew, so Everett is likely to be at sea for several weeks.

511 *pigs carrying straws*: proverbial: 'When pigs carry sticks, the clouds will play tricks; when they lie in the mud, no fear of a flood.'

513 *that which was worse*: 'Video meliora, proboque; | Deteriora sequor' ('I see the better way, and approve it; I follow the worse'), Ovid, *Metamorphoses*, 7. 20.

516 *power does corrupt*: 'Unlimited power is apt to corrupt the minds of those who possess it' (William Pitt, House of Lords, 9 January 1770). Lord Acton's more famous formulation, 'Power tends to corrupt and absolute power corrupts absolutely', would not be uttered until 1887.

518 *little Lady Glencora*: the size of Plantagenet Palliser and Lady Glencora's family varies slightly from novel to novel. In chapter 48 of *Phineas Finn*, Phineas remarks that 'I know there are three or four babies,' and in chapter 60 we are told that, 'Since the future little Lord Silverbridge had been born . . . from year to year, a little brother was added'. In *The Prime Minister* things are clearer: there are two boys, Lord Silverbridge and his brother Lord Gerald Palliser, and 'two little girls' (p. 140), one of whom is called Glencora after her mother. In *The Duke's Children*, however, there are two sons but only one daughter, Lady Mary; 'little' Glencora appears to have vanished.

519 *boroughs*: see note to p. 540.

521 *four hundred and fifty*: about £21,000 in modern money.

twopence: about 40p in modern money.

523 *two sovereigns*: about £92 in modern money.

524 *two pounds weekly*: in modern money, Mr Wharton gives Mrs Parker a 'pension' of about £5,000 a year.

527 *Niobe*: in Greek myth the daughter of Tantalus and the mother of seven sons and seven daughters. She claimed to be superior to the goddess Leto, who had only two children: Apollo and Artemis. When punished by the deaths of her fourteen offspring, she wept until she turned into a pillar of stone from which water continued to drip.

528 *£60,000*: about £2,750,000 in modern money.

529 *Irish Land Bill*: the Irish Land Act (1870) had given greater protection to Irish tenants, including compensation for improvements they had made to the property during their tenancy and loans to help tenants purchase freeholds, but left both tenants and landlords dissatisfied. Gladstone would introduce a new Land Bill in 1881.

Corpus Christi: Corpus Christi College, Cambridge, was founded in 1352 without a chapel, so originally used St Benet's (Benedict's) Church next door. During the Reformation it became known by its nickname of 'St Benet's' or 'Bene't', to avoid the Catholic implications of 'corpus Christi' (body of Christ). It began to use its original name again in the late 1820s, just after Sir Alured Wharton's time as an undergraduate.

532 *Lord Chancellor*: the Lord Chancellor is the senior English judge, the Speaker of the House of Lords, and a member of the cabinet. He wears his wig in the first two of those capacities but not the third, which may explain Mrs Fletcher's confusion.

Bradshaw: railway timetable. George Bradshaw (1801–53) was a Manchester publisher who began to produce his *Railway Time Tables* in 1839. It became an indispensable handbook in the railway age, with monthly updates coordinating the schedules of the numerous train companies.

540 *County Suffrage Bill*: the forty English counties had traditionally been single constituencies, each returning two MPs (a total of eighty) while the

203 boroughs (towns) had returned 415 MPs. Though the First Reform Act in 1832 redistributed 143 seats from 'rotten' boroughs, these went chiefly to the new large towns: by 1865 each county member represented 70,000 people, each borough member only 26,000. The Second Reform Act of 1867 redistributed fifty-three seats but, again, only a minority of them went to the counties, which also retained a more demanding property qualification for voters. This created a grievance about unequal representation which would not be addressed until the Reform and Representation Acts of 1884–5 created a uniform franchise and awarded sixty-six more seats to English and Welsh counties. (See note to p. 58.)

540 *American system*: one man one vote.

541 *second reading*: the Second Reading is the debate on the principles of a bill (the First Reading merely constitutes an order to have the bill printed; the Second Reading is followed by the detailed scrutiny of the Committee and Report Stages, and by the Third or final Reading).

send it up to you: a bill which starts in the House of Commons (like this one) must be 'sent up' to the House of Lords for similar consideration there. It must pass through both Houses to become law.

542 *address was voted*: an address of thanks to the Sovereign is moved as a response to the Queen's Speech at the beginning of the parliamentary session. This provides an opportunity for a general debate on the government's performance and policy.

543 *not to put his trust in princes*: Psalm 146: 3: 'Put not your trust in princes'.

544 *Mr Bott*: in *Can You Forgive Her?* the Liberal MP for St Helens in Lancashire; before that a cotton manufacturer (see chapters 23 and 24). Elected as a Manchester School Radical, he became an ally of the Whigs and shared Palliser's interest in the technicalities of financial policy. Lady Glencora suspected him of spying on her encounters with Burgo Fitzgerald.

546 *Downing Street*: 10 Downing Street has been the Prime Minister's official residence since 1732 but that is not what is referred to here. Many nineteenth-century prime ministers, including Trollope's Duke of Omnium, preferred to use their own, grander London Houses. St Bungay is calling on Omnium in Carlton House Terrace on his way to the new Government Offices on the other side of Downing Street (see note to p. 78).

548 *Pompey*: Pompey (Gnaeus Pompeius, 106–48 BC), Roman general and politician. In 60 BC he formed a triumvirate with Caesar and Crassus. But Crassus died and in 52 BC Pompey became sole consul and sought to end Caesar's powers. This led to the first Civil War; in 49 BC Caesar led a legion into Italy and expelled Pompey. Trollope published a translation of *The Commentaries of Caesar* in 1870.

551 *Othello*: see Shakespeare's *Othello*, III. iii. 353–62: 'Farewell the tranquil mind, farewell content, | Farewell the plumèd troops and the big

wars | That make ambition virtue . . . Farewell! Othello's occupation's gone.' Trollope's note on *Othello*, made on 30 June 1871, states, 'The plot, performance, and language of this play are alike perfect. It is assuredly one of the grandest works of human genius.'

554 *The Spartan boy*: in the famous story, originally found in Plutarch's life of Lycurgus (the legendary legislator of the state of Sparta), the boy stoically conceals a fox, rather than a wolf.

555 *new Liberal club*: the City Liberal Club was founded in 1874 but this is more probably a fictitious West End club. The National Liberal Club in Whitehall Place would not be founded until 1882.

Jove-born intellect: Minerva (Greek, Athena), goddess of wisdom, was born from the head of her father, Jove (Greek, Zeus), the supreme god.

559 *Wolsey*: Thomas Wolsey (1475–1530), Cardinal and statesman who lost favour in 1529 after failing to advance Henry VIII's divorce from Catherine of Aragon and marriage with Anne Bullen (or Boleyn, beheaded for adultery in 1536). Trollope is probably remembering the account of Wolsey's fall in the play *Henry VIII* (now also known as *All Is True*) by Shakespeare and John Fletcher, especially Wolsey's speech at III. ii. 351–73: 'Farewell, a long farewell, to all my greatness!' Trollope's note on *Henry VIII*, made on 30 June 1871, reads, 'This is, I think, the finest of the historical pieces, possessing higher dramatic interest than any of the others.'

562 *take the County hounds*: become Master of the local hunt.

571 *bench at Ross*: Ross-on-Wye in Herefordshire, where Sir Alured sits as a magistrate (on 'the bench').

572 *subscription*: the fees paid for membership of a hunt. In modern money '£1500' would be about £69,000. Running the hunt costs (in modern money) more like £115,000 a year, as John Fletcher will have to spend 'a thousand a year' (£46,000) out of his own pocket to subsidize it.

574 *Howell and James's*: Howell and James of Regent Street held royal warrants as jewellers to the Royal Family and silk mercers to the Queen. Like Lewis and Allenby (see note to p. 376) they helped to make the trousseaux of the Queen's daughters, so were a very smart and expensive firm. Muddocks and Cramble's, the provincial alternative, seem to have been invented: 'cramble' is a dialect word meaning 'branches of crooked or angular growth, used for rustic work or firewood' (*OED*).

579 *Mr Mildmay doing it twice*: William Mildmay is Prime Minister only once in Trollope's Palliser novels, in *Phineas Finn*, though with a hint (in chapter 9) that he had held the office before: his appointment involves a willingness to 'once more buckle on his ancient armour'. This would mean a premiership before that of Lord Brock (see Appendix). It remains hard to see how he can have returned 'twice'. The real politician on whom he is often thought to have been based, Lord John Russell, was Prime Minister 1846–52 and again in 1865–6. But he is known to have had 'Caesar cannot serve under Pompey' thoughts when his government

fell in 1852 and overcame them to serve as Foreign Secretary in the Aberdeen coalition: this may constitute the returning 'twice' (once as Foreign Secretary, once as Prime Minister) which Lady Glencora is supposed to have in mind.

582 *boody*: sulk (French, *bouder*). An unusual word which Trollope had used before in *Barchester Towers*, chapter 27.

Lama: (Tibetan) spiritual teacher. Here used to suggest the withdrawn and remote quality of the Dalai Lama, the priestly ruler of nineteenth-century Tibet.

583 *Ne peccet ad extremum ridendus*: Horace, *Epistles*, I. I. 8–9: 'Solve senescentem mature sanus equem, ne | peccet ad extremum ridendus, et ilia ducat' ('Be wise as the years pass and get rid of the horse which has become weak with age, lest it fails and becomes a laughing stock, broken-winded').

586 *appanage*: a province, dependency, or adjunct.

590 *bar*: a barrister who becomes a Queen's Counsel is no longer directly briefed by a solicitor but acts as the senior counsel in cases for which the preliminary work has been done by a more junior barrister. In practice, a QC spends much of his time giving opinions on issues which will not come to court.

595 *pachydermatous*: thick-skinned (like a hippopotamus).

597 *to march through Coventry with!*: Shakespeare, *Henry IV, Part 1*, IV. ii. 11–42. Falstaff is embarrassed to be seen with the feeble soldiers he has recruited: 'If I be not ashamed of my soldiers, I am a soused gurnet . . . No eye hath seen such scarecrows. I'll not march through Coventry with them, that's flat.'

an Attorney-General of my own: the Duchy of Lancaster, whose Chancellor sits in the cabinet, is responsible for the administration of Crown estates, the appointment of justices of the peace, and ecclesiastical patronage in Lancashire; it has its own Attorney-General to handle its legal matters.

608 *days now long passed*: in *Can You Forgive Her?*, about fifteen years before the events of this novel.

609 *all the woods of Gatherum should come to Matching*: the last of the *Macbeth* allusions, with their serio-comic linking of Omnium and Glencora to Lord and Lady Macbeth. The Duke of St Bungay has played the part of the three witches by suggesting that Omnium should become Prime Minister; unlike the Macbeths, the Omniums have not committed 'absolute' murder (though they could be said to have played a part in Lopez's suicide); unlike Lady Macbeth, Glencora has not gone mad. The moving woods are from *Macbeth*, IV. i. 108–10, V. v. 42–4 ('Fear not till Birnam Wood | Do come to Dunsinane'), and V. x. 30, where the wood does move, in the sense that King Malcom's army cuts down its branches and carries them as camouflage.

611 *needy knife-grinder*: see 'The Friend of Humanity and the Knife Grinder', a poem mocking sympathizers with the French Revolution, first printed in *The Anti-Jacobin* (1797–98), a journal founded by George Canning and John Hookham Frere, and edited by William Gifford. Having failed to rouse the knife grinder (who prefers an evening in the pub) to a state of revolutionary indignation, the Friend of Humanity 'Kicks the Knife-grinder, overturns his wheel, and exit[s] in a transport of Republican enthusiasm and universal philanthropy'.

Late Victorian Gothic Tales

JANE AUSTEN
Emma
Mansfield Park
Persuasion
Pride and Prejudice
Selected Letters
Sense and Sensibility

MRS BEETON
Book of Household Management

MARY ELIZABETH BRADDON
Lady Audley's Secret

ANNE BRONTË
The Tenant of Wildfell Hall

CHARLOTTE BRONTË
Jane Eyre
Shirley
Villette

EMILY BRONTË
Wuthering Heights

ROBERT BROWNING
The Major Works

JOHN CLARE
The Major Works

SAMUEL TAYLOR COLERIDGE
The Major Works

WILKIE COLLINS
The Moonstone
No Name
The Woman in White

CHARLES DARWIN
The Origin of Species

THOMAS DE QUINCEY
The Confessions of an English Opium-Eater
On Murder

CHARLES DICKENS
The Adventures of Oliver Twist
Barnaby Rudge
Bleak House
David Copperfield
Great Expectations
Nicholas Nickleby
The Old Curiosity Shop
Our Mutual Friend
The Pickwick Papers

CHARLES DICKENS	A Tale of Two Cities
GEORGE DU MAURIER	Trilby
MARIA EDGEWORTH	Castle Rackrent
GEORGE ELIOT	Daniel Deronda The Lifted Veil and Brother Jacob Middlemarch The Mill on the Floss Silas Marner
SUSAN FERRIER	Marriage
ELIZABETH GASKELL	Cranford The Life of Charlotte Brontë Mary Barton North and South Wives and Daughters
GEORGE GISSING	New Grub Street The Odd Women
EDMUND GOSSE	Father and Son
THOMAS HARDY	Far from the Madding Crowd Jude the Obscure The Mayor of Casterbridge The Return of the Native Tess of the d'Urbervilles The Woodlanders
WILLIAM HAZLITT	Selected Writings
JAMES HOGG	The Private Memoirs and Confessions of a Justified Sinner
JOHN KEATS	The Major Works Selected Letters
CHARLES MATURIN	Melmoth the Wanderer
JOHN RUSKIN	Selected Writings
WALTER SCOTT	The Antiquary Ivanhoe

GUY DE MAUPASSANT	A Day in the Country and Other Stories
	A Life
	Bel-Ami
	Mademoiselle Fifi and Other Stories
	Pierre et Jean
PROSPER MÉRIMÉE	Carmen and Other Stories
MOLIÈRE	Don Juan and Other Plays
	The Misanthrope, Tartuffe, and Other Plays
BLAISE PASCAL	Pensées and Other Writings
ABBÉ PRÉVOST	Manon Lescaut
JEAN RACINE	Britannicus, Phaedra, and Athaliah
ARTHUR RIMBAUD	Collected Poems
EDMOND ROSTAND	Cyrano de Bergerac
MARQUIS DE SADE	The Crimes of Love
	The Misfortunes of Virtue and Other Early Tales
GEORGE SAND	Indiana
MME DE STAËL	Corinne
STENDHAL	The Red and the Black
	The Charterhouse of Parma
PAUL VERLAINE	Selected Poems
JULES VERNE	Around the World in Eighty Days
	Captain Hatteras
	Journey to the Centre of the Earth
	Twenty Thousand Leagues under the Seas
VOLTAIRE	Candide and Other Stories
	Letters concerning the English Nation

ÉMILE ZOLA

L'Assommoir
The Attack on the Mill
La Bête humaine
La Débâcle
Germinal
The Kill
The Ladies' Paradise
The Masterpiece
Nana
Pot Luck
Thérèse Raquin